BUNT!

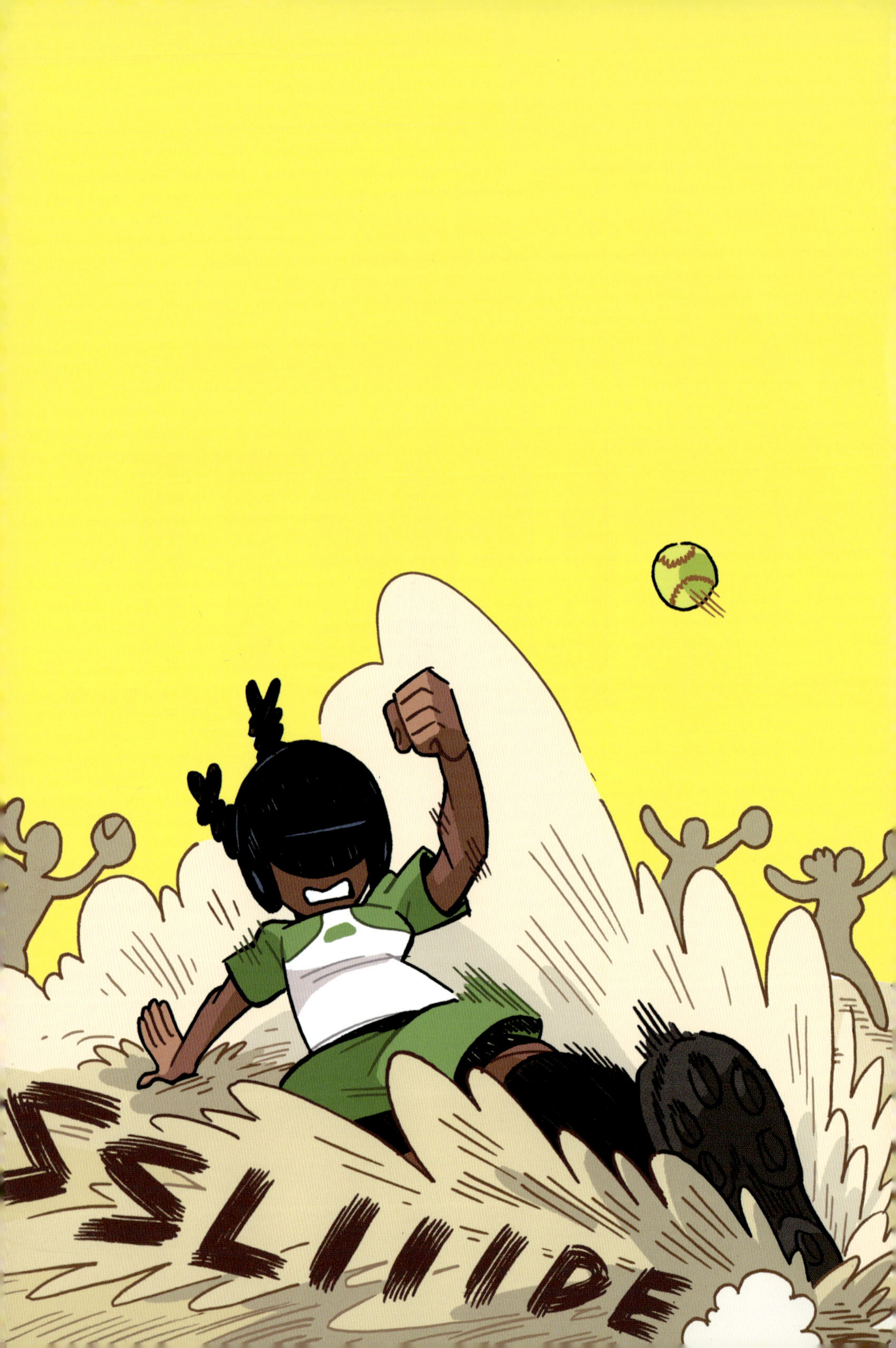
SSLIIIDE

BUNT!
STRIKING OUT ON FINANCIAL AID

WRITTEN BY NGOZI UKAZU
ART BY MAD RUPERT
COLOR BY K CZAP

:01
First Second
NEW YORK

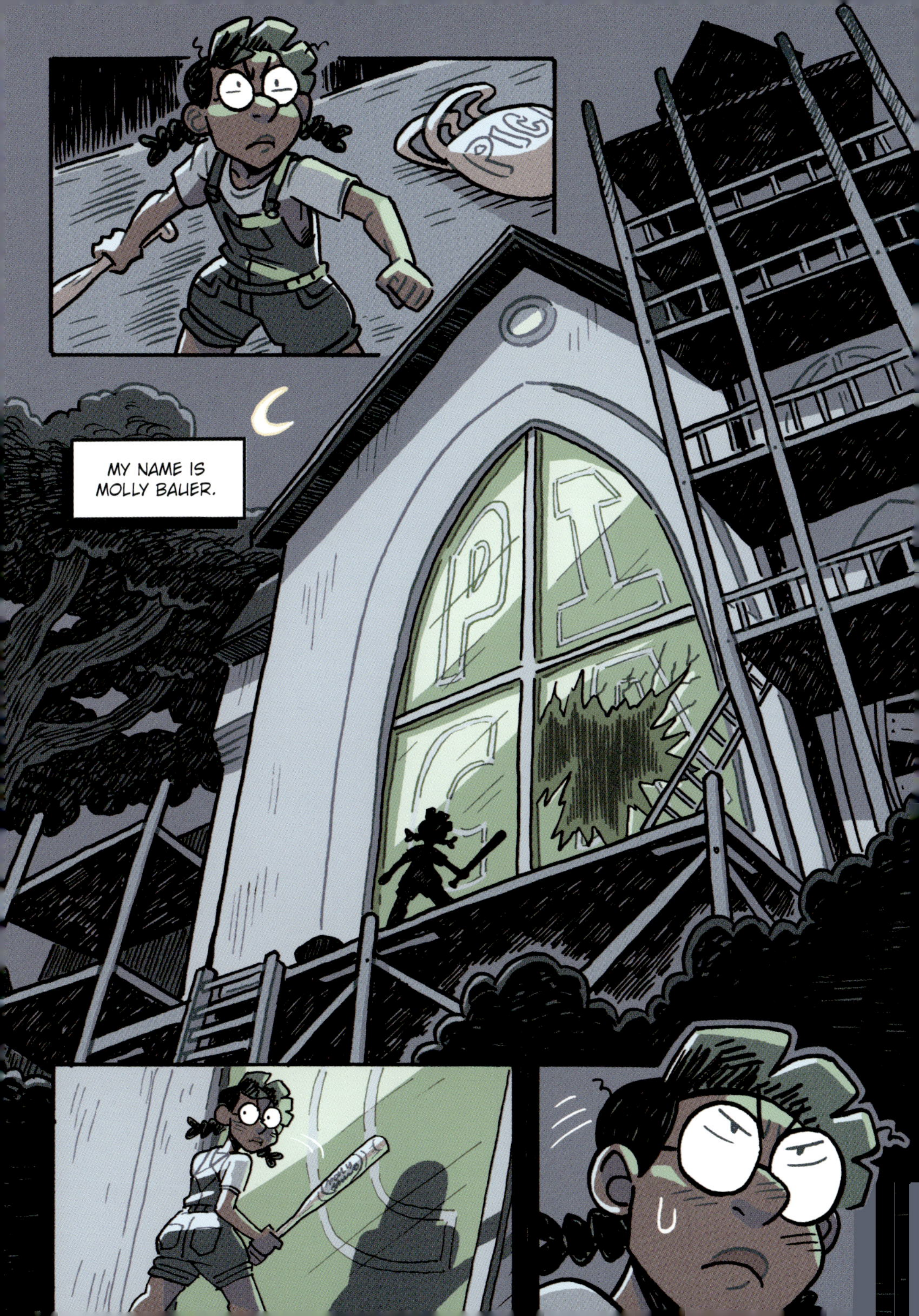
PIG
MY NAME IS MOLLY BAUER.

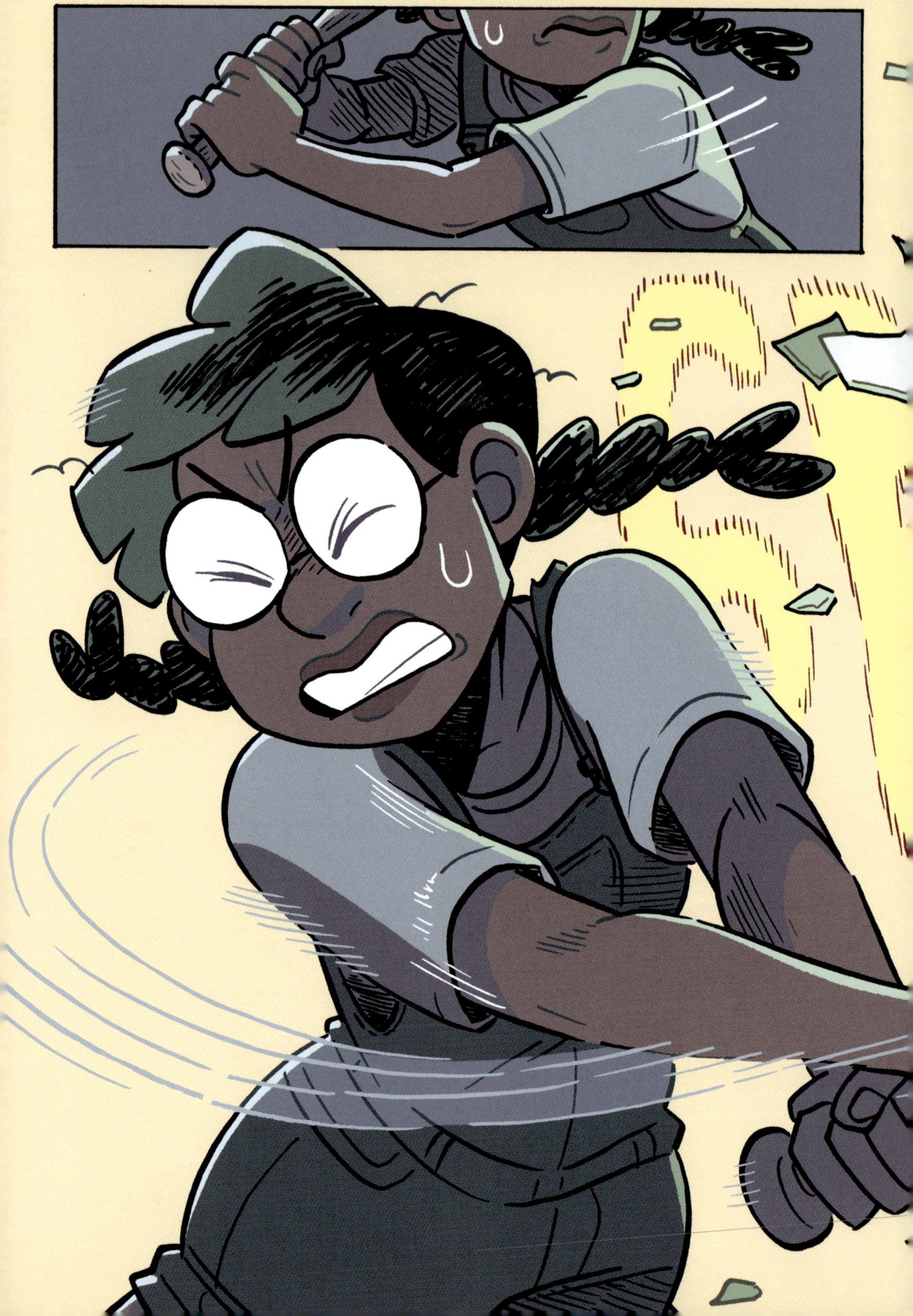

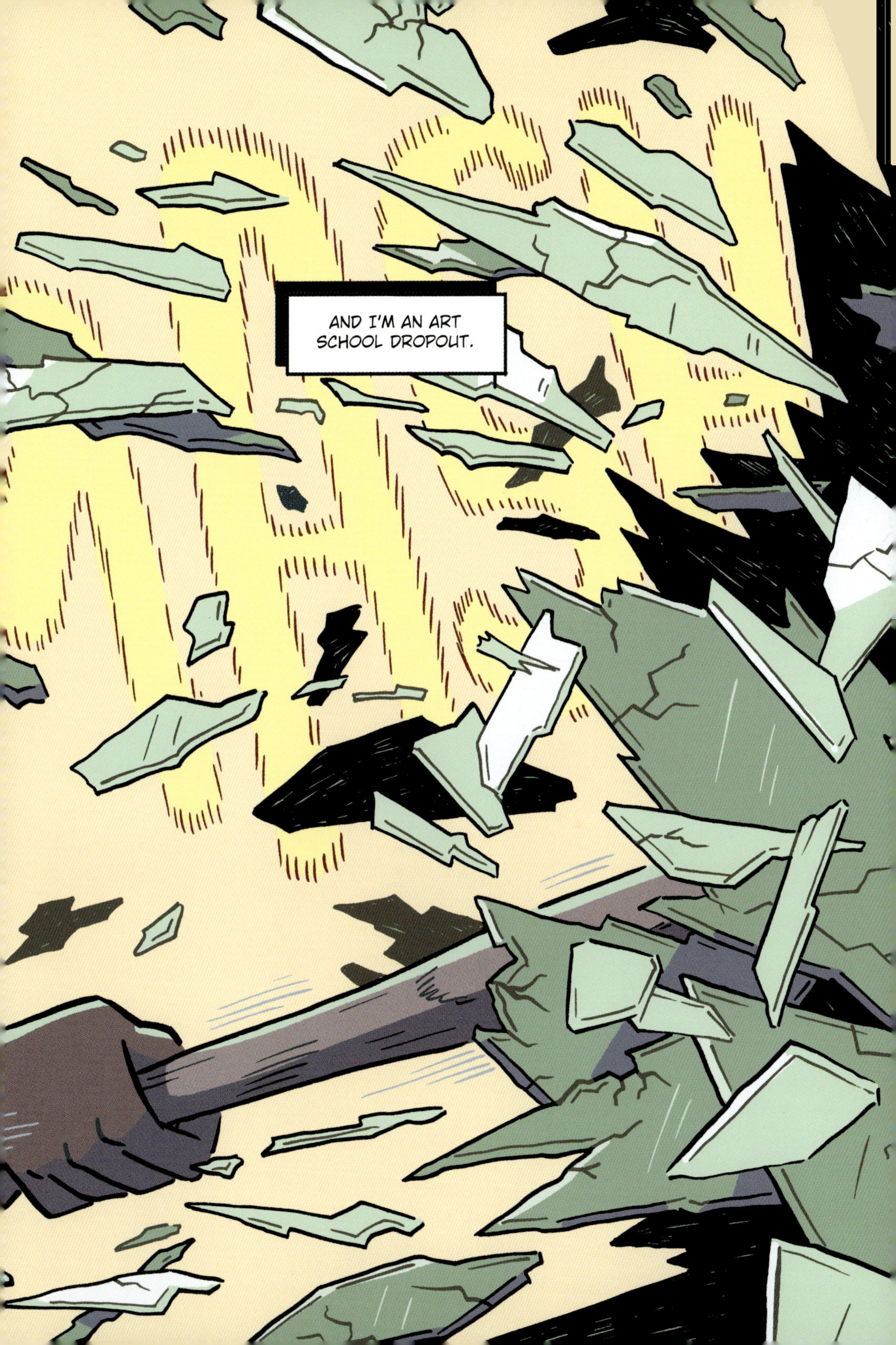
AND I'M AN ART SCHOOL DROPOUT.

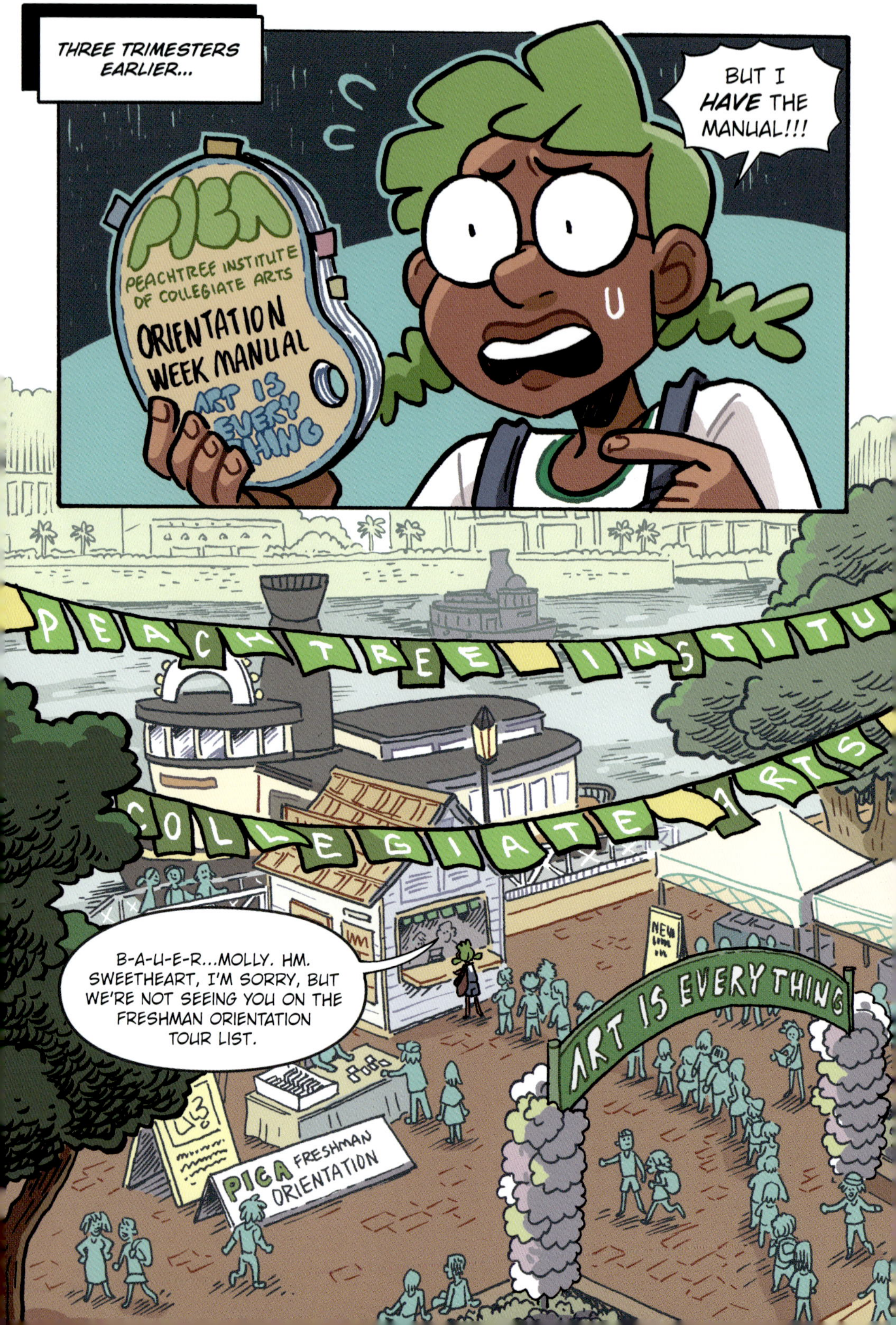
THREE TRIMESTERS EARLIER...
BUT I HAVE THE MANUAL!!!
PICA PEACHTREE INSTITUTE OF COLLEGIATE ARTS ORIENTATION WEEK MANUAL ART IS EVERYTHING
PEACHTREE INSTITUTE COLLEGIATE ARTS
B-A-U-E-R...MOLLY. HM. SWEETHEART, I'M SORRY, BUT WE'RE NOT SEEING YOU ON THE FRESHMAN ORIENTATION TOUR LIST.
ART IS EVERYTHING
PICA FRESHMAN ORIENTATION

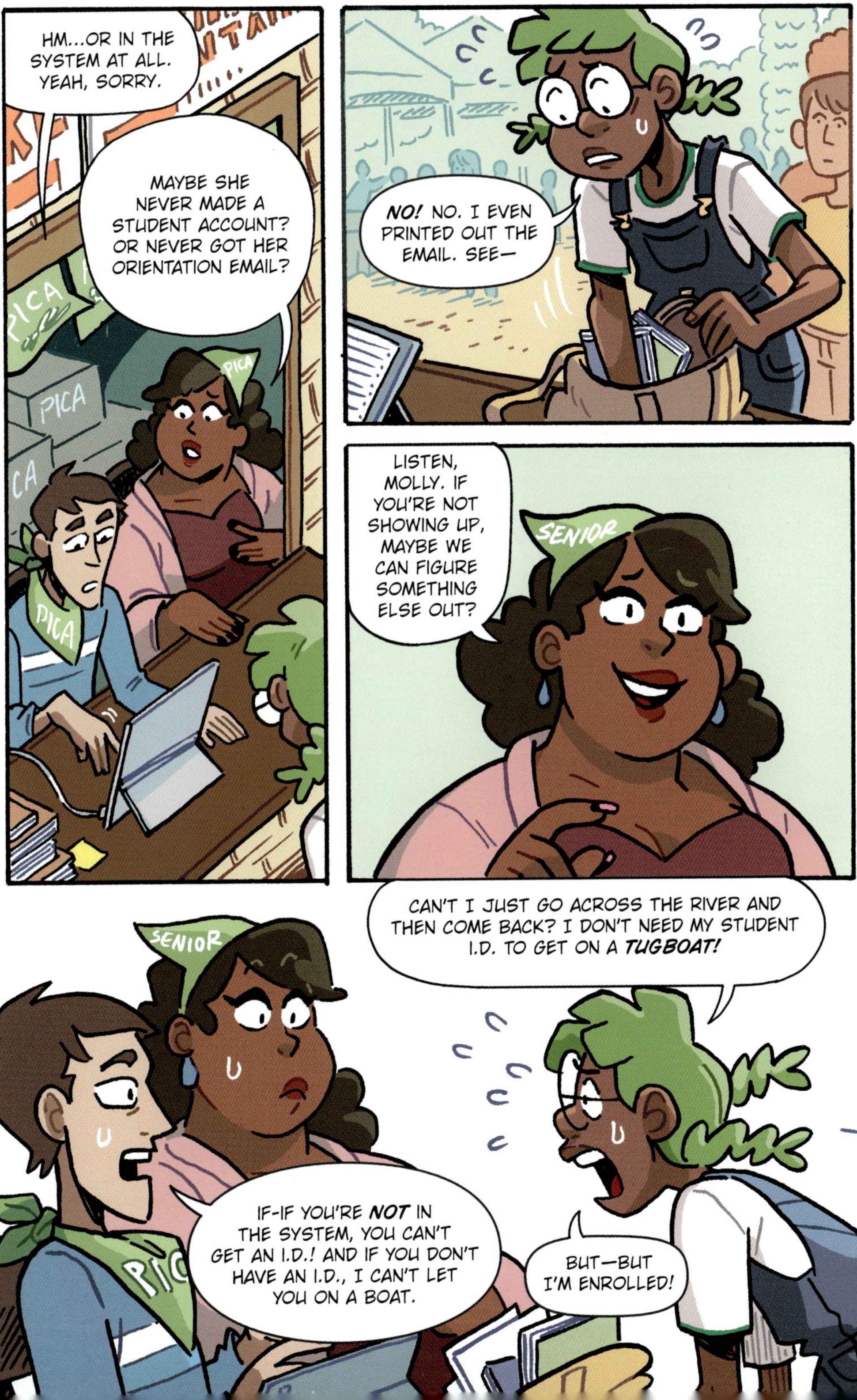
HM...OR IN THE SYSTEM AT ALL. YEAH, SORRY.
MAYBE SHE NEVER MADE A STUDENT ACCOUNT? OR NEVER GOT HER ORIENTATION EMAIL?
PICA
NO! NO. I EVEN PRINTED OUT THE EMAIL. SEE—
LISTEN, MOLLY. IF YOU'RE NOT SHOWING UP, MAYBE WE CAN FIGURE SOMETHING ELSE OUT?
SENIOR
CAN'T I JUST GO ACROSS THE RIVER AND THEN COME BACK? I DON'T NEED MY STUDENT I.D. TO GET ON A TUGBOAT!
SENIOR
IF-IF YOU'RE NOT IN THE SYSTEM, YOU CAN'T GET AN I.D.! AND IF YOU DON'T HAVE AN I.D., I CAN'T LET YOU ON A BOAT.
BUT—BUT I'M ENROLLED!

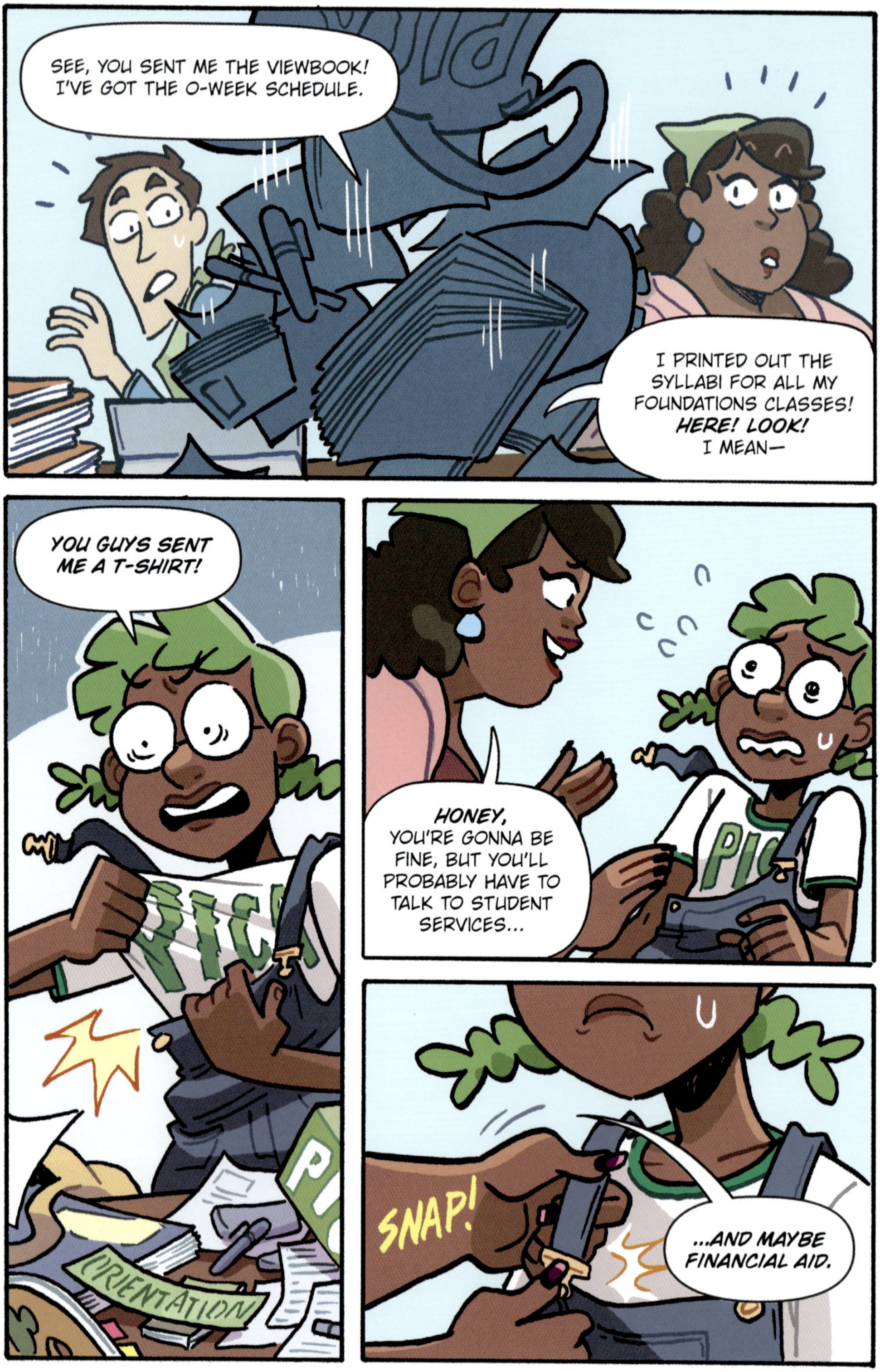
SEE, YOU SENT ME THE VIEWBOOK! I'VE GOT THE O-WEEK SCHEDULE.
I PRINTED OUT THE SYLLABI FOR ALL MY FOUNDATIONS CLASSES! *HERE! LOOK!* I MEAN—
YOU GUYS SENT ME A T-SHIRT!
PIC
ORIENTATION
HONEY, YOU'RE GONNA BE FINE, BUT YOU'LL PROBABLY HAVE TO TALK TO STUDENT SERVICES...
SNAP!
...AND MAYBE FINANCIAL AID.

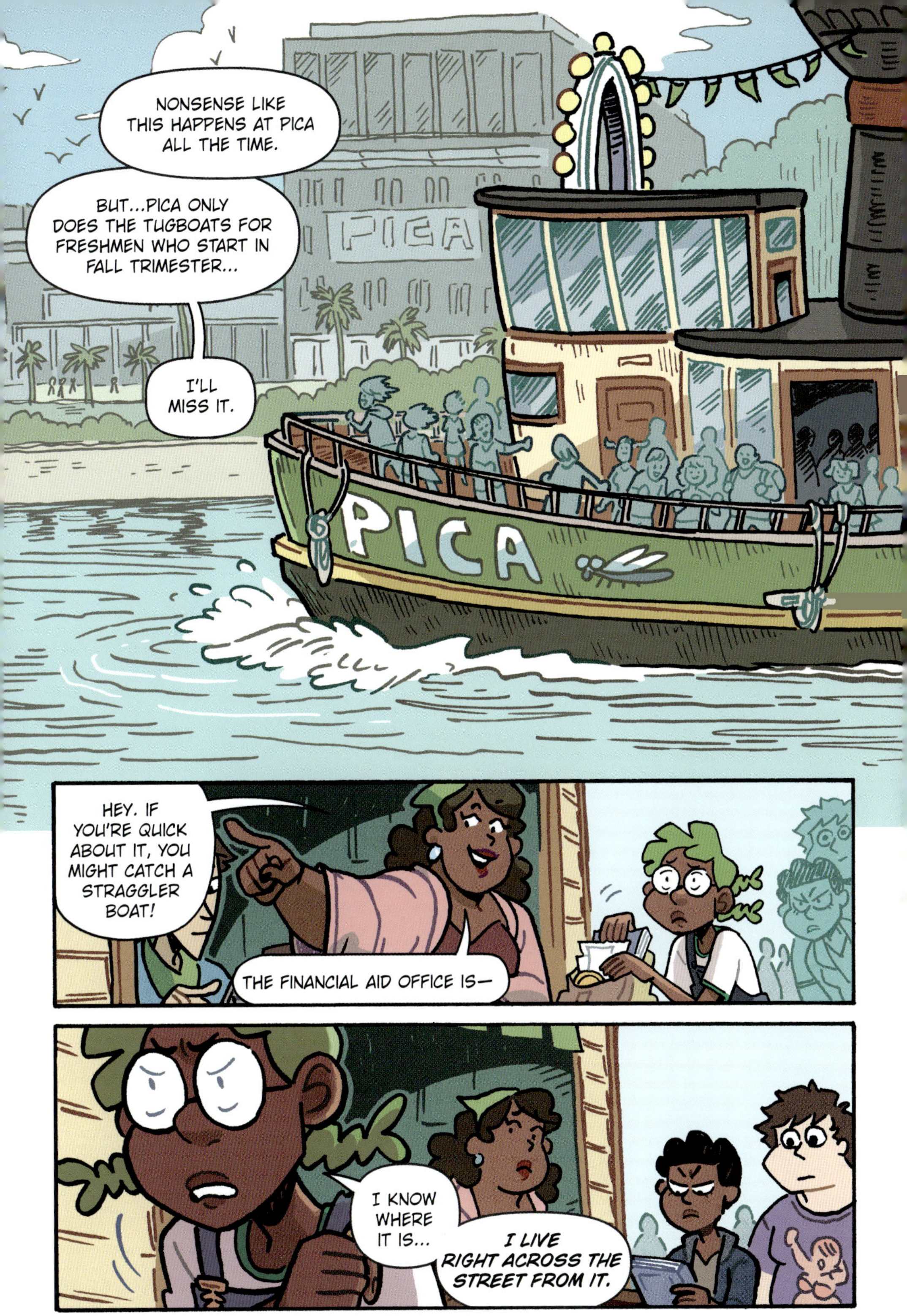
NONSENSE LIKE THIS HAPPENS AT PICA ALL THE TIME.
BUT...PICA ONLY DOES THE TUGBOATS FOR FRESHMEN WHO START IN FALL TRIMESTER...
I'LL MISS IT.
PICA
PICA
HEY. IF YOU'RE QUICK ABOUT IT, YOU MIGHT CATCH A STRAGGLER BOAT!
THE FINANCIAL AID OFFICE IS—
I KNOW WHERE IT IS...
I LIVE RIGHT ACROSS THE STREET FROM IT.

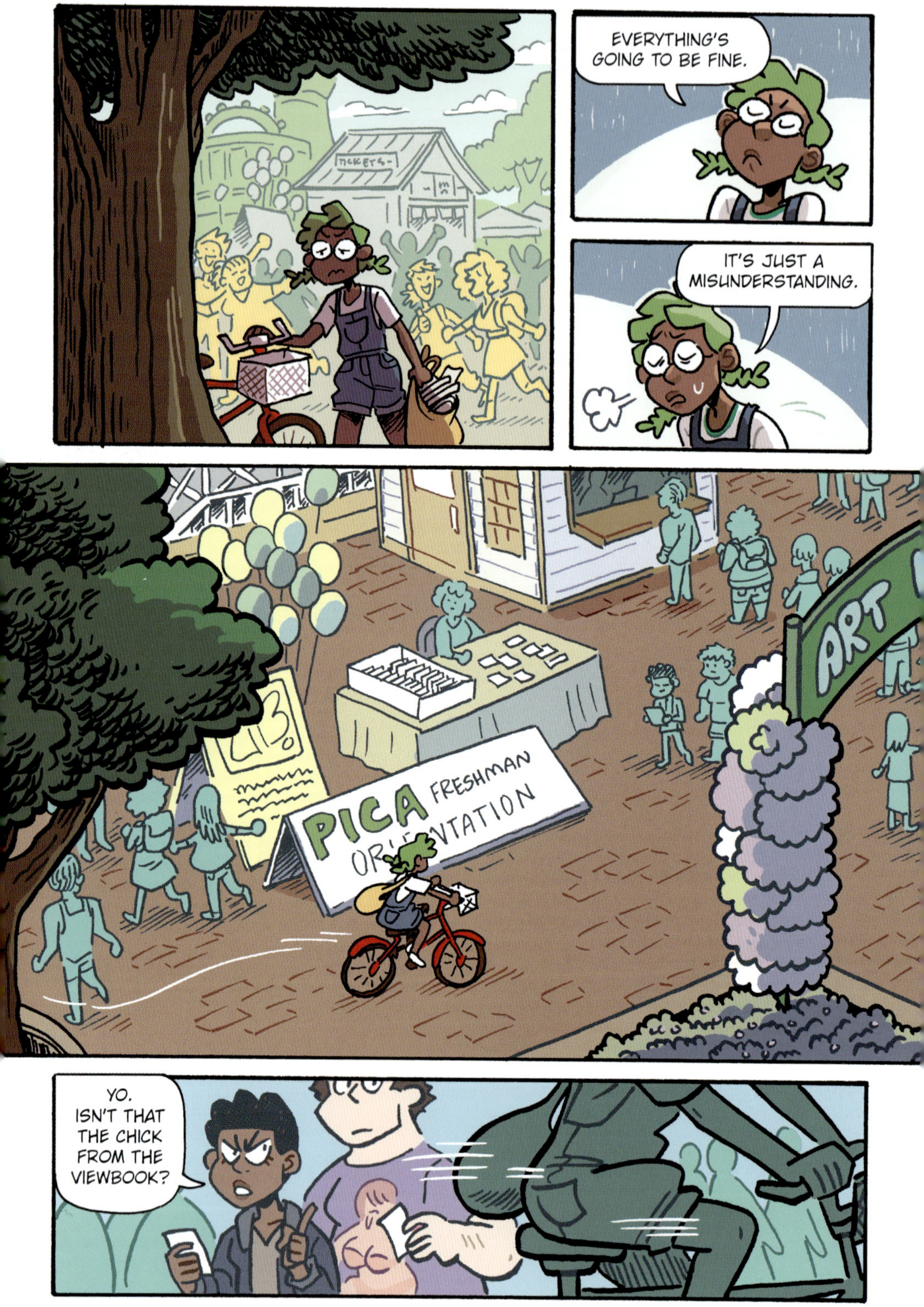
TICKETS
EVERYTHING'S GOING TO BE FINE.
IT'S JUST A MISUNDERSTANDING.
PICA FRESHMAN ORIENTATION
ART
YO. ISN'T THAT THE CHICK FROM THE VIEWBOOK?

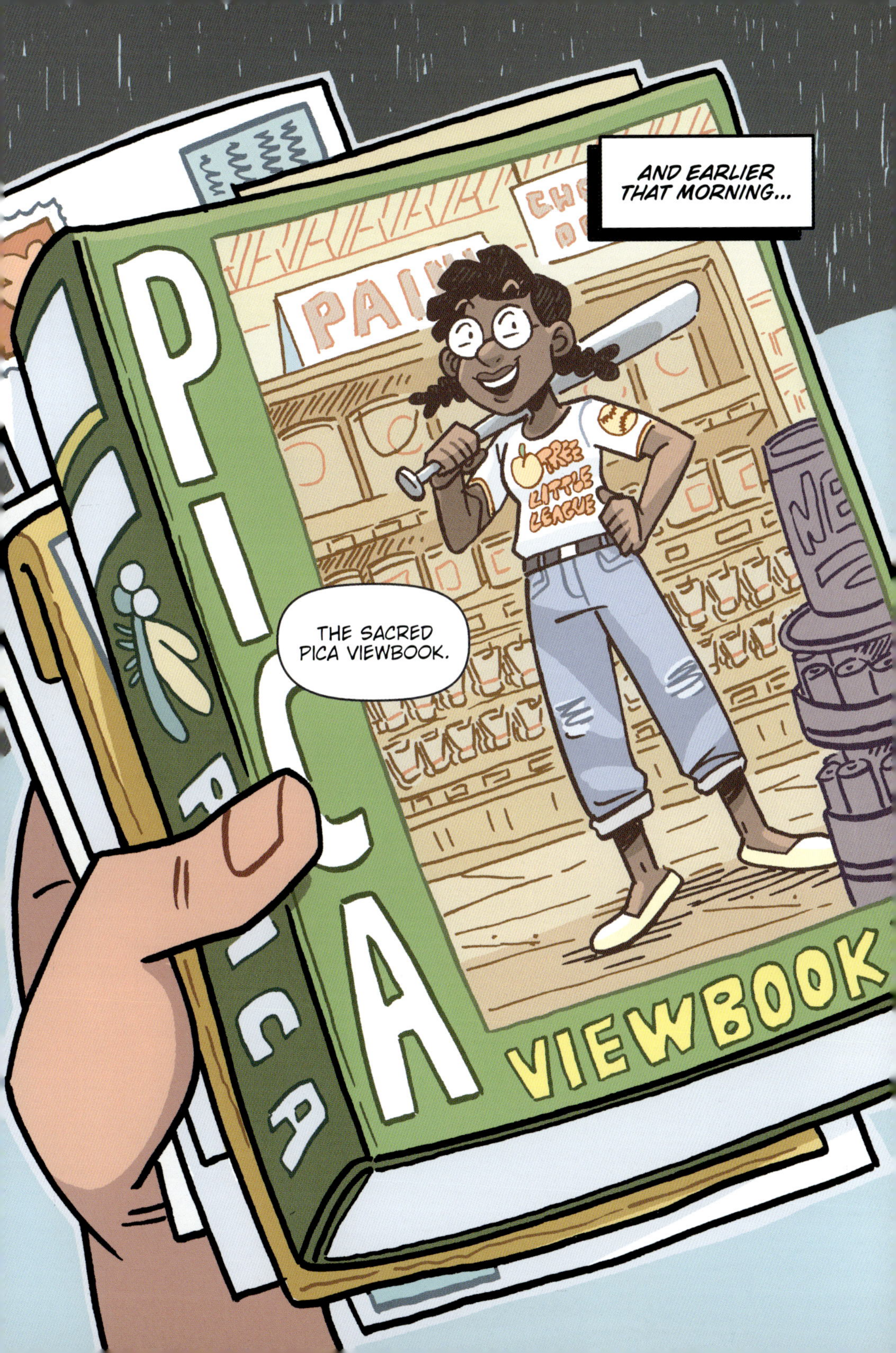
AND EARLIER THAT MORNING...
THE SACRED PICA VIEWBOOK.
PICA
VIEWBOOK
PICA
TREE LITTLE LEAGUE

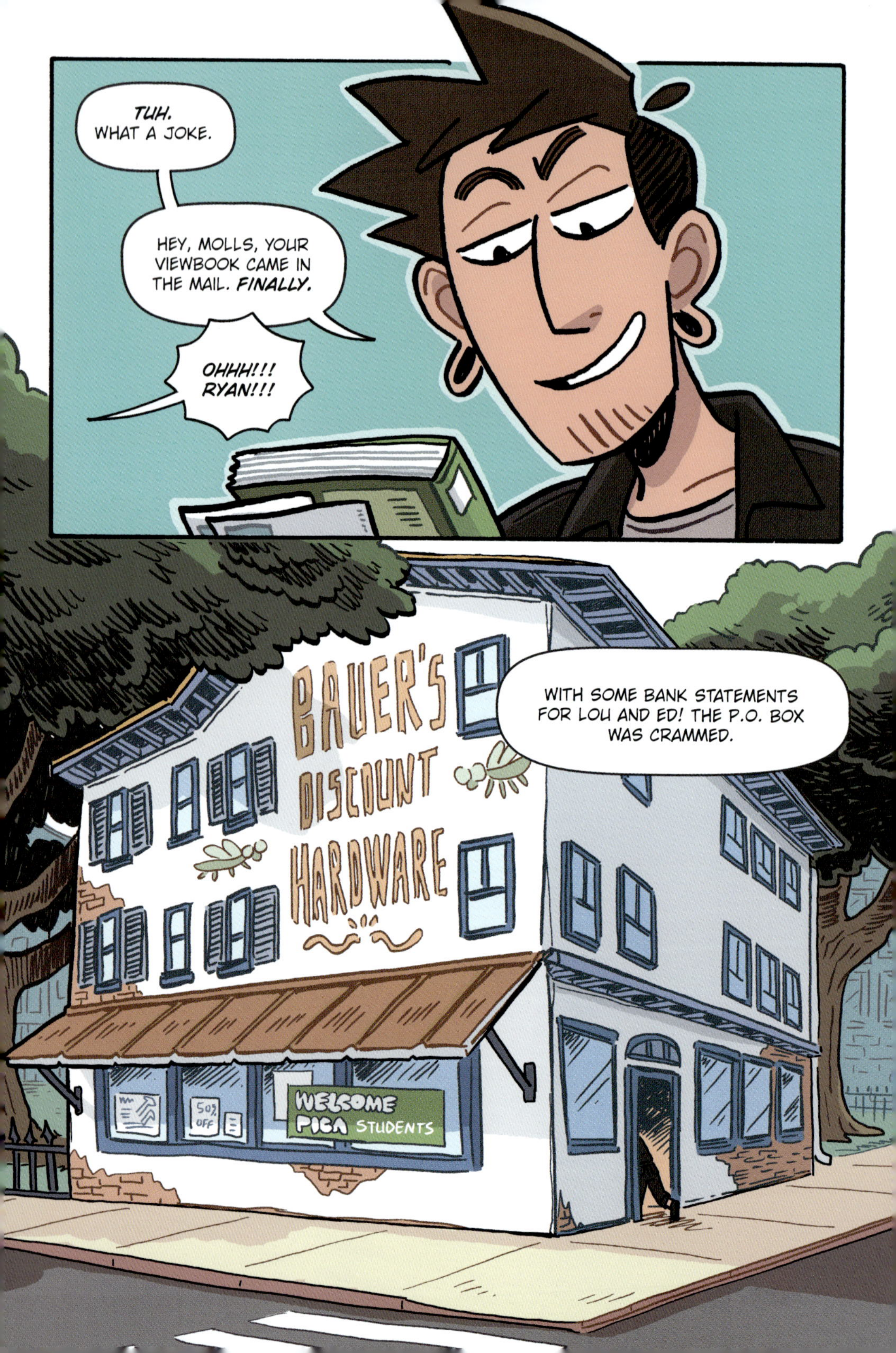
TUH.
WHAT A JOKE.
HEY, MOLLS, YOUR VIEWBOOK CAME IN THE MAIL. FINALLY.
OHHH!!! RYAN!!!
BAUER'S DISCOUNT HARDWARE
WITH SOME BANK STATEMENTS FOR LOU AND ED! THE P.O. BOX WAS CRAMMED.
50% OFF
WELCOME PICA STUDENTS

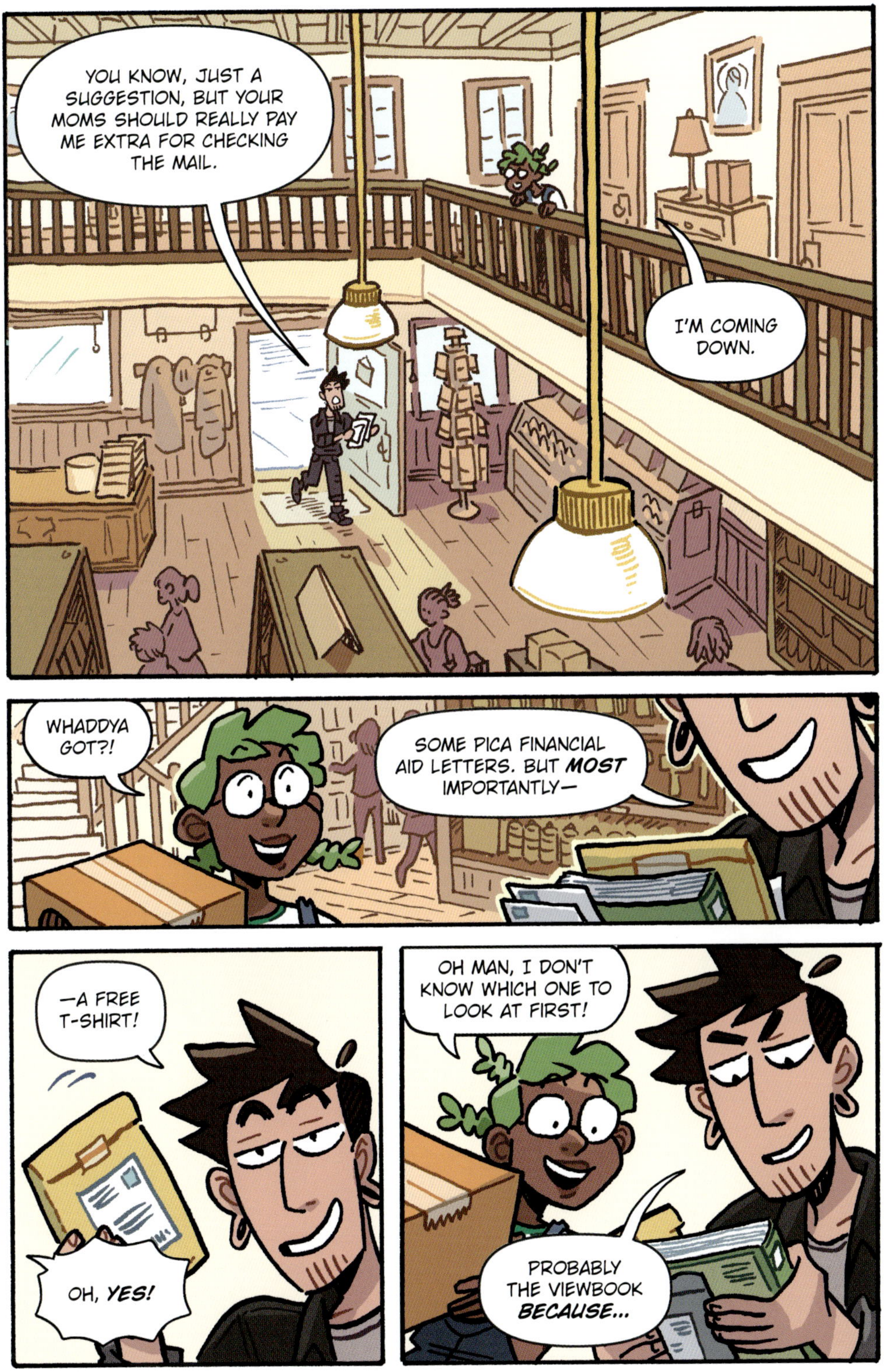

YOU KNOW, JUST A SUGGESTION, BUT YOUR MOMS SHOULD REALLY PAY ME EXTRA FOR CHECKING THE MAIL.
I'M COMING DOWN.
WHADDYA GOT?!
SOME PICA FINANCIAL AID LETTERS. BUT *MOST* IMPORTANTLY—
—A FREE T-SHIRT!
OH, *YES!*
OH MAN, I DON'T KNOW WHICH ONE TO LOOK AT FIRST!
PROBABLY THE VIEWBOOK *BECAUSE...*

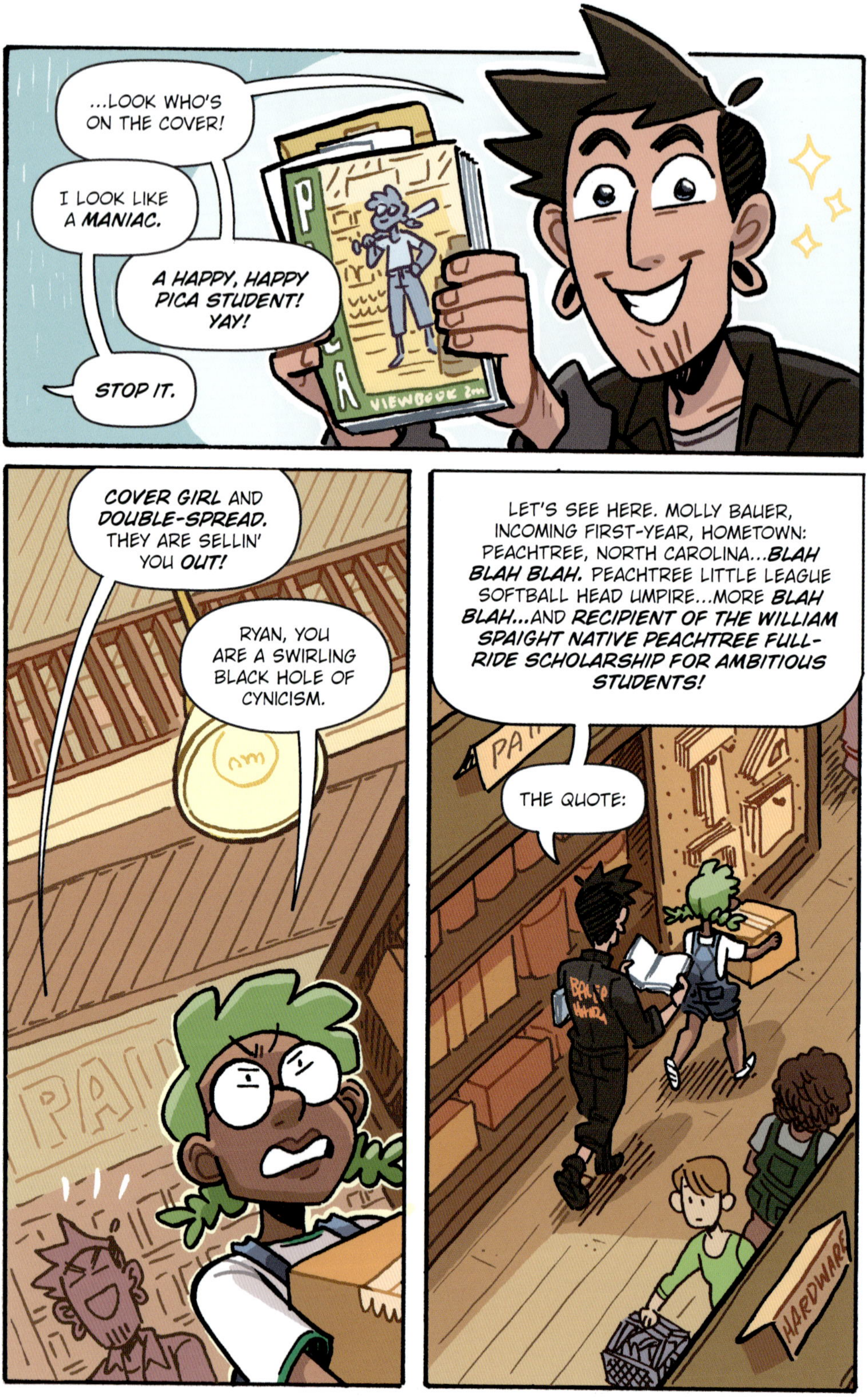
...LOOK WHO'S ON THE COVER!
I LOOK LIKE A MANIAC.
A HAPPY, HAPPY PICA STUDENT! YAY!
STOP IT.
VIEWBOOK
COVER GIRL AND DOUBLE-SPREAD. THEY ARE SELLIN' YOU OUT!
RYAN, YOU ARE A SWIRLING BLACK HOLE OF CYNICISM.
LET'S SEE HERE. MOLLY BAUER, INCOMING FIRST-YEAR, HOMETOWN: PEACHTREE, NORTH CAROLINA...BLAH BLAH BLAH. PEACHTREE LITTLE LEAGUE SOFTBALL HEAD UMPIRE...MORE BLAH BLAH...AND RECIPIENT OF THE WILLIAM SPAIGHT NATIVE PEACHTREE FULL-RIDE SCHOLARSHIP FOR AMBITIOUS STUDENTS!
THE QUOTE:
HARDWARE

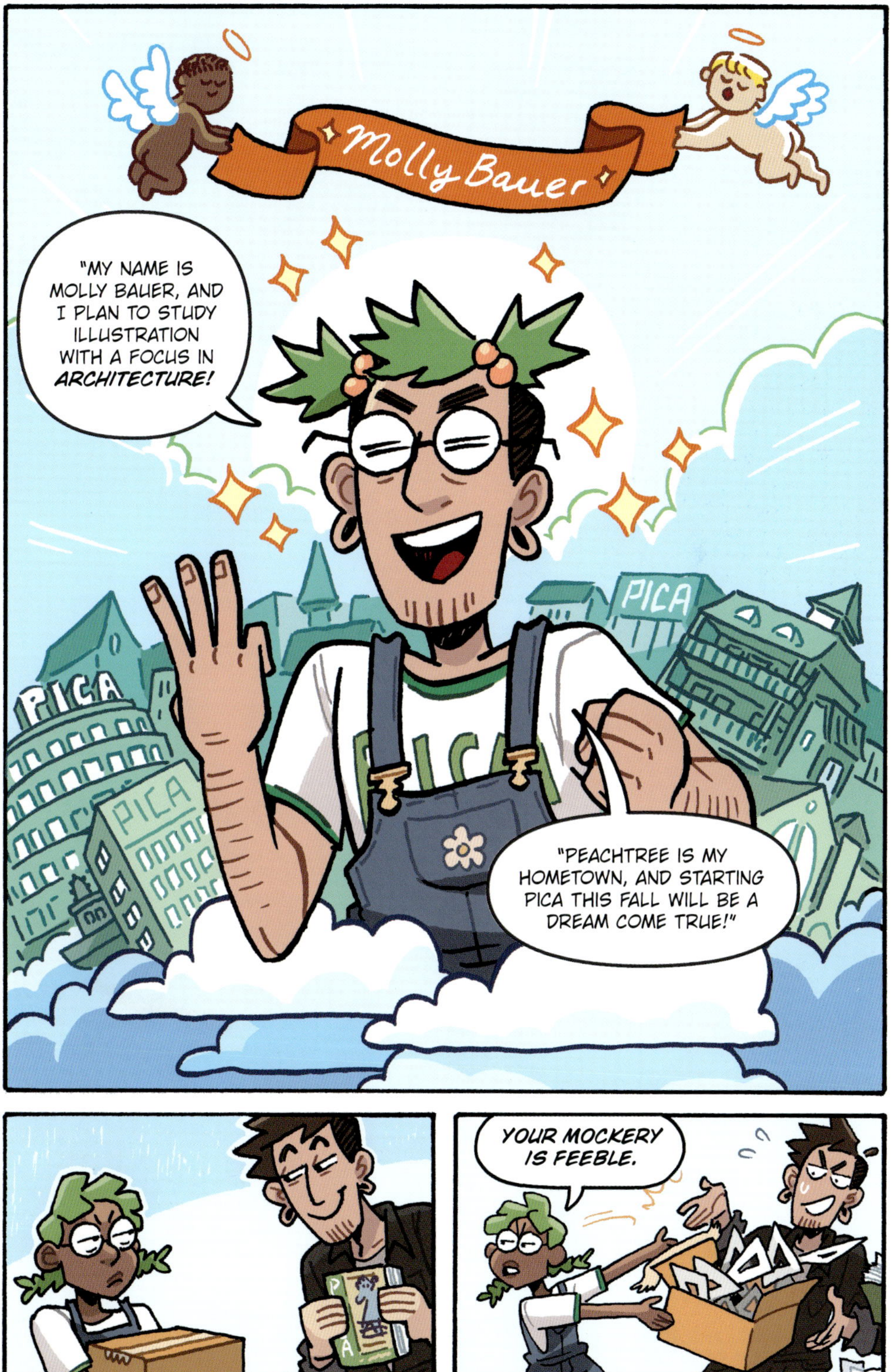
Molly Bauer
"MY NAME IS MOLLY BAUER, AND I PLAN TO STUDY ILLUSTRATION WITH A FOCUS IN ARCHITECTURE!
"PEACHTREE IS MY HOMETOWN, AND STARTING PICA THIS FALL WILL BE A DREAM COME TRUE!"
YOUR MOCKERY IS FEEBLE.

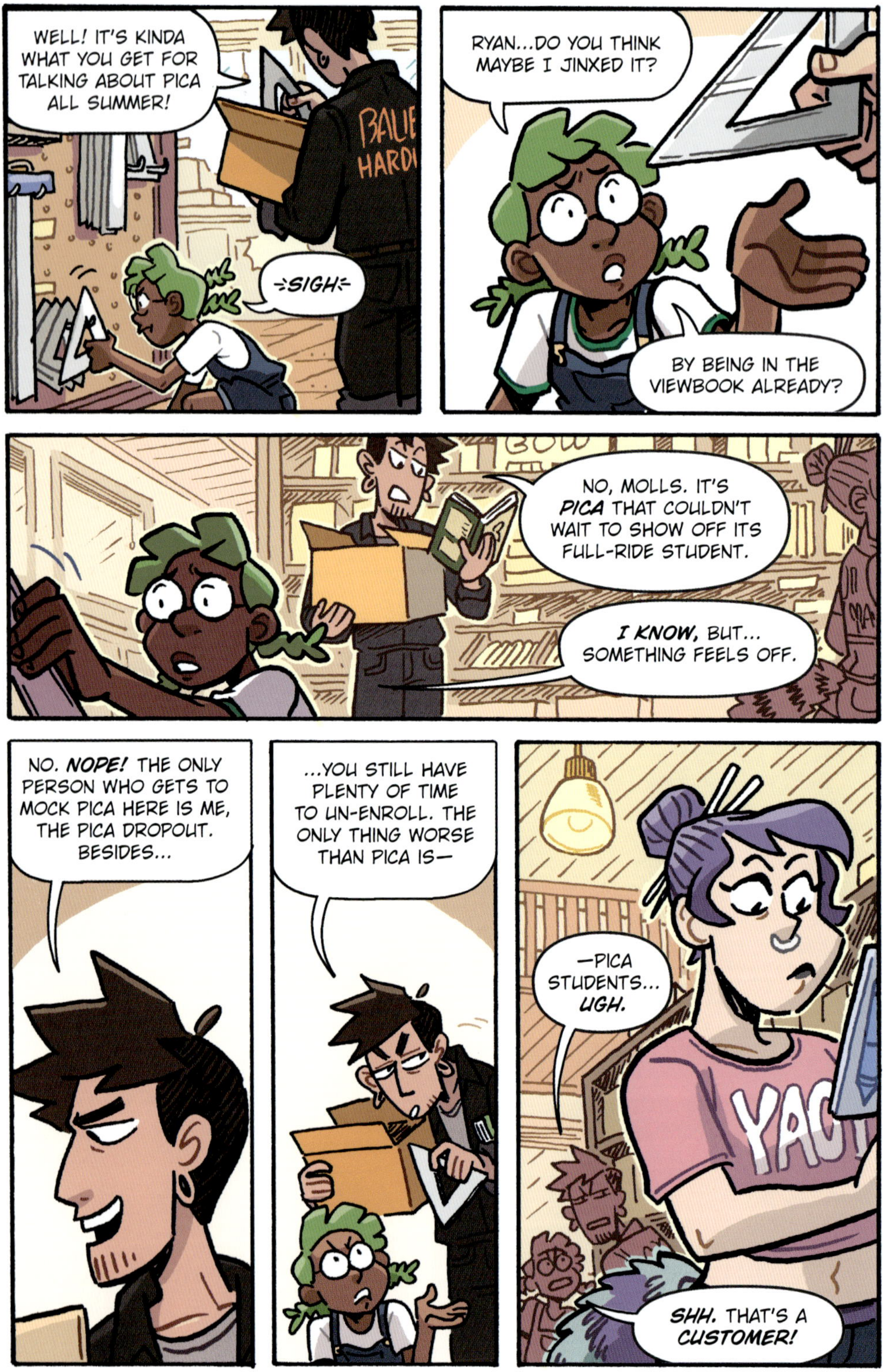
WELL! IT'S KINDA WHAT YOU GET FOR TALKING ABOUT PICA ALL SUMMER!
BALIE
HARD
SIGH
RYAN...DO YOU THINK MAYBE I JINXED IT?
BY BEING IN THE VIEWBOOK ALREADY?
NO, MOLLS. IT'S PICA THAT COULDN'T WAIT TO SHOW OFF ITS FULL-RIDE STUDENT.
I KNOW, BUT... SOMETHING FEELS OFF.
NO. NOPE! THE ONLY PERSON WHO GETS TO MOCK PICA HERE IS ME, THE PICA DROPOUT. BESIDES...
...YOU STILL HAVE PLENTY OF TIME TO UN-ENROLL. THE ONLY THING WORSE THAN PICA IS—
—PICA STUDENTS... UGH.
YAC
SHH. THAT'S A CUSTOMER!

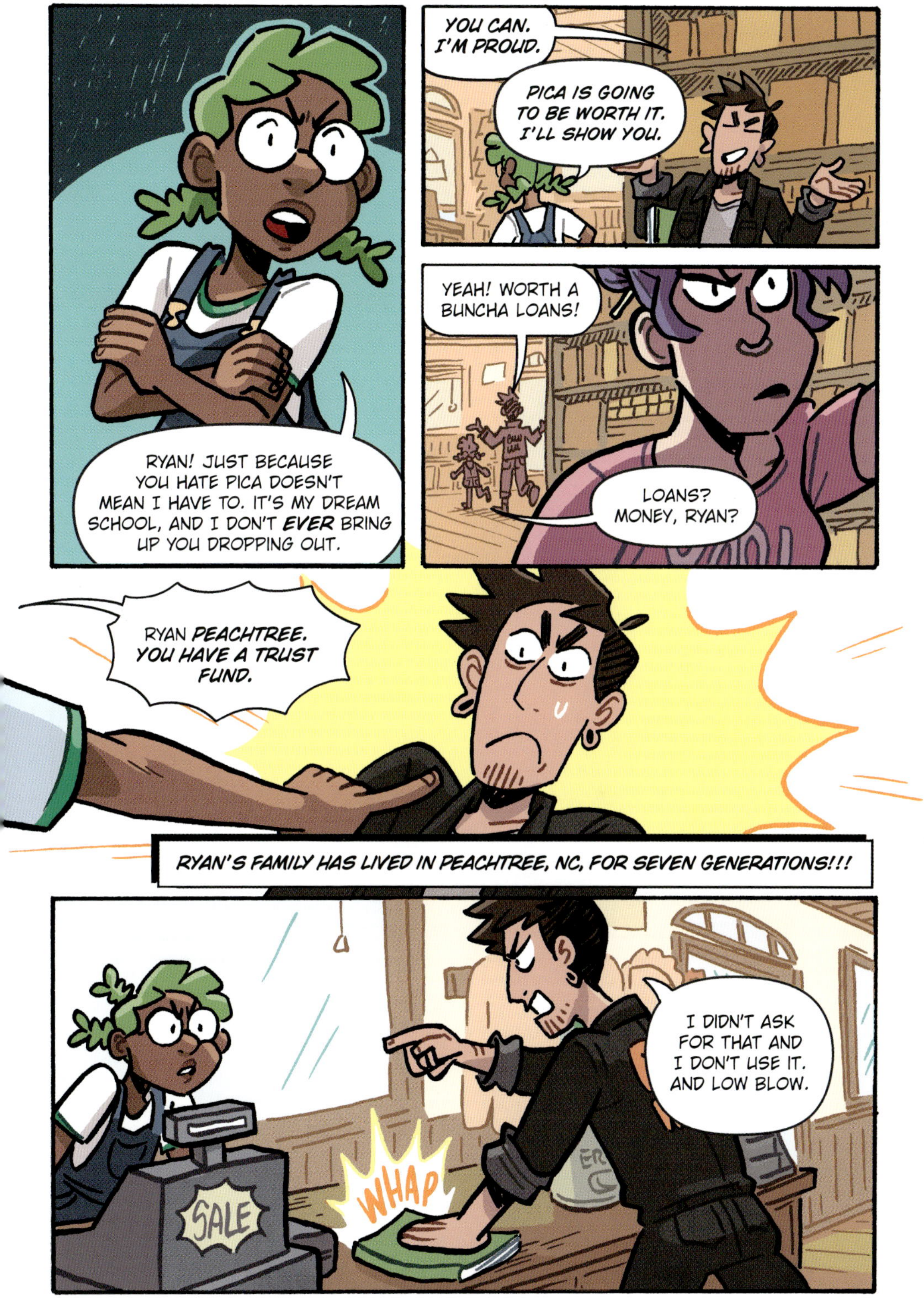
RYAN! JUST BECAUSE YOU HATE PICA DOESN'T MEAN I HAVE TO. IT'S MY DREAM SCHOOL, AND I DON'T *EVER* BRING UP YOU DROPPING OUT.
YOU CAN. I'M PROUD.
PICA IS GOING TO BE WORTH IT. I'LL SHOW YOU.
YEAH! WORTH A BUNCHA LOANS!
LOANS? MONEY, RYAN?
RYAN *PEACHTREE. YOU HAVE A TRUST FUND.*
RYAN'S FAMILY HAS LIVED IN PEACHTREE, NC, FOR SEVEN GENERATIONS!!!
I DIDN'T ASK FOR THAT AND I DON'T USE IT. AND LOW BLOW.
SALE
WHAP

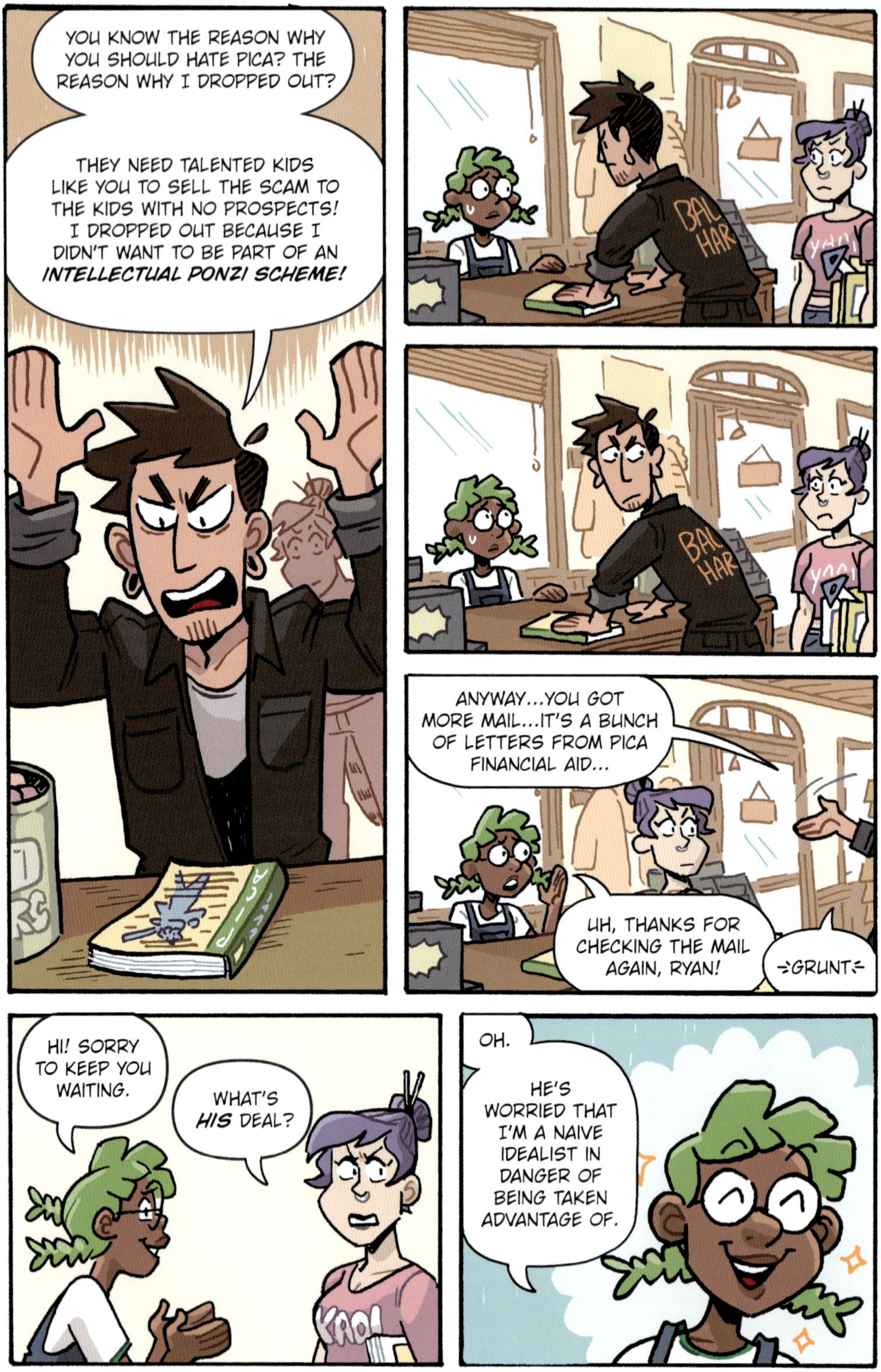

YOU KNOW THE REASON WHY YOU SHOULD HATE PICA? THE REASON WHY I DROPPED OUT?
THEY NEED TALENTED KIDS LIKE YOU TO SELL THE SCAM TO THE KIDS WITH NO PROSPECTS! I DROPPED OUT BECAUSE I DIDN'T WANT TO BE PART OF AN ***INTELLECTUAL PONZI SCHEME!***
BAL HAR
BAL HAR
ANYWAY... YOU GOT MORE MAIL... IT'S A BUNCH OF LETTERS FROM PICA FINANCIAL AID...
UH, THANKS FOR CHECKING THE MAIL AGAIN, RYAN!
GRUNT
HI! SORRY TO KEEP YOU WAITING.
WHAT'S ***HIS*** DEAL?
OH.
HE'S WORRIED THAT I'M A NAIVE IDEALIST IN DANGER OF BEING TAKEN ADVANTAGE OF.

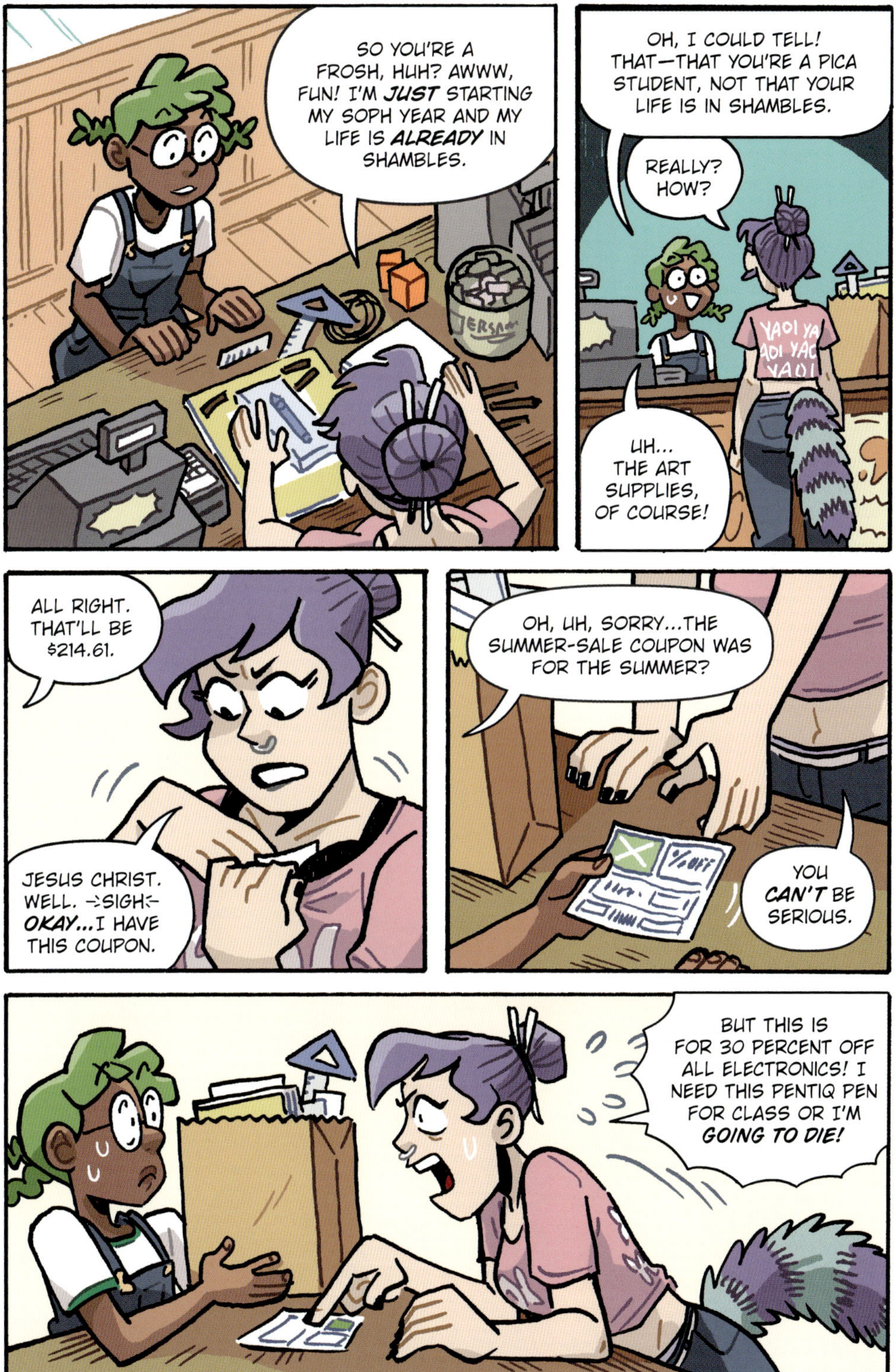
SO YOU'RE A FROSH, HUH? AWWW, FUN! I'M JUST STARTING MY SOPH YEAR AND MY LIFE IS ALREADY IN SHAMBLES.
OH, I COULD TELL! THAT—THAT YOU'RE A PICA STUDENT, NOT THAT YOUR LIFE IS IN SHAMBLES.
REALLY? HOW?
YAOI YAOI YAOI YAOI
UH... THE ART SUPPLIES, OF COURSE!
ALL RIGHT. THAT'LL BE $214.61.
JESUS CHRIST. WELL. ⇒SIGH⇐ OKAY...I HAVE THIS COUPON.
OH, UH, SORRY...THE SUMMER-SALE COUPON WAS FOR THE SUMMER?
YOU CAN'T BE SERIOUS.
BUT THIS IS FOR 30 PERCENT OFF ALL ELECTRONICS! I NEED THIS PENTIQ PEN FOR CLASS OR I'M GOING TO DIE!

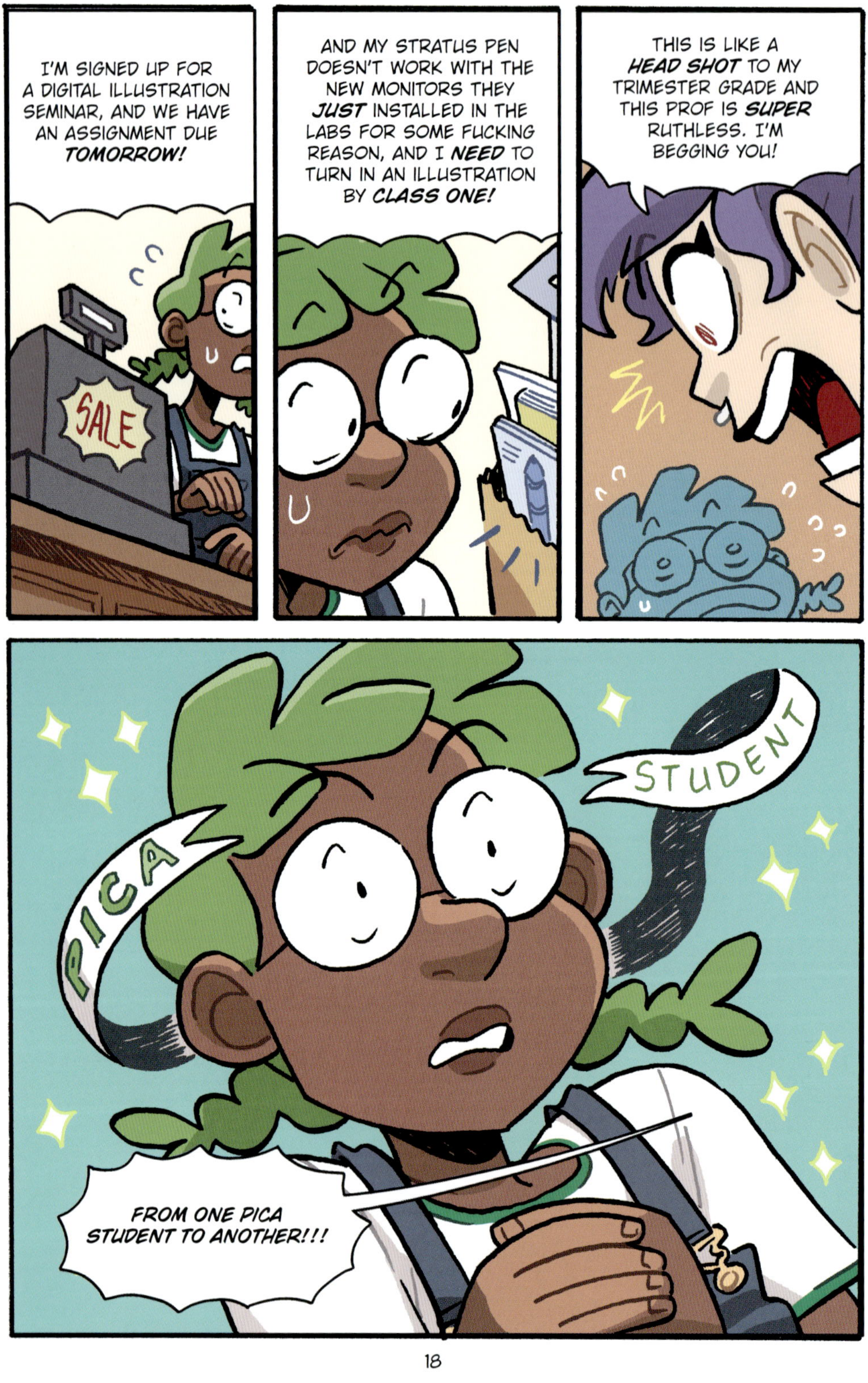
I'M SIGNED UP FOR A DIGITAL ILLUSTRATION SEMINAR, AND WE HAVE AN ASSIGNMENT DUE ***TOMORROW!***
SALE
AND MY STRATUS PEN DOESN'T WORK WITH THE NEW MONITORS THEY ***JUST*** INSTALLED IN THE LABS FOR SOME FUCKING REASON, AND I ***NEED*** TO TURN IN AN ILLUSTRATION BY ***CLASS ONE!***
THIS IS LIKE A ***HEAD SHOT*** TO MY TRIMESTER GRADE AND THIS PROF IS ***SUPER*** RUTHLESS. I'M BEGGING YOU!
PICA
STUDENT
FROM ONE PICA STUDENT TO ANOTHER!!!

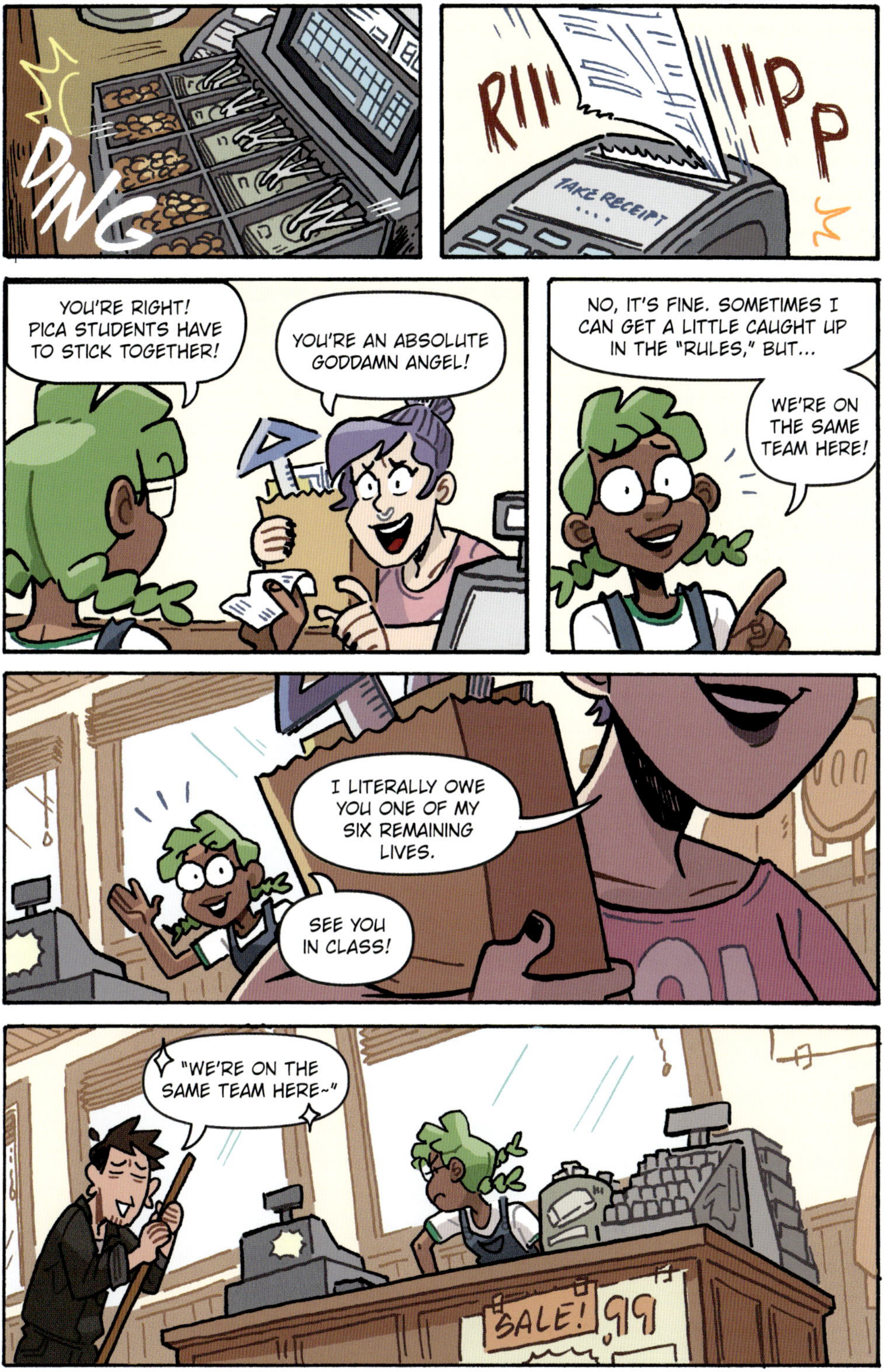
DING
RIIIIPP
TAKE RECEIPT
YOU'RE RIGHT! PICA STUDENTS HAVE TO STICK TOGETHER!
YOU'RE AN ABSOLUTE GODDAMN ANGEL!
NO, IT'S FINE. SOMETIMES I CAN GET A LITTLE CAUGHT UP IN THE "RULES," BUT...
WE'RE ON THE SAME TEAM HERE!
I LITERALLY OWE YOU ONE OF MY SIX REMAINING LIVES.
SEE YOU IN CLASS!
"WE'RE ON THE SAME TEAM HERE~"
SALE! .99

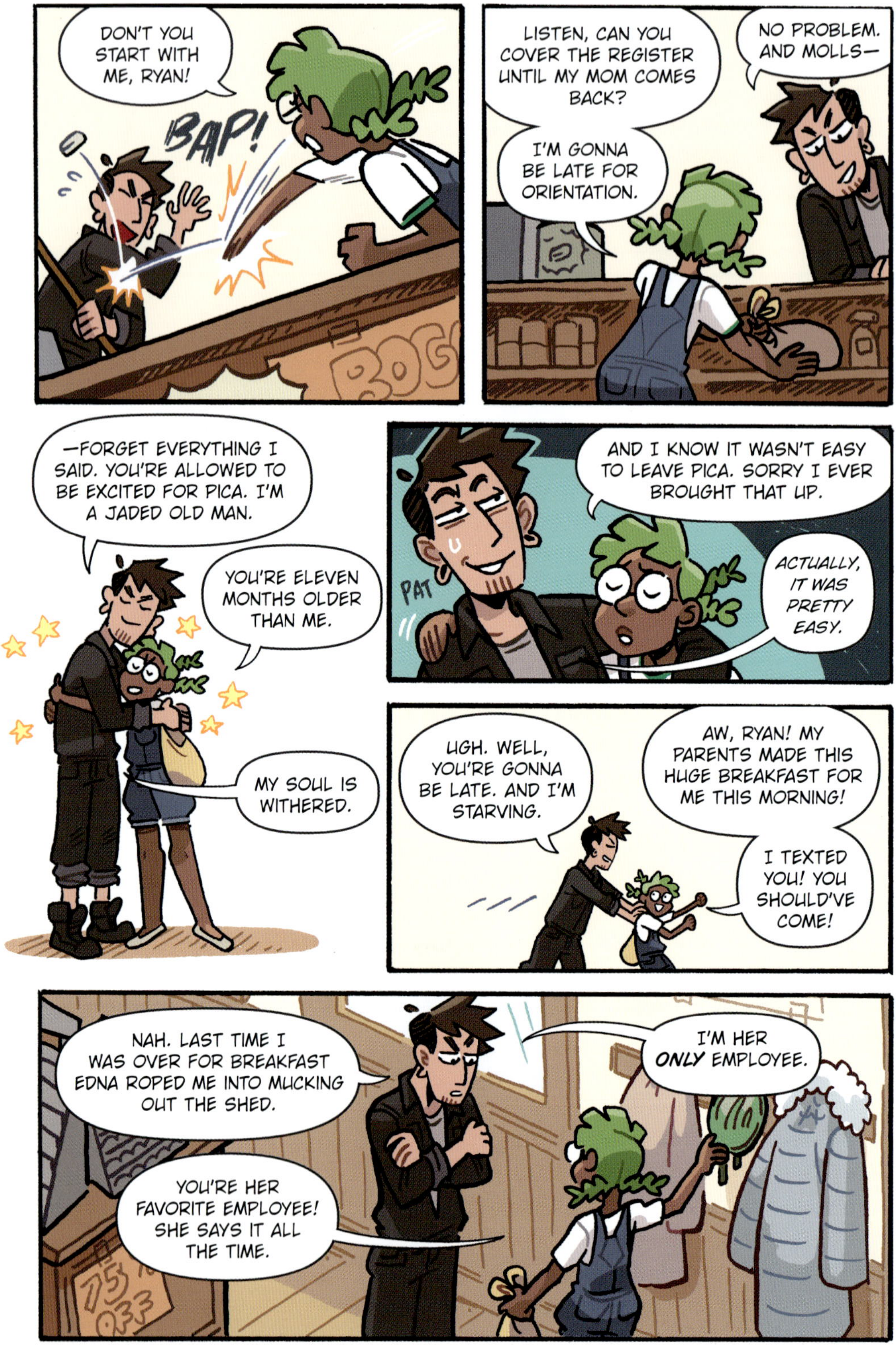
DON'T YOU START WITH ME, RYAN!
BAP!
LISTEN, CAN YOU COVER THE REGISTER UNTIL MY MOM COMES BACK?
I'M GONNA BE LATE FOR ORIENTATION.
NO PROBLEM. AND MOLLS—
—FORGET EVERYTHING I SAID. YOU'RE ALLOWED TO BE EXCITED FOR PICA. I'M A JADED OLD MAN.
YOU'RE ELEVEN MONTHS OLDER THAN ME.
MY SOUL IS WITHERED.
AND I KNOW IT WASN'T EASY TO LEAVE PICA. SORRY I EVER BROUGHT THAT UP.
PAT
ACTUALLY, IT WAS PRETTY EASY.
UGH. WELL, YOU'RE GONNA BE LATE. AND I'M STARVING.
AW, RYAN! MY PARENTS MADE THIS HUGE BREAKFAST FOR ME THIS MORNING!
I TEXTED YOU! YOU SHOULD'VE COME!
NAH. LAST TIME I WAS OVER FOR BREAKFAST EDNA ROPED ME INTO MUCKING OUT THE SHED.
YOU'RE HER FAVORITE EMPLOYEE! SHE SAYS IT ALL THE TIME.
I'M HER *ONLY* EMPLOYEE.

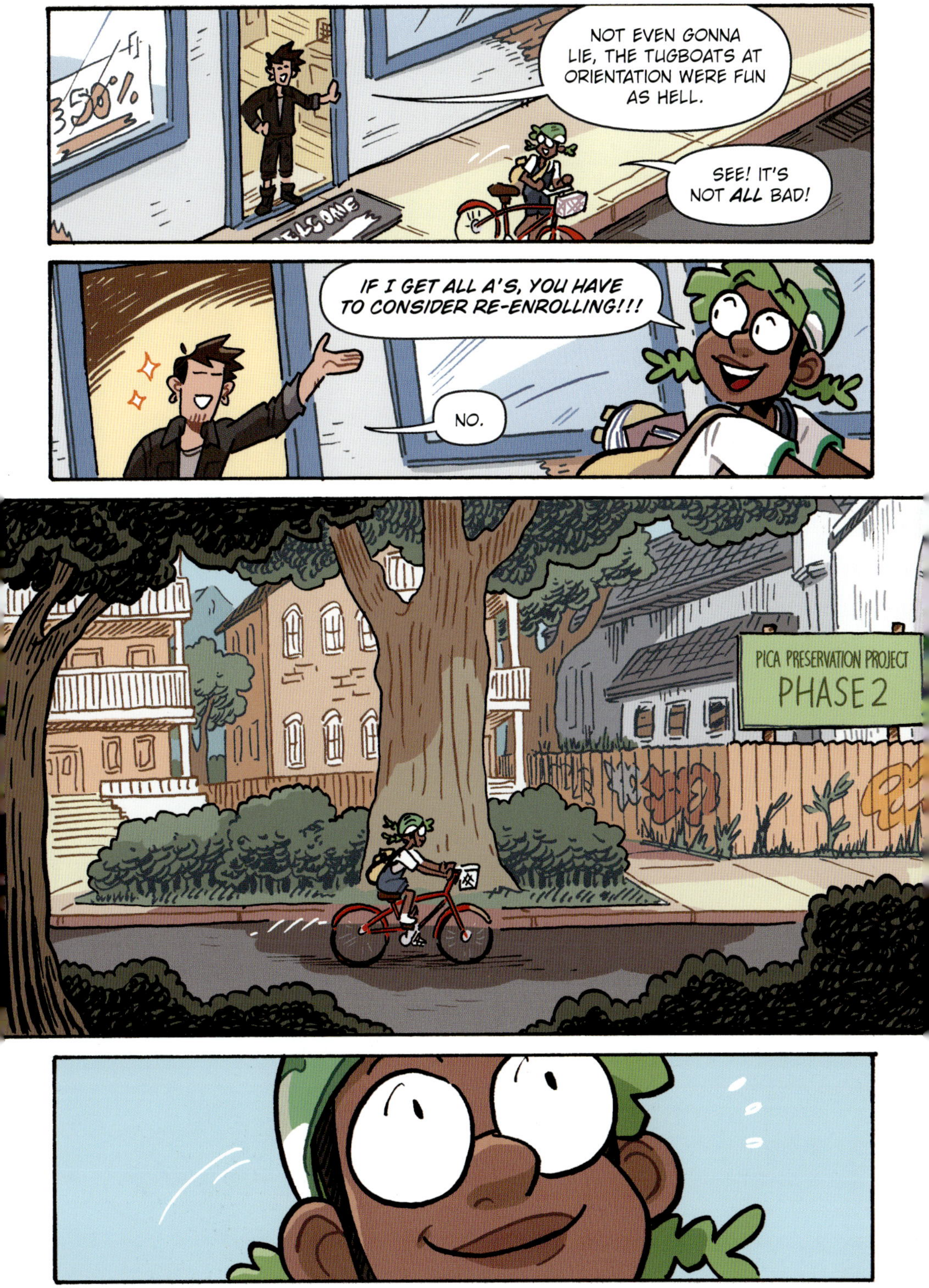

350%
WELCOME
NOT EVEN GONNA LIE, THE TUGBOATS AT ORIENTATION WERE FUN AS HELL.
SEE! IT'S NOT ALL BAD!
IF I GET ALL A'S, YOU HAVE TO CONSIDER RE-ENROLLING!!!
NO.
PICA PRESERVATION PROJECT
PHASE 2

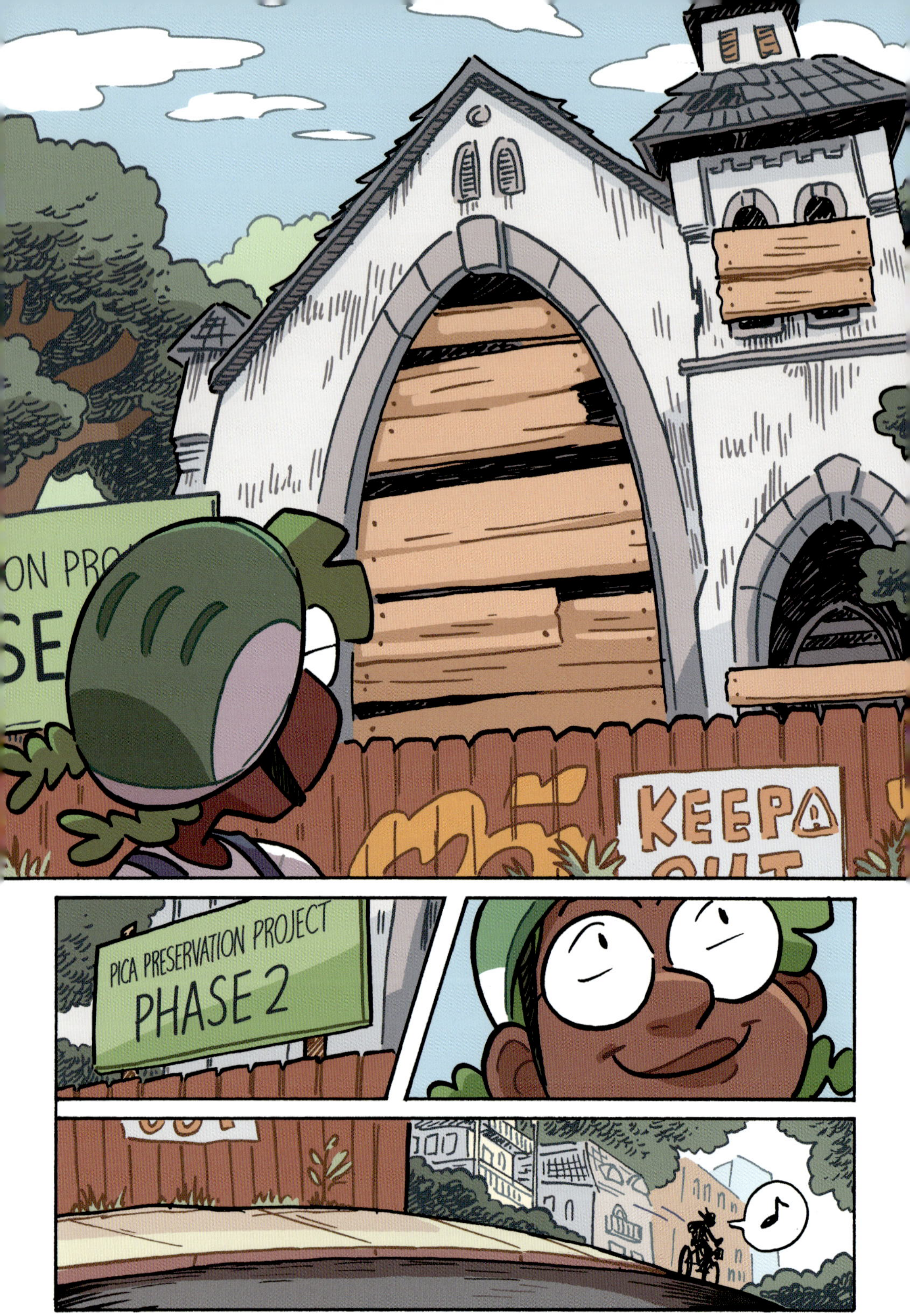
KEEP
PICA PRESERVATION PROJECT
PHASE 2

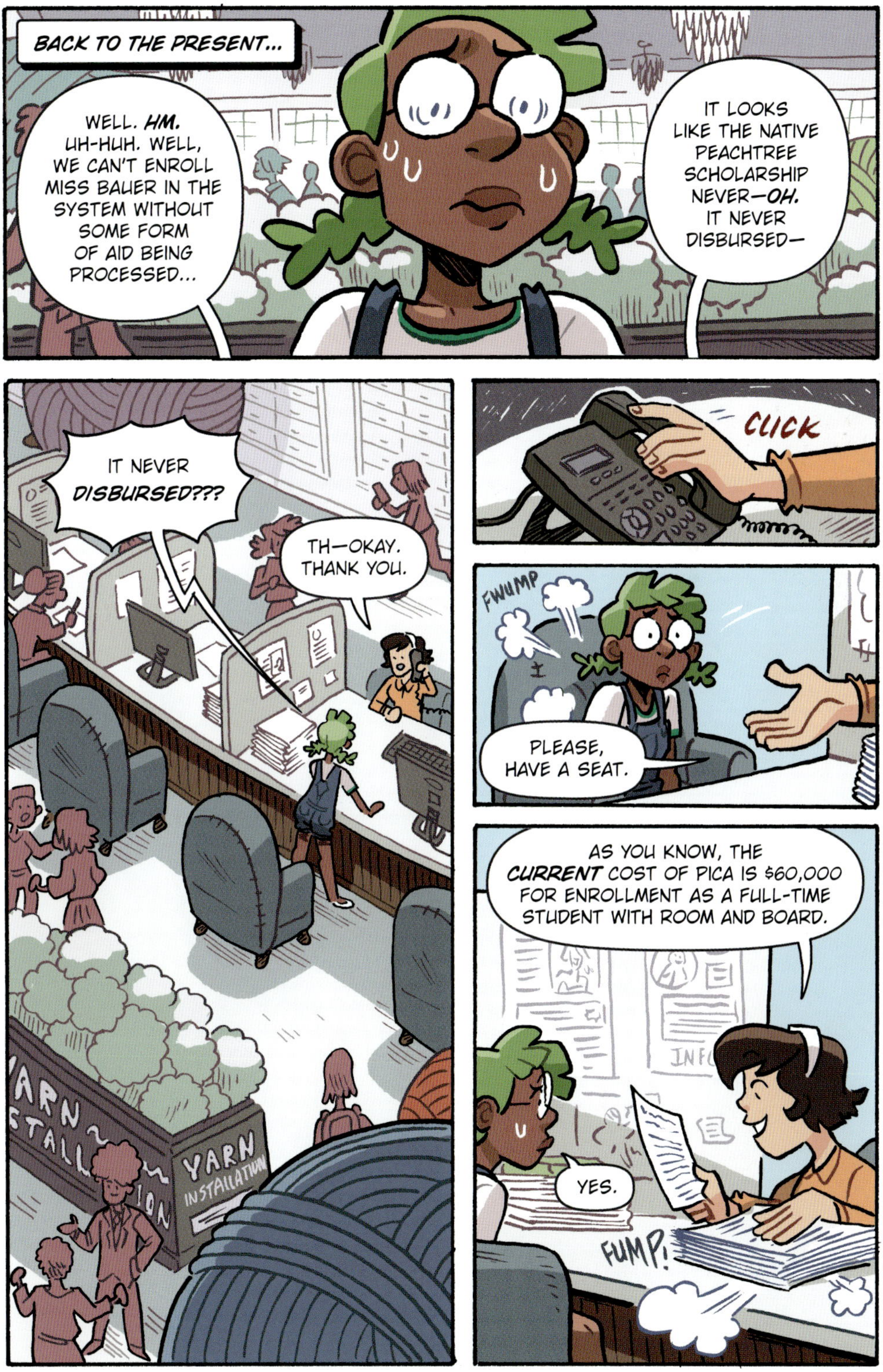
BACK TO THE PRESENT...
WELL. HM. UH-HUH. WELL, WE CAN'T ENROLL MISS BAUER IN THE SYSTEM WITHOUT SOME FORM OF AID BEING PROCESSED...
IT LOOKS LIKE THE NATIVE PEACHTREE SCHOLARSHIP NEVER—OH. IT NEVER DISBURSED—
IT NEVER DISBURSED???
TH—OKAY. THANK YOU.
YARN INSTALLATION
YARN INSTALLATION
CLICK
FWUMP
PLEASE, HAVE A SEAT.
AS YOU KNOW, THE CURRENT COST OF PICA IS $60,000 FOR ENROLLMENT AS A FULL-TIME STUDENT WITH ROOM AND BOARD.
YES.
FUMP!

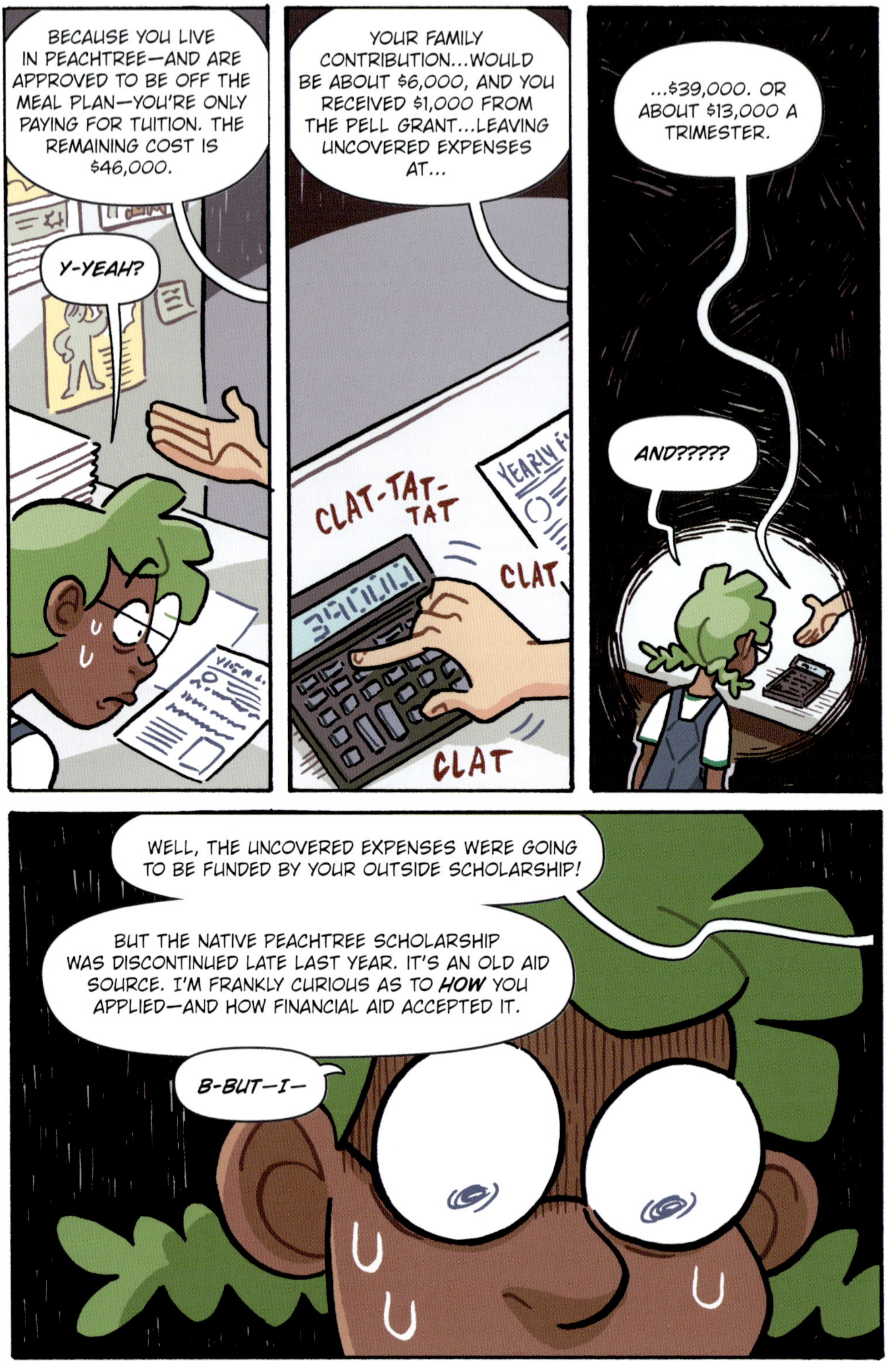
BECAUSE YOU LIVE IN PEACHTREE—AND ARE APPROVED TO BE OFF THE MEAL PLAN—YOU'RE ONLY PAYING FOR TUITION. THE REMAINING COST IS $46,000.
Y-YEAH?
YOUR FAMILY CONTRIBUTION...WOULD BE ABOUT $6,000, AND YOU RECEIVED $1,000 FROM THE PELL GRANT...LEAVING UNCOVERED EXPENSES AT...
CLAT-TAT-TAT
CLAT
CLAT
...$39,000. OR ABOUT $13,000 A TRIMESTER.
AND?????
WELL, THE UNCOVERED EXPENSES WERE GOING TO BE FUNDED BY YOUR OUTSIDE SCHOLARSHIP!
BUT THE NATIVE PEACHTREE SCHOLARSHIP WAS DISCONTINUED LATE LAST YEAR. IT'S AN OLD AID SOURCE. I'M FRANKLY CURIOUS AS TO HOW YOU APPLIED—AND HOW FINANCIAL AID ACCEPTED IT.
B-BUT—I—

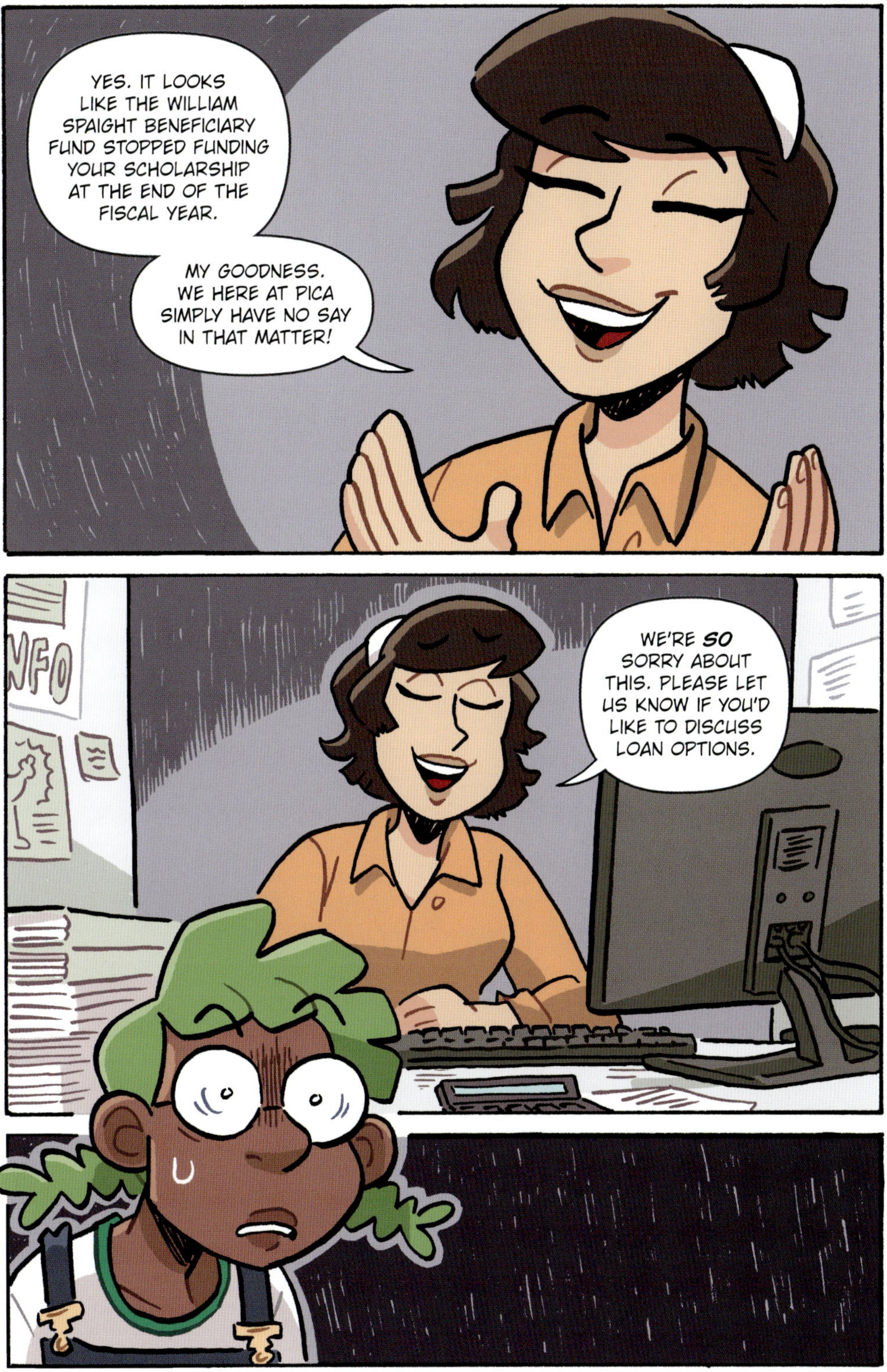
YES. IT LOOKS LIKE THE WILLIAM SPAIGHT BENEFICIARY FUND STOPPED FUNDING YOUR SCHOLARSHIP AT THE END OF THE FISCAL YEAR.
MY GOODNESS. WE HERE AT PICA SIMPLY HAVE NO SAY IN THAT MATTER!
NFO
WE'RE **SO** SORRY ABOUT THIS. PLEASE LET US KNOW IF YOU'D LIKE TO DISCUSS LOAN OPTIONS.

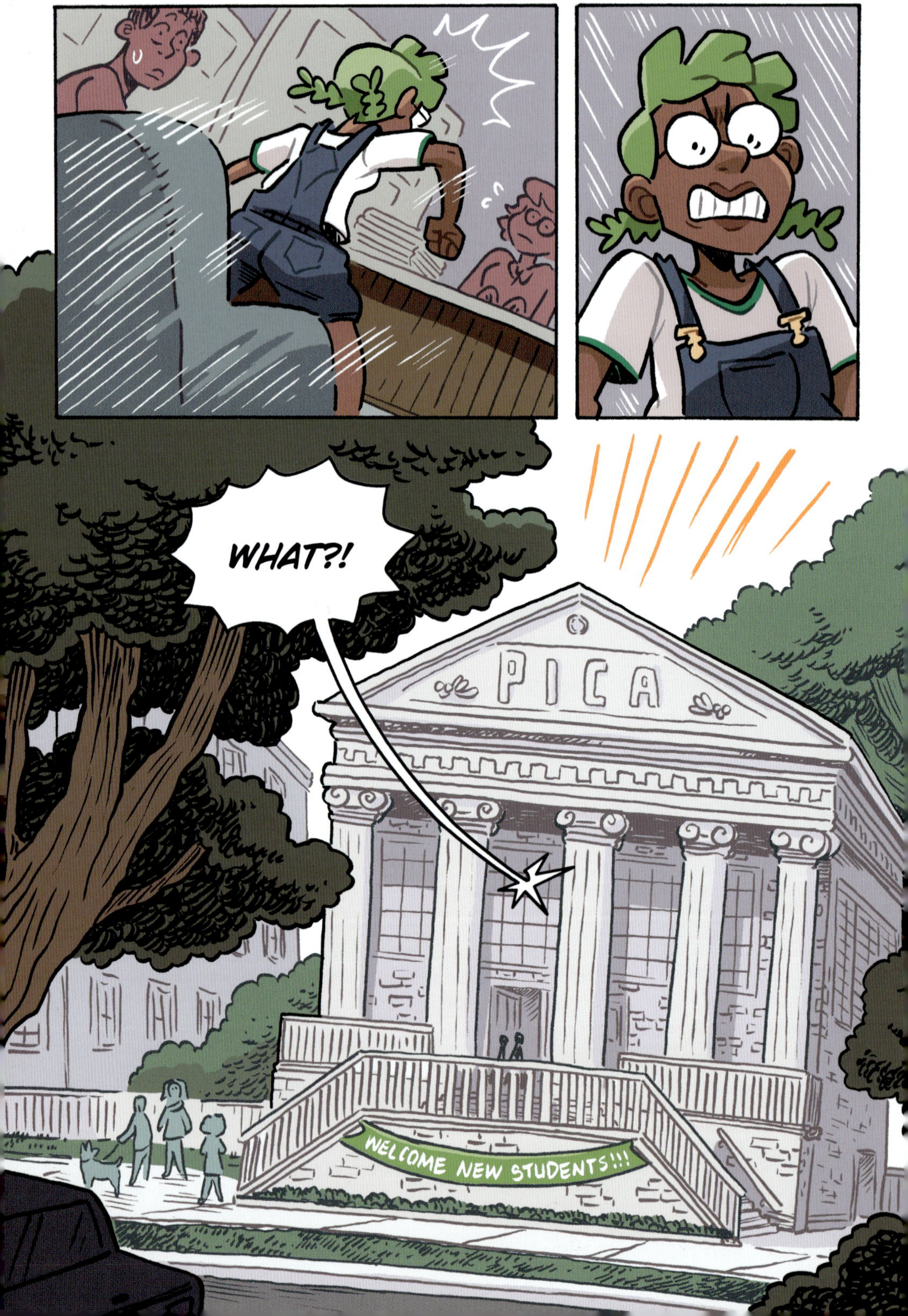
WHAT?!
PICA
WELCOME NEW STUDENTS!!!

WHAT HAPPENED TO MOLLY'S FINANCIAL AID?

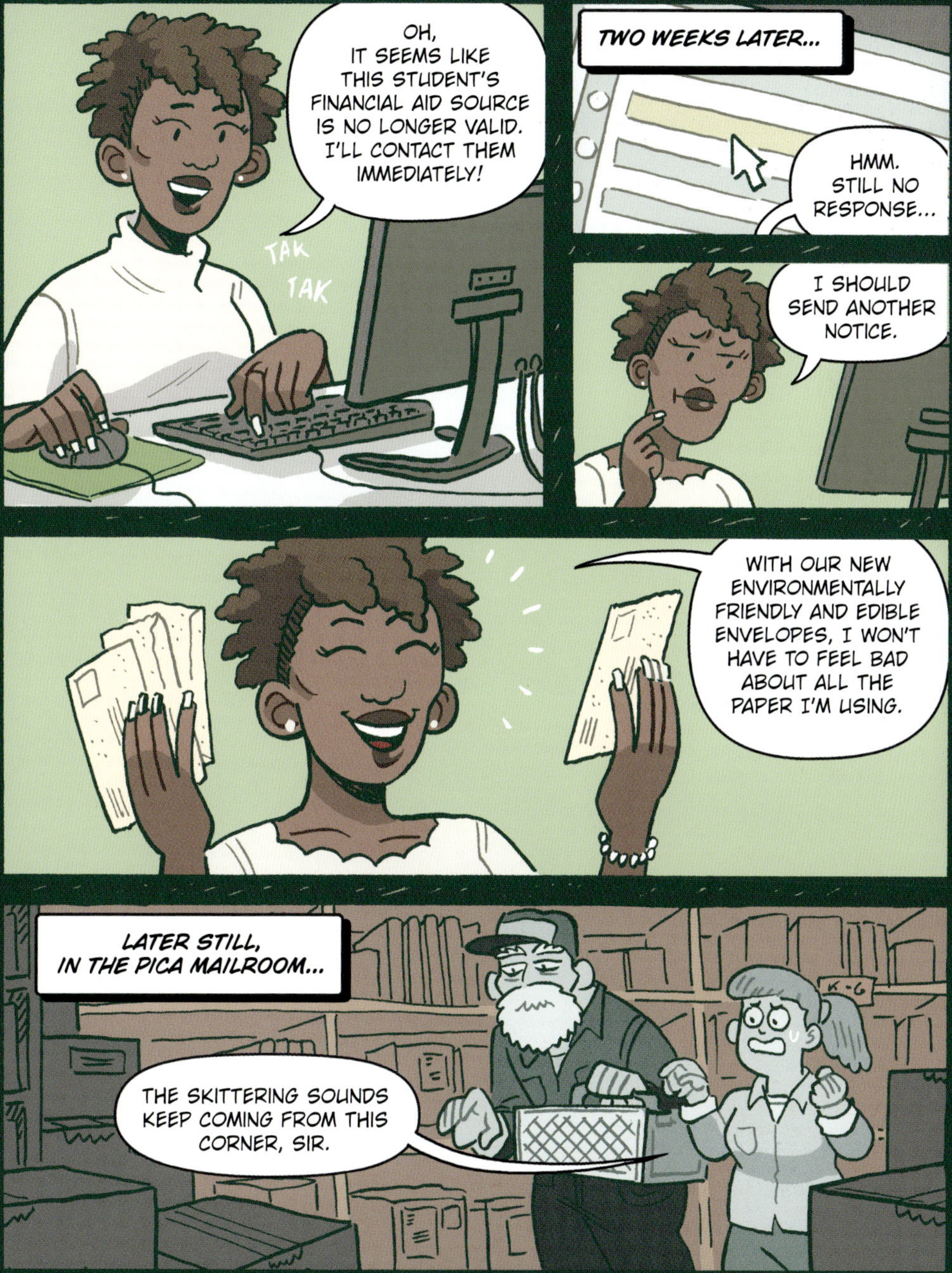

OH, IT SEEMS LIKE THIS STUDENT'S FINANCIAL AID SOURCE IS NO LONGER VALID. I'LL CONTACT THEM IMMEDIATELY!
TAK TAK
TWO WEEKS LATER...
HMM. STILL NO RESPONSE...
I SHOULD SEND ANOTHER NOTICE.
WITH OUR NEW ENVIRONMENTALLY FRIENDLY AND EDIBLE ENVELOPES, I WON'T HAVE TO FEEL BAD ABOUT ALL THE PAPER I'M USING.
LATER STILL, IN THE PICA MAILROOM...
K-G
THE SKITTERING SOUNDS KEEP COMING FROM THIS CORNER, SIR.

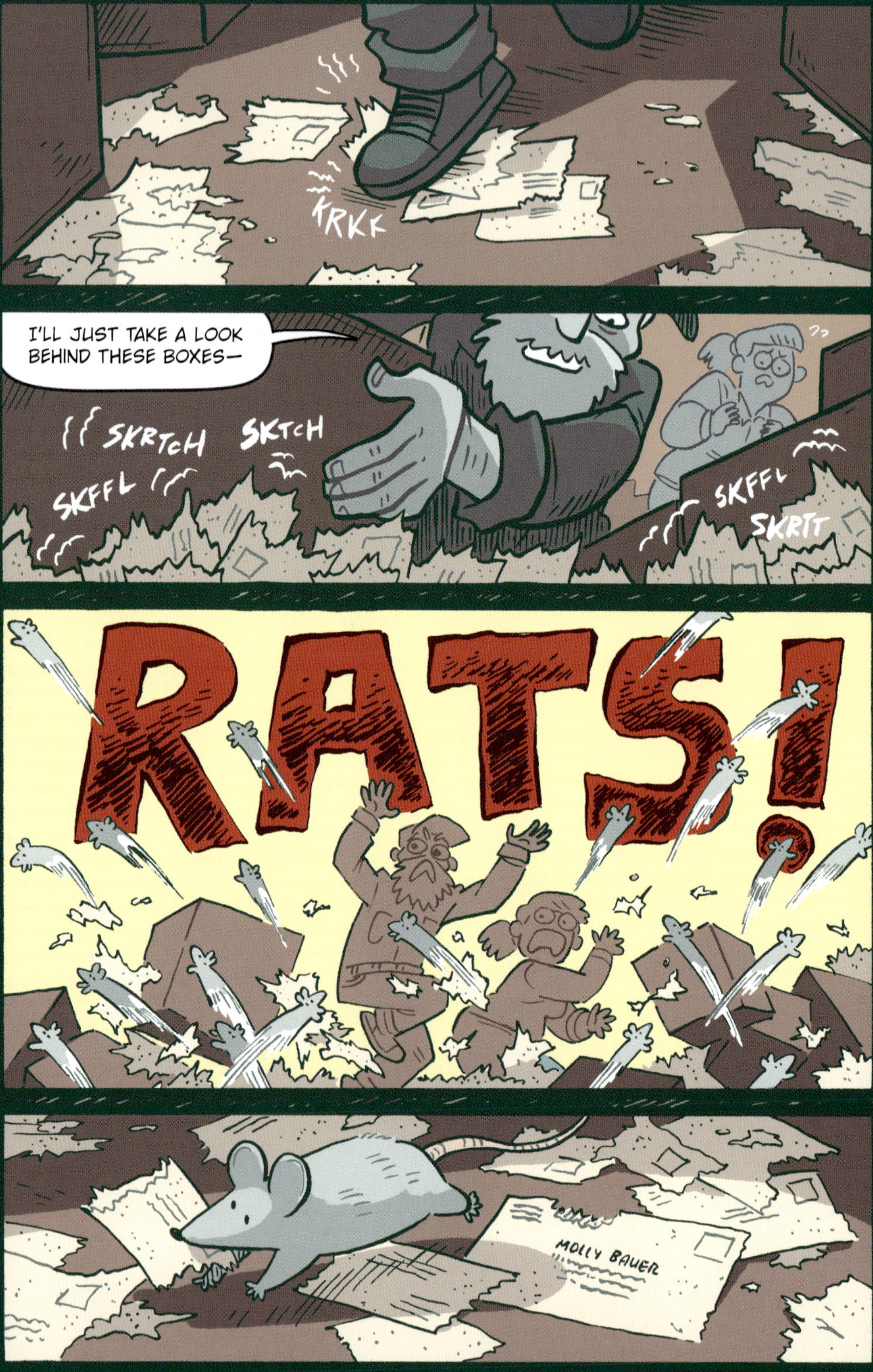
KRKK
I'LL JUST TAKE A LOOK BEHIND THESE BOXES—
SKRTCH
SKTCH
SKFFL
SKFFL
SKRTT
RATS!
MOLLY BAUER

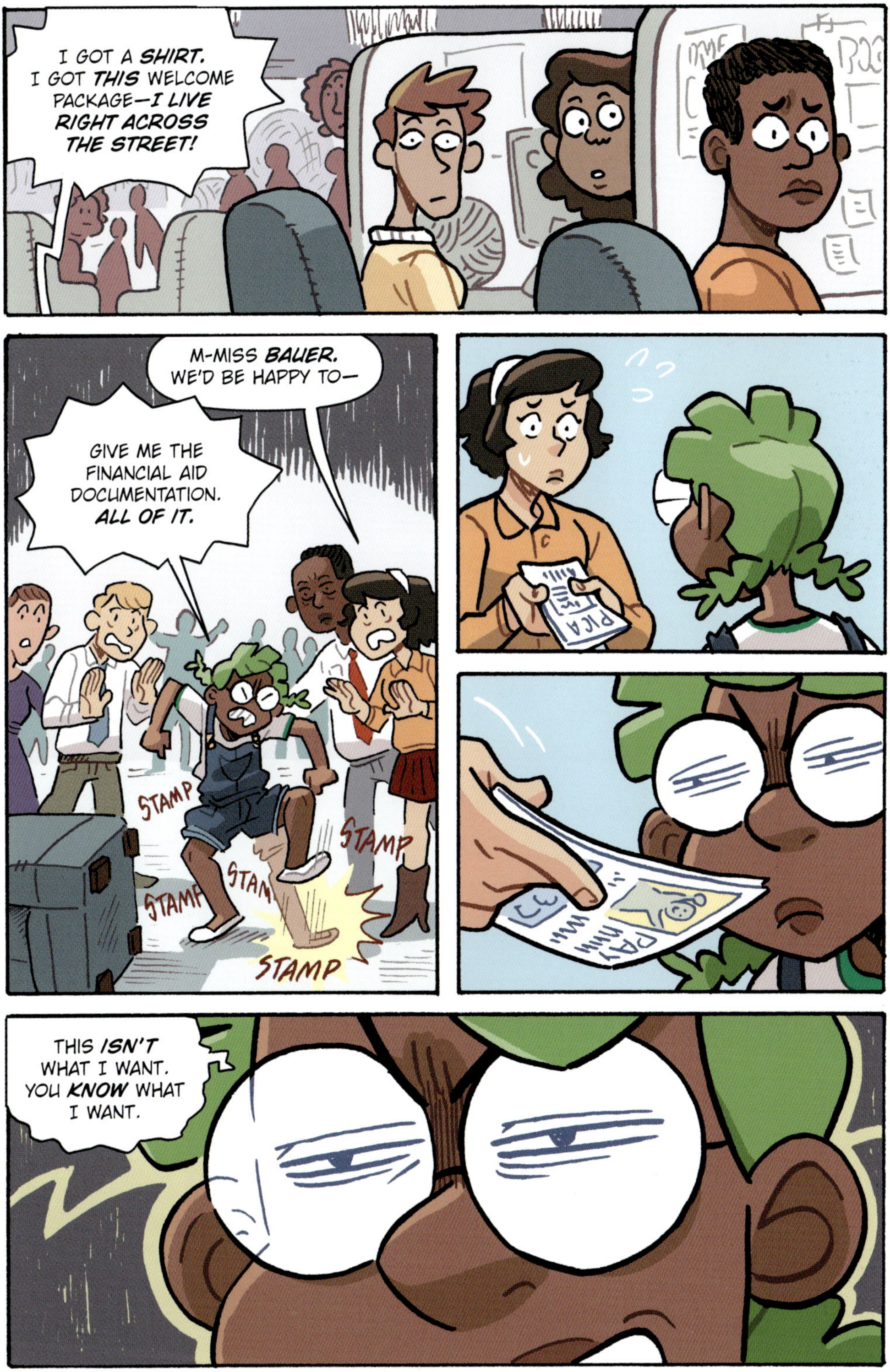
I GOT A SHIRT. I GOT THIS WELCOME PACKAGE—I LIVE RIGHT ACROSS THE STREET!
M-MISS BAUER. WE'D BE HAPPY TO—
GIVE ME THE FINANCIAL AID DOCUMENTATION. ALL OF IT.
STAMP
STAMP
STAM
STAMP
STAMP
PICA
PAY
THIS ISN'T WHAT I WANT. YOU KNOW WHAT I WANT.

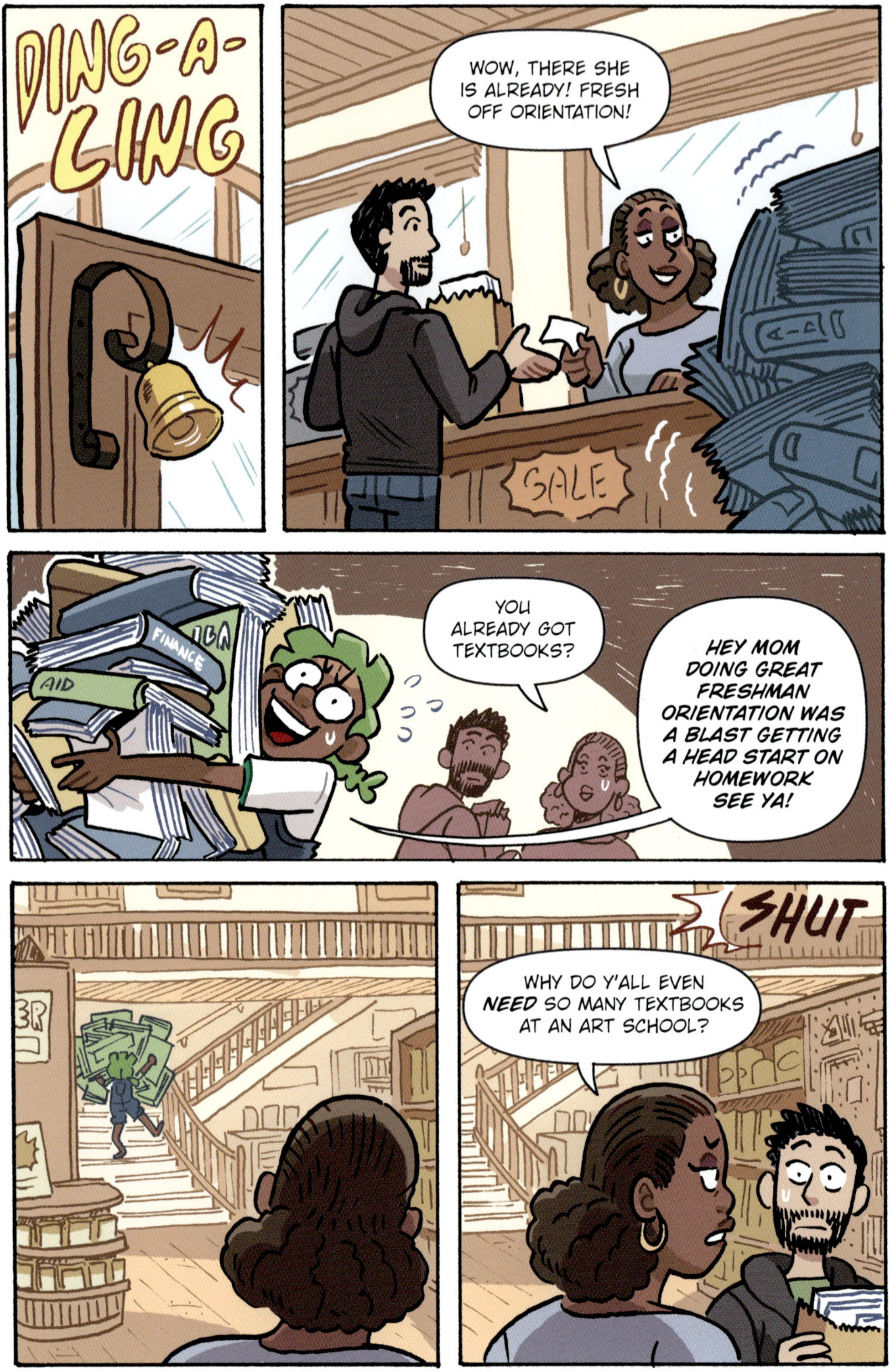
DING-A-LING
WOW, THERE SHE IS ALREADY! FRESH OFF ORIENTATION!
SALE
FINANCE
AID
YOU ALREADY GOT TEXTBOOKS?
HEY MOM DOING GREAT FRESHMAN ORIENTATION WAS A BLAST GETTING A HEAD START ON HOMEWORK SEE YA!
SHUT
WHY DO Y'ALL EVEN *NEED* SO MANY TEXTBOOKS AT AN ART SCHOOL?

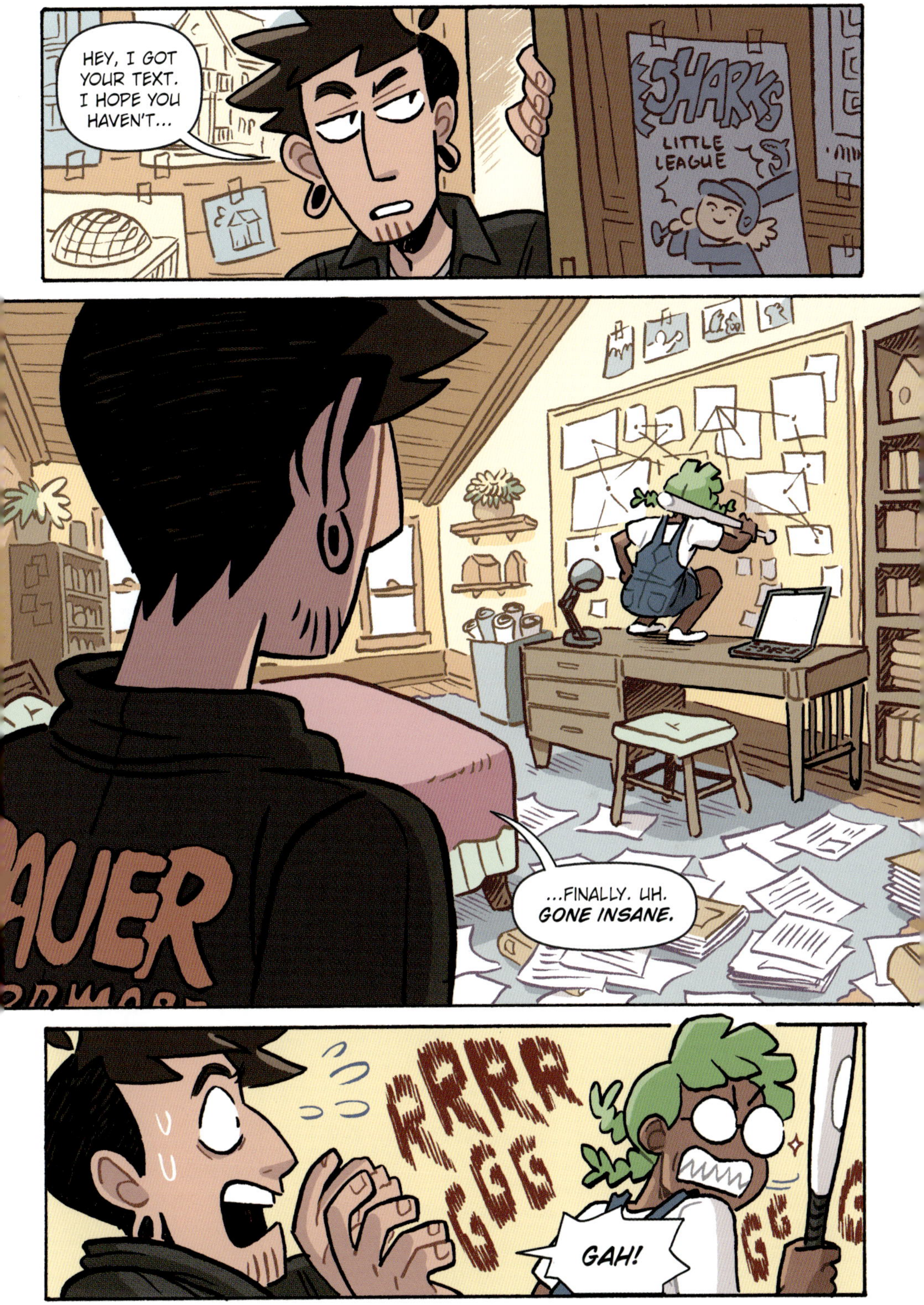
HEY, I GOT YOUR TEXT. I HOPE YOU HAVEN'T...
SHARKS
LITTLE LEAGUE
...FINALLY. UH. *GONE INSANE.*
RRRRGGG
GAH!

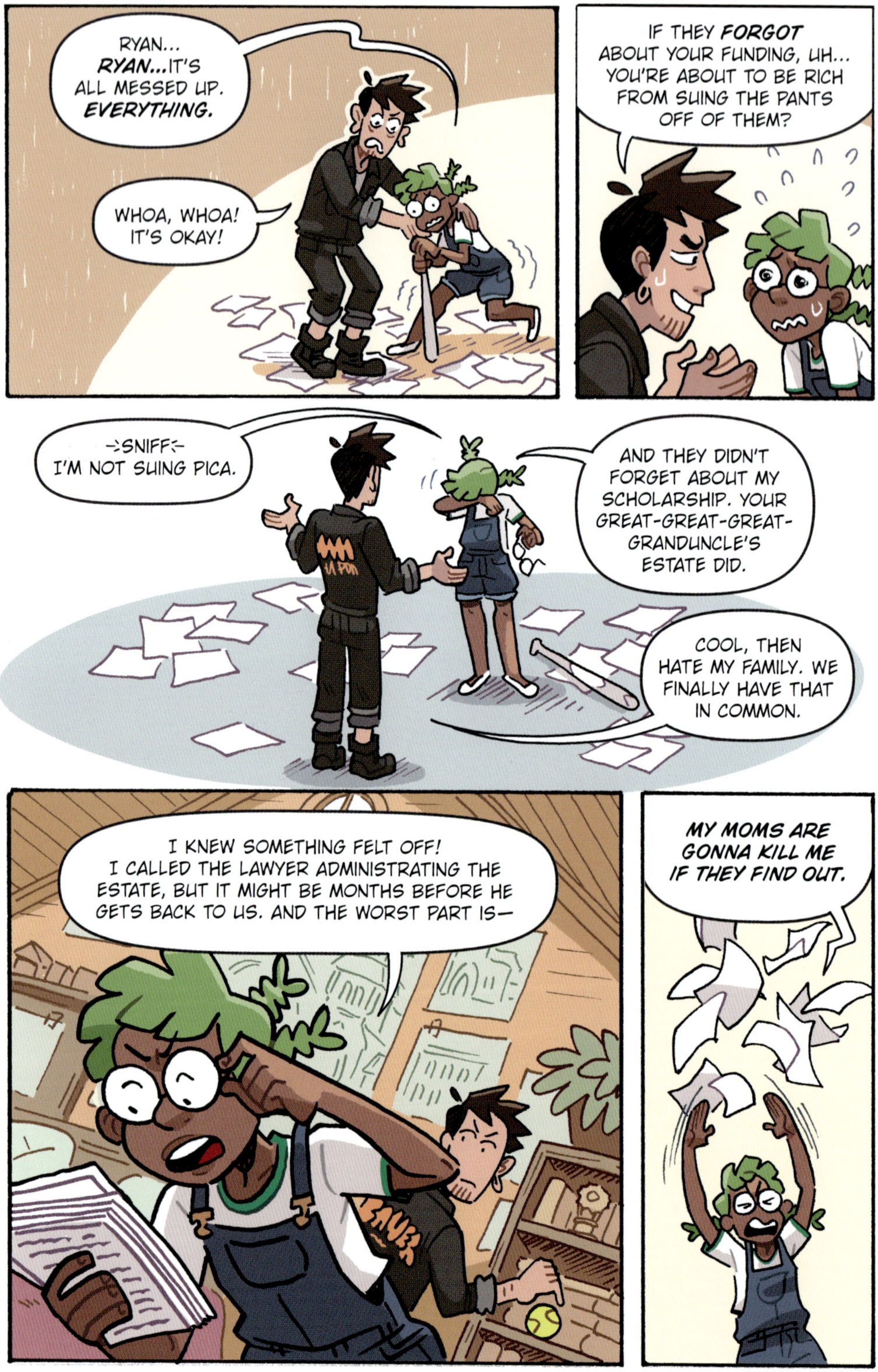
RYAN... *RYAN...* IT'S ALL MESSED UP. *EVERYTHING.*
WHOA, WHOA! IT'S OKAY!
IF THEY *FORGOT* ABOUT YOUR FUNDING, UH... YOU'RE ABOUT TO BE RICH FROM SUING THE PANTS OFF OF THEM?
SNIFF
I'M NOT SUING PICA.
AND THEY DIDN'T FORGET ABOUT MY SCHOLARSHIP. YOUR GREAT-GREAT-GREAT-GRANDUNCLE'S ESTATE DID.
COOL, THEN HATE MY FAMILY. WE FINALLY HAVE THAT IN COMMON.
I KNEW SOMETHING FELT OFF! I CALLED THE LAWYER ADMINISTRATING THE ESTATE, BUT IT MIGHT BE MONTHS BEFORE HE GETS BACK TO US. AND THE WORST PART IS—
MY MOMS ARE GONNA KILL ME IF THEY FIND OUT.

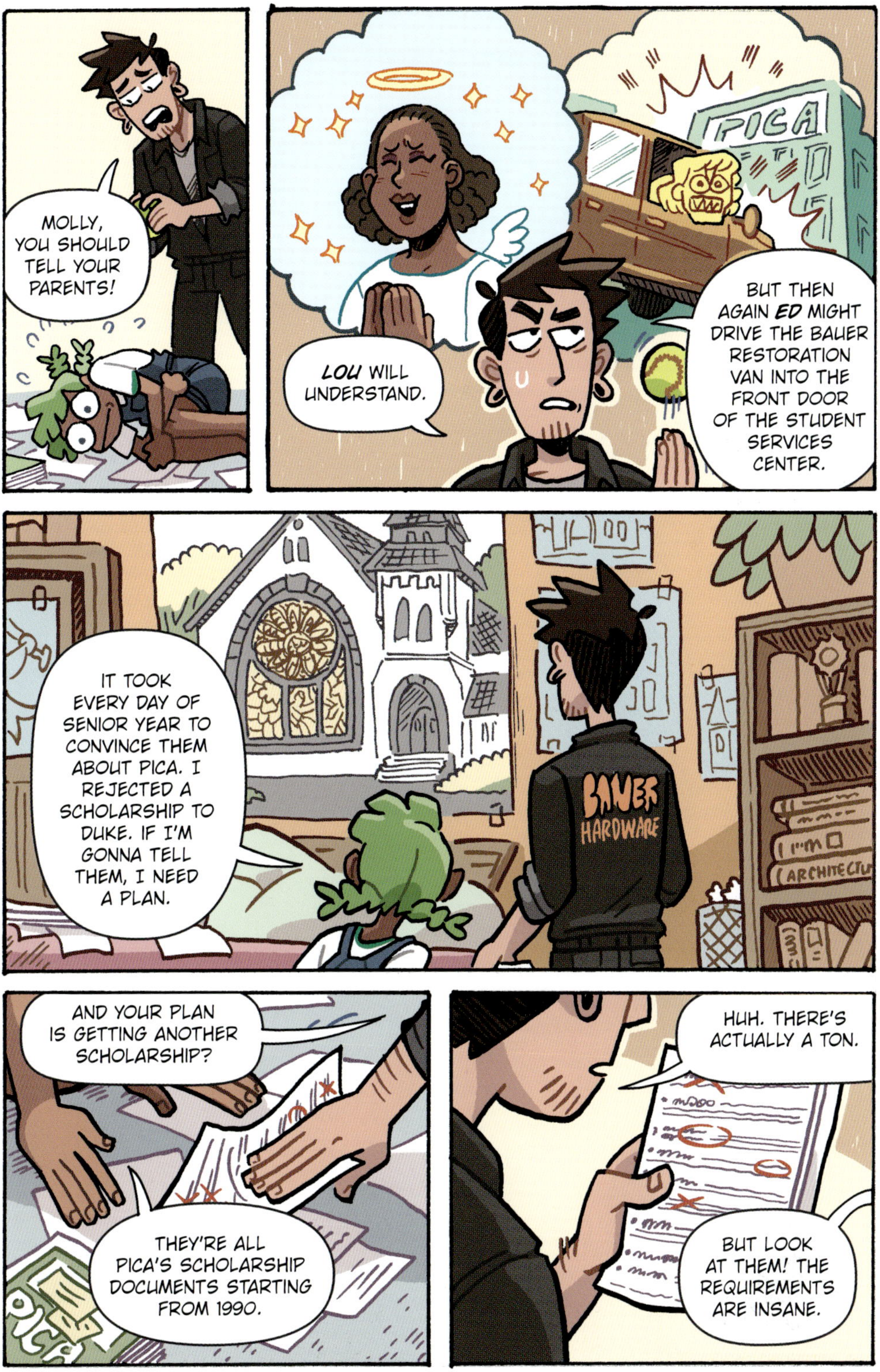

MOLLY, YOU SHOULD TELL YOUR PARENTS!
LOU WILL UNDERSTAND.
PICA
BUT THEN AGAIN ED MIGHT DRIVE THE BAUER RESTORATION VAN INTO THE FRONT DOOR OF THE STUDENT SERVICES CENTER.
IT TOOK EVERY DAY OF SENIOR YEAR TO CONVINCE THEM ABOUT PICA. I REJECTED A SCHOLARSHIP TO DUKE. IF I'M GONNA TELL THEM, I NEED A PLAN.
BAUER HARDWARE
AND YOUR PLAN IS GETTING ANOTHER SCHOLARSHIP?
THEY'RE ALL PICA'S SCHOLARSHIP DOCUMENTS STARTING FROM 1990.
HUH. THERE'S ACTUALLY A TON.
BUT LOOK AT THEM! THE REQUIREMENTS ARE INSANE.

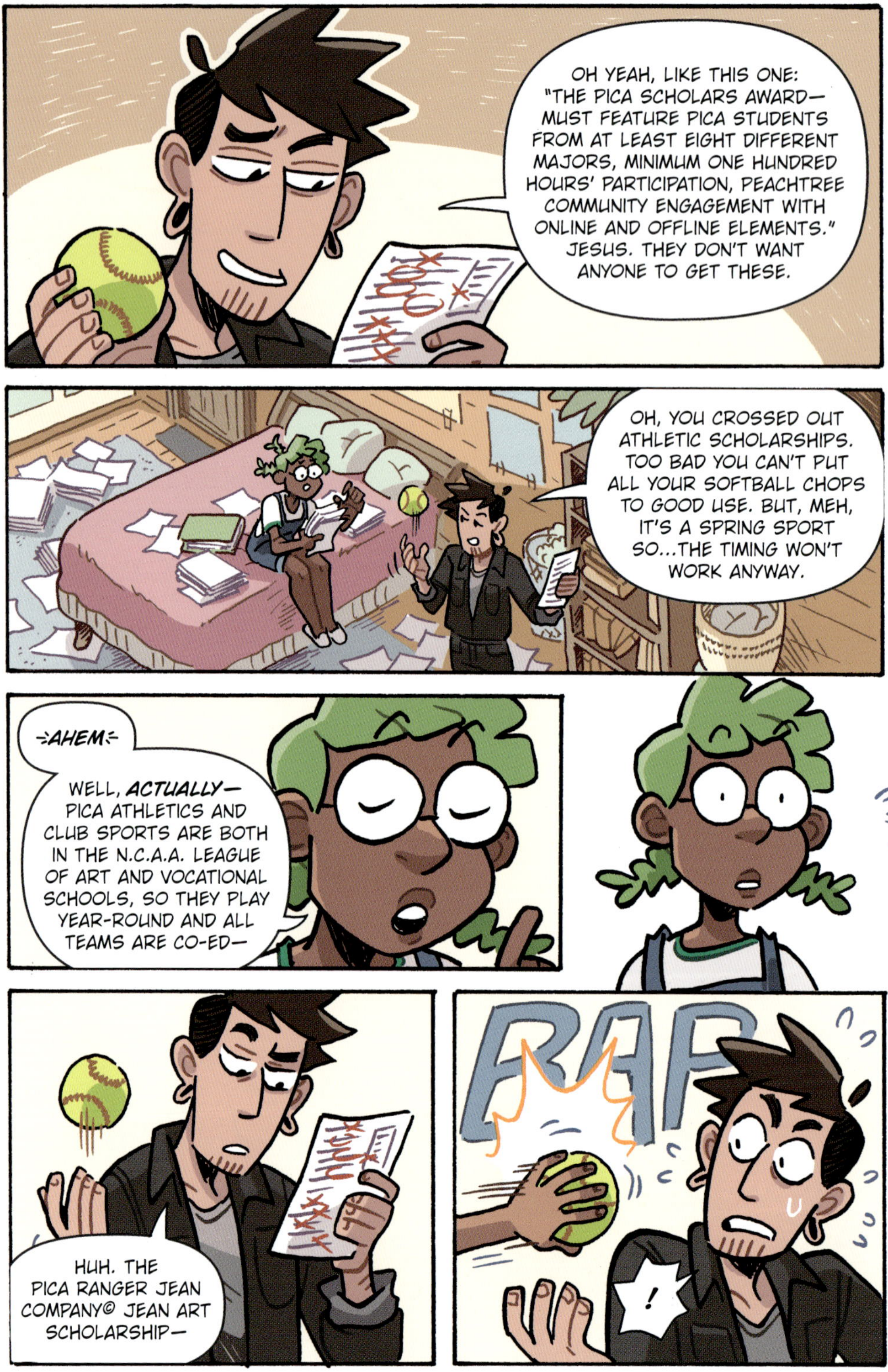
OH YEAH, LIKE THIS ONE: "THE PICA SCHOLARS AWARD— MUST FEATURE PICA STUDENTS FROM AT LEAST EIGHT DIFFERENT MAJORS, MINIMUM ONE HUNDRED HOURS' PARTICIPATION, PEACHTREE COMMUNITY ENGAGEMENT WITH ONLINE AND OFFLINE ELEMENTS." JESUS. THEY DON'T WANT ANYONE TO GET THESE.
OH, YOU CROSSED OUT ATHLETIC SCHOLARSHIPS. TOO BAD YOU CAN'T PUT ALL YOUR SOFTBALL CHOPS TO GOOD USE. BUT, MEH, IT'S A SPRING SPORT SO...THE TIMING WON'T WORK ANYWAY.
AHEM
WELL, ***ACTUALLY***— PICA ATHLETICS AND CLUB SPORTS ARE BOTH IN THE N.C.A.A. LEAGUE OF ART AND VOCATIONAL SCHOOLS, SO THEY PLAY YEAR-ROUND AND ALL TEAMS ARE CO-ED—
HUH. THE PICA RANGER JEAN COMPANY© JEAN ART SCHOLARSHIP—
RAP
!

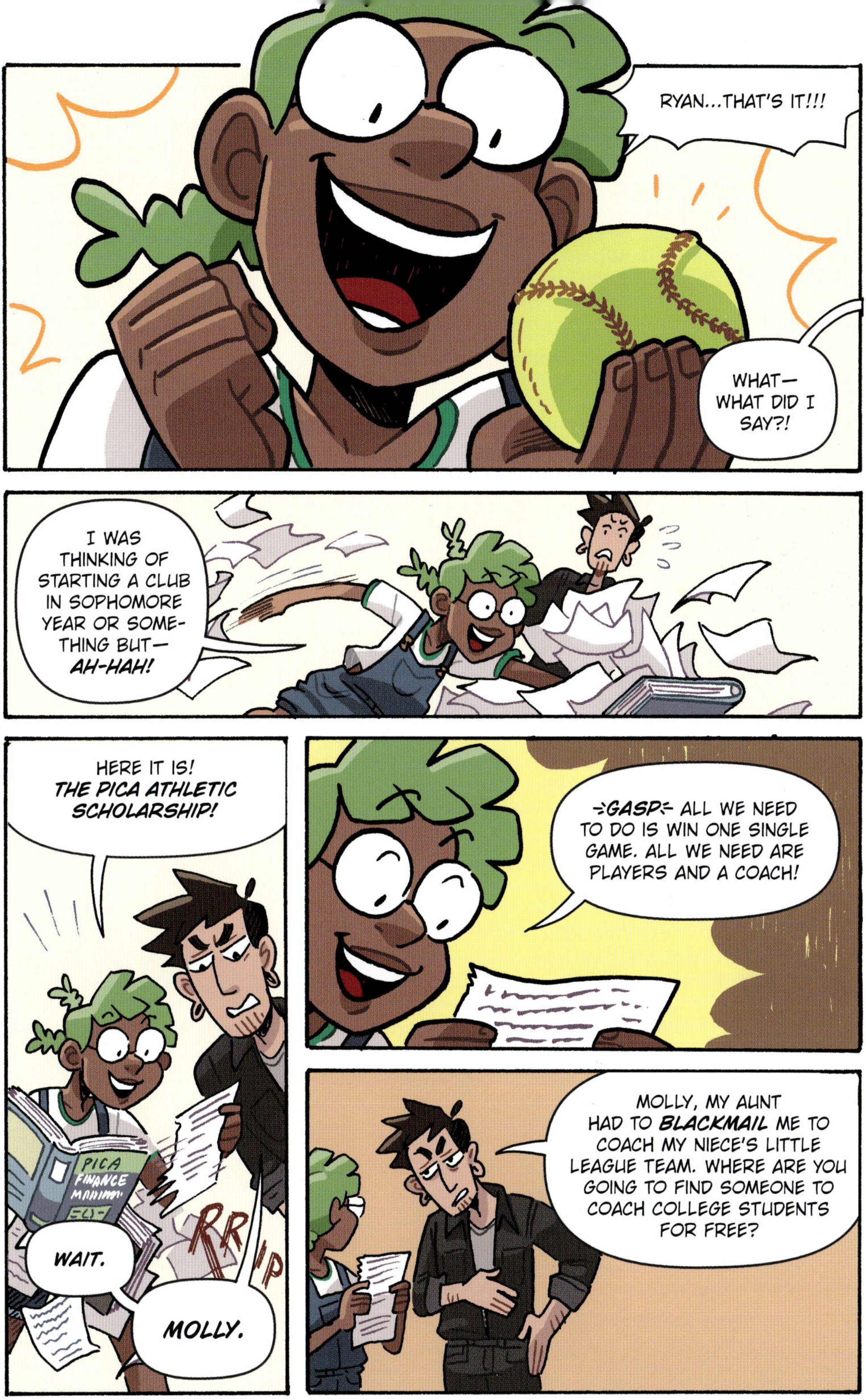
RYAN...THAT'S IT!!!
WHAT— WHAT DID I SAY?!
I WAS THINKING OF STARTING A CLUB IN SOPHOMORE YEAR OR SOMETHING BUT— AH-HAH!
HERE IT IS! THE PICA ATHLETIC SCHOLARSHIP!
PICA FINANCE
WAIT.
RRRIP
MOLLY.
GASP ALL WE NEED TO DO IS WIN ONE SINGLE GAME. ALL WE NEED ARE PLAYERS AND A COACH!
MOLLY, MY AUNT HAD TO BLACKMAIL ME TO COACH MY NIECE'S LITTLE LEAGUE TEAM. WHERE ARE YOU GOING TO FIND SOMEONE TO COACH COLLEGE STUDENTS FOR FREE?

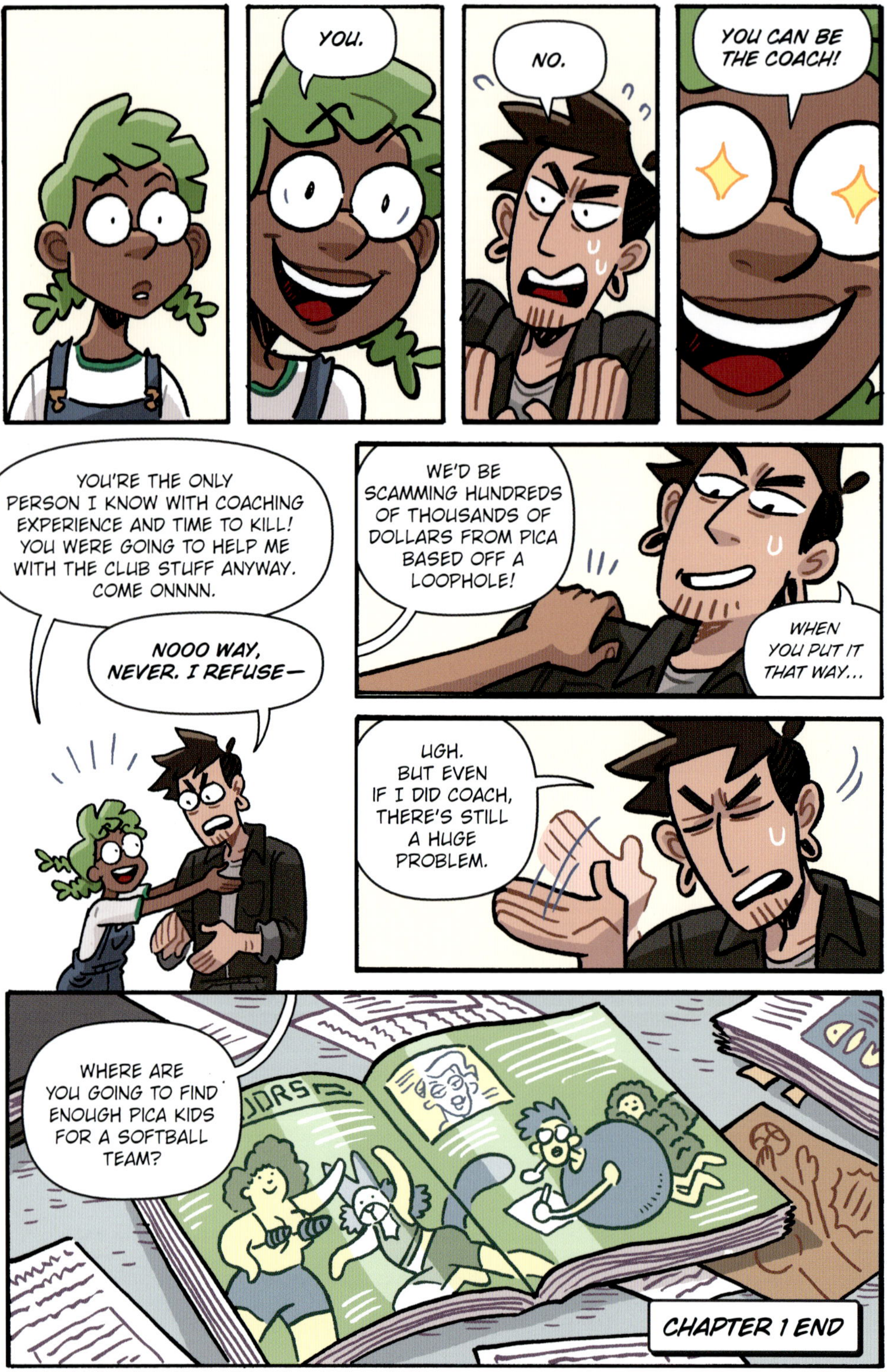
YOU.
NO.
YOU CAN BE THE COACH!
YOU'RE THE ONLY PERSON I KNOW WITH COACHING EXPERIENCE AND TIME TO KILL! YOU WERE GOING TO HELP ME WITH THE CLUB STUFF ANYWAY. COME ONNNN.
NOOO WAY, NEVER. I REFUSE—
WE'D BE SCAMMING HUNDREDS OF THOUSANDS OF DOLLARS FROM PICA BASED OFF A LOOPHOLE!
WHEN YOU PUT IT THAT WAY...
UGH. BUT EVEN IF I DID COACH, THERE'S STILL A HUGE PROBLEM.
WHERE ARE YOU GOING TO FIND ENOUGH PICA KIDS FOR A SOFTBALL TEAM?
CHAPTER 1 END

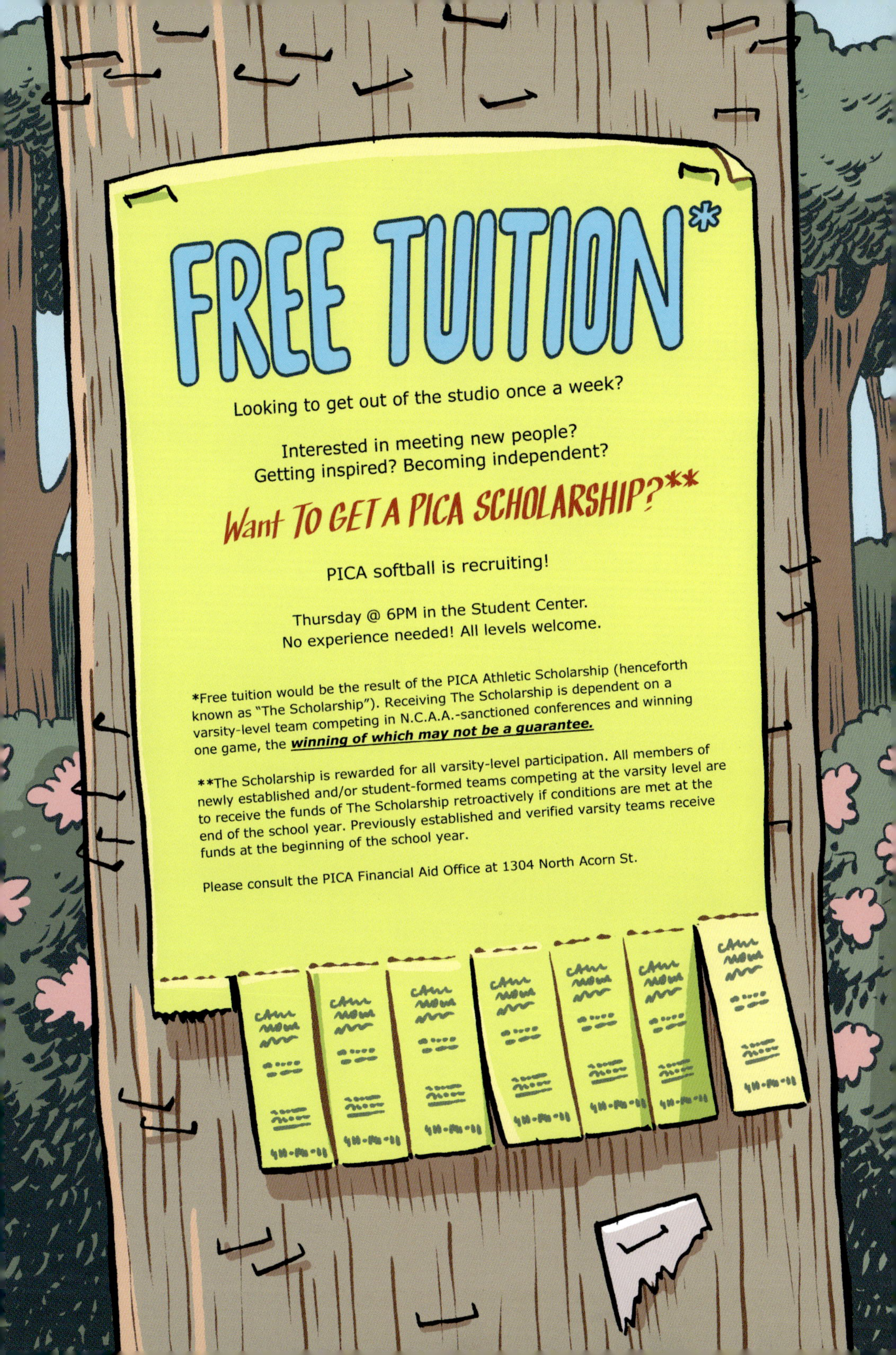
FREE TUITION*
Looking to get out of the studio once a week?
Interested in meeting new people?
Getting inspired? Becoming independent?
Want TO GET A PICA SCHOLARSHIP?**
PICA softball is recruiting!
Thursday @ 6PM in the Student Center.
No experience needed! All levels welcome.
*Free tuition would be the result of the PICA Athletic Scholarship (henceforth known as "The Scholarship"). Receiving The Scholarship is dependent on a varsity-level team competing in N.C.A.A.-sanctioned conferences and winning one game, the winning of which may not be a guarantee.
**The Scholarship is rewarded for all varsity-level participation. All members of newly established and/or student-formed teams competing at the varsity level are to receive the funds of The Scholarship retroactively if conditions are met at the end of the school year. Previously established and verified varsity teams receive funds at the beginning of the school year.
Please consult the PICA Financial Aid Office at 1304 North Acorn St.

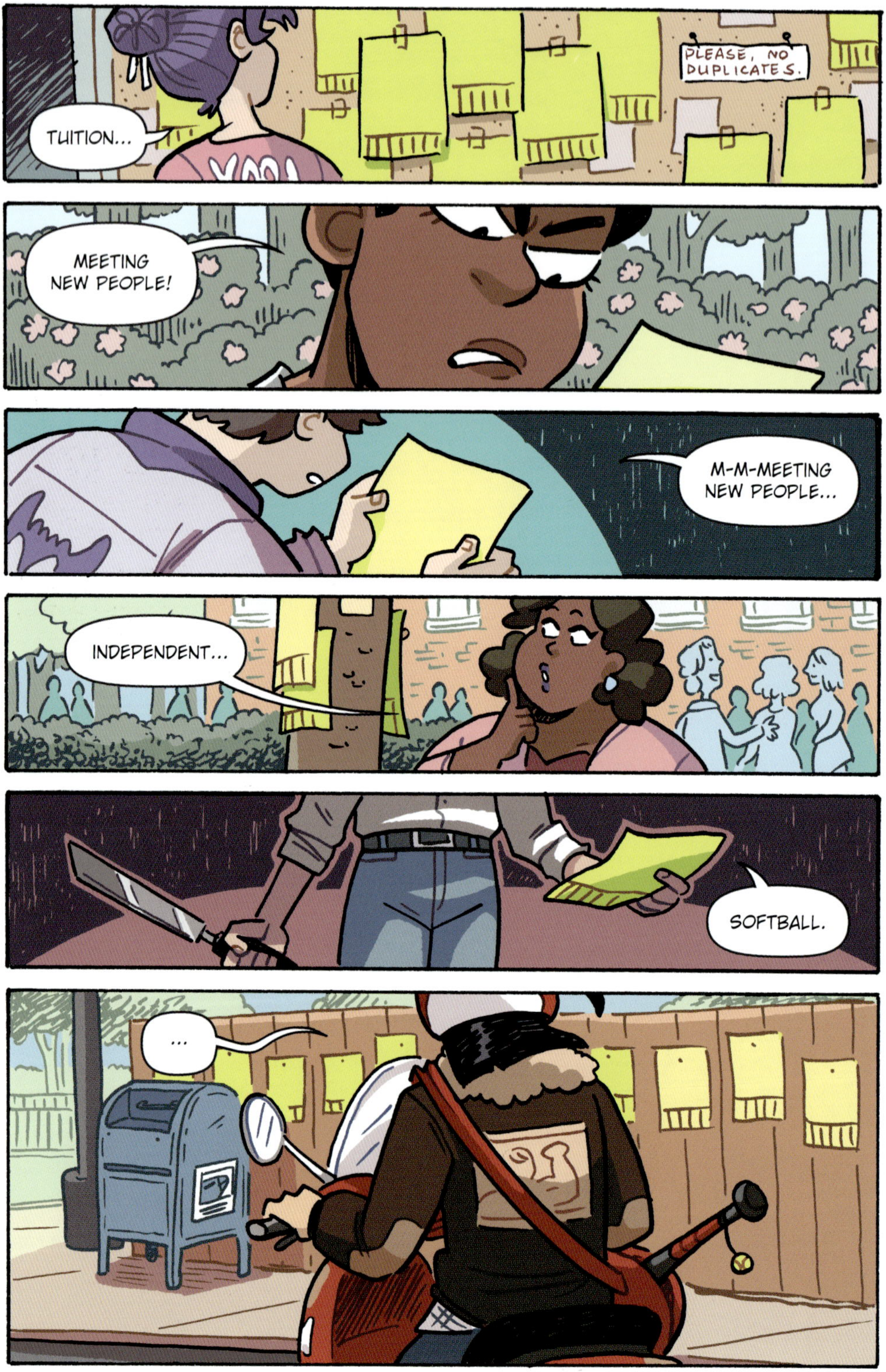
TUITION...
PLEASE, NO DUPLICATES.
MEETING NEW PEOPLE!
M-M-MEETING NEW PEOPLE...
INDEPENDENT...
SOFTBALL.
...

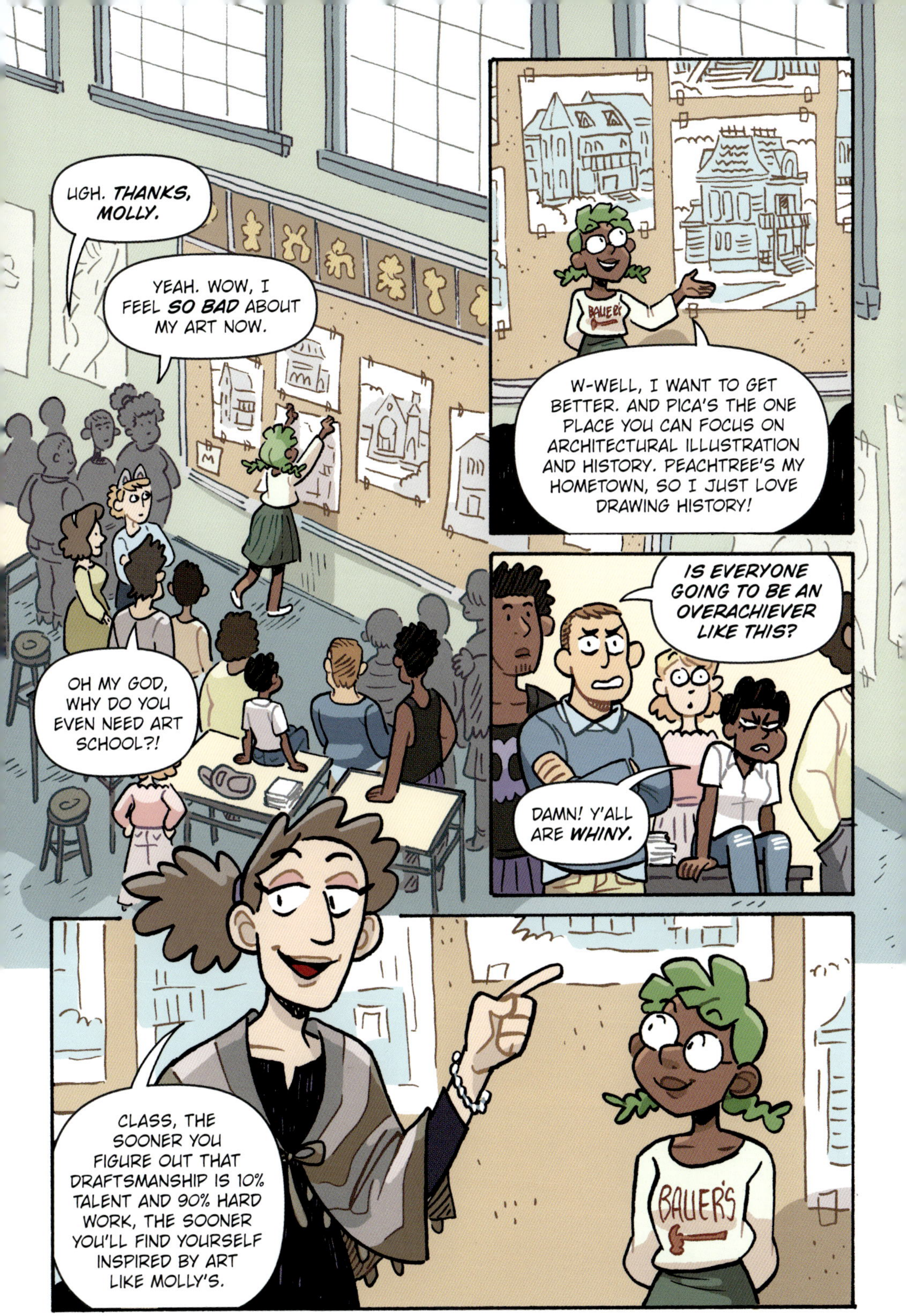
UGH. THANKS, MOLLY.
YEAH. WOW, I FEEL SO BAD ABOUT MY ART NOW.
W-WELL, I WANT TO GET BETTER. AND PICA'S THE ONE PLACE YOU CAN FOCUS ON ARCHITECTURAL ILLUSTRATION AND HISTORY. PEACHTREE'S MY HOMETOWN, SO I JUST LOVE DRAWING HISTORY!
BAUER'S
OH MY GOD, WHY DO YOU EVEN NEED ART SCHOOL?!
IS EVERYONE GOING TO BE AN OVERACHIEVER LIKE THIS?
DAMN! Y'ALL ARE WHINY.
CLASS, THE SOONER YOU FIGURE OUT THAT DRAFTSMANSHIP IS 10% TALENT AND 90% HARD WORK, THE SOONER YOU'LL FIND YOURSELF INSPIRED BY ART LIKE MOLLY'S.
BAUER'S

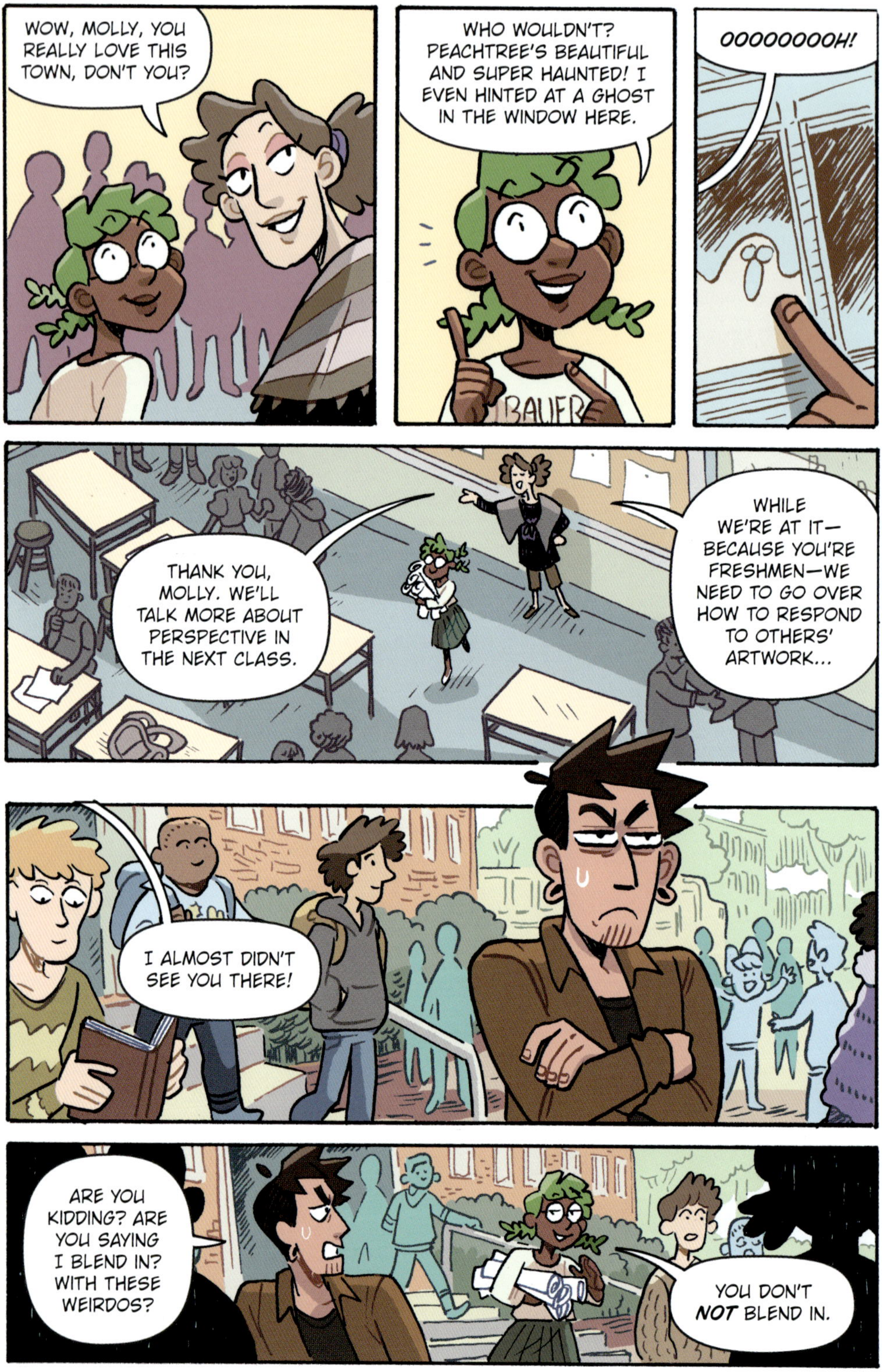
WOW, MOLLY, YOU REALLY LOVE THIS TOWN, DON'T YOU?
WHO WOULDN'T? PEACHTREE'S BEAUTIFUL AND SUPER HAUNTED! I EVEN HINTED AT A GHOST IN THE WINDOW HERE.
BAUER
OOOOOOOOH!
THANK YOU, MOLLY. WE'LL TALK MORE ABOUT PERSPECTIVE IN THE NEXT CLASS.
WHILE WE'RE AT IT—BECAUSE YOU'RE FRESHMEN—WE NEED TO GO OVER HOW TO RESPOND TO OTHERS' ARTWORK...
I ALMOST DIDN'T SEE YOU THERE!
ARE YOU KIDDING? ARE YOU SAYING I BLEND IN? WITH THESE WEIRDOS?
YOU DON'T *NOT* BLEND IN.

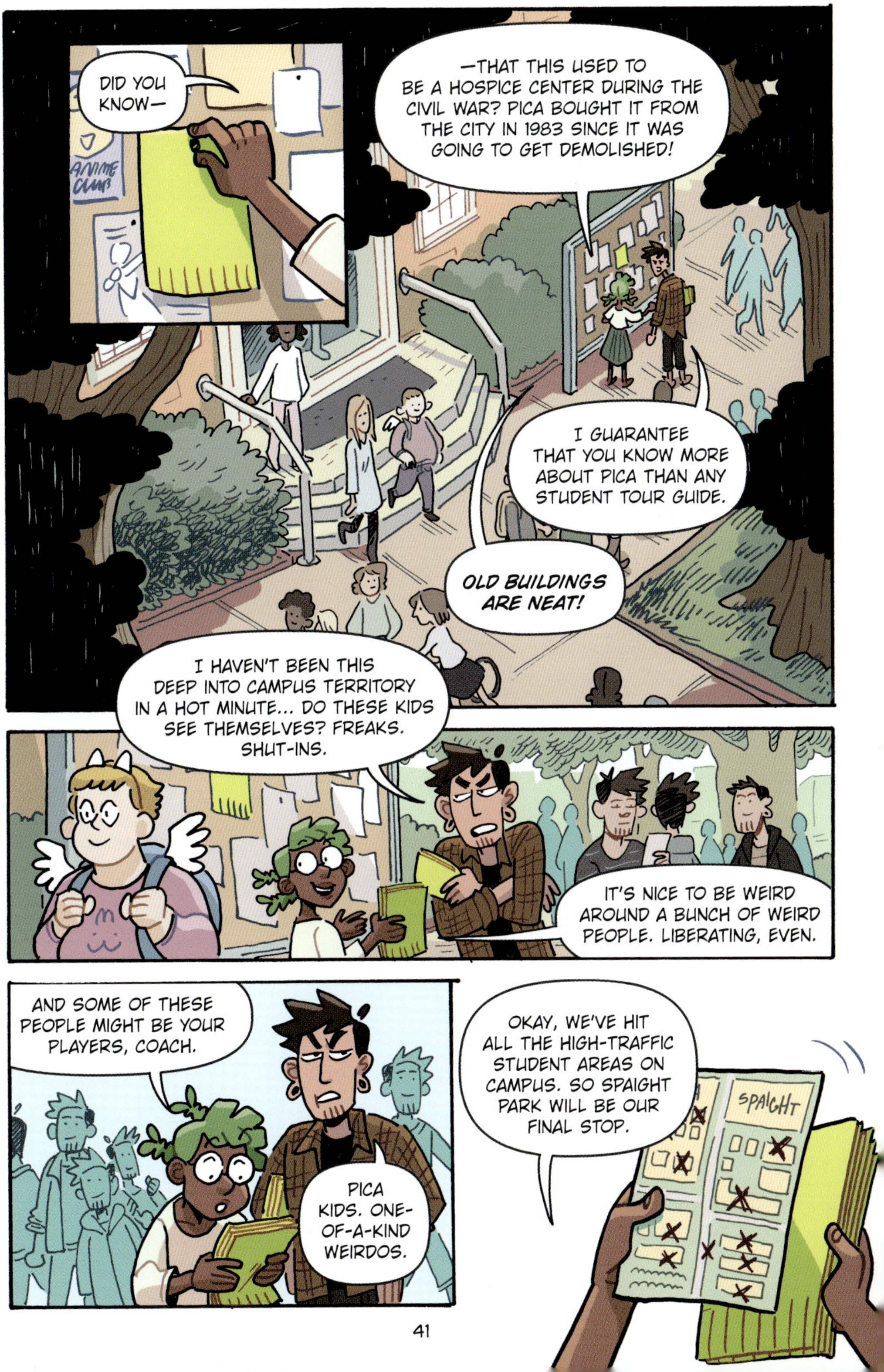

ANIME CLUB
DID YOU KNOW—
—THAT THIS USED TO BE A HOSPICE CENTER DURING THE CIVIL WAR? PICA BOUGHT IT FROM THE CITY IN 1983 SINCE IT WAS GOING TO GET DEMOLISHED!
I GUARANTEE THAT YOU KNOW MORE ABOUT PICA THAN ANY STUDENT TOUR GUIDE.
OLD BUILDINGS ARE NEAT!
I HAVEN'T BEEN THIS DEEP INTO CAMPUS TERRITORY IN A HOT MINUTE... DO THESE KIDS SEE THEMSELVES? FREAKS. SHUT-INS.
IT'S NICE TO BE WEIRD AROUND A BUNCH OF WEIRD PEOPLE. LIBERATING, EVEN.
AND SOME OF THESE PEOPLE MIGHT BE YOUR PLAYERS, COACH.
PICA KIDS. ONE-OF-A-KIND WEIRDOS.
OKAY, WE'VE HIT ALL THE HIGH-TRAFFIC STUDENT AREAS ON CAMPUS. SO SPAIGHT PARK WILL BE OUR FINAL STOP.
SPAIGHT

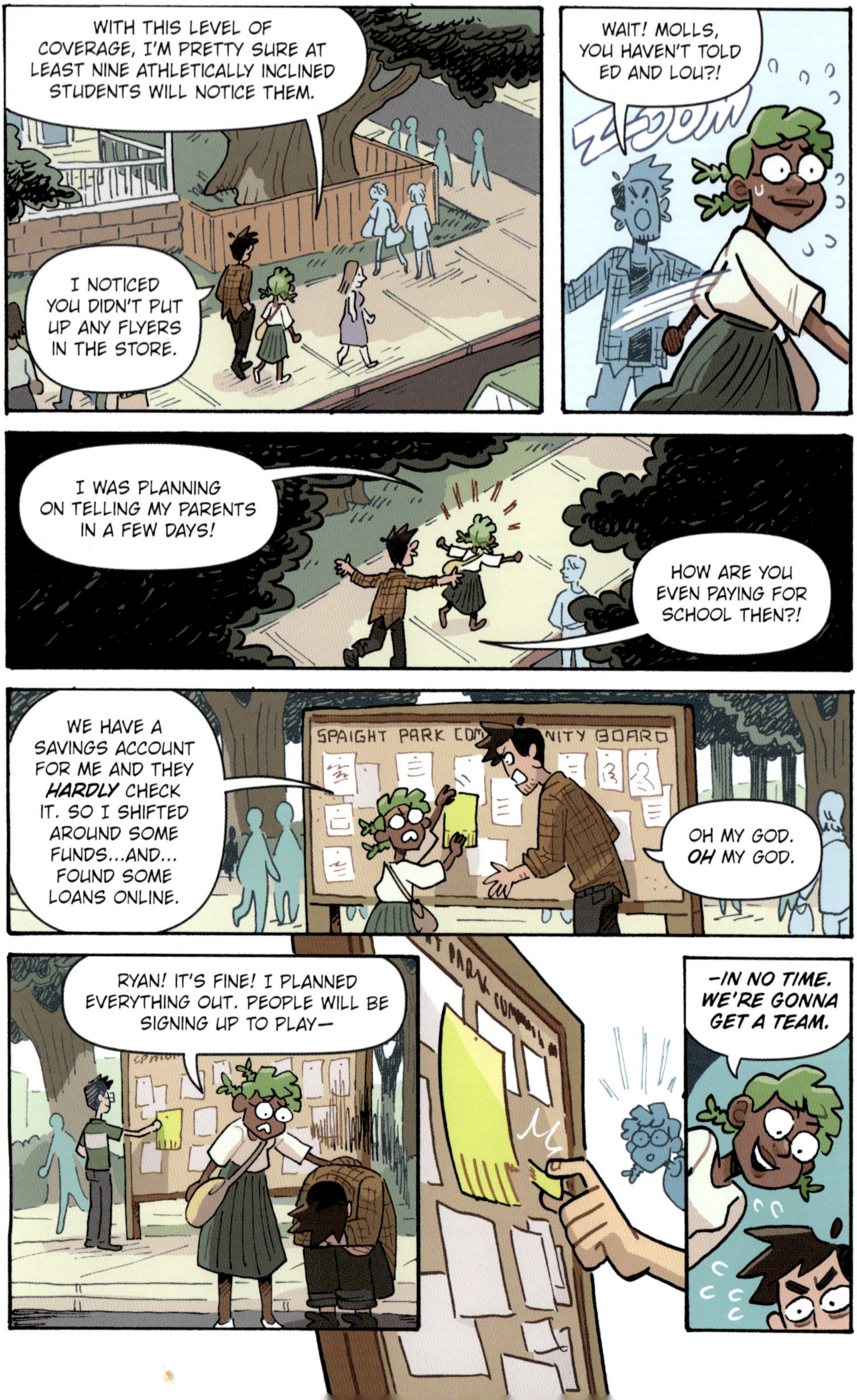
WITH THIS LEVEL OF COVERAGE, I'M PRETTY SURE AT LEAST NINE ATHLETICALLY INCLINED STUDENTS WILL NOTICE THEM.
I NOTICED YOU DIDN'T PUT UP ANY FLYERS IN THE STORE.
WAIT! MOLLS, YOU HAVEN'T TOLD ED AND LOU?!
ZOOM
I WAS PLANNING ON TELLING MY PARENTS IN A FEW DAYS!
HOW ARE YOU EVEN PAYING FOR SCHOOL THEN?!
WE HAVE A SAVINGS ACCOUNT FOR ME AND THEY *HARDLY* CHECK IT. SO I SHIFTED AROUND SOME FUNDS...AND... FOUND SOME LOANS ONLINE.
SPAIGHT PARK COM NITY BOARD
OH MY GOD. *OH* MY GOD.
RYAN! IT'S FINE! I PLANNED EVERYTHING OUT. PEOPLE WILL BE SIGNING UP TO PLAY—
—IN NO TIME. WE'RE GONNA GET A TEAM.

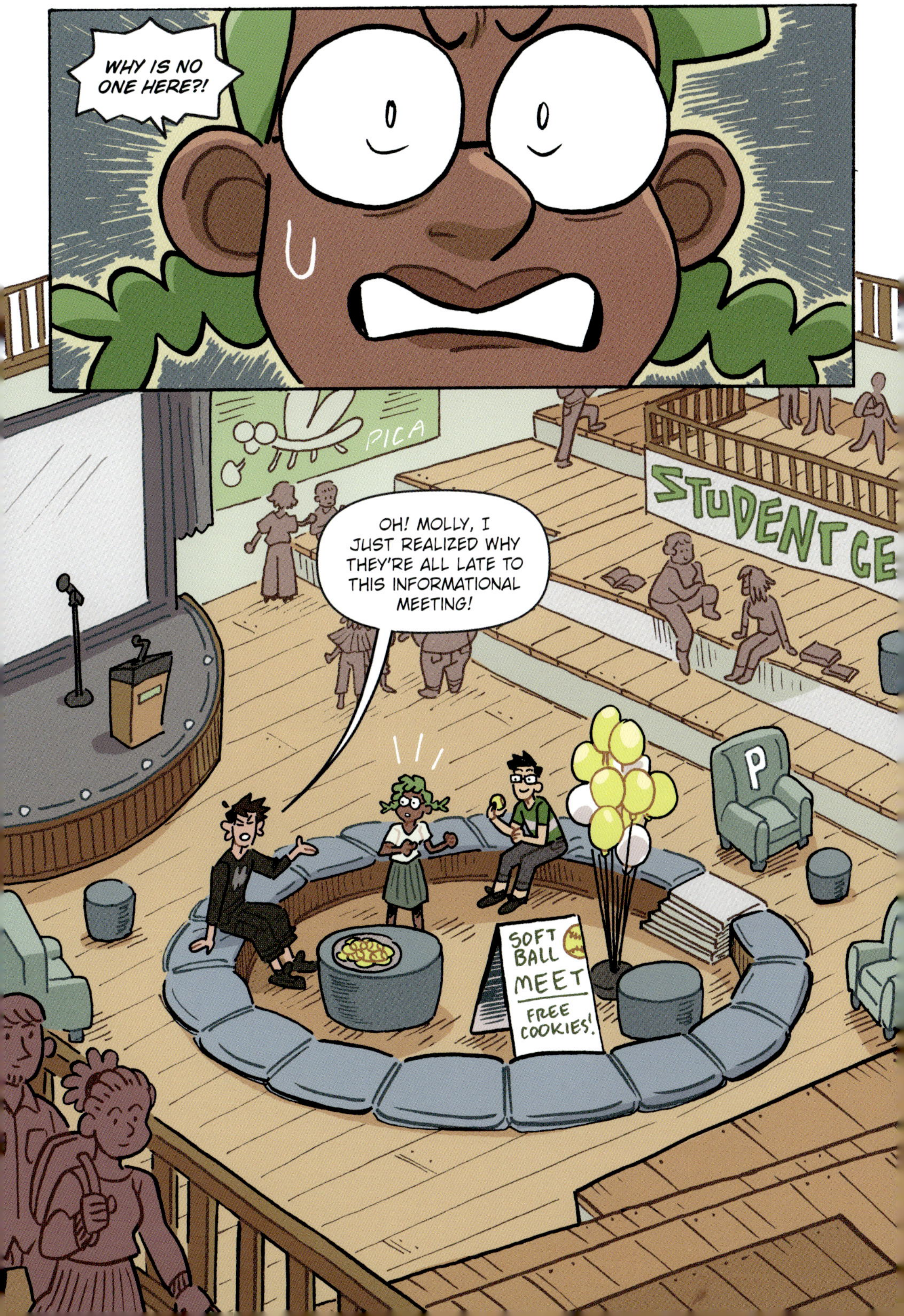
WHY IS NO ONE HERE?!
PICA
OH! MOLLY, I JUST REALIZED WHY THEY'RE ALL LATE TO THIS INFORMATIONAL MEETING!
STUDENT CE
P
SOFT BALL MEET
FREE COOKIES!

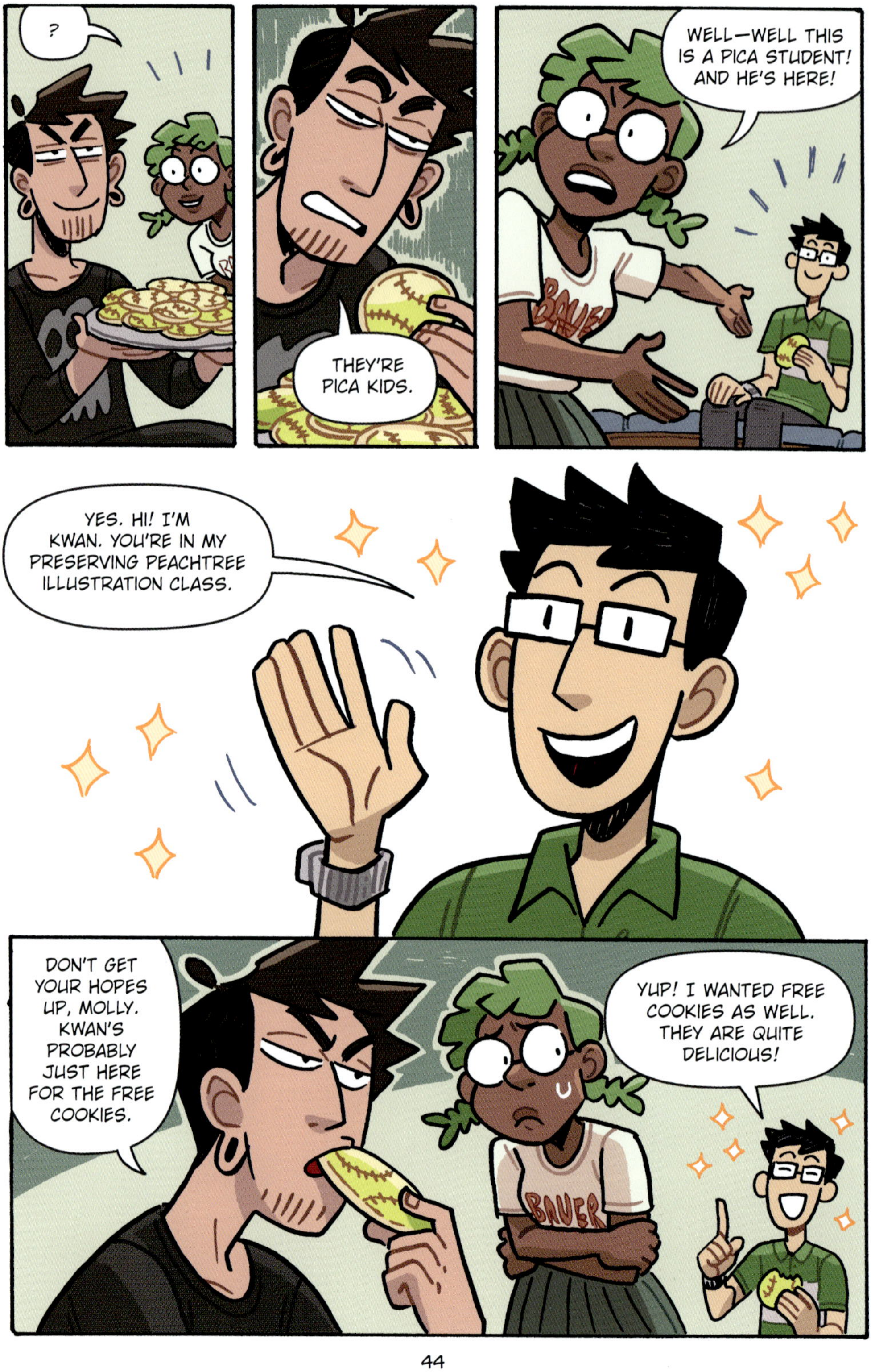
?
THEY'RE PICA KIDS.
WELL—WELL THIS IS A PICA STUDENT! AND HE'S HERE!
YES. HI! I'M KWAN. YOU'RE IN MY PRESERVING PEACHTREE ILLUSTRATION CLASS.
DON'T GET YOUR HOPES UP, MOLLY. KWAN'S PROBABLY JUST HERE FOR THE FREE COOKIES.
YUP! I WANTED FREE COOKIES AS WELL. THEY ARE QUITE DELICIOUS!

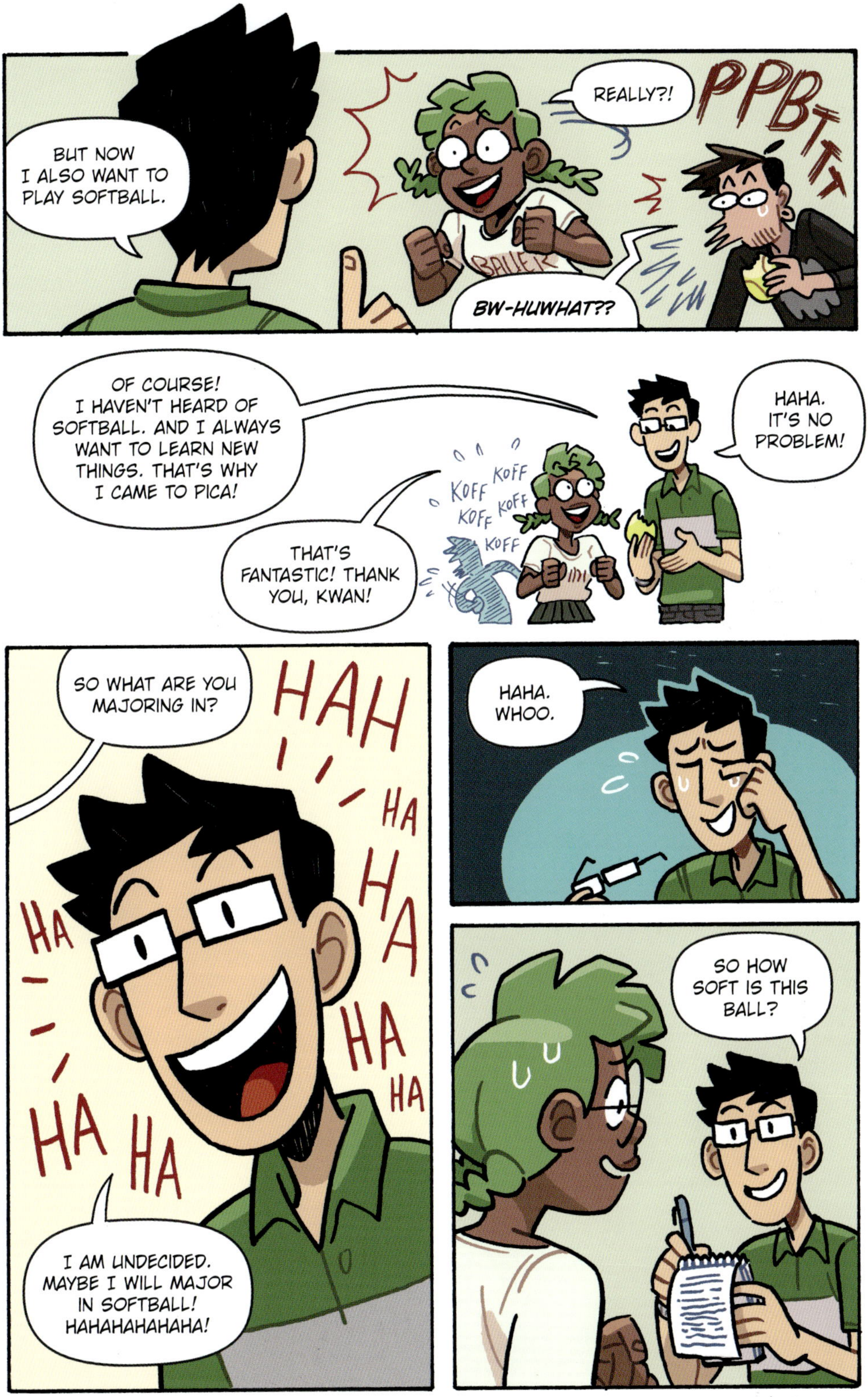
BUT NOW I ALSO WANT TO PLAY SOFTBALL.
REALLY?!
PPBTTT
BW-HUWHAT??
OF COURSE! I HAVEN'T HEARD OF SOFTBALL. AND I ALWAYS WANT TO LEARN NEW THINGS. THAT'S WHY I CAME TO PICA!
HAHA. IT'S NO PROBLEM!
KOFF KOFF KOFF KOFF KOFF
THAT'S FANTASTIC! THANK YOU, KWAN!
SO WHAT ARE YOU MAJORING IN?
HAH
HA HA HA HA HA HA HA HA
I AM UNDECIDED. MAYBE I WILL MAJOR IN SOFTBALL! HAHAHAHAHAHA!
HAHA. WHOO.
SO HOW SOFT IS THIS BALL?

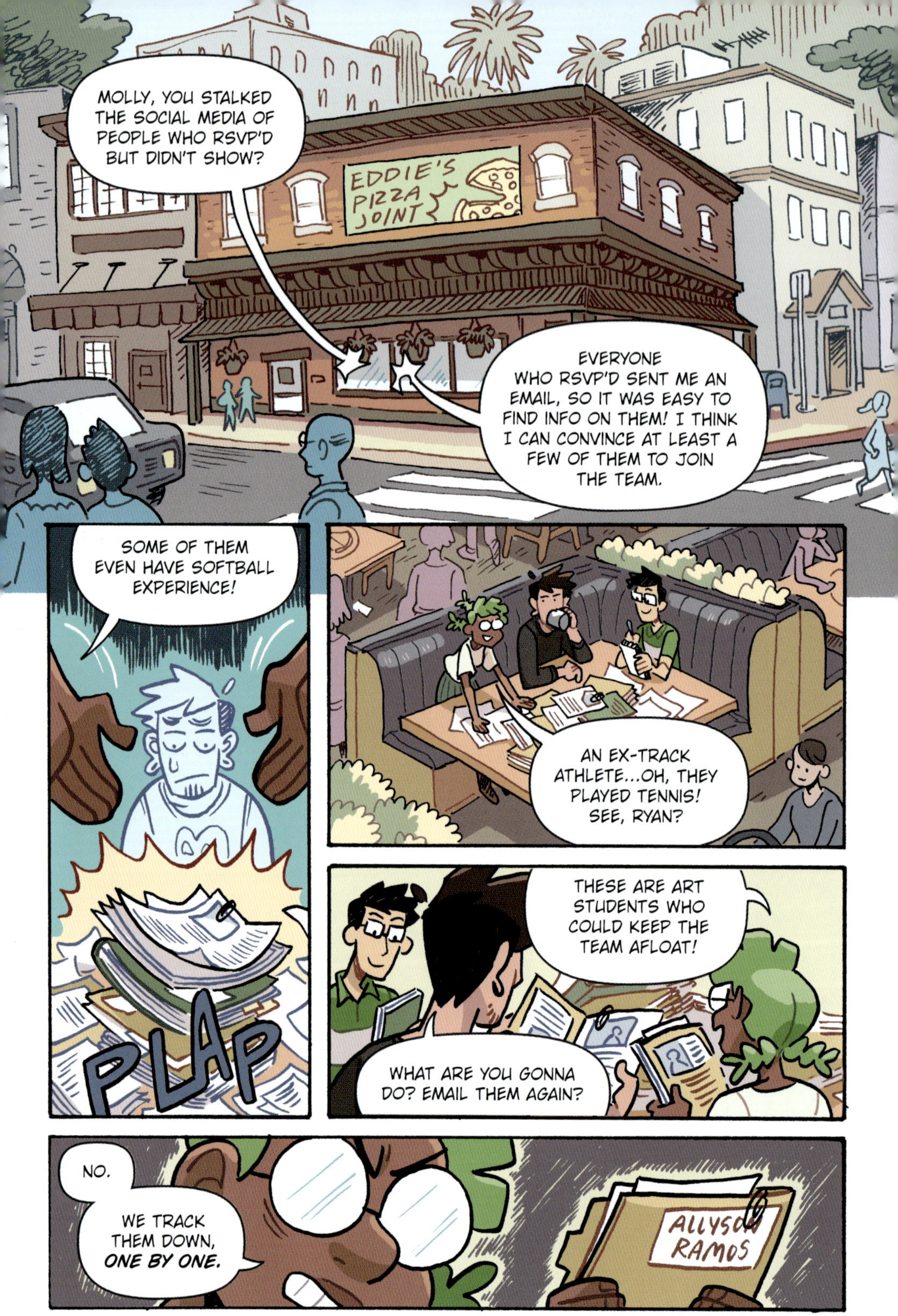
MOLLY, YOU STALKED THE SOCIAL MEDIA OF PEOPLE WHO RSVP'D BUT DIDN'T SHOW?
EDDIE'S PIZZA JOINT
EVERYONE WHO RSVP'D SENT ME AN EMAIL, SO IT WAS EASY TO FIND INFO ON THEM! I THINK I CAN CONVINCE AT LEAST A FEW OF THEM TO JOIN THE TEAM.
SOME OF THEM EVEN HAVE SOFTBALL EXPERIENCE!
PLAP
AN EX-TRACK ATHLETE...OH, THEY PLAYED TENNIS! SEE, RYAN?
THESE ARE ART STUDENTS WHO COULD KEEP THE TEAM AFLOAT!
WHAT ARE YOU GONNA DO? EMAIL THEM AGAIN?
NO.
WE TRACK THEM DOWN, *ONE BY ONE.*
ALLYSON RAMOS

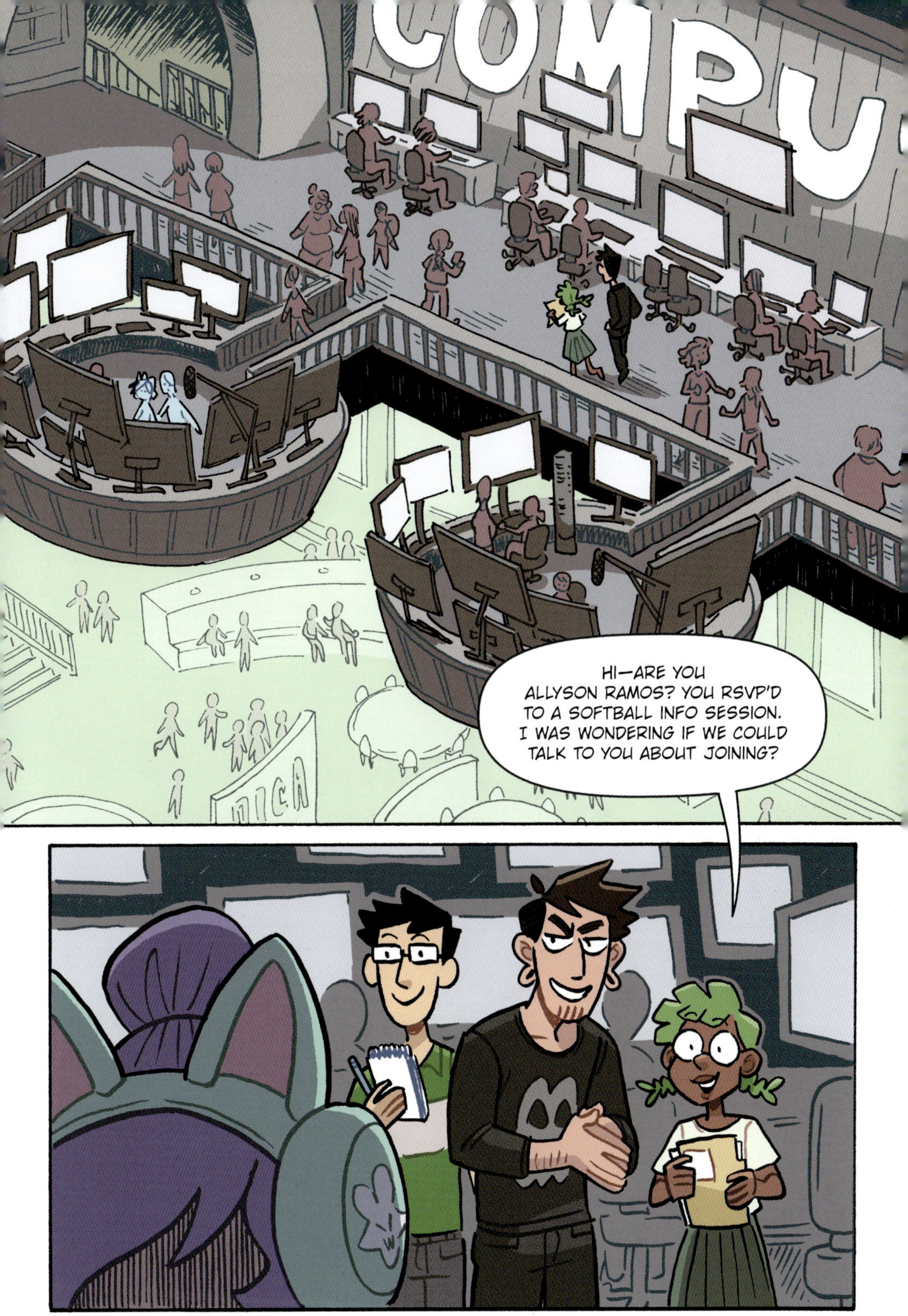
COMPU
HI—ARE YOU ALLYSON RAMOS? YOU RSVP'D TO A SOFTBALL INFO SESSION. I WAS WONDERING IF WE COULD TALK TO YOU ABOUT JOINING?

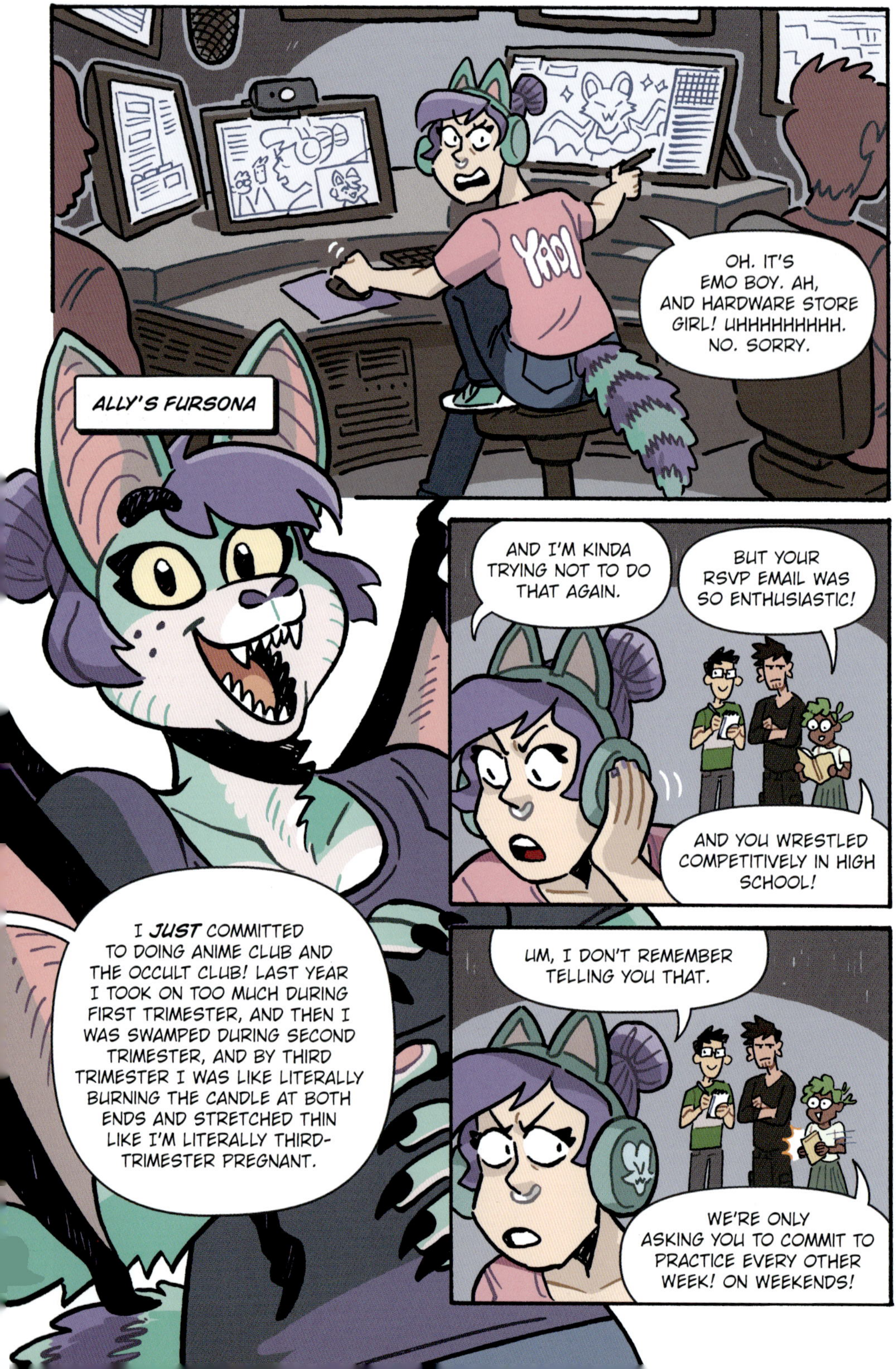
OH. IT'S EMO BOY. AH, AND HARDWARE STORE GIRL! UHHHHHHHHH. NO. SORRY.
ALLY'S FURSONA
I *JUST* COMMITTED TO DOING ANIME CLUB AND THE OCCULT CLUB! LAST YEAR I TOOK ON TOO MUCH DURING FIRST TRIMESTER, AND THEN I WAS SWAMPED DURING SECOND TRIMESTER, AND BY THIRD TRIMESTER I WAS LIKE LITERALLY BURNING THE CANDLE AT BOTH ENDS AND STRETCHED THIN LIKE I'M LITERALLY THIRD-TRIMESTER PREGNANT.
AND I'M KINDA TRYING NOT TO DO THAT AGAIN.
BUT YOUR RSVP EMAIL WAS SO ENTHUSIASTIC!
AND YOU WRESTLED COMPETITIVELY IN HIGH SCHOOL!
UM, I DON'T REMEMBER TELLING YOU THAT.
WE'RE ONLY ASKING YOU TO COMMIT TO PRACTICE EVERY OTHER WEEK! ON WEEKENDS!

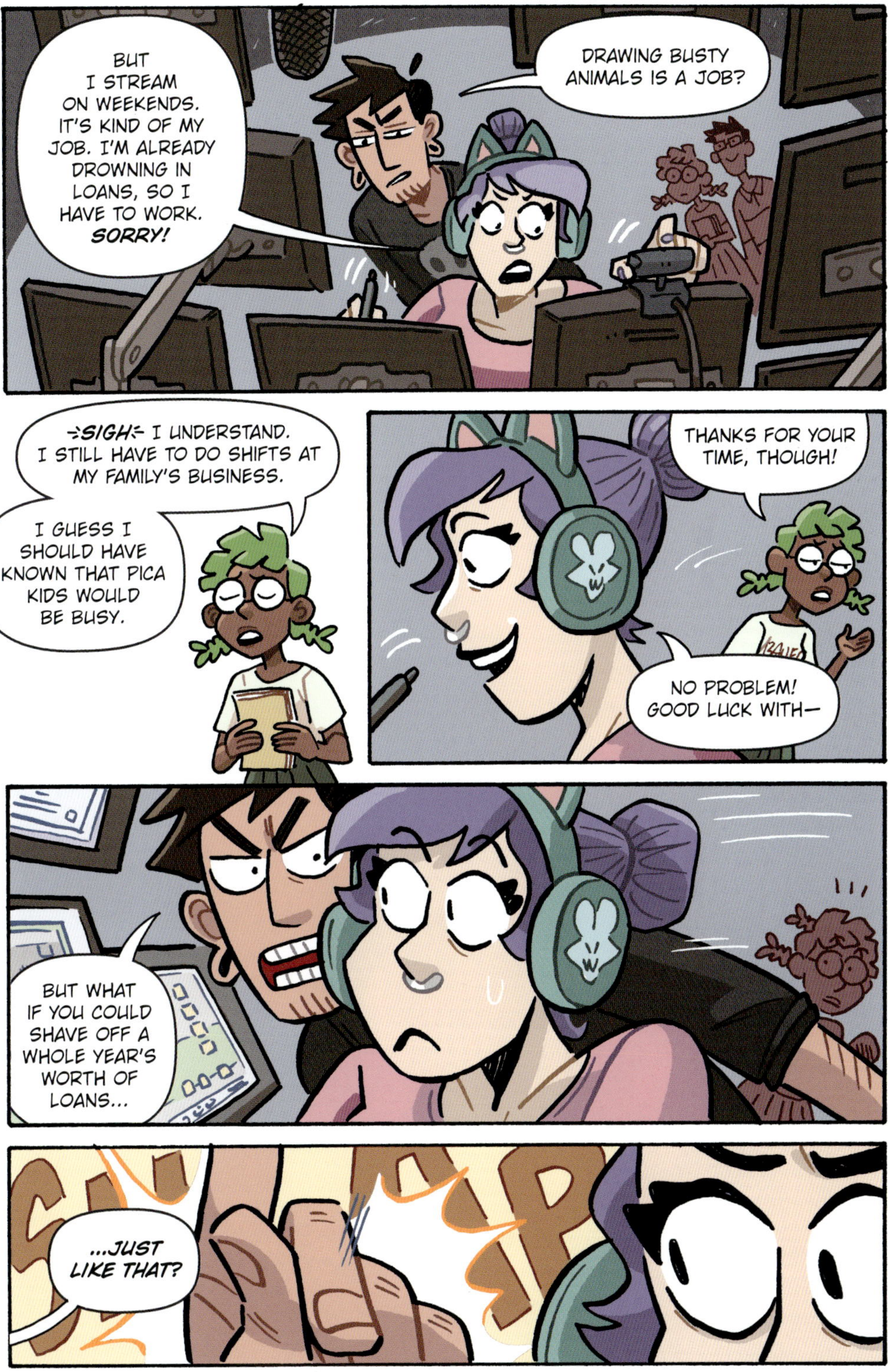

BUT I STREAM ON WEEKENDS. IT'S KIND OF MY JOB. I'M ALREADY DROWNING IN LOANS, SO I HAVE TO WORK. SORRY!
DRAWING BUSTY ANIMALS IS A JOB?
=SIGH= I UNDERSTAND. I STILL HAVE TO DO SHIFTS AT MY FAMILY'S BUSINESS.
I GUESS I SHOULD HAVE KNOWN THAT PICA KIDS WOULD BE BUSY.
THANKS FOR YOUR TIME, THOUGH!
NO PROBLEM! GOOD LUCK WITH—
BUT WHAT IF YOU COULD SHAVE OFF A WHOLE YEAR'S WORTH OF LOANS...
...JUST LIKE THAT?

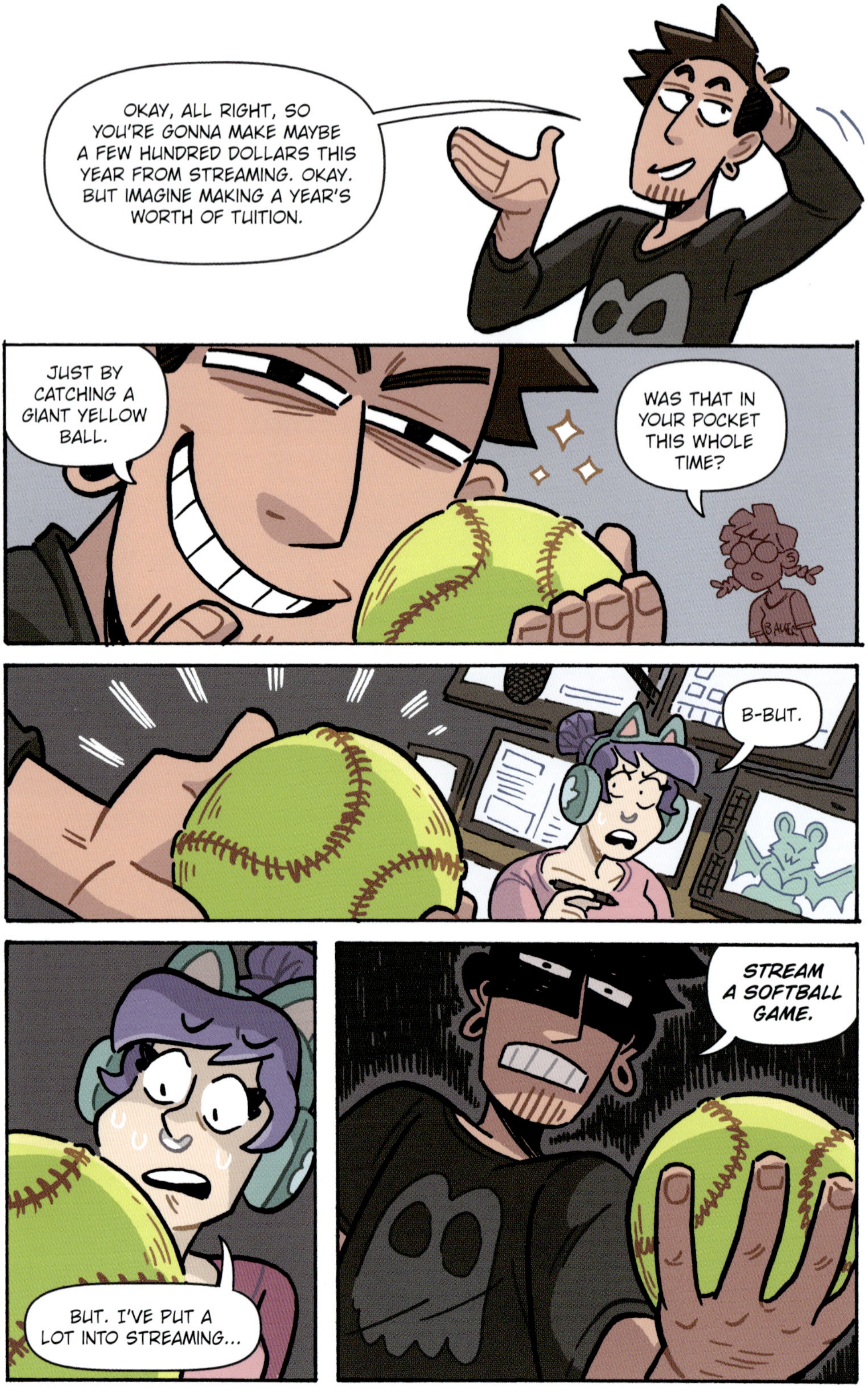
OKAY, ALL RIGHT, SO YOU'RE GONNA MAKE MAYBE A FEW HUNDRED DOLLARS THIS YEAR FROM STREAMING. OKAY. BUT IMAGINE MAKING A YEAR'S WORTH OF TUITION.
JUST BY CATCHING A GIANT YELLOW BALL.
WAS THAT IN YOUR POCKET THIS WHOLE TIME?
B-BUT.
BUT. I'VE PUT A LOT INTO STREAMING...
STREAM A SOFTBALL GAME.

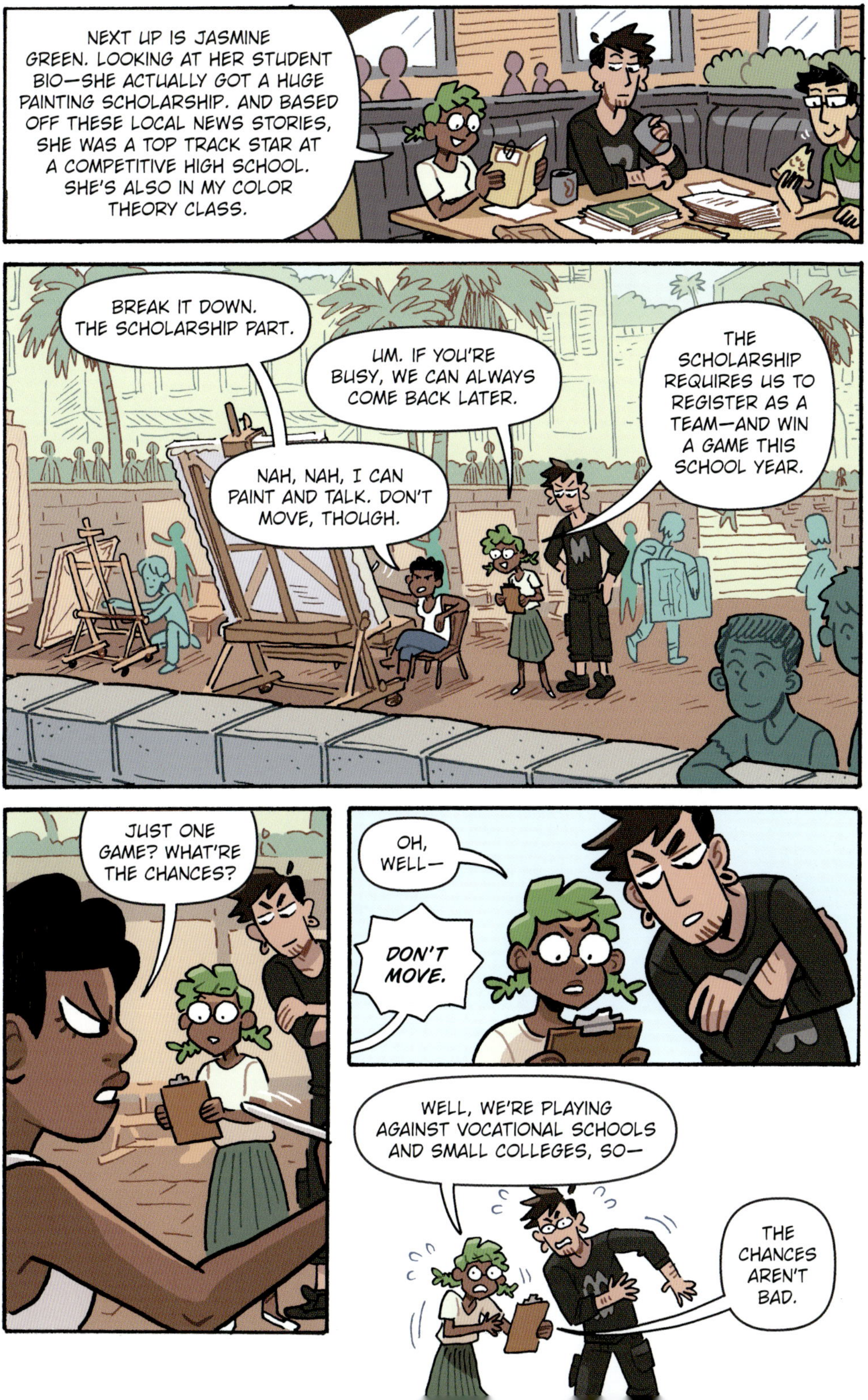
NEXT UP IS JASMINE GREEN. LOOKING AT HER STUDENT BIO—SHE ACTUALLY GOT A HUGE PAINTING SCHOLARSHIP. AND BASED OFF THESE LOCAL NEWS STORIES, SHE WAS A TOP TRACK STAR AT A COMPETITIVE HIGH SCHOOL. SHE'S ALSO IN MY COLOR THEORY CLASS.
BREAK IT DOWN. THE SCHOLARSHIP PART.
UM. IF YOU'RE BUSY, WE CAN ALWAYS COME BACK LATER.
NAH, NAH, I CAN PAINT AND TALK. DON'T MOVE, THOUGH.
THE SCHOLARSHIP REQUIRES US TO REGISTER AS A TEAM—AND WIN A GAME THIS SCHOOL YEAR.
JUST ONE GAME? WHAT'RE THE CHANCES?
OH, WELL—
DON'T MOVE.
WELL, WE'RE PLAYING AGAINST VOCATIONAL SCHOOLS AND SMALL COLLEGES, SO—
THE CHANCES AREN'T BAD.

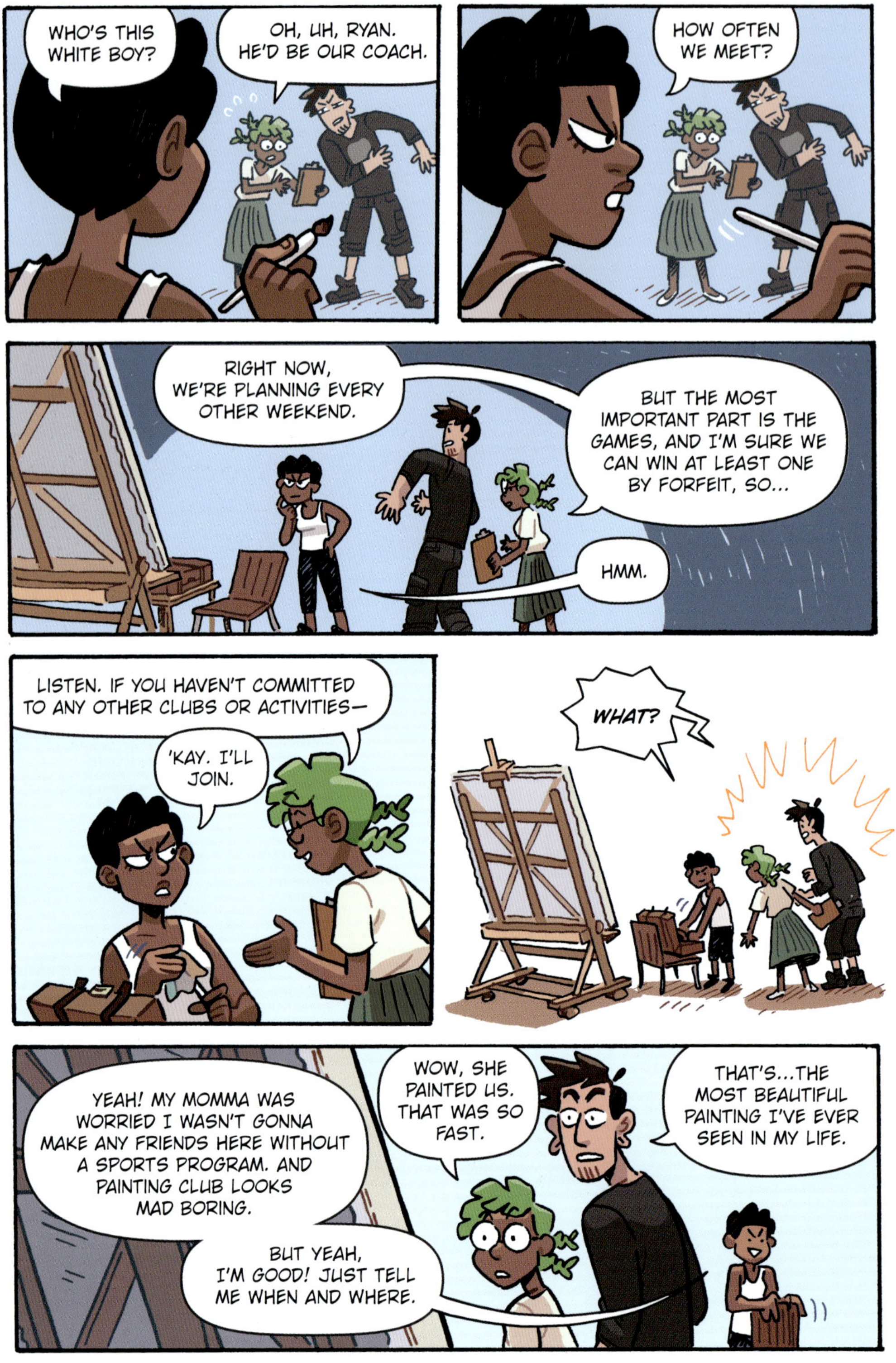
WHO'S THIS WHITE BOY?
OH, UH, RYAN. HE'D BE OUR COACH.
HOW OFTEN WE MEET?
RIGHT NOW, WE'RE PLANNING EVERY OTHER WEEKEND.
BUT THE MOST IMPORTANT PART IS THE GAMES, AND I'M SURE WE CAN WIN AT LEAST ONE BY FORFEIT, SO...
HMM.
LISTEN. IF YOU HAVEN'T COMMITTED TO ANY OTHER CLUBS OR ACTIVITIES—
'KAY. I'LL JOIN.
WHAT?
YEAH! MY MOMMA WAS WORRIED I WASN'T GONNA MAKE ANY FRIENDS HERE WITHOUT A SPORTS PROGRAM. AND PAINTING CLUB LOOKS MAD BORING.
BUT YEAH, I'M GOOD! JUST TELL ME WHEN AND WHERE.
WOW, SHE PAINTED US. THAT WAS SO FAST.
THAT'S...THE MOST BEAUTIFUL PAINTING I'VE EVER SEEN IN MY LIFE.

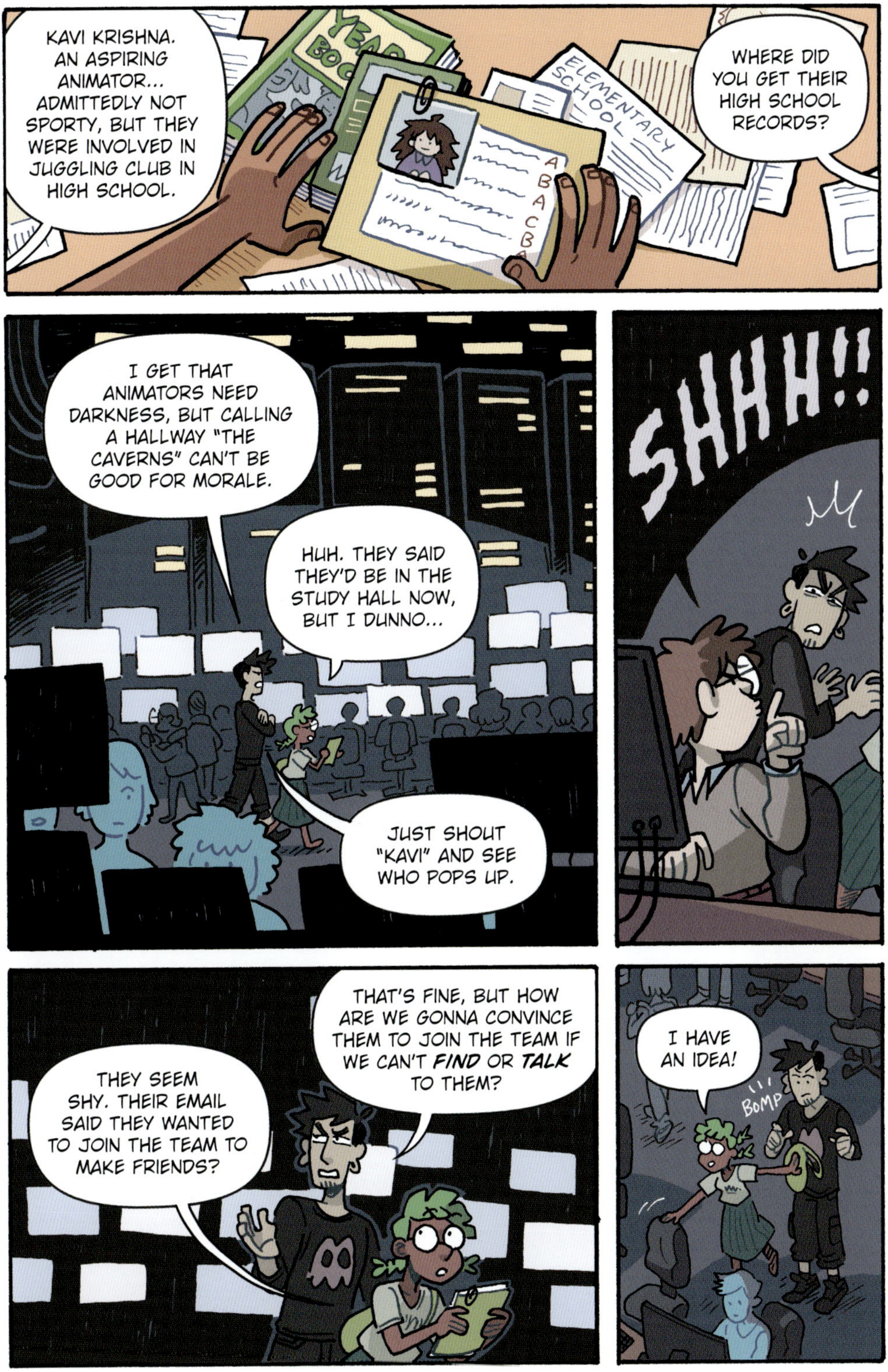
KAVI KRISHNA. AN ASPIRING ANIMATOR... ADMITTEDLY NOT SPORTY, BUT THEY WERE INVOLVED IN JUGGLING CLUB IN HIGH SCHOOL.
ELEMENTARY SCHOOL
WHERE DID YOU GET THEIR HIGH SCHOOL RECORDS?
I GET THAT ANIMATORS NEED DARKNESS, BUT CALLING A HALLWAY "THE CAVERNS" CAN'T BE GOOD FOR MORALE.
HUH. THEY SAID THEY'D BE IN THE STUDY HALL NOW, BUT I DUNNO...
JUST SHOUT "KAVI" AND SEE WHO POPS UP.
SHHH!!
THEY SEEM SHY. THEIR EMAIL SAID THEY WANTED TO JOIN THE TEAM TO MAKE FRIENDS?
THAT'S FINE, BUT HOW ARE WE GONNA CONVINCE THEM TO JOIN THE TEAM IF WE CAN'T *FIND* OR *TALK* TO THEM?
I HAVE AN IDEA!
BOMP

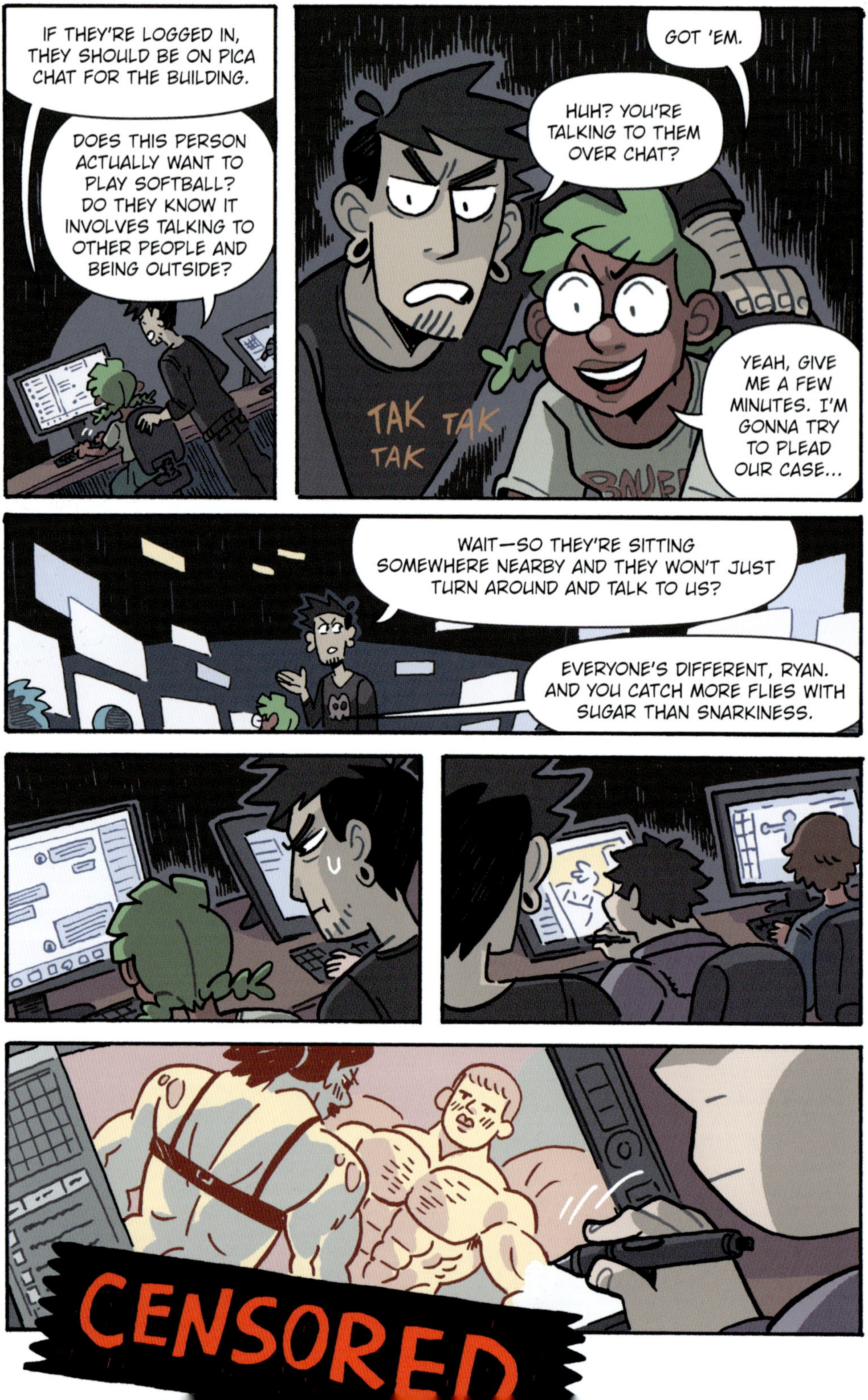
IF THEY'RE LOGGED IN, THEY SHOULD BE ON PICA CHAT FOR THE BUILDING.
DOES THIS PERSON ACTUALLY WANT TO PLAY SOFTBALL? DO THEY KNOW IT INVOLVES TALKING TO OTHER PEOPLE AND BEING OUTSIDE?
GOT 'EM.
HUH? YOU'RE TALKING TO THEM OVER CHAT?
TAK TAK TAK
YEAH, GIVE ME A FEW MINUTES. I'M GONNA TRY TO PLEAD OUR CASE...
WAIT—SO THEY'RE SITTING SOMEWHERE NEARBY AND THEY WON'T JUST TURN AROUND AND TALK TO US?
EVERYONE'S DIFFERENT, RYAN. AND YOU CATCH MORE FLIES WITH SUGAR THAN SNARKINESS.
CENSORED

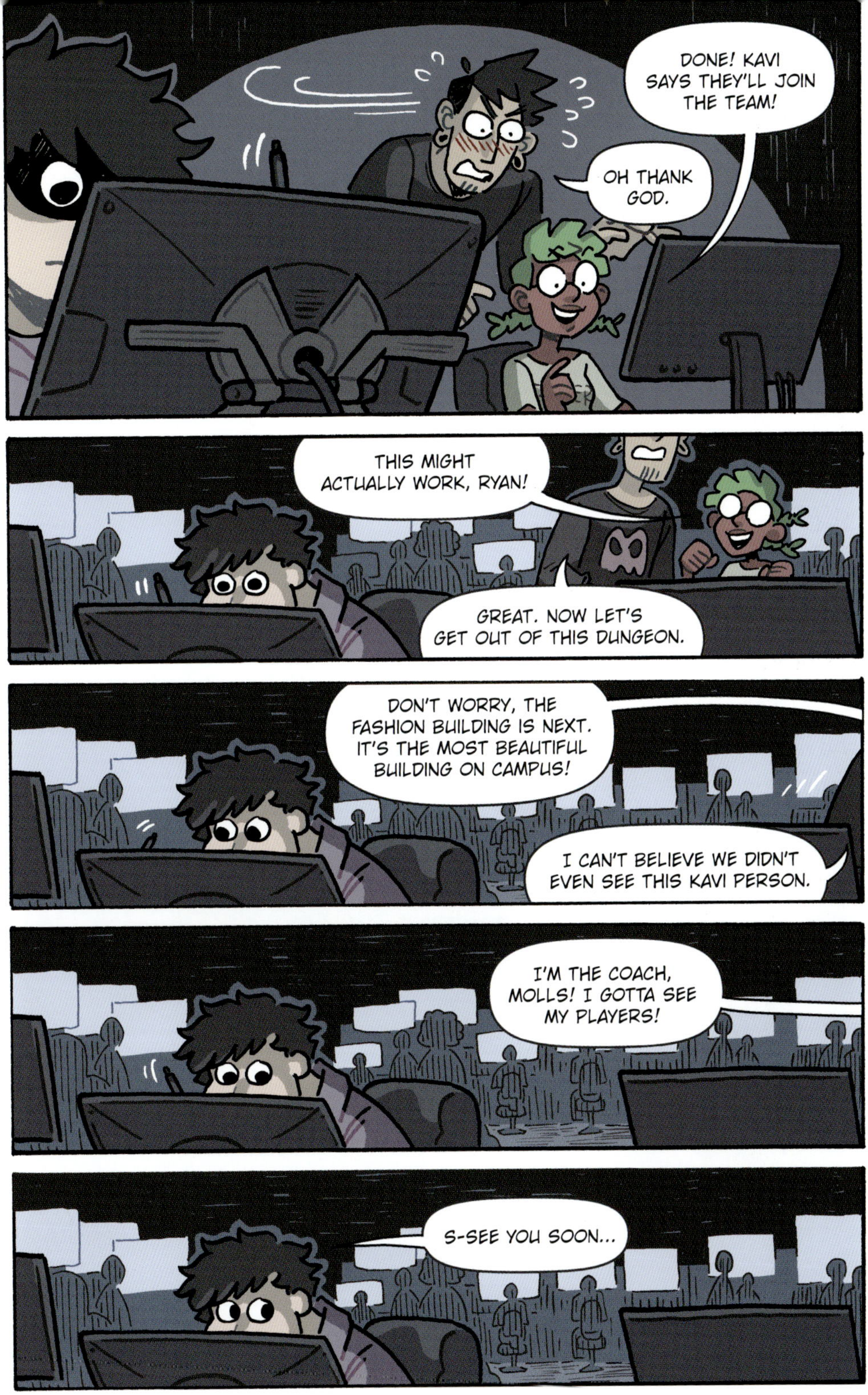
DONE! KAVI SAYS THEY'LL JOIN THE TEAM!
OH THANK GOD.
THIS MIGHT ACTUALLY WORK, RYAN!
GREAT. NOW LET'S GET OUT OF THIS DUNGEON.
DON'T WORRY, THE FASHION BUILDING IS NEXT. IT'S THE MOST BEAUTIFUL BUILDING ON CAMPUS!
I CAN'T BELIEVE WE DIDN'T EVEN SEE THIS KAVI PERSON.
I'M THE COACH, MOLLS! I GOTTA SEE MY PLAYERS!
S-SEE YOU SOON...

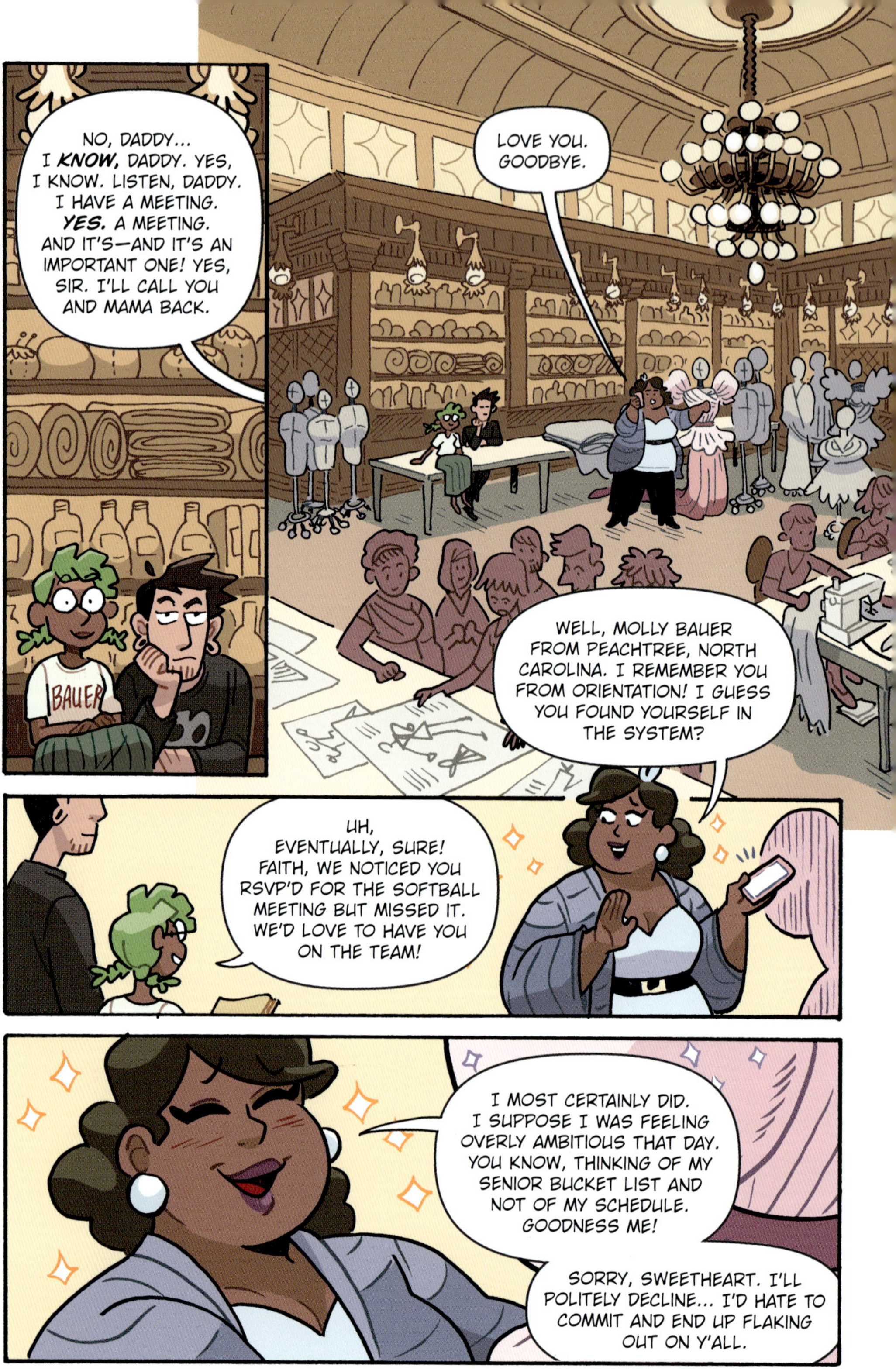
NO, DADDY... I **KNOW,** DADDY. YES, I KNOW. LISTEN, DADDY. I HAVE A MEETING. **YES.** A MEETING. AND IT'S—AND IT'S AN IMPORTANT ONE! YES, SIR. I'LL CALL YOU AND MAMA BACK.
LOVE YOU. GOODBYE.
BAUER
WELL, MOLLY BAUER FROM PEACHTREE, NORTH CAROLINA. I REMEMBER YOU FROM ORIENTATION! I GUESS YOU FOUND YOURSELF IN THE SYSTEM?
UH, EVENTUALLY, SURE! FAITH, WE NOTICED YOU RSVP'D FOR THE SOFTBALL MEETING BUT MISSED IT. WE'D LOVE TO HAVE YOU ON THE TEAM!
I MOST CERTAINLY DID. I SUPPOSE I WAS FEELING OVERLY AMBITIOUS THAT DAY. YOU KNOW, THINKING OF MY SENIOR BUCKET LIST AND NOT OF MY SCHEDULE. GOODNESS ME!
SORRY, SWEETHEART. I'LL POLITELY DECLINE... I'D HATE TO COMMIT AND END UP FLAKING OUT ON Y'ALL.

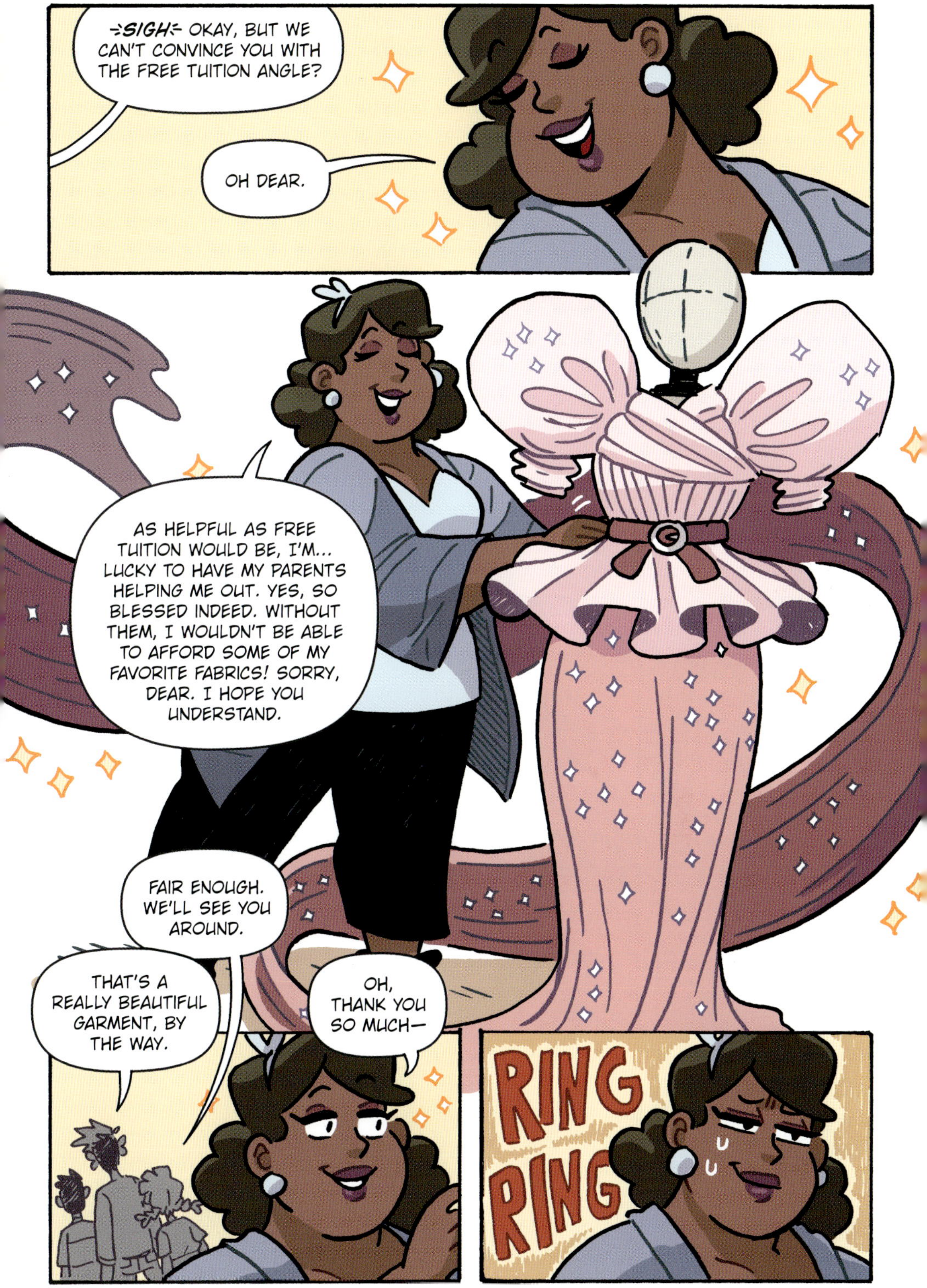

-SIGH- OKAY, BUT WE CAN'T CONVINCE YOU WITH THE FREE TUITION ANGLE?
OH DEAR.
AS HELPFUL AS FREE TUITION WOULD BE, I'M... LUCKY TO HAVE MY PARENTS HELPING ME OUT. YES, SO BLESSED INDEED. WITHOUT THEM, I WOULDN'T BE ABLE TO AFFORD SOME OF MY FAVORITE FABRICS! SORRY, DEAR. I HOPE YOU UNDERSTAND.
FAIR ENOUGH. WE'LL SEE YOU AROUND.
THAT'S A REALLY BEAUTIFUL GARMENT, BY THE WAY.
OH, THANK YOU SO MUCH—
RING RING

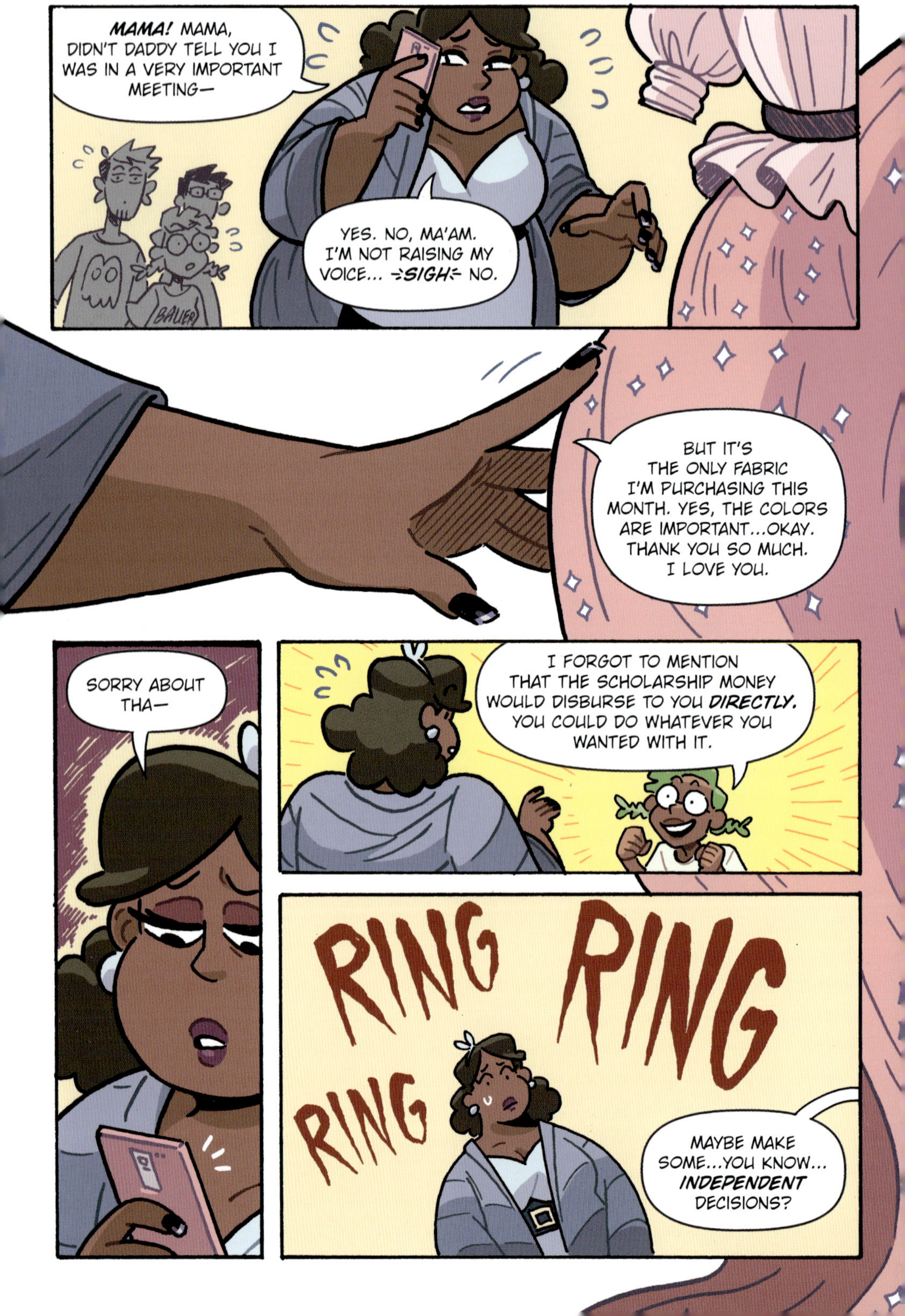
MAMA! MAMA, DIDN'T DADDY TELL YOU I WAS IN A VERY IMPORTANT MEETING—
YES. NO, MA'AM. I'M NOT RAISING MY VOICE... SIGH NO.
BUT IT'S THE ONLY FABRIC I'M PURCHASING THIS MONTH. YES, THE COLORS ARE IMPORTANT...OKAY. THANK YOU SO MUCH. I LOVE YOU.
SORRY ABOUT THA—
I FORGOT TO MENTION THAT THE SCHOLARSHIP MONEY WOULD DISBURSE TO YOU DIRECTLY. YOU COULD DO WHATEVER YOU WANTED WITH IT.
RING RING
RING
MAYBE MAKE SOME...YOU KNOW... INDEPENDENT DECISIONS?

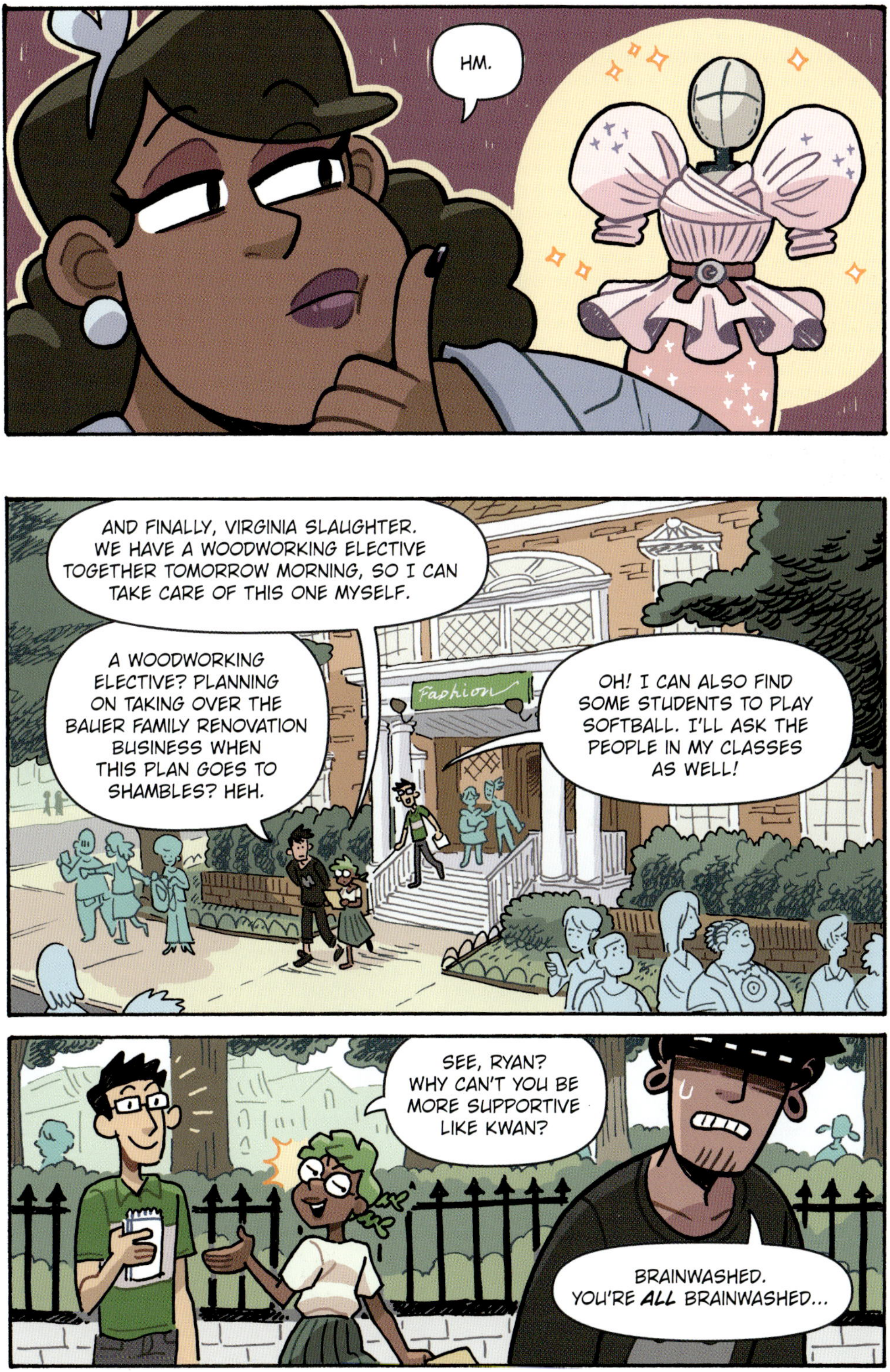
HM.
AND FINALLY, VIRGINIA SLAUGHTER. WE HAVE A WOODWORKING ELECTIVE TOGETHER TOMORROW MORNING, SO I CAN TAKE CARE OF THIS ONE MYSELF.
A WOODWORKING ELECTIVE? PLANNING ON TAKING OVER THE BAUER FAMILY RENOVATION BUSINESS WHEN THIS PLAN GOES TO SHAMBLES? HEH.
OH! I CAN ALSO FIND SOME STUDENTS TO PLAY SOFTBALL. I'LL ASK THE PEOPLE IN MY CLASSES AS WELL!
Fashion
SEE, RYAN? WHY CAN'T YOU BE MORE SUPPORTIVE LIKE KWAN?
BRAINWASHED. YOU'RE ***ALL*** BRAINWASHED...

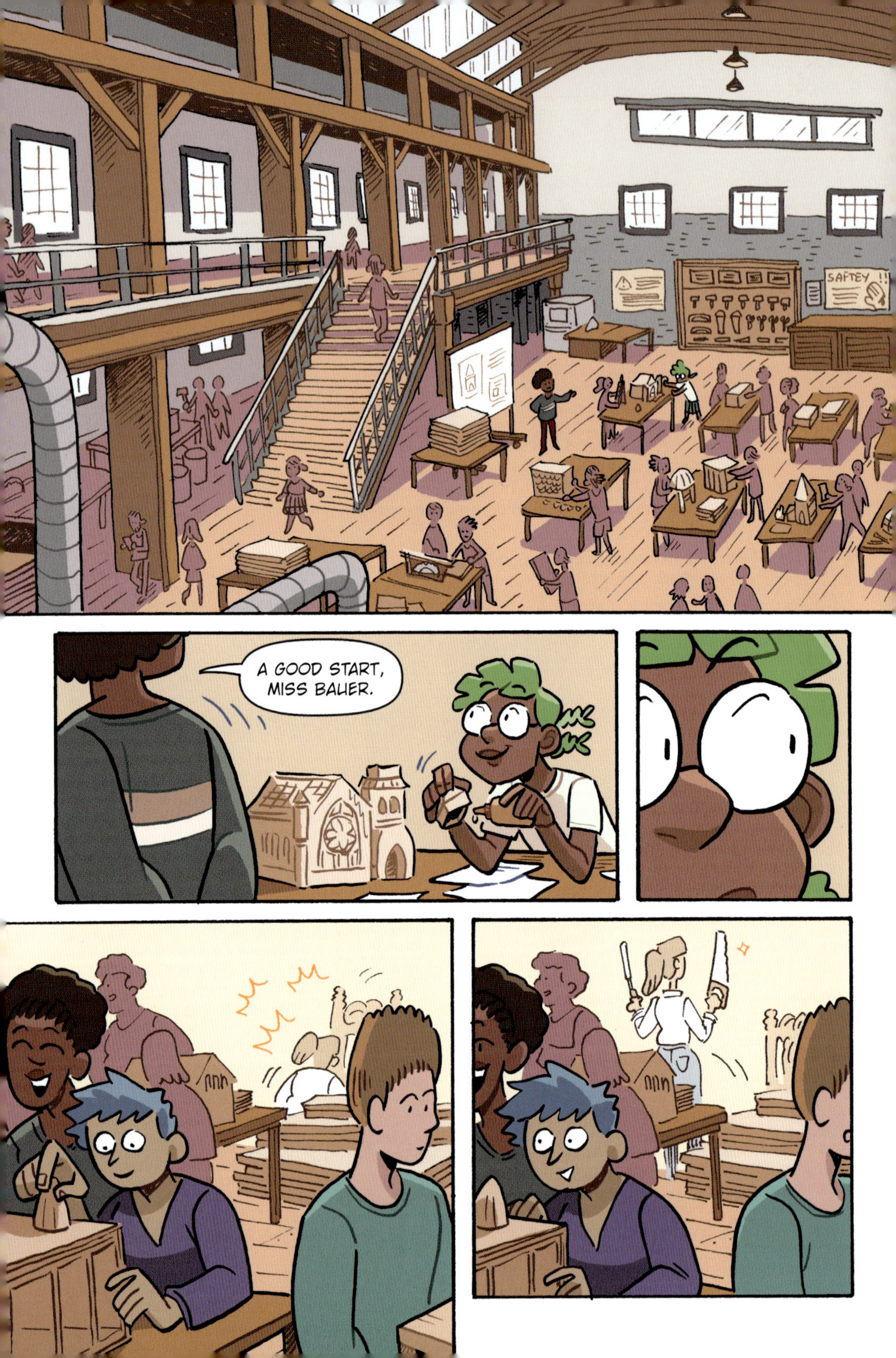
SAFTEY !!
A GOOD START, MISS BAUER.

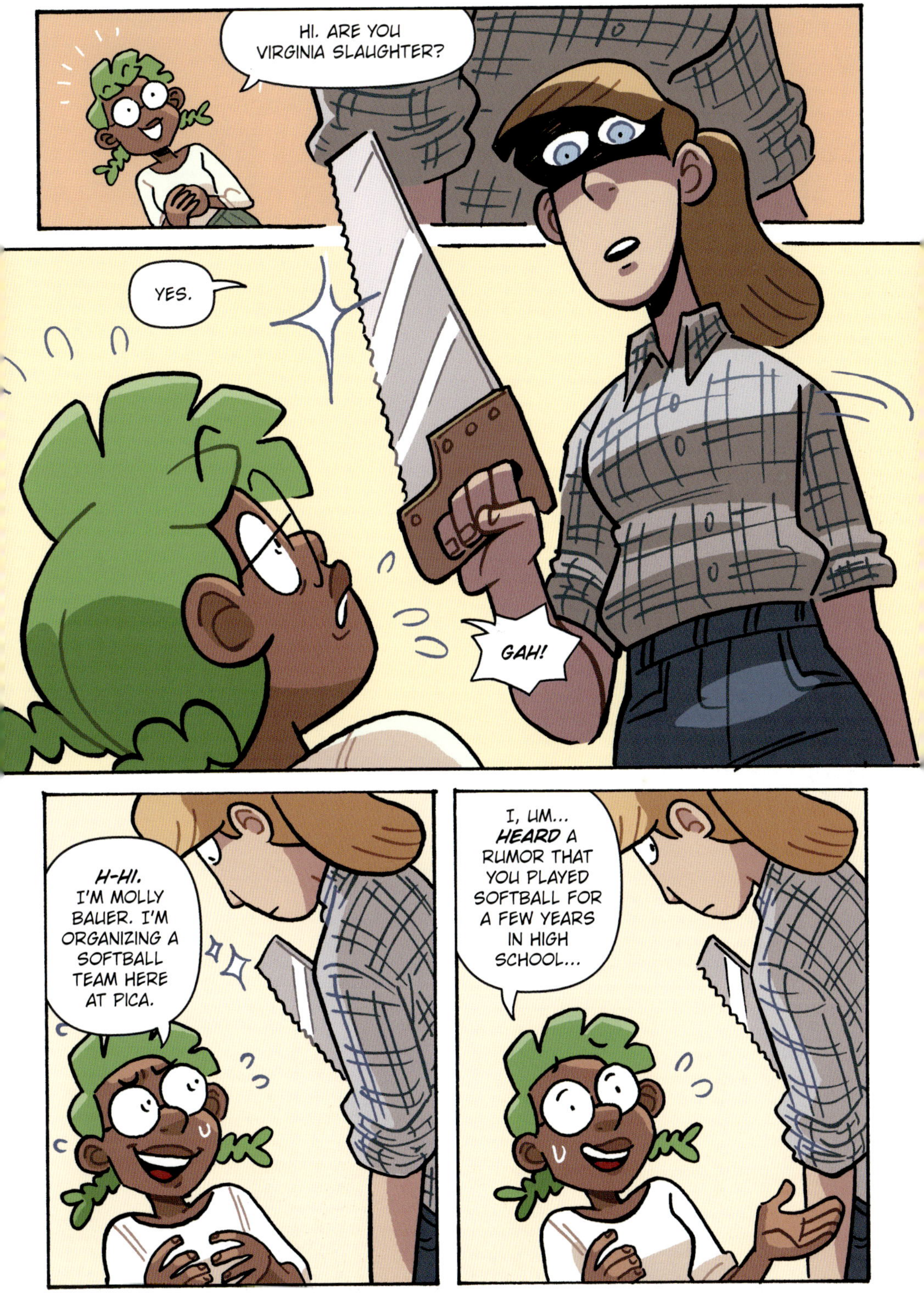
HI. ARE YOU VIRGINIA SLAUGHTER?
YES.
GAH!
H-HI. I'M MOLLY BAUER. I'M ORGANIZING A SOFTBALL TEAM HERE AT PICA.
I, UM... HEARD A RUMOR THAT YOU PLAYED SOFTBALL FOR A FEW YEARS IN HIGH SCHOOL...

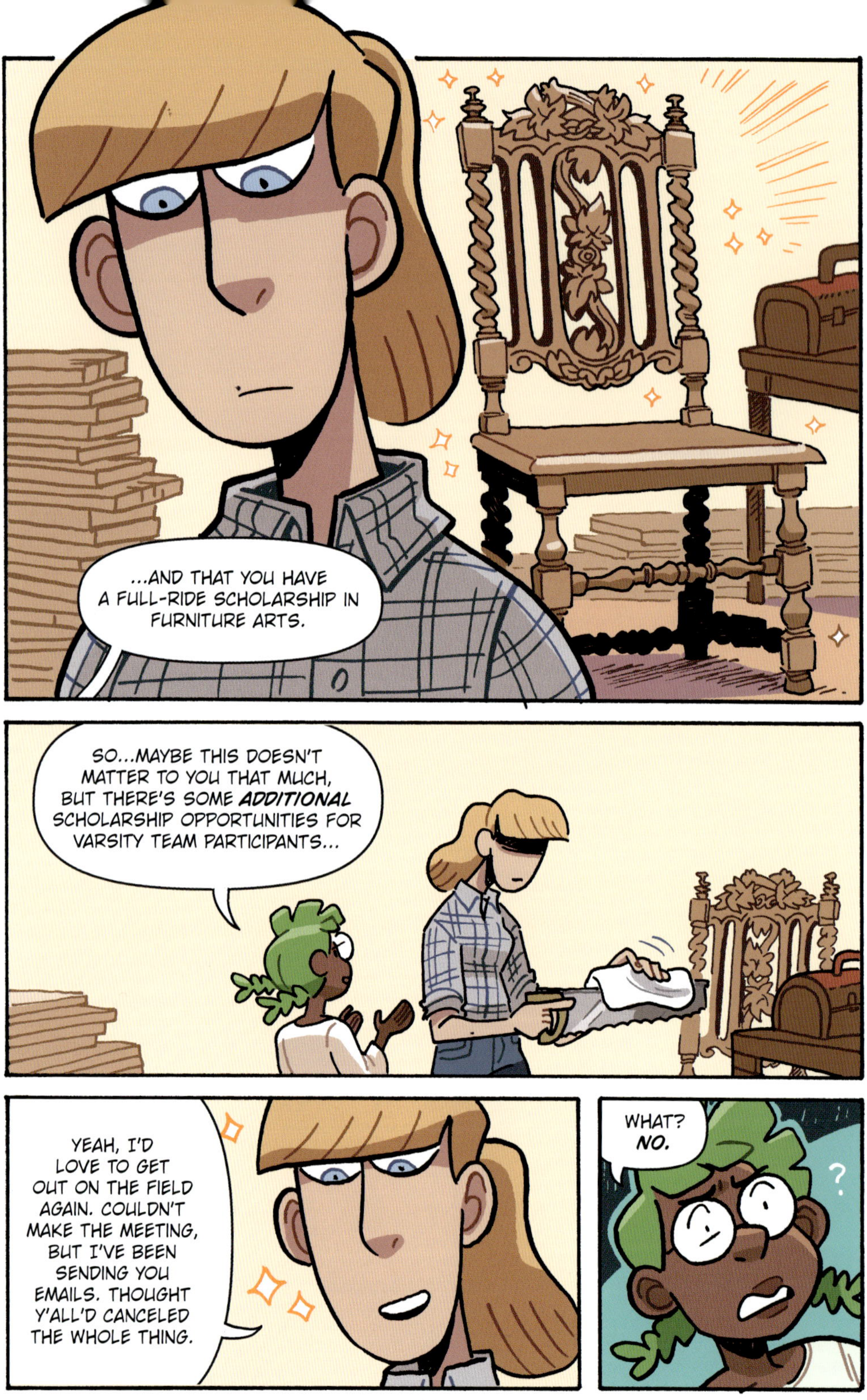
...AND THAT YOU HAVE A FULL-RIDE SCHOLARSHIP IN FURNITURE ARTS.
SO...MAYBE THIS DOESN'T MATTER TO YOU THAT MUCH, BUT THERE'S SOME *ADDITIONAL* SCHOLARSHIP OPPORTUNITIES FOR VARSITY TEAM PARTICIPANTS...
YEAH, I'D LOVE TO GET OUT ON THE FIELD AGAIN. COULDN'T MAKE THE MEETING, BUT I'VE BEEN SENDING YOU EMAILS. THOUGHT Y'ALL'D CANCELED THE WHOLE THING.
WHAT? *NO.*
?

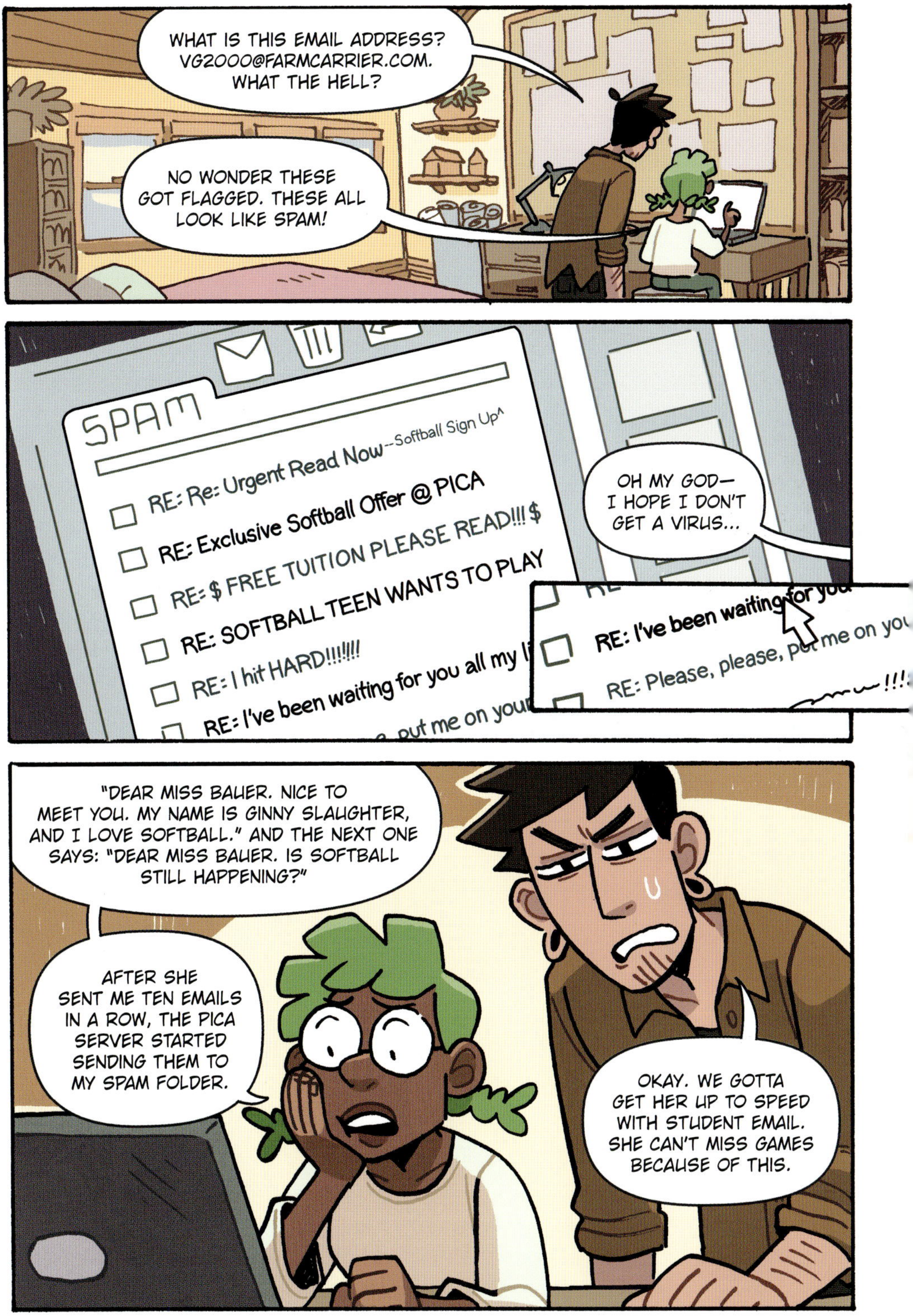

WHAT IS THIS EMAIL ADDRESS? VG2000@FARMCARRIER.COM. WHAT THE HELL?
NO WONDER THESE GOT FLAGGED. THESE ALL LOOK LIKE SPAM!
SPAM
--Softball Sign Up^
RE: Re: Urgent Read Now
RE: Exclusive Softball Offer @ PICA
RE: $ FREE TUITION PLEASE READ!!! $
RE: SOFTBALL TEEN WANTS TO PLAY
RE: I hit HARD!!!!!!
RE: I've been waiting for you all my
OH MY GOD— I HOPE I DON'T GET A VIRUS...
RE: I've been waiting
RE: Please, please,
"DEAR MISS BAUER. NICE TO MEET YOU. MY NAME IS GINNY SLAUGHTER, AND I LOVE SOFTBALL." AND THE NEXT ONE SAYS: "DEAR MISS BAUER. IS SOFTBALL STILL HAPPENING?"
AFTER SHE SENT ME TEN EMAILS IN A ROW, THE PICA SERVER STARTED SENDING THEM TO MY SPAM FOLDER.
OKAY. WE GOTTA GET HER UP TO SPEED WITH STUDENT EMAIL. SHE CAN'T MISS GAMES BECAUSE OF THIS.

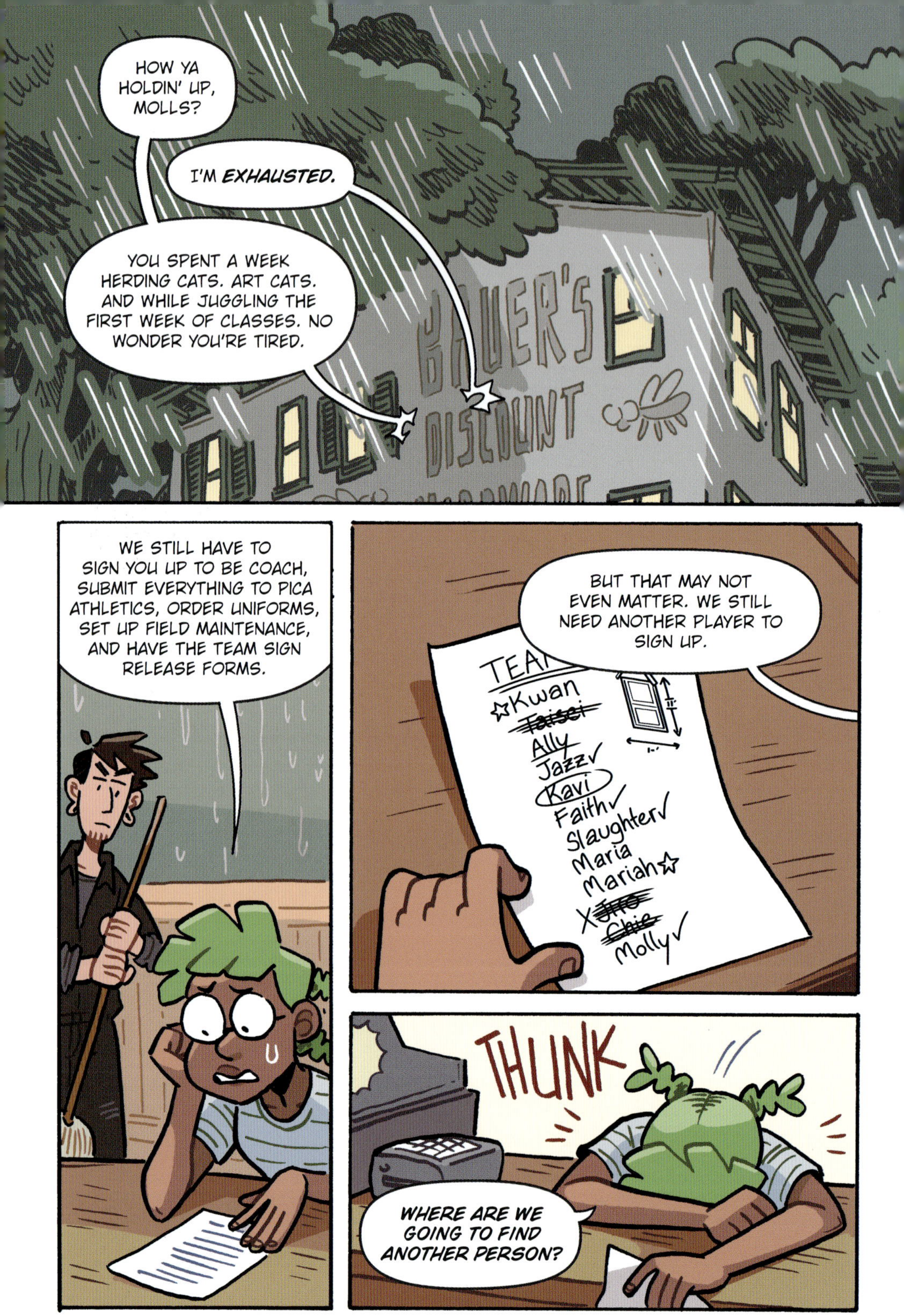
HOW YA HOLDIN' UP, MOLLS?
I'M *EXHAUSTED.*
YOU SPENT A WEEK HERDING CATS. ART CATS. AND WHILE JUGGLING THE FIRST WEEK OF CLASSES. NO WONDER YOU'RE TIRED.
DISCOUNT
WE STILL HAVE TO SIGN YOU UP TO BE COACH, SUBMIT EVERYTHING TO PICA ATHLETICS, ORDER UNIFORMS, SET UP FIELD MAINTENANCE, AND HAVE THE TEAM SIGN RELEASE FORMS.
BUT THAT MAY NOT EVEN MATTER. WE STILL NEED ANOTHER PLAYER TO SIGN UP.
Kwan
Ally
Jazz
Kavi
Faith
Slaughter
Maria
Mariah
Molly
THUNK
WHERE ARE WE GOING TO FIND ANOTHER PERSON?

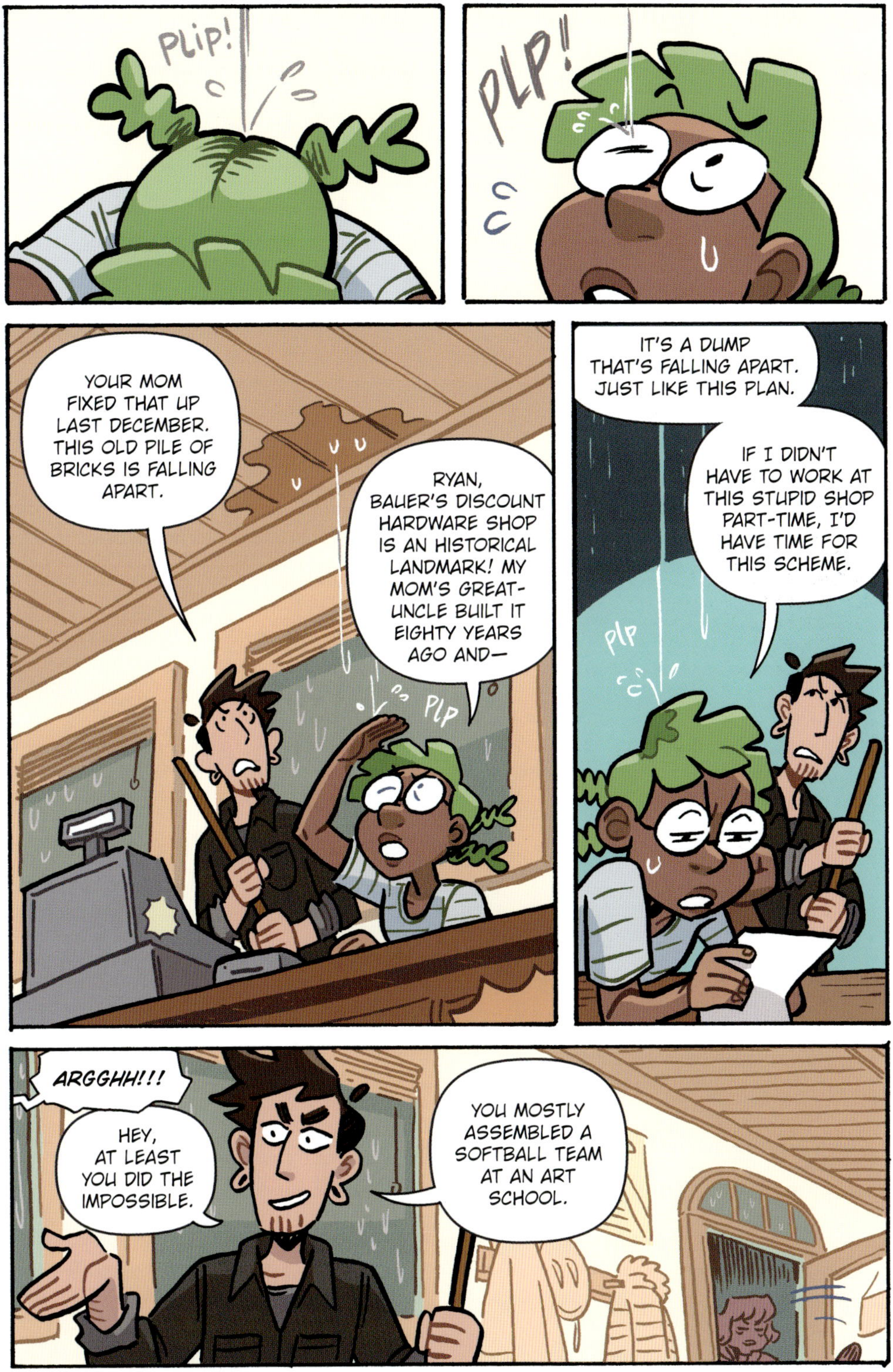
PLIP!
PLP!
YOUR MOM FIXED THAT UP LAST DECEMBER. THIS OLD PILE OF BRICKS IS FALLING APART.
RYAN, BAUER'S DISCOUNT HARDWARE SHOP IS AN HISTORICAL LANDMARK! MY MOM'S GREAT-UNCLE BUILT IT EIGHTY YEARS AGO AND—
PLP
IT'S A DUMP THAT'S FALLING APART. JUST LIKE THIS PLAN.
IF I DIDN'T HAVE TO WORK AT THIS STUPID SHOP PART-TIME, I'D HAVE TIME FOR THIS SCHEME.
PLP
ARGGHH!!!
HEY, AT LEAST YOU DID THE IMPOSSIBLE.
YOU MOSTLY ASSEMBLED A SOFTBALL TEAM AT AN ART SCHOOL.

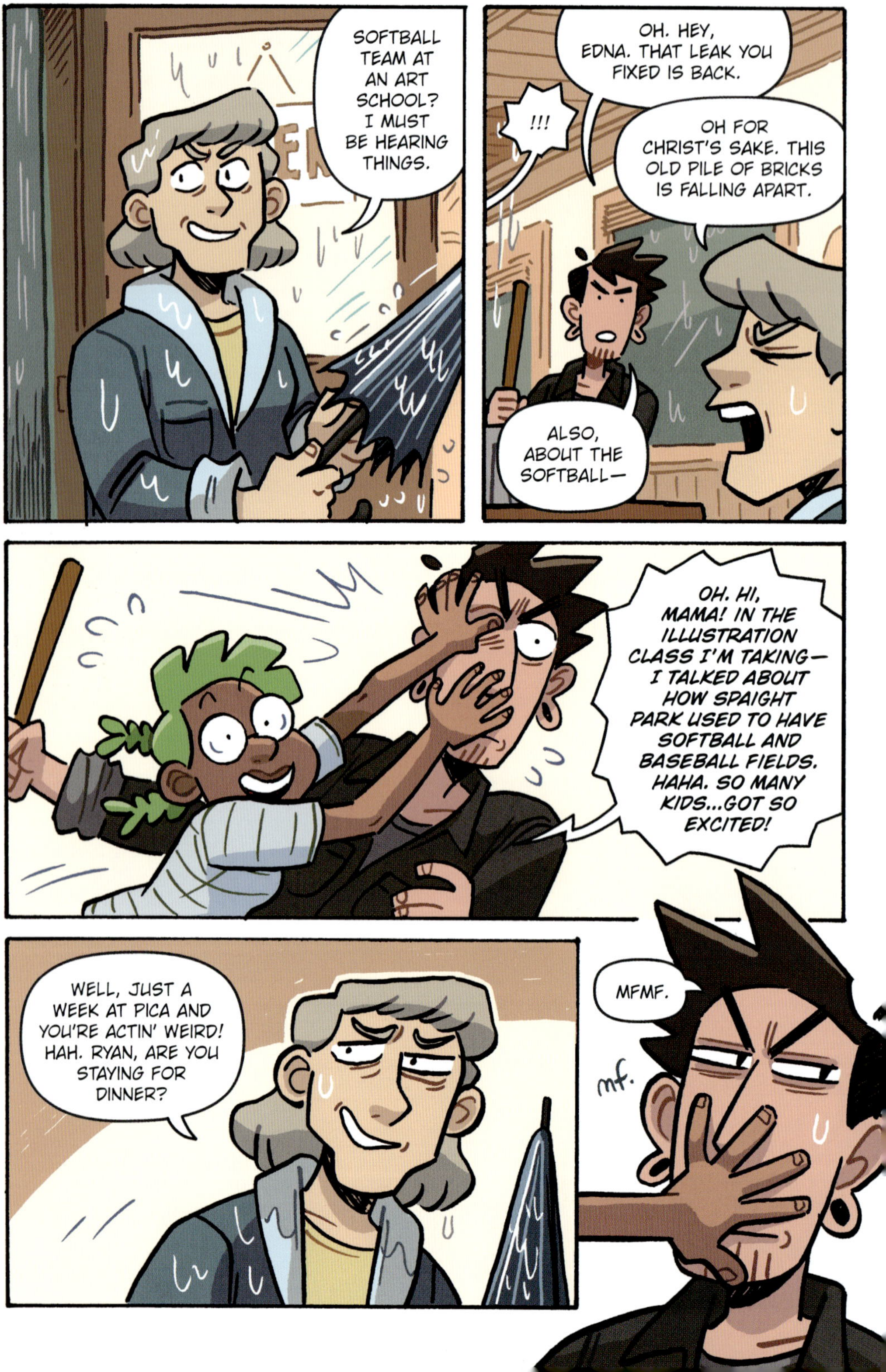
SOFTBALL TEAM AT AN ART SCHOOL? I MUST BE HEARING THINGS.
OH. HEY, EDNA. THAT LEAK YOU FIXED IS BACK.
!!!
OH FOR CHRIST'S SAKE. THIS OLD PILE OF BRICKS IS FALLING APART.
ALSO, ABOUT THE SOFTBALL—
OH. HI, MAMA! IN THE ILLUSTRATION CLASS I'M TAKING— I TALKED ABOUT HOW SPAIGHT PARK USED TO HAVE SOFTBALL AND BASEBALL FIELDS. HAHA. SO MANY KIDS...GOT SO EXCITED!
WELL, JUST A WEEK AT PICA AND YOU'RE ACTIN' WEIRD! HAH. RYAN, ARE YOU STAYING FOR DINNER?
MFMF.
mf.

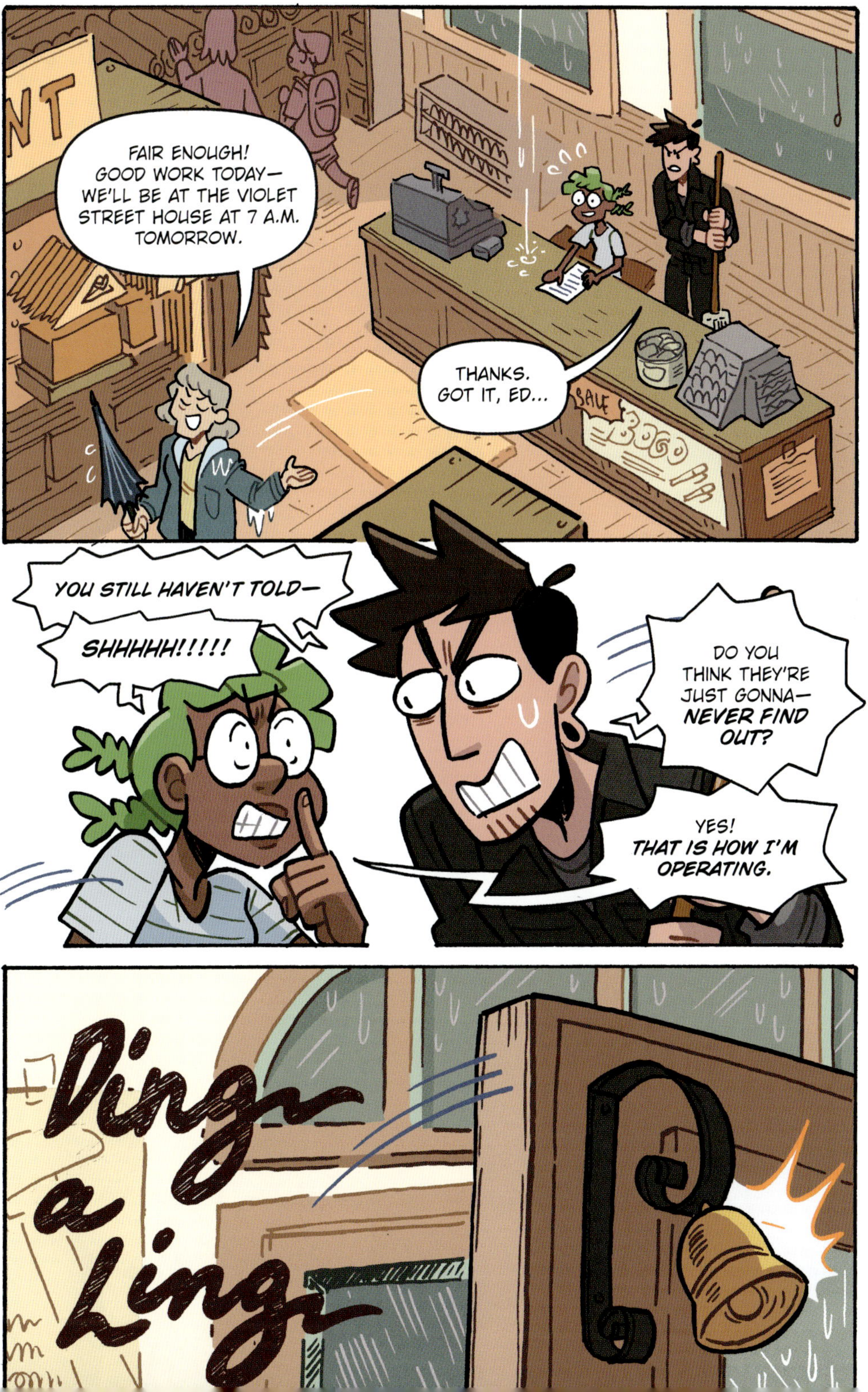

FAIR ENOUGH! GOOD WORK TODAY— WE'LL BE AT THE VIOLET STREET HOUSE AT 7 A.M. TOMORROW.
THANKS. GOT IT, ED...
SALE
BOGO
YOU STILL HAVEN'T TOLD—
SHHHHH!!!!!
DO YOU THINK THEY'RE JUST GONNA— NEVER FIND OUT?
YES! THAT IS HOW I'M OPERATING.
Ding a Ling

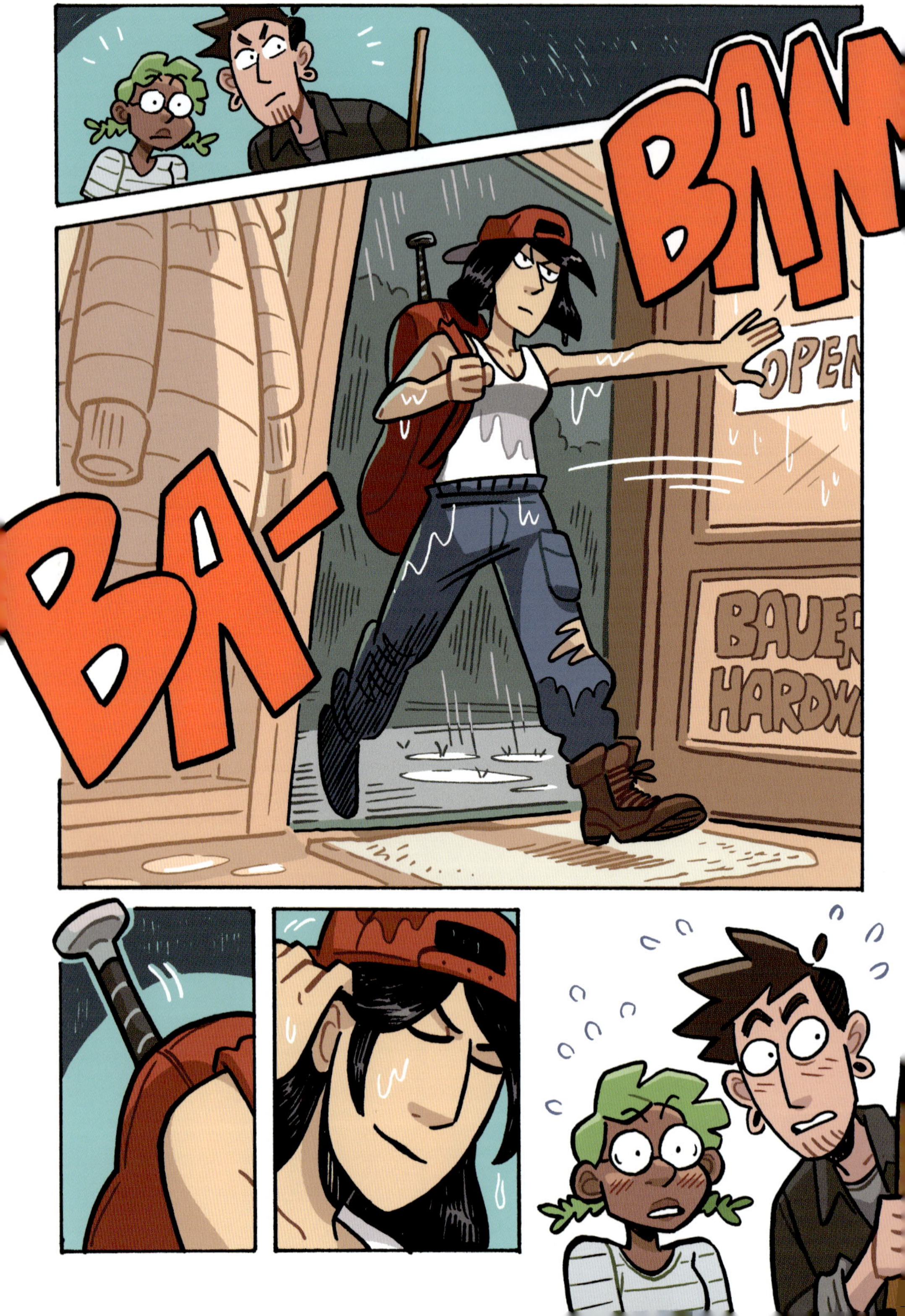
BAM
OPEN
BA-
BAUER
HARDW

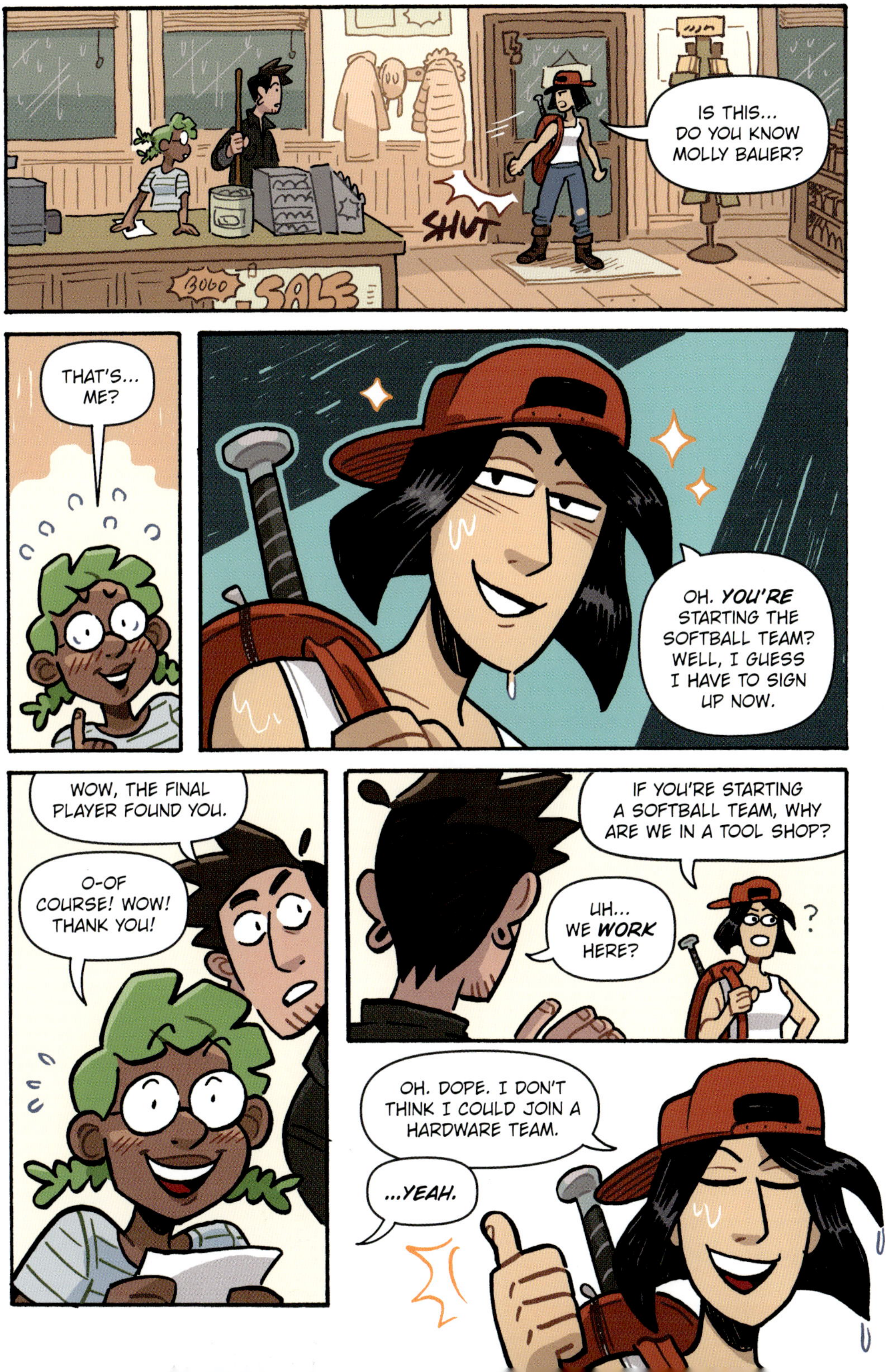
IS THIS... DO YOU KNOW MOLLY BAUER?
SHUT
BOGO
SALE
THAT'S... ME?
OH. YOU'RE STARTING THE SOFTBALL TEAM? WELL, I GUESS I HAVE TO SIGN UP NOW.
WOW, THE FINAL PLAYER FOUND YOU.
O-OF COURSE! WOW! THANK YOU!
IF YOU'RE STARTING A SOFTBALL TEAM, WHY ARE WE IN A TOOL SHOP?
UH... WE WORK HERE?
?
OH. DOPE. I DON'T THINK I COULD JOIN A HARDWARE TEAM.
...YEAH.

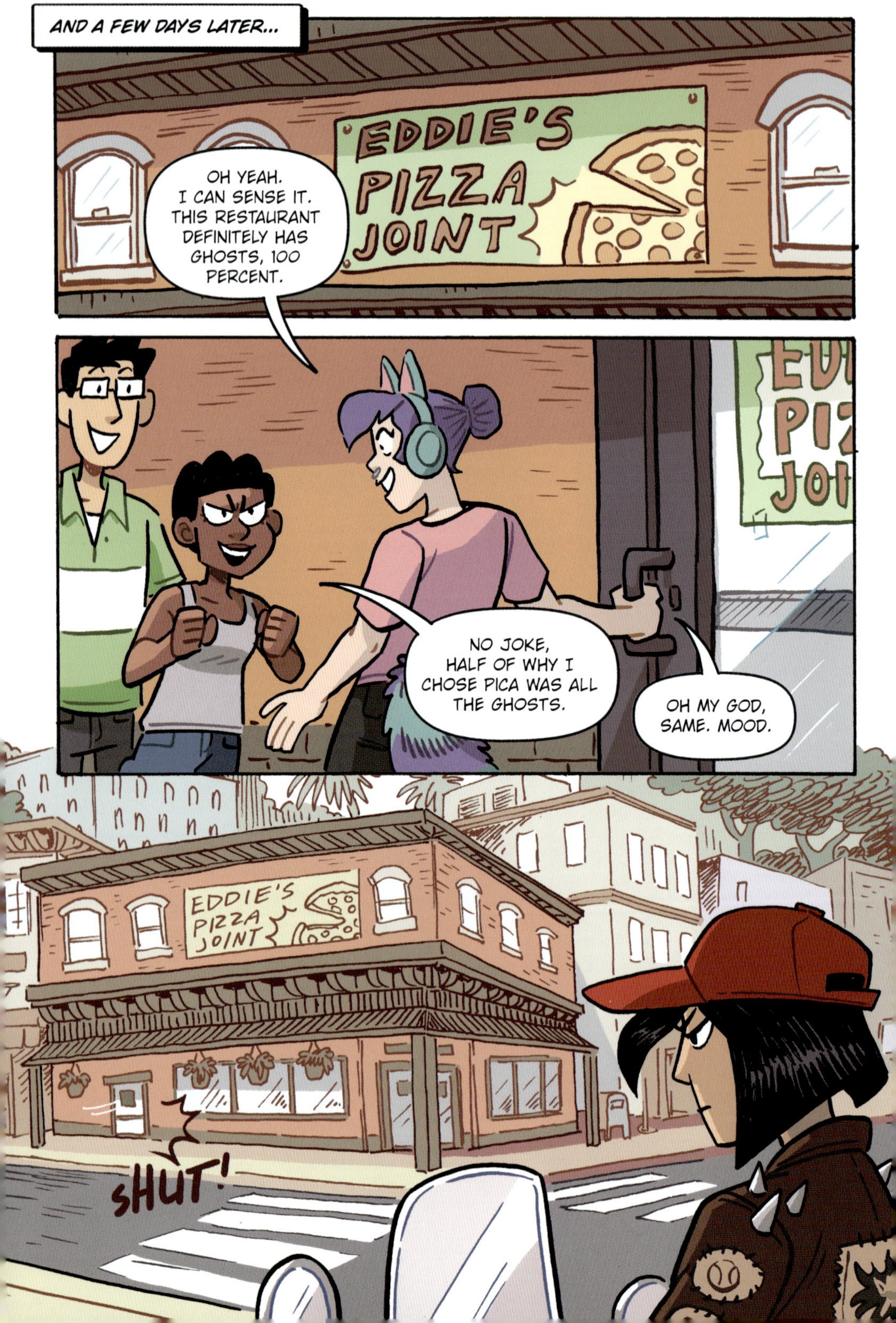
AND A FEW DAYS LATER...
EDDIE'S PIZZA JOINT
OH YEAH. I CAN SENSE IT. THIS RESTAURANT DEFINITELY HAS GHOSTS, 100 PERCENT.
NO JOKE, HALF OF WHY I CHOSE PICA WAS ALL THE GHOSTS.
OH MY GOD, SAME. MOOD.
EDDIE'S PIZZA JOINT
SHUT!

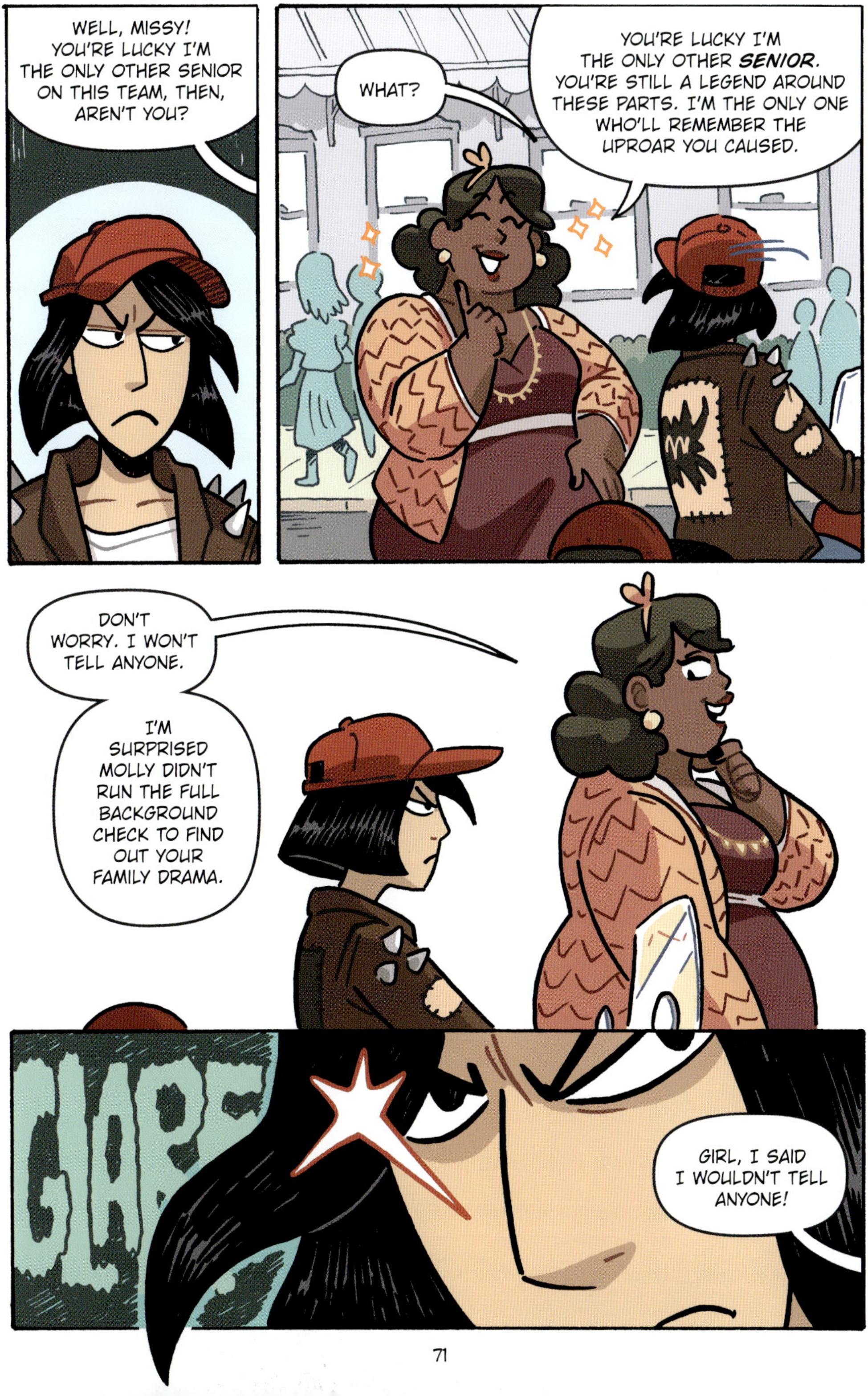
WELL, MISSY! YOU'RE LUCKY I'M THE ONLY OTHER SENIOR ON THIS TEAM, THEN, AREN'T YOU?
WHAT?
YOU'RE LUCKY I'M THE ONLY OTHER **SENIOR**. YOU'RE STILL A LEGEND AROUND THESE PARTS. I'M THE ONLY ONE WHO'LL REMEMBER THE UPROAR YOU CAUSED.
DON'T WORRY. I WON'T TELL ANYONE.
I'M SURPRISED MOLLY DIDN'T RUN THE FULL BACKGROUND CHECK TO FIND OUT YOUR FAMILY DRAMA.
GLARE
GIRL, I SAID I WOULDN'T TELL ANYONE!

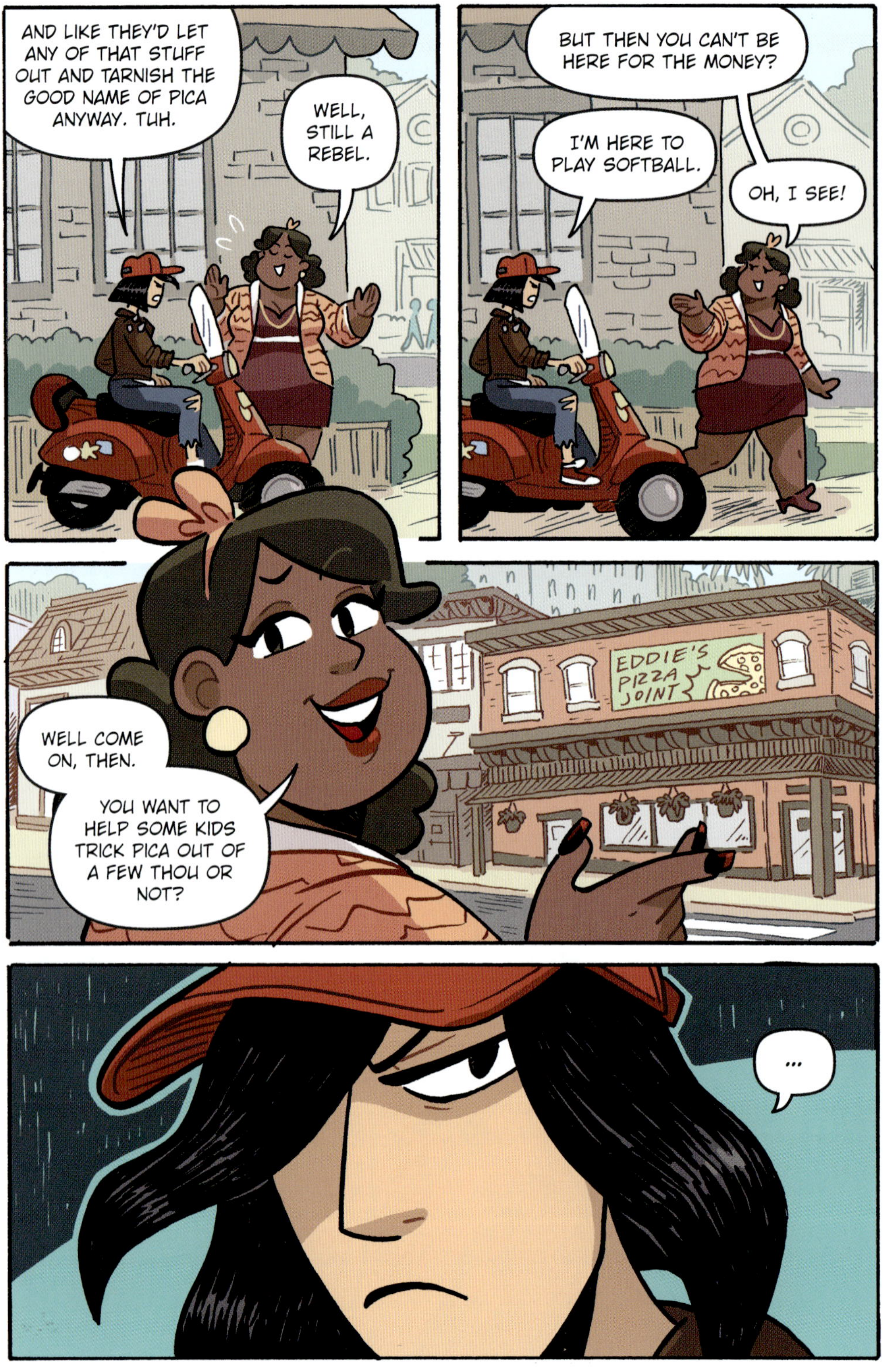
AND LIKE THEY'D LET ANY OF THAT STUFF OUT AND TARNISH THE GOOD NAME OF PICA ANYWAY. TUH.
WELL, STILL A REBEL.
BUT THEN YOU CAN'T BE HERE FOR THE MONEY?
I'M HERE TO PLAY SOFTBALL.
OH, I SEE!
EDDIE'S PIZZA JOINT
WELL COME ON, THEN.
YOU WANT TO HELP SOME KIDS TRICK PICA OUT OF A FEW THOU OR NOT?
...

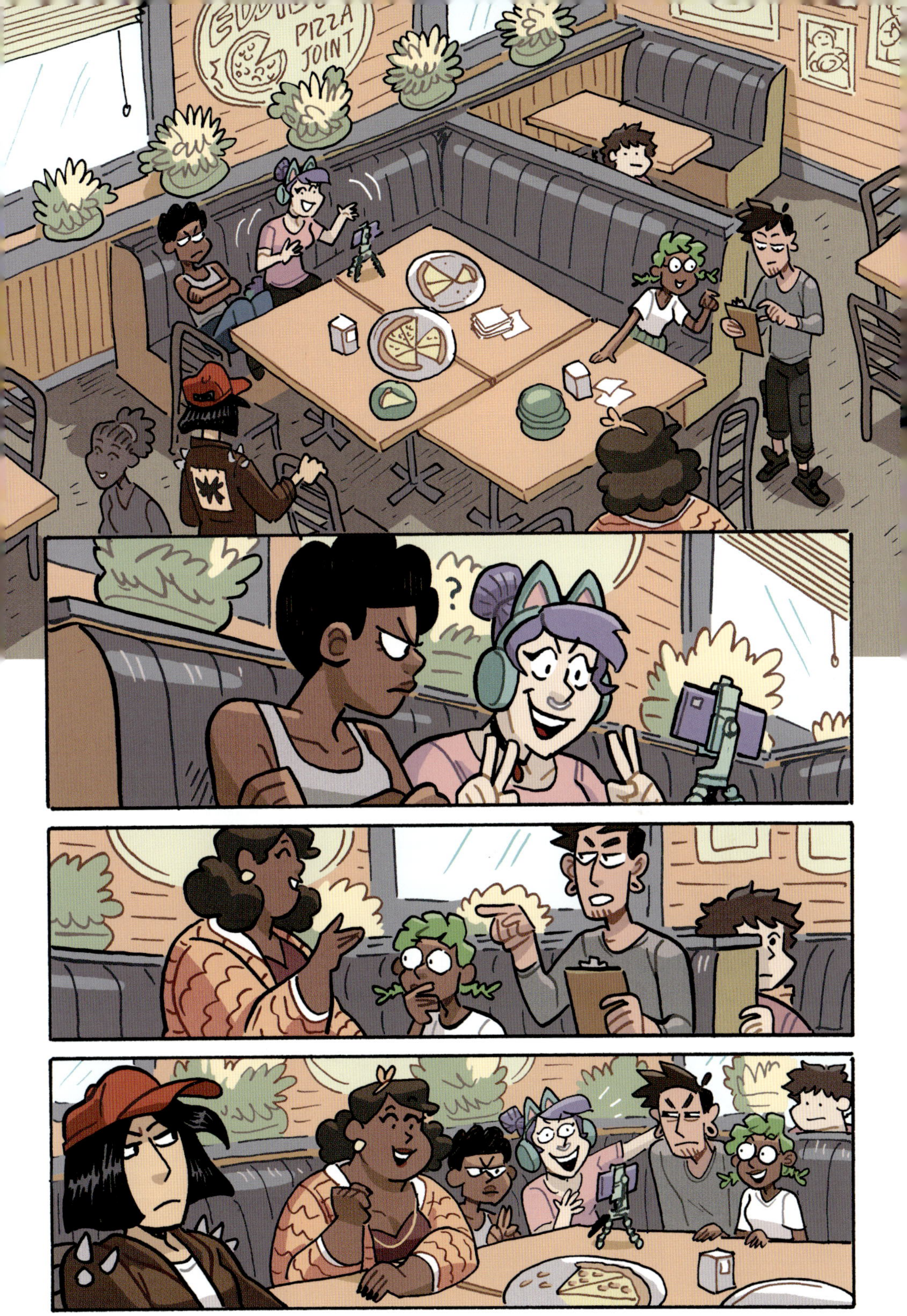
PIZZA JOINT

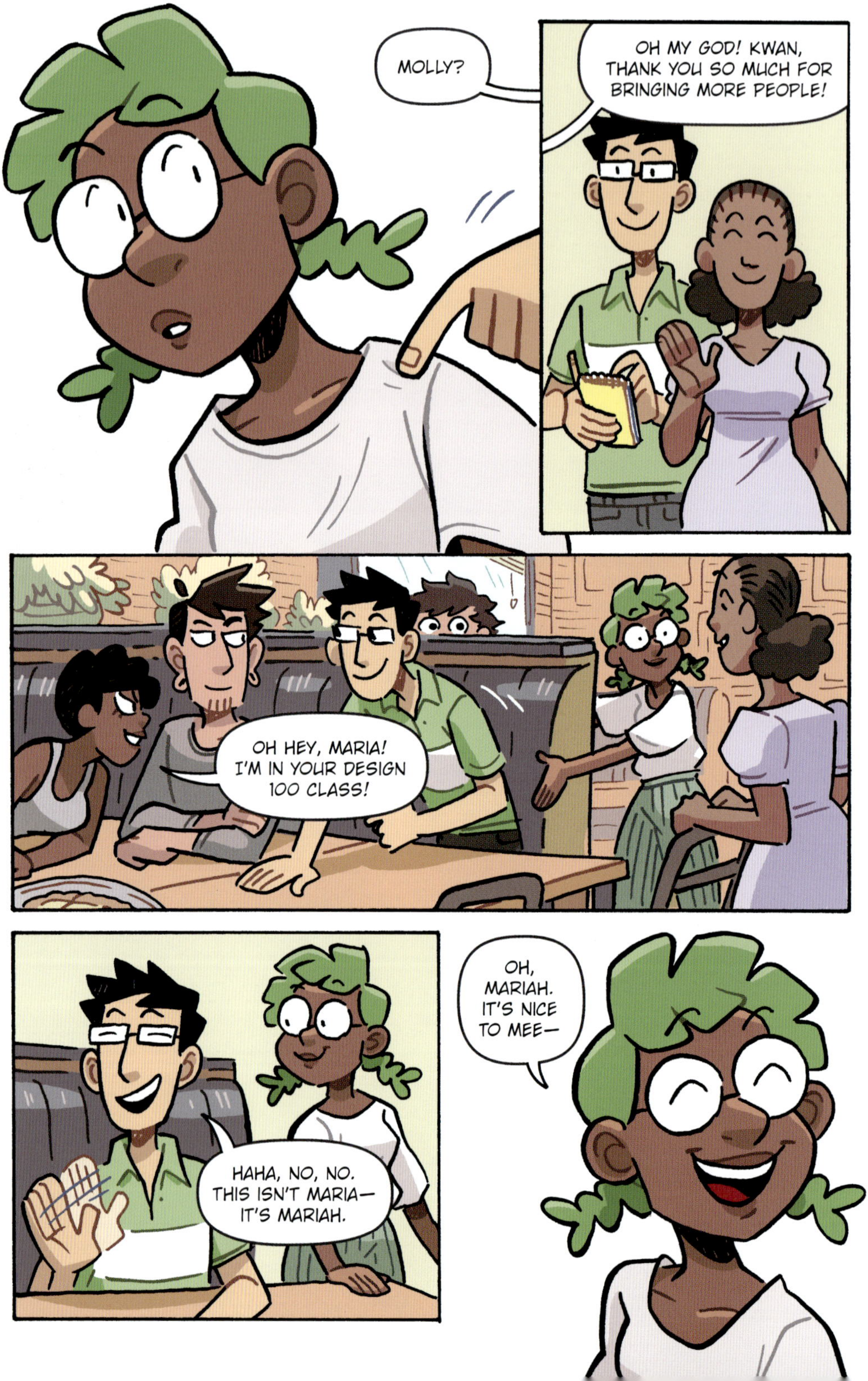
MOLLY?
OH MY GOD! KWAN, THANK YOU SO MUCH FOR BRINGING MORE PEOPLE!
OH HEY, MARIA! I'M IN YOUR DESIGN 100 CLASS!
HAHA, NO, NO. THIS ISN'T MARIA— IT'S MARIAH.
OH, MARIAH. IT'S NICE TO MEE—

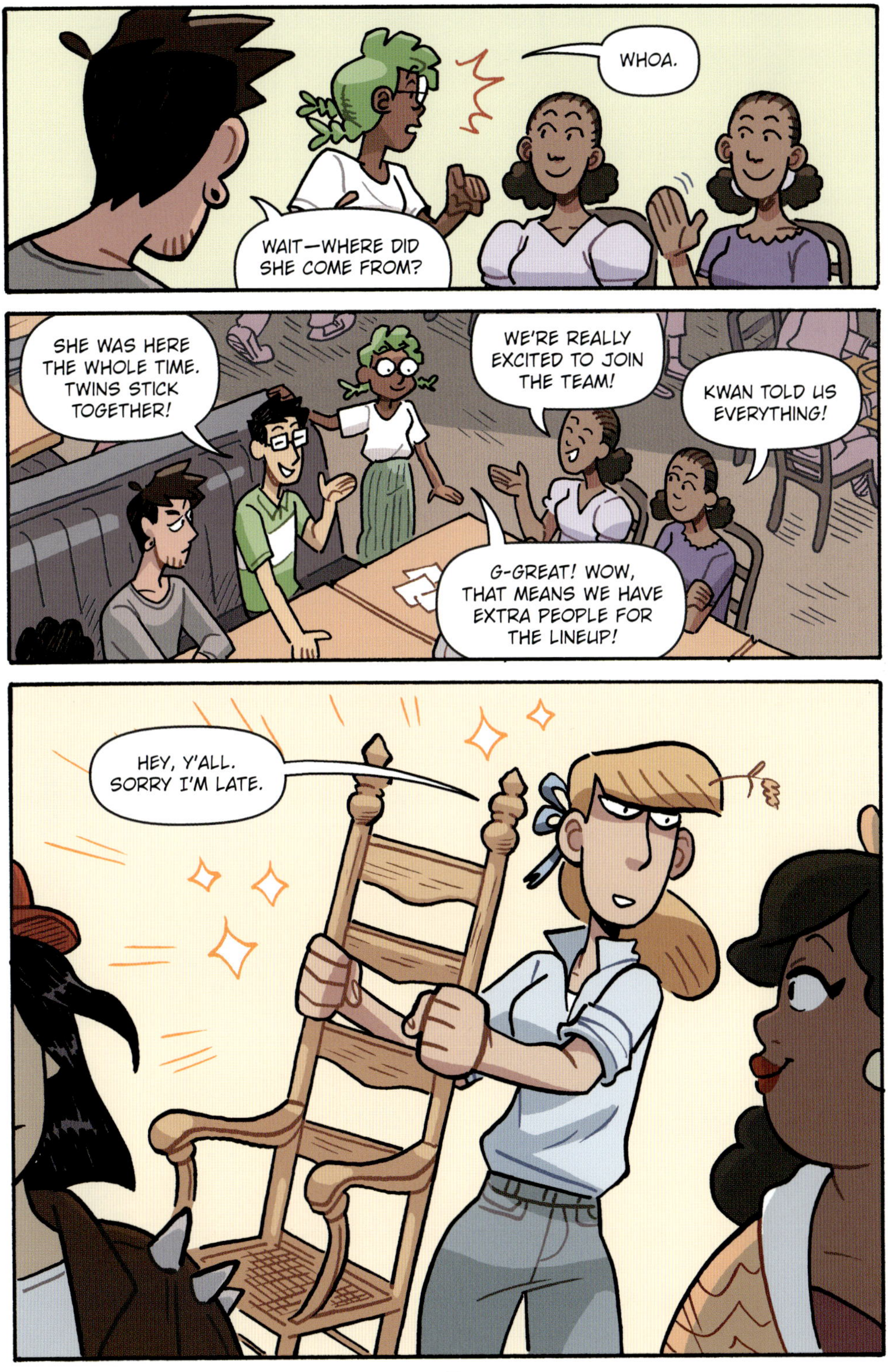
WHOA.
WAIT—WHERE DID SHE COME FROM?
SHE WAS HERE THE WHOLE TIME. TWINS STICK TOGETHER!
WE'RE REALLY EXCITED TO JOIN THE TEAM!
KWAN TOLD US EVERYTHING!
G-GREAT! WOW, THAT MEANS WE HAVE EXTRA PEOPLE FOR THE LINEUP!
HEY, Y'ALL. SORRY I'M LATE.

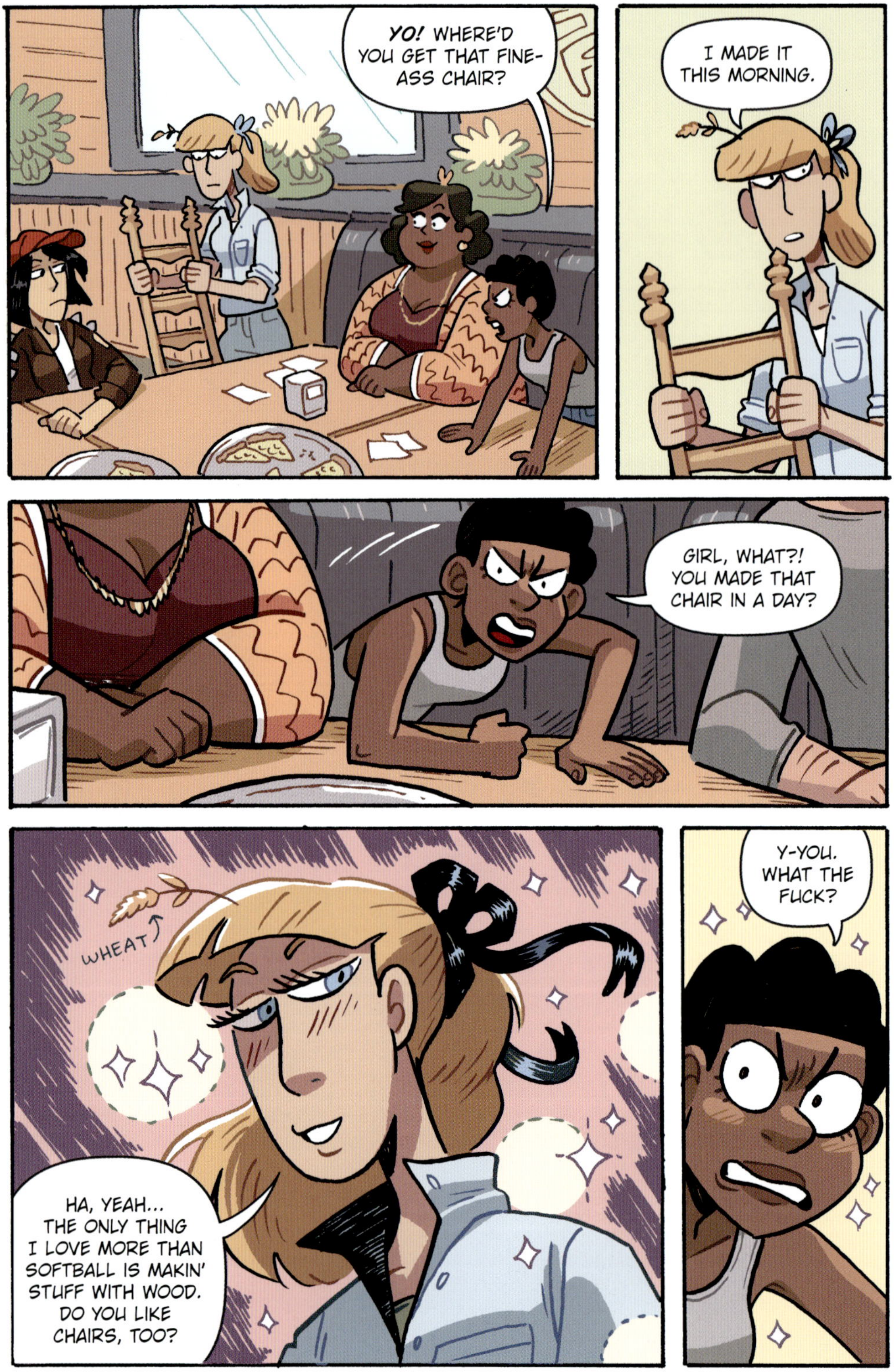
YO! WHERE'D YOU GET THAT FINE-ASS CHAIR?
I MADE IT THIS MORNING.
GIRL, WHAT?! YOU MADE THAT CHAIR IN A DAY?
WHEAT
HA, YEAH... THE ONLY THING I LOVE MORE THAN SOFTBALL IS MAKIN' STUFF WITH WOOD. DO YOU LIKE CHAIRS, TOO?
Y-YOU. WHAT THE FUCK?

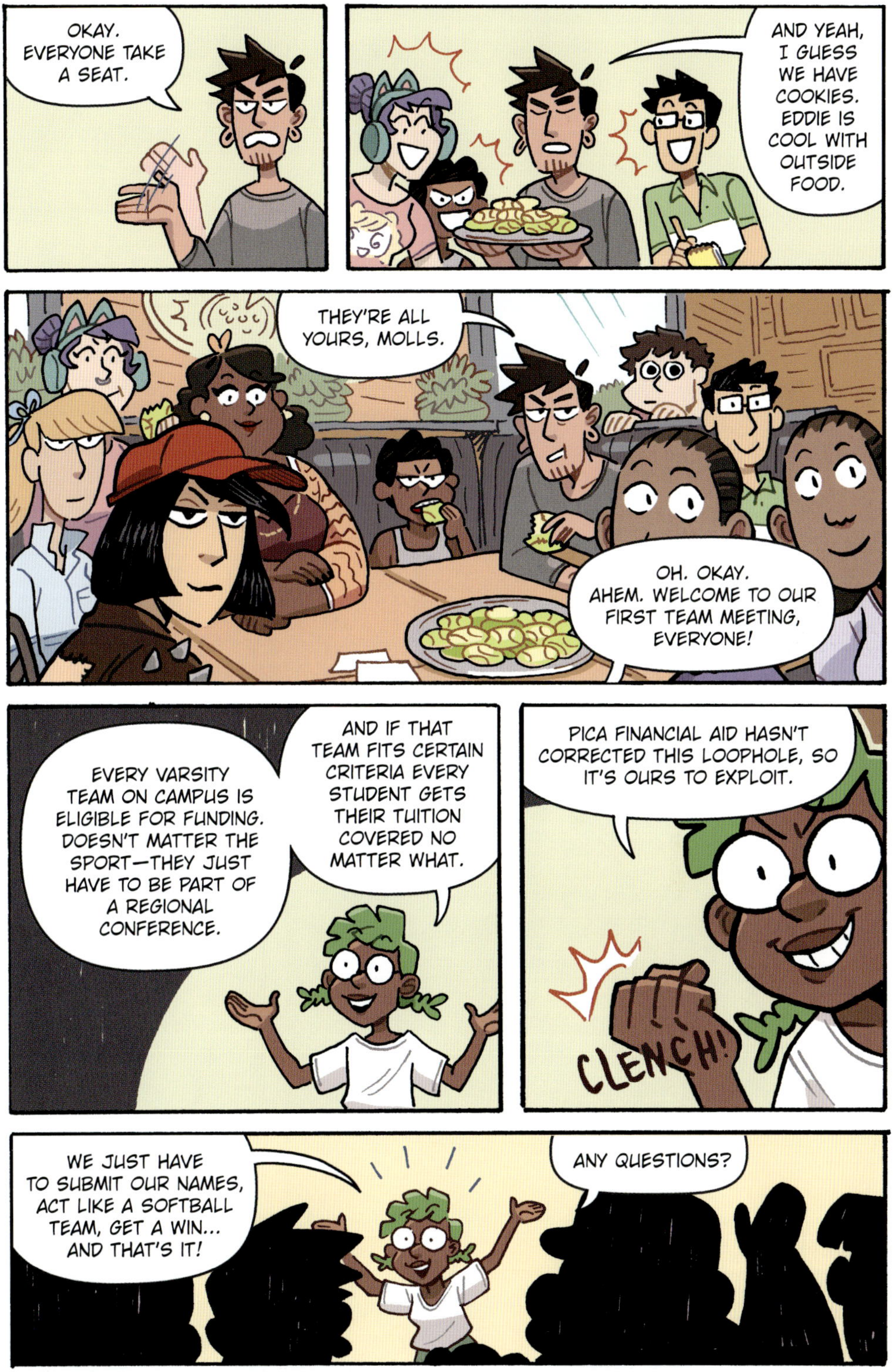
OKAY. EVERYONE TAKE A SEAT.
AND YEAH, I GUESS WE HAVE COOKIES. EDDIE IS COOL WITH OUTSIDE FOOD.
THEY'RE ALL YOURS, MOLLS.
OH. OKAY. AHEM. WELCOME TO OUR FIRST TEAM MEETING, EVERYONE!
EVERY VARSITY TEAM ON CAMPUS IS ELIGIBLE FOR FUNDING. DOESN'T MATTER THE SPORT—THEY JUST HAVE TO BE PART OF A REGIONAL CONFERENCE.
AND IF THAT TEAM FITS CERTAIN CRITERIA EVERY STUDENT GETS THEIR TUITION COVERED NO MATTER WHAT.
PICA FINANCIAL AID HASN'T CORRECTED THIS LOOPHOLE, SO IT'S OURS TO EXPLOIT.
CLENCH!
WE JUST HAVE TO SUBMIT OUR NAMES, ACT LIKE A SOFTBALL TEAM, GET A WIN... AND THAT'S IT!
ANY QUESTIONS?

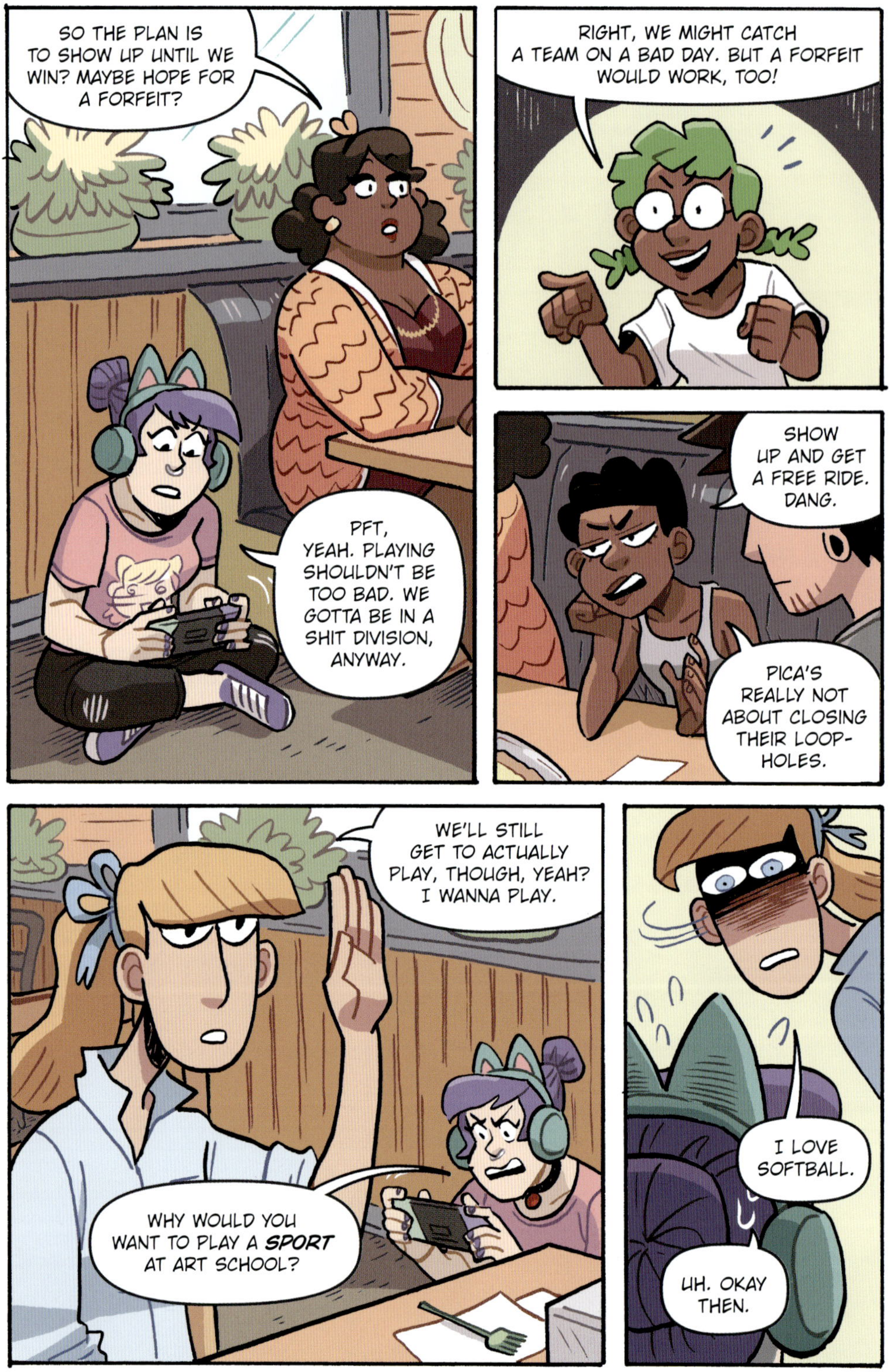
SO THE PLAN IS TO SHOW UP UNTIL WE WIN? MAYBE HOPE FOR A FORFEIT?
PFT, YEAH. PLAYING SHOULDN'T BE TOO BAD. WE GOTTA BE IN A SHIT DIVISION, ANYWAY.
RIGHT, WE MIGHT CATCH A TEAM ON A BAD DAY. BUT A FORFEIT WOULD WORK, TOO!
SHOW UP AND GET A FREE RIDE. DANG.
PICA'S REALLY NOT ABOUT CLOSING THEIR LOOP-HOLES.
WE'LL STILL GET TO ACTUALLY PLAY, THOUGH, YEAH? I WANNA PLAY.
WHY WOULD YOU WANT TO PLAY A **SPORT** AT ART SCHOOL?
I LOVE SOFTBALL.
UH. OKAY THEN.

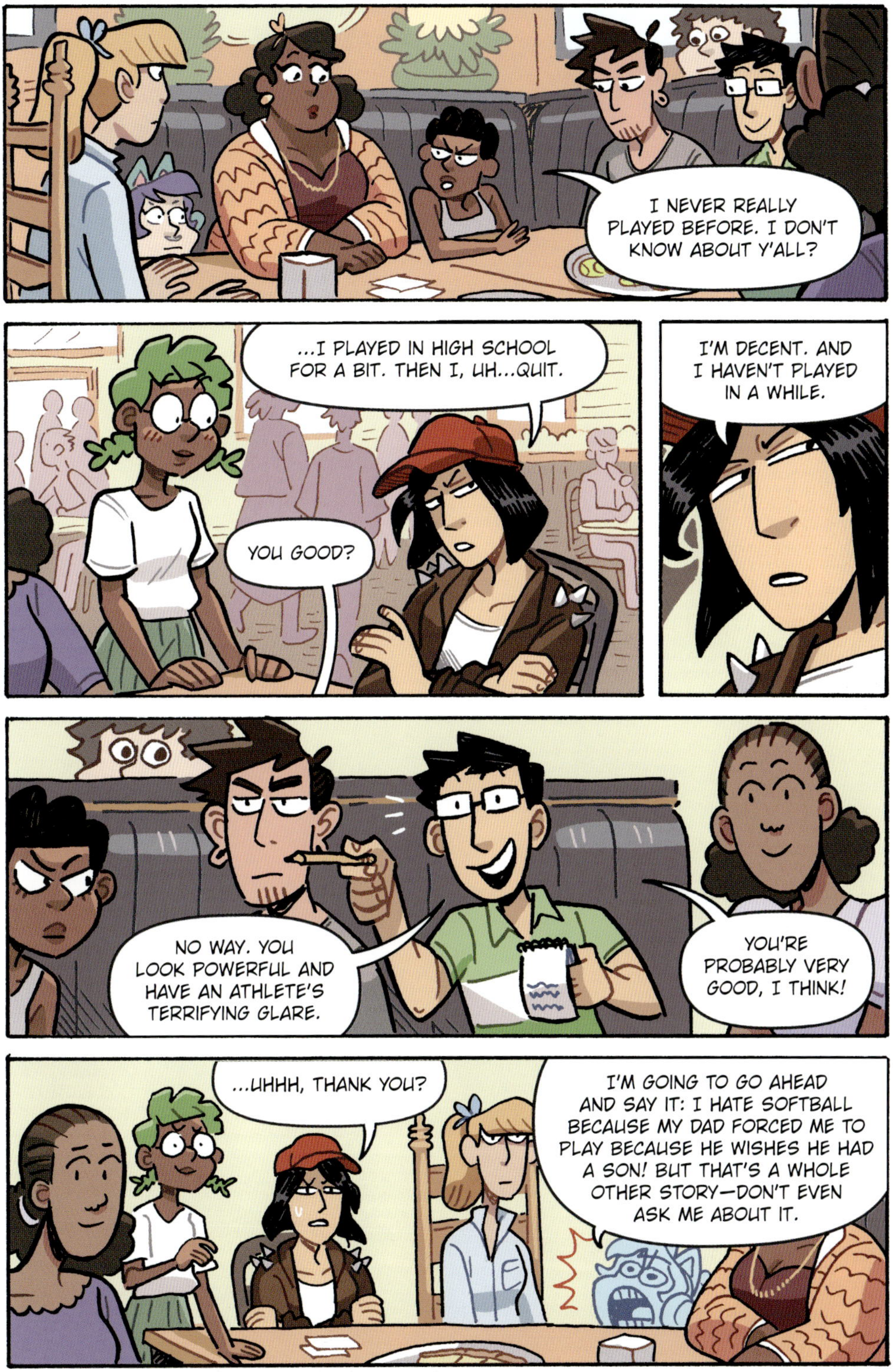
I NEVER REALLY PLAYED BEFORE. I DON'T KNOW ABOUT Y'ALL?
...I PLAYED IN HIGH SCHOOL FOR A BIT. THEN I, UH...QUIT.
YOU GOOD?
I'M DECENT. AND I HAVEN'T PLAYED IN A WHILE.
NO WAY. YOU LOOK POWERFUL AND HAVE AN ATHLETE'S TERRIFYING GLARE.
YOU'RE PROBABLY VERY GOOD, I THINK!
...UHHH, THANK YOU?
I'M GOING TO GO AHEAD AND SAY IT: I HATE SOFTBALL BECAUSE MY DAD FORCED ME TO PLAY BECAUSE HE WISHES HE HAD A SON! BUT THAT'S A WHOLE OTHER STORY—DON'T EVEN ASK ME ABOUT IT.

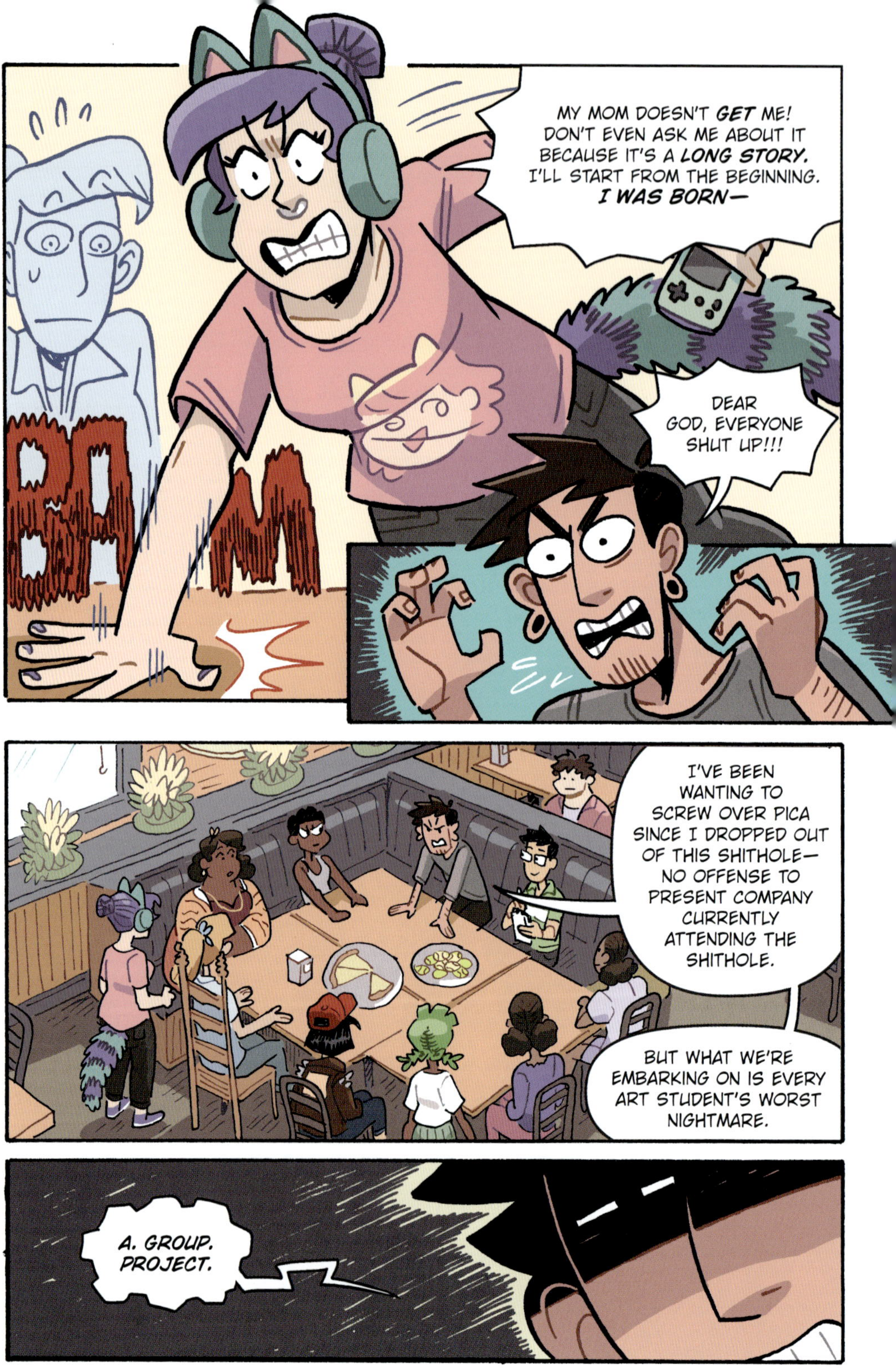
MY MOM DOESN'T GET ME! DON'T EVEN ASK ME ABOUT IT BECAUSE IT'S A LONG STORY. I'LL START FROM THE BEGINNING. I WAS BORN—
BAM
DEAR GOD, EVERYONE SHUT UP!!!
I'VE BEEN WANTING TO SCREW OVER PICA SINCE I DROPPED OUT OF THIS SHITHOLE—NO OFFENSE TO PRESENT COMPANY CURRENTLY ATTENDING THE SHITHOLE.
BUT WHAT WE'RE EMBARKING ON IS EVERY ART STUDENT'S WORST NIGHTMARE.
A. GROUP. PROJECT.

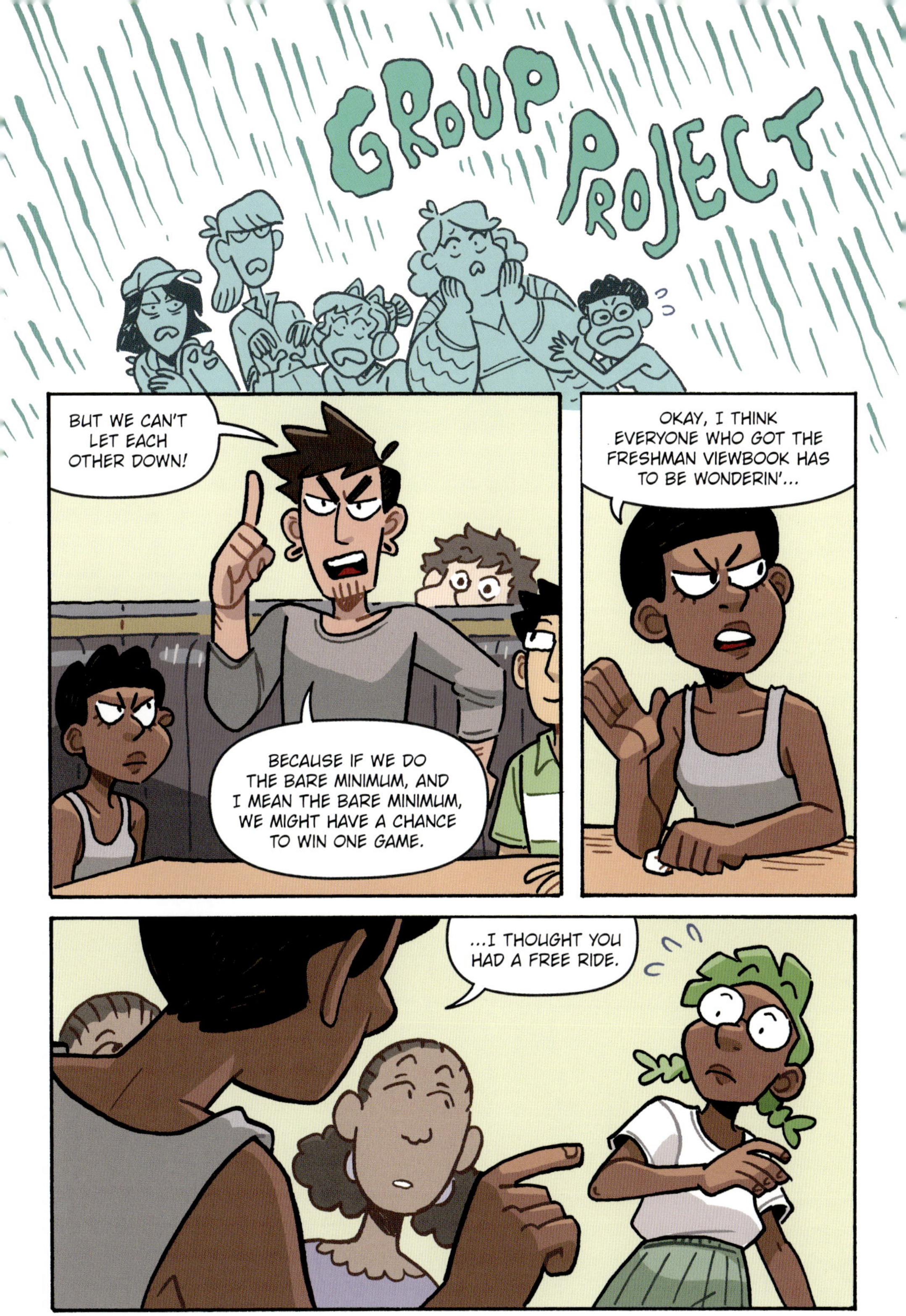
GROUP PROJECT
BUT WE CAN'T LET EACH OTHER DOWN!
BECAUSE IF WE DO THE BARE MINIMUM, AND I MEAN THE BARE MINIMUM, WE MIGHT HAVE A CHANCE TO WIN ONE GAME.
OKAY, I THINK EVERYONE WHO GOT THE FRESHMAN VIEWBOOK HAS TO BE WONDERIN'...
...I THOUGHT YOU HAD A FREE RIDE.

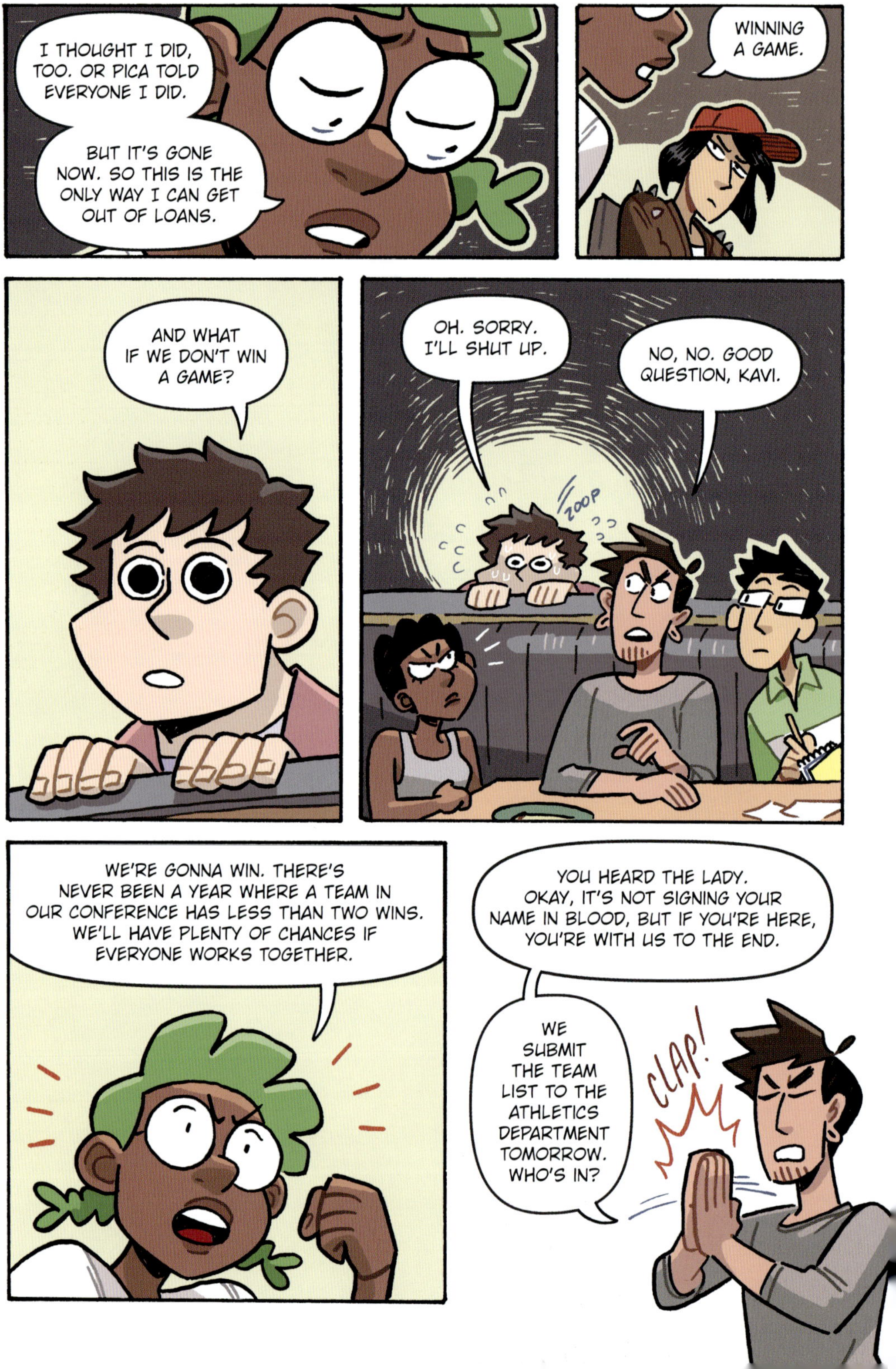

I THOUGHT I DID, TOO. OR PICA TOLD EVERYONE I DID.
BUT IT'S GONE NOW. SO THIS IS THE ONLY WAY I CAN GET OUT OF LOANS.
WINNING A GAME.
AND WHAT IF WE DON'T WIN A GAME?
OH. SORRY. I'LL SHUT UP.
ZOOP
NO, NO. GOOD QUESTION, KAVI.
WE'RE GONNA WIN. THERE'S NEVER BEEN A YEAR WHERE A TEAM IN OUR CONFERENCE HAS LESS THAN TWO WINS. WE'LL HAVE PLENTY OF CHANCES IF EVERYONE WORKS TOGETHER.
YOU HEARD THE LADY. OKAY, IT'S NOT SIGNING YOUR NAME IN BLOOD, BUT IF YOU'RE HERE, YOU'RE WITH US TO THE END.
WE SUBMIT THE TEAM LIST TO THE ATHLETICS DEPARTMENT TOMORROW. WHO'S IN?
CLAP!

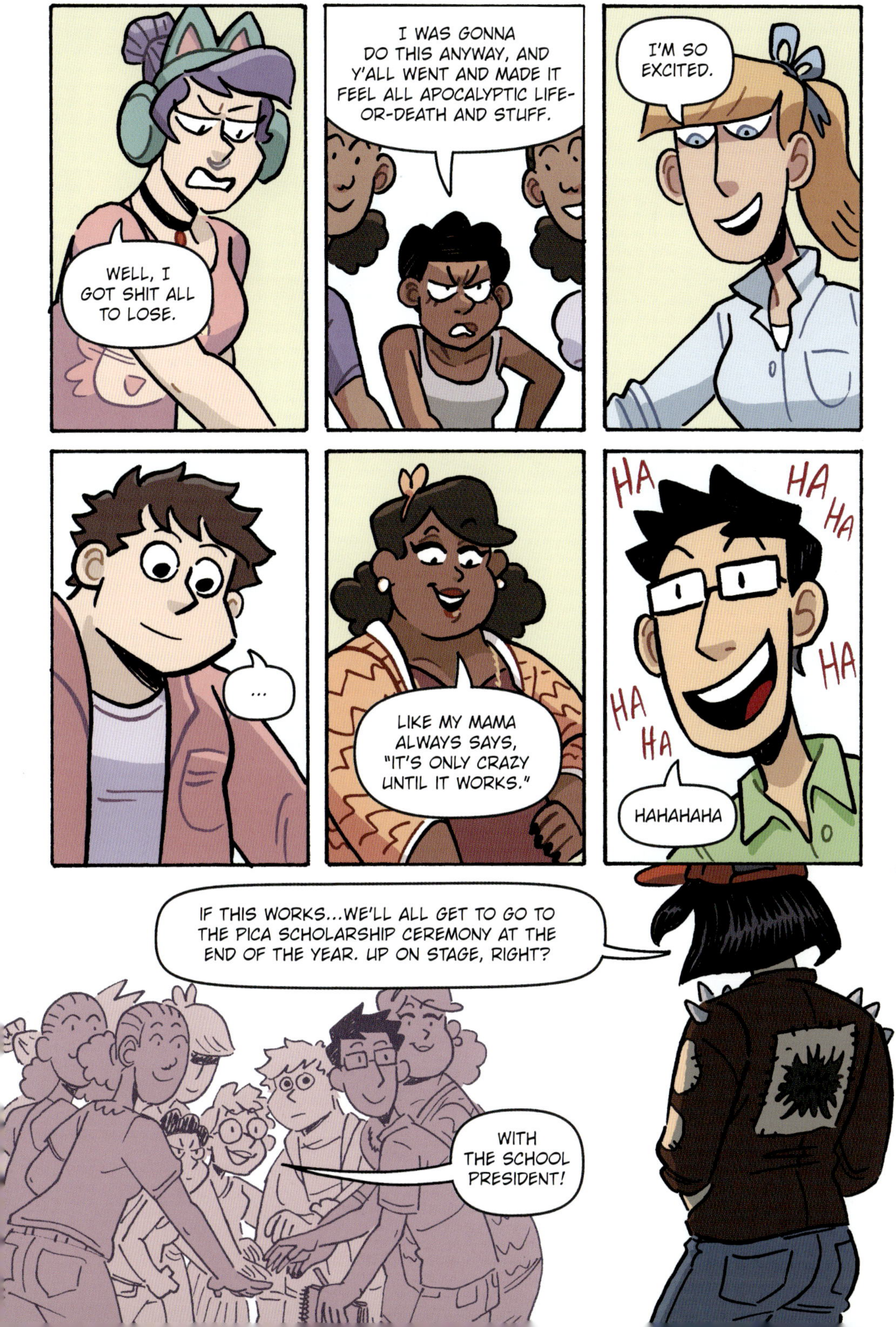
WELL, I GOT SHIT ALL TO LOSE.
I WAS GONNA DO THIS ANYWAY, AND Y'ALL WENT AND MADE IT FEEL ALL APOCALYPTIC LIFE-OR-DEATH AND STUFF.
I'M SO EXCITED.
...
LIKE MY MAMA ALWAYS SAYS, "IT'S ONLY CRAZY UNTIL IT WORKS."
HA HA HA HA HA HA
HAHAHAHA
IF THIS WORKS...WE'LL ALL GET TO GO TO THE PICA SCHOLARSHIP CEREMONY AT THE END OF THE YEAR. UP ON STAGE, RIGHT?
WITH THE SCHOOL PRESIDENT!

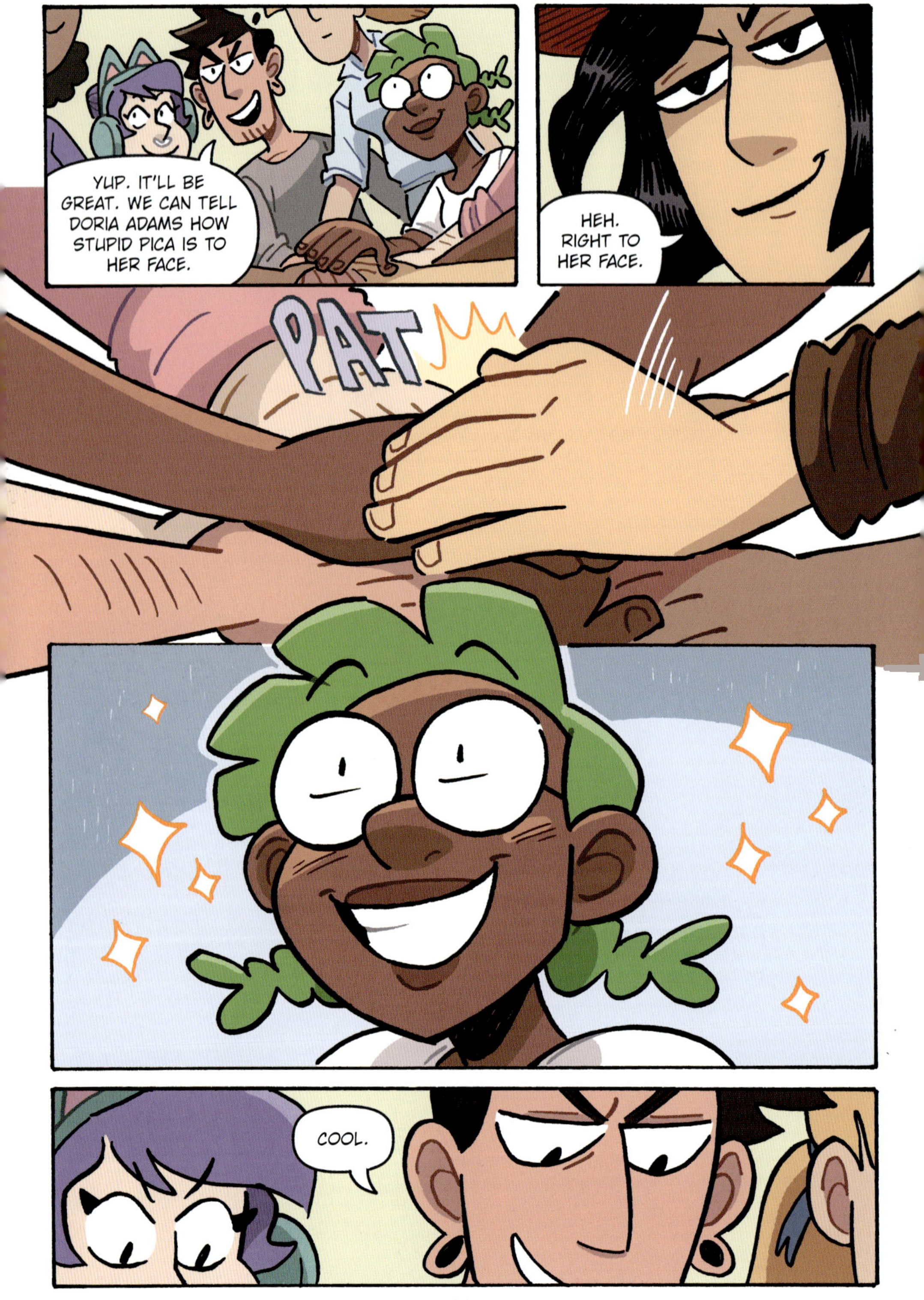
YUP. IT'LL BE GREAT. WE CAN TELL DORIA ADAMS HOW STUPID PICA IS TO HER FACE.
HEH. RIGHT TO HER FACE.
PAT
COOL.

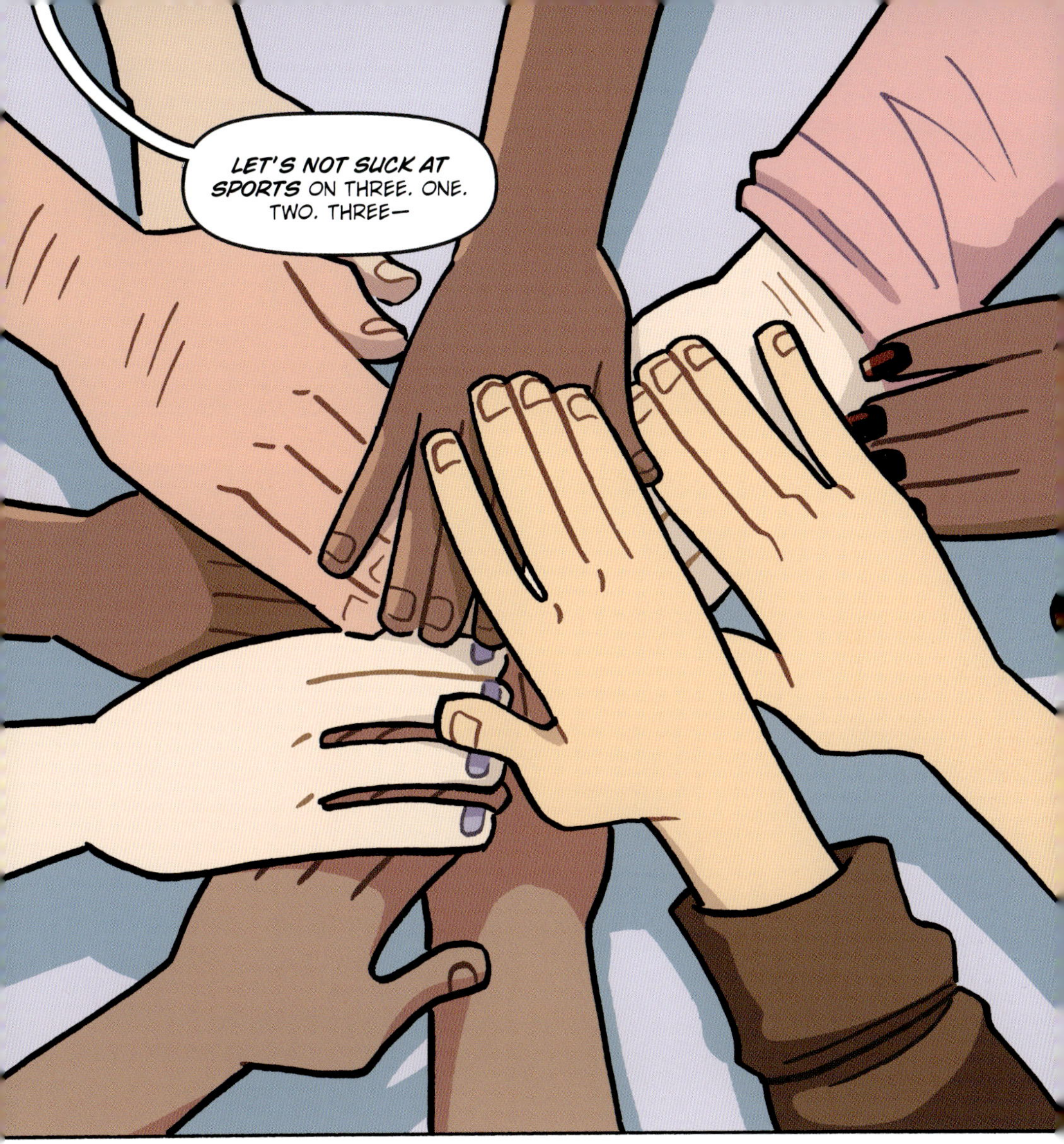
LET'S NOT SUCK AT SPORTS ON THREE. ONE. TWO. THREE—

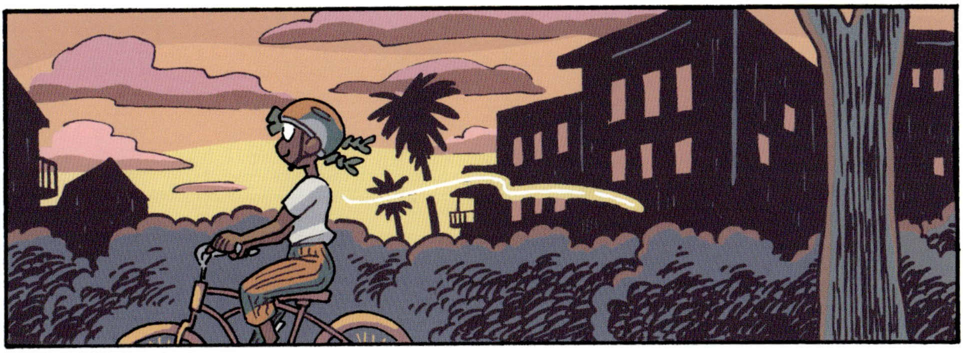

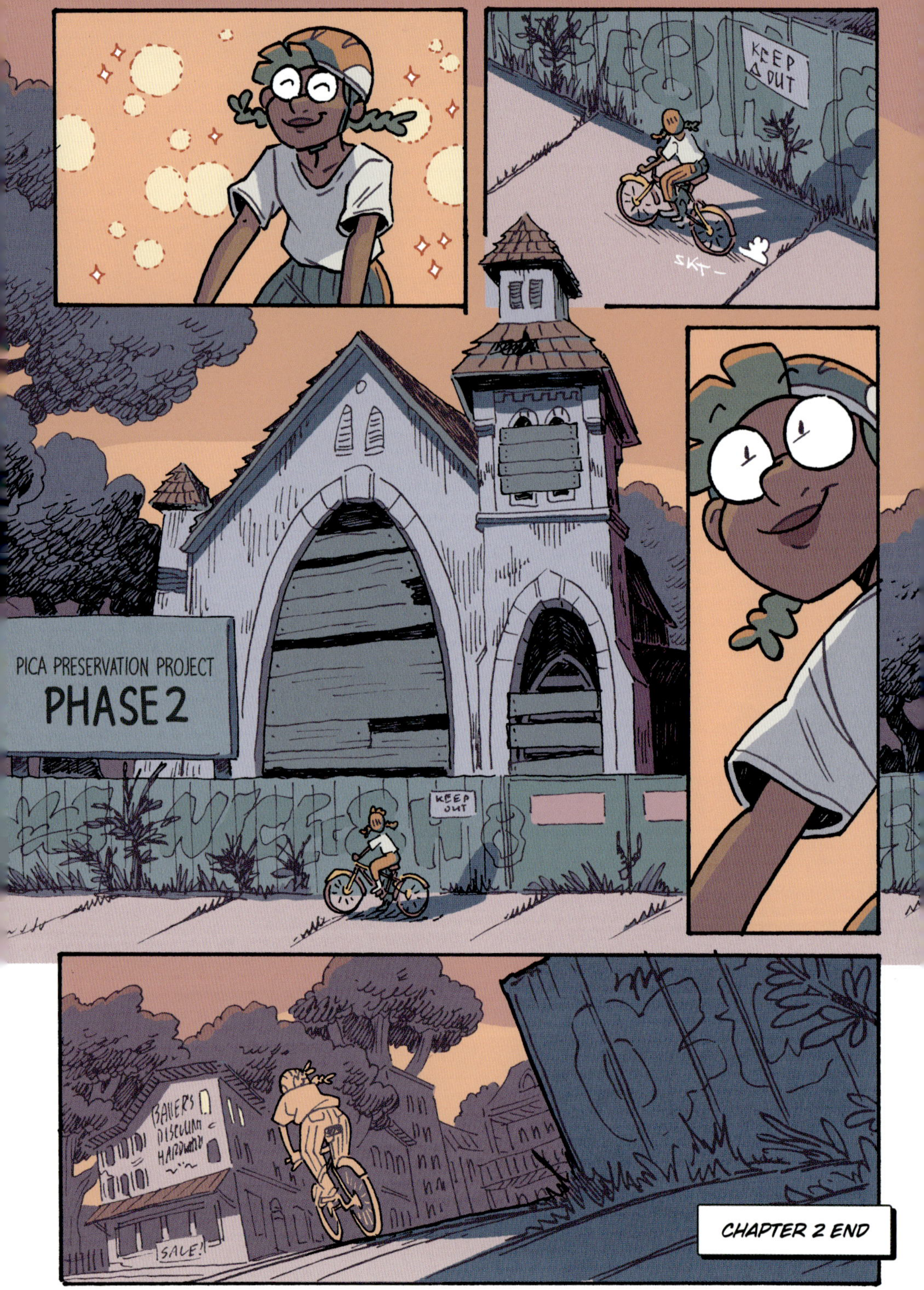
KEEP OUT
SKT–
PICA PRESERVATION PROJECT
PHASE 2
KEEP OUT
BAUER'S DISCOUNT HARDWARE
SALE!
CHAPTER 2 END

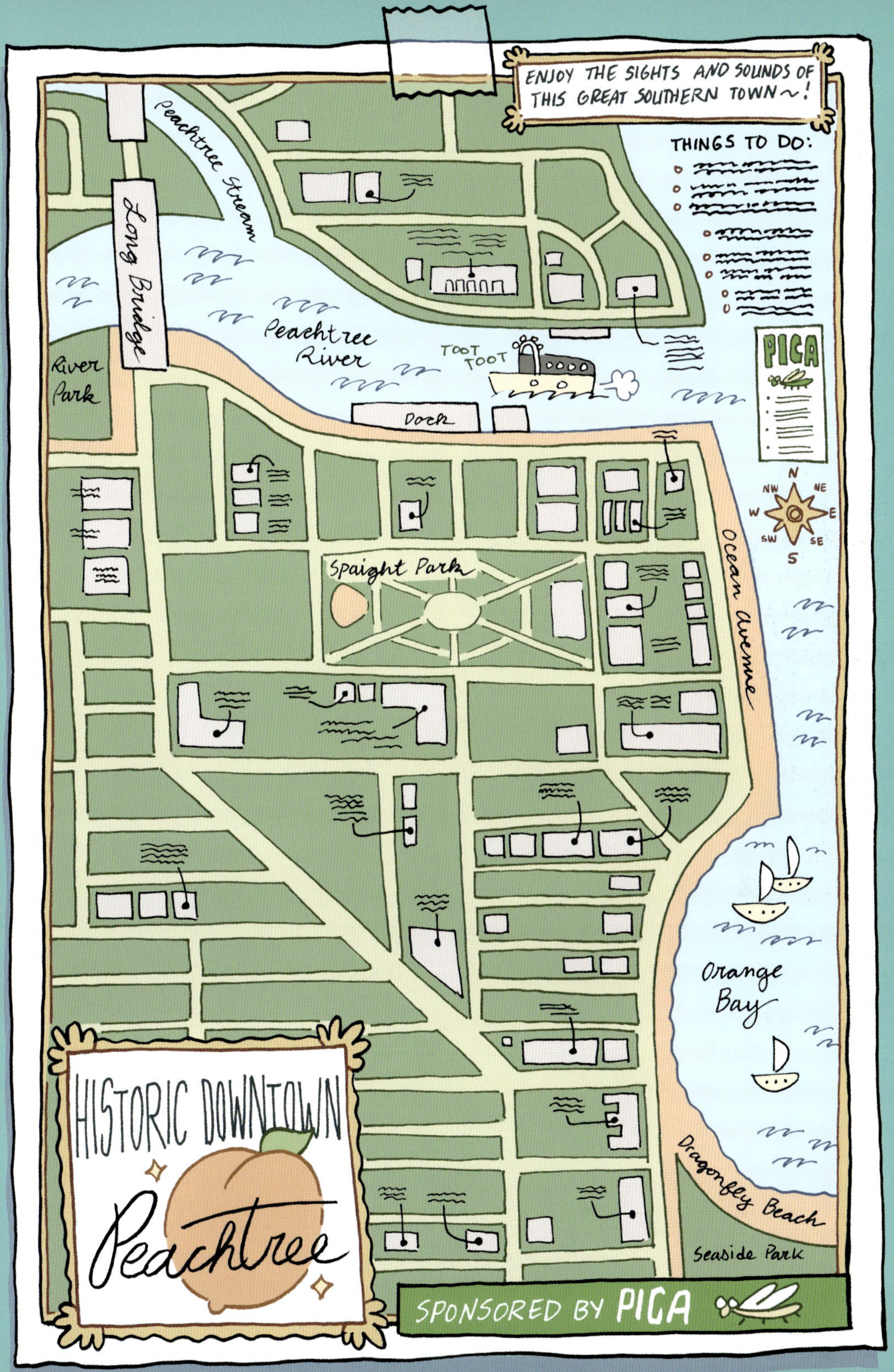

ENJOY THE SIGHTS AND SOUNDS OF THIS GREAT SOUTHERN TOWN~!
THINGS TO DO:
PIGA
Peachtree Stream
Long Bridge
Peachtree River
River Park
TOOT TOOT
Dock
N
NE
E
SE
S
SW
W
NW
Spaight Park
Ocean Avenue
Orange Bay
Dragonfly Beach
Seaside Park
HISTORIC DOWNTOWN
Peachtree
SPONSORED BY PIGA

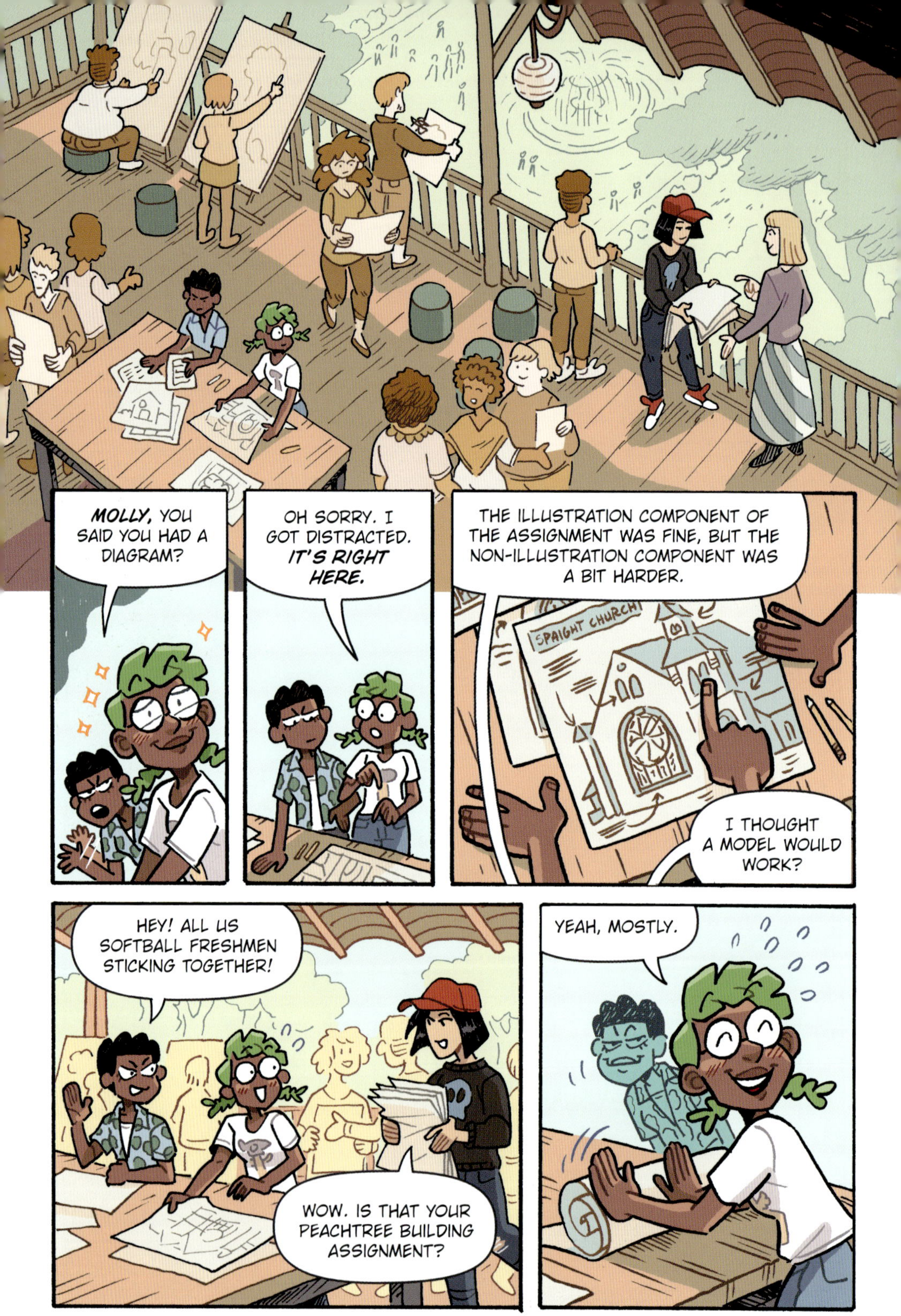
MOLLY, YOU SAID YOU HAD A DIAGRAM?
OH SORRY. I GOT DISTRACTED. IT'S RIGHT HERE.
THE ILLUSTRATION COMPONENT OF THE ASSIGNMENT WAS FINE, BUT THE NON-ILLUSTRATION COMPONENT WAS A BIT HARDER.
SPAIGHT CHURCH
I THOUGHT A MODEL WOULD WORK?
HEY! ALL US SOFTBALL FRESHMEN STICKING TOGETHER!
WOW. IS THAT YOUR PEACHTREE BUILDING ASSIGNMENT?
YEAH, MOSTLY.

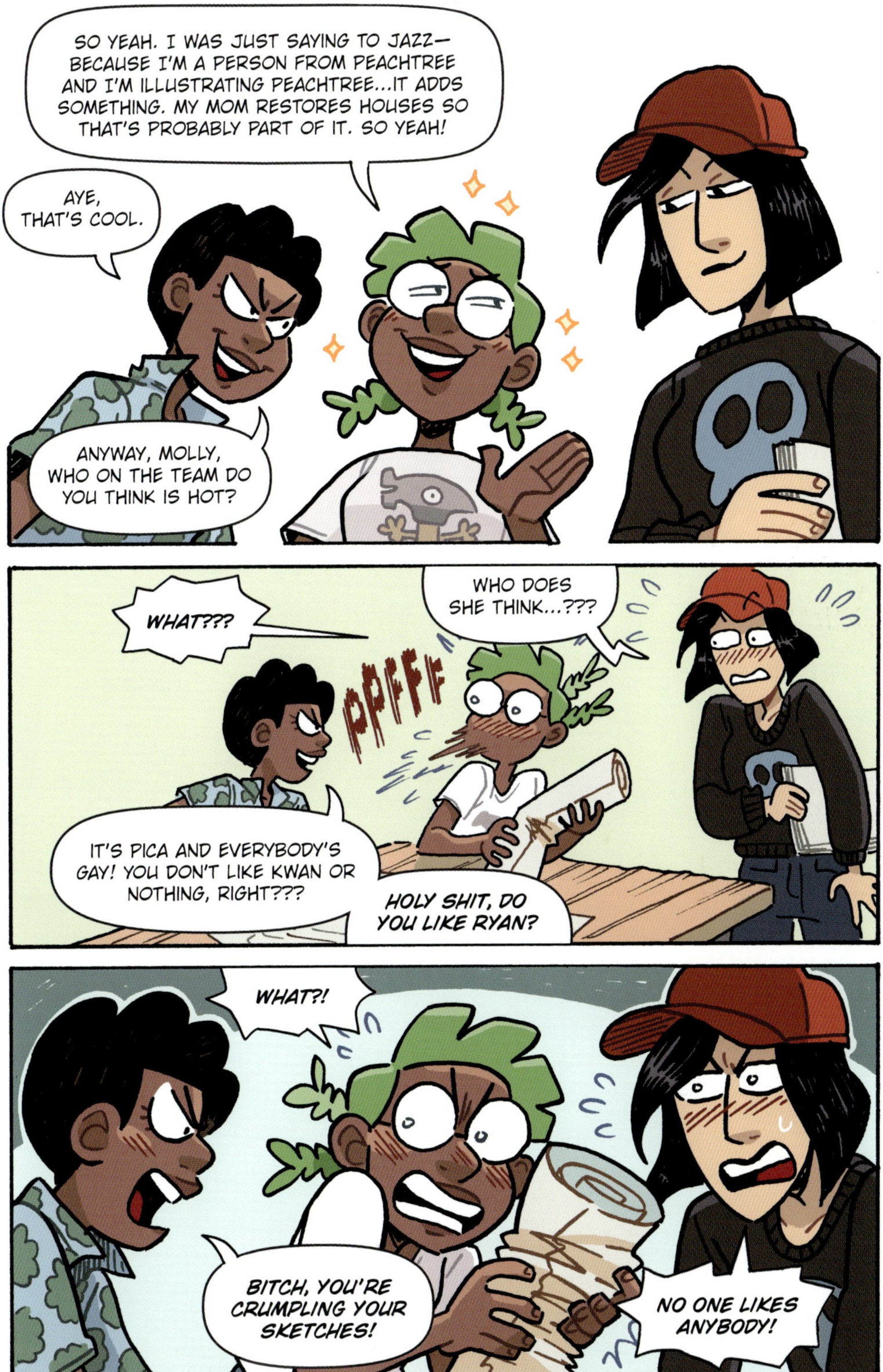
SO YEAH. I WAS JUST SAYING TO JAZZ—BECAUSE I'M A PERSON FROM PEACHTREE AND I'M ILLUSTRATING PEACHTREE...IT ADDS SOMETHING. MY MOM RESTORES HOUSES SO THAT'S PROBABLY PART OF IT. SO YEAH!
AYE, THAT'S COOL.
ANYWAY, MOLLY, WHO ON THE TEAM DO YOU THINK IS HOT?
WHAT???
WHO DOES SHE THINK...???
PPFFF
IT'S PICA AND EVERYBODY'S GAY! YOU DON'T LIKE KWAN OR NOTHING, RIGHT???
HOLY SHIT, DO YOU LIKE RYAN?
WHAT?!
BITCH, YOU'RE CRUMPLING YOUR SKETCHES!
NO ONE LIKES ANYBODY!

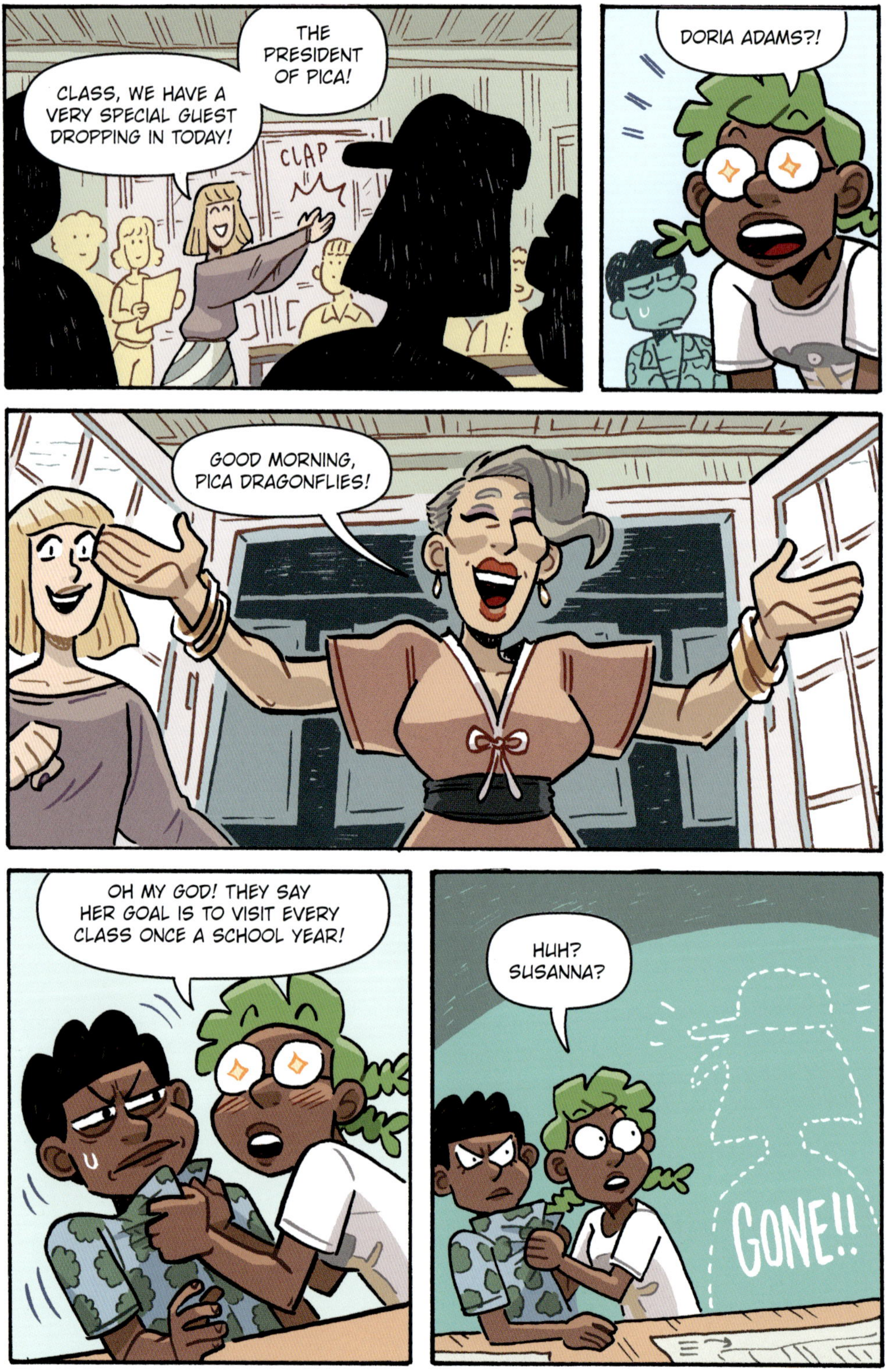
CLASS, WE HAVE A VERY SPECIAL GUEST DROPPING IN TODAY!
THE PRESIDENT OF PICA!
CLAP
DORIA ADAMS?!
GOOD MORNING, PICA DRAGONFLIES!
OH MY GOD! THEY SAY HER GOAL IS TO VISIT EVERY CLASS ONCE A SCHOOL YEAR!
HUH? SUSANNA?
GONE!!

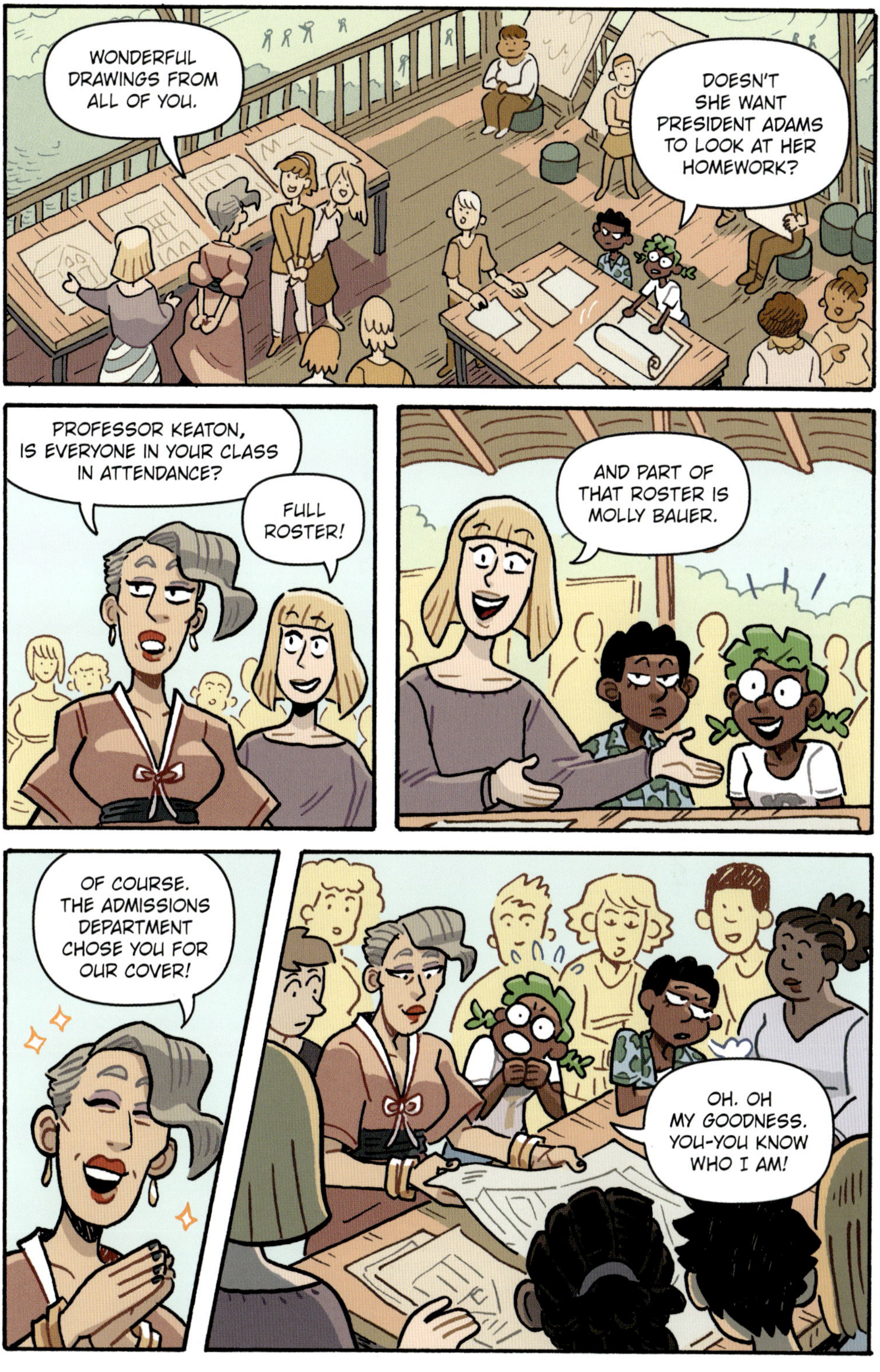
WONDERFUL DRAWINGS FROM ALL OF YOU.
DOESN'T SHE WANT PRESIDENT ADAMS TO LOOK AT HER HOMEWORK?
PROFESSOR KEATON, IS EVERYONE IN YOUR CLASS IN ATTENDANCE?
FULL ROSTER!
AND PART OF THAT ROSTER IS MOLLY BAUER.
OF COURSE. THE ADMISSIONS DEPARTMENT CHOSE YOU FOR OUR COVER!
OH. OH MY GOODNESS. YOU-YOU KNOW WHO I AM!

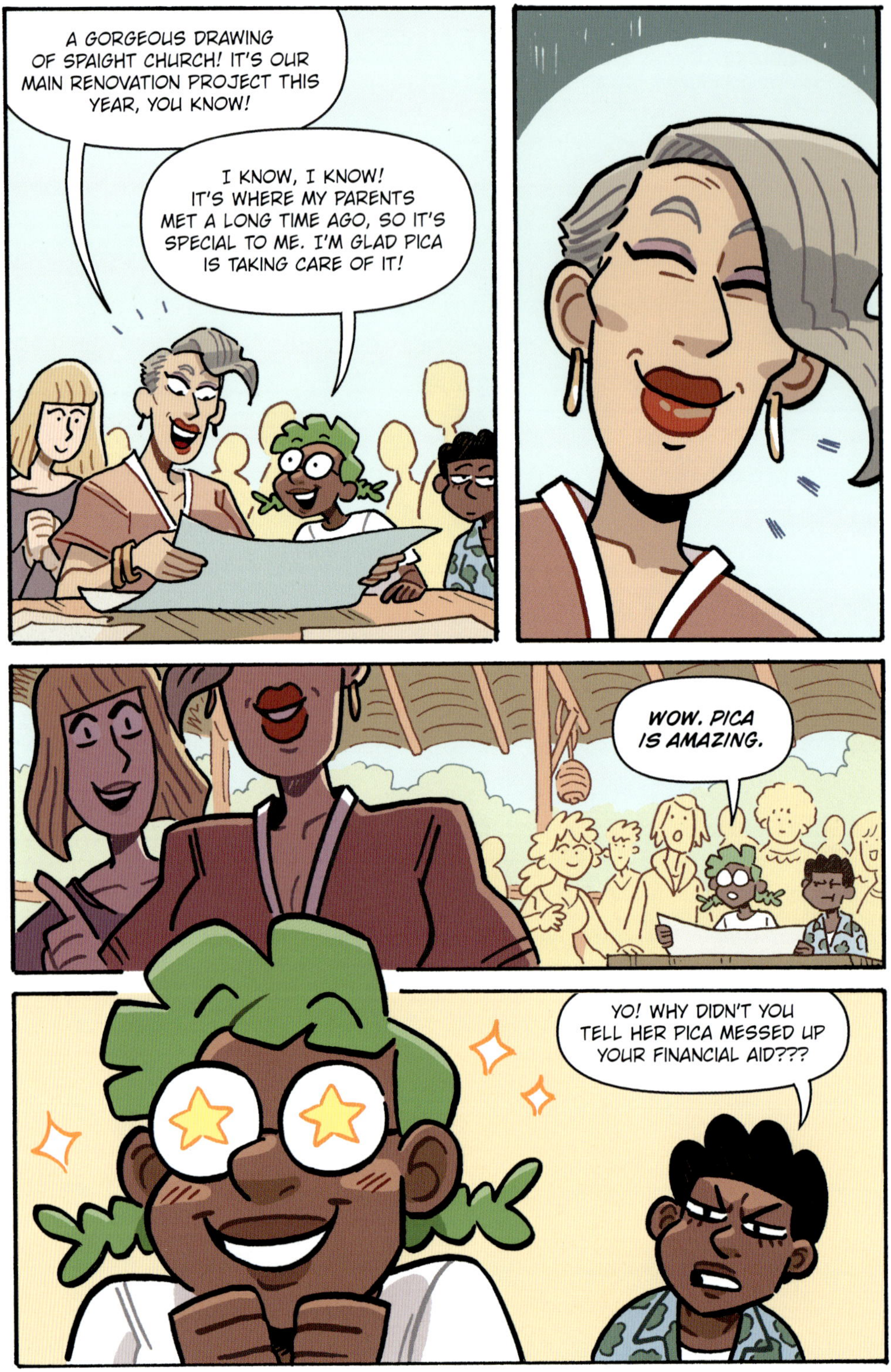
A GORGEOUS DRAWING OF SPAIGHT CHURCH! IT'S OUR MAIN RENOVATION PROJECT THIS YEAR, YOU KNOW!
I KNOW, I KNOW! IT'S WHERE MY PARENTS MET A LONG TIME AGO, SO IT'S SPECIAL TO ME. I'M GLAD PICA IS TAKING CARE OF IT!
WOW. PICA IS AMAZING.
YO! WHY DIDN'T YOU TELL HER PICA MESSED UP YOUR FINANCIAL AID???

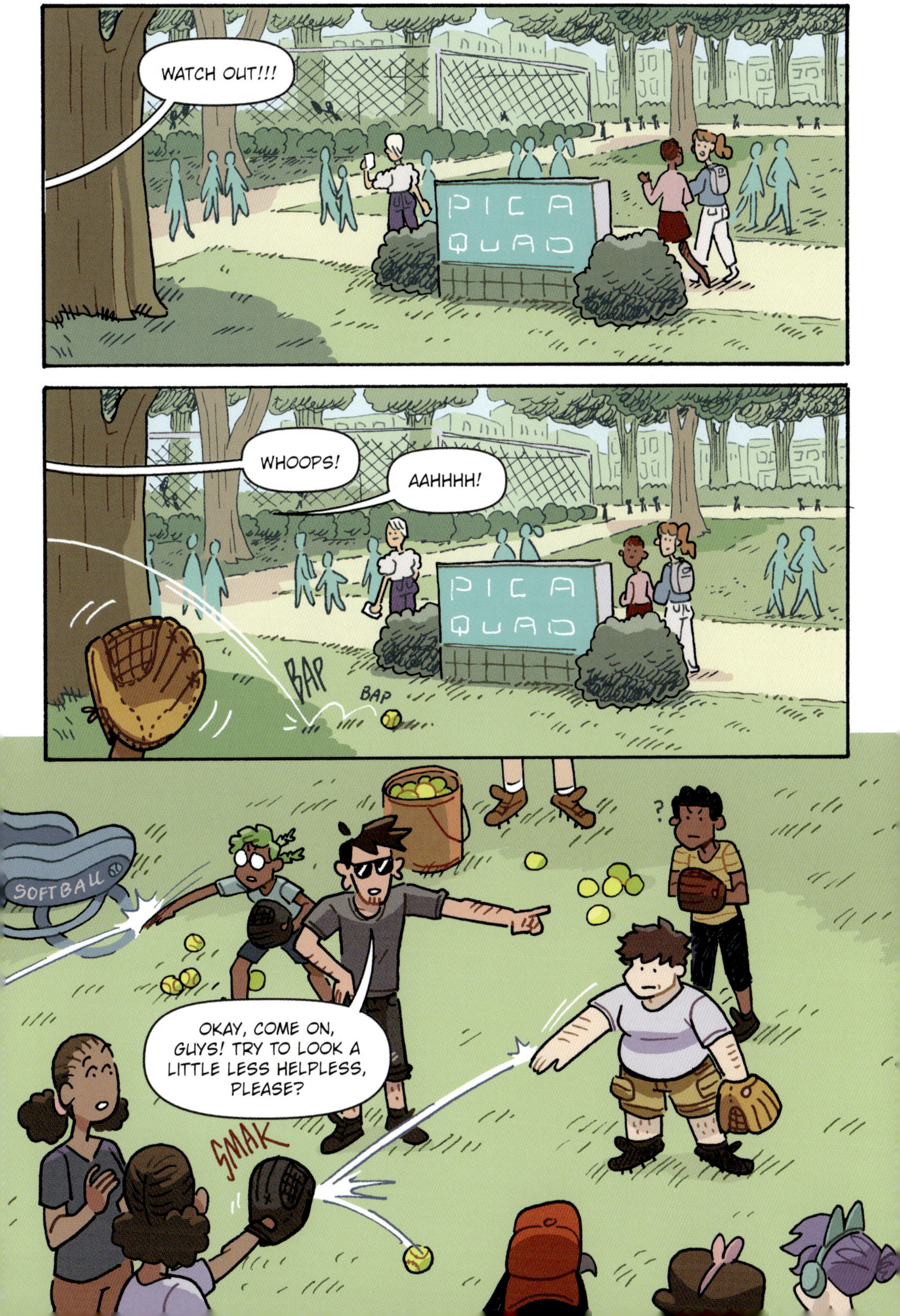
WATCH OUT!!!
PICA QUAD
WHOOPS!
AAHHHH!
PICA QUAD
BAP
BAP
?
SOFTBALL
OKAY, COME ON, GUYS! TRY TO LOOK A LITTLE LESS HELPLESS, PLEASE?
SMAK

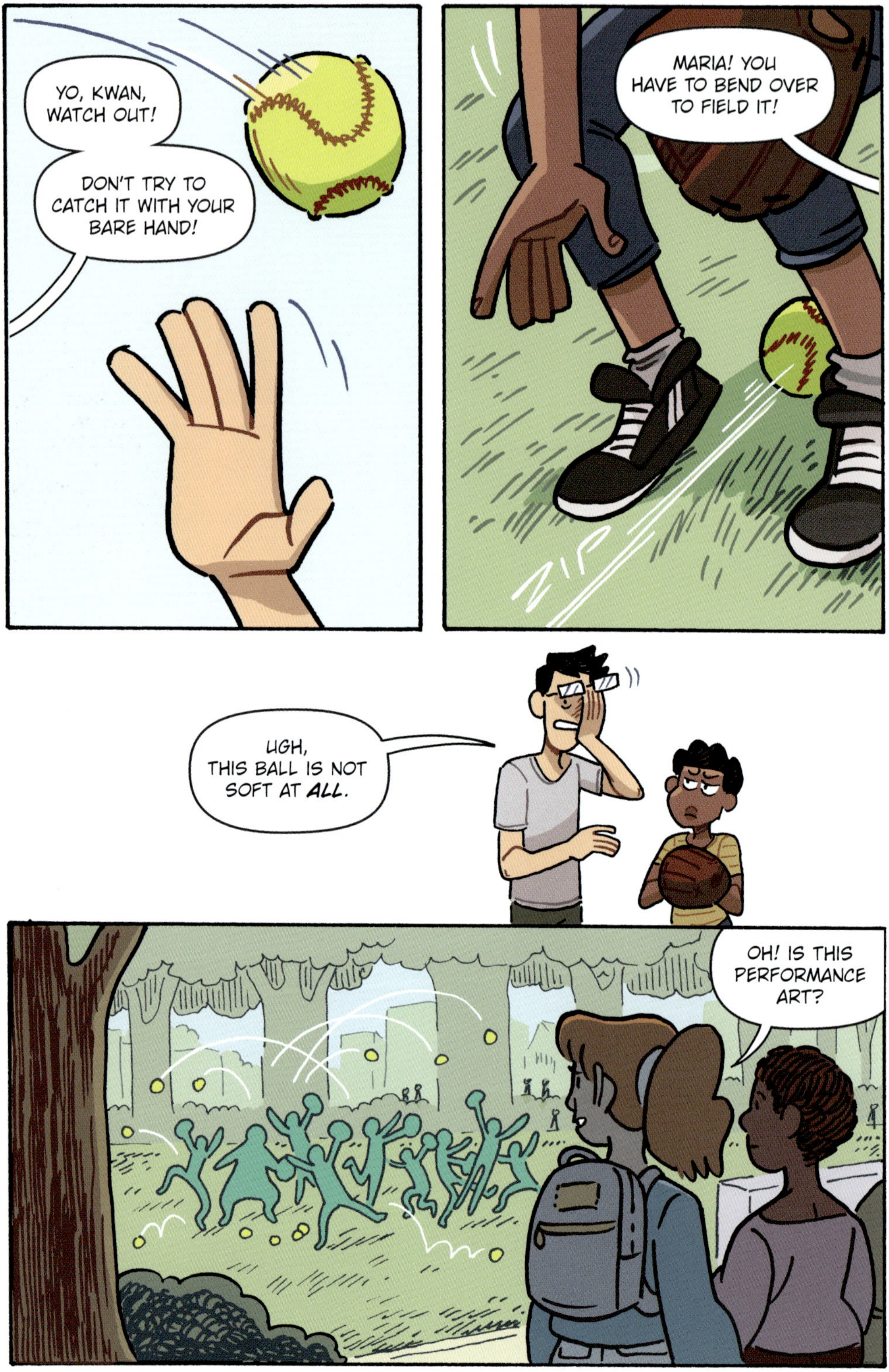
YO, KWAN, WATCH OUT!
DON'T TRY TO CATCH IT WITH YOUR BARE HAND!
MARIA! YOU HAVE TO BEND OVER TO FIELD IT!
ZIP
UGH, THIS BALL IS NOT SOFT AT ALL.
OH! IS THIS PERFORMANCE ART?

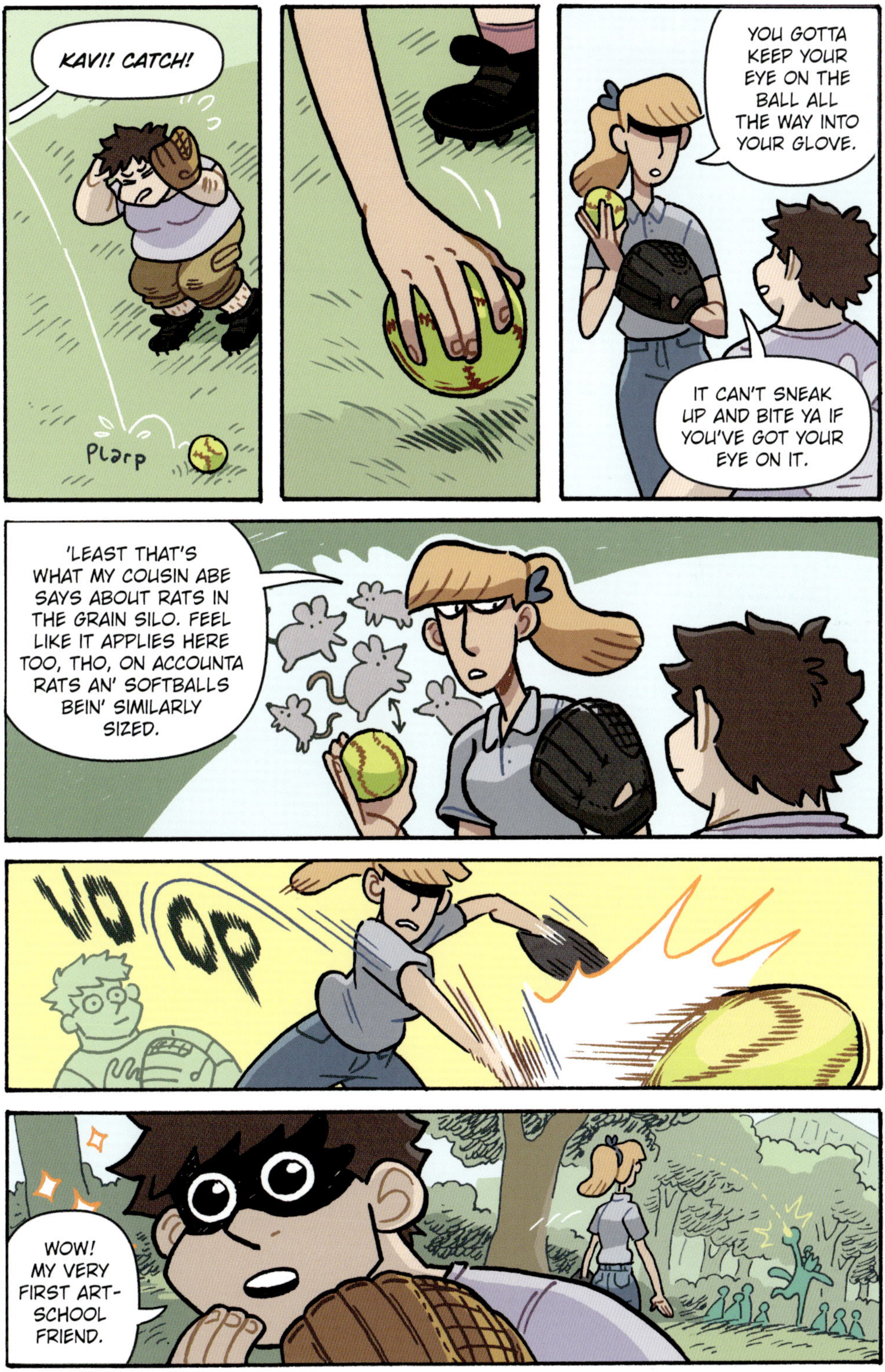
KAVI! CATCH!
Plarp
YOU GOTTA KEEP YOUR EYE ON THE BALL ALL THE WAY INTO YOUR GLOVE.
IT CAN'T SNEAK UP AND BITE YA IF YOU'VE GOT YOUR EYE ON IT.
'LEAST THAT'S WHAT MY COUSIN ABE SAYS ABOUT RATS IN THE GRAIN SILO. FEEL LIKE IT APPLIES HERE TOO, THO, ON ACCOUNTA RATS AN' SOFTBALLS BEIN' SIMILARLY SIZED.
WOOP
WOW! MY VERY FIRST ART-SCHOOL FRIEND.

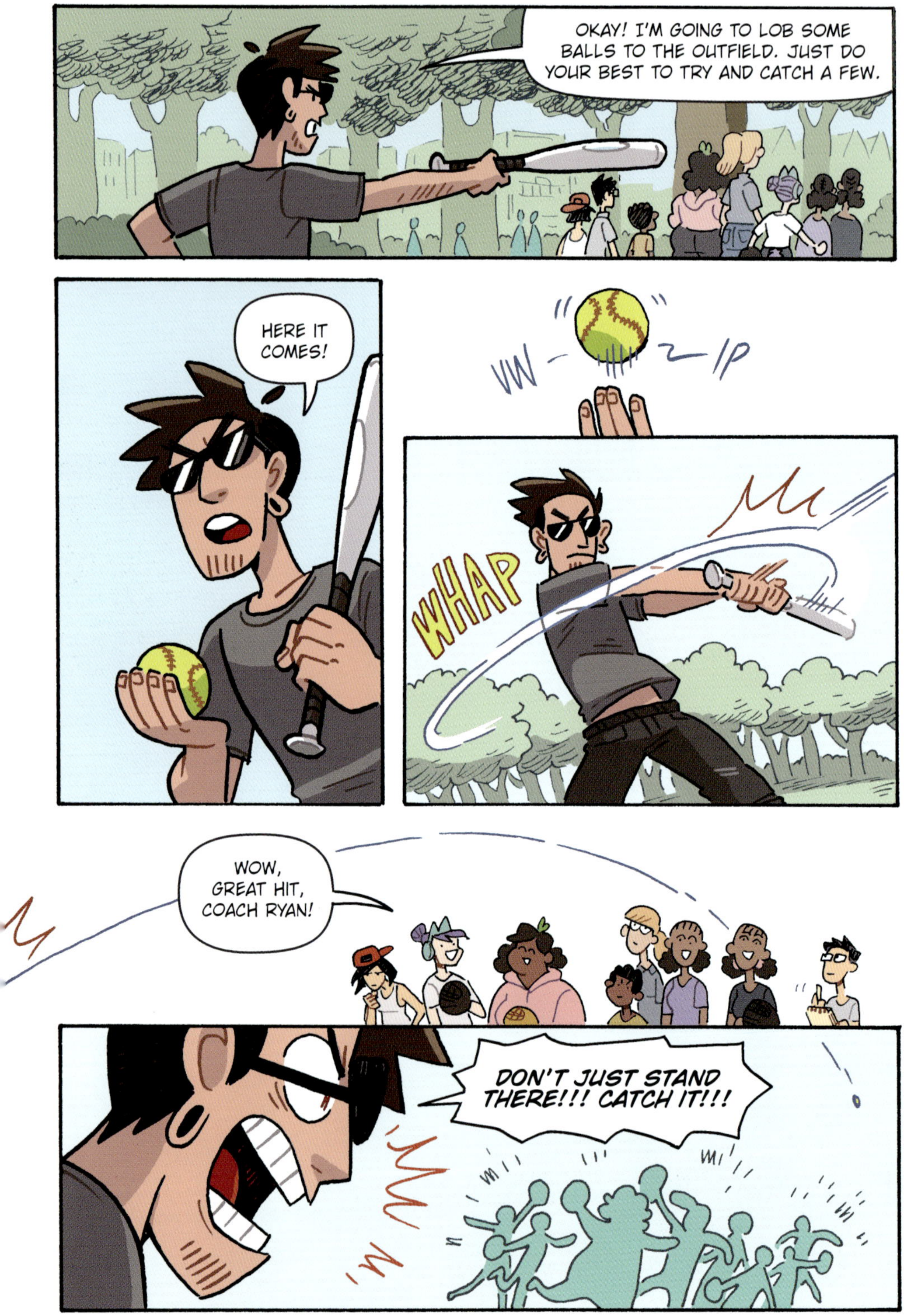
OKAY! I'M GOING TO LOB SOME BALLS TO THE OUTFIELD. JUST DO YOUR BEST TO TRY AND CATCH A FEW.
HERE IT COMES!
WHAP
WOW, GREAT HIT, COACH RYAN!
DON'T JUST STAND THERE!!! CATCH IT!!!

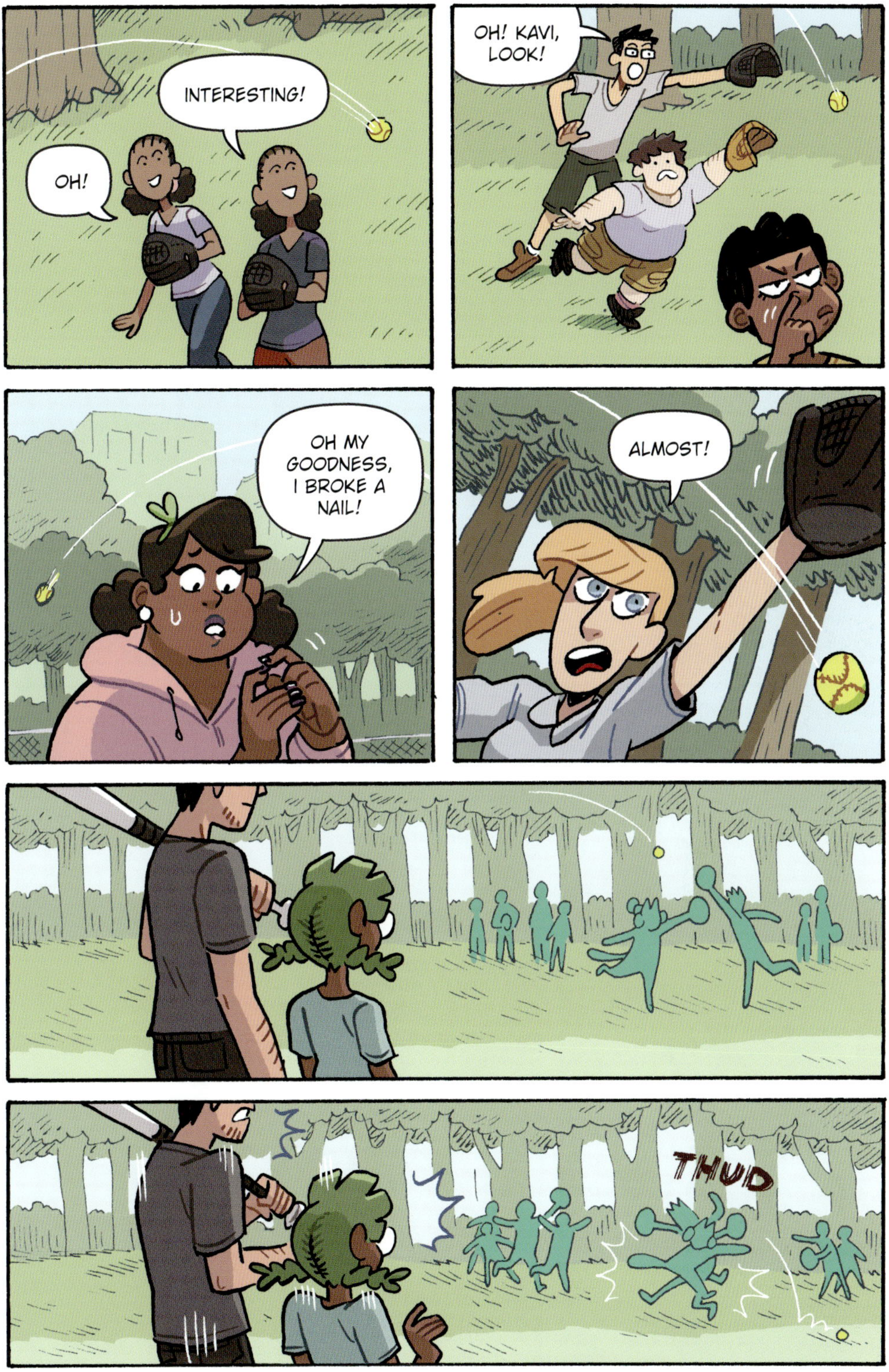
OH!
INTERESTING!
OH! KAVI, LOOK!
OH MY GOODNESS, I BROKE A NAIL!
ALMOST!
THUD

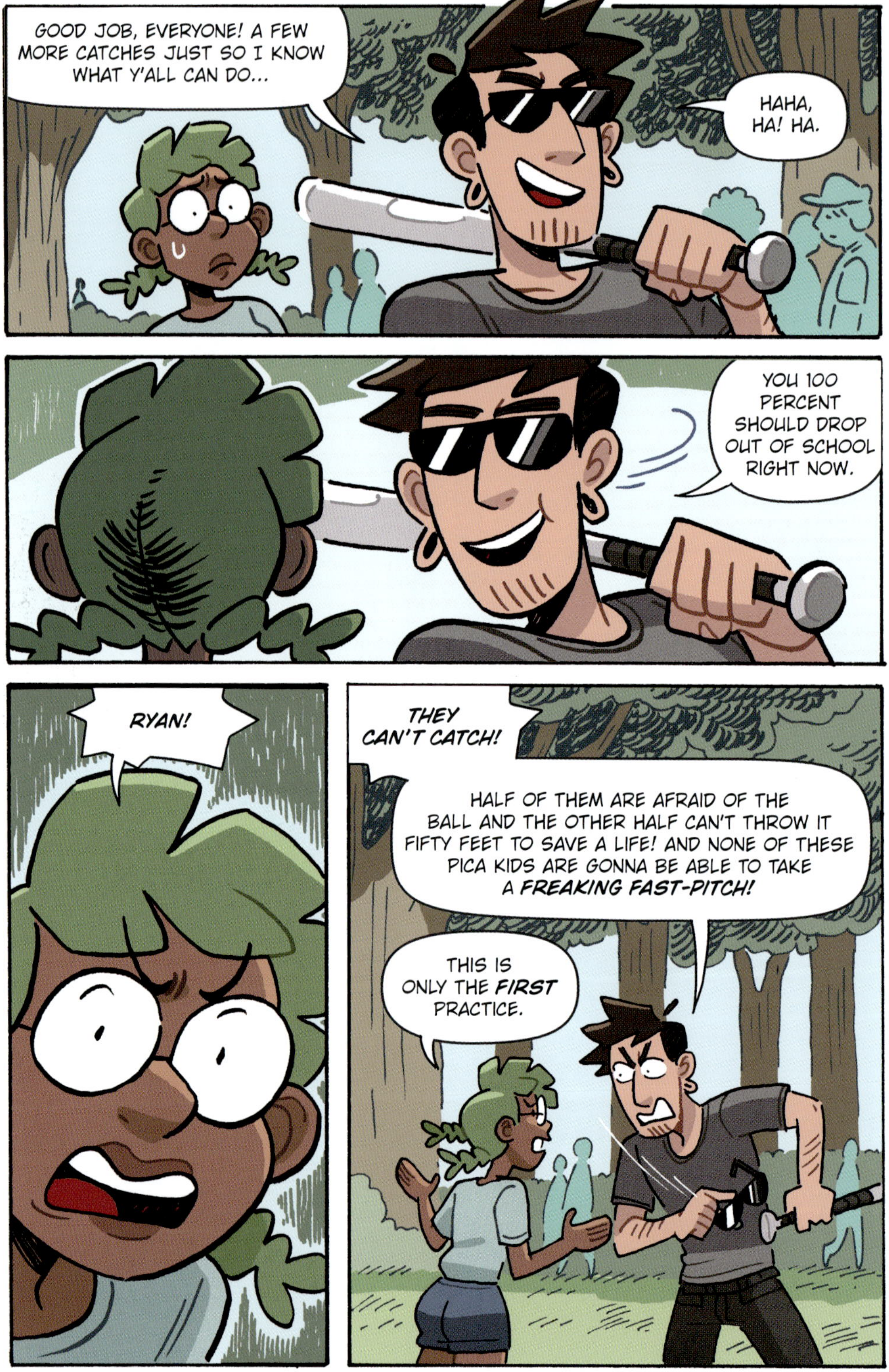
GOOD JOB, EVERYONE! A FEW MORE CATCHES JUST SO I KNOW WHAT Y'ALL CAN DO...
HAHA, HA! HA.
YOU 100 PERCENT SHOULD DROP OUT OF SCHOOL RIGHT NOW.
RYAN!
THEY CAN'T CATCH!
HALF OF THEM ARE AFRAID OF THE BALL AND THE OTHER HALF CAN'T THROW IT FIFTY FEET TO SAVE A LIFE! AND NONE OF THESE PICA KIDS ARE GONNA BE ABLE TO TAKE A FREAKING FAST-PITCH!
THIS IS ONLY THE FIRST PRACTICE.

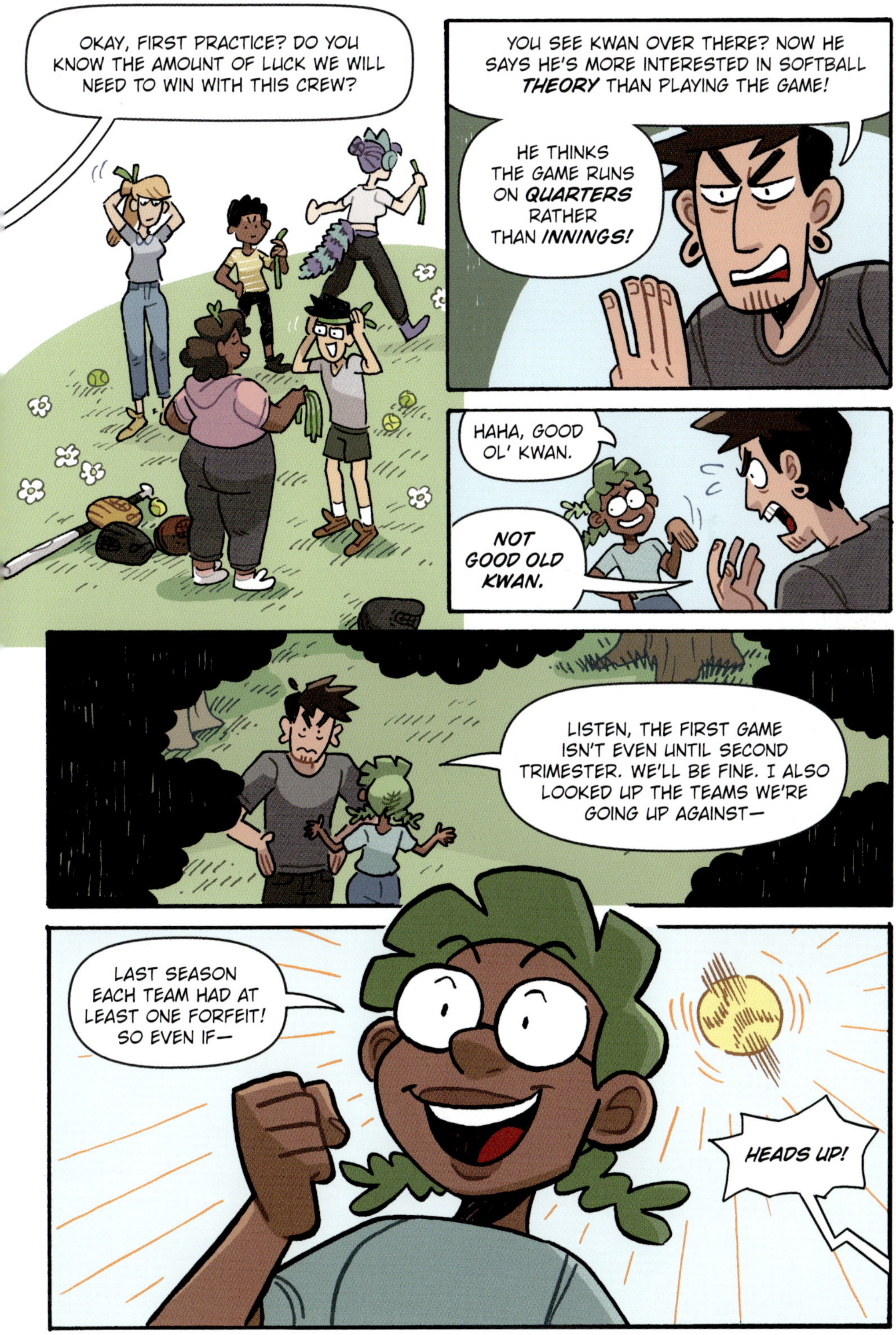
OKAY, FIRST PRACTICE? DO YOU KNOW THE AMOUNT OF LUCK WE WILL NEED TO WIN WITH THIS CREW?
YOU SEE KWAN OVER THERE? NOW HE SAYS HE'S MORE INTERESTED IN SOFTBALL THEORY THAN PLAYING THE GAME!
HE THINKS THE GAME RUNS ON QUARTERS RATHER THAN INNINGS!
HAHA, GOOD OL' KWAN.
NOT GOOD OLD KWAN.
LISTEN, THE FIRST GAME ISN'T EVEN UNTIL SECOND TRIMESTER. WE'LL BE FINE. I ALSO LOOKED UP THE TEAMS WE'RE GOING UP AGAINST—
LAST SEASON EACH TEAM HAD AT LEAST ONE FORFEIT! SO EVEN IF—
HEADS UP!

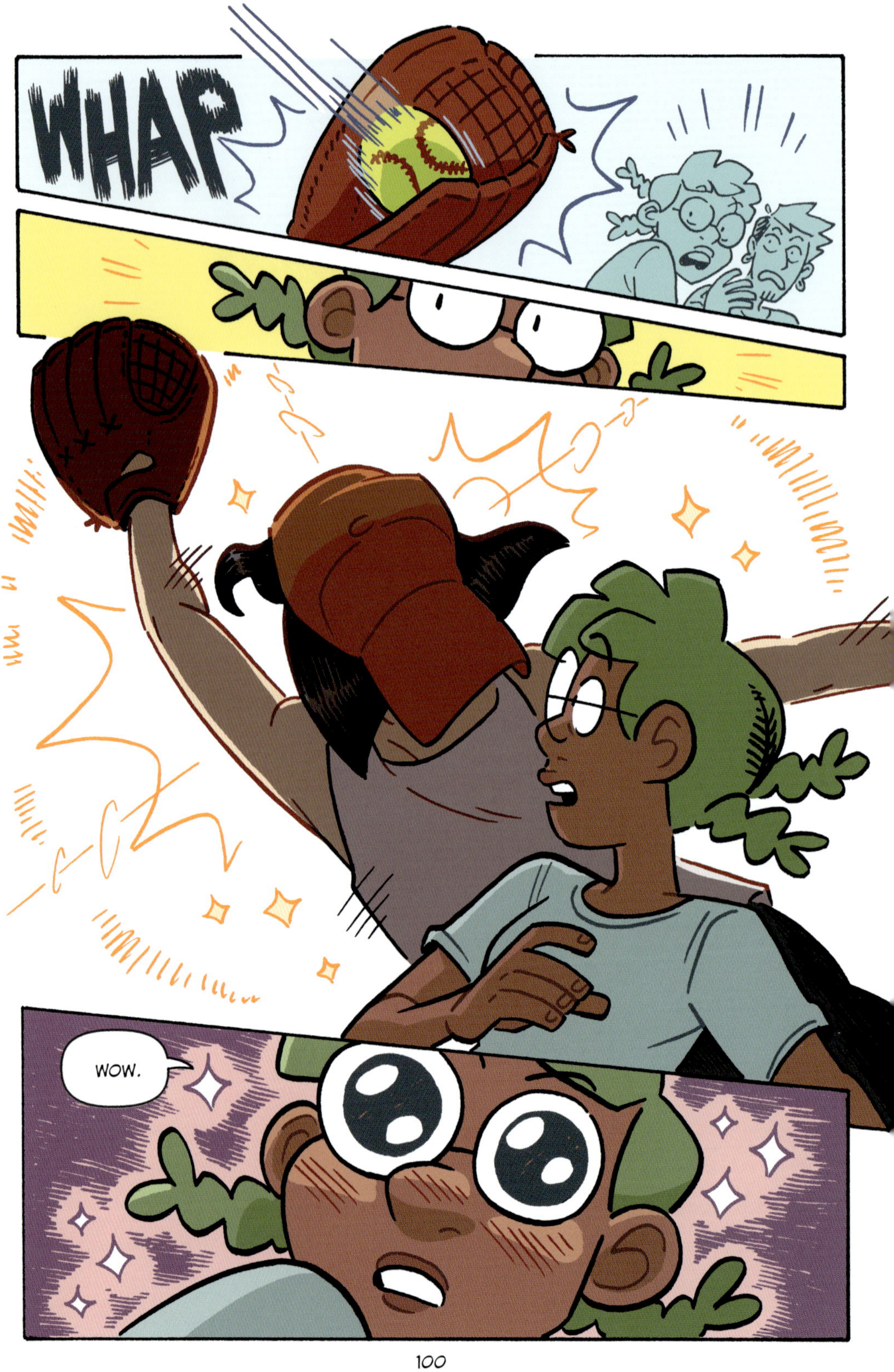
WHAP
WOW.

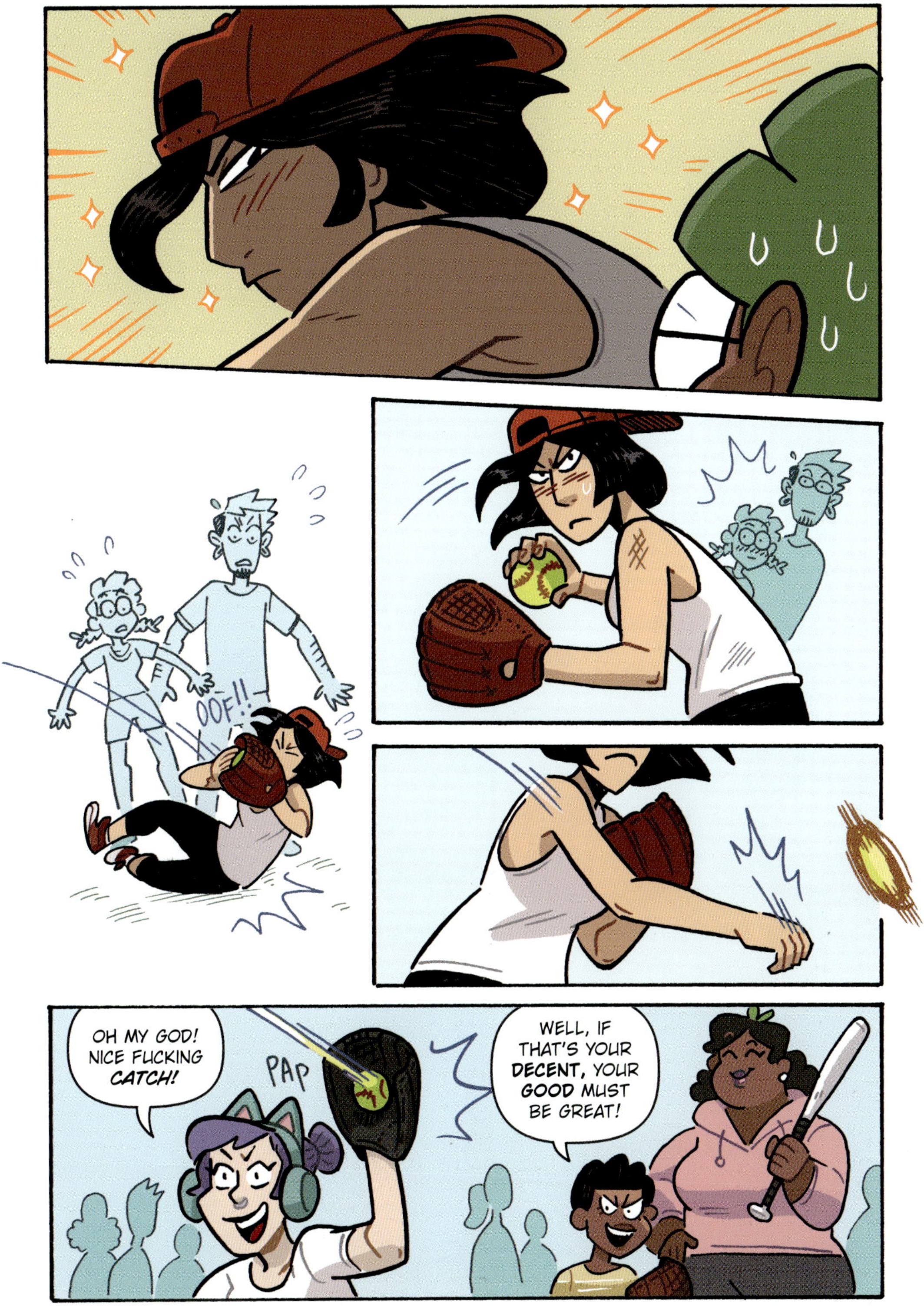

OOF!!
OH MY GOD! NICE FUCKING CATCH!
PAP
WELL, IF THAT'S YOUR DECENT, YOUR GOOD MUST BE GREAT!

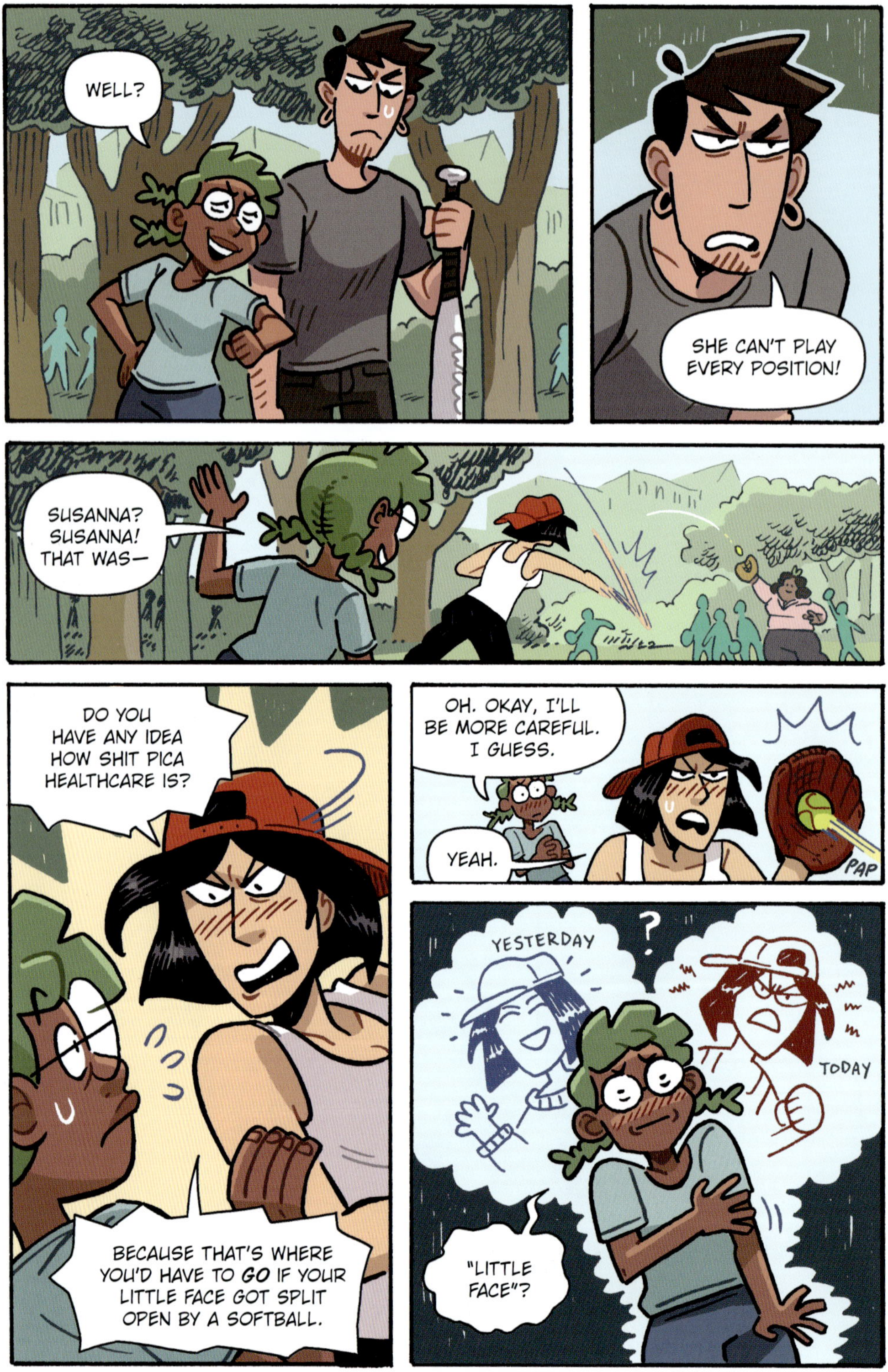
WELL?
SHE CAN'T PLAY EVERY POSITION!
SUSANNA? SUSANNA! THAT WAS—
DO YOU HAVE ANY IDEA HOW SHIT PICA HEALTHCARE IS?
BECAUSE THAT'S WHERE YOU'D HAVE TO GO IF YOUR LITTLE FACE GOT SPLIT OPEN BY A SOFTBALL.
OH. OKAY, I'LL BE MORE CAREFUL. I GUESS.
YEAH.
PAP
?
YESTERDAY
TODAY
"LITTLE FACE"?

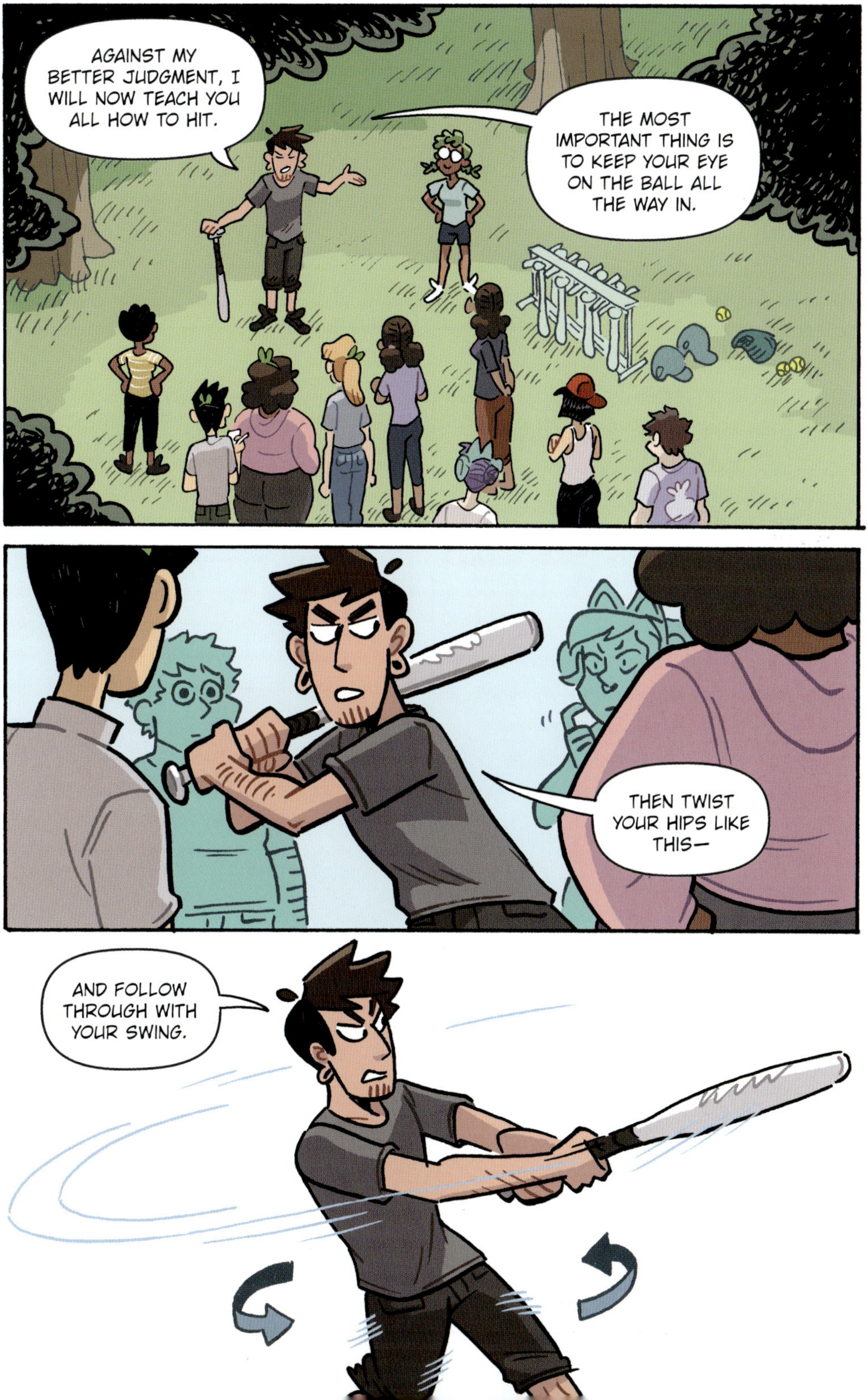
AGAINST MY BETTER JUDGMENT, I WILL NOW TEACH YOU ALL HOW TO HIT.
THE MOST IMPORTANT THING IS TO KEEP YOUR EYE ON THE BALL ALL THE WAY IN.
THEN TWIST YOUR HIPS LIKE THIS—
AND FOLLOW THROUGH WITH YOUR SWING.

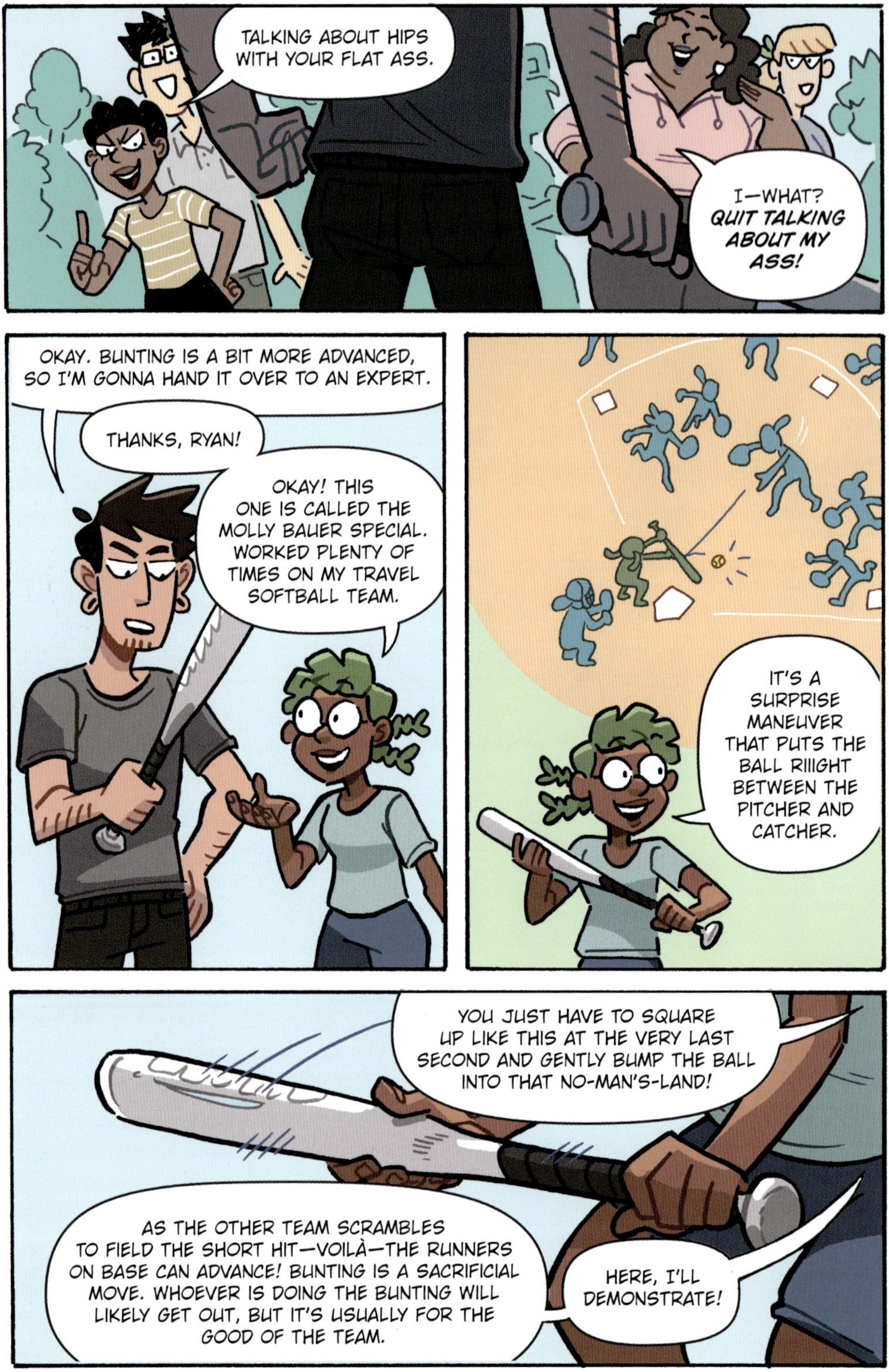
TALKING ABOUT HIPS WITH YOUR FLAT ASS.
I—WHAT? *QUIT TALKING ABOUT MY ASS!*
OKAY. BUNTING IS A BIT MORE ADVANCED, SO I'M GONNA HAND IT OVER TO AN EXPERT.
THANKS, RYAN!
OKAY! THIS ONE IS CALLED THE MOLLY BAUER SPECIAL. WORKED PLENTY OF TIMES ON MY TRAVEL SOFTBALL TEAM.
IT'S A SURPRISE MANEUVER THAT PUTS THE BALL RIIIGHT BETWEEN THE PITCHER AND CATCHER.
YOU JUST HAVE TO SQUARE UP LIKE THIS AT THE VERY LAST SECOND AND GENTLY BUMP THE BALL INTO THAT NO-MAN'S-LAND!
AS THE OTHER TEAM SCRAMBLES TO FIELD THE SHORT HIT—VOILÀ—THE RUNNERS ON BASE CAN ADVANCE! BUNTING IS A SACRIFICIAL MOVE. WHOEVER IS DOING THE BUNTING WILL LIKELY GET OUT, BUT IT'S USUALLY FOR THE GOOD OF THE TEAM.
HERE, I'LL DEMONSTRATE!

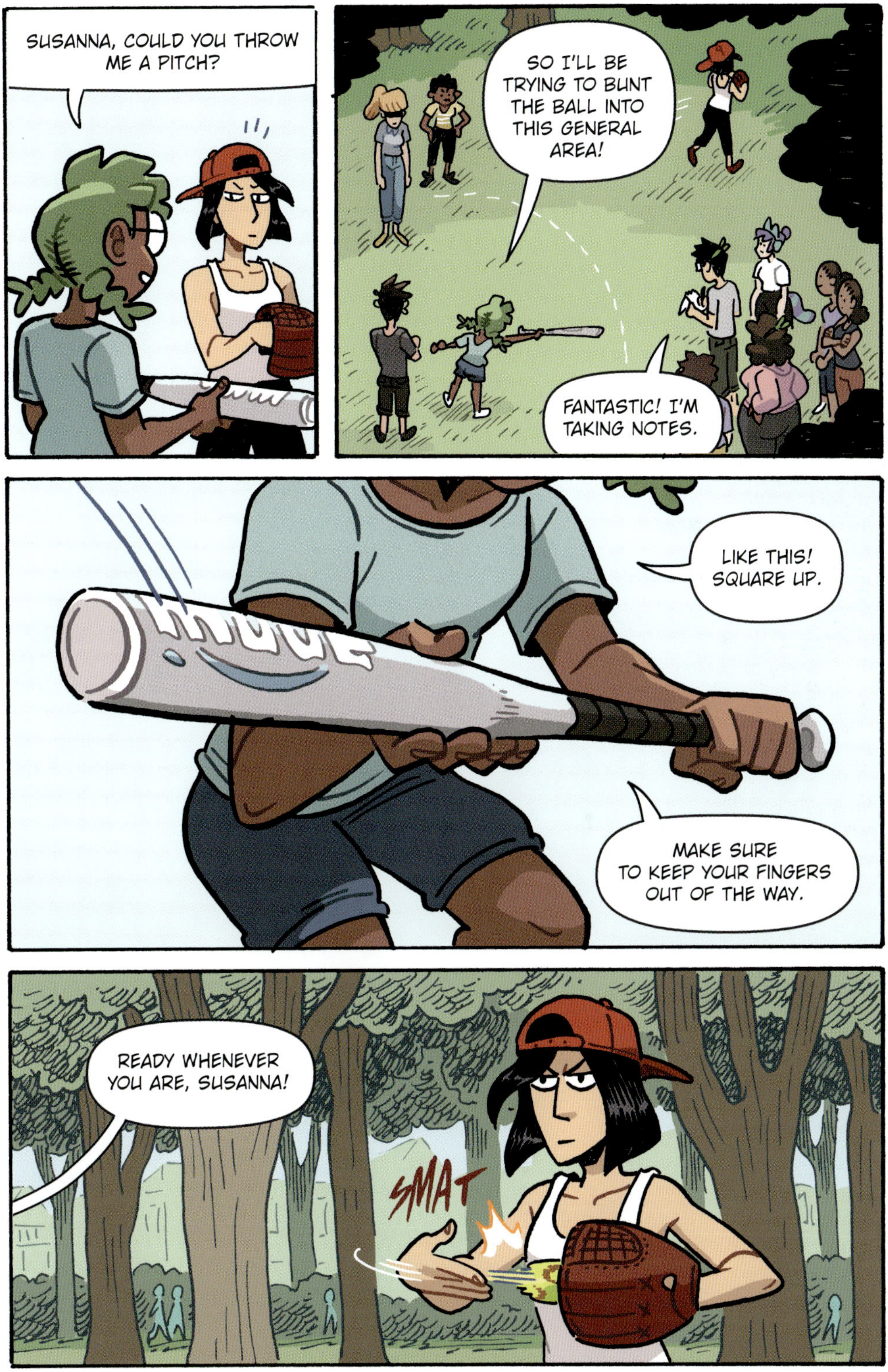
SUSANNA, COULD YOU THROW ME A PITCH?
SO I'LL BE TRYING TO BUNT THE BALL INTO THIS GENERAL AREA!
FANTASTIC! I'M TAKING NOTES.
LIKE THIS! SQUARE UP.
MAKE SURE TO KEEP YOUR FINGERS OUT OF THE WAY.
READY WHENEVER YOU ARE, SUSANNA!
SMAT

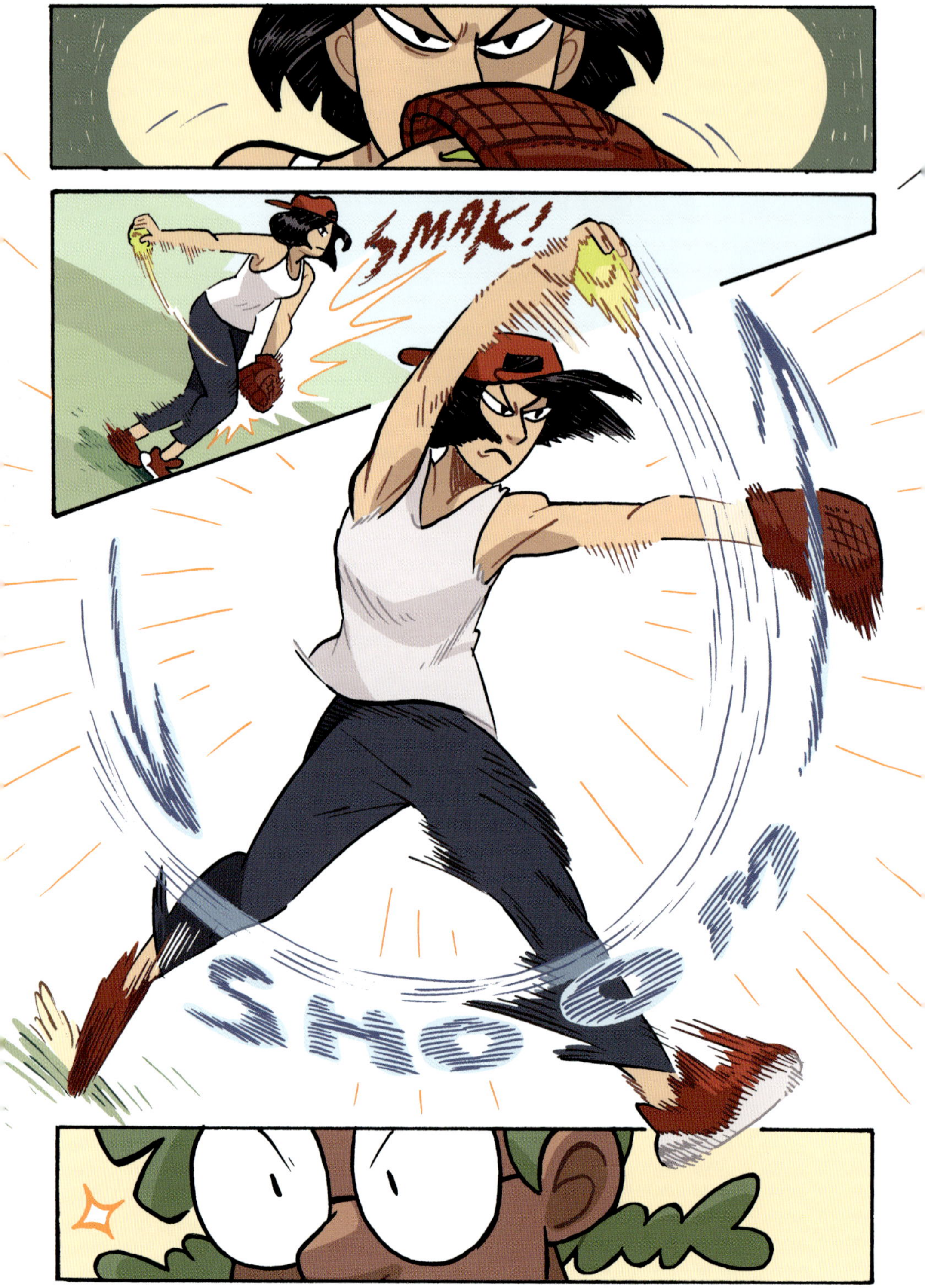
SMAK!
SHOOM

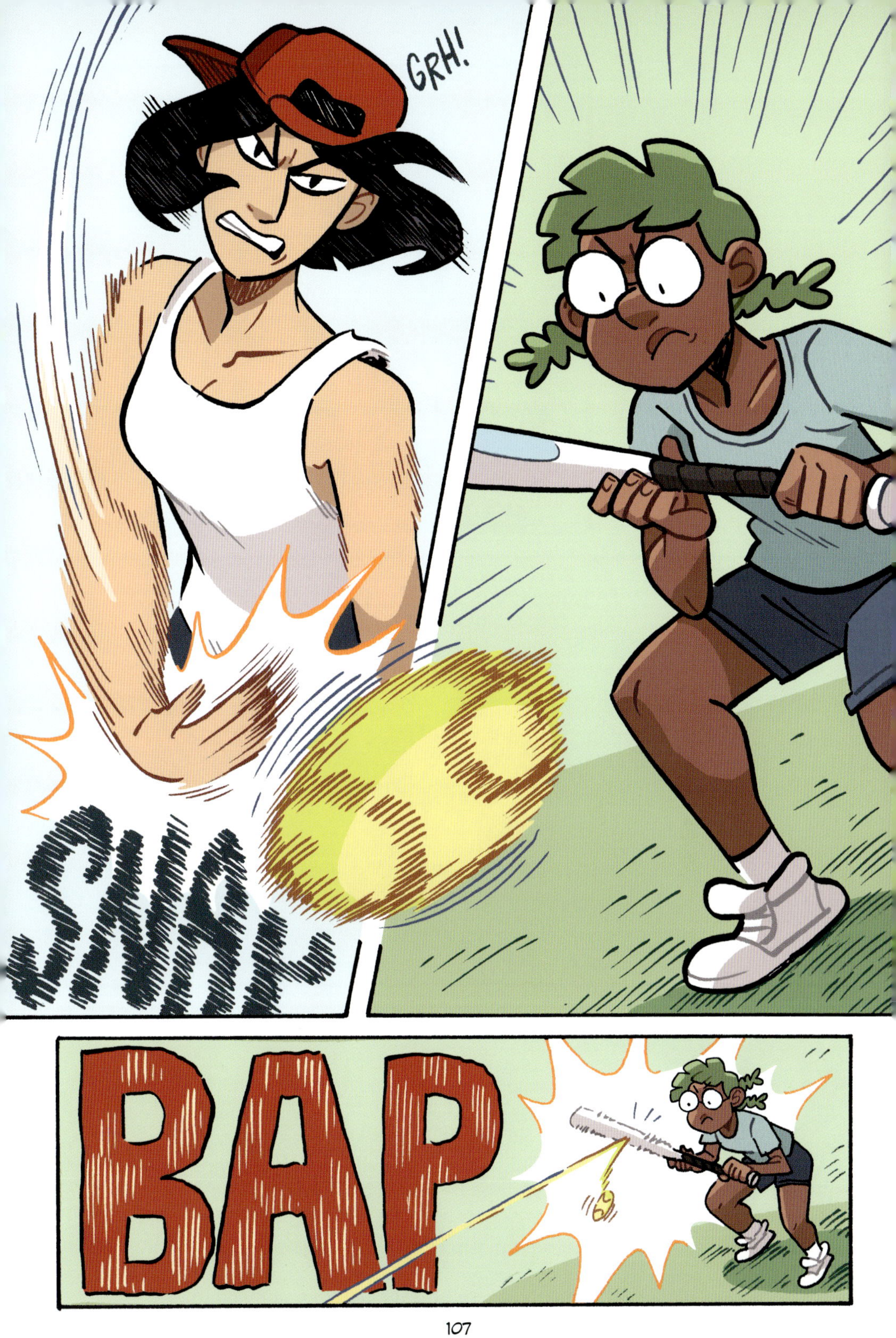
GRH!
SNAP
BAP

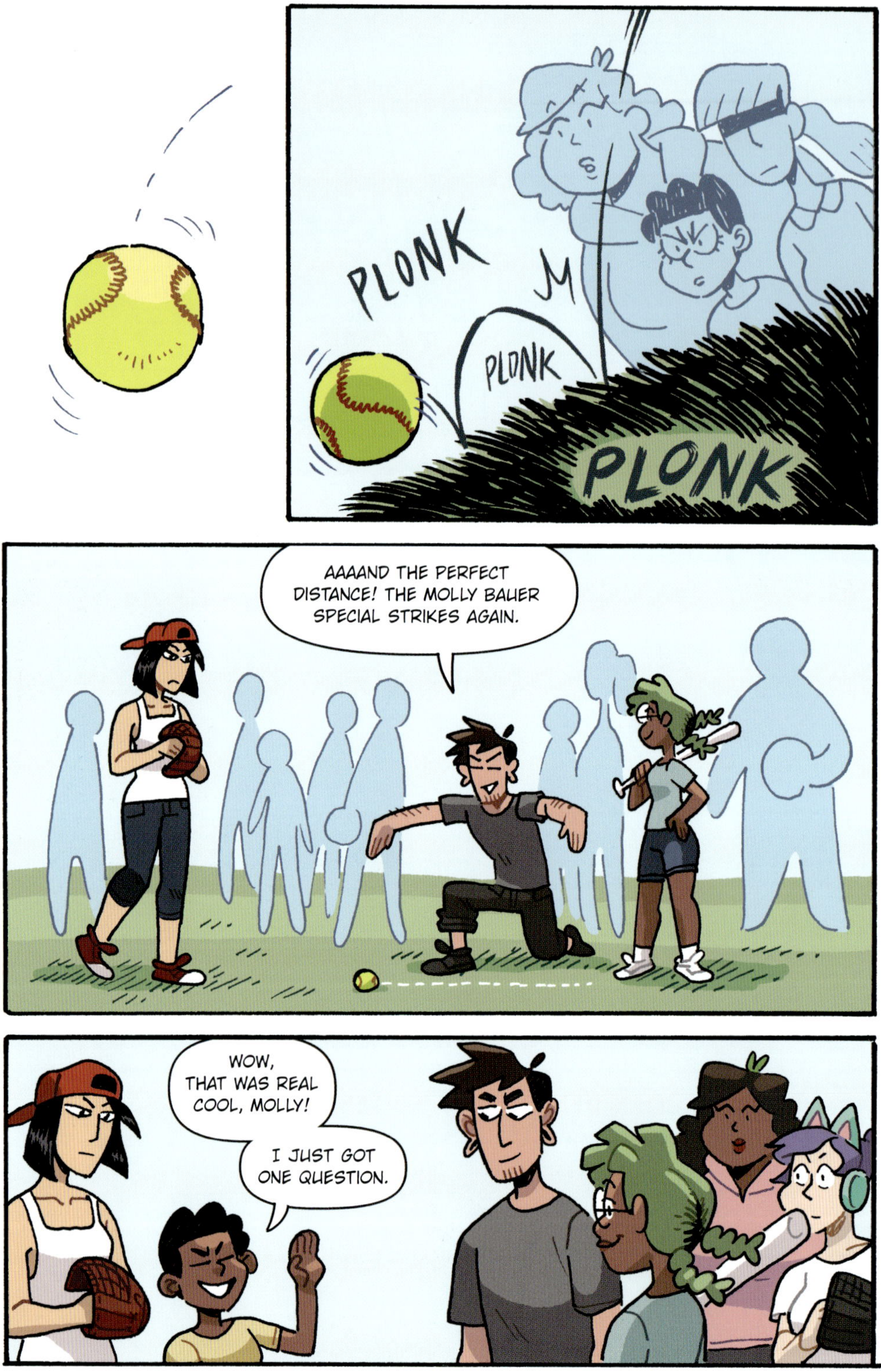
PLONK
PLONK
PLONK
AAAAND THE PERFECT DISTANCE! THE MOLLY BAUER SPECIAL STRIKES AGAIN.
WOW, THAT WAS REAL COOL, MOLLY!
I JUST GOT ONE QUESTION.

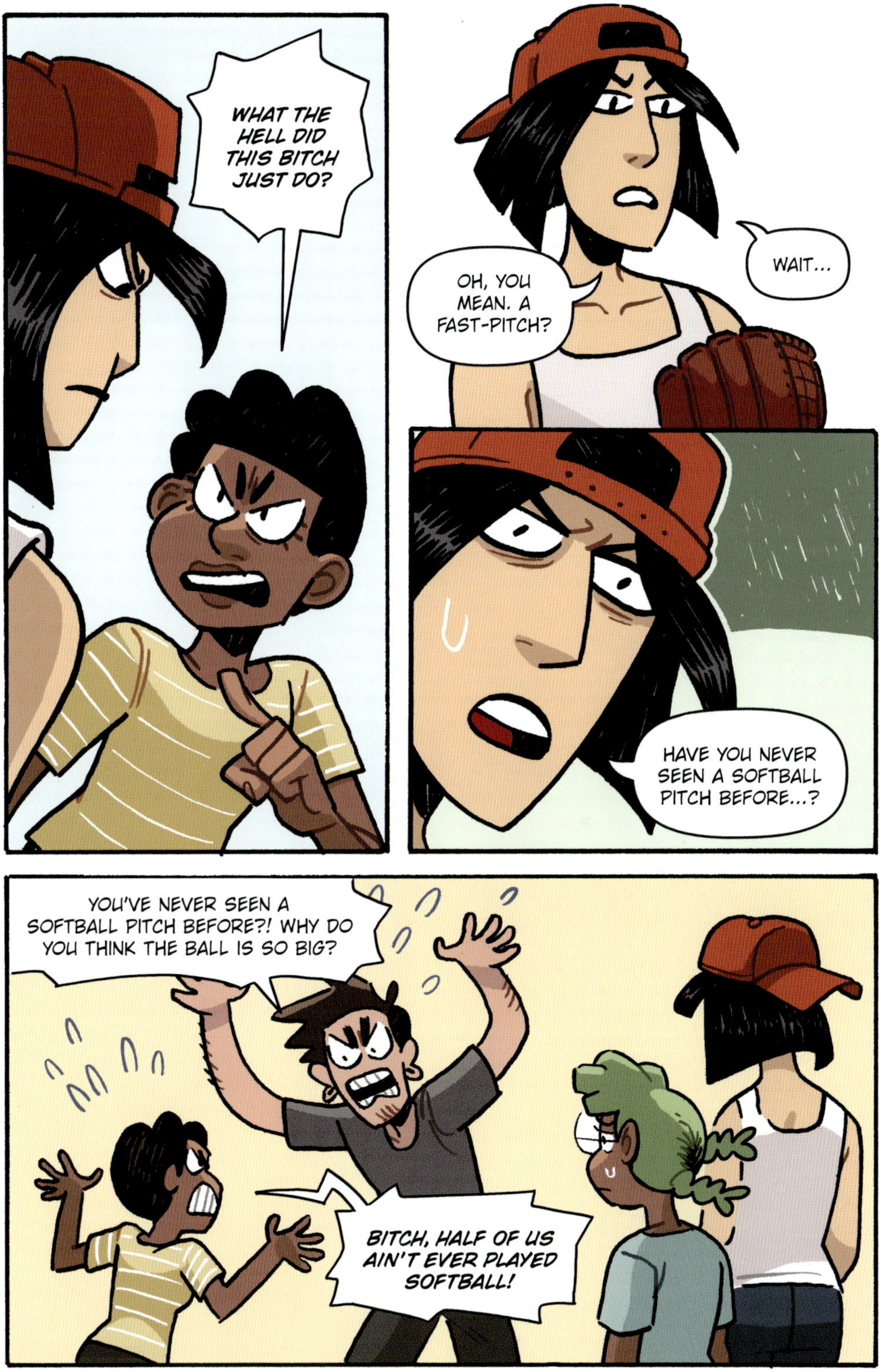
WHAT THE HELL DID THIS BITCH JUST DO?
OH, YOU MEAN. A FAST-PITCH?
WAIT...
HAVE YOU NEVER SEEN A SOFTBALL PITCH BEFORE...?
YOU'VE NEVER SEEN A SOFTBALL PITCH BEFORE?! WHY DO YOU THINK THE BALL IS SO BIG?
BITCH, HALF OF US AIN'T EVER PLAYED SOFTBALL!

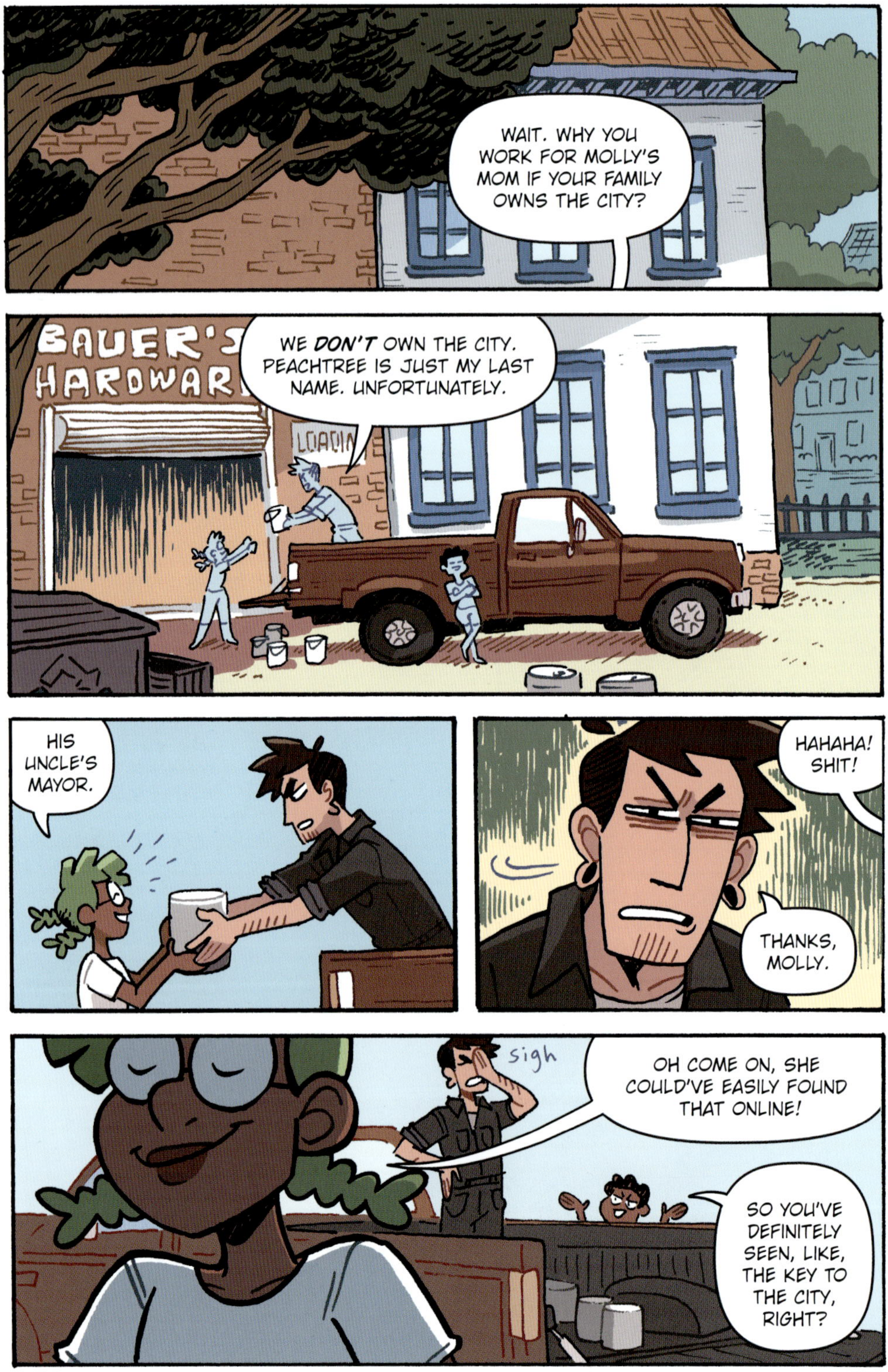
WAIT. WHY YOU WORK FOR MOLLY'S MOM IF YOUR FAMILY OWNS THE CITY?
BAUER'S HARDWAR
WE *DON'T* OWN THE CITY. PEACHTREE IS JUST MY LAST NAME. UNFORTUNATELY.
HIS UNCLE'S MAYOR.
HAHAHA! SHIT!
THANKS, MOLLY.
sigh
OH COME ON, SHE COULD'VE EASILY FOUND THAT ONLINE!
SO YOU'VE DEFINITELY SEEN, LIKE, THE KEY TO THE CITY, RIGHT?

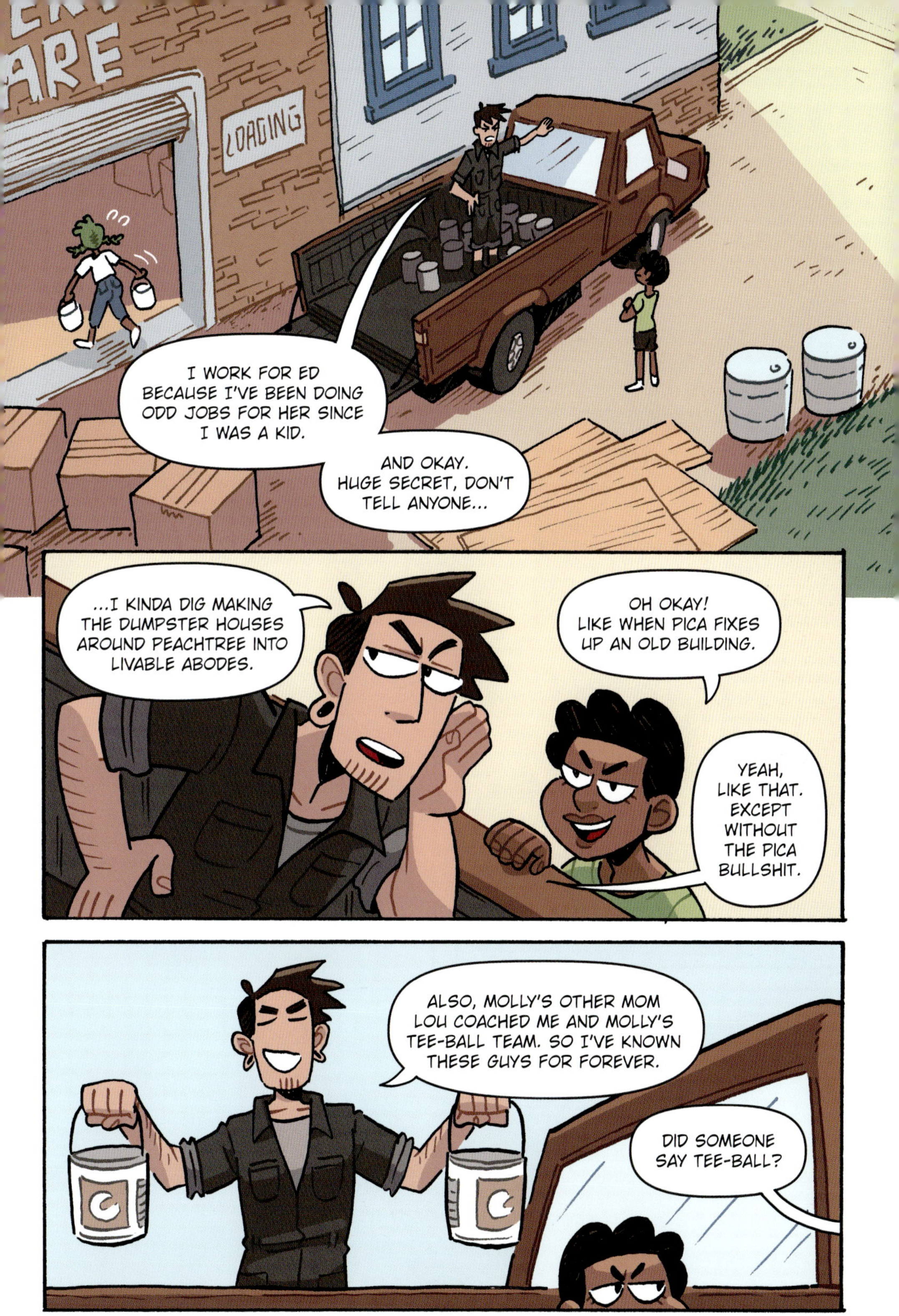
LOADING
I WORK FOR ED BECAUSE I'VE BEEN DOING ODD JOBS FOR HER SINCE I WAS A KID.
AND OKAY. HUGE SECRET, DON'T TELL ANYONE...
...I KINDA DIG MAKING THE DUMPSTER HOUSES AROUND PEACHTREE INTO LIVABLE ABODES.
OH OKAY! LIKE WHEN PICA FIXES UP AN OLD BUILDING.
YEAH, LIKE THAT. EXCEPT WITHOUT THE PICA BULLSHIT.
ALSO, MOLLY'S OTHER MOM LOU COACHED ME AND MOLLY'S TEE-BALL TEAM. SO I'VE KNOWN THESE GUYS FOR FOREVER.
DID SOMEONE SAY TEE-BALL?

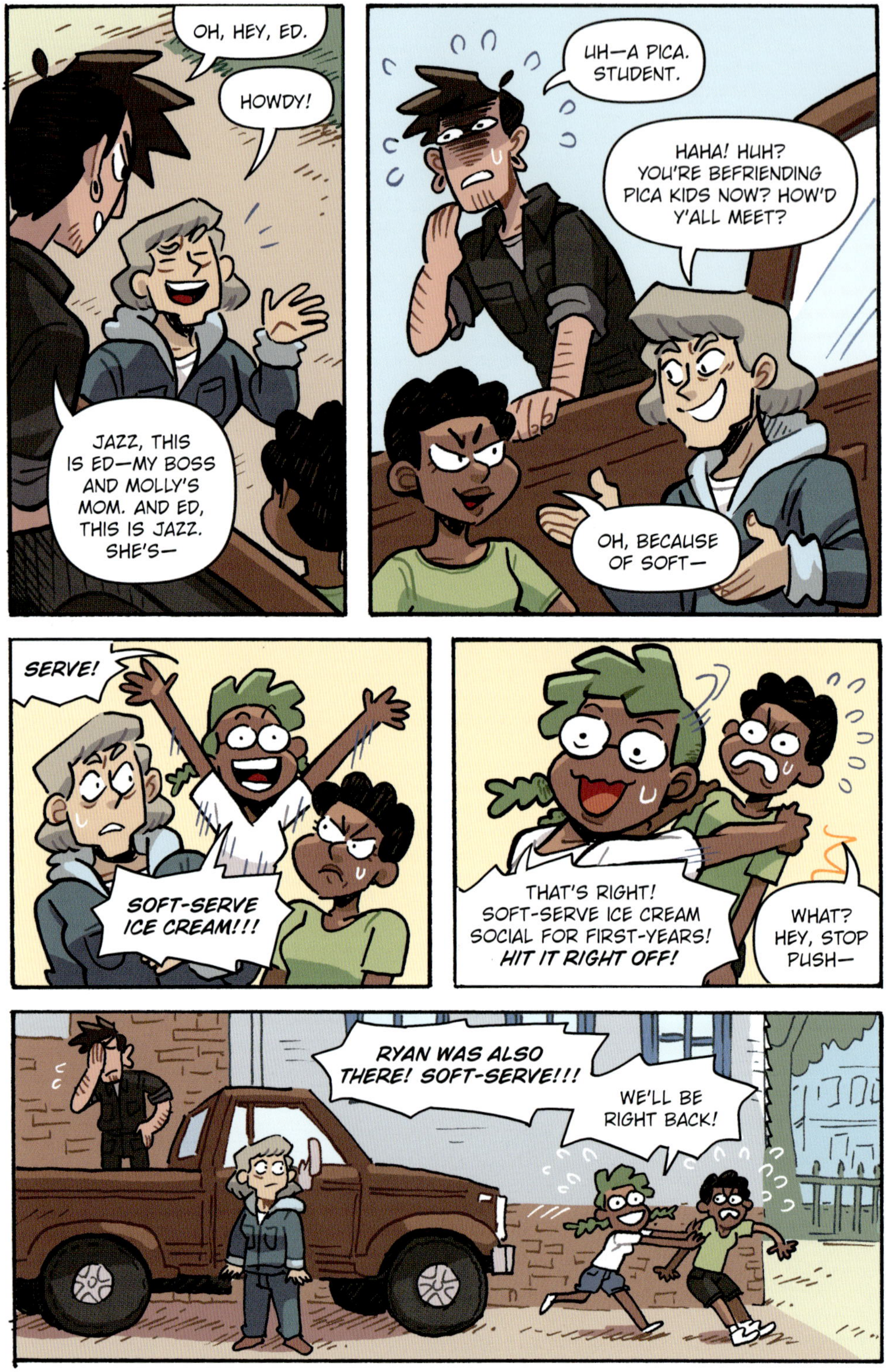
OH, HEY, ED.
HOWDY!
JAZZ, THIS IS ED—MY BOSS AND MOLLY'S MOM. AND ED, THIS IS JAZZ. SHE'S—
UH—A PICA. STUDENT.
HAHA! HUH? YOU'RE BEFRIENDING PICA KIDS NOW? HOW'D Y'ALL MEET?
OH, BECAUSE OF SOFT—
SERVE!
SOFT-SERVE ICE CREAM!!!
THAT'S RIGHT! SOFT-SERVE ICE CREAM SOCIAL FOR FIRST-YEARS! HIT IT RIGHT OFF!
WHAT? HEY, STOP PUSH—
RYAN WAS ALSO THERE! SOFT-SERVE!!!
WE'LL BE RIGHT BACK!

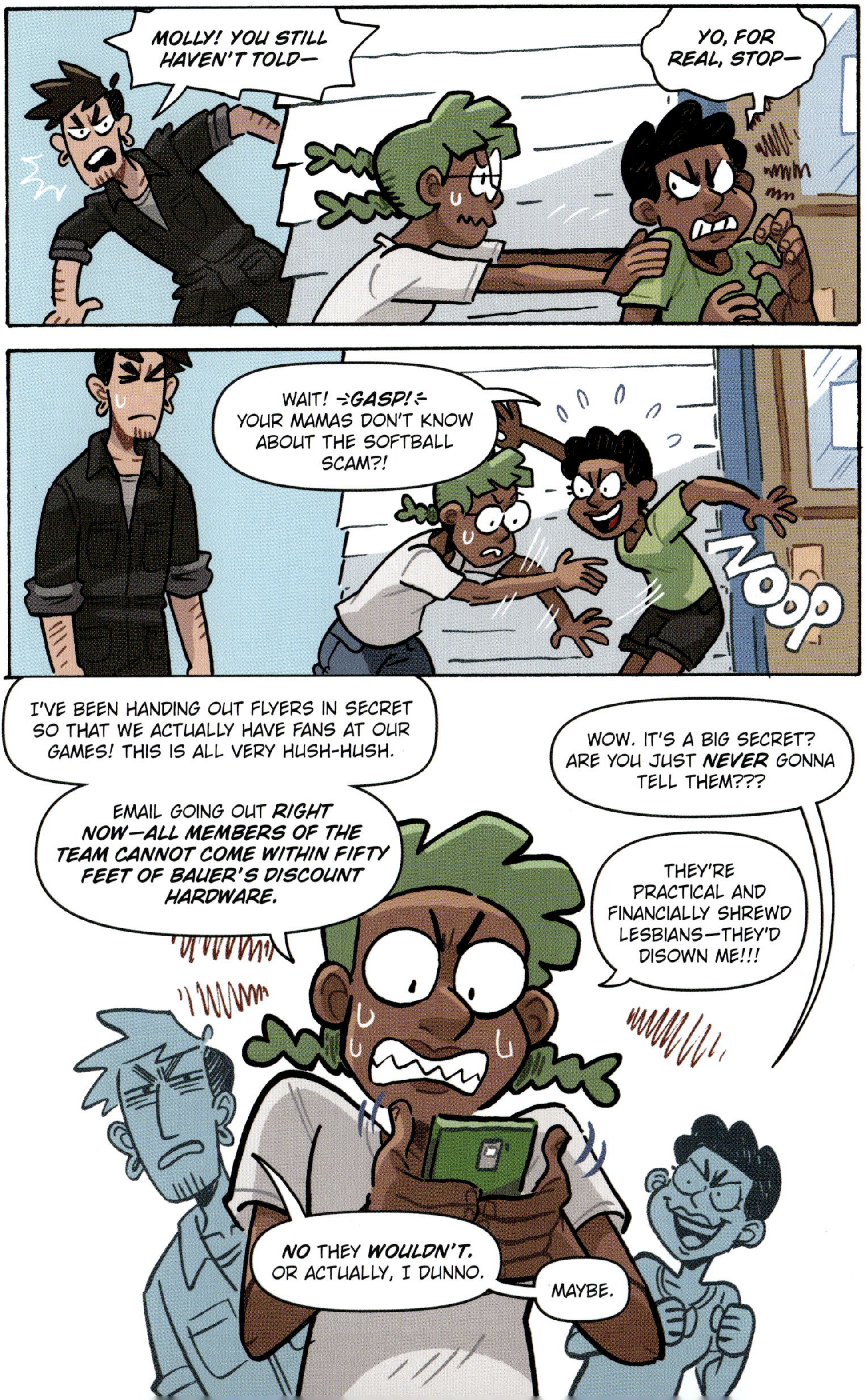
MOLLY! YOU STILL HAVEN'T TOLD—
YO, FOR REAL, STOP—
WAIT! GASP! YOUR MAMAS DON'T KNOW ABOUT THE SOFTBALL SCAM?!
NOOP
I'VE BEEN HANDING OUT FLYERS IN SECRET SO THAT WE ACTUALLY HAVE FANS AT OUR GAMES! THIS IS ALL VERY HUSH-HUSH.
EMAIL GOING OUT RIGHT NOW—ALL MEMBERS OF THE TEAM CANNOT COME WITHIN FIFTY FEET OF BAUER'S DISCOUNT HARDWARE.
WOW. IT'S A BIG SECRET? ARE YOU JUST NEVER GONNA TELL THEM???
THEY'RE PRACTICAL AND FINANCIALLY SHREWD LESBIANS—THEY'D DISOWN ME!!!
NO THEY WOULDN'T. OR ACTUALLY, I DUNNO.
MAYBE.

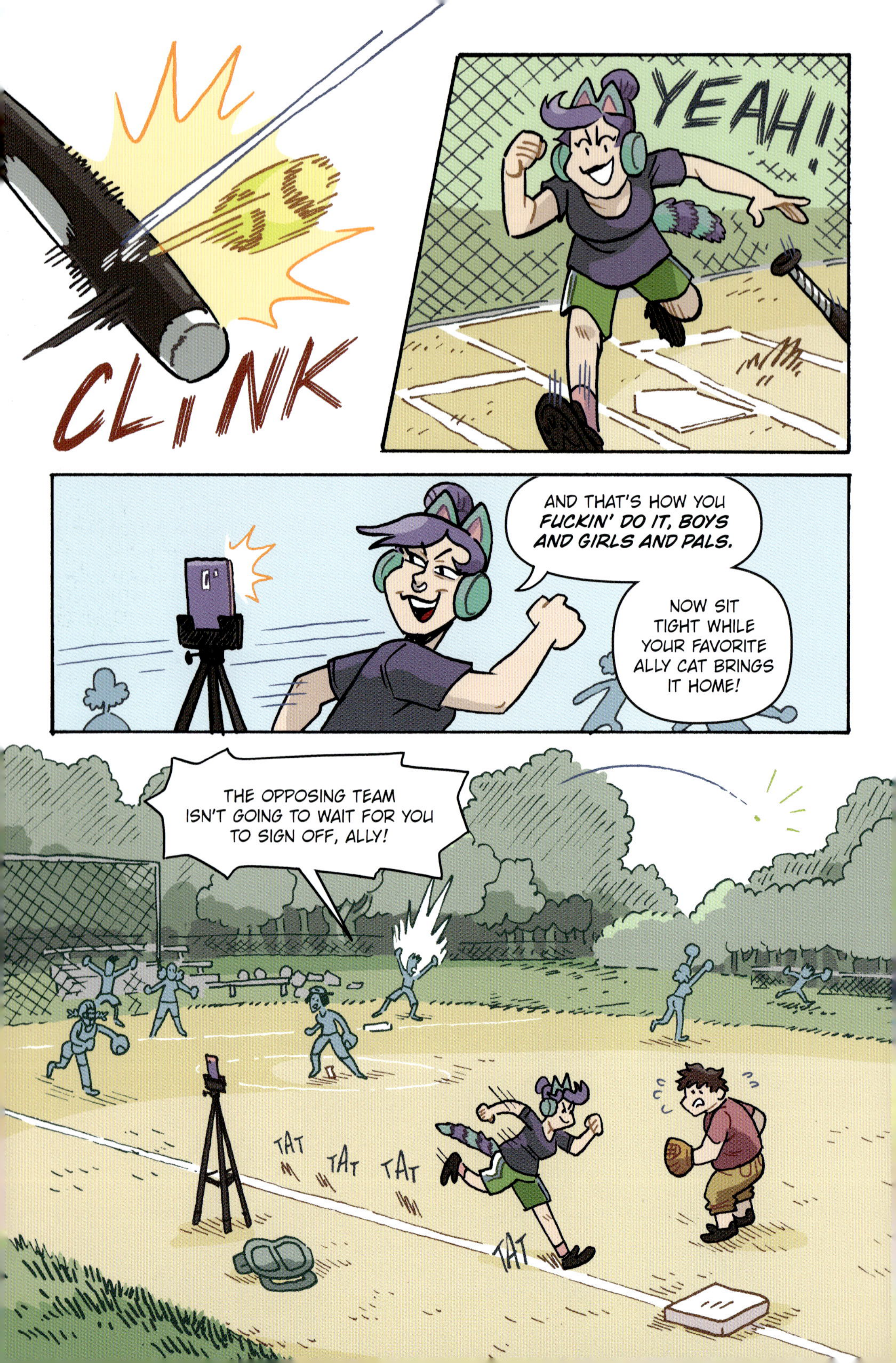
CLINK
YEAH!
AND THAT'S HOW YOU *FUCKIN' DO IT, BOYS AND GIRLS AND PALS.*
NOW SIT TIGHT WHILE YOUR FAVORITE ALLY CAT BRINGS IT HOME!
THE OPPOSING TEAM ISN'T GOING TO WAIT FOR YOU TO SIGN OFF, ALLY!
TAT TAT TAT
TAT

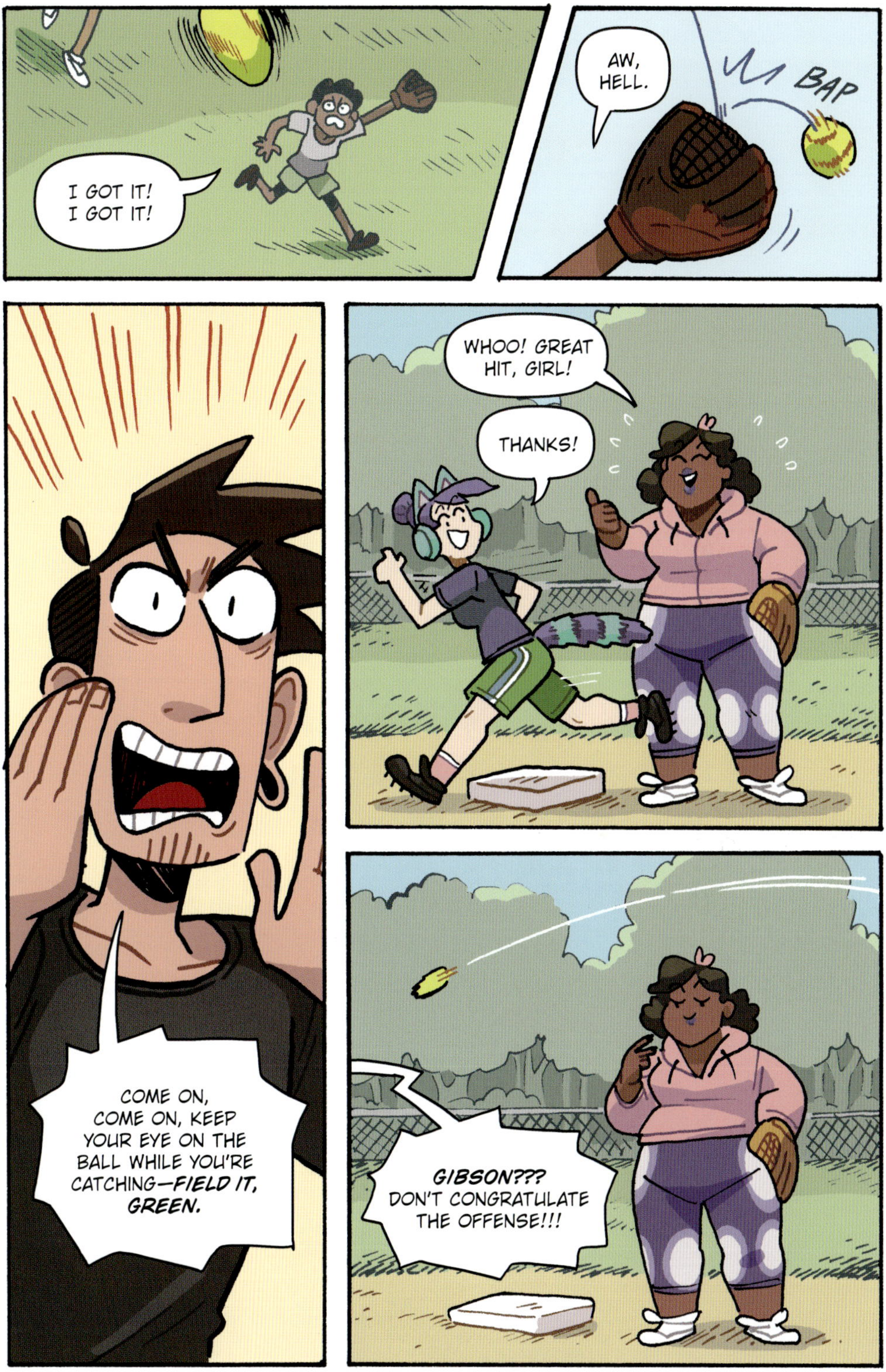
I GOT IT! I GOT IT!
AW, HELL.
BAP
COME ON, COME ON, KEEP YOUR EYE ON THE BALL WHILE YOU'RE CATCHING—**FIELD IT, GREEN.**
WHOO! GREAT HIT, GIRL!
THANKS!
GIBSON??? DON'T CONGRATULATE THE OFFENSE!!!

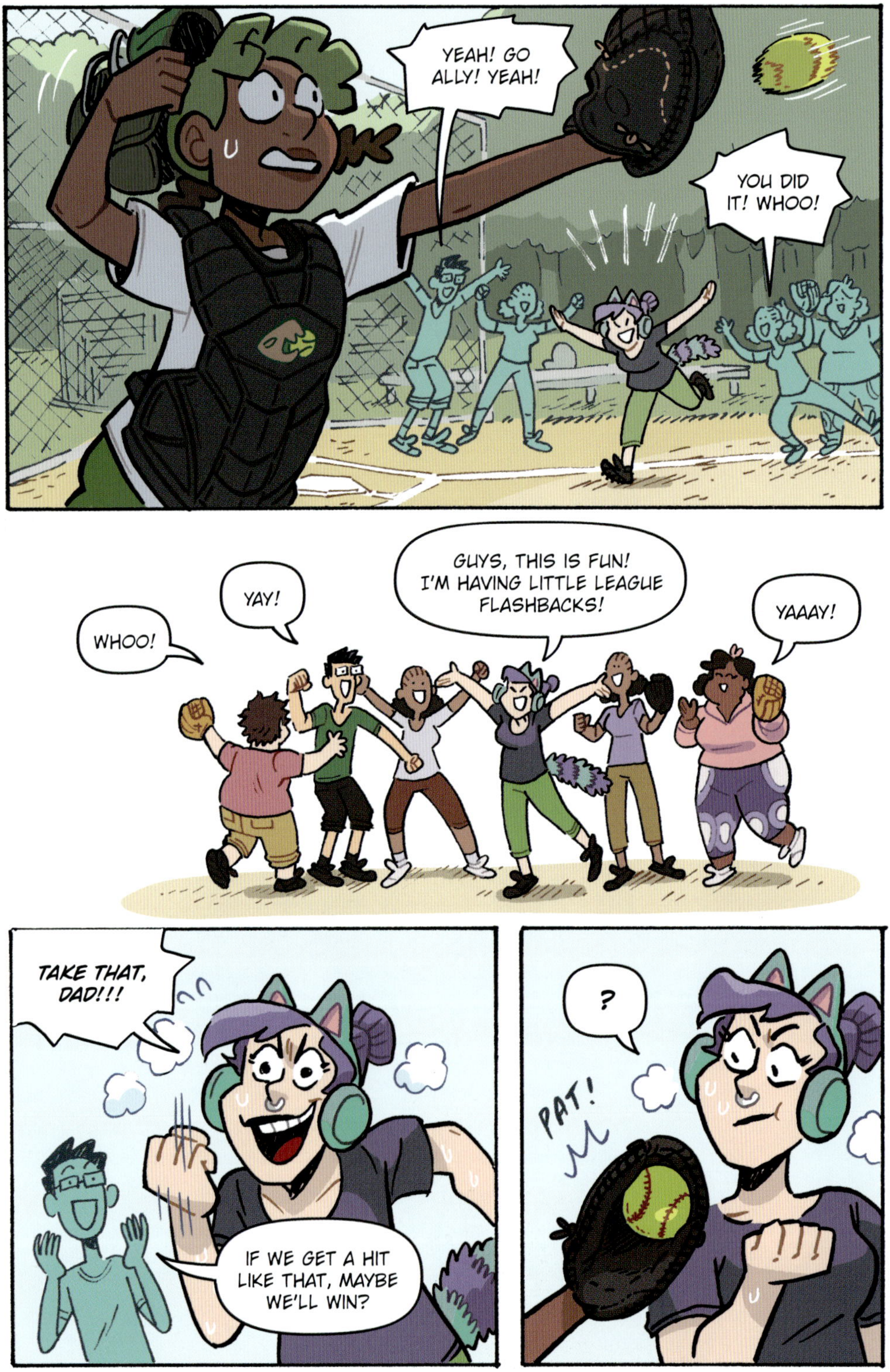
YEAH! GO ALLY! YEAH!
YOU DID IT! WHOO!
WHOO!
YAY!
GUYS, THIS IS FUN! I'M HAVING LITTLE LEAGUE FLASHBACKS!
YAAAY!
TAKE THAT, DAD!!!
IF WE GET A HIT LIKE THAT, MAYBE WE'LL WIN?
?
PAT!

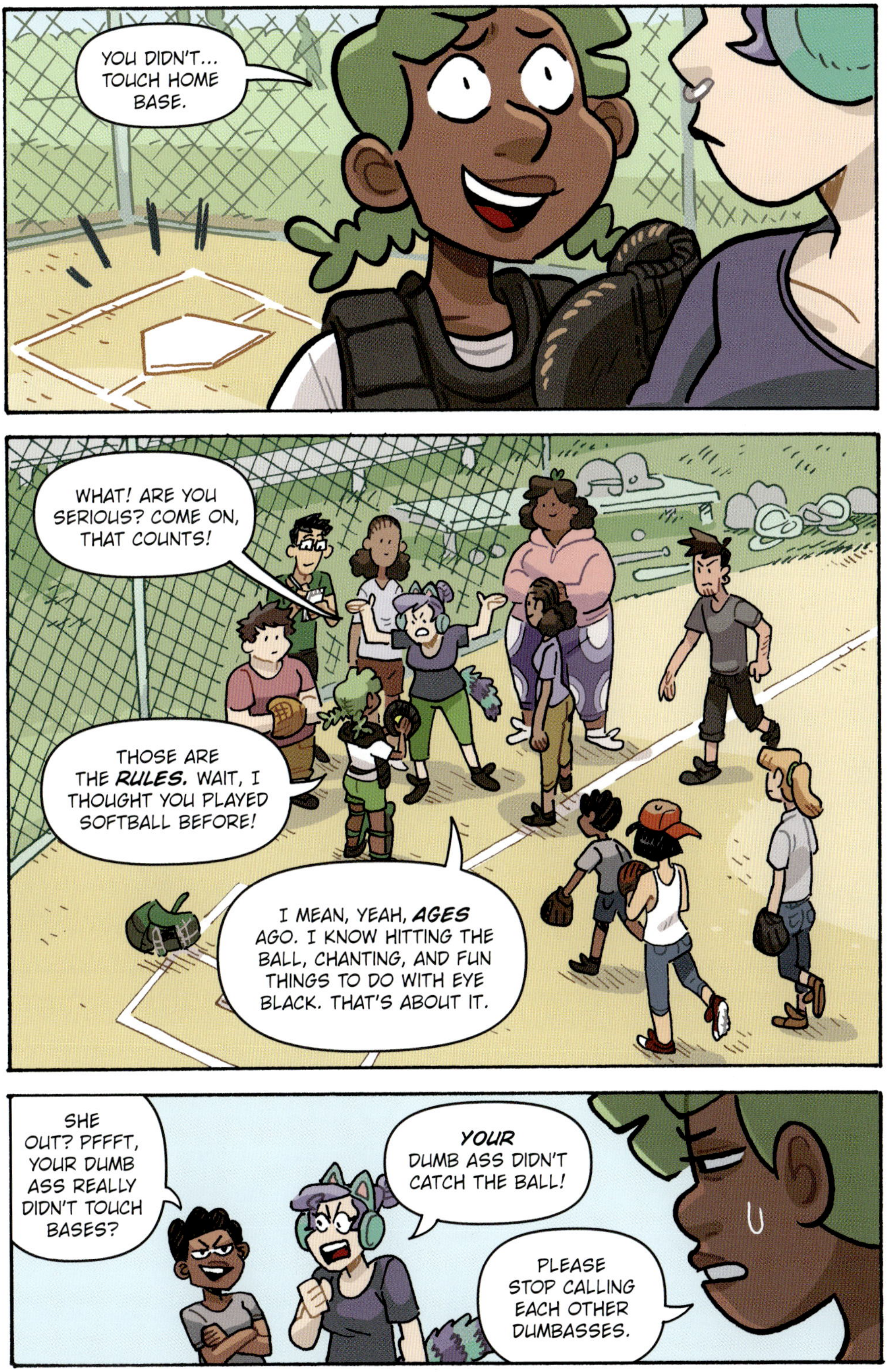
YOU DIDN'T... TOUCH HOME BASE.
WHAT! ARE YOU SERIOUS? COME ON, THAT COUNTS!
THOSE ARE THE **RULES.** WAIT, I THOUGHT YOU PLAYED SOFTBALL BEFORE!
I MEAN, YEAH, ***AGES*** AGO. I KNOW HITTING THE BALL, CHANTING, AND FUN THINGS TO DO WITH EYE BLACK. THAT'S ABOUT IT.
SHE OUT? PFFFT, YOUR DUMB ASS REALLY DIDN'T TOUCH BASES?
YOUR DUMB ASS DIDN'T CATCH THE BALL!
PLEASE STOP CALLING EACH OTHER DUMBASSES.

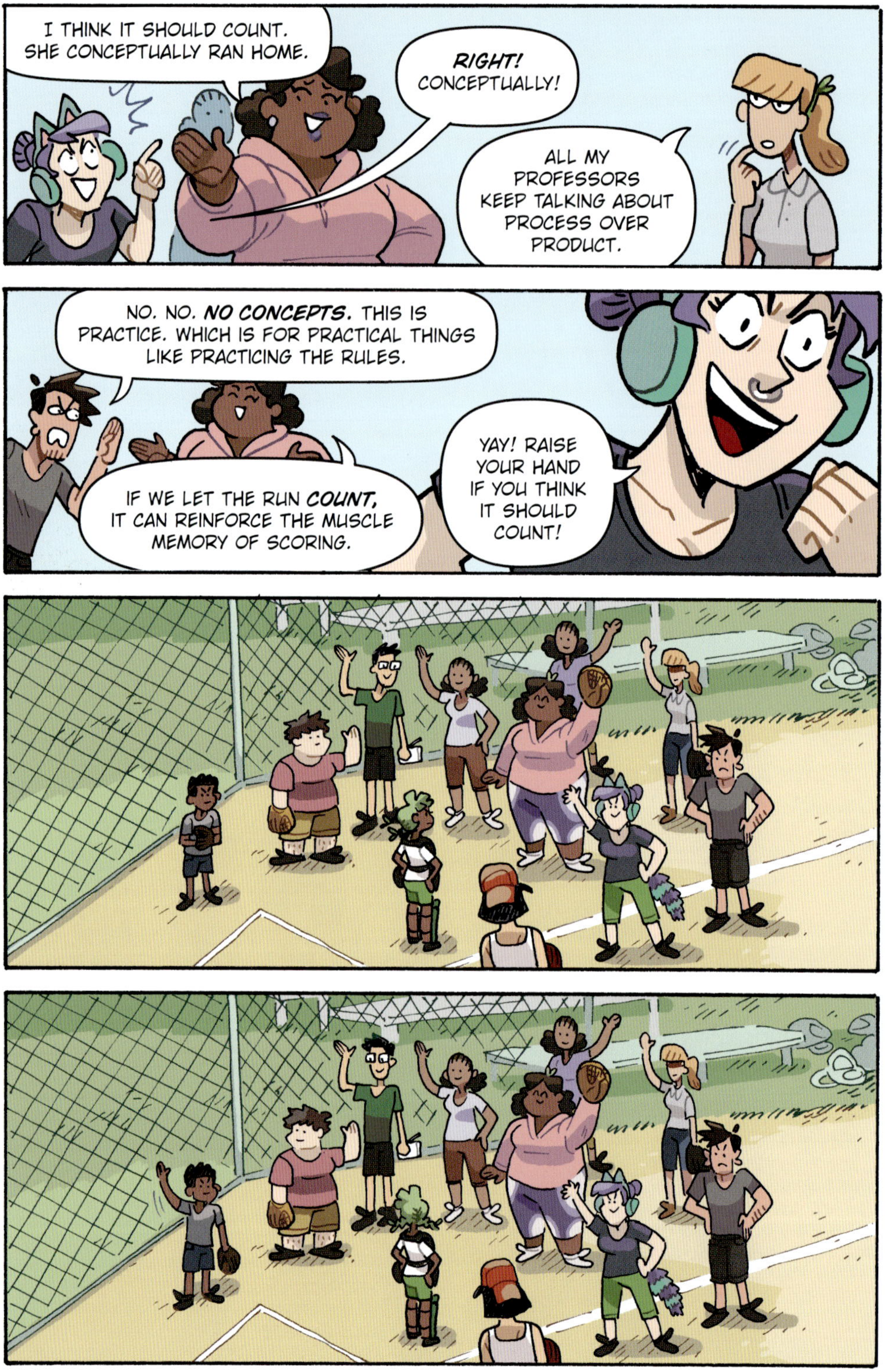
I THINK IT SHOULD COUNT. SHE CONCEPTUALLY RAN HOME.
RIGHT! CONCEPTUALLY!
ALL MY PROFESSORS KEEP TALKING ABOUT PROCESS OVER PRODUCT.
NO. NO. NO CONCEPTS. THIS IS PRACTICE. WHICH IS FOR PRACTICAL THINGS LIKE PRACTICING THE RULES.
IF WE LET THE RUN COUNT, IT CAN REINFORCE THE MUSCLE MEMORY OF SCORING.
YAY! RAISE YOUR HAND IF YOU THINK IT SHOULD COUNT!

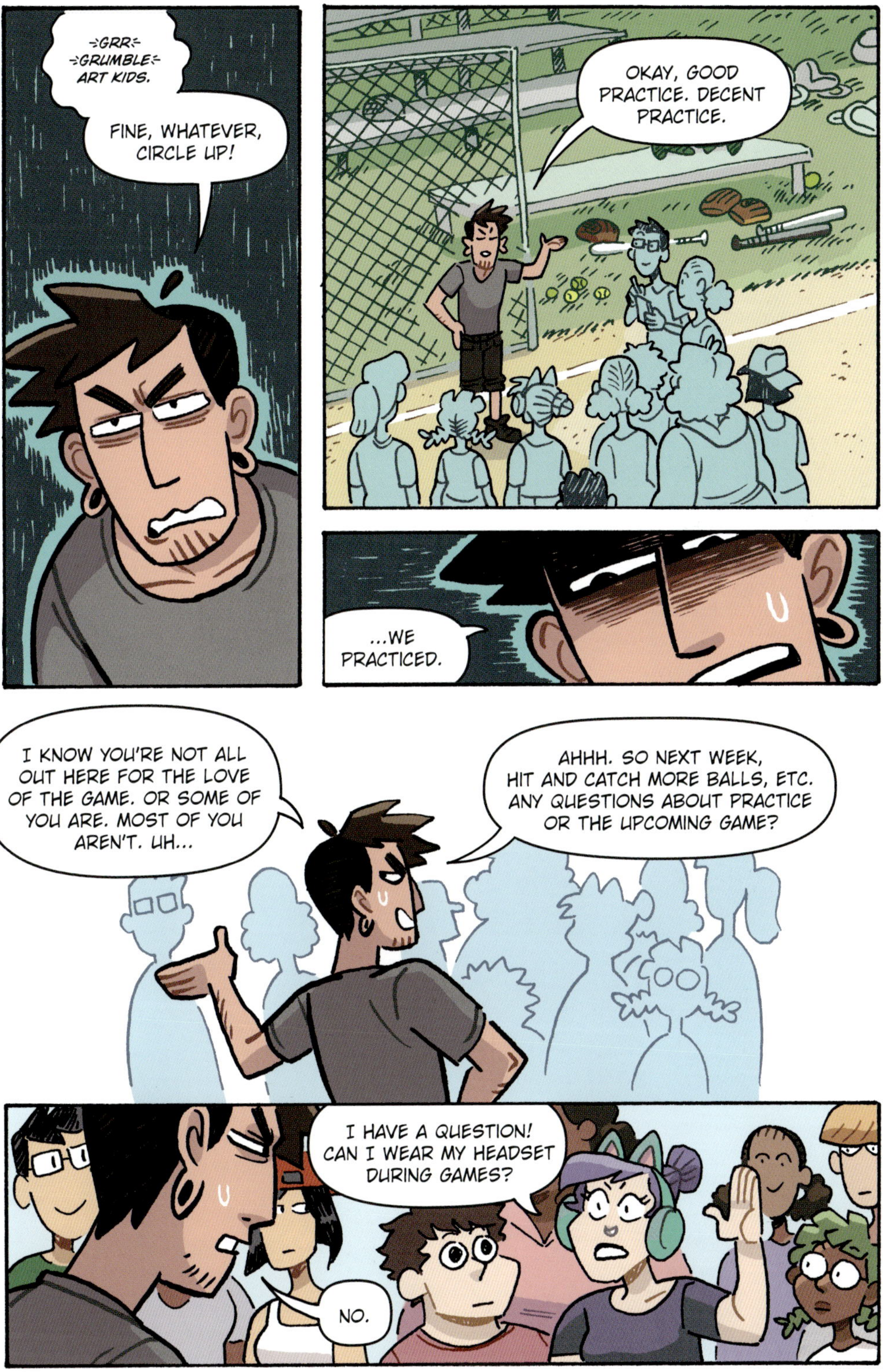

GRR
GRUMBLE
ART KIDS.
FINE, WHATEVER, CIRCLE UP!
OKAY, GOOD PRACTICE. DECENT PRACTICE.
...WE PRACTICED.
I KNOW YOU'RE NOT ALL OUT HERE FOR THE LOVE OF THE GAME. OR SOME OF YOU ARE. MOST OF YOU AREN'T. UH...
AHHH. SO NEXT WEEK, HIT AND CATCH MORE BALLS, ETC. ANY QUESTIONS ABOUT PRACTICE OR THE UPCOMING GAME?
I HAVE A QUESTION! CAN I WEAR MY HEADSET DURING GAMES?
NO.

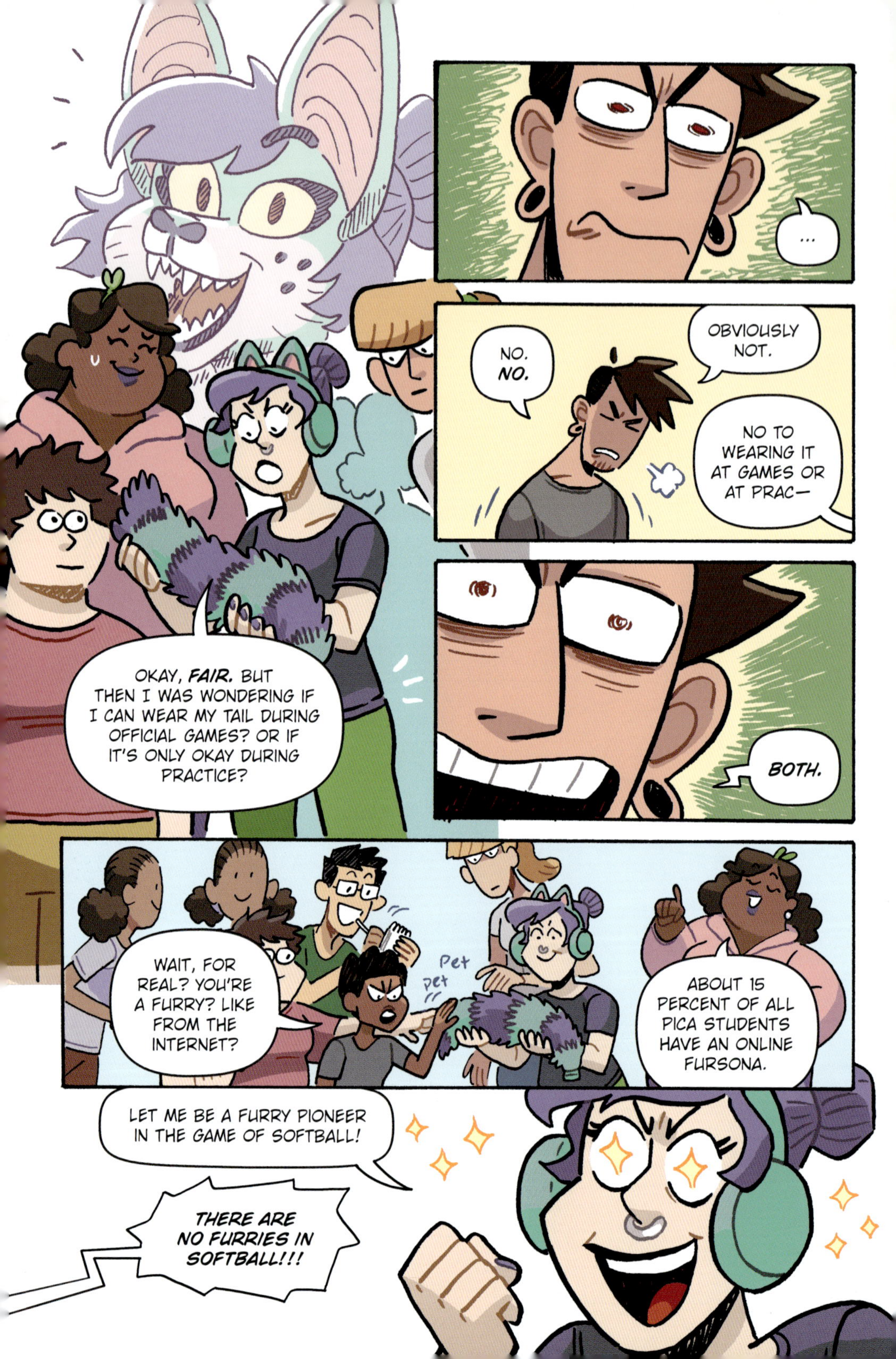
...
OKAY, FAIR. BUT THEN I WAS WONDERING IF I CAN WEAR MY TAIL DURING OFFICIAL GAMES? OR IF IT'S ONLY OKAY DURING PRACTICE?
NO. NO.
OBVIOUSLY NOT.
NO TO WEARING IT AT GAMES OR AT PRAC—
BOTH.
WAIT, FOR REAL? YOU'RE A FURRY? LIKE FROM THE INTERNET?
pet
pet
ABOUT 15 PERCENT OF ALL PICA STUDENTS HAVE AN ONLINE FURSONA.
LET ME BE A FURRY PIONEER IN THE GAME OF SOFTBALL!
THERE ARE NO FURRIES IN SOFTBALL!!!

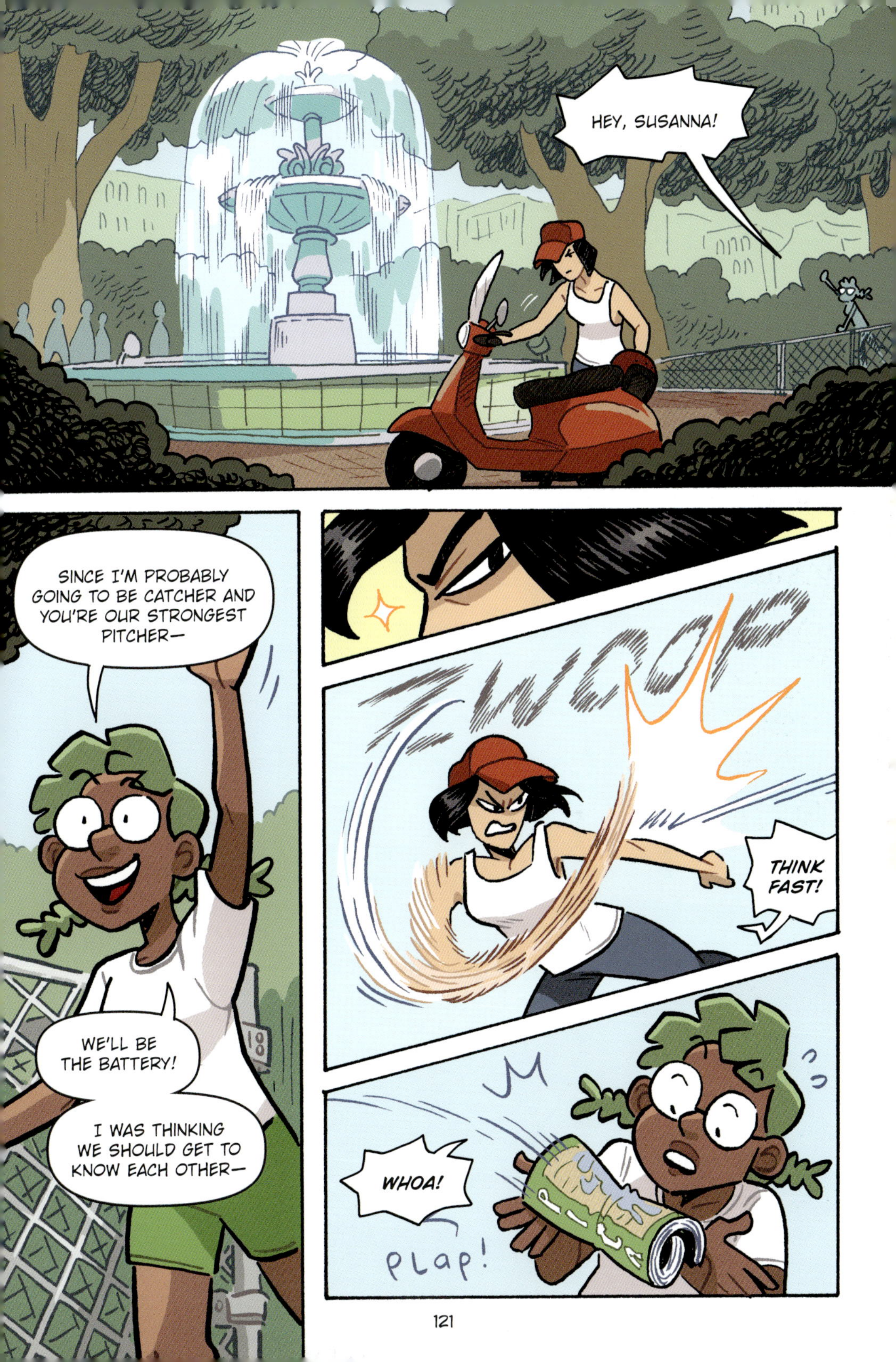
HEY, SUSANNA!
SINCE I'M PROBABLY GOING TO BE CATCHER AND YOU'RE OUR STRONGEST PITCHER—
WE'LL BE THE BATTERY!
I WAS THINKING WE SHOULD GET TO KNOW EACH OTHER—
ZWOOP
THINK FAST!
WHOA!
PLAP!

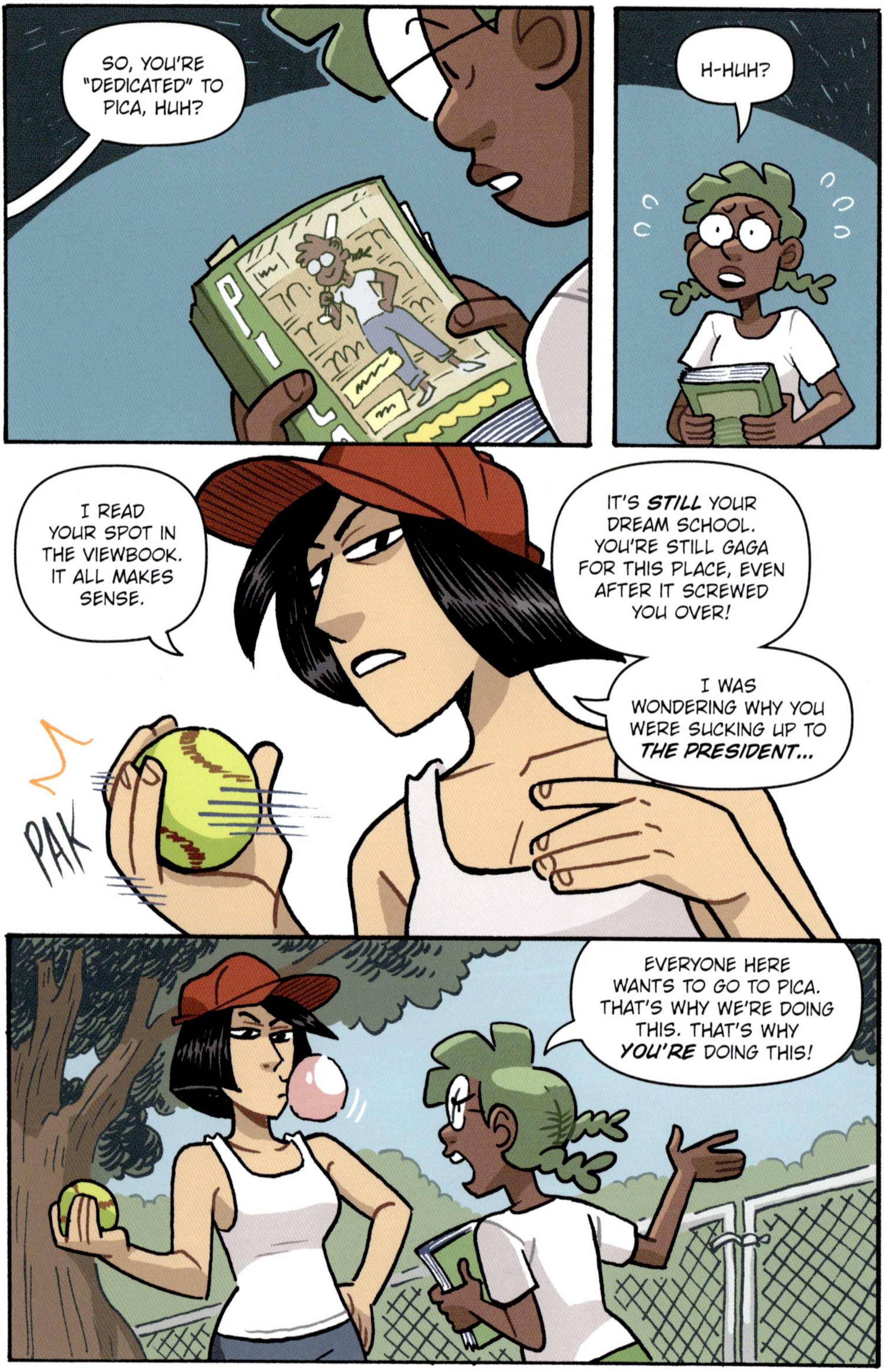

SO, YOU'RE "DEDICATED" TO PICA, HUH?
H-HUH?
I READ YOUR SPOT IN THE VIEWBOOK. IT ALL MAKES SENSE.
IT'S *STILL* YOUR DREAM SCHOOL. YOU'RE STILL GAGA FOR THIS PLACE, EVEN AFTER IT SCREWED YOU OVER!
I WAS WONDERING WHY YOU WERE SUCKING UP TO ***THE PRESIDENT...***
PAK
EVERYONE HERE WANTS TO GO TO PICA. THAT'S WHY WE'RE DOING THIS. THAT'S WHY ***YOU'RE*** DOING THIS!

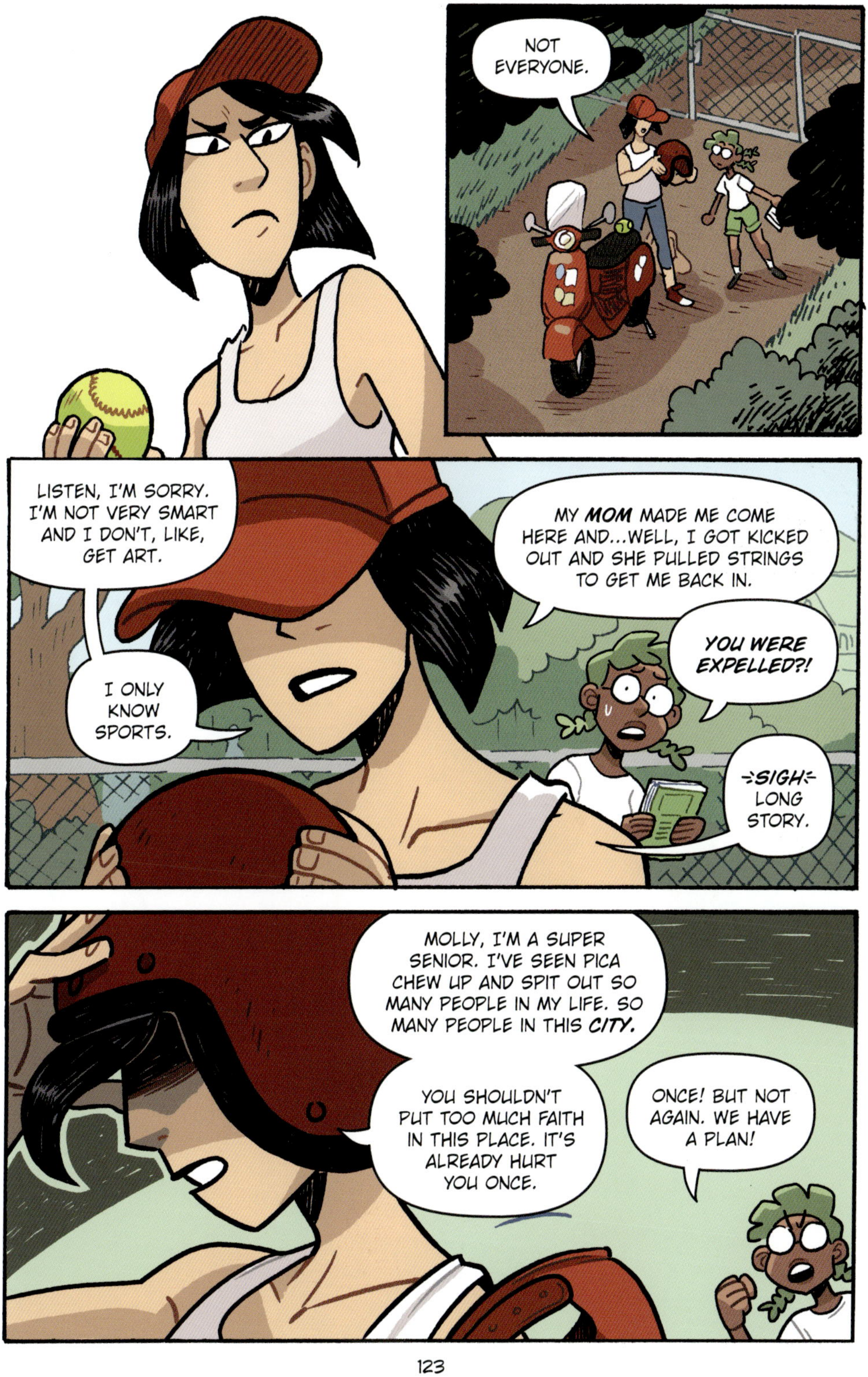

NOT EVERYONE.
LISTEN, I'M SORRY. I'M NOT VERY SMART AND I DON'T, LIKE, GET ART.
I ONLY KNOW SPORTS.
MY **MOM** MADE ME COME HERE AND...WELL, I GOT KICKED OUT AND SHE PULLED STRINGS TO GET ME BACK IN.
YOU WERE EXPELLED?!
SIGH LONG STORY.
MOLLY, I'M A SUPER SENIOR. I'VE SEEN PICA CHEW UP AND SPIT OUT SO MANY PEOPLE IN MY LIFE. SO MANY PEOPLE IN THIS *CITY.*
YOU SHOULDN'T PUT TOO MUCH FAITH IN THIS PLACE. IT'S ALREADY HURT YOU ONCE.
ONCE! BUT NOT AGAIN. WE HAVE A PLAN!

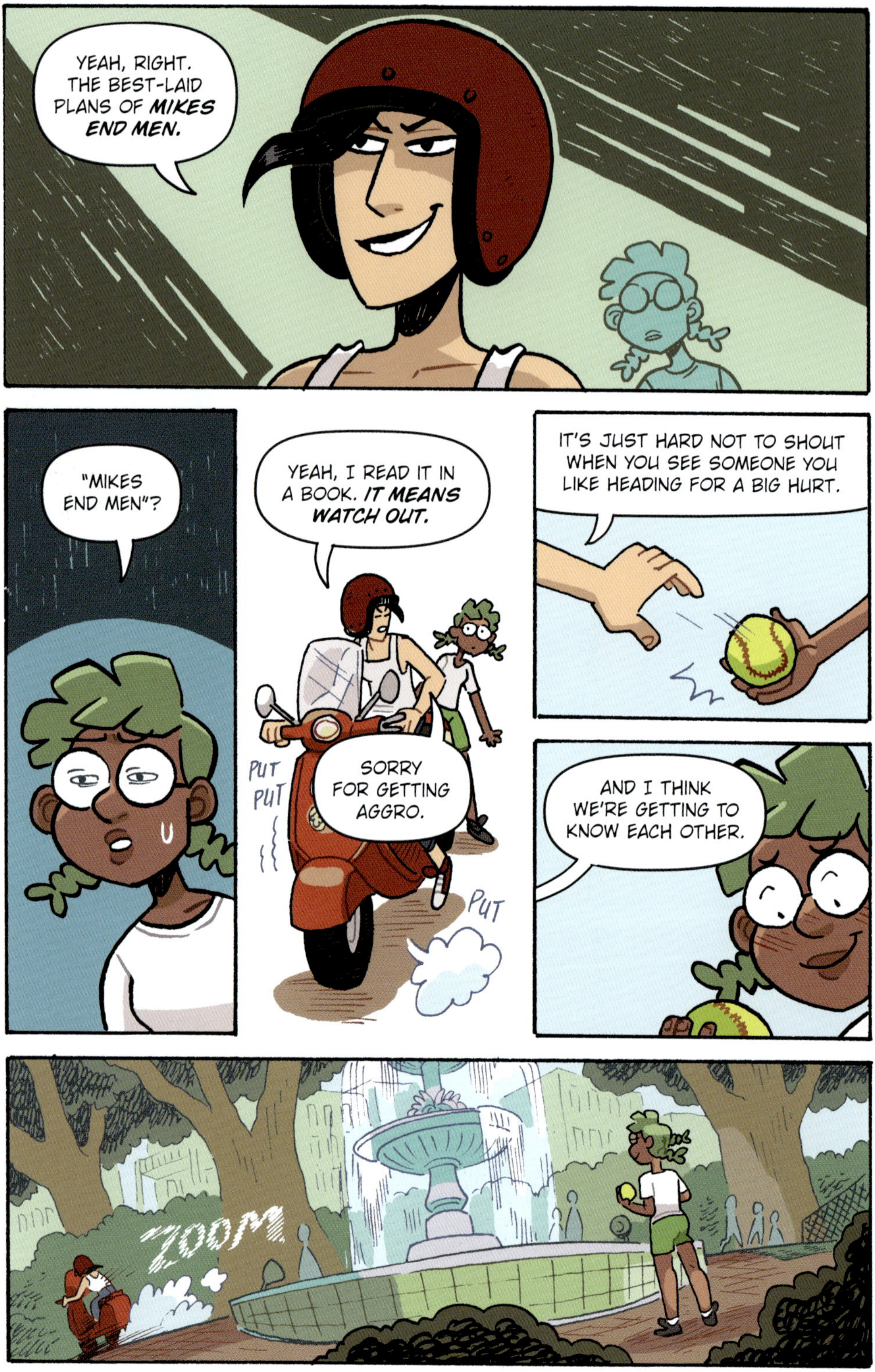
YEAH, RIGHT. THE BEST-LAID PLANS OF MIKES END MEN.
"MIKES END MEN"?
YEAH, I READ IT IN A BOOK. IT MEANS WATCH OUT.
PUT PUT
SORRY FOR GETTING AGGRO.
PUT
IT'S JUST HARD NOT TO SHOUT WHEN YOU SEE SOMEONE YOU LIKE HEADING FOR A BIG HURT.
AND I THINK WE'RE GETTING TO KNOW EACH OTHER.
ZOOM

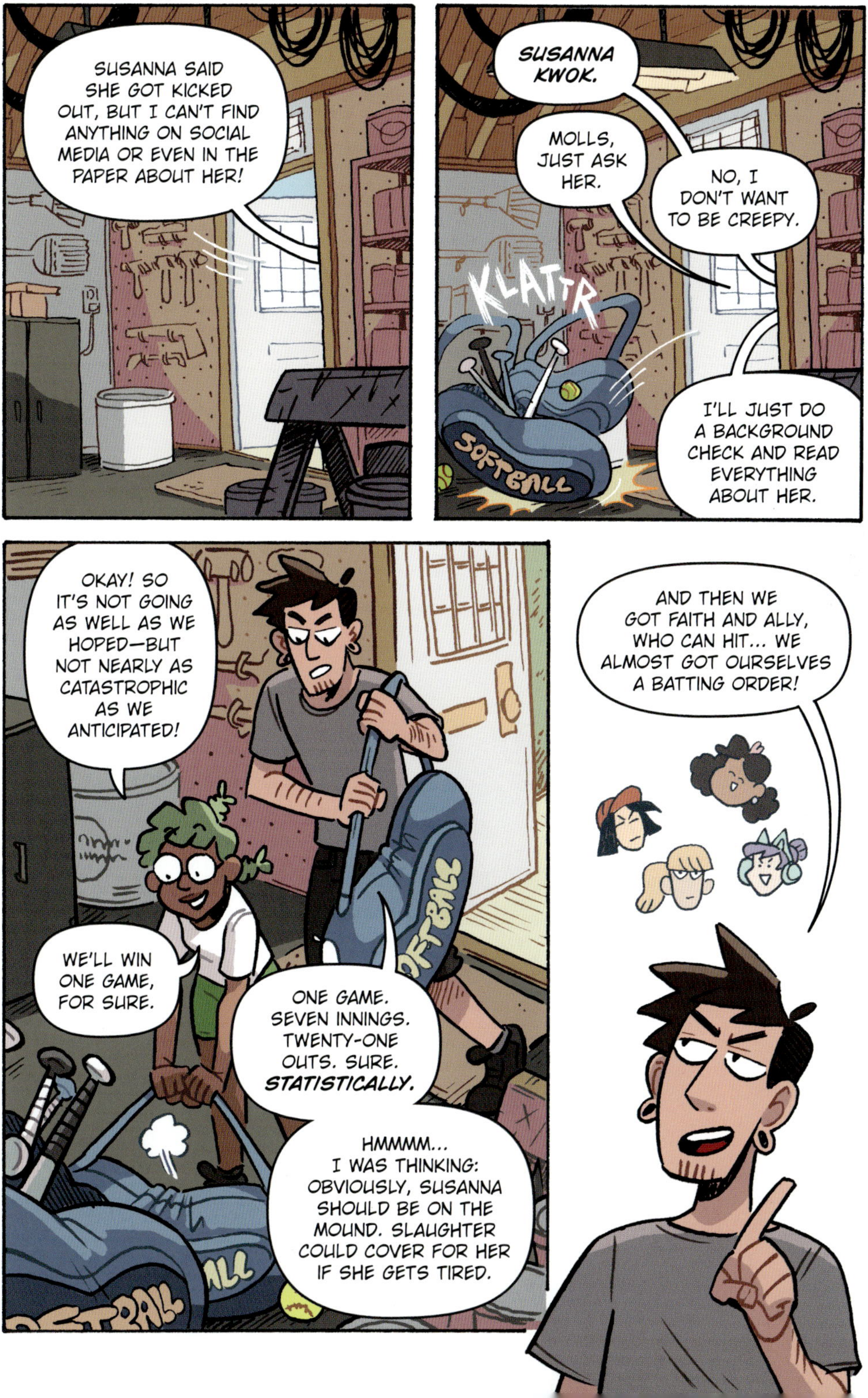
SUSANNA SAID SHE GOT KICKED OUT, BUT I CAN'T FIND ANYTHING ON SOCIAL MEDIA OR EVEN IN THE PAPER ABOUT HER!
SUSANNA KWOK.
MOLLS, JUST ASK HER.
NO, I DON'T WANT TO BE CREEPY.
KLATTR
SOFTBALL
I'LL JUST DO A BACKGROUND CHECK AND READ EVERYTHING ABOUT HER.
OKAY! SO IT'S NOT GOING AS WELL AS WE HOPED—BUT NOT NEARLY AS CATASTROPHIC AS WE ANTICIPATED!
WE'LL WIN ONE GAME, FOR SURE.
ONE GAME. SEVEN INNINGS. TWENTY-ONE OUTS. SURE. STATISTICALLY.
HMMMM... I WAS THINKING: OBVIOUSLY, SUSANNA SHOULD BE ON THE MOUND. SLAUGHTER COULD COVER FOR HER IF SHE GETS TIRED.
AND THEN WE GOT FAITH AND ALLY, WHO CAN HIT... WE ALMOST GOT OURSELVES A BATTING ORDER!

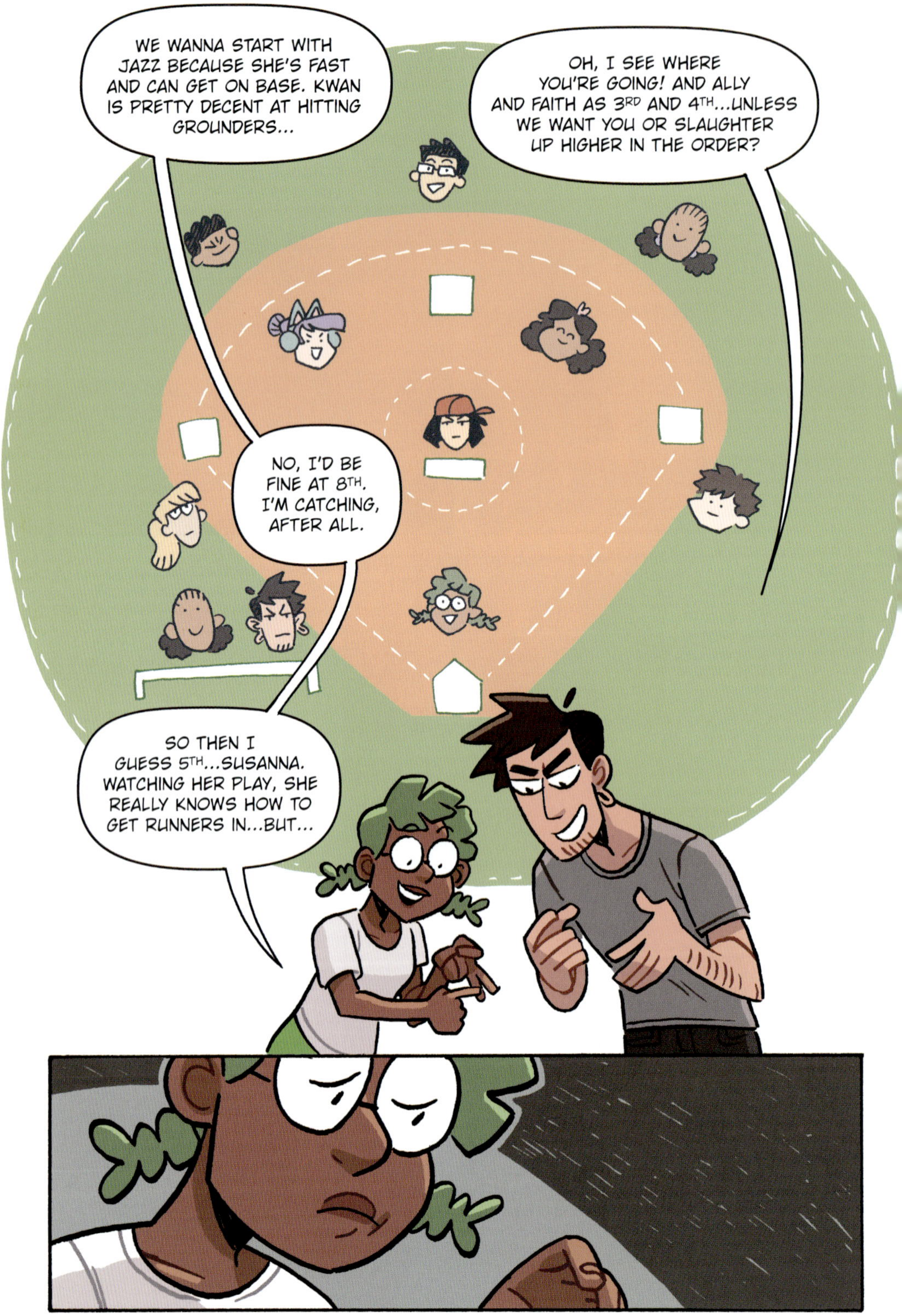
WE WANNA START WITH JAZZ BECAUSE SHE'S FAST AND CAN GET ON BASE. KWAN IS PRETTY DECENT AT HITTING GROUNDERS...
OH, I SEE WHERE YOU'RE GOING! AND ALLY AND FAITH AS 3RD AND 4TH...UNLESS WE WANT YOU OR SLAUGHTER UP HIGHER IN THE ORDER?
NO, I'D BE FINE AT 8TH. I'M CATCHING, AFTER ALL.
SO THEN I GUESS 5TH...SUSANNA. WATCHING HER PLAY, SHE REALLY KNOWS HOW TO GET RUNNERS IN...BUT...

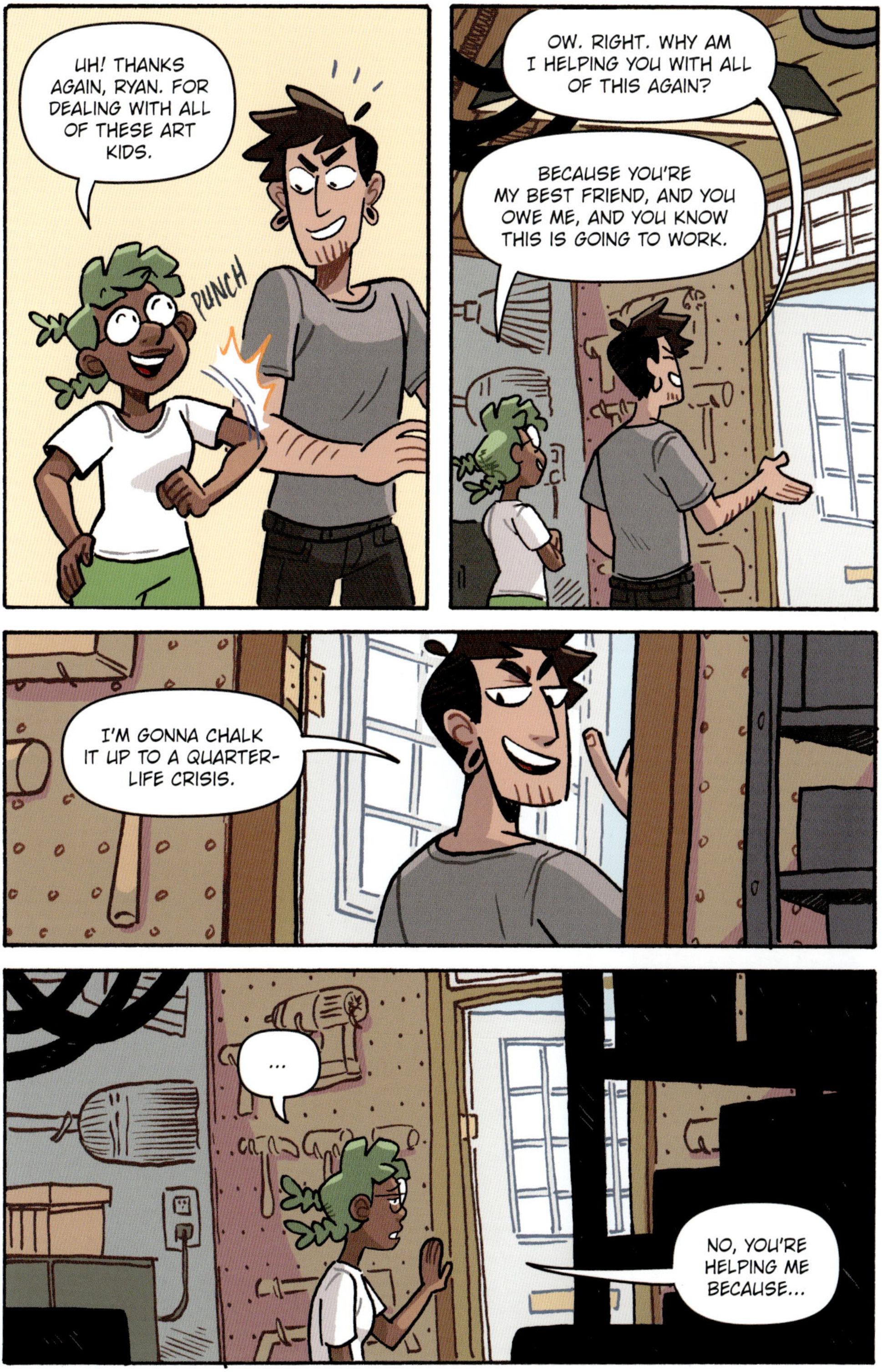
UH! THANKS AGAIN, RYAN. FOR DEALING WITH ALL OF THESE ART KIDS.
PUNCH
OW. RIGHT. WHY AM I HELPING YOU WITH ALL OF THIS AGAIN?
BECAUSE YOU'RE MY BEST FRIEND, AND YOU OWE ME, AND YOU KNOW THIS IS GOING TO WORK.
I'M GONNA CHALK IT UP TO A QUARTER-LIFE CRISIS.
...
NO, YOU'RE HELPING ME BECAUSE...

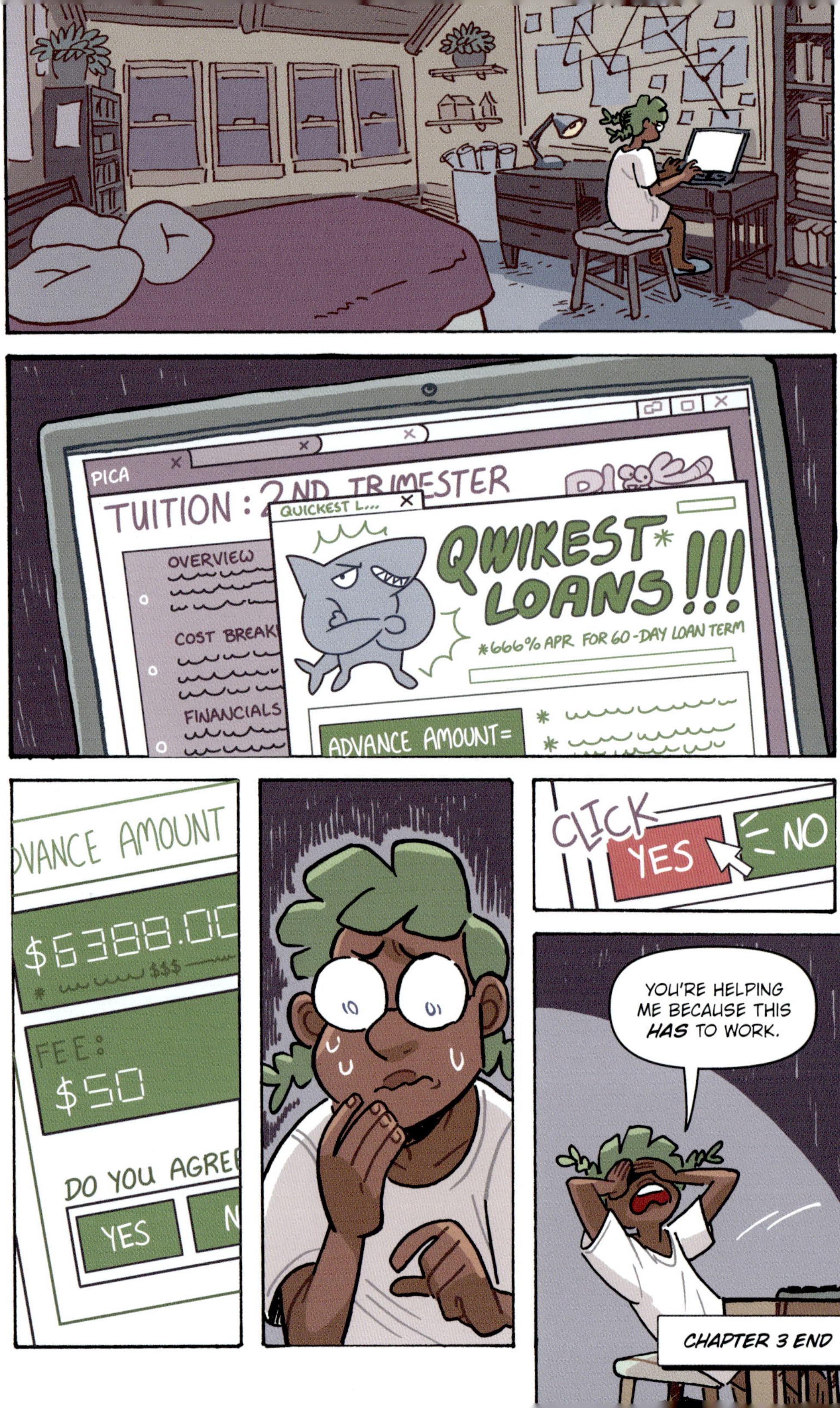
PICA
TUITION : 2ND TRIMESTER
OVERVIEW
COST BREAK
FINANCIALS
QUICKEST L...
QWIKEST LOANS!!!
*666% APR FOR 60-DAY LOAN TERM
ADVANCE AMOUNT=
VANCE AMOUNT
$6388.00
$$$
FEE:
$50
DO YOU AGRE
YES
CLICK
YES
NO
YOU'RE HELPING ME BECAUSE THIS HAS TO WORK.
CHAPTER 3 END

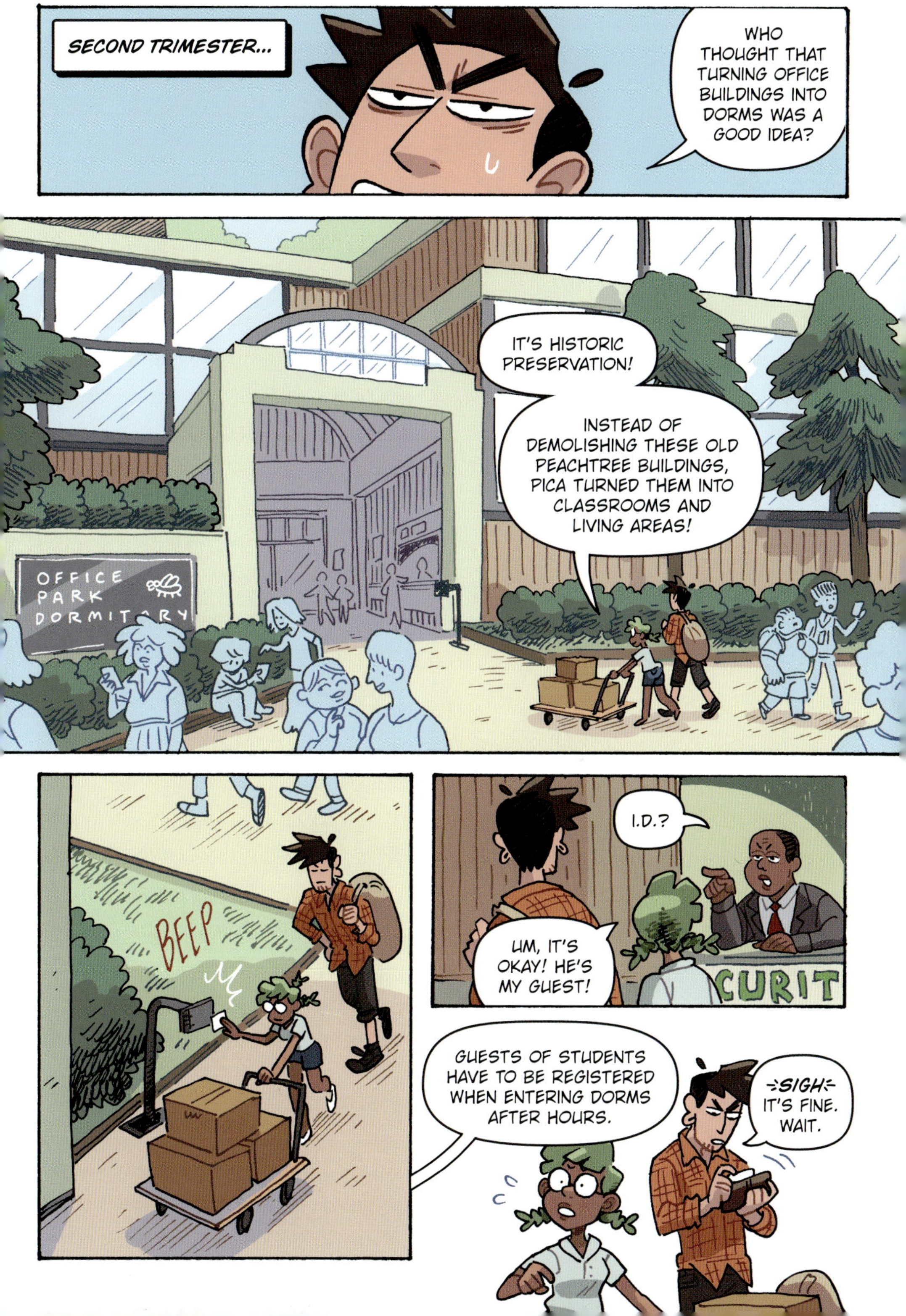
SECOND TRIMESTER...
WHO THOUGHT THAT TURNING OFFICE BUILDINGS INTO DORMS WAS A GOOD IDEA?
IT'S HISTORIC PRESERVATION!
INSTEAD OF DEMOLISHING THESE OLD PEACHTREE BUILDINGS, PICA TURNED THEM INTO CLASSROOMS AND LIVING AREAS!
OFFICE PARK DORMITORY
BEEP
I.D.?
UM, IT'S OKAY! HE'S MY GUEST!
CURIT
GUESTS OF STUDENTS HAVE TO BE REGISTERED WHEN ENTERING DORMS AFTER HOURS.
SIGH IT'S FINE. WAIT.

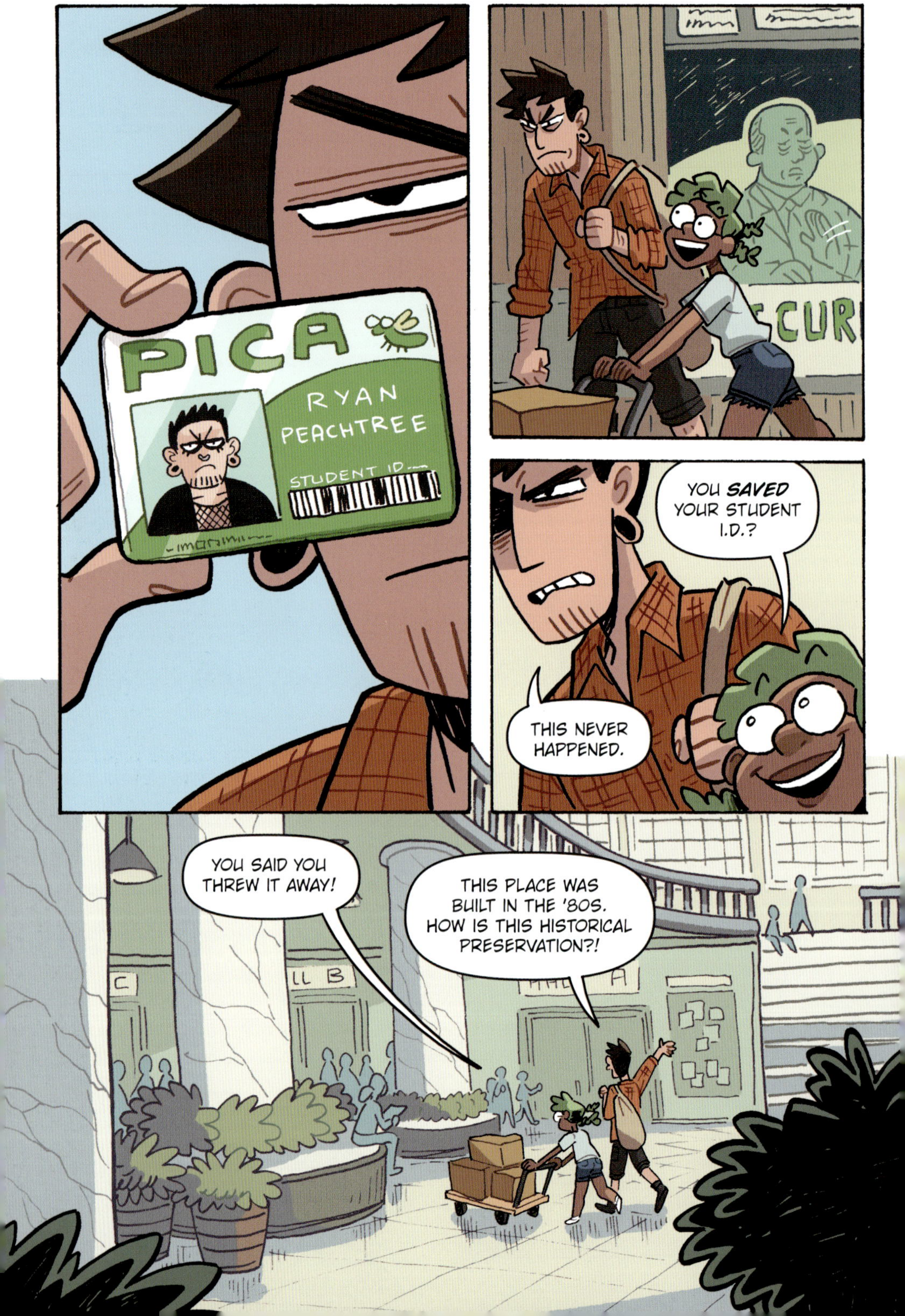
PICA
RYAN PEACHTREE
STUDENT ID
YOU SAVED YOUR STUDENT I.D.?
THIS NEVER HAPPENED.
YOU SAID YOU THREW IT AWAY!
THIS PLACE WAS BUILT IN THE '80S. HOW IS THIS HISTORICAL PRESERVATION?!

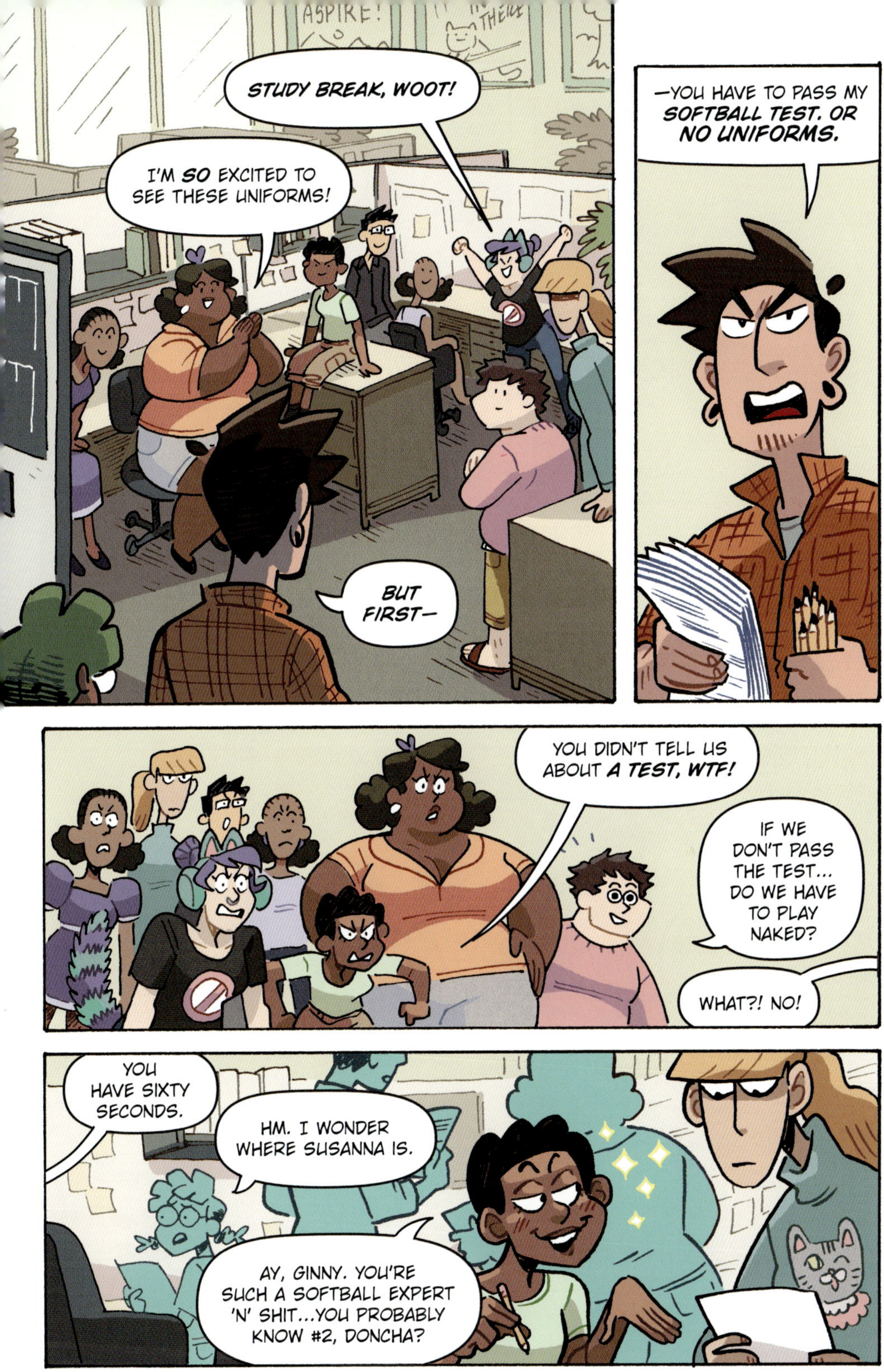
ASPIRE!
STUDY BREAK, WOOT!
I'M SO EXCITED TO SEE THESE UNIFORMS!
BUT FIRST—
—YOU HAVE TO PASS MY SOFTBALL TEST. OR NO UNIFORMS.
YOU DIDN'T TELL US ABOUT A TEST, WTF!
IF WE DON'T PASS THE TEST... DO WE HAVE TO PLAY NAKED?
WHAT?! NO!
YOU HAVE SIXTY SECONDS.
HM. I WONDER WHERE SUSANNA IS.
AY, GINNY. YOU'RE SUCH A SOFTBALL EXPERT 'N' SHIT...YOU PROBABLY KNOW #2, DONCHA?

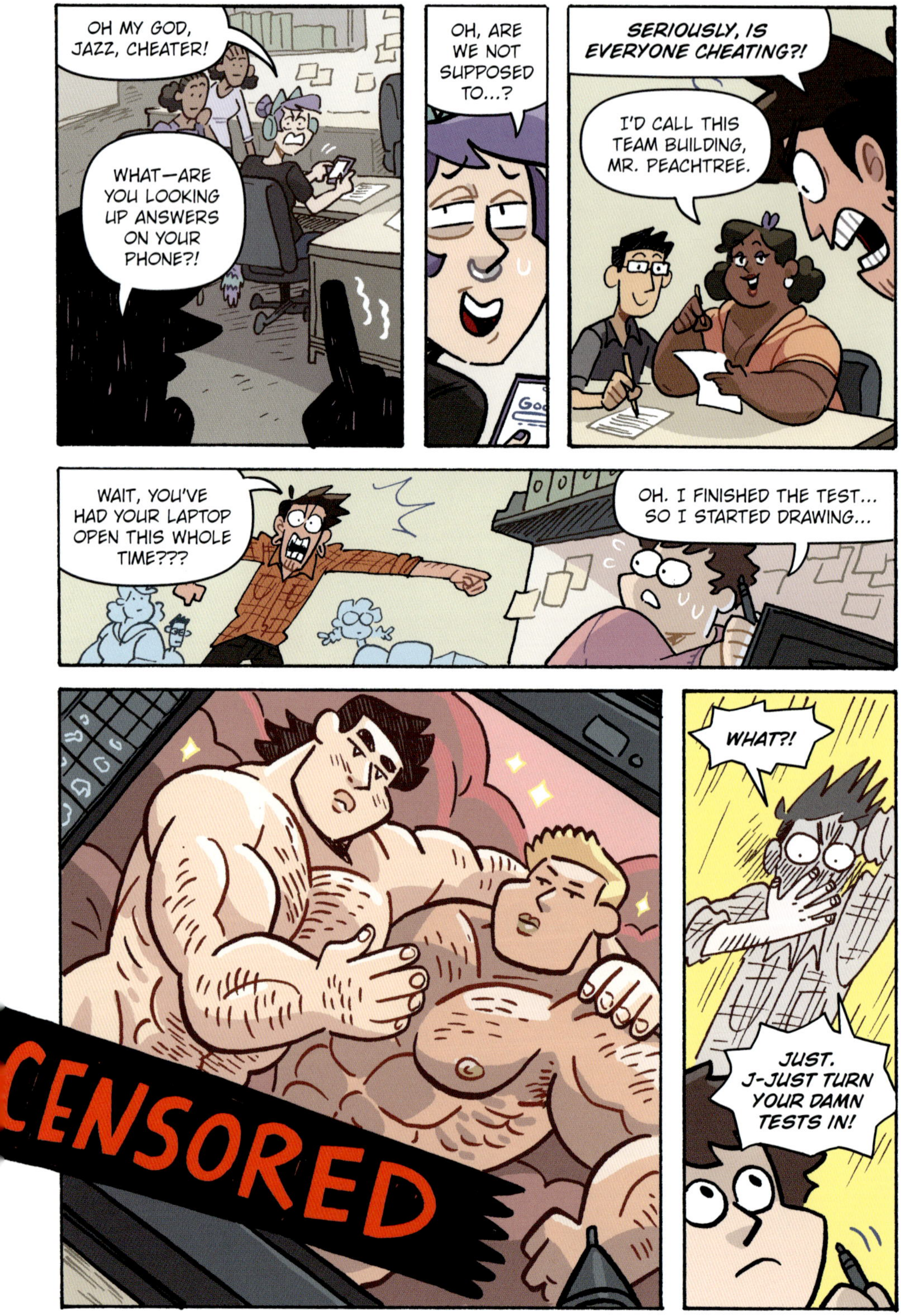
OH MY GOD, JAZZ, CHEATER!
WHAT—ARE YOU LOOKING UP ANSWERS ON YOUR PHONE?!
OH, ARE WE NOT SUPPOSED TO...?
SERIOUSLY, IS EVERYONE CHEATING?!
I'D CALL THIS TEAM BUILDING, MR. PEACHTREE.
WAIT, YOU'VE HAD YOUR LAPTOP OPEN THIS WHOLE TIME???
OH. I FINISHED THE TEST... SO I STARTED DRAWING...
CENSORED
WHAT?!
JUST. J-JUST TURN YOUR DAMN TESTS IN!

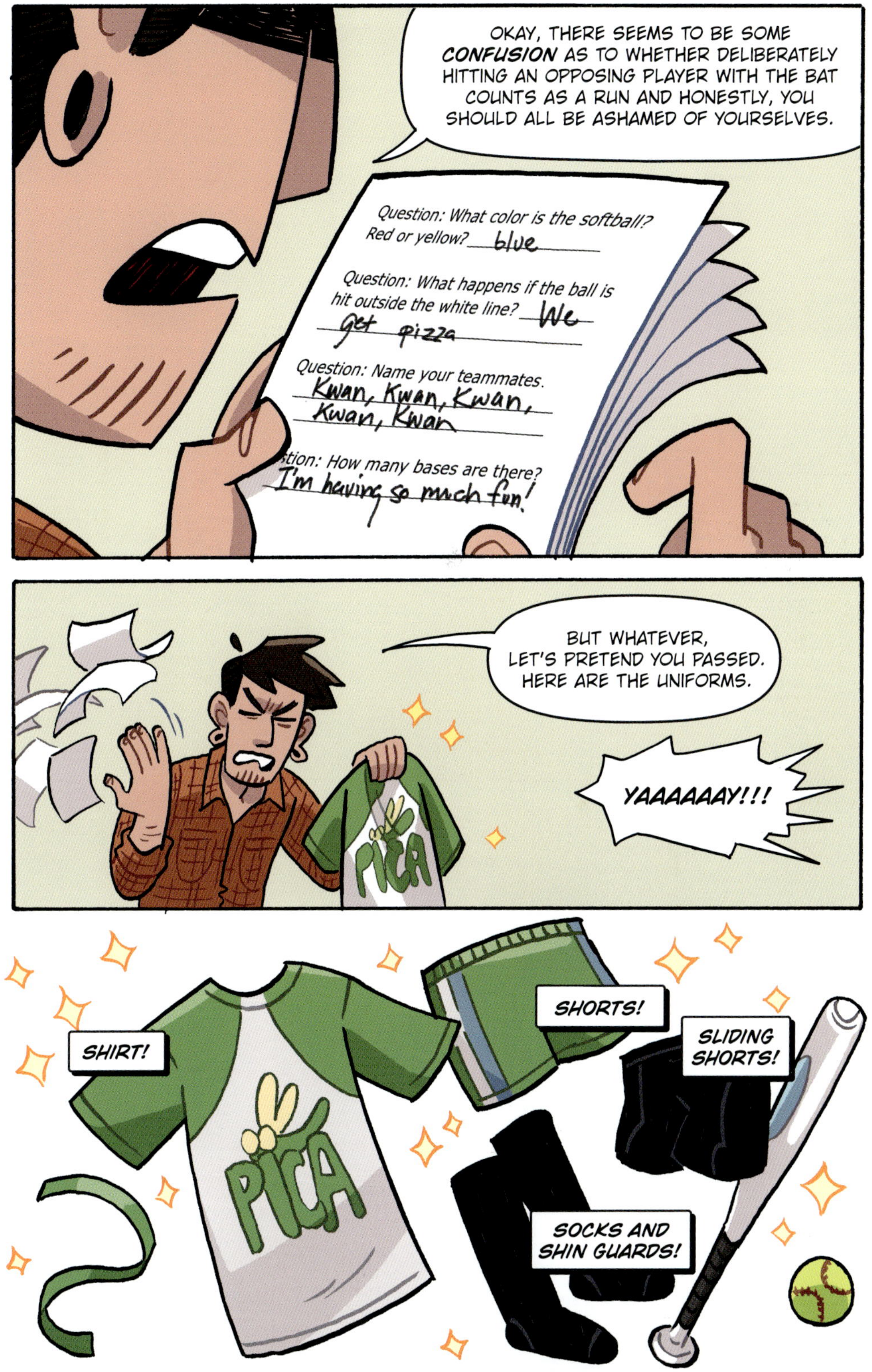

OKAY, THERE SEEMS TO BE SOME CONFUSION AS TO WHETHER DELIBERATELY HITTING AN OPPOSING PLAYER WITH THE BAT COUNTS AS A RUN AND HONESTLY, YOU SHOULD ALL BE ASHAMED OF YOURSELVES.
Question: What color is the softball? Red or yellow? blue
Question: What happens if the ball is hit outside the white line? We get pizza
Question: Name your teammates. Kwan, Kwan, Kwan, Kwan, Kwan
stion: How many bases are there? I'm having so much fun!
BUT WHATEVER, LET'S PRETEND YOU PASSED. HERE ARE THE UNIFORMS.
YAAAAAAY!!!
PICA
SHIRT!
SHORTS!
SLIDING SHORTS!
SOCKS AND SHIN GUARDS!

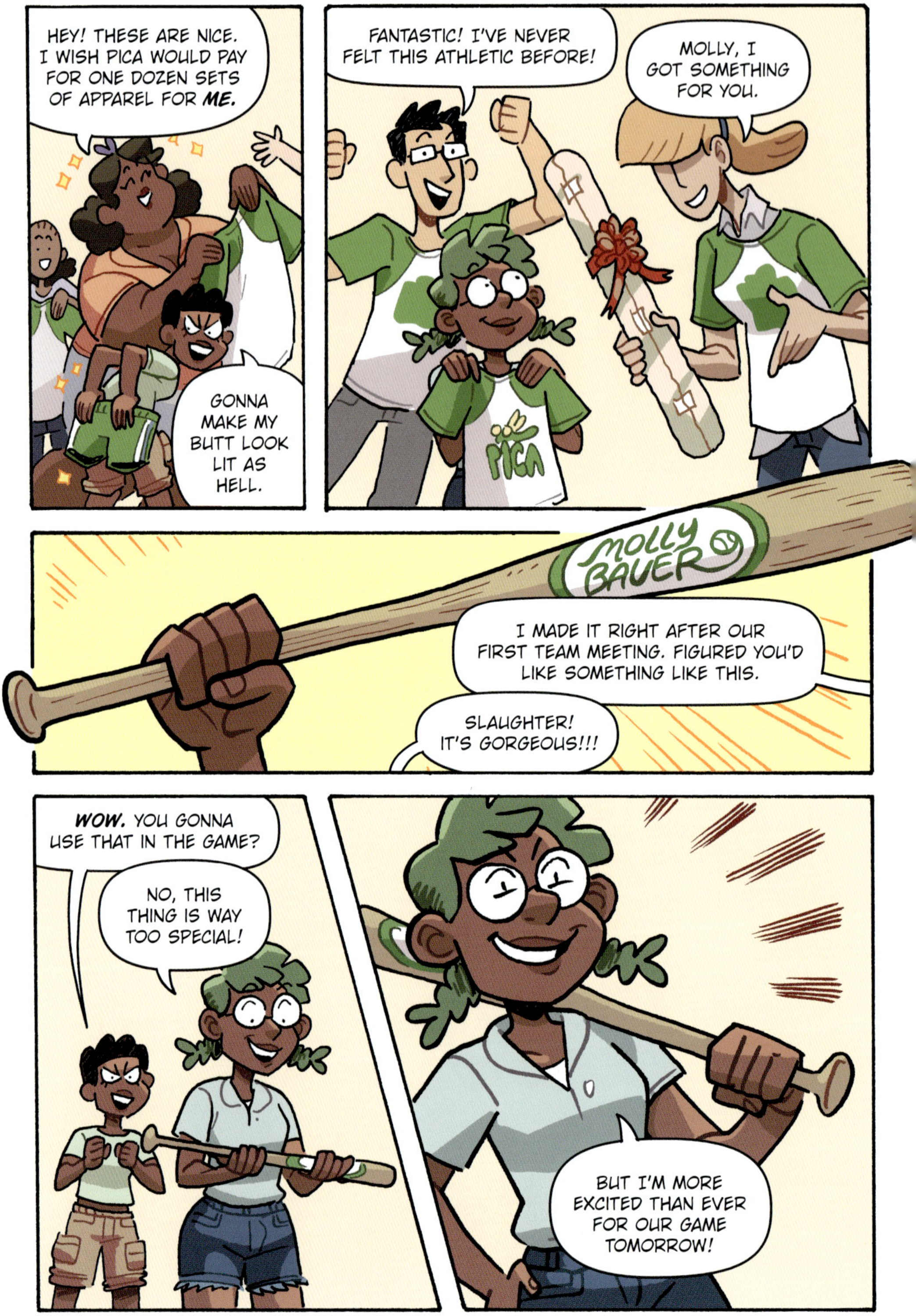
HEY! THESE ARE NICE. I WISH PICA WOULD PAY FOR ONE DOZEN SETS OF APPAREL FOR ***ME.***
GONNA MAKE MY BUTT LOOK LIT AS HELL.
FANTASTIC! I'VE NEVER FELT THIS ATHLETIC BEFORE!
MOLLY, I GOT SOMETHING FOR YOU.
PICA
MOLLY BAUER
I MADE IT RIGHT AFTER OUR FIRST TEAM MEETING. FIGURED YOU'D LIKE SOMETHING LIKE THIS.
SLAUGHTER! IT'S GORGEOUS!!!
WOW. YOU GONNA USE THAT IN THE GAME?
NO, THIS THING IS WAY TOO SPECIAL!
BUT I'M MORE EXCITED THAN EVER FOR OUR GAME TOMORROW!

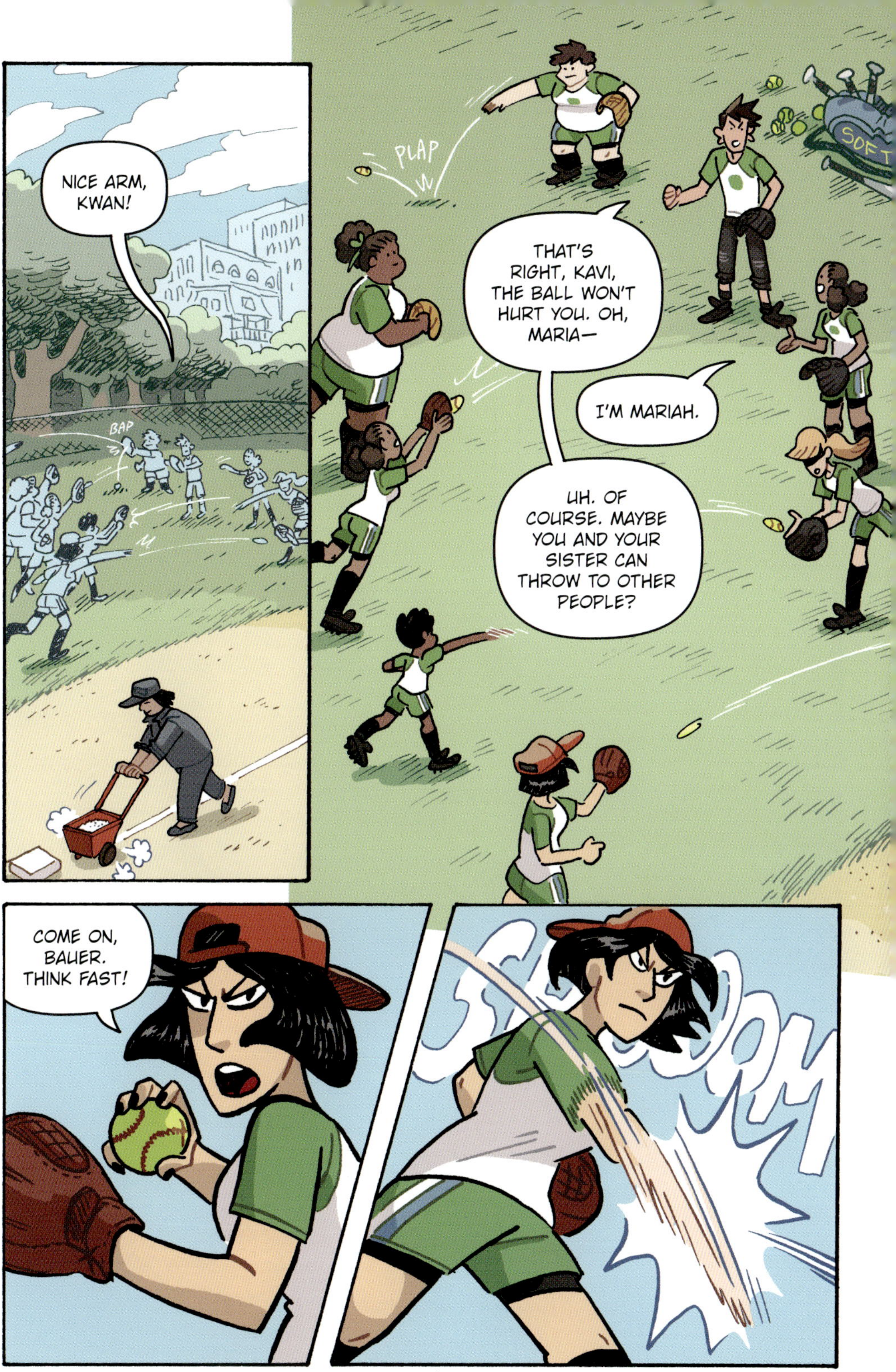
NICE ARM, KWAN!
BAP
PLAP
SOFT
THAT'S RIGHT, KAVI, THE BALL WON'T HURT YOU. OH, MARIA—
I'M MARIAH.
UH. OF COURSE. MAYBE YOU AND YOUR SISTER CAN THROW TO OTHER PEOPLE?
COME ON, BAUER. THINK FAST!

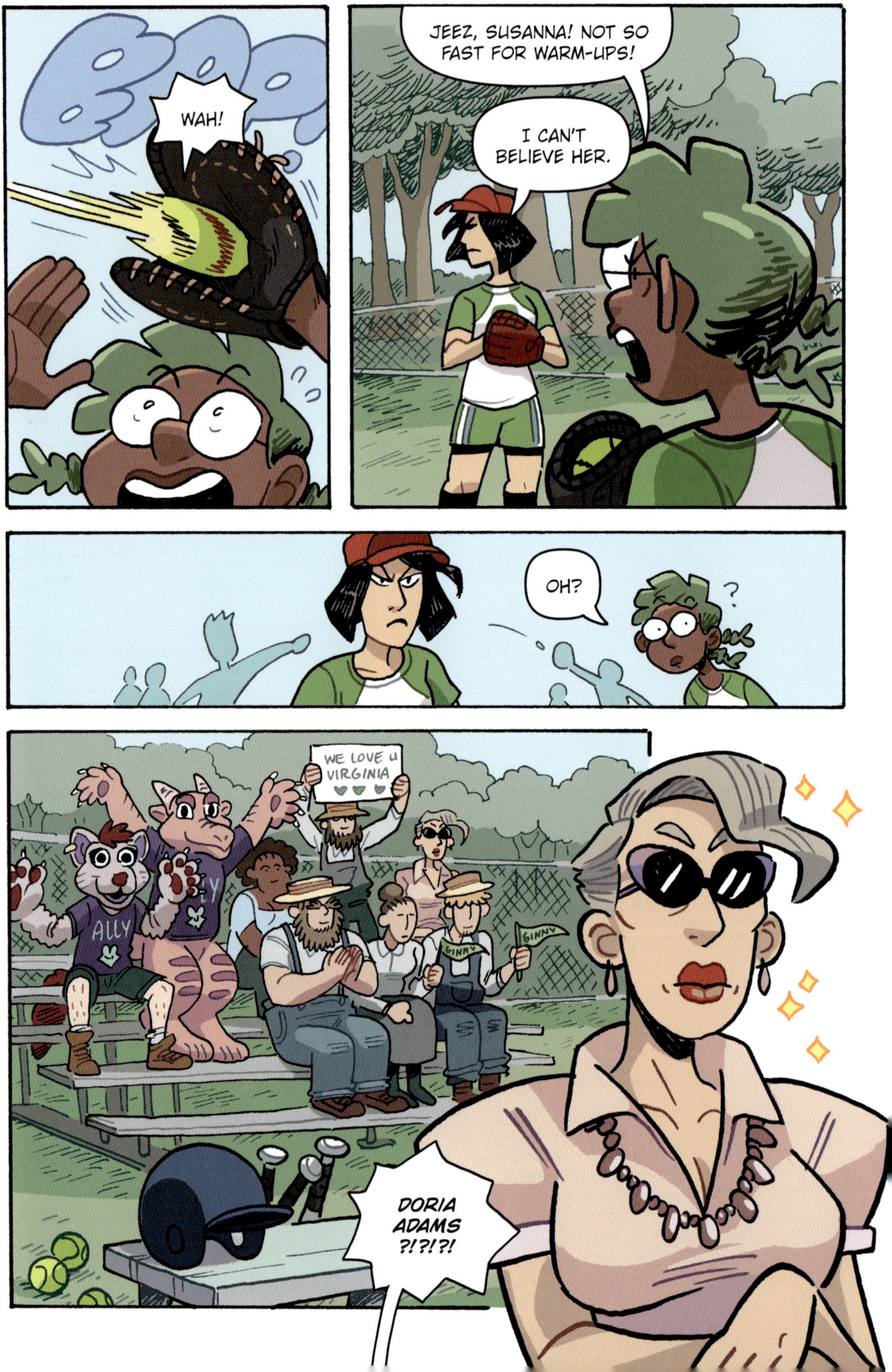
WAH!
JEEZ, SUSANNA! NOT SO FAST FOR WARM-UPS!
I CAN'T BELIEVE HER.
OH?
?
WE LOVE U VIRGINIA
ALLY
GINNY
GINNY
DORIA ADAMS ?!?!?!

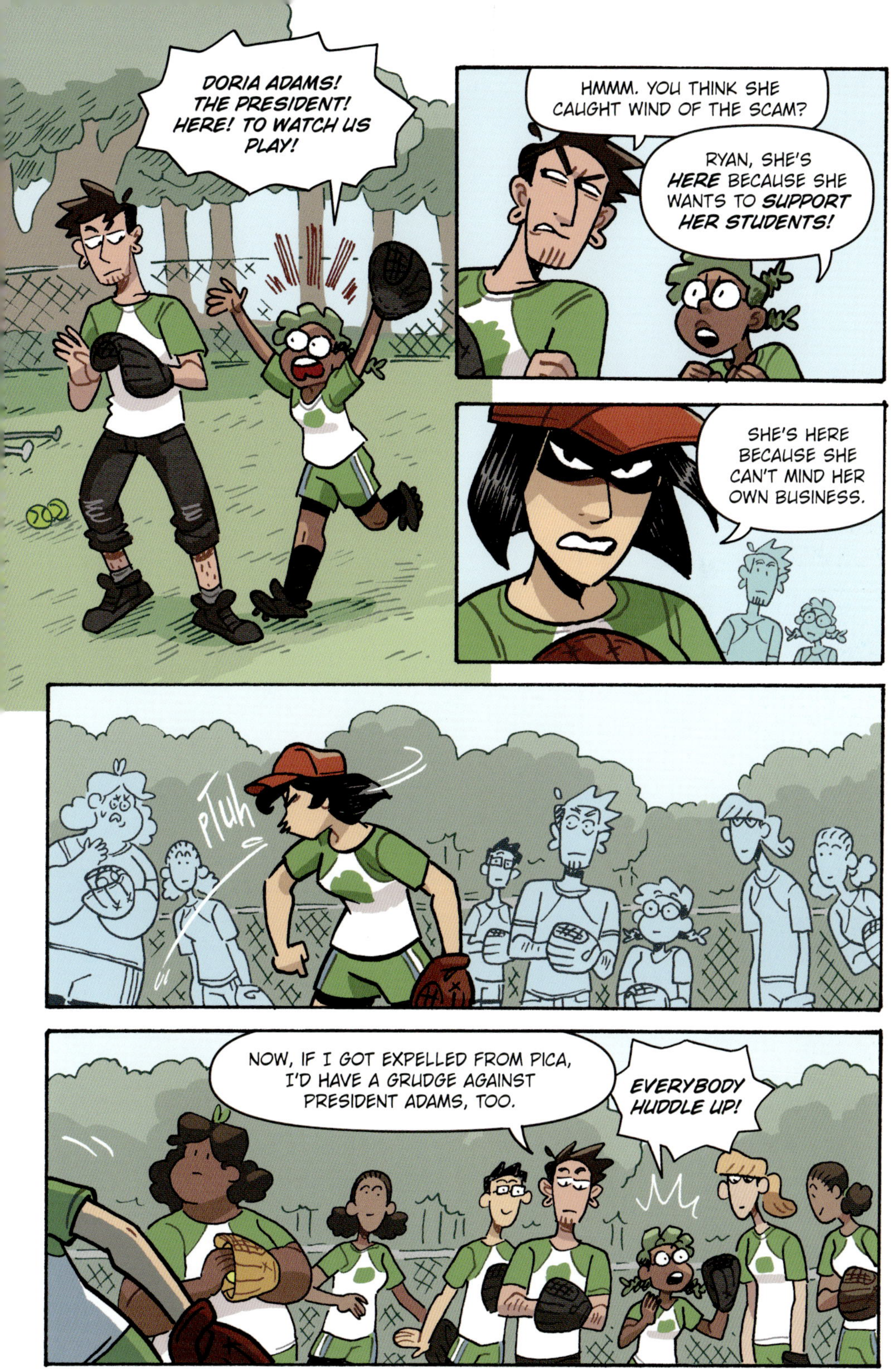
DORIA ADAMS! THE PRESIDENT! HERE! TO WATCH US PLAY!
HMMM. YOU THINK SHE CAUGHT WIND OF THE SCAM?
RYAN, SHE'S *HERE* BECAUSE SHE WANTS TO *SUPPORT HER STUDENTS!*
SHE'S HERE BECAUSE SHE CAN'T MIND HER OWN BUSINESS.
PTUH
NOW, IF I GOT EXPELLED FROM PICA, I'D HAVE A GRUDGE AGAINST PRESIDENT ADAMS, TOO.
EVERYBODY HUDDLE UP!

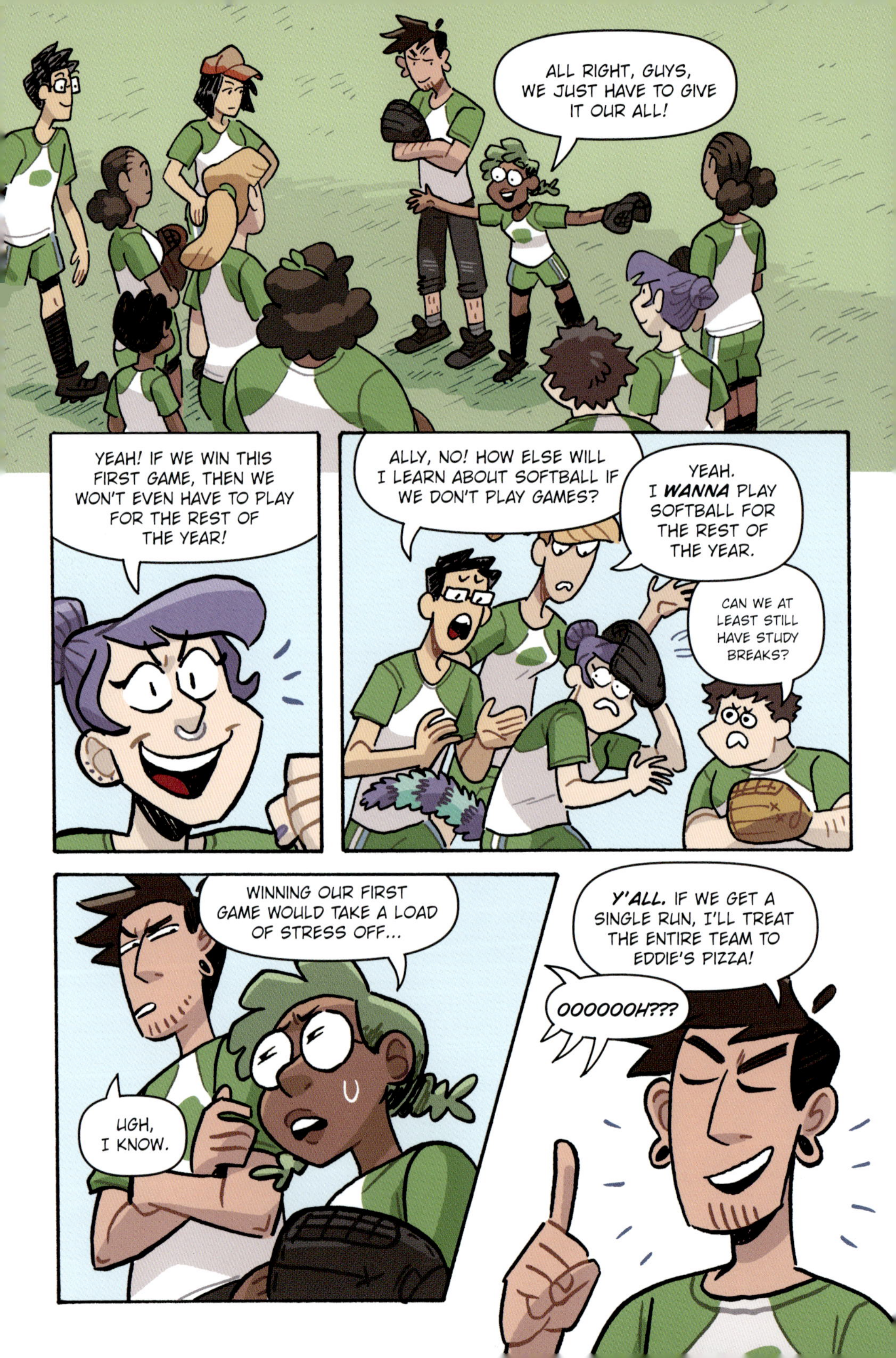
ALL RIGHT, GUYS, WE JUST HAVE TO GIVE IT OUR ALL!
YEAH! IF WE WIN THIS FIRST GAME, THEN WE WON'T EVEN HAVE TO PLAY FOR THE REST OF THE YEAR!
ALLY, NO! HOW ELSE WILL I LEARN ABOUT SOFTBALL IF WE DON'T PLAY GAMES?
YEAH. I **WANNA** PLAY SOFTBALL FOR THE REST OF THE YEAR.
CAN WE AT LEAST STILL HAVE STUDY BREAKS?
WINNING OUR FIRST GAME WOULD TAKE A LOAD OF STRESS OFF...
UGH, I KNOW.
Y'ALL. IF WE GET A SINGLE RUN, I'LL TREAT THE ENTIRE TEAM TO EDDIE'S PIZZA!
OOOOOOH???

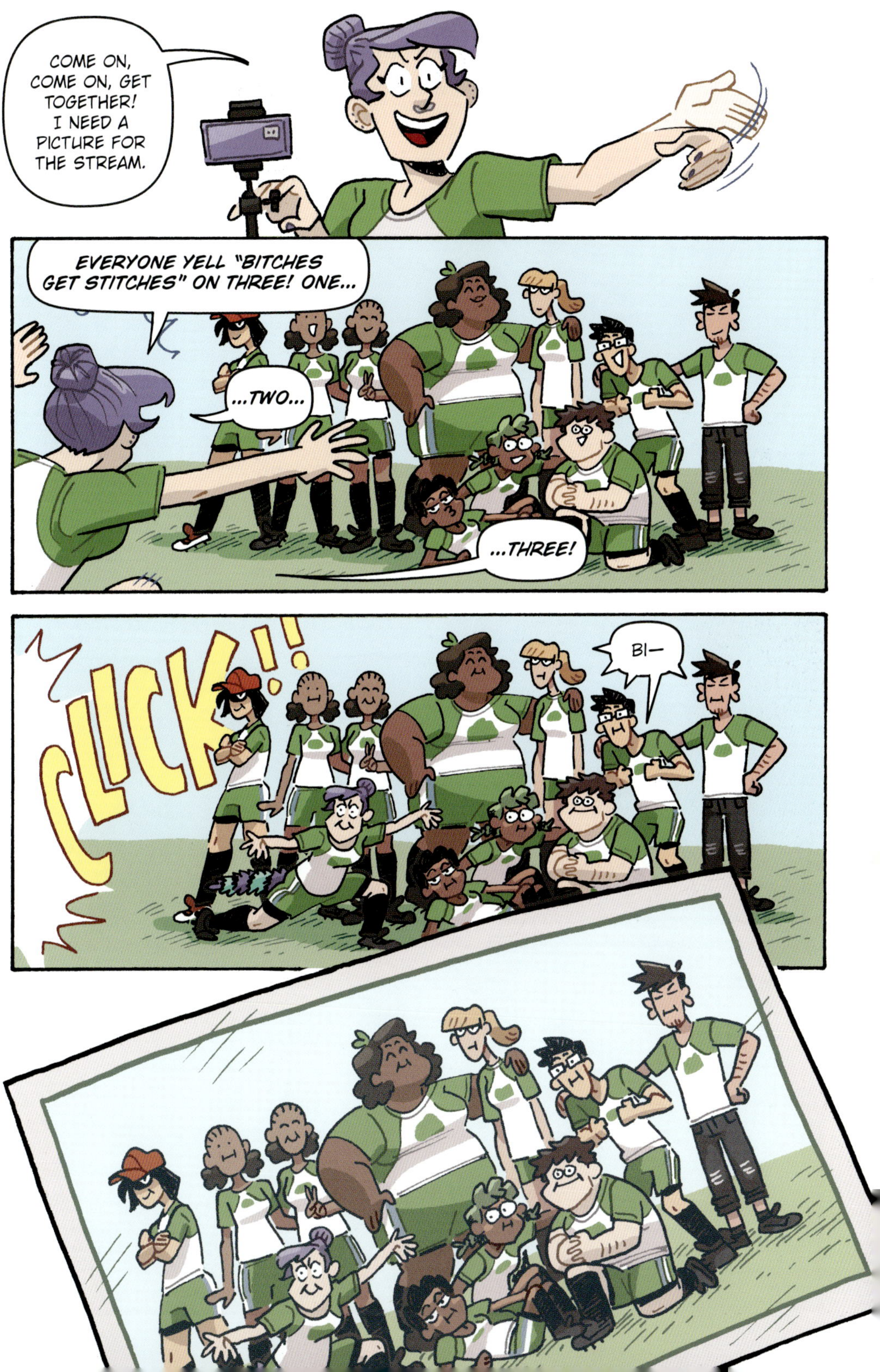
COME ON, COME ON, GET TOGETHER! I NEED A PICTURE FOR THE STREAM.
EVERYONE YELL "BITCHES GET STITCHES" ON THREE! ONE...
...TWO...
...THREE!
CLICK!!
BI—

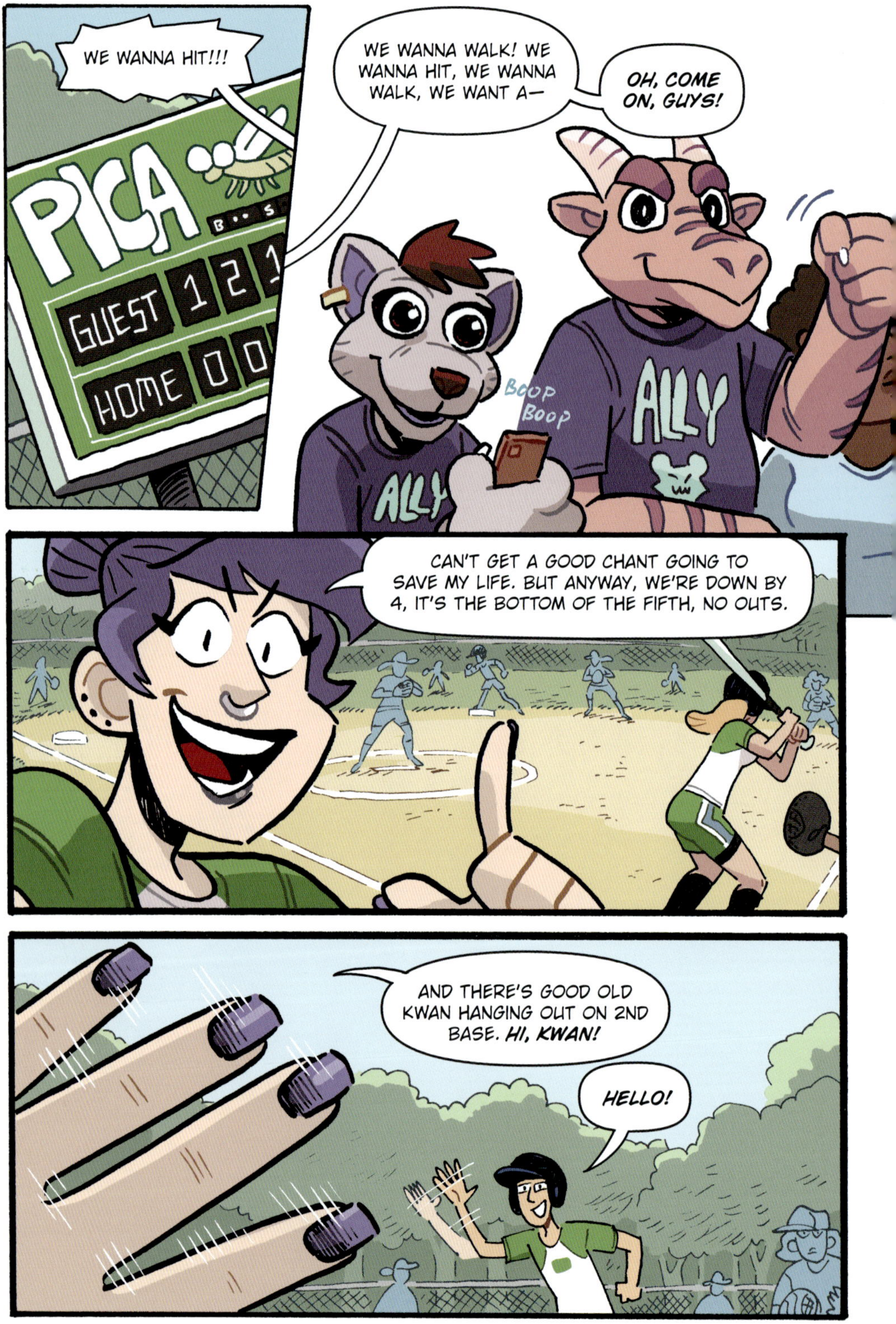

WE WANNA HIT!!!
PICA
GUEST
HOME
WE WANNA WALK! WE WANNA HIT, WE WANNA WALK, WE WANT A—
OH, COME ON, GUYS!
ALLY
BOOP BOOP
ALLY
CAN'T GET A GOOD CHANT GOING TO SAVE MY LIFE. BUT ANYWAY, WE'RE DOWN BY 4, IT'S THE BOTTOM OF THE FIFTH, NO OUTS.
AND THERE'S GOOD OLD KWAN HANGING OUT ON 2ND BASE. *HI, KWAN!*
HELLO!

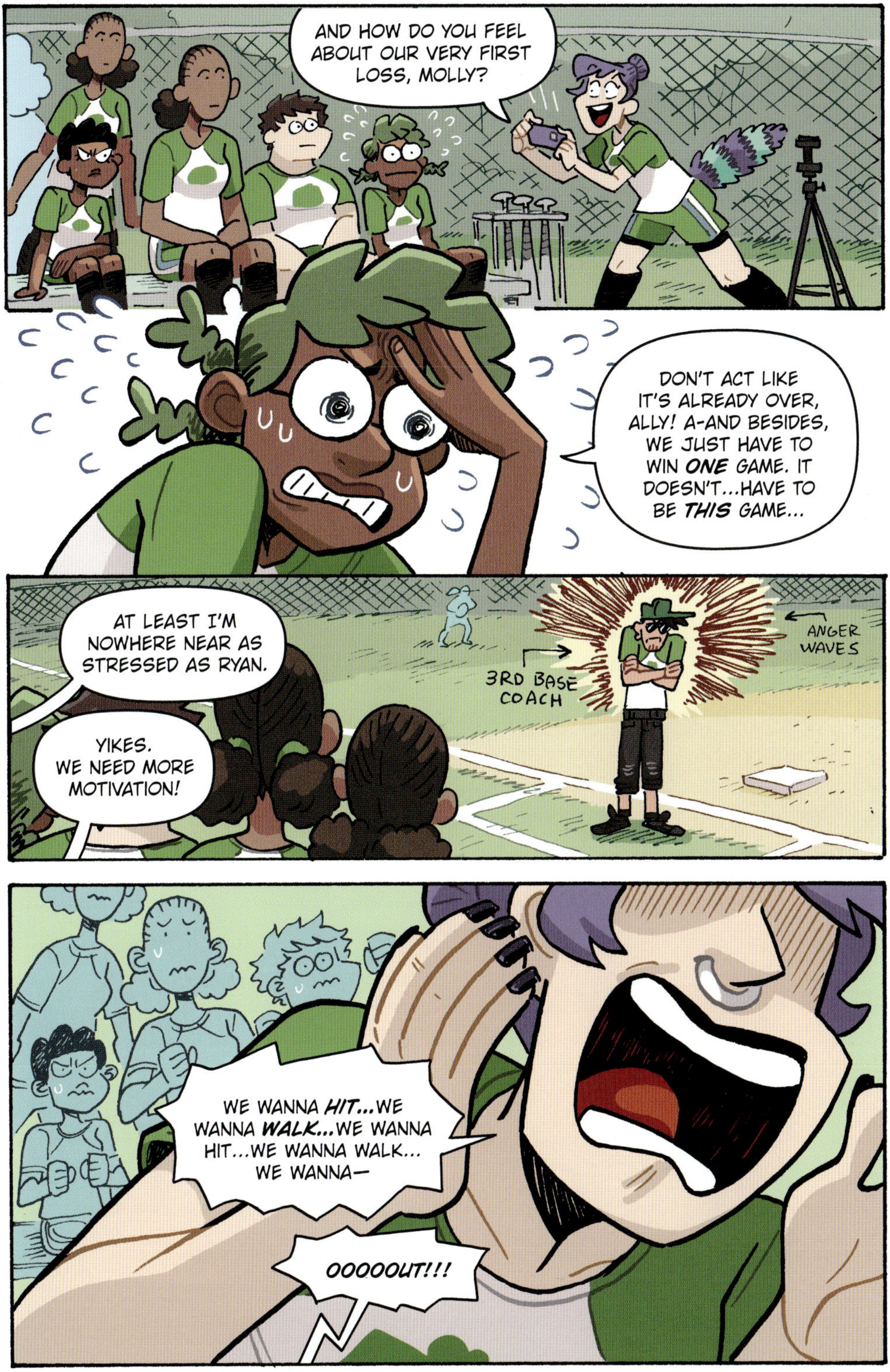
AND HOW DO YOU FEEL ABOUT OUR VERY FIRST LOSS, MOLLY?
DON'T ACT LIKE IT'S ALREADY OVER, ALLY! A-AND BESIDES, WE JUST HAVE TO WIN **ONE** GAME. IT DOESN'T...HAVE TO BE **THIS** GAME...
AT LEAST I'M NOWHERE NEAR AS STRESSED AS RYAN.
3RD BASE COACH
ANGER WAVES
YIKES. WE NEED MORE MOTIVATION!
WE WANNA **HIT...** WE WANNA **WALK...** WE WANNA HIT...WE WANNA WALK... WE WANNA—
OOOOOUT!!!

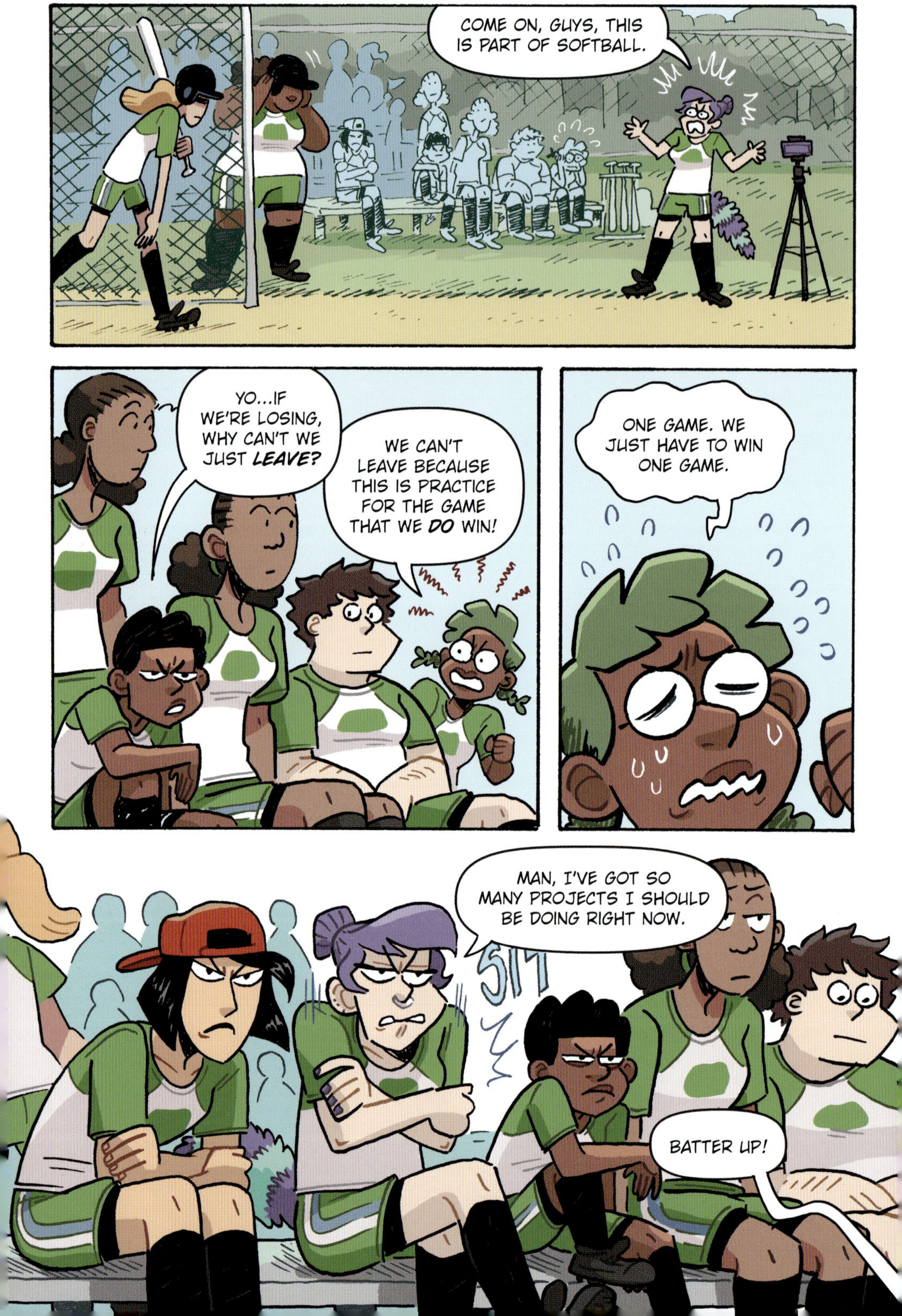
COME ON, GUYS, THIS IS PART OF SOFTBALL.
YO...IF WE'RE LOSING, WHY CAN'T WE JUST *LEAVE?*
WE CAN'T LEAVE BECAUSE THIS IS PRACTICE FOR THE GAME THAT WE *DO* WIN!
ONE GAME. WE JUST HAVE TO WIN ONE GAME.
MAN, I'VE GOT SO MANY PROJECTS I SHOULD BE DOING RIGHT NOW.
SIT
BATTER UP!

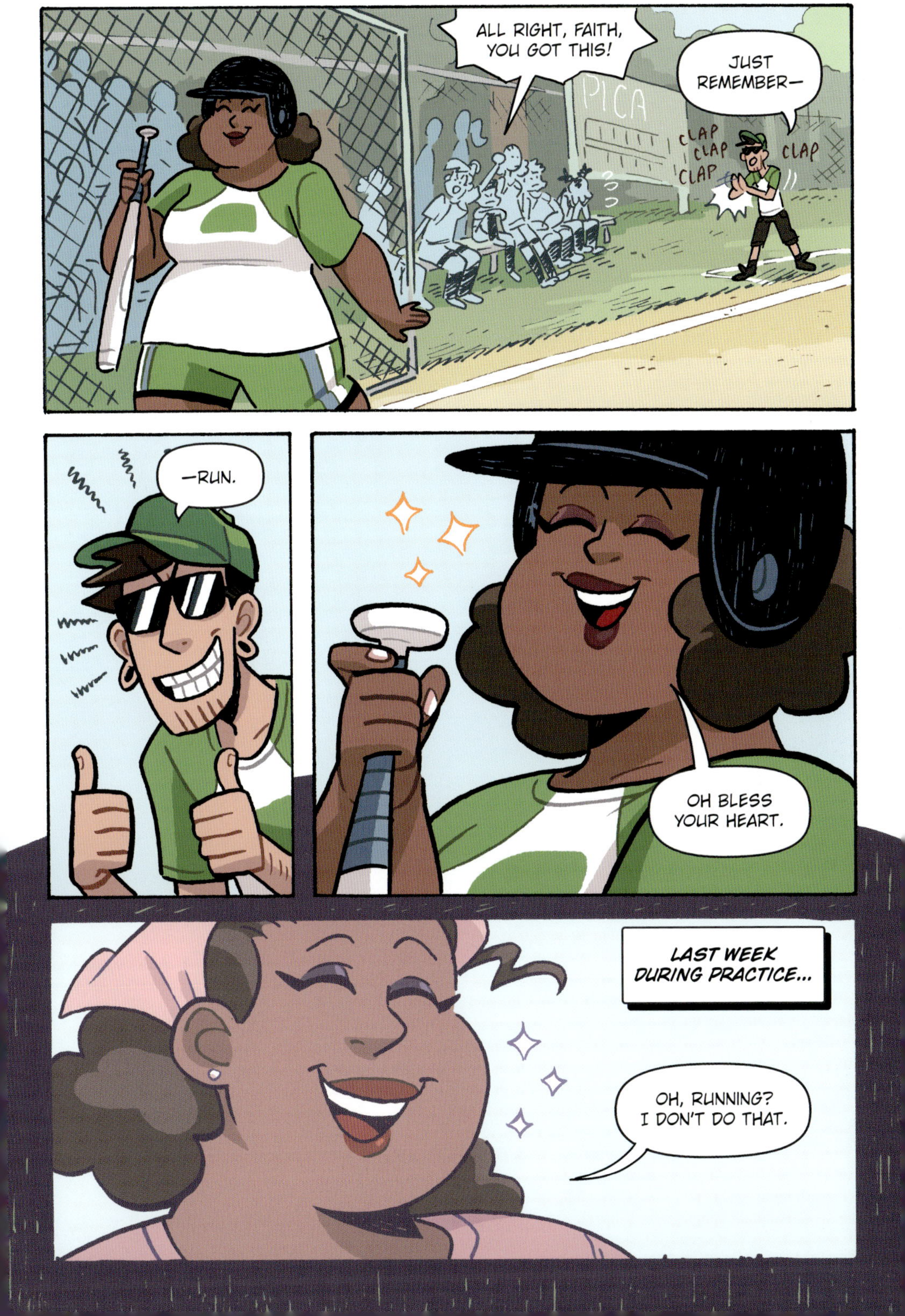
ALL RIGHT, FAITH, YOU GOT THIS!
JUST REMEMBER—
CLAP CLAP CLAP
CLAP
—RUN.
OH BLESS YOUR HEART.
LAST WEEK DURING PRACTICE...
OH, RUNNING? I DON'T DO THAT.

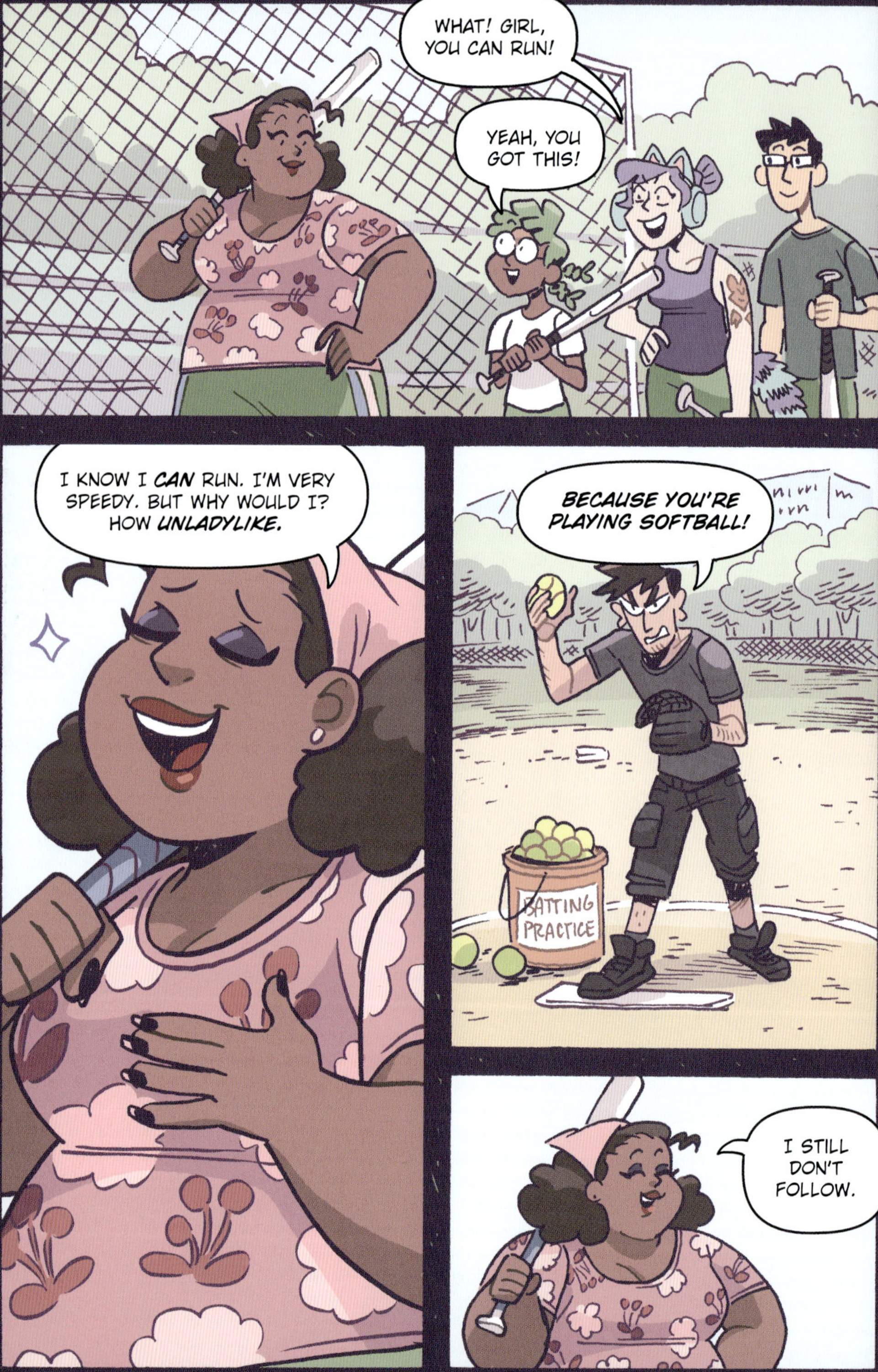
WHAT! GIRL, YOU CAN RUN!
YEAH, YOU GOT THIS!
I KNOW I CAN RUN. I'M VERY SPEEDY. BUT WHY WOULD I? HOW UNLADYLIKE.
BECAUSE YOU'RE PLAYING SOFTBALL!
BATTING PRACTICE
I STILL DON'T FOLLOW.

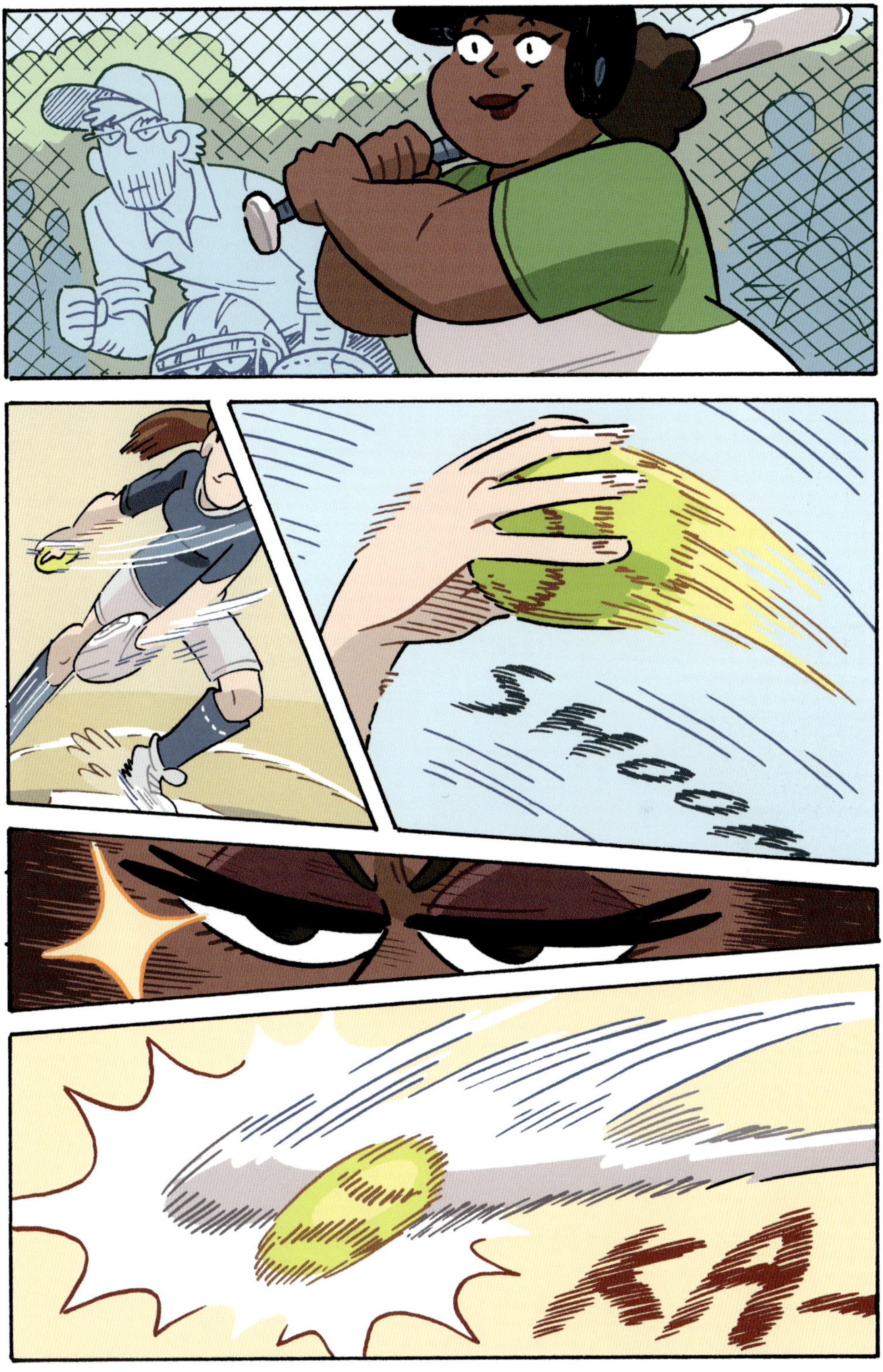
SHOOO
KA-

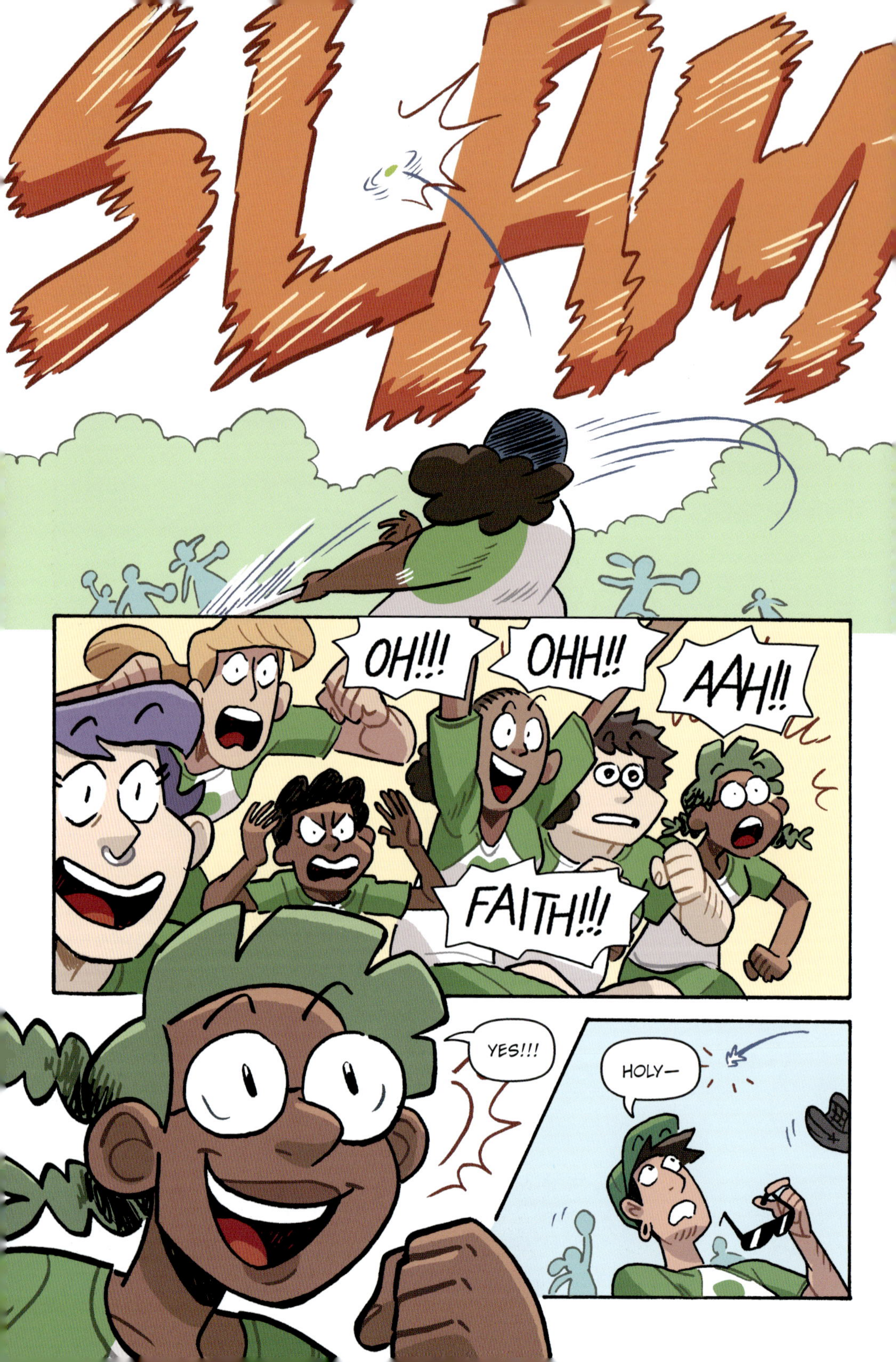
SLAM
OH!!!
OHH!!
AAH!!
FAITH!!!
YES!!!
HOLY—

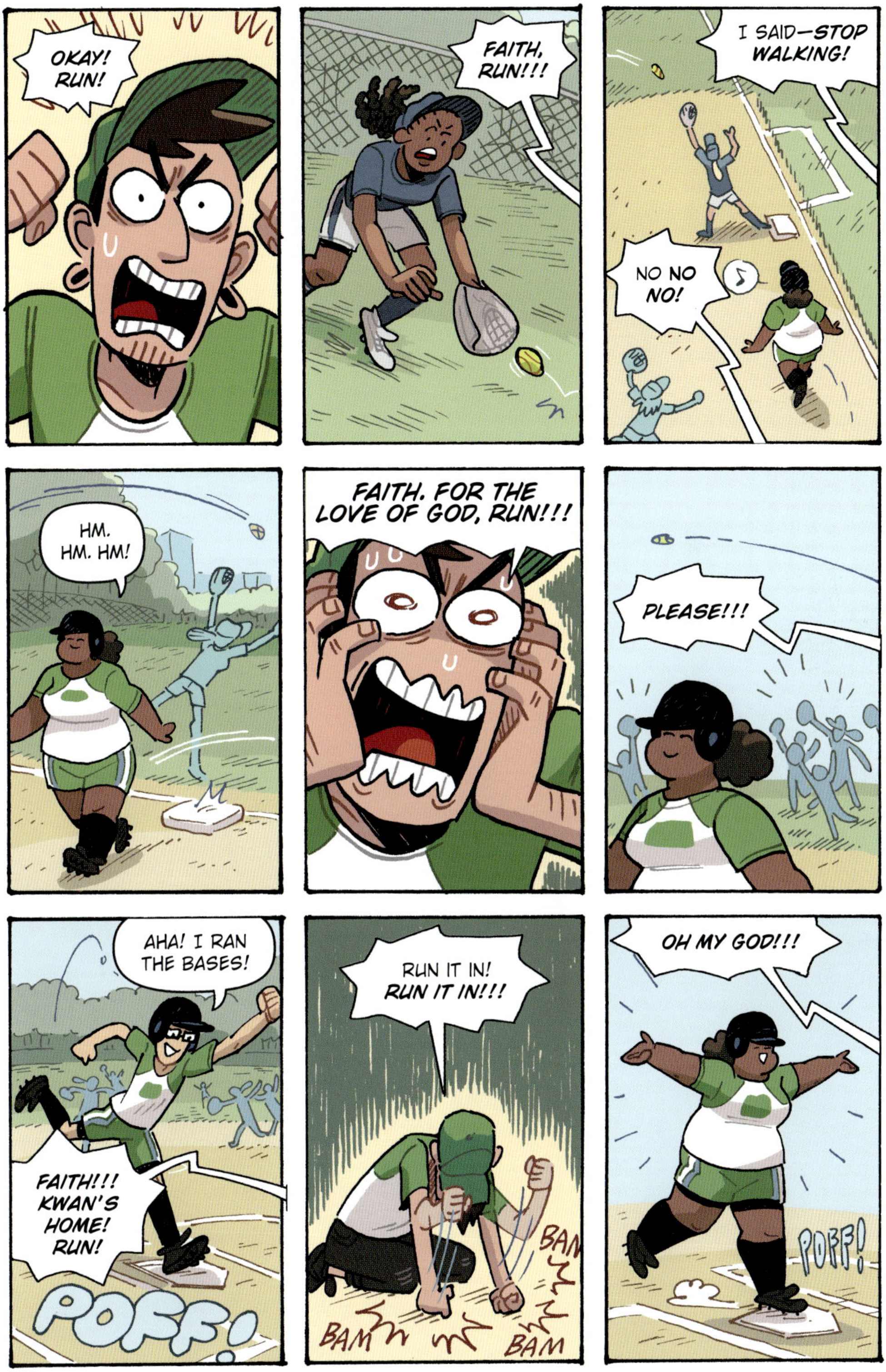
OKAY! RUN!
FAITH, RUN!!!
I SAID—STOP WALKING!
NO NO NO!
HM. HM. HM!
FAITH. FOR THE LOVE OF GOD, RUN!!!
PLEASE!!!
AHA! I RAN THE BASES!
FAITH!!! KWAN'S HOME! RUN!
POFF!
RUN IT IN! RUN IT IN!!!
BAM
BAM
BAM
OH MY GOD!!!
POFF!

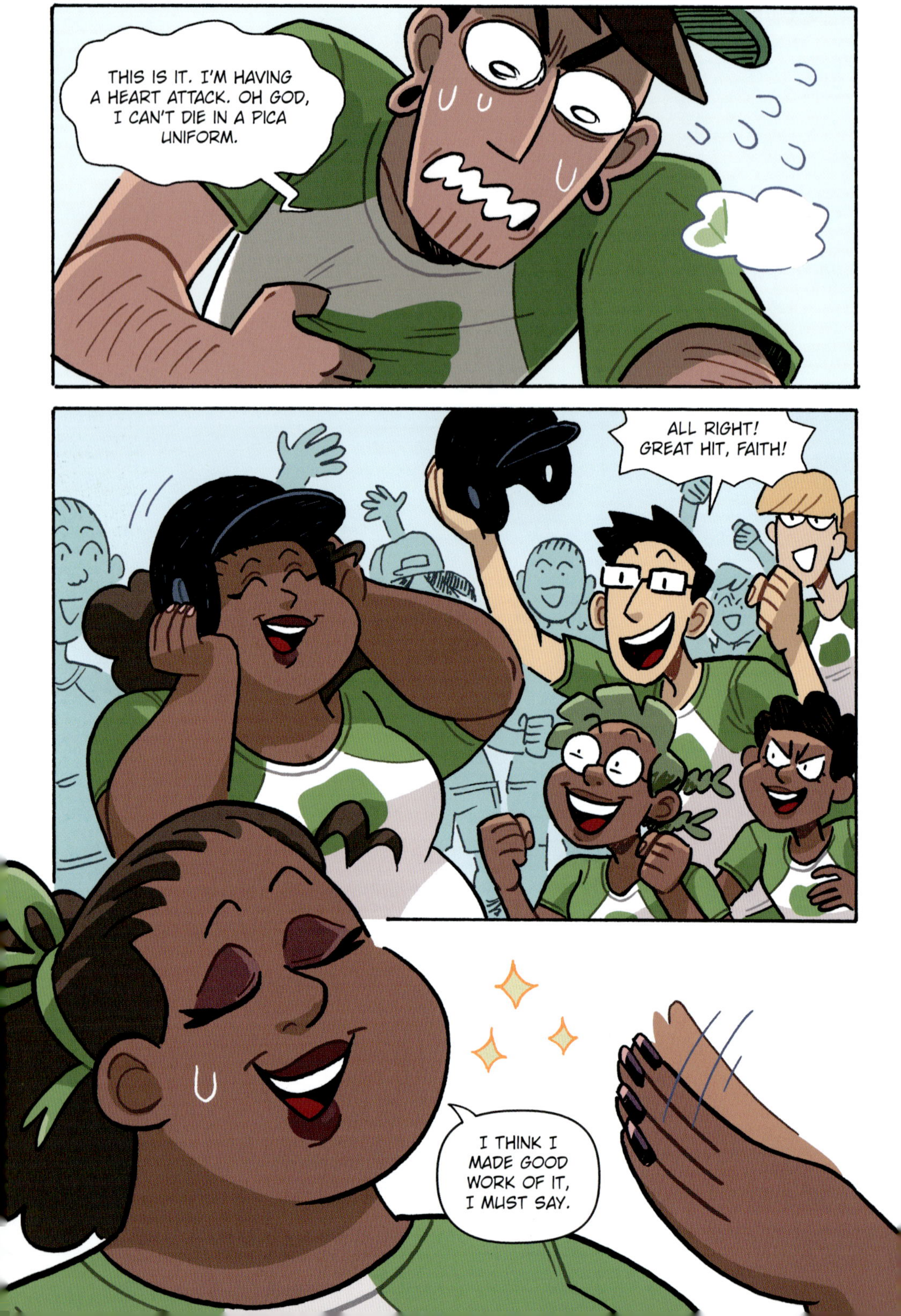
THIS IS IT. I'M HAVING A HEART ATTACK. OH GOD, I CAN'T DIE IN A PICA UNIFORM.
ALL RIGHT! GREAT HIT, FAITH!
I THINK I MADE GOOD WORK OF IT, I MUST SAY.

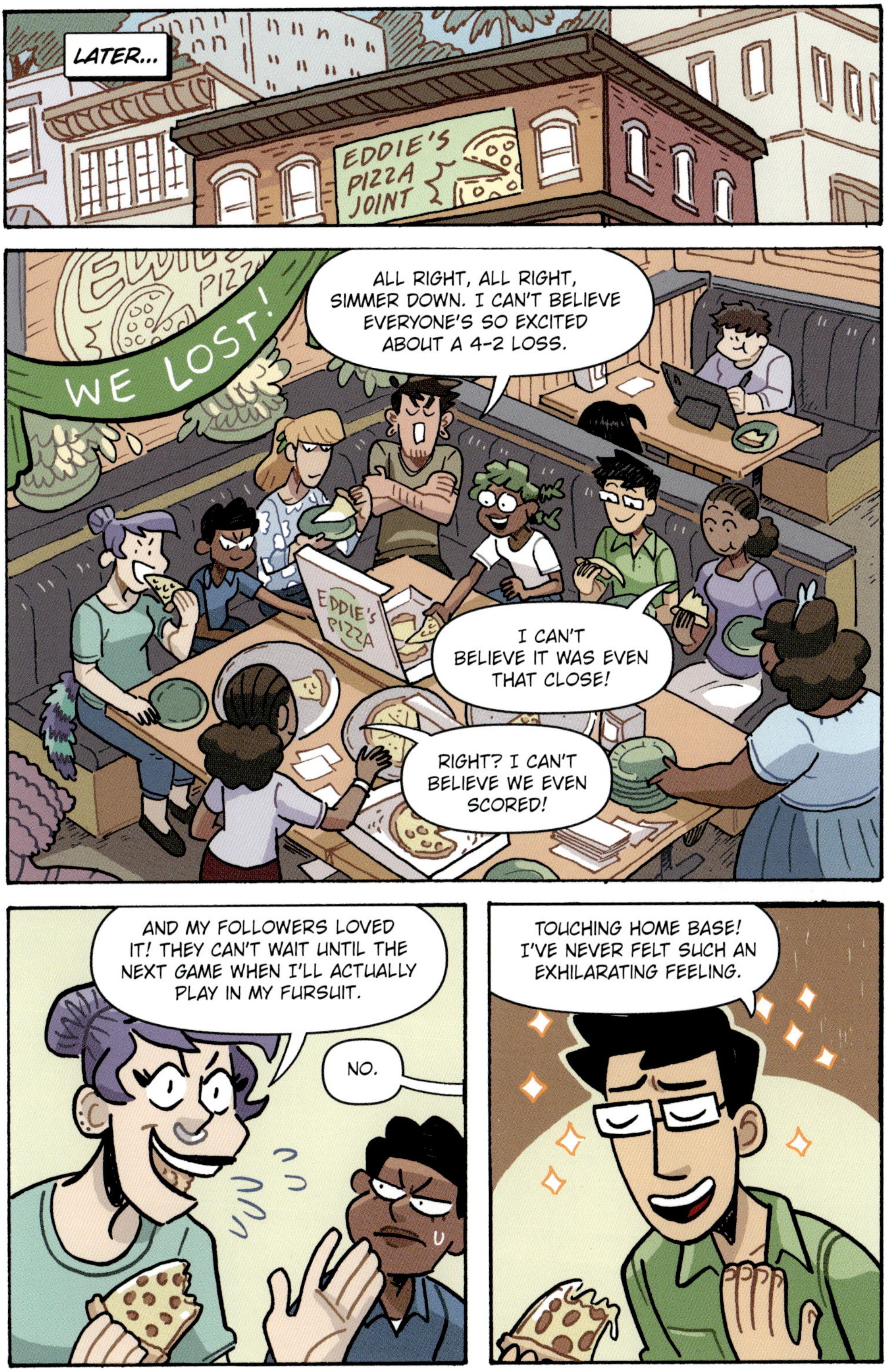
LATER...
EDDIE'S PIZZA JOINT
WE LOST!
ALL RIGHT, ALL RIGHT, SIMMER DOWN. I CAN'T BELIEVE EVERYONE'S SO EXCITED ABOUT A 4-2 LOSS.
EDDIE'S PIZZA
I CAN'T BELIEVE IT WAS EVEN THAT CLOSE!
RIGHT? I CAN'T BELIEVE WE EVEN SCORED!
AND MY FOLLOWERS LOVED IT! THEY CAN'T WAIT UNTIL THE NEXT GAME WHEN I'LL ACTUALLY PLAY IN MY FURSUIT.
NO.
TOUCHING HOME BASE! I'VE NEVER FELT SUCH AN EXHILARATING FEELING.

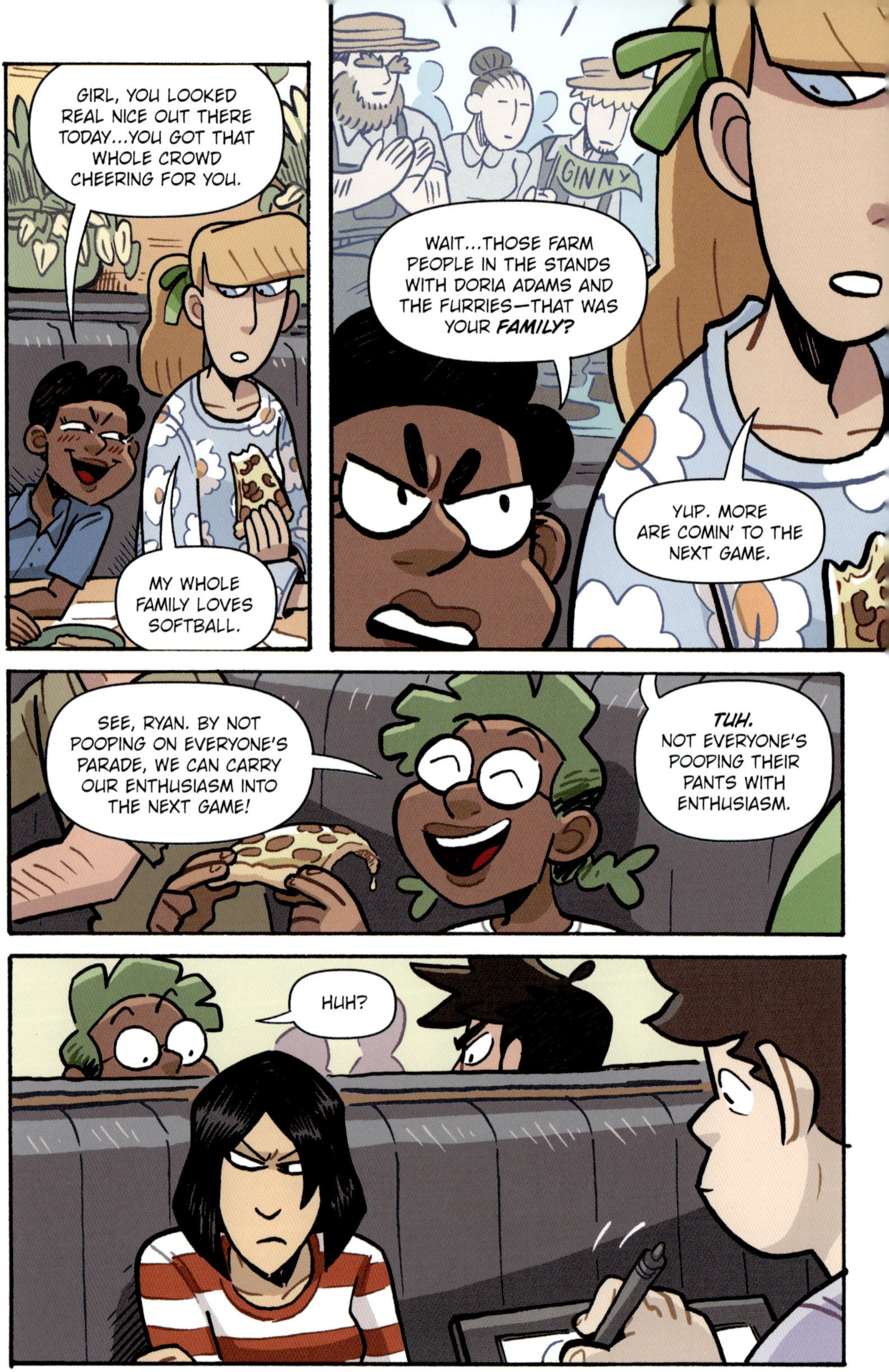
GIRL, YOU LOOKED REAL NICE OUT THERE TODAY...YOU GOT THAT WHOLE CROWD CHEERING FOR YOU.
MY WHOLE FAMILY LOVES SOFTBALL.
GINNY
WAIT...THOSE FARM PEOPLE IN THE STANDS WITH DORIA ADAMS AND THE FURRIES—THAT WAS YOUR *FAMILY?*
YUP. MORE ARE COMIN' TO THE NEXT GAME.
SEE, RYAN. BY NOT POOPING ON EVERYONE'S PARADE, WE CAN CARRY OUR ENTHUSIASM INTO THE NEXT GAME!
TUH.
NOT EVERYONE'S POOPING THEIR PANTS WITH ENTHUSIASM.
HUH?

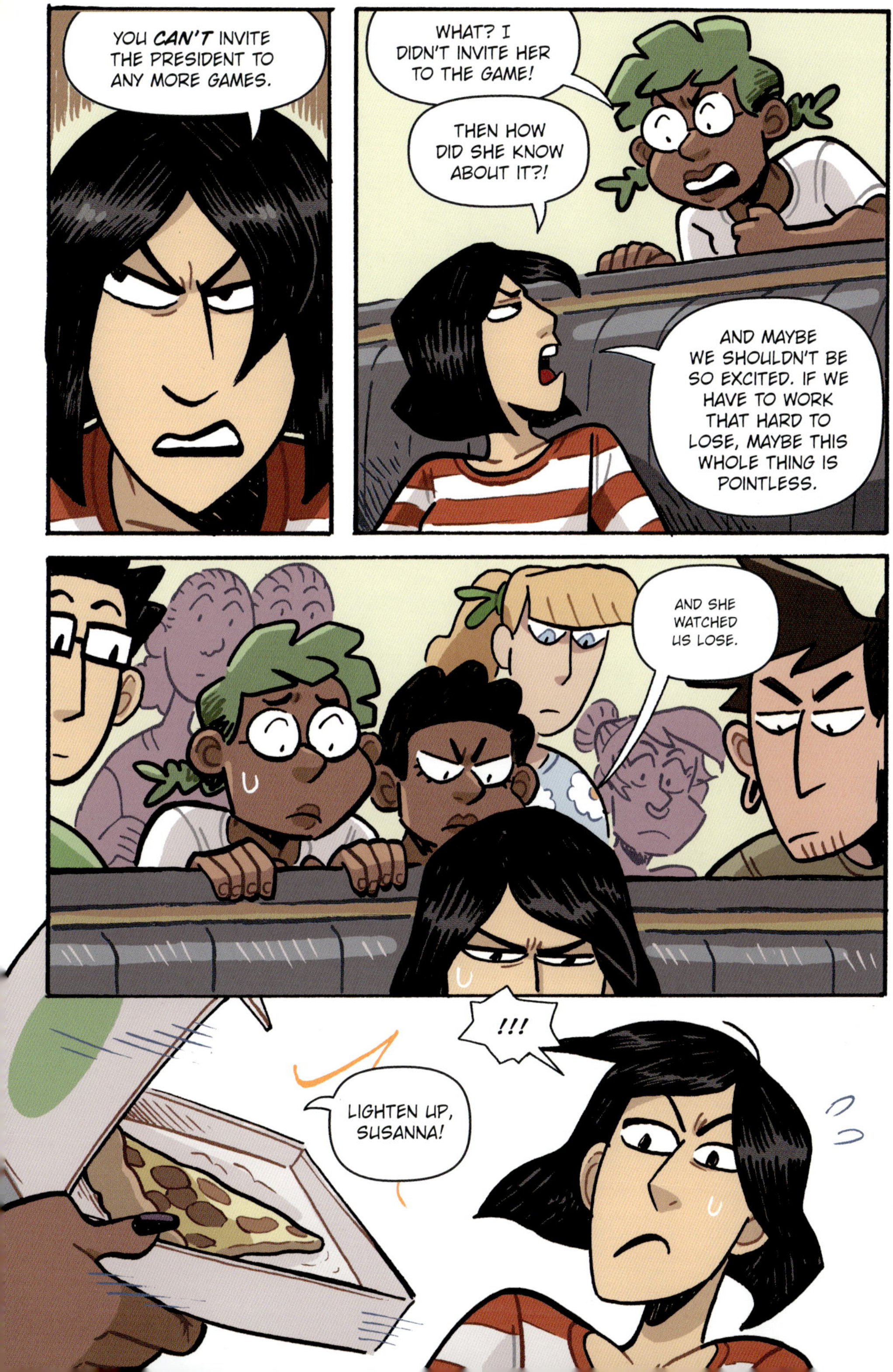
YOU CAN'T INVITE THE PRESIDENT TO ANY MORE GAMES.
WHAT? I DIDN'T INVITE HER TO THE GAME!
THEN HOW DID SHE KNOW ABOUT IT?!
AND MAYBE WE SHOULDN'T BE SO EXCITED. IF WE HAVE TO WORK THAT HARD TO LOSE, MAYBE THIS WHOLE THING IS POINTLESS.
AND SHE WATCHED US LOSE.
!!!
LIGHTEN UP, SUSANNA!

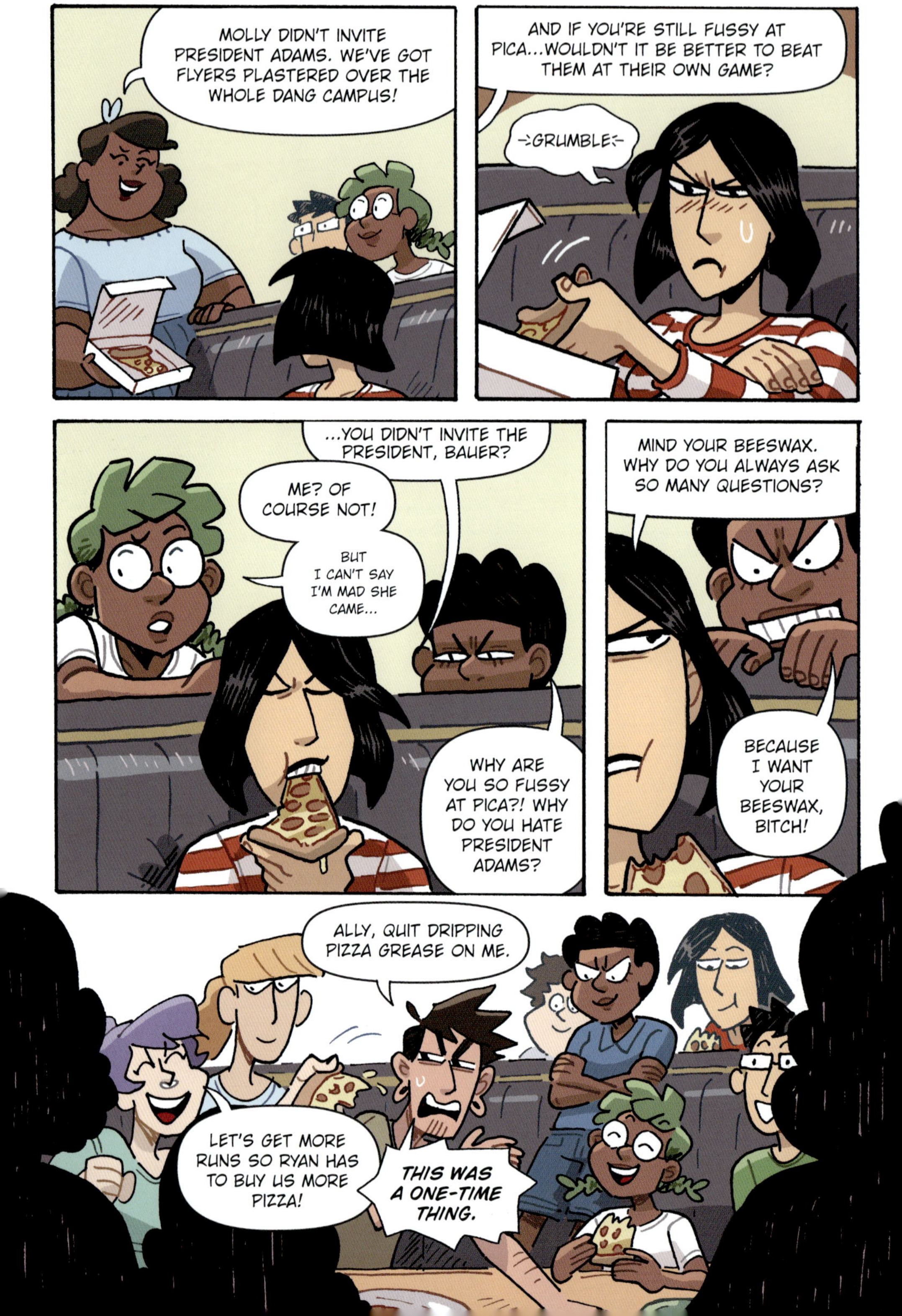
MOLLY DIDN'T INVITE PRESIDENT ADAMS. WE'VE GOT FLYERS PLASTERED OVER THE WHOLE DANG CAMPUS!
AND IF YOU'RE STILL FUSSY AT PICA...WOULDN'T IT BE BETTER TO BEAT THEM AT THEIR OWN GAME?
GRUMBLE
...YOU DIDN'T INVITE THE PRESIDENT, BAUER?
ME? OF COURSE NOT!
BUT I CAN'T SAY I'M MAD SHE CAME...
WHY ARE YOU SO FUSSY AT PICA?! WHY DO YOU HATE PRESIDENT ADAMS?
MIND YOUR BEESWAX. WHY DO YOU ALWAYS ASK SO MANY QUESTIONS?
BECAUSE I WANT YOUR BEESWAX, BITCH!
ALLY, QUIT DRIPPING PIZZA GREASE ON ME.
LET'S GET MORE RUNS SO RYAN HAS TO BUY US MORE PIZZA!
THIS WAS A ONE-TIME THING.

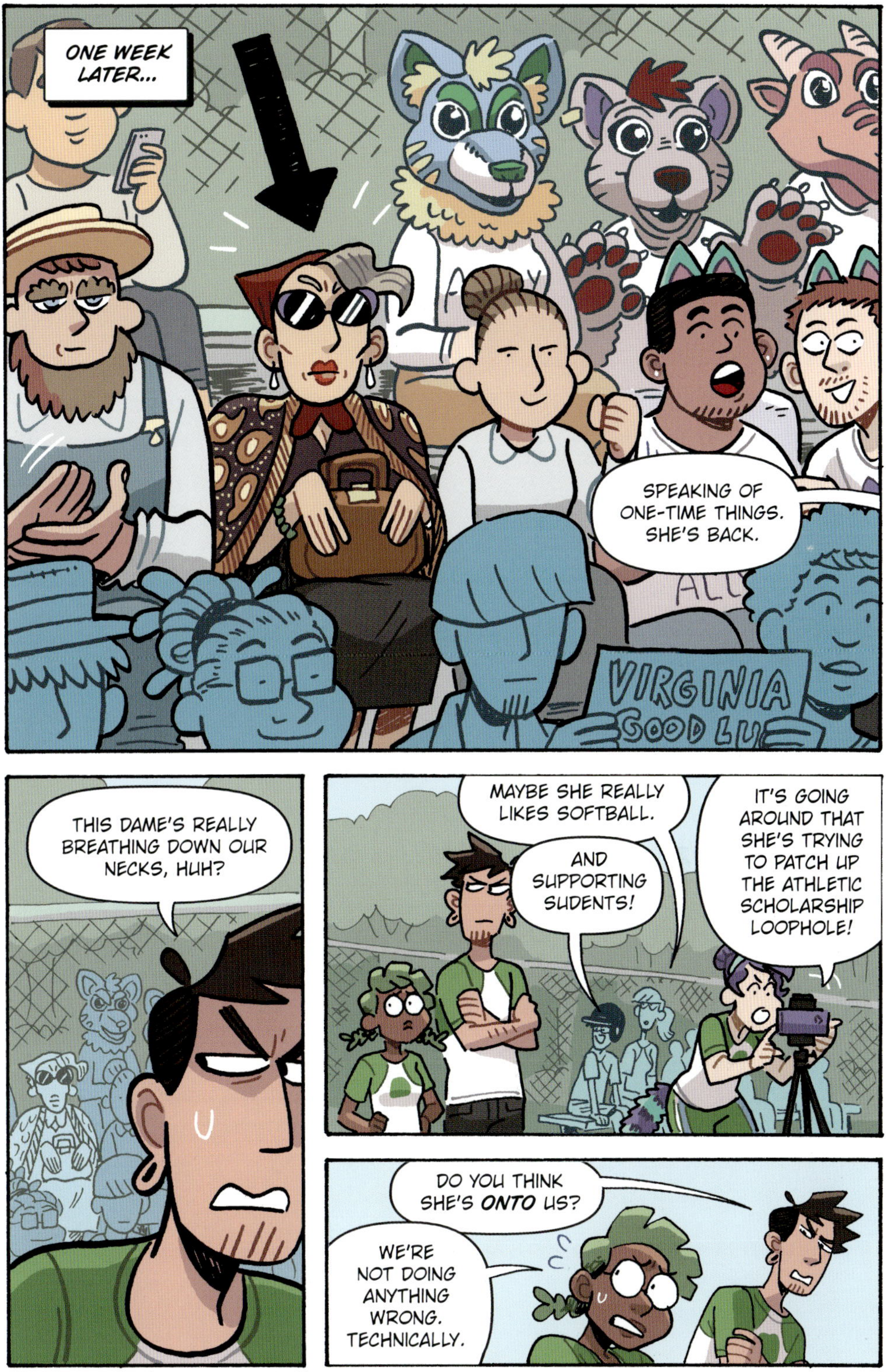
ONE WEEK LATER...
SPEAKING OF ONE-TIME THINGS. SHE'S BACK.
VIRGINIA
GOOD LU
THIS DAME'S REALLY BREATHING DOWN OUR NECKS, HUH?
MAYBE SHE REALLY LIKES SOFTBALL.
AND SUPPORTING SUDENTS!
IT'S GOING AROUND THAT SHE'S TRYING TO PATCH UP THE ATHLETIC SCHOLARSHIP LOOPHOLE!
DO YOU THINK SHE'S *ONTO* US?
WE'RE NOT DOING ANYTHING WRONG. TECHNICALLY.

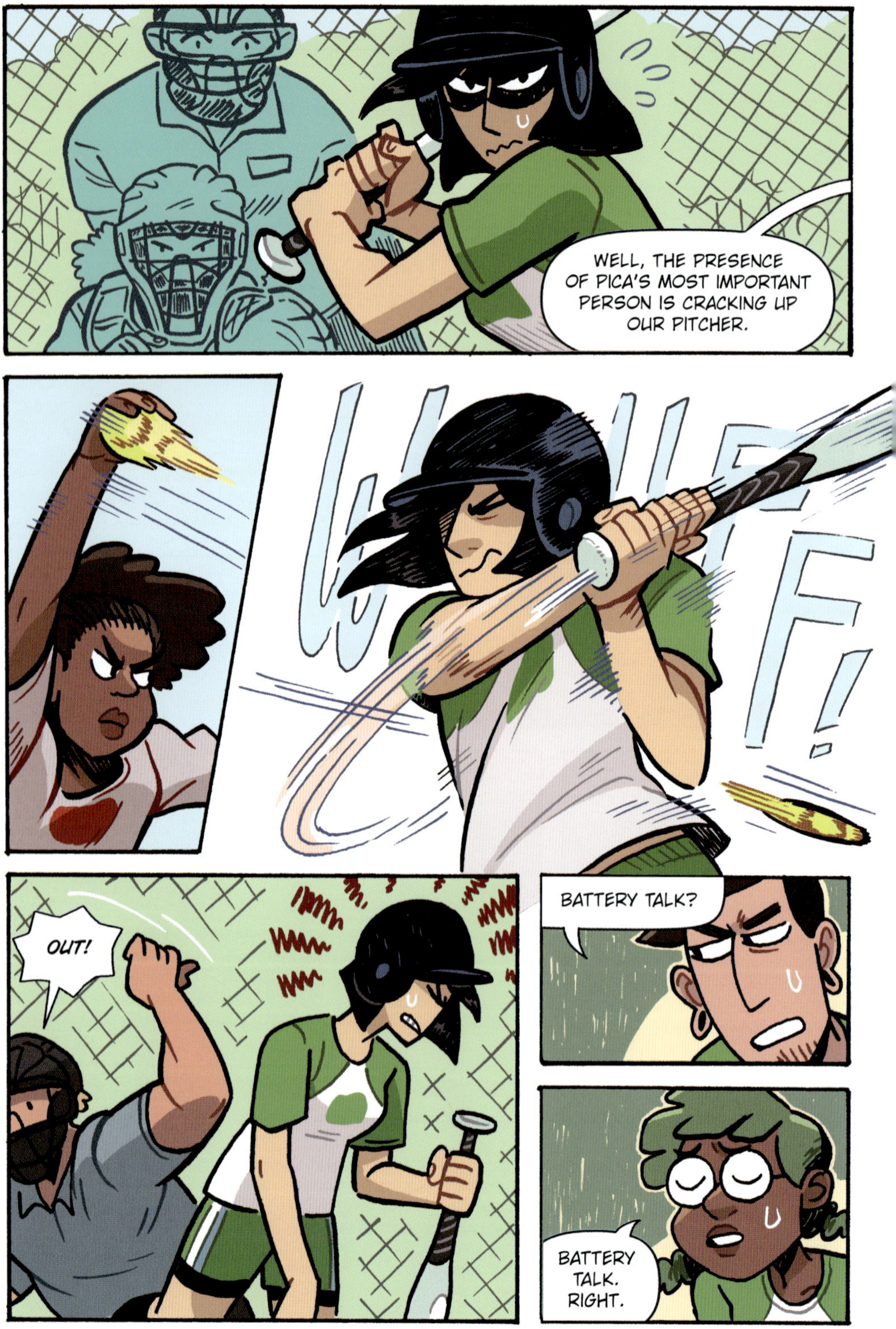
WELL, THE PRESENCE OF PICA'S MOST IMPORTANT PERSON IS CRACKING UP OUR PITCHER.
WHIFF!
OUT!
BATTERY TALK?
BATTERY TALK. RIGHT.

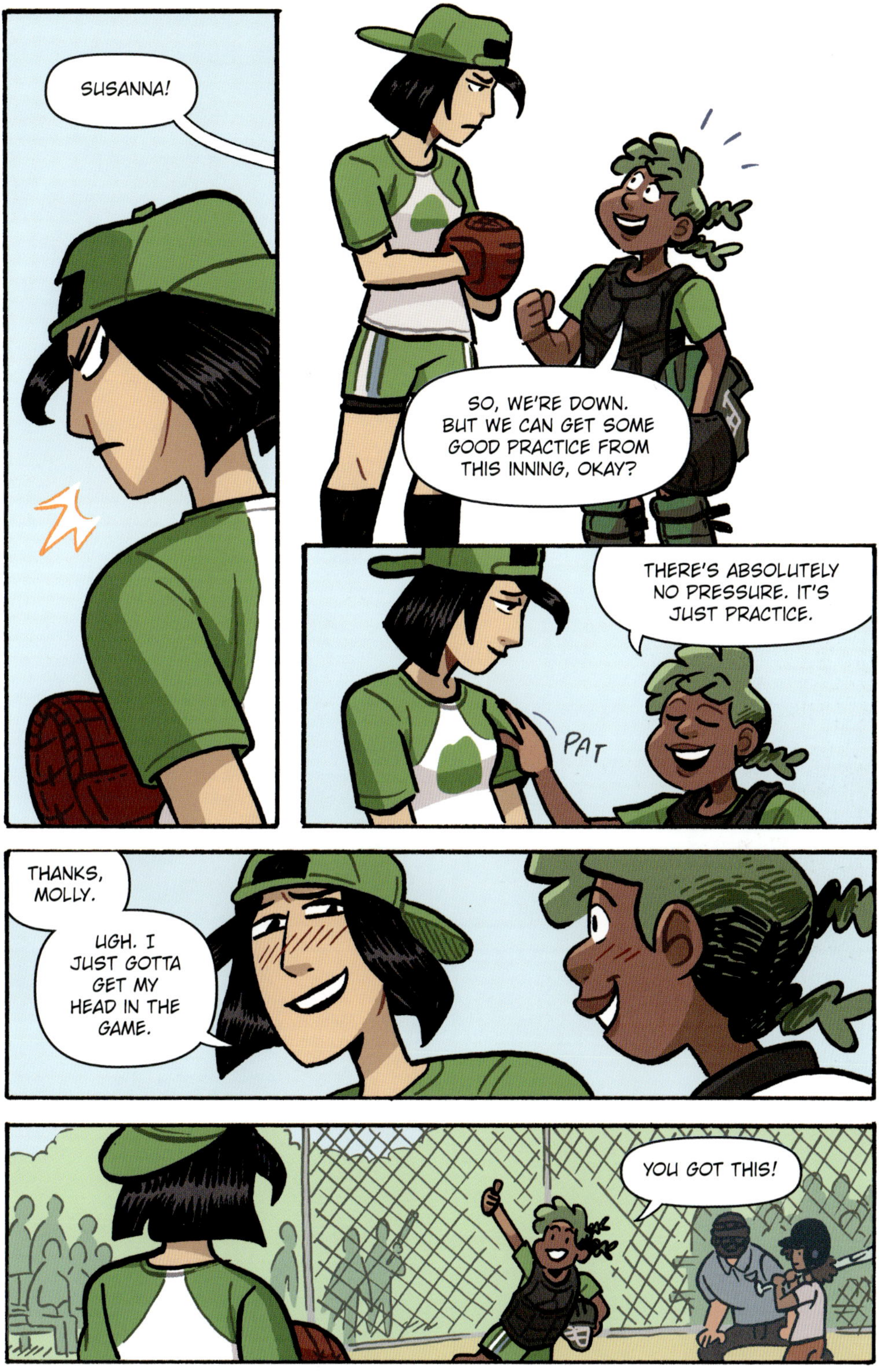
SUSANNA!
SO, WE'RE DOWN. BUT WE CAN GET SOME GOOD PRACTICE FROM THIS INNING, OKAY?
THERE'S ABSOLUTELY NO PRESSURE. IT'S JUST PRACTICE.
PAT
THANKS, MOLLY.
UGH. I JUST GOTTA GET MY HEAD IN THE GAME.
YOU GOT THIS!

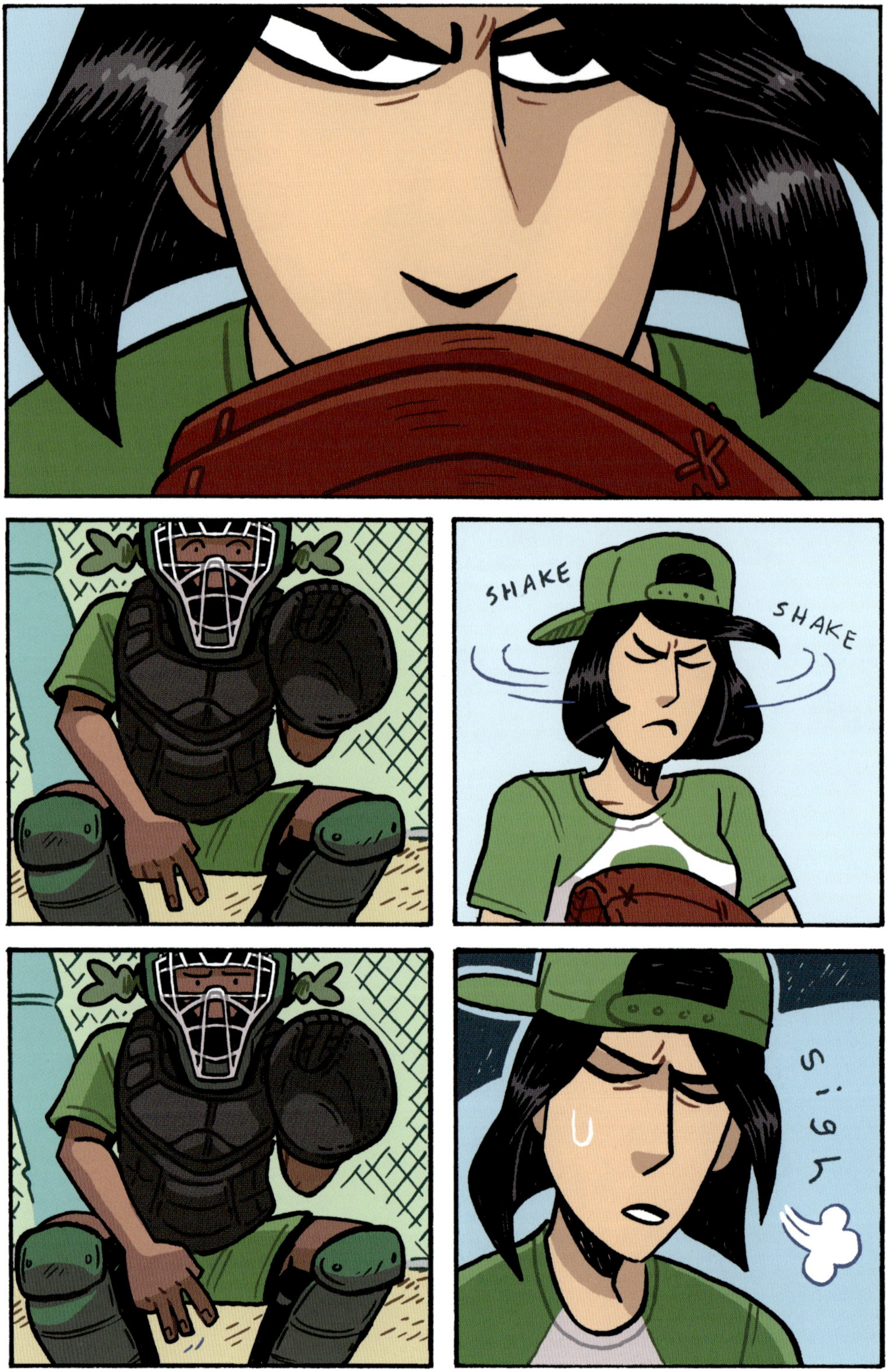
SHAKE
SHAKE
sigh

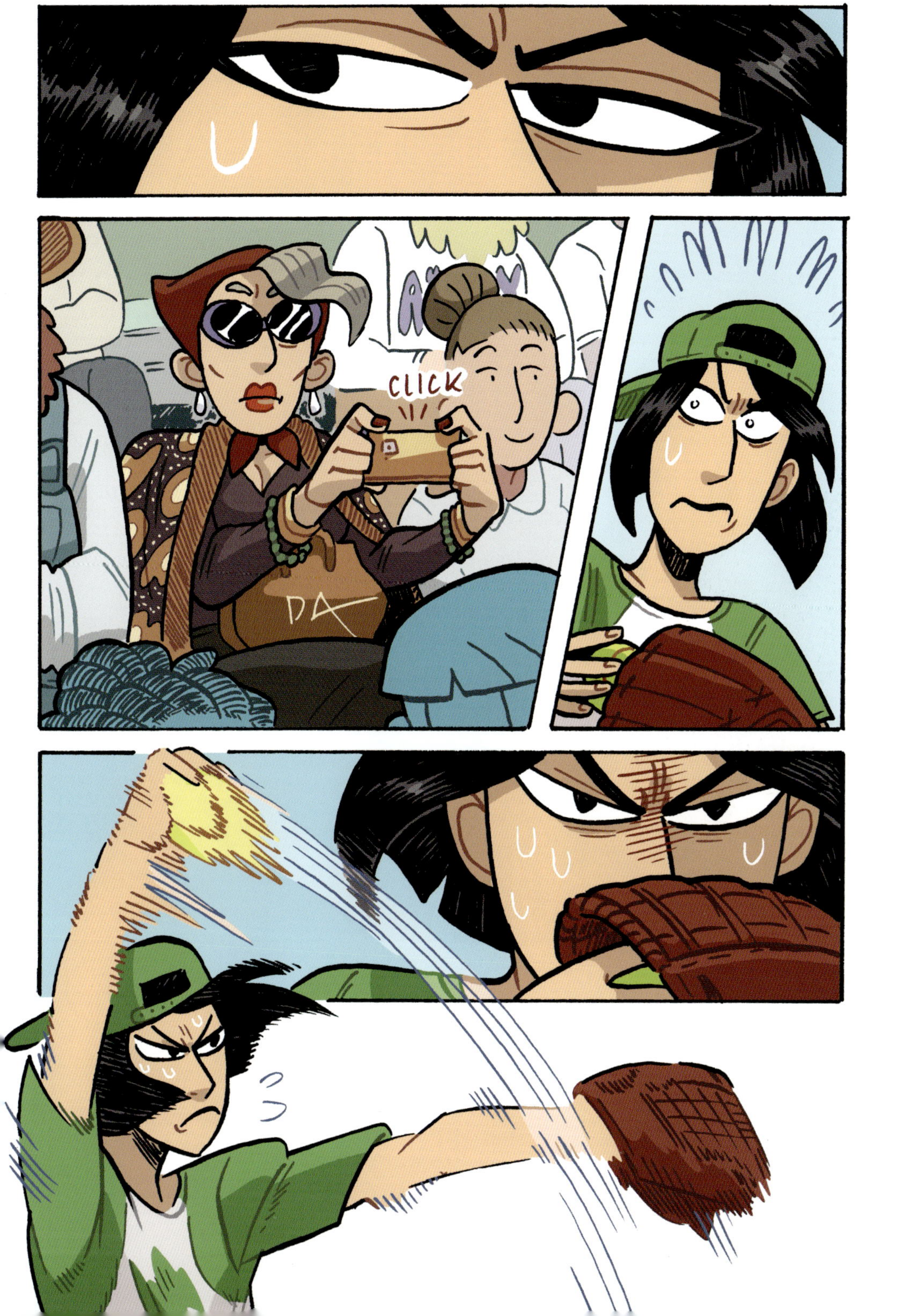
CLICK

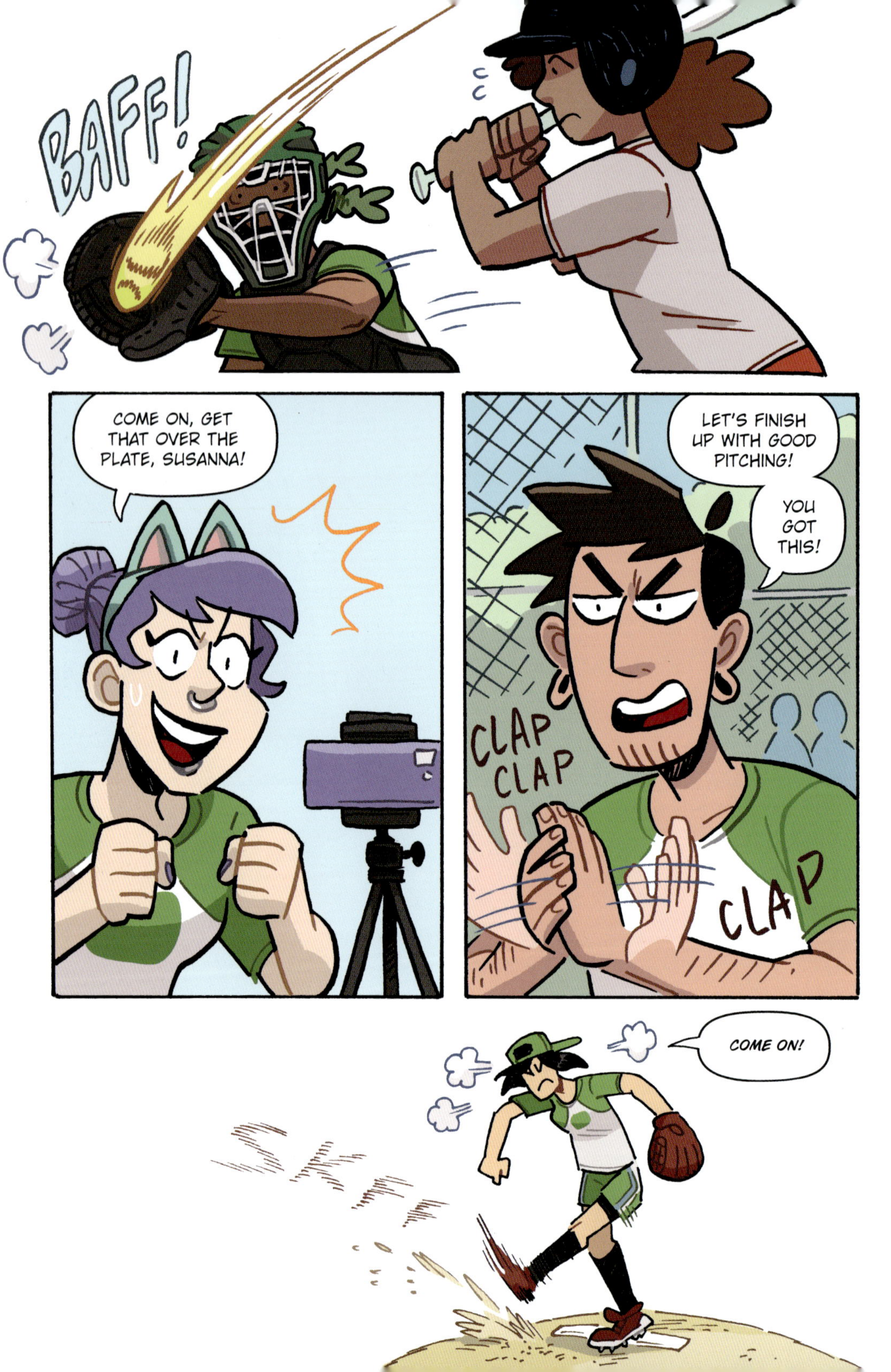
BAFF!
COME ON, GET THAT OVER THE PLATE, SUSANNA!
LET'S FINISH UP WITH GOOD PITCHING!
YOU GOT THIS!
CLAP
CLAP
CLAP
COME ON!

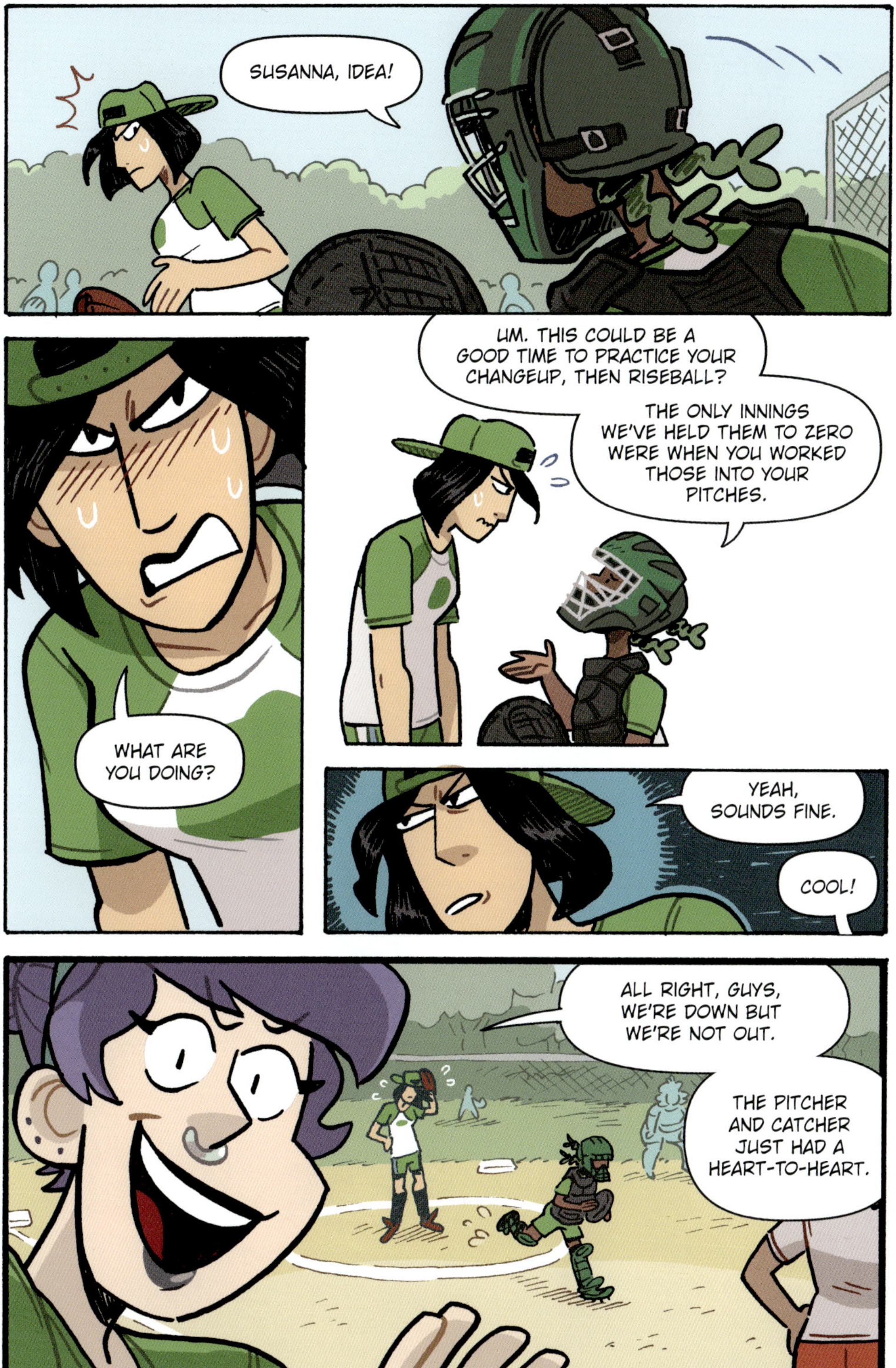
SUSANNA, IDEA!
WHAT ARE YOU DOING?
UM. THIS COULD BE A GOOD TIME TO PRACTICE YOUR CHANGEUP, THEN RISEBALL?
THE ONLY INNINGS WE'VE HELD THEM TO ZERO WERE WHEN YOU WORKED THOSE INTO YOUR PITCHES.
YEAH, SOUNDS FINE.
COOL!
ALL RIGHT, GUYS, WE'RE DOWN BUT WE'RE NOT OUT.
THE PITCHER AND CATCHER JUST HAD A HEART-TO-HEART.

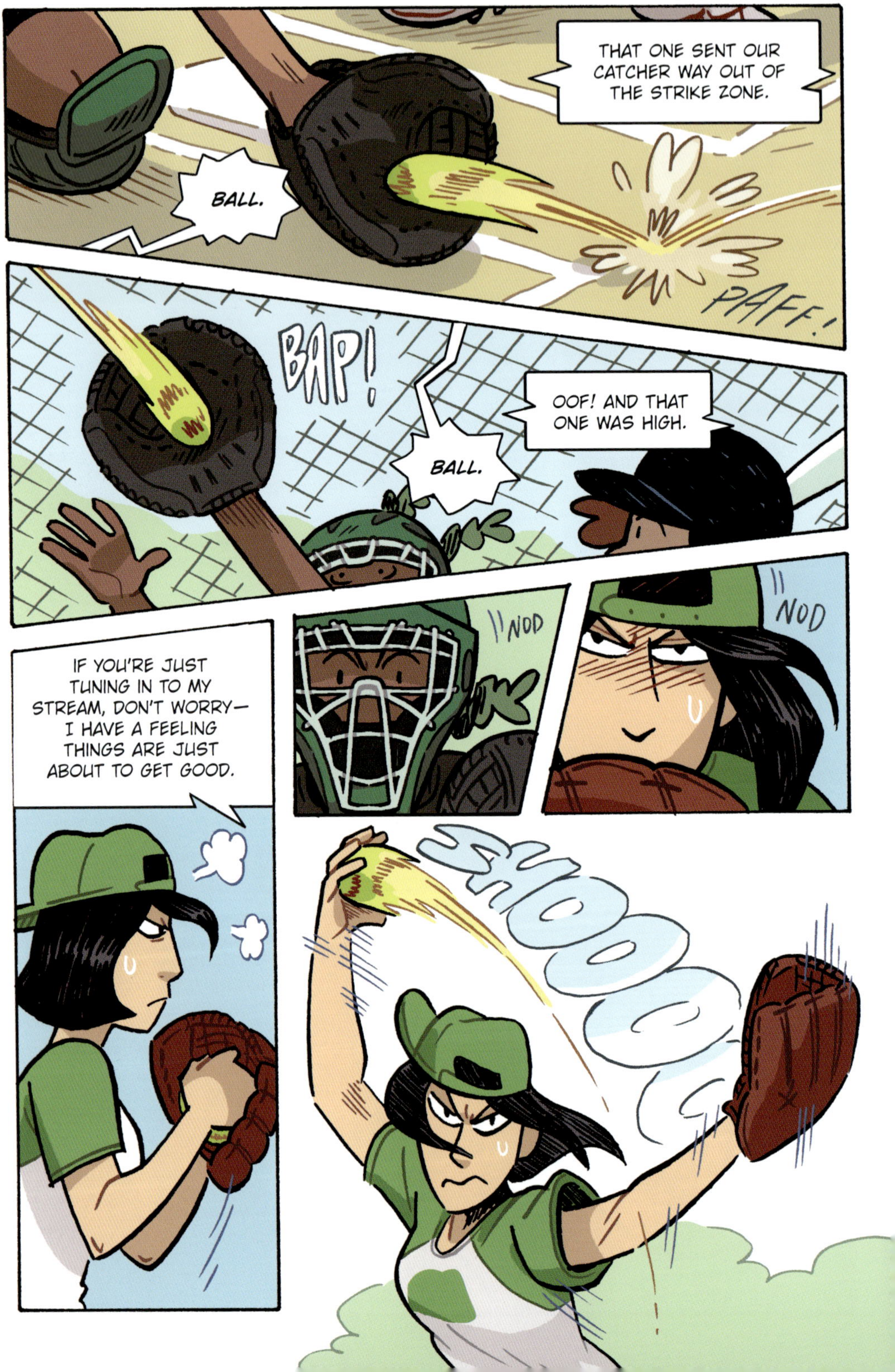
THAT ONE SENT OUR CATCHER WAY OUT OF THE STRIKE ZONE.
BALL.
PAFF!
BAP!
BALL.
OOF! AND THAT ONE WAS HIGH.
NOD
NOD
IF YOU'RE JUST TUNING IN TO MY STREAM, DON'T WORRY— I HAVE A FEELING THINGS ARE JUST ABOUT TO GET GOOD.
SHOOO

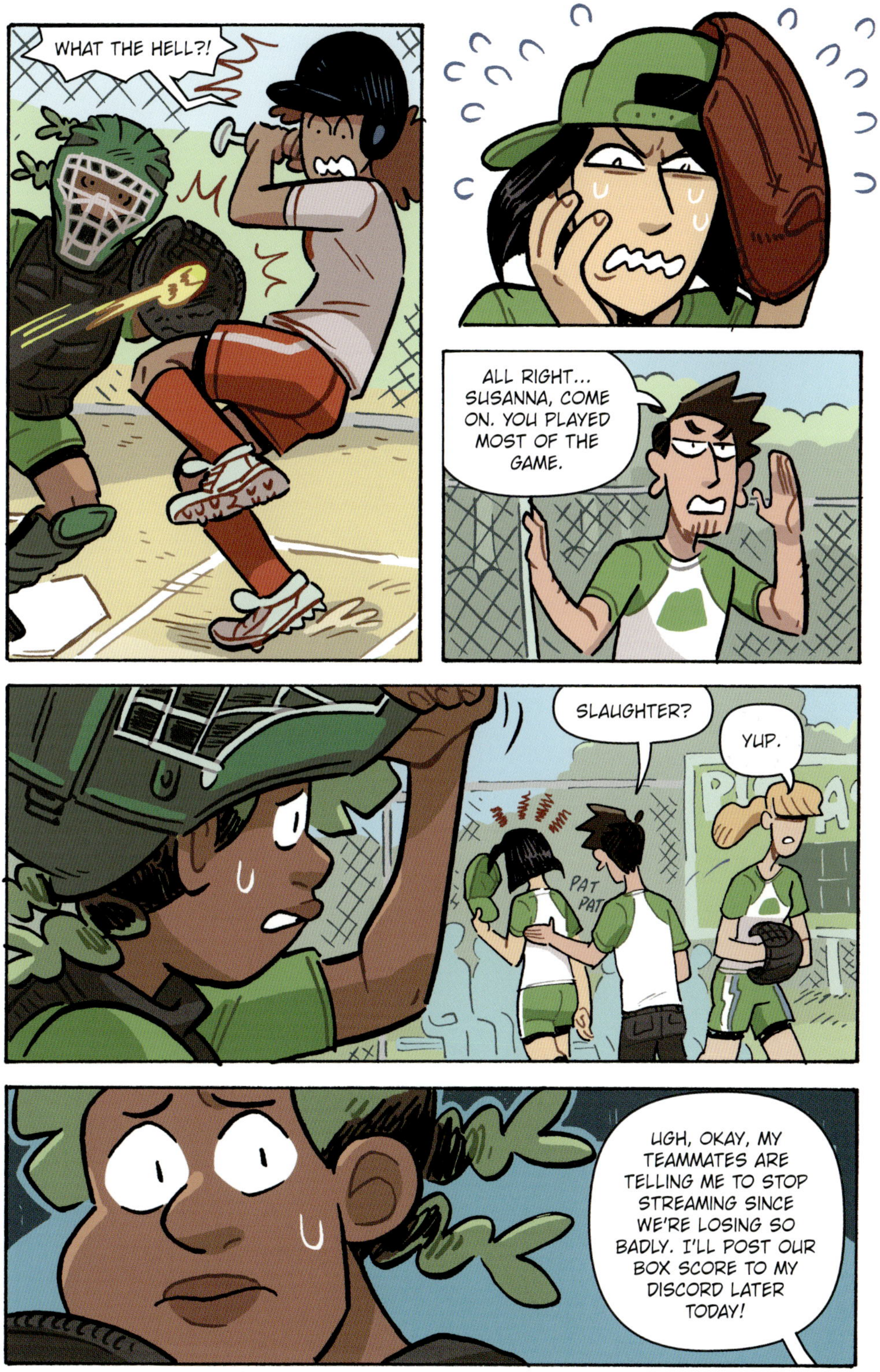
WHAT THE HELL?!
ALL RIGHT... SUSANNA, COME ON. YOU PLAYED MOST OF THE GAME.
SLAUGHTER?
YUP.
PAT PAT
UGH, OKAY, MY TEAMMATES ARE TELLING ME TO STOP STREAMING SINCE WE'RE LOSING SO BADLY. I'LL POST OUR BOX SCORE TO MY DISCORD LATER TODAY!

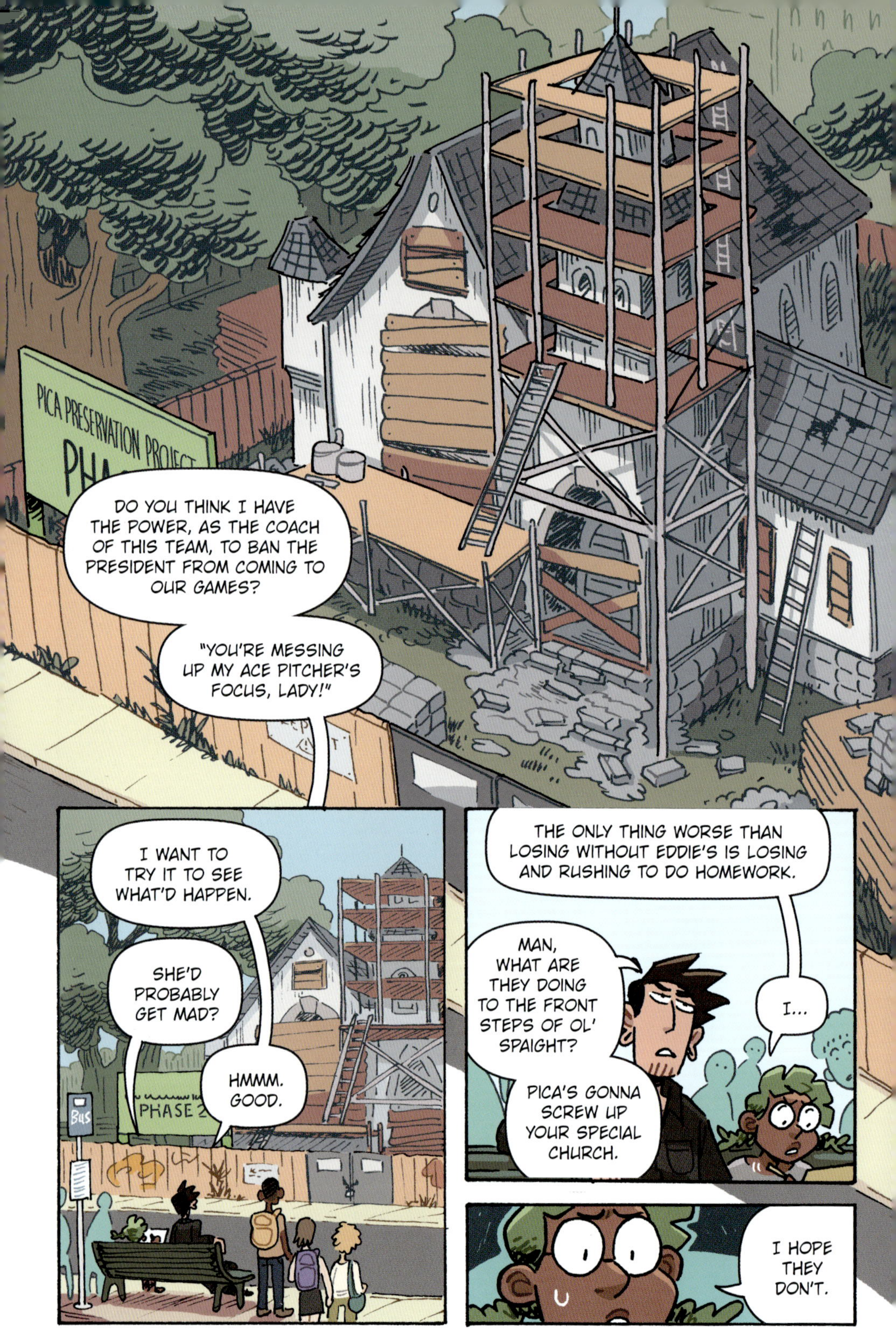
PICA PRESERVATION PROJECT
PHA
DO YOU THINK I HAVE THE POWER, AS THE COACH OF THIS TEAM, TO BAN THE PRESIDENT FROM COMING TO OUR GAMES?
"YOU'RE MESSING UP MY ACE PITCHER'S FOCUS, LADY!"
I WANT TO TRY IT TO SEE WHAT'D HAPPEN.
SHE'D PROBABLY GET MAD?
HMMM. GOOD.
PHASE 2
BUS
THE ONLY THING WORSE THAN LOSING WITHOUT EDDIE'S IS LOSING AND RUSHING TO DO HOMEWORK.
MAN, WHAT ARE THEY DOING TO THE FRONT STEPS OF OL' SPAIGHT?
I...
PICA'S GONNA SCREW UP YOUR SPECIAL CHURCH.
I HOPE THEY DON'T.

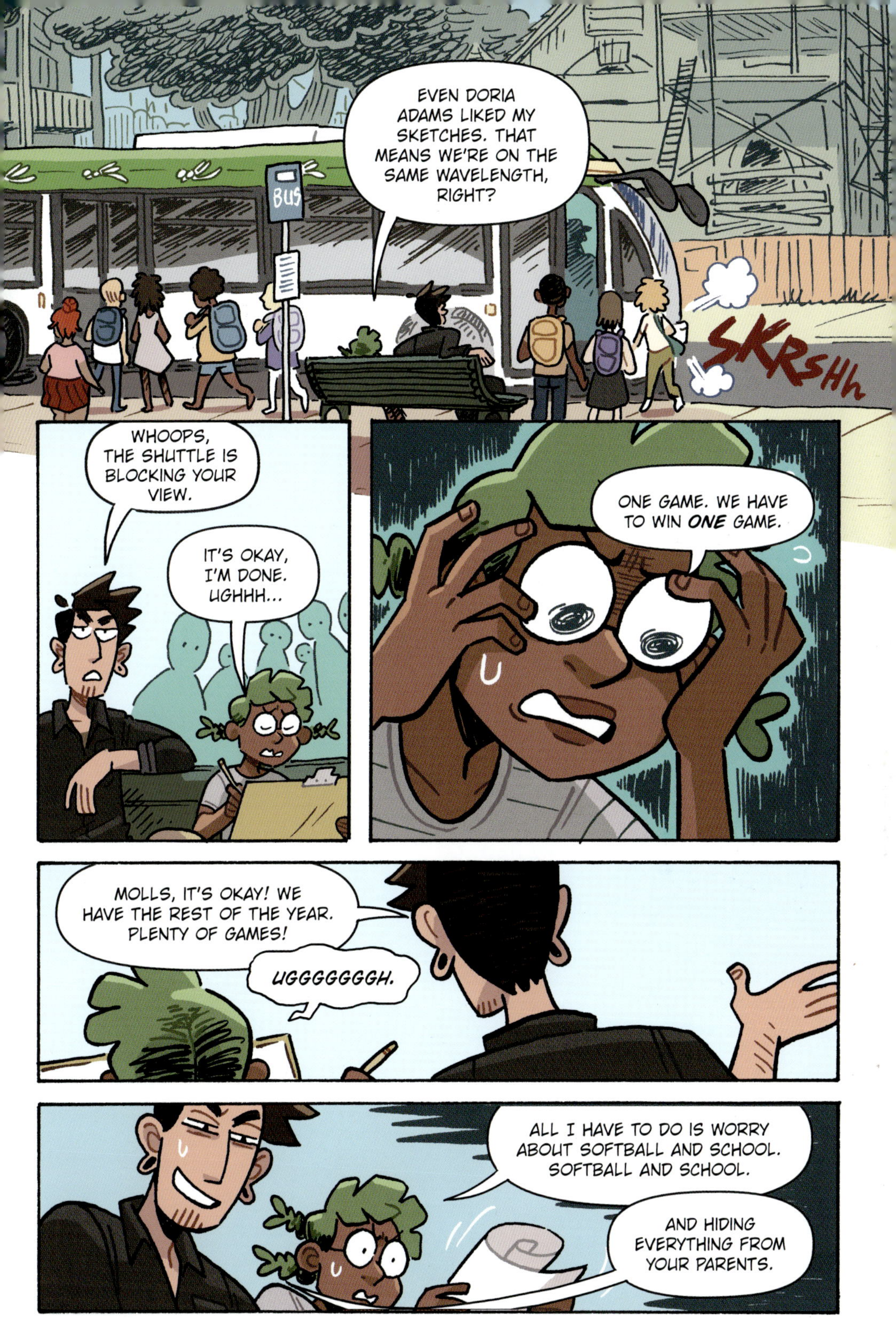
EVEN DORIA ADAMS LIKED MY SKETCHES. THAT MEANS WE'RE ON THE SAME WAVELENGTH, RIGHT?
BUS
SKRSHH
WHOOPS, THE SHUTTLE IS BLOCKING YOUR VIEW.
IT'S OKAY, I'M DONE. UGHHH...
ONE GAME. WE HAVE TO WIN *ONE* GAME.
MOLLS, IT'S OKAY! WE HAVE THE REST OF THE YEAR. PLENTY OF GAMES!
UGGGGGGGH.
ALL I HAVE TO DO IS WORRY ABOUT SOFTBALL AND SCHOOL. SOFTBALL AND SCHOOL.
AND HIDING EVERYTHING FROM YOUR PARENTS.

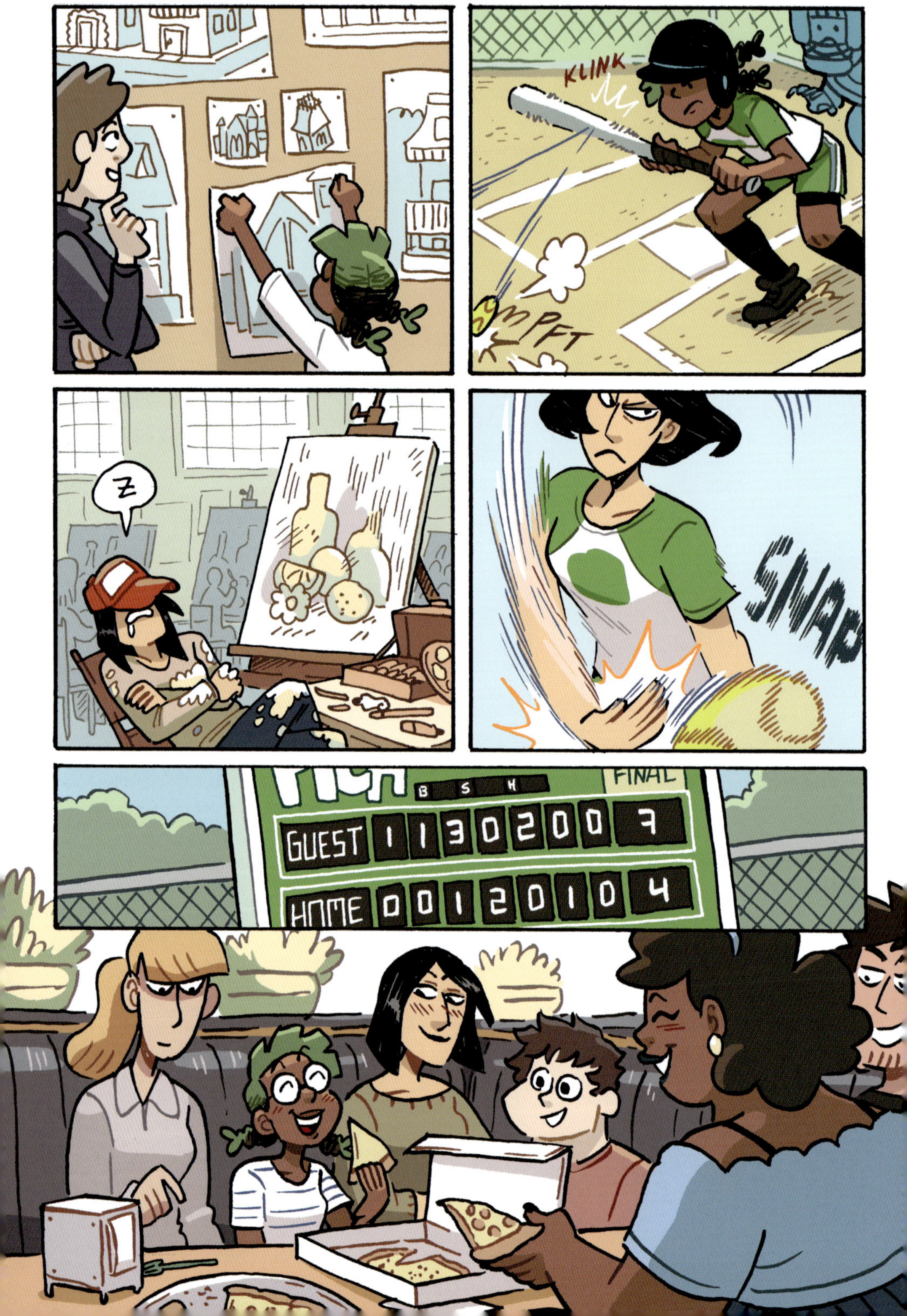
KLINK
MPFT
Z
SNAP
B S H
FINAL
GUEST 1 1 3 0 2 0 0 7
HOME 0 0 1 2 0 1 0 4

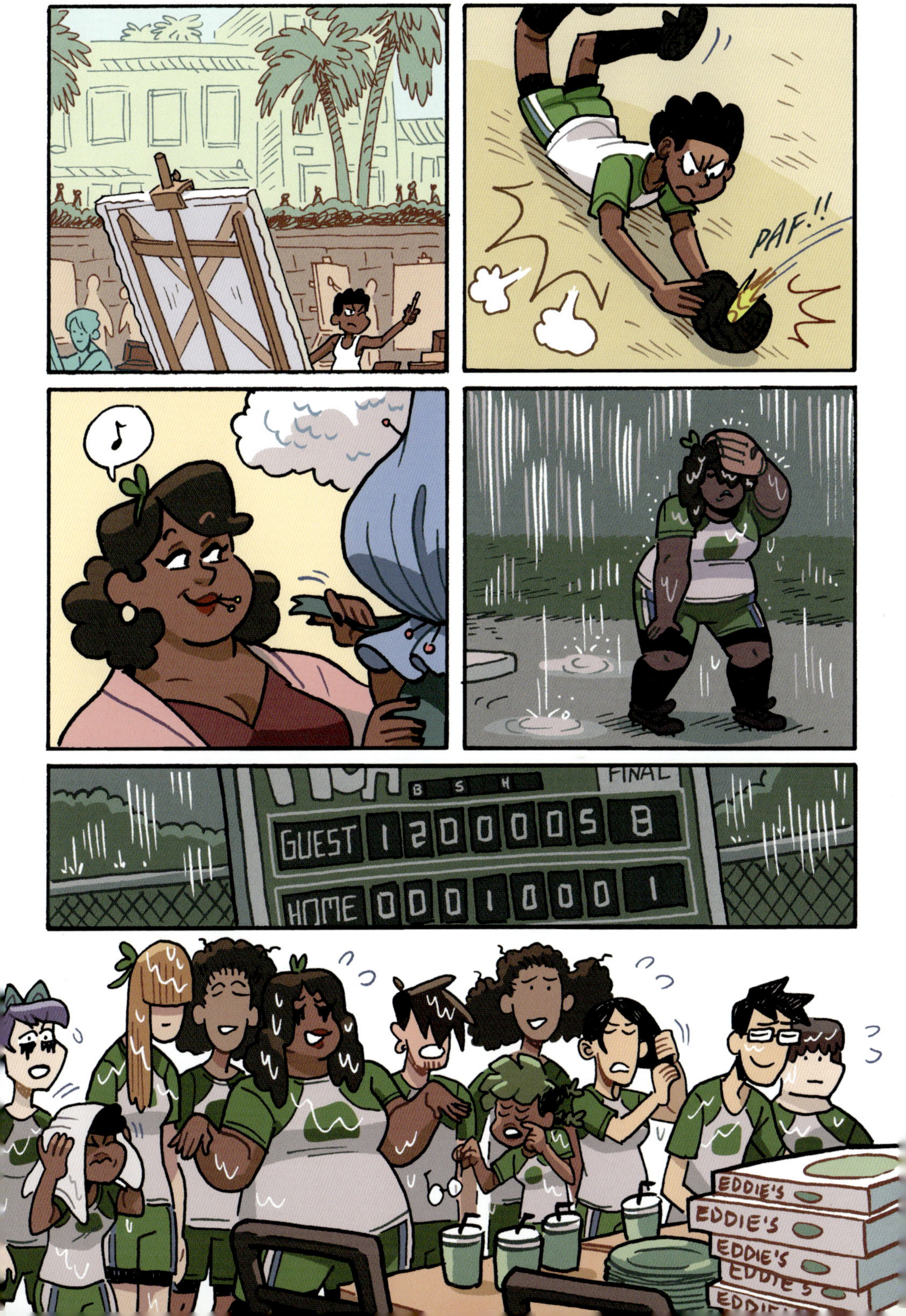
PAF!!
♪
B S H
FINAL
GUEST 1 2 0 0 0 0 5 8
HOME 0 0 0 1 0 0 0 1
EDDIE'S
EDDIE'S
EDDIE'S

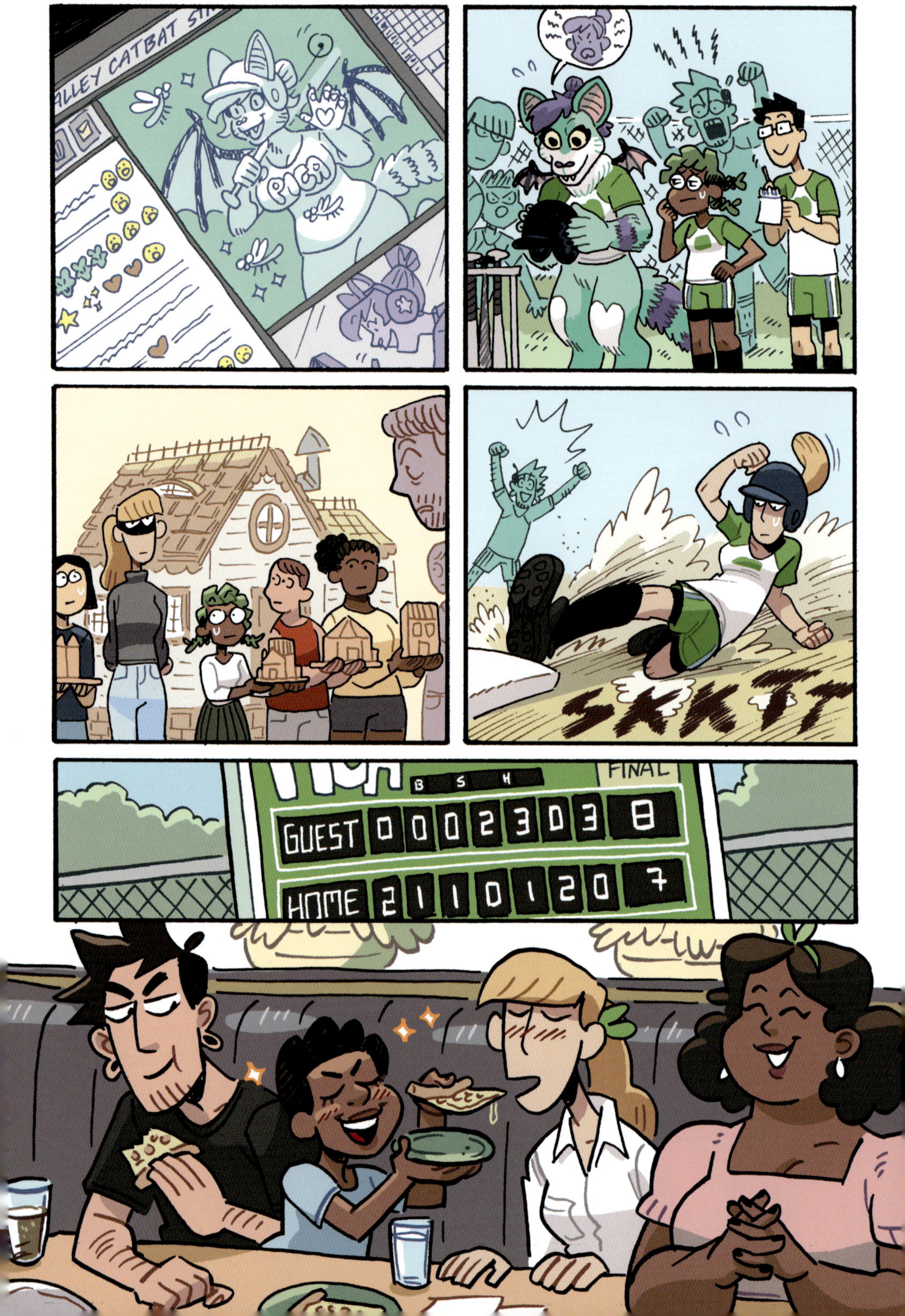
ALLEY CATBAT
PICA
SKKTT
B S H
FINAL
GUEST 0 0 0 2 3 0 3 8
HOME 2 1 1 0 1 2 0 7

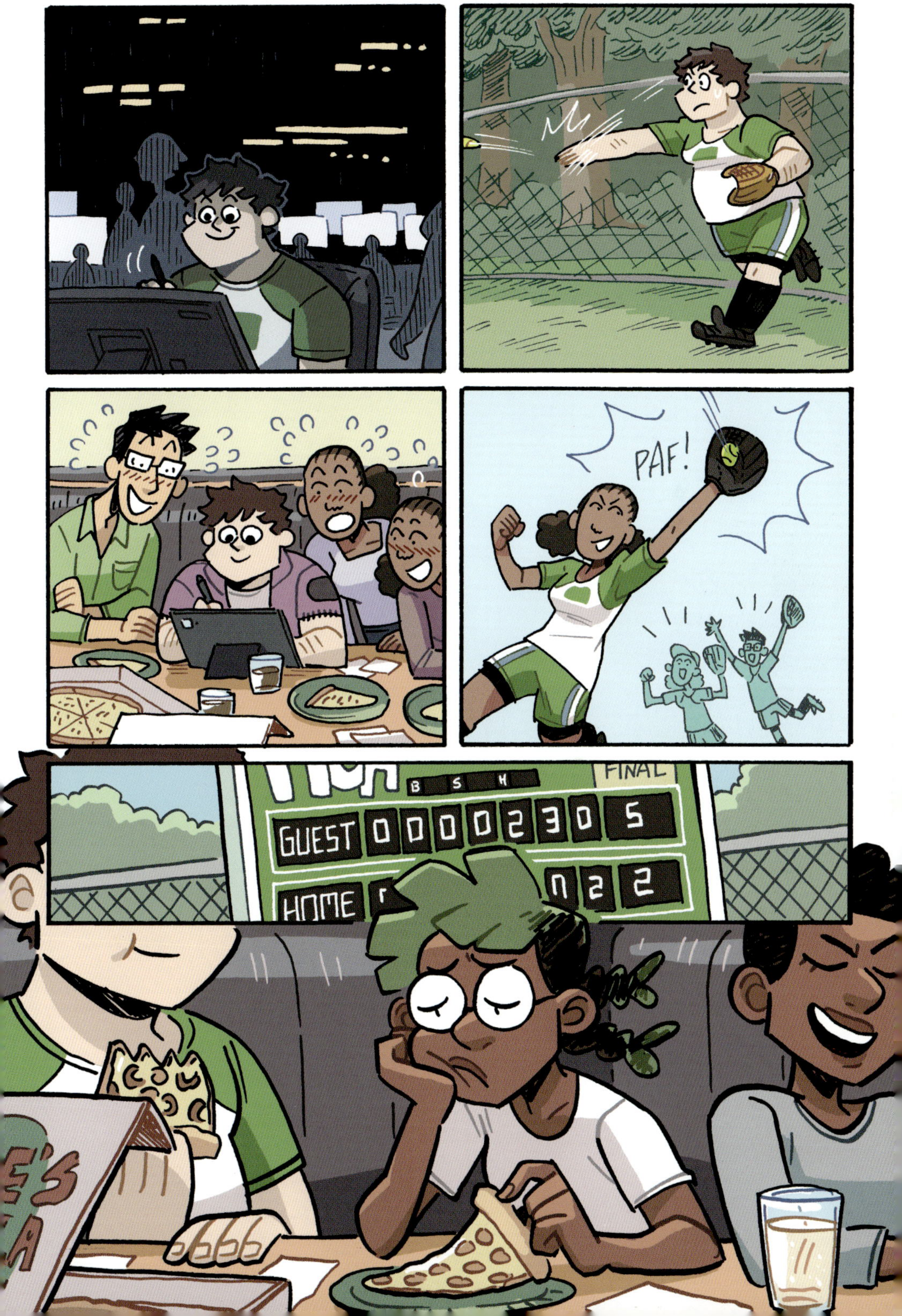
PAF!
FINAL
B S H
GUEST 0 0 0 0 2 3 0 5
HOME
0 2 2

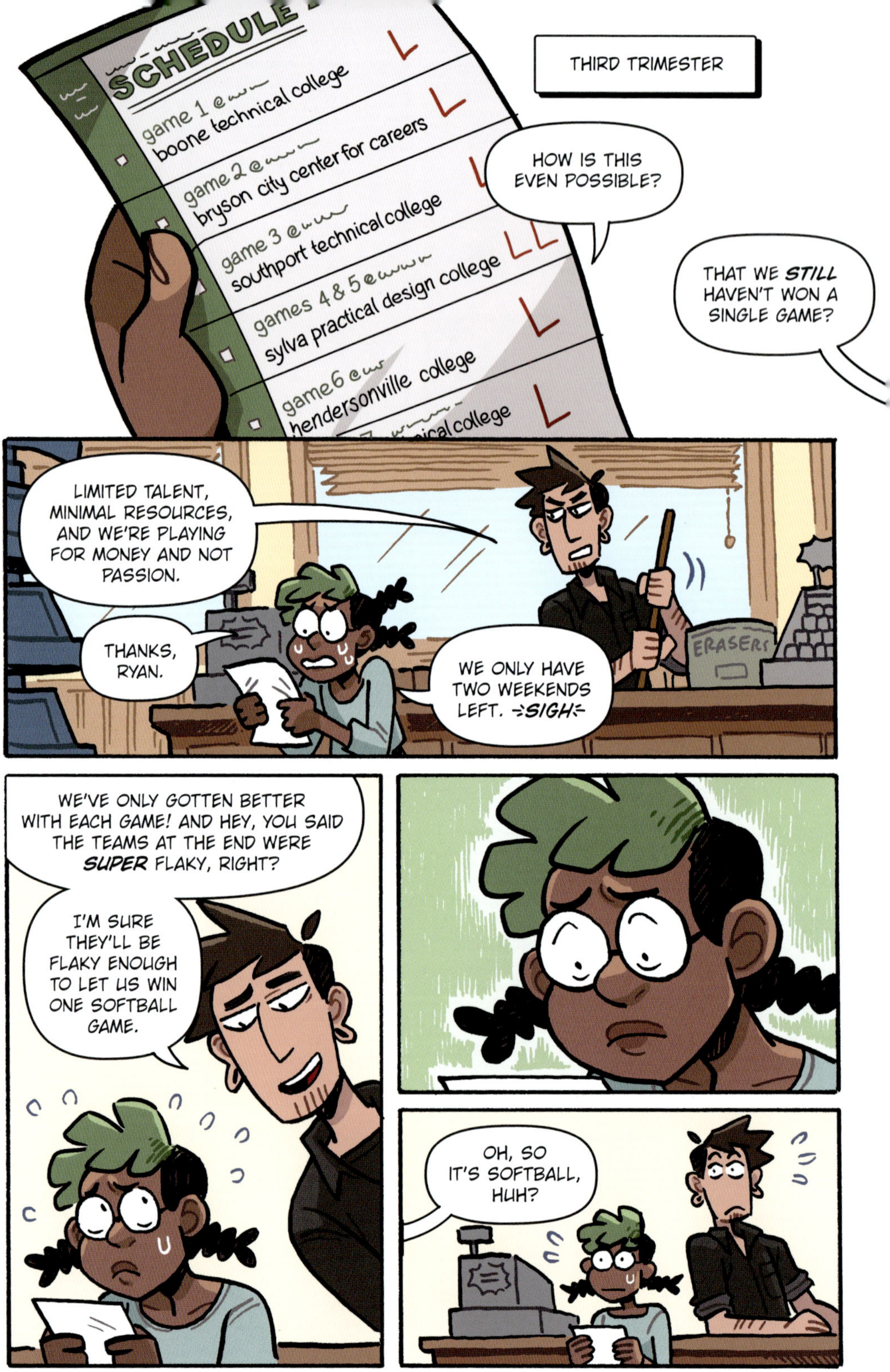
SCHEDULE
game 1 @
boone technical college
game 2 @
bryson city center for careers
game 3 @
southport technical college
games 4 & 5 @
sylva practical design college
game 6 @
hendersonville college
THIRD TRIMESTER
HOW IS THIS EVEN POSSIBLE?
THAT WE *STILL* HAVEN'T WON A SINGLE GAME?
LIMITED TALENT, MINIMAL RESOURCES, AND WE'RE PLAYING FOR MONEY AND NOT PASSION.
THANKS, RYAN.
WE ONLY HAVE TWO WEEKENDS LEFT. *SIGH*
ERASERS
WE'VE ONLY GOTTEN BETTER WITH EACH GAME! AND HEY, YOU SAID THE TEAMS AT THE END WERE *SUPER* FLAKY, RIGHT?
I'M SURE THEY'LL BE FLAKY ENOUGH TO LET US WIN ONE SOFTBALL GAME.
OH, SO IT'S SOFTBALL, HUH?

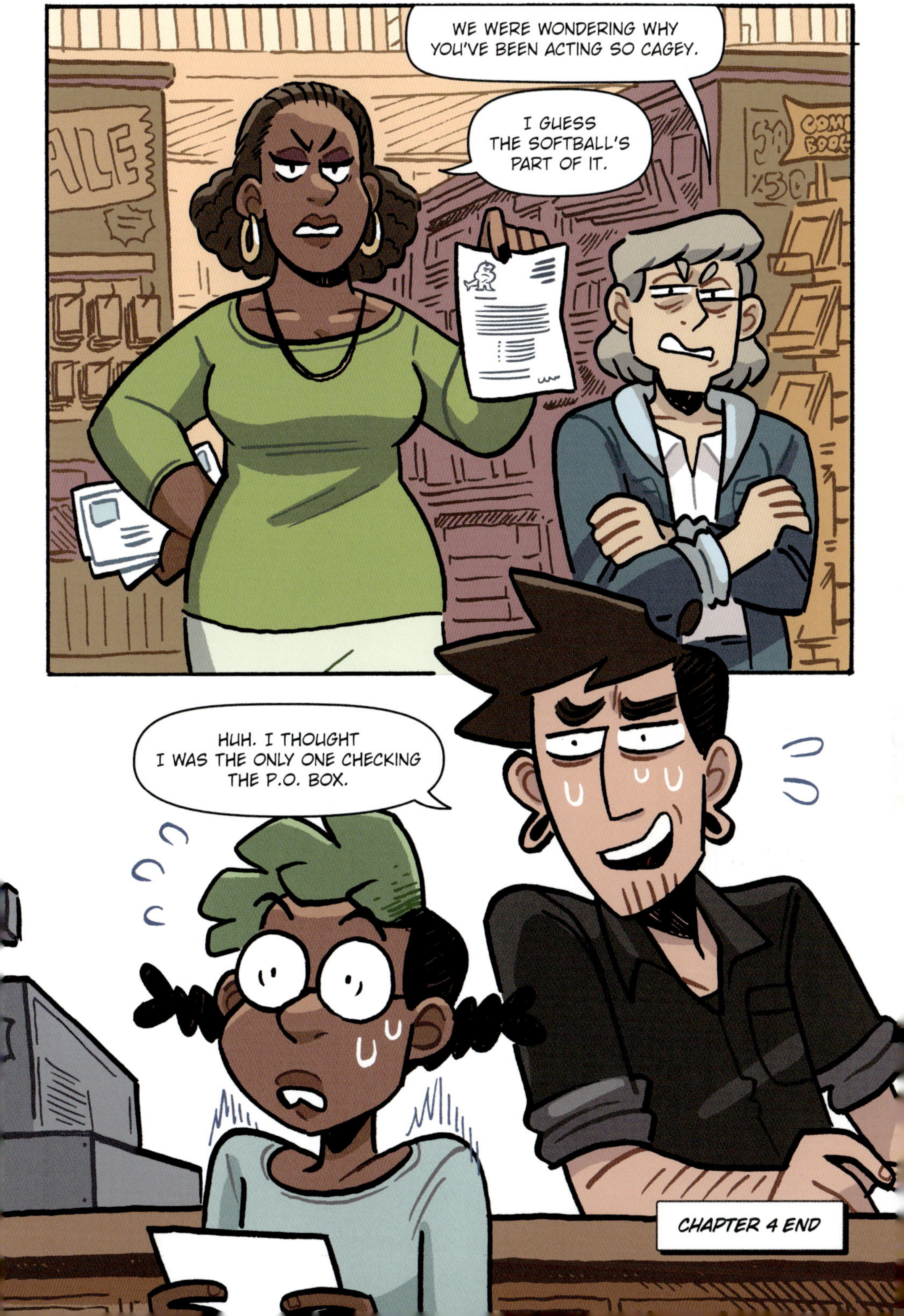
WE WERE WONDERING WHY YOU'VE BEEN ACTING SO CAGEY.
I GUESS THE SOFTBALL'S PART OF IT.
HUH. I THOUGHT I WAS THE ONLY ONE CHECKING THE P.O. BOX.
CHAPTER 4 END

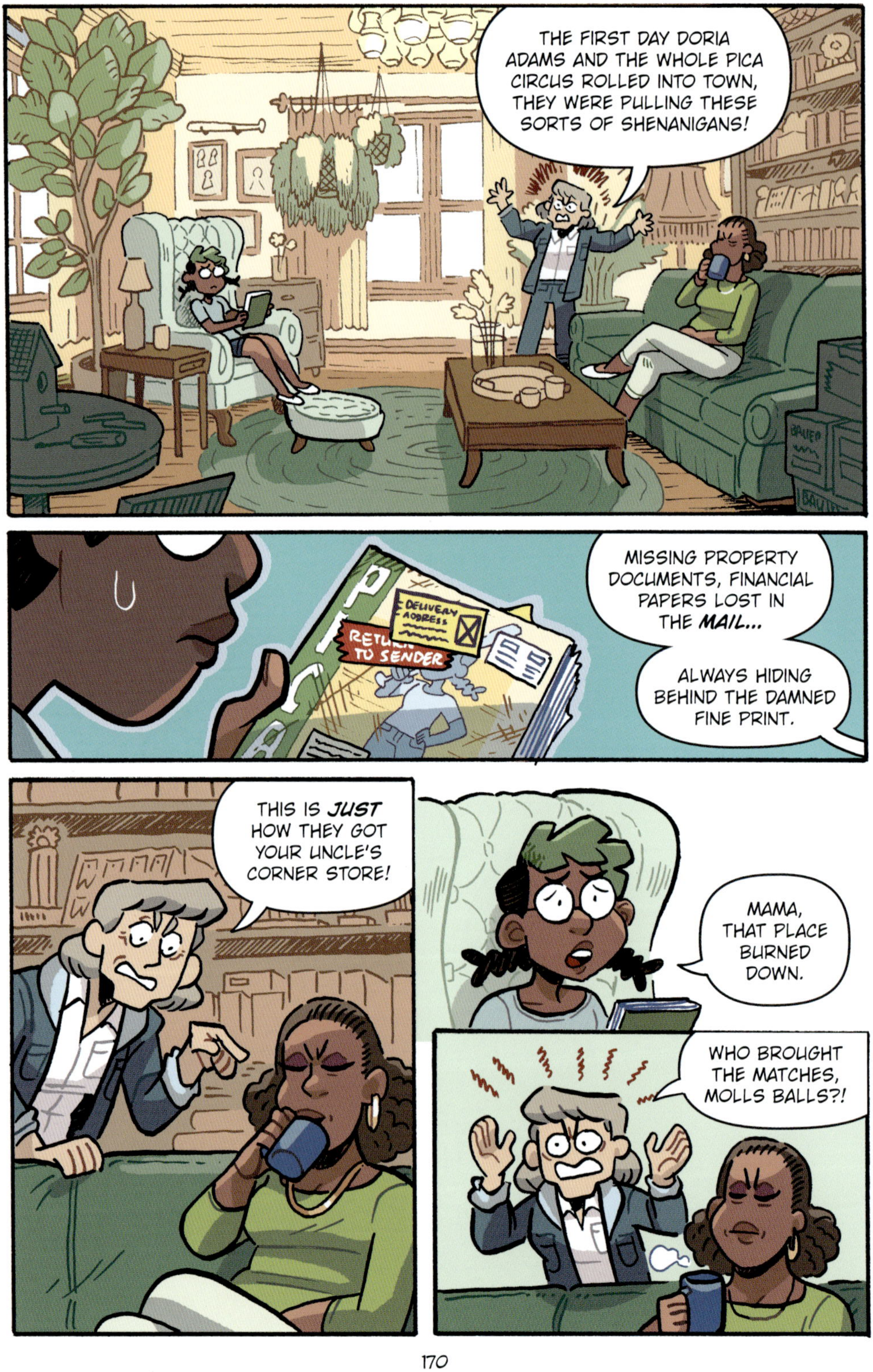
THE FIRST DAY DORIA ADAMS AND THE WHOLE PICA CIRCUS ROLLED INTO TOWN, THEY WERE PULLING THESE SORTS OF SHENANIGANS!
MISSING PROPERTY DOCUMENTS, FINANCIAL PAPERS LOST IN THE *MAIL...*
ALWAYS HIDING BEHIND THE DAMNED FINE PRINT.
DELIVERY ADDRESS
TO SENDER
THIS IS *JUST* HOW THEY GOT YOUR UNCLE'S CORNER STORE!
MAMA, THAT PLACE BURNED DOWN.
WHO BROUGHT THE MATCHES, MOLLS BALLS?!

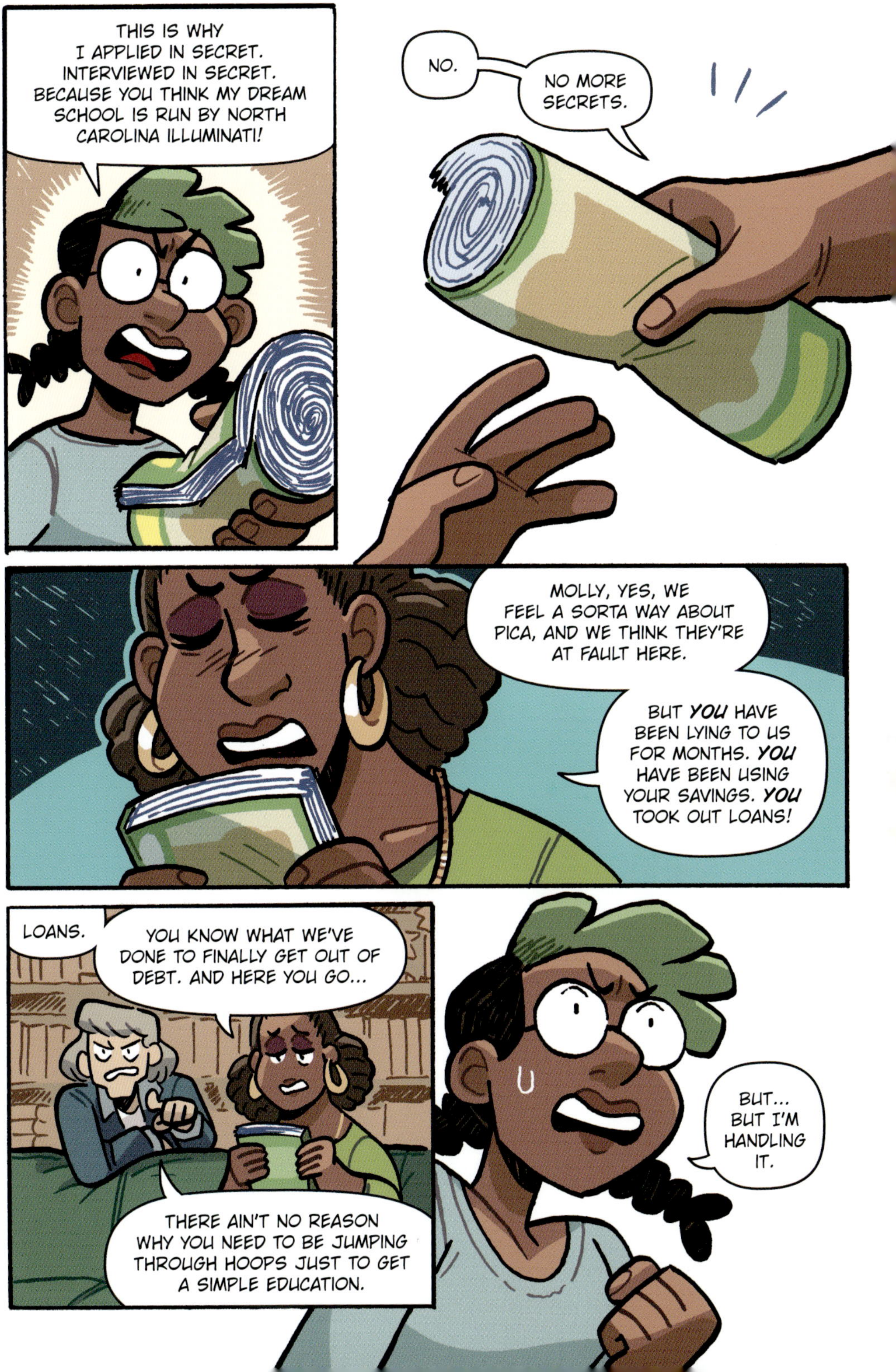

THIS IS WHY I APPLIED IN SECRET. INTERVIEWED IN SECRET. BECAUSE YOU THINK MY DREAM SCHOOL IS RUN BY NORTH CAROLINA ILLUMINATI!
NO.
NO MORE SECRETS.
MOLLY, YES, WE FEEL A SORTA WAY ABOUT PICA, AND WE THINK THEY'RE AT FAULT HERE.
BUT YOU HAVE BEEN LYING TO US FOR MONTHS. YOU HAVE BEEN USING YOUR SAVINGS. YOU TOOK OUT LOANS!
LOANS.
YOU KNOW WHAT WE'VE DONE TO FINALLY GET OUT OF DEBT. AND HERE YOU GO...
THERE AIN'T NO REASON WHY YOU NEED TO BE JUMPING THROUGH HOOPS JUST TO GET A SIMPLE EDUCATION.
BUT... BUT I'M HANDLING IT.

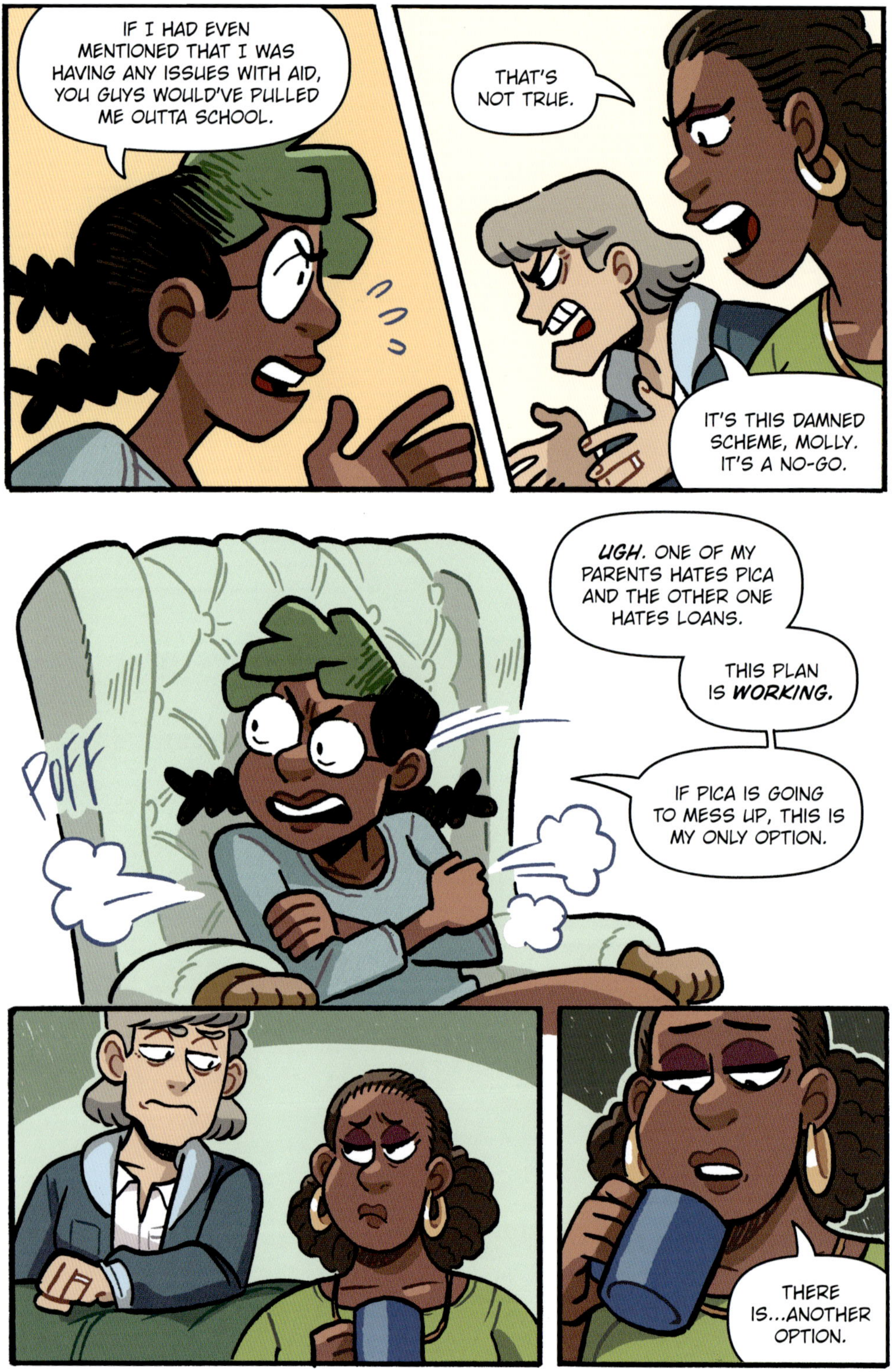
IF I HAD EVEN MENTIONED THAT I WAS HAVING ANY ISSUES WITH AID, YOU GUYS WOULD'VE PULLED ME OUTTA SCHOOL.
THAT'S NOT TRUE.
IT'S THIS DAMNED SCHEME, MOLLY. IT'S A NO-GO.
UGH. ONE OF MY PARENTS HATES PICA AND THE OTHER ONE HATES LOANS.
THIS PLAN IS WORKING.
IF PICA IS GOING TO MESS UP, THIS IS MY ONLY OPTION.
POFF
THERE IS...ANOTHER OPTION.

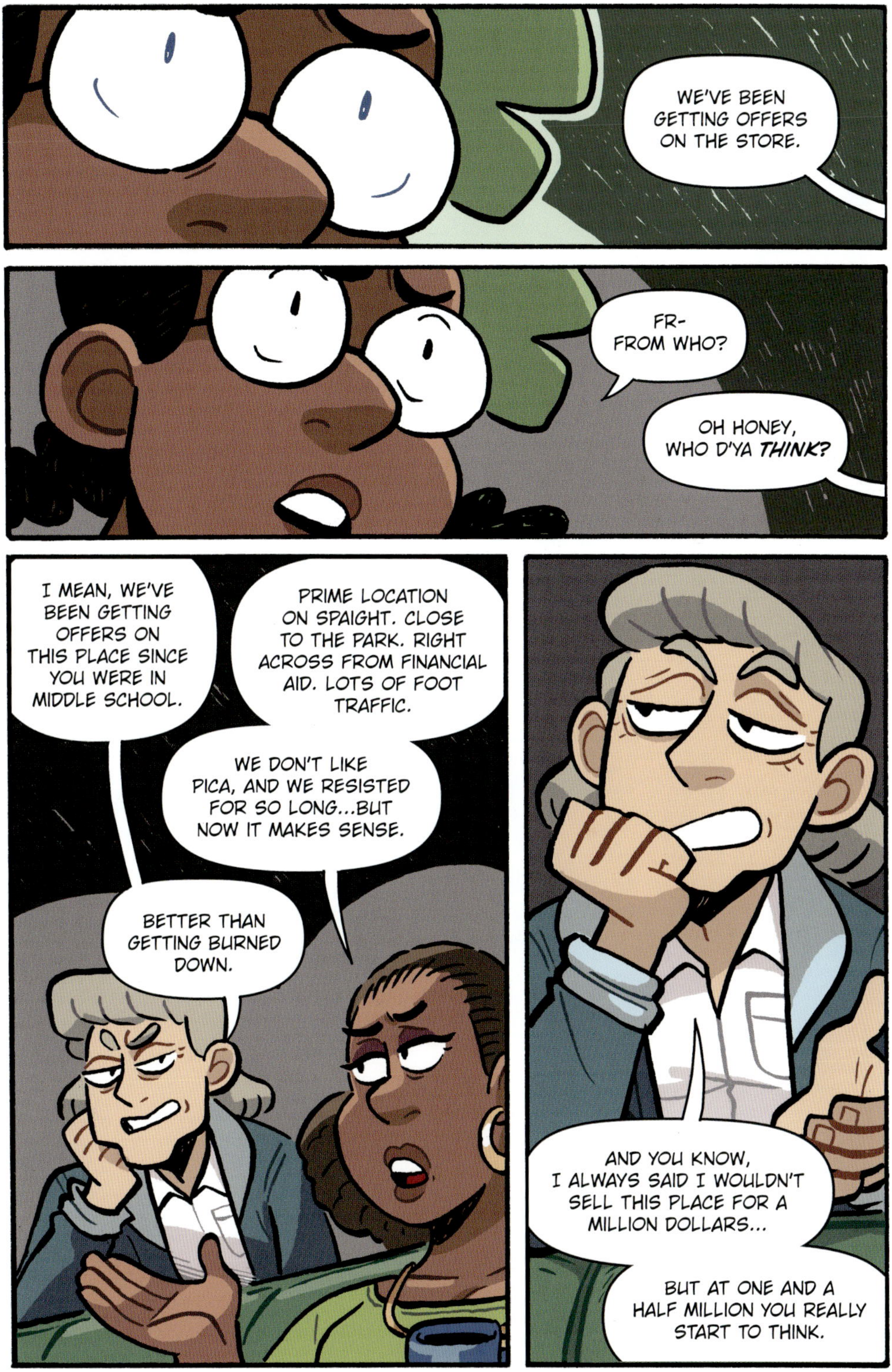
WE'VE BEEN GETTING OFFERS ON THE STORE.
FR- FROM WHO?
OH HONEY, WHO D'YA *THINK?*
I MEAN, WE'VE BEEN GETTING OFFERS ON THIS PLACE SINCE YOU WERE IN MIDDLE SCHOOL.
PRIME LOCATION ON SPAIGHT. CLOSE TO THE PARK. RIGHT ACROSS FROM FINANCIAL AID. LOTS OF FOOT TRAFFIC.
WE DON'T LIKE PICA, AND WE RESISTED FOR SO LONG...BUT NOW IT MAKES SENSE.
BETTER THAN GETTING BURNED DOWN.
AND YOU KNOW, I ALWAYS SAID I WOULDN'T SELL THIS PLACE FOR A MILLION DOLLARS...
BUT AT ONE AND A HALF MILLION YOU REALLY START TO THINK.

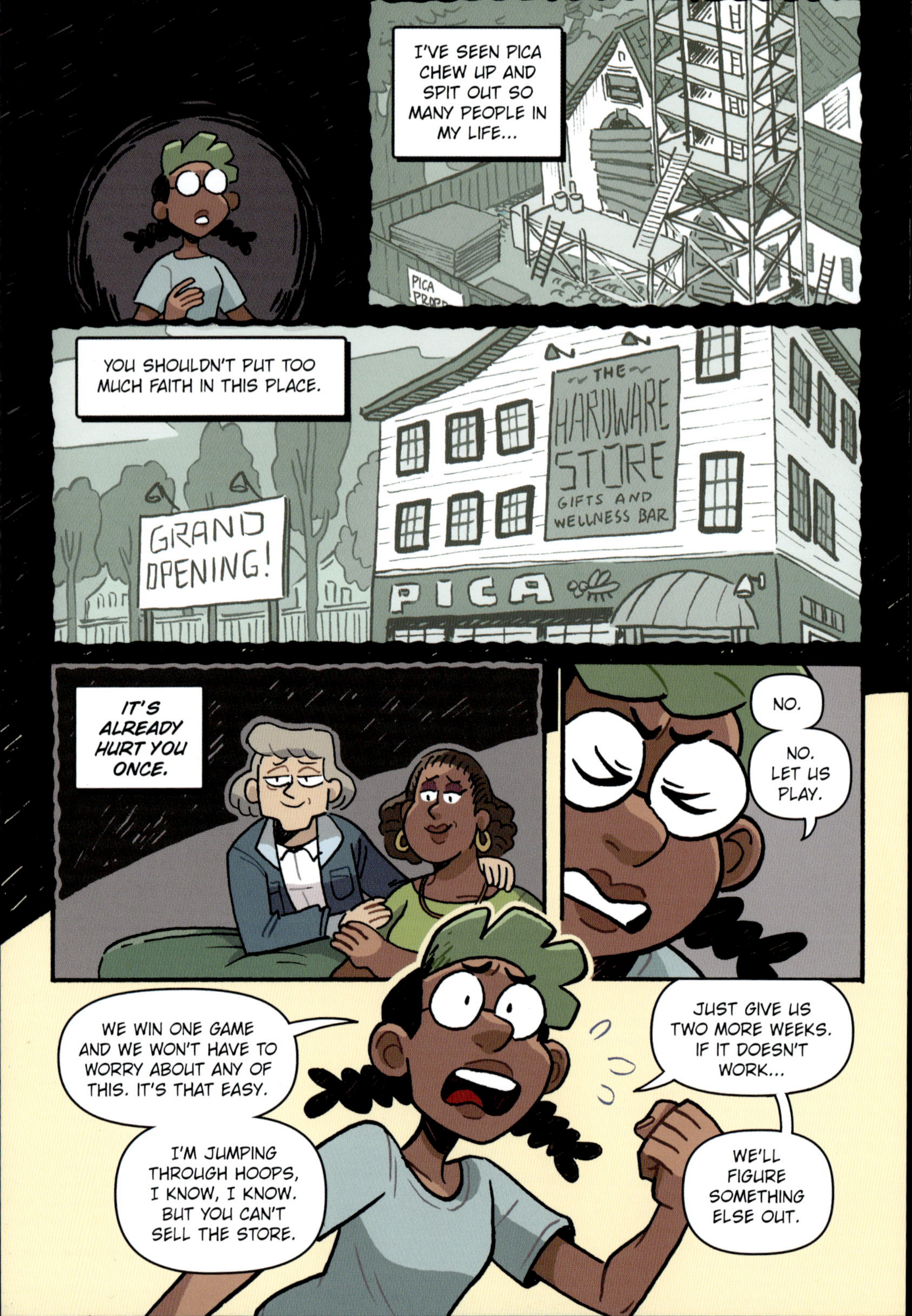
I'VE SEEN PICA CHEW UP AND SPIT OUT SO MANY PEOPLE IN MY LIFE...
PICA
YOU SHOULDN'T PUT TOO MUCH FAITH IN THIS PLACE.
THE HARDWARE STORE
GIFTS AND WELLNESS BAR
GRAND OPENING!
PICA
IT'S ALREADY HURT YOU ONCE.
NO.
NO. LET US PLAY.
WE WIN ONE GAME AND WE WON'T HAVE TO WORRY ABOUT ANY OF THIS. IT'S THAT EASY.
I'M JUMPING THROUGH HOOPS, I KNOW, I KNOW. BUT YOU CAN'T SELL THE STORE.
JUST GIVE US TWO MORE WEEKS. IF IT DOESN'T WORK...
WE'LL FIGURE SOMETHING ELSE OUT.

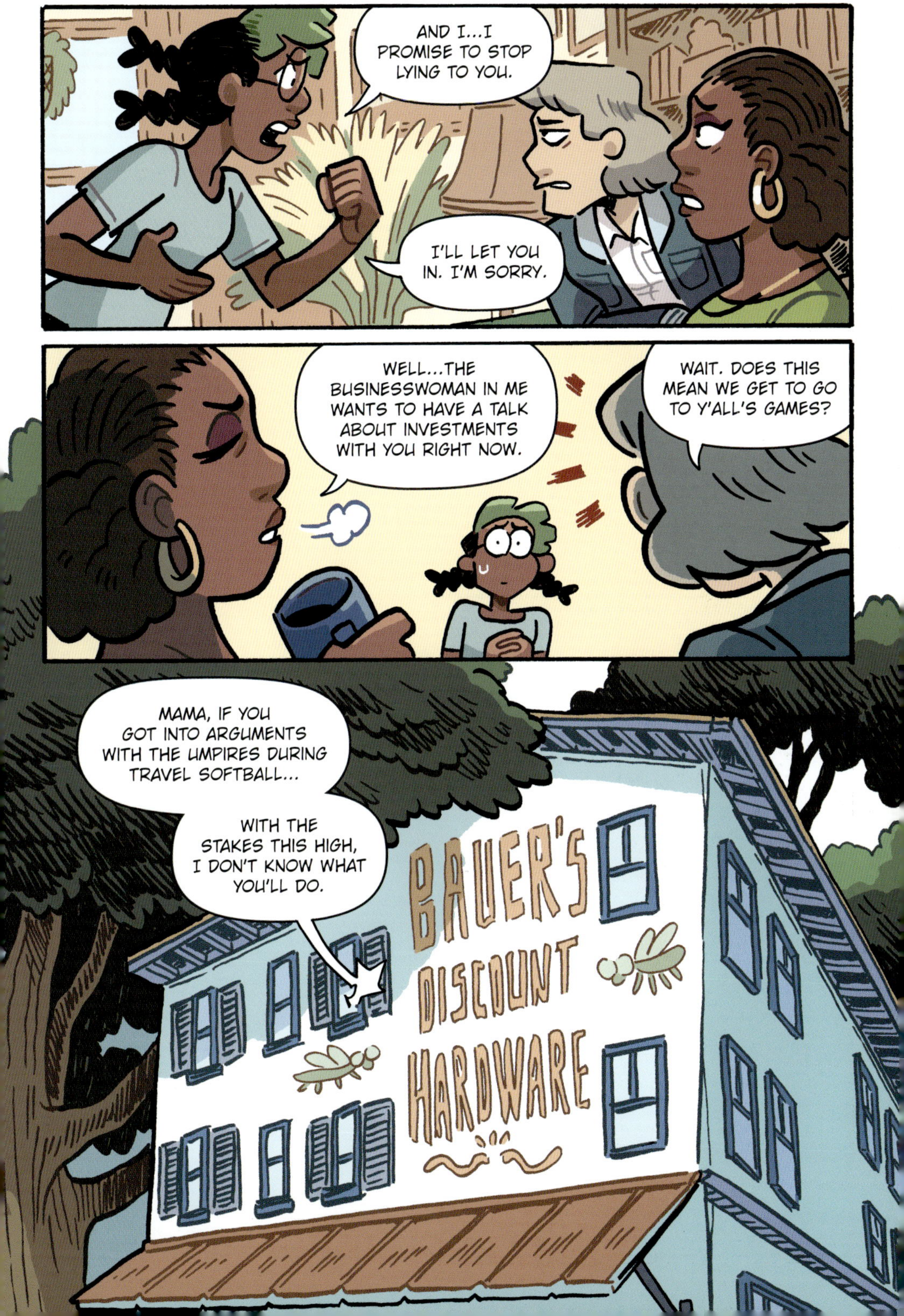
AND I...I PROMISE TO STOP LYING TO YOU.
I'LL LET YOU IN. I'M SORRY.
WELL...THE BUSINESSWOMAN IN ME WANTS TO HAVE A TALK ABOUT INVESTMENTS WITH YOU RIGHT NOW.
WAIT. DOES THIS MEAN WE GET TO GO TO Y'ALL'S GAMES?
MAMA, IF YOU GOT INTO ARGUMENTS WITH THE UMPIRES DURING TRAVEL SOFTBALL...
WITH THE STAKES THIS HIGH, I DON'T KNOW WHAT YOU'LL DO.
BAUER'S DISCOUNT HARDWARE

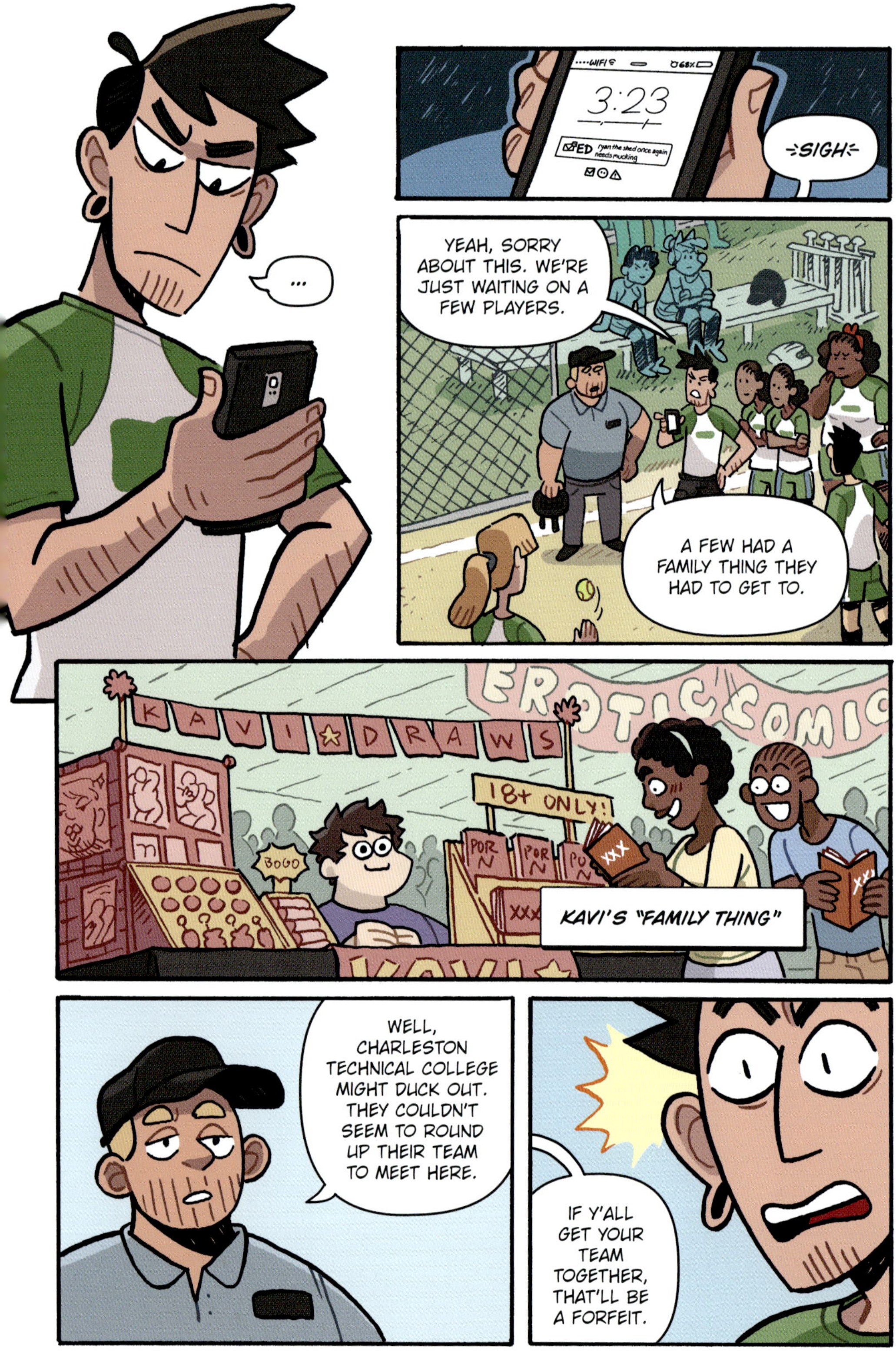
...
3:23
ED ryan the shed once again needs mucking
SIGH
YEAH, SORRY ABOUT THIS. WE'RE JUST WAITING ON A FEW PLAYERS.
A FEW HAD A FAMILY THING THEY HAD TO GET TO.
KAVI DRAWS
EROTIC COMIC
18+ ONLY!
BOGO
PORN
XXX
KAVI'S "FAMILY THING"
WELL, CHARLESTON TECHNICAL COLLEGE MIGHT DUCK OUT. THEY COULDN'T SEEM TO ROUND UP THEIR TEAM TO MEET HERE.
IF Y'ALL GET YOUR TEAM TOGETHER, THAT'LL BE A FORFEIT.

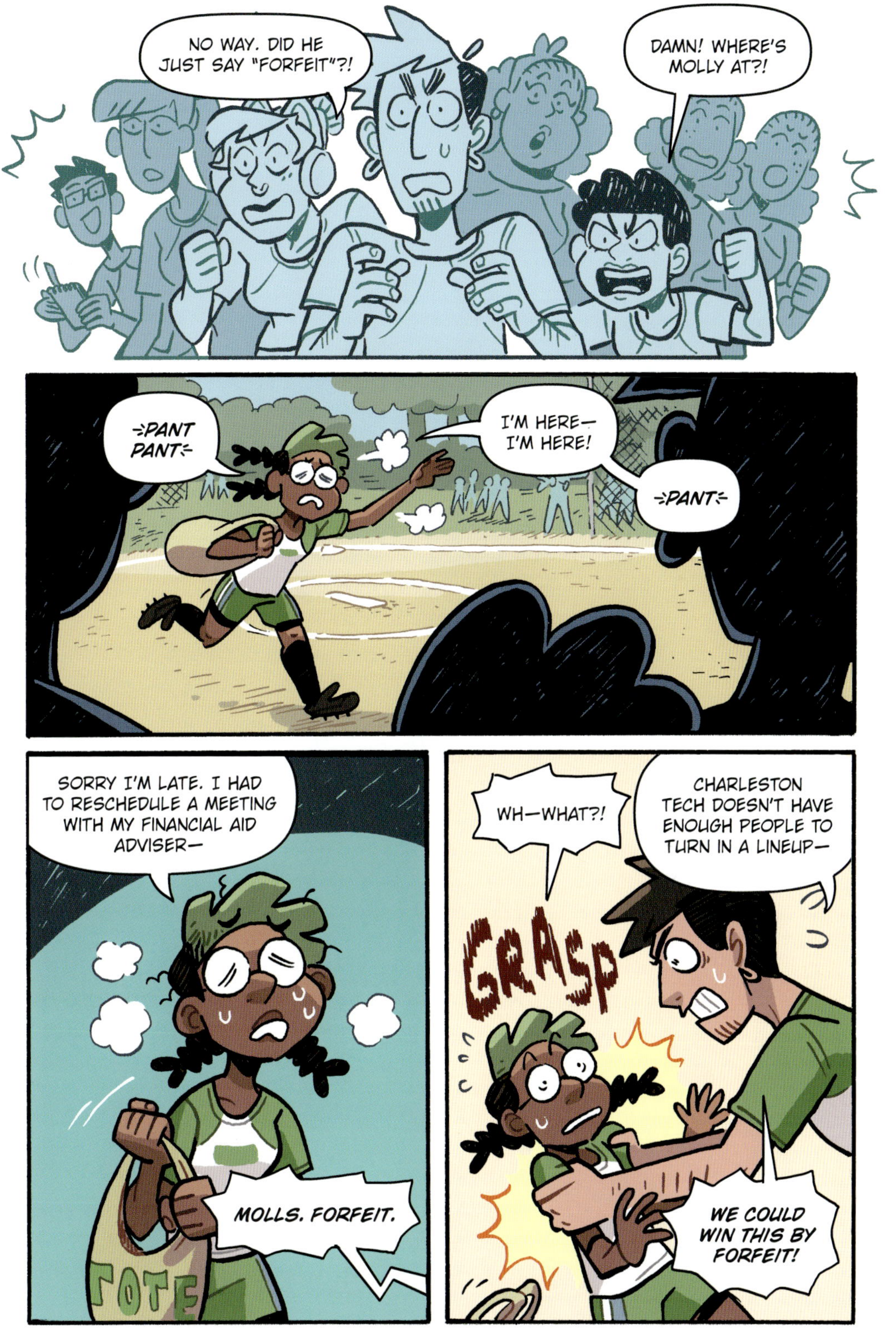
NO WAY. DID HE JUST SAY "FORFEIT"?!
DAMN! WHERE'S MOLLY AT?!
PANT PANT
I'M HERE— I'M HERE!
PANT
SORRY I'M LATE. I HAD TO RESCHEDULE A MEETING WITH MY FINANCIAL AID ADVISER—
MOLLS. FORFEIT.
TOTE
WH—WHAT?!
CHARLESTON TECH DOESN'T HAVE ENOUGH PEOPLE TO TURN IN A LINEUP—
GRASP
WE COULD WIN THIS BY FORFEIT!

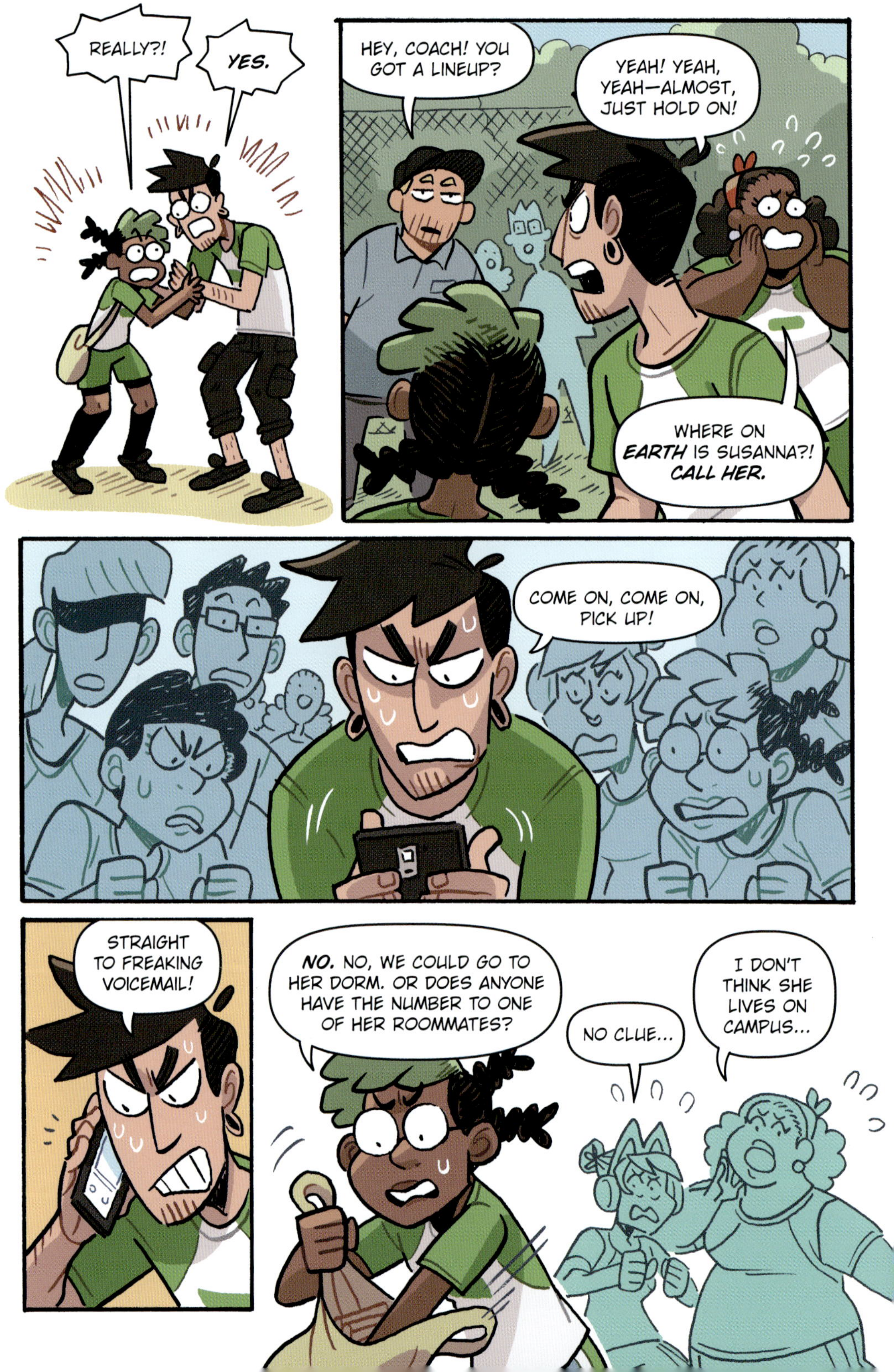
REALLY?!
YES.
HEY, COACH! YOU GOT A LINEUP?
YEAH! YEAH, YEAH—ALMOST, JUST HOLD ON!
WHERE ON EARTH IS SUSANNA?! CALL HER.
COME ON, COME ON, PICK UP!
STRAIGHT TO FREAKING VOICEMAIL!
NO. NO, WE COULD GO TO HER DORM. OR DOES ANYONE HAVE THE NUMBER TO ONE OF HER ROOMMATES?
NO CLUE...
I DON'T THINK SHE LIVES ON CAMPUS...

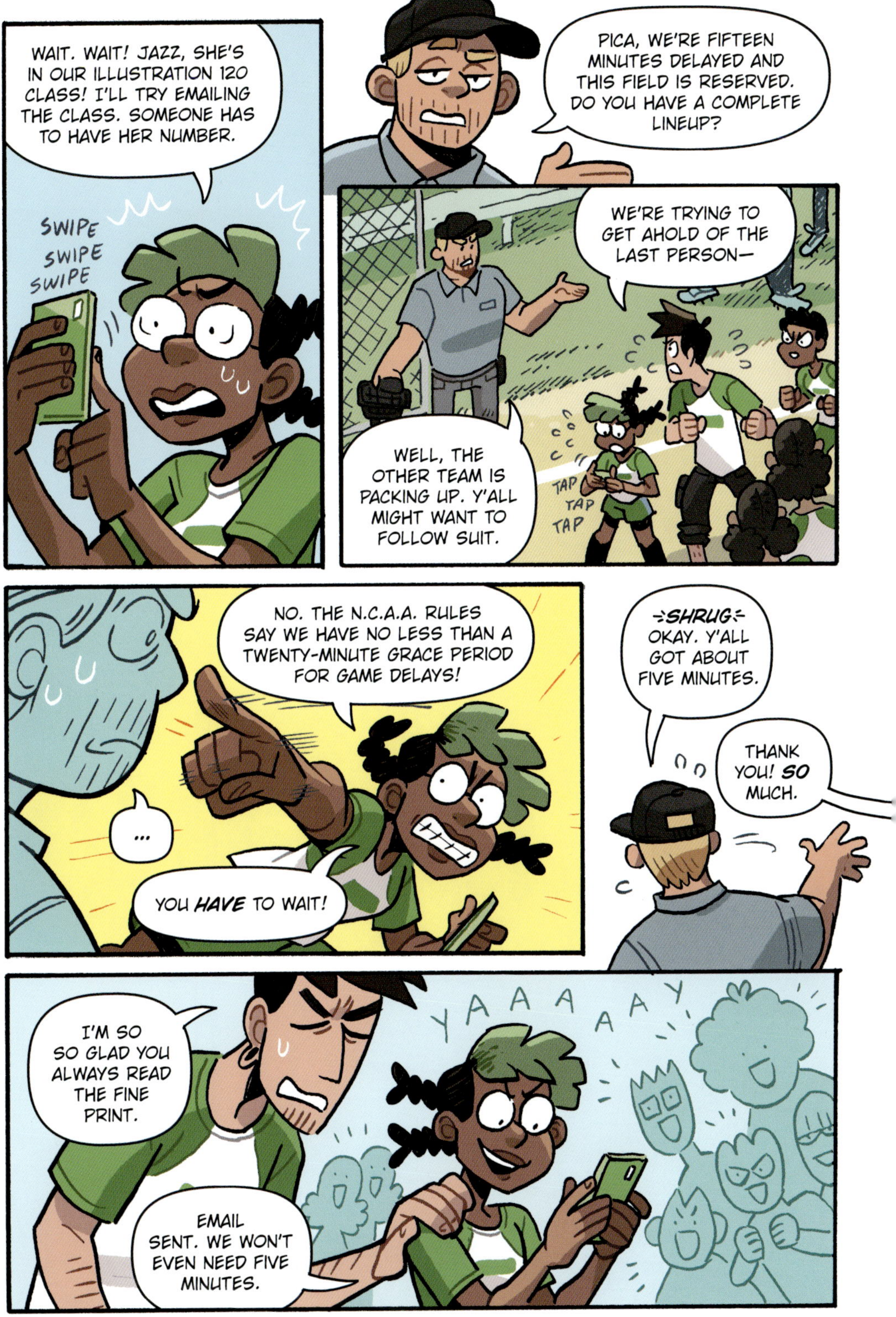
WAIT. WAIT! JAZZ, SHE'S IN OUR ILLUSTRATION 120 CLASS! I'LL TRY EMAILING THE CLASS. SOMEONE HAS TO HAVE HER NUMBER.
SWIPE SWIPE SWIPE
PICA, WE'RE FIFTEEN MINUTES DELAYED AND THIS FIELD IS RESERVED. DO YOU HAVE A COMPLETE LINEUP?
WE'RE TRYING TO GET AHOLD OF THE LAST PERSON—
WELL, THE OTHER TEAM IS PACKING UP. Y'ALL MIGHT WANT TO FOLLOW SUIT.
TAP TAP TAP
NO. THE N.C.A.A. RULES SAY WE HAVE NO LESS THAN A TWENTY-MINUTE GRACE PERIOD FOR GAME DELAYS!
...
YOU *HAVE* TO WAIT!
SHRUG OKAY. Y'ALL GOT ABOUT FIVE MINUTES.
THANK YOU! *SO* MUCH.
I'M SO SO GLAD YOU ALWAYS READ THE FINE PRINT.
YAAAAAY
EMAIL SENT. WE WON'T EVEN NEED FIVE MINUTES.

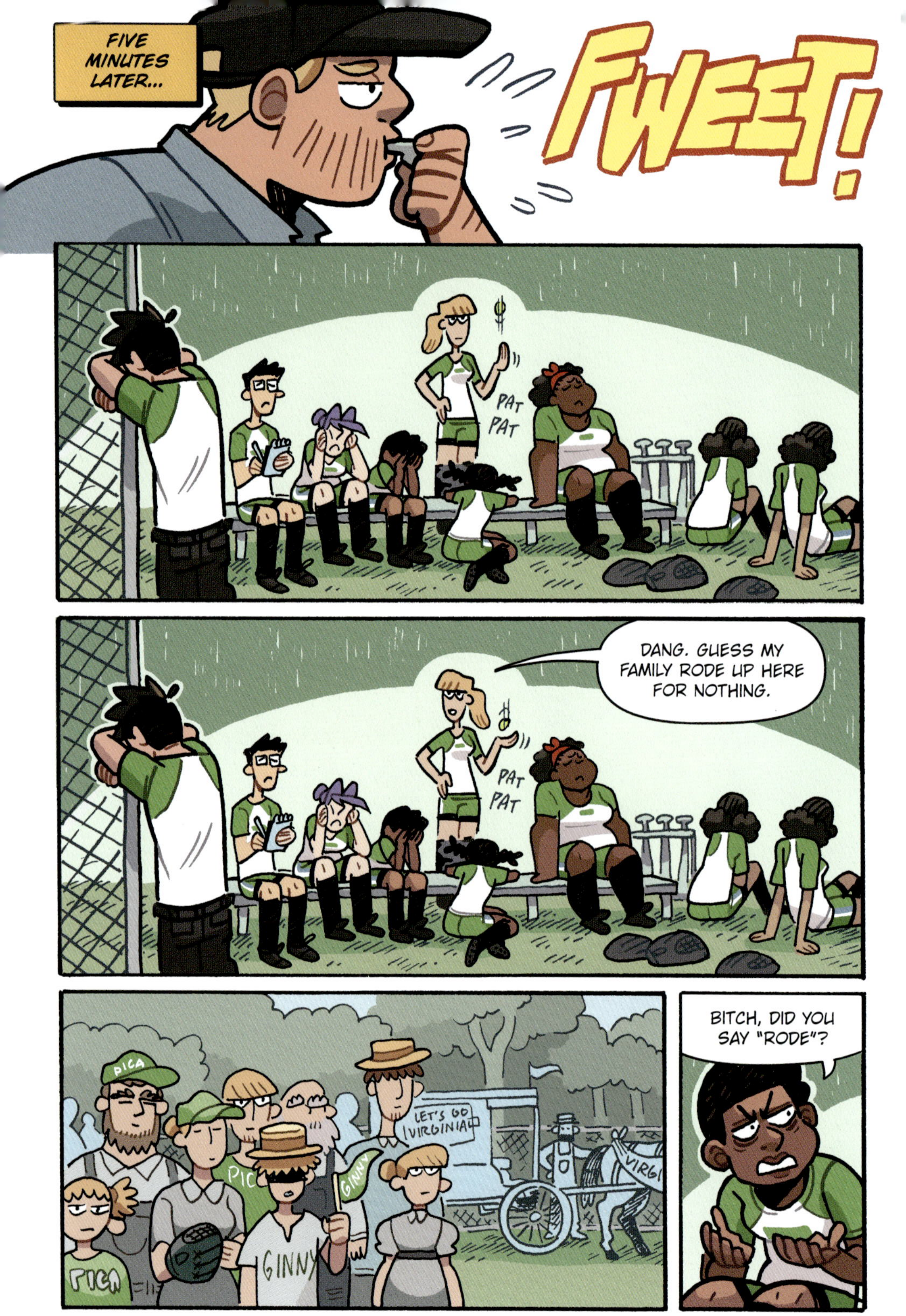
FIVE MINUTES LATER...
FWEET!
PAT PAT
PAT PAT
DANG. GUESS MY FAMILY RODE UP HERE FOR NOTHING.
PICA
LET'S GO VIRGINIA!
PIC
GINNY
VIRGI
GINNY
PICA
BITCH, DID YOU SAY "RODE"?

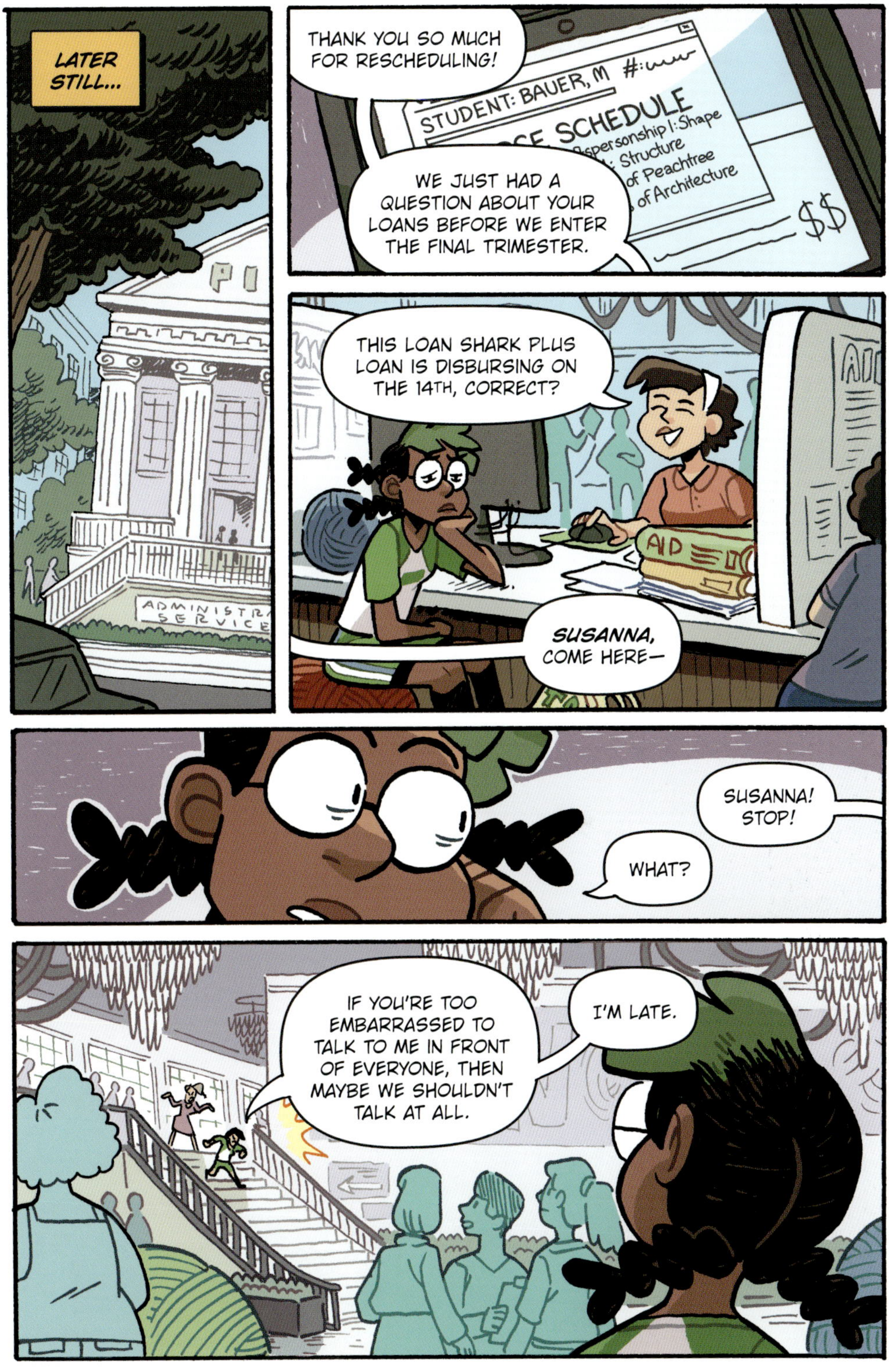
LATER STILL...
PI
ADMINISTRA
SERVICE
THANK YOU SO MUCH FOR RESCHEDULING!
STUDENT: BAUER, M
SCHEDULE
WE JUST HAD A QUESTION ABOUT YOUR LOANS BEFORE WE ENTER THE FINAL TRIMESTER.
THIS LOAN SHARK PLUS LOAN IS DISBURSING ON THE 14TH, CORRECT?
AID
SUSANNA, COME HERE—
SUSANNA! STOP!
WHAT?
IF YOU'RE TOO EMBARRASSED TO TALK TO ME IN FRONT OF EVERYONE, THEN MAYBE WE SHOULDN'T TALK AT ALL.
I'M LATE.

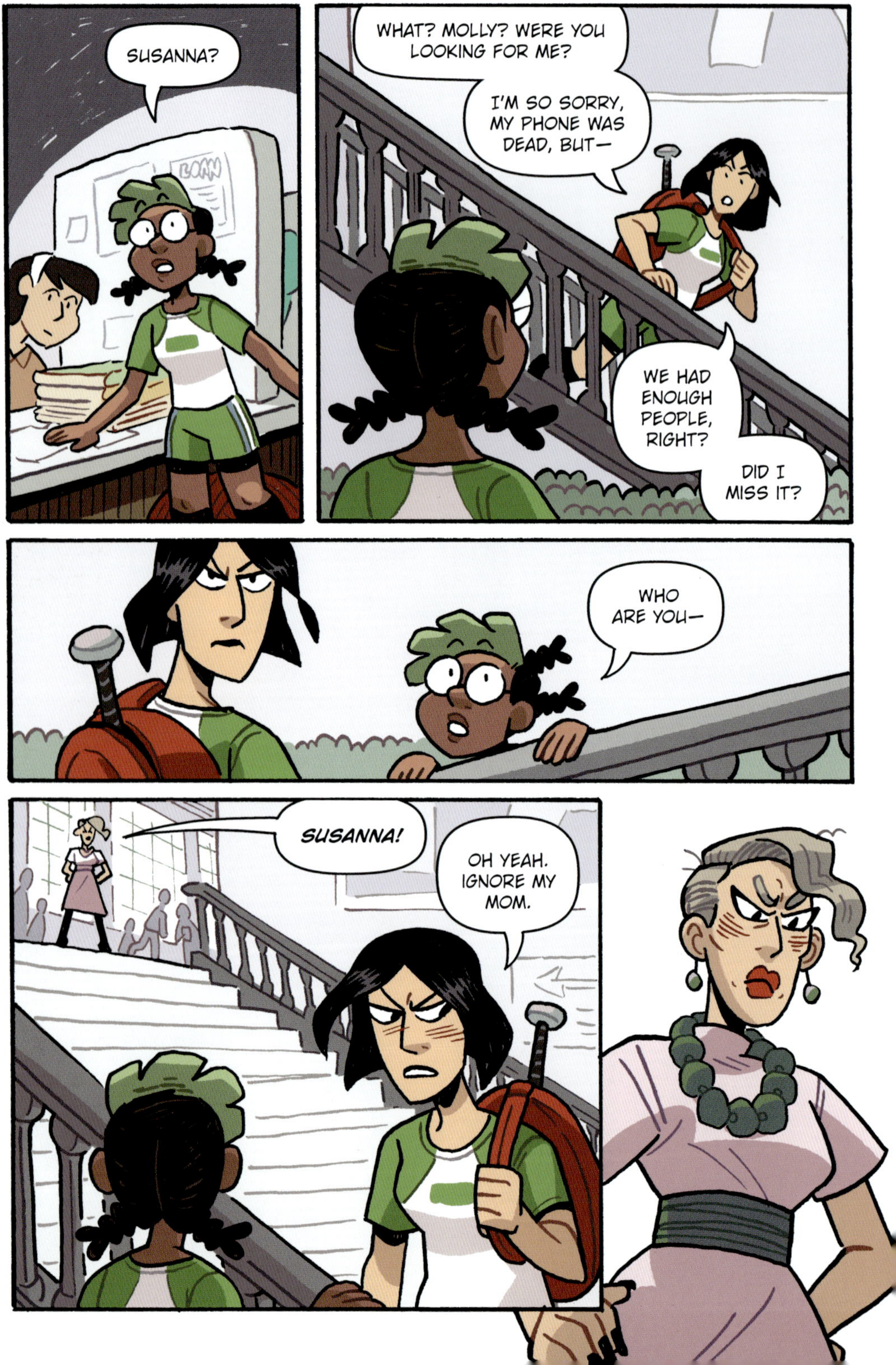
SUSANNA?
WHAT? MOLLY? WERE YOU LOOKING FOR ME?
I'M SO SORRY, MY PHONE WAS DEAD, BUT—
WE HAD ENOUGH PEOPLE, RIGHT?
DID I MISS IT?
WHO ARE YOU—
SUSANNA!
OH YEAH. IGNORE MY MOM.

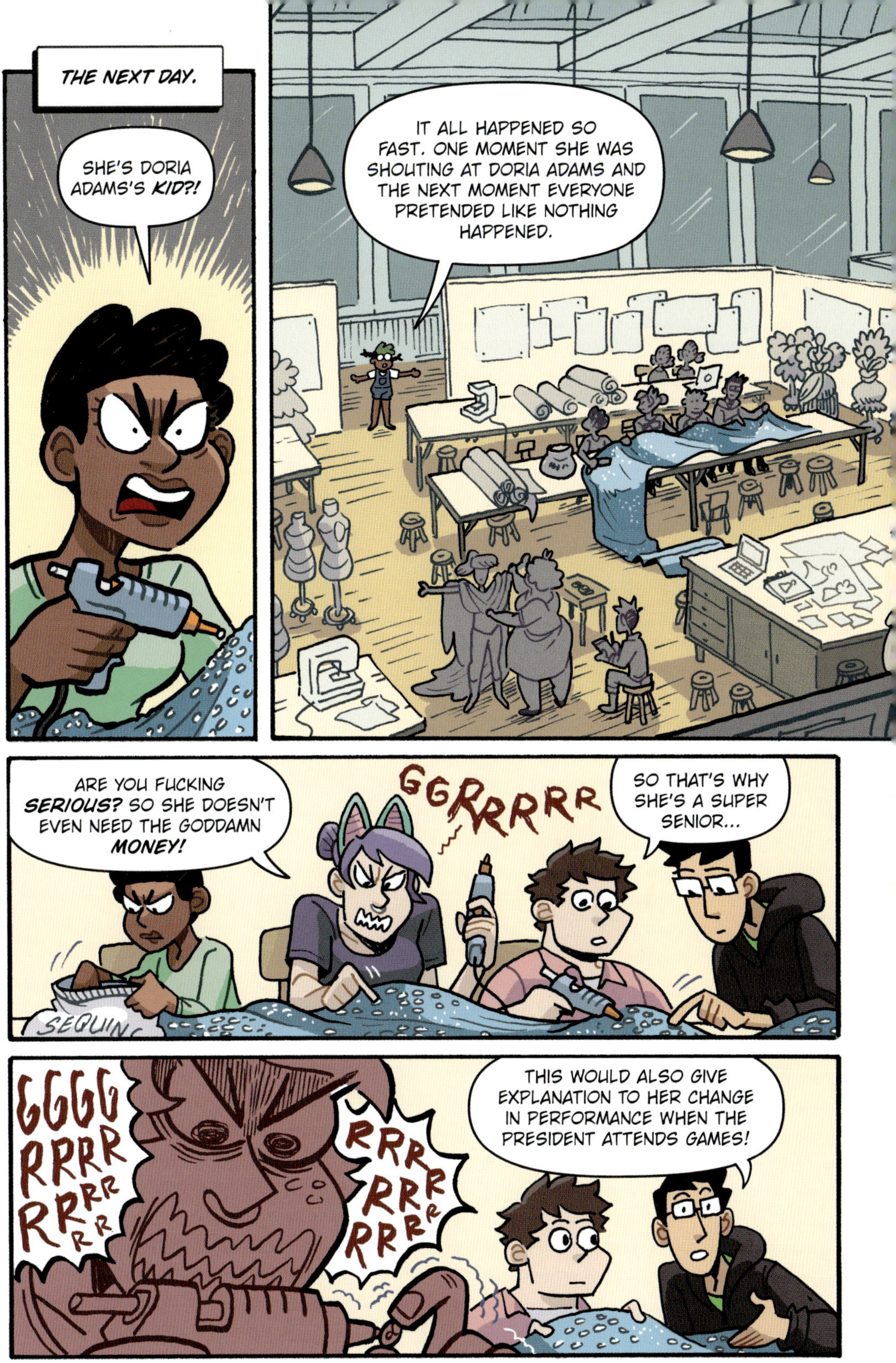

THE NEXT DAY.
SHE'S DORIA ADAMS'S *KID?!*
IT ALL HAPPENED SO FAST. ONE MOMENT SHE WAS SHOUTING AT DORIA ADAMS AND THE NEXT MOMENT EVERYONE PRETENDED LIKE NOTHING HAPPENED.
ARE YOU FUCKING ***SERIOUS?*** SO SHE DOESN'T EVEN NEED THE GODDAMN ***MONEY!***
GGRRRRRR
SO THAT'S WHY SHE'S A SUPER SENIOR...
SEQUIN
GGGGRRRRRRRRR
RRRRRRRRR
THIS WOULD ALSO GIVE EXPLANATION TO HER CHANGE IN PERFORMANCE WHEN THE PRESIDENT ATTENDS GAMES!

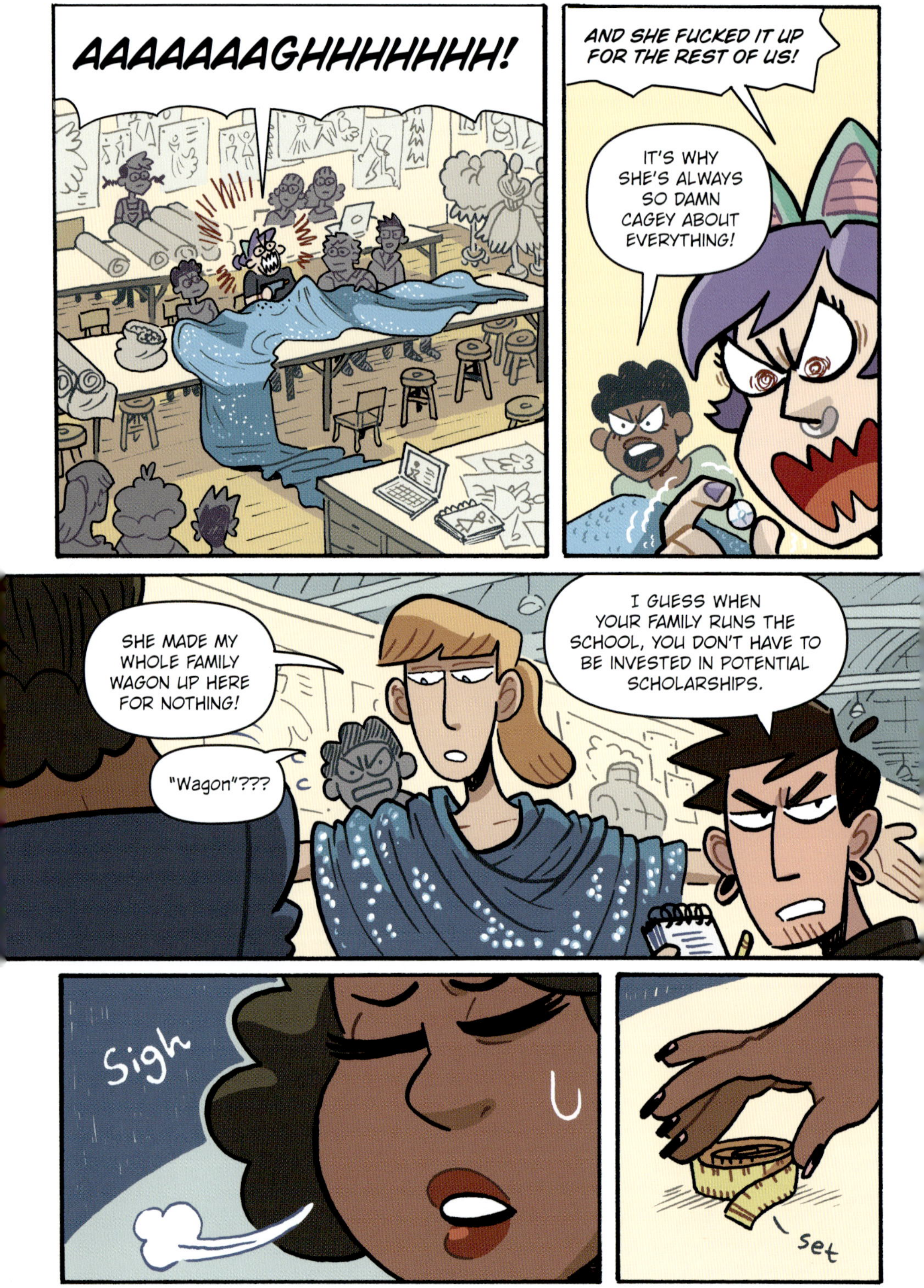
AAAAAAAGHHHHHHH!
AND SHE FUCKED IT UP FOR THE REST OF US!
IT'S WHY SHE'S ALWAYS SO DAMN CAGEY ABOUT EVERYTHING!
SHE MADE MY WHOLE FAMILY WAGON UP HERE FOR NOTHING!
"Wagon"???
I GUESS WHEN YOUR FAMILY RUNS THE SCHOOL, YOU DON'T HAVE TO BE INVESTED IN POTENTIAL SCHOLARSHIPS.
Sigh
set

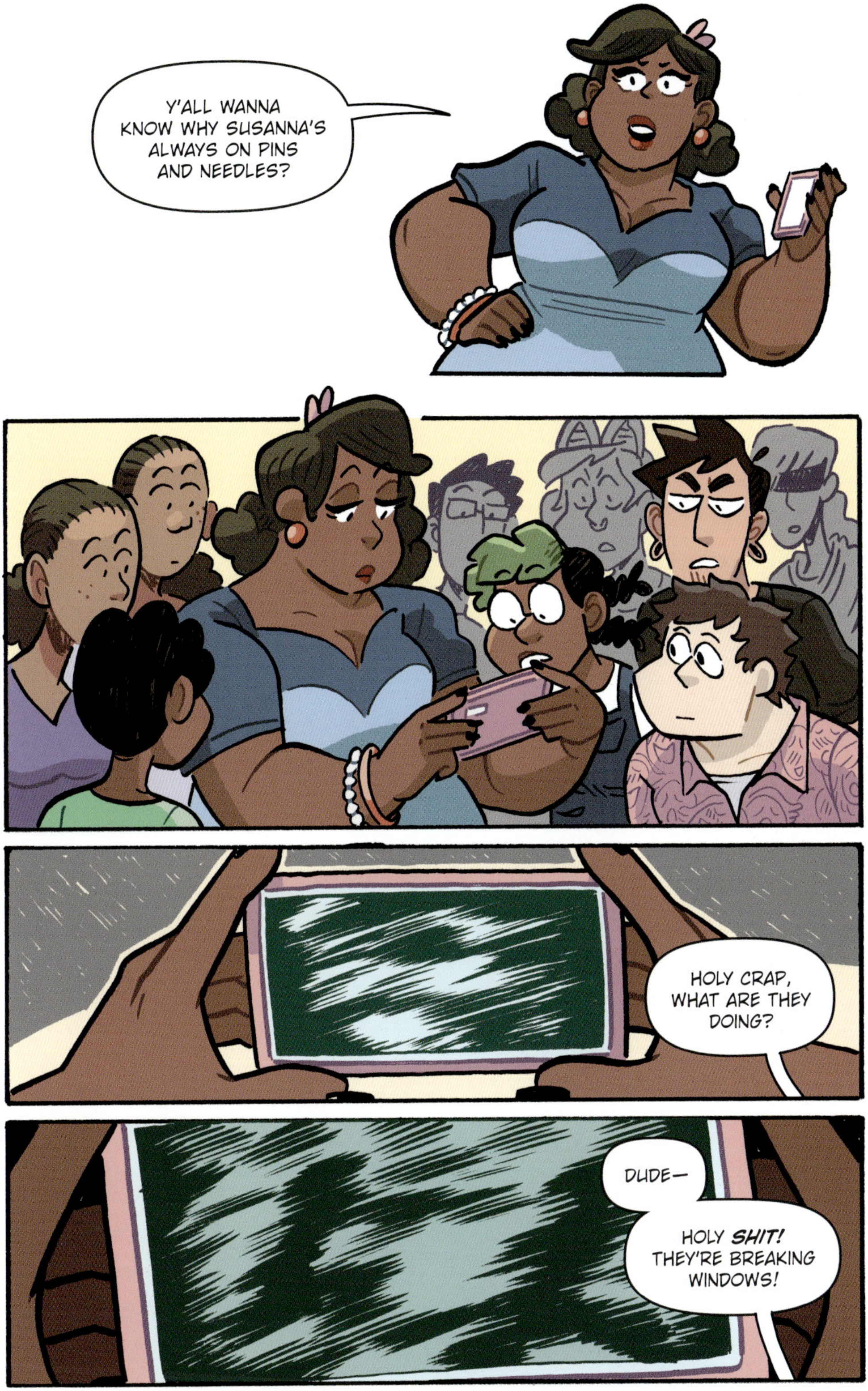
Y'ALL WANNA KNOW WHY SUSANNA'S ALWAYS ON PINS AND NEEDLES?
HOLY CRAP, WHAT ARE THEY DOING?
DUDE—
HOLY *SHIT!* THEY'RE BREAKING WINDOWS!

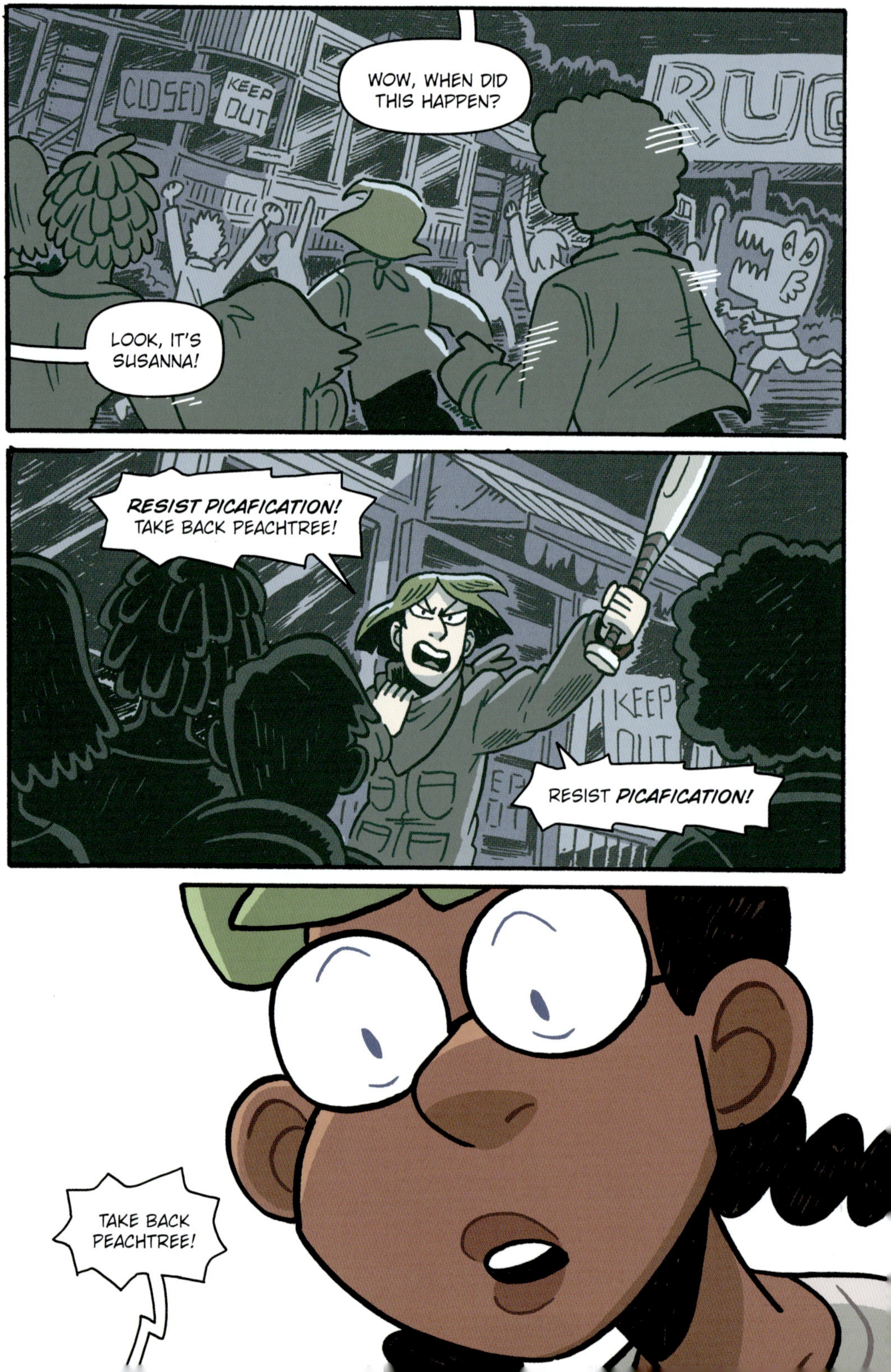
CLOSED
KEEP OUT
WOW, WHEN DID THIS HAPPEN?
RUG
LOOK, IT'S SUSANNA!
RESIST PICAFICATION! TAKE BACK PEACHTREE!
KEEP OUT
RESIST PICAFICATION!
TAKE BACK PEACHTREE!

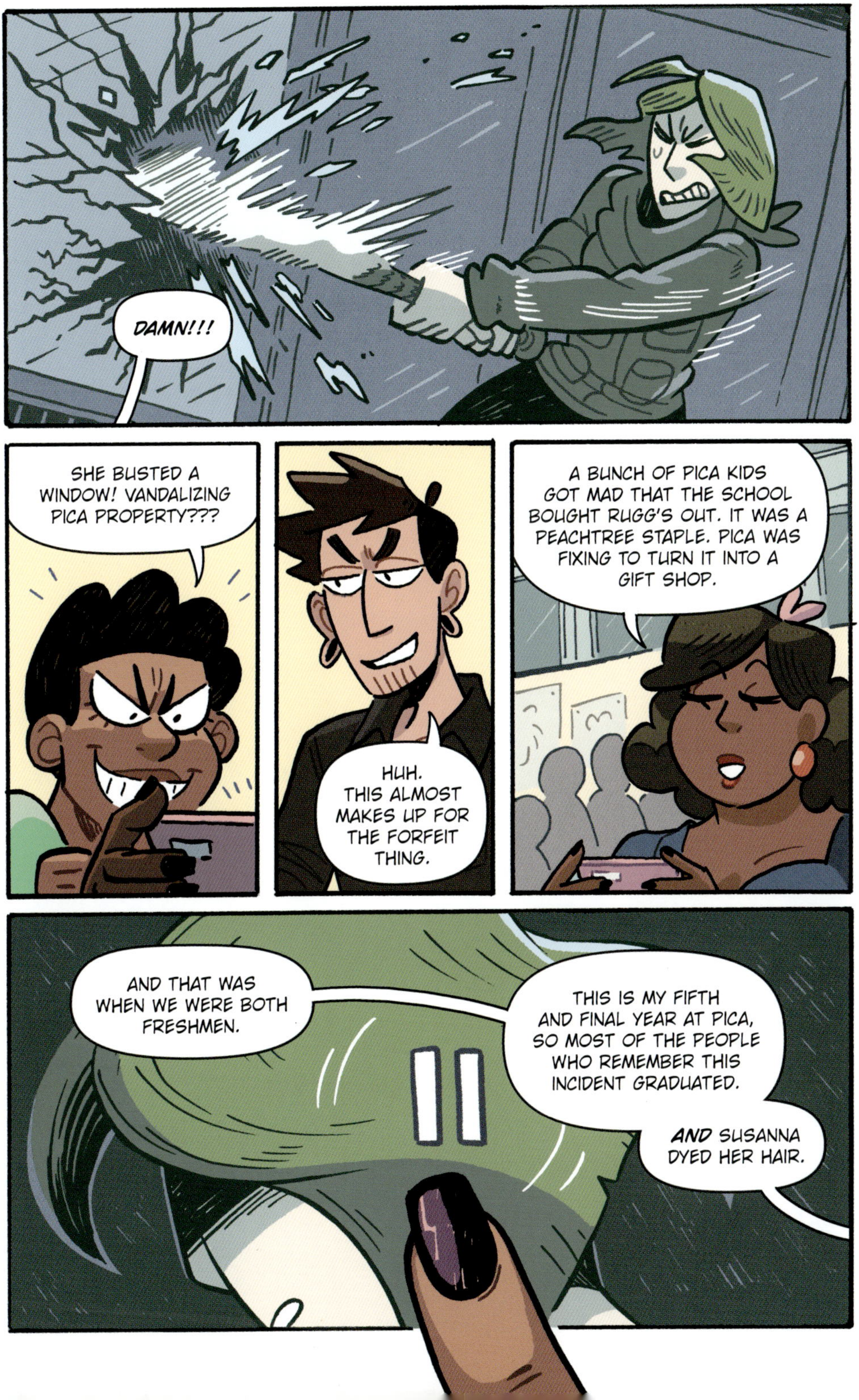
DAMN!!!
SHE BUSTED A WINDOW! VANDALIZING PICA PROPERTY???
HUH. THIS ALMOST MAKES UP FOR THE FORFEIT THING.
A BUNCH OF PICA KIDS GOT MAD THAT THE SCHOOL BOUGHT RUGG'S OUT. IT WAS A PEACHTREE STAPLE. PICA WAS FIXING TO TURN IT INTO A GIFT SHOP.
AND THAT WAS WHEN WE WERE BOTH FRESHMEN.
THIS IS MY FIFTH AND FINAL YEAR AT PICA, SO MOST OF THE PEOPLE WHO REMEMBER THIS INCIDENT GRADUATED.
AND SUSANNA DYED HER HAIR.

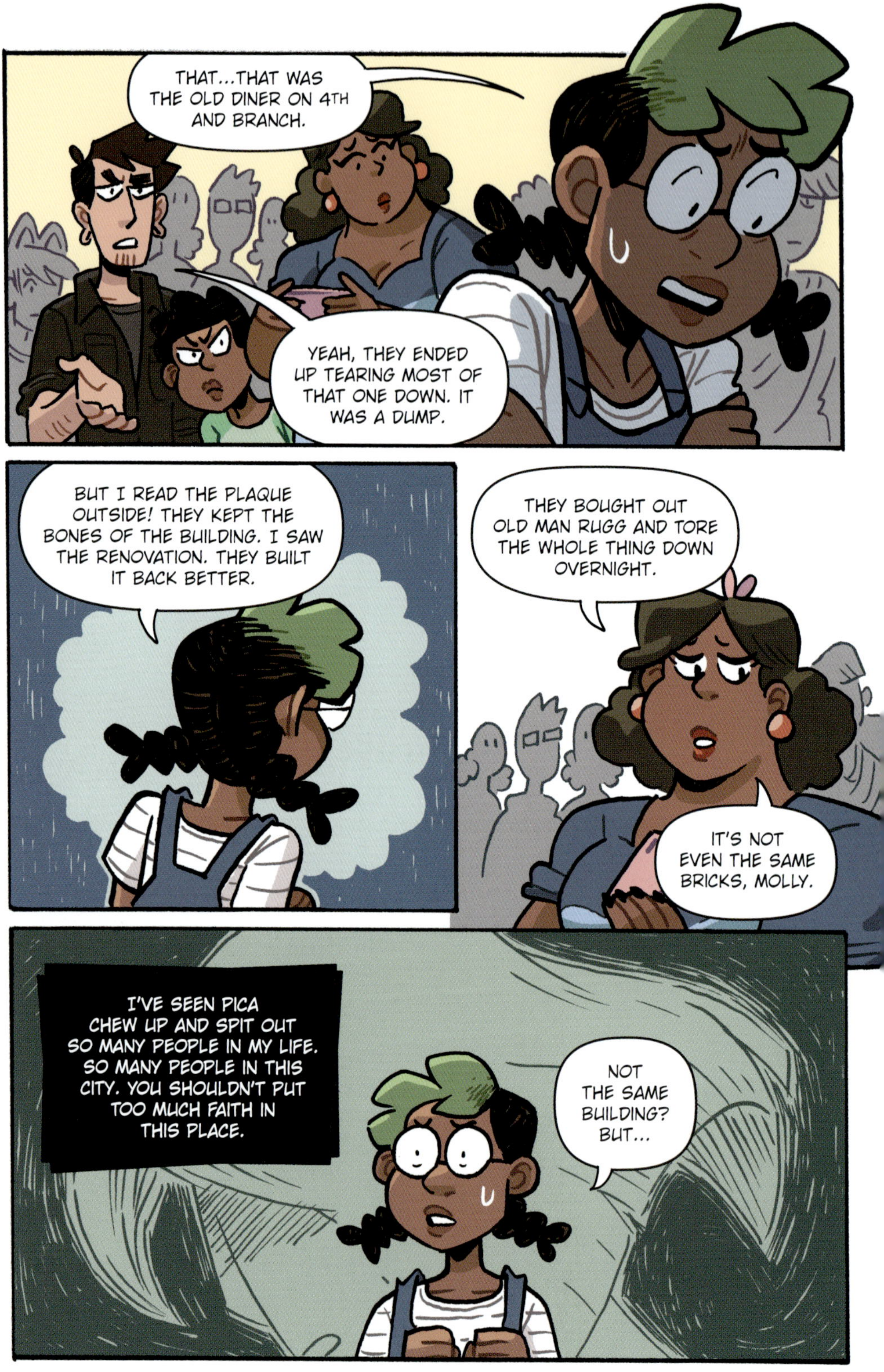
THAT...THAT WAS THE OLD DINER ON 4TH AND BRANCH.
YEAH, THEY ENDED UP TEARING MOST OF THAT ONE DOWN. IT WAS A DUMP.
BUT I READ THE PLAQUE OUTSIDE! THEY KEPT THE BONES OF THE BUILDING. I SAW THE RENOVATION. THEY BUILT IT BACK BETTER.
THEY BOUGHT OUT OLD MAN RUGG AND TORE THE WHOLE THING DOWN OVERNIGHT.
IT'S NOT EVEN THE SAME BRICKS, MOLLY.
I'VE SEEN PICA CHEW UP AND SPIT OUT SO MANY PEOPLE IN MY LIFE. SO MANY PEOPLE IN THIS CITY. YOU SHOULDN'T PUT TOO MUCH FAITH IN THIS PLACE.
NOT THE SAME BUILDING? BUT...

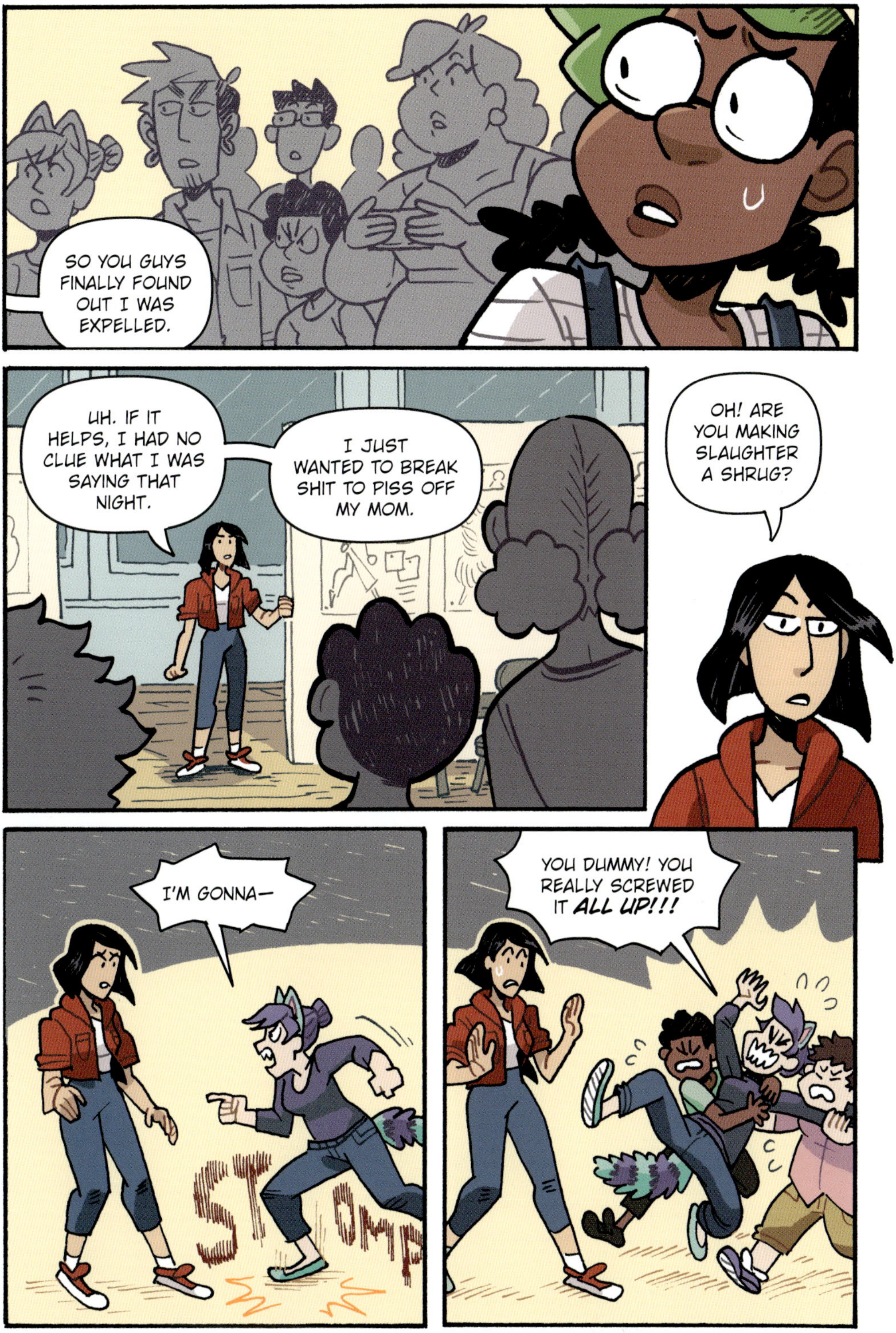
SO YOU GUYS FINALLY FOUND OUT I WAS EXPELLED.
UH. IF IT HELPS, I HAD NO CLUE WHAT I WAS SAYING THAT NIGHT.
I JUST WANTED TO BREAK SHIT TO PISS OFF MY MOM.
OH! ARE YOU MAKING SLAUGHTER A SHRUG?
I'M GONNA—
STOMP
YOU DUMMY! YOU REALLY SCREWED IT **ALL UP!!!**

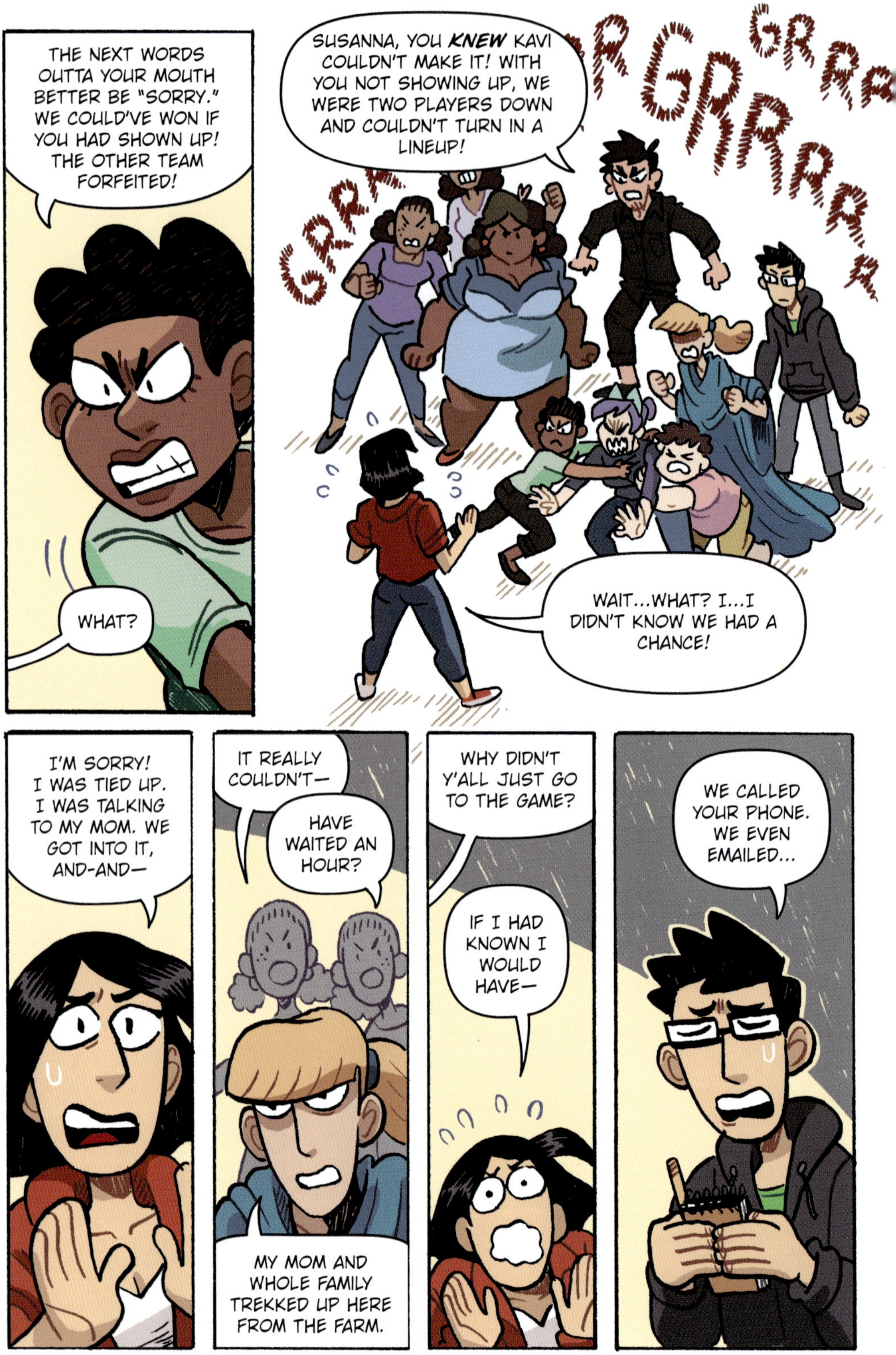
THE NEXT WORDS OUTTA YOUR MOUTH BETTER BE "SORRY." WE COULD'VE WON IF YOU HAD SHOWN UP! THE OTHER TEAM FORFEITED!
WHAT?
SUSANNA, YOU ***KNEW*** KAVI COULDN'T MAKE IT! WITH YOU NOT SHOWING UP, WE WERE TWO PLAYERS DOWN AND COULDN'T TURN IN A LINEUP!
GRRR
GRRRRRRR
GRRR
WAIT...WHAT? I...I DIDN'T KNOW WE HAD A CHANCE!
I'M SORRY! I WAS TIED UP. I WAS TALKING TO MY MOM. WE GOT INTO IT, AND-AND—
IT REALLY COULDN'T—
HAVE WAITED AN HOUR?
MY MOM AND WHOLE FAMILY TREKKED UP HERE FROM THE FARM.
WHY DIDN'T Y'ALL JUST GO TO THE GAME?
IF I HAD KNOWN I WOULD HAVE—
WE CALLED YOUR PHONE. WE EVEN EMAILED...

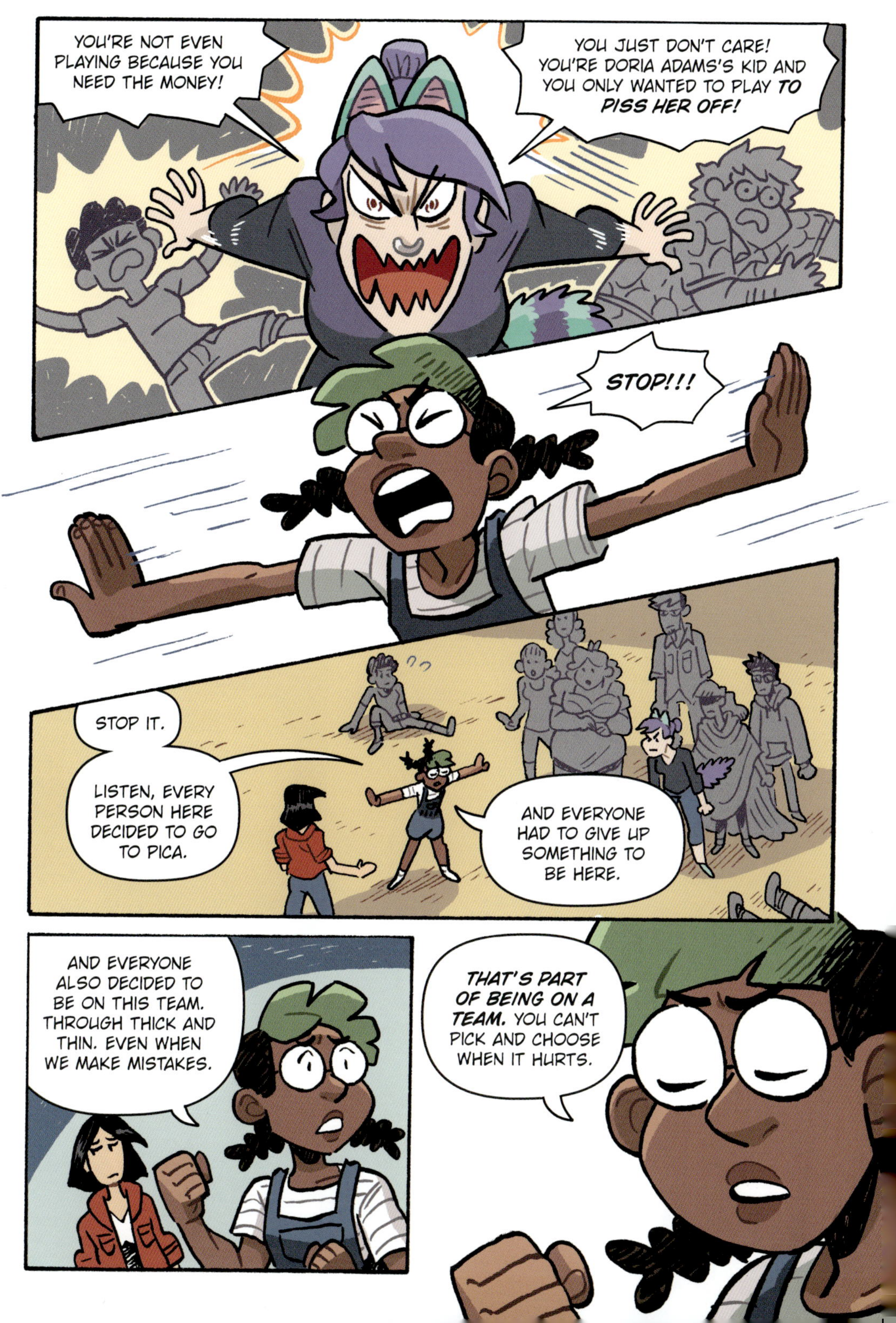
YOU'RE NOT EVEN PLAYING BECAUSE YOU NEED THE MONEY!
YOU JUST DON'T CARE! YOU'RE DORIA ADAMS'S KID AND YOU ONLY WANTED TO PLAY *TO PISS HER OFF!*
STOP!!!
STOP IT.
LISTEN, EVERY PERSON HERE DECIDED TO GO TO PICA.
AND EVERYONE HAD TO GIVE UP SOMETHING TO BE HERE.
AND EVERYONE ALSO DECIDED TO BE ON THIS TEAM. THROUGH THICK AND THIN. EVEN WHEN WE MAKE MISTAKES.
THAT'S PART OF BEING ON A TEAM. YOU CAN'T PICK AND CHOOSE WHEN IT HURTS.

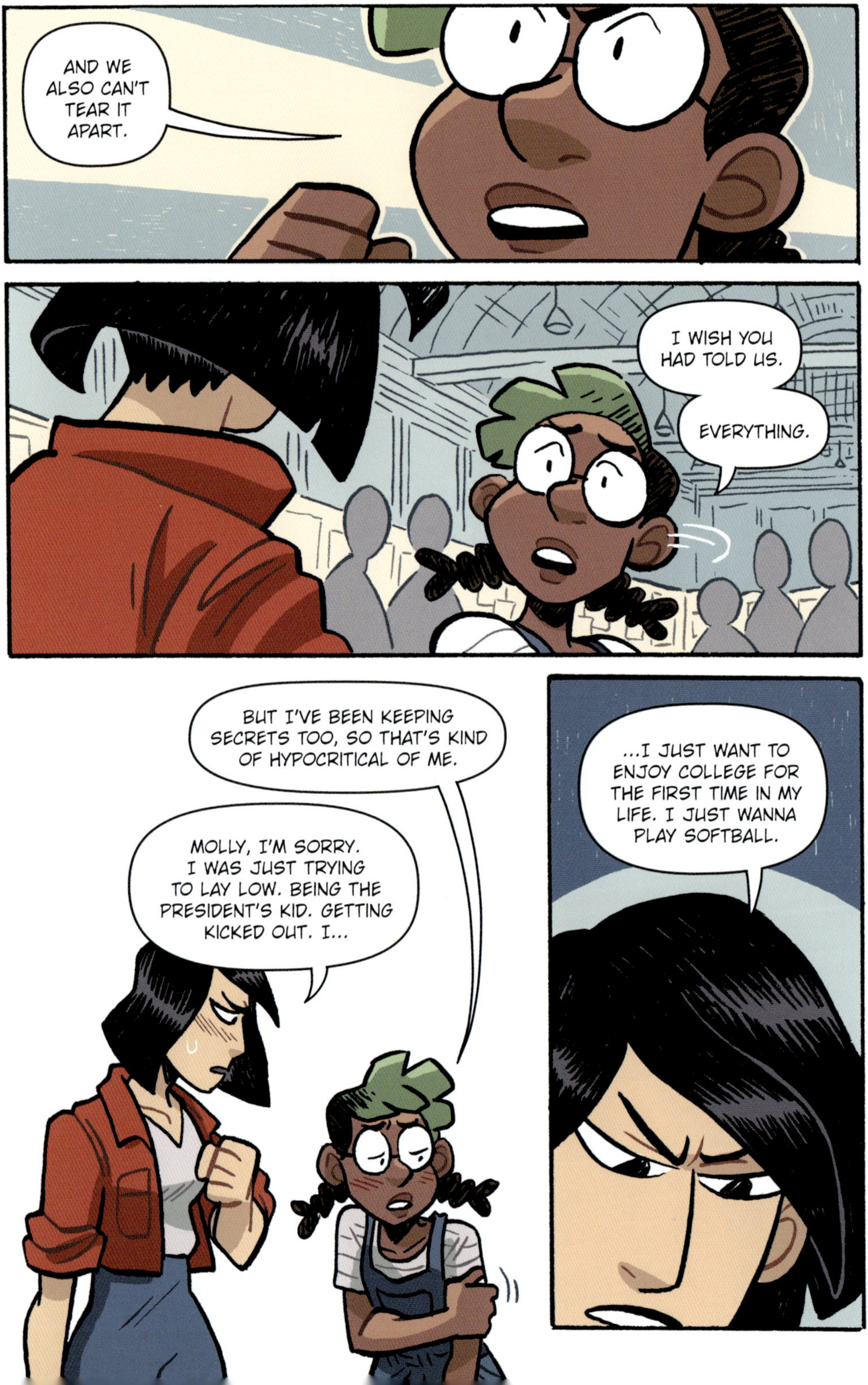
AND WE ALSO CAN'T TEAR IT APART.
I WISH YOU HAD TOLD US.
EVERYTHING.
BUT I'VE BEEN KEEPING SECRETS TOO, SO THAT'S KIND OF HYPOCRITICAL OF ME.
MOLLY, I'M SORRY. I WAS JUST TRYING TO LAY LOW. BEING THE PRESIDENT'S KID. GETTING KICKED OUT. I...
...I JUST WANT TO ENJOY COLLEGE FOR THE FIRST TIME IN MY LIFE. I JUST WANNA PLAY SOFTBALL.

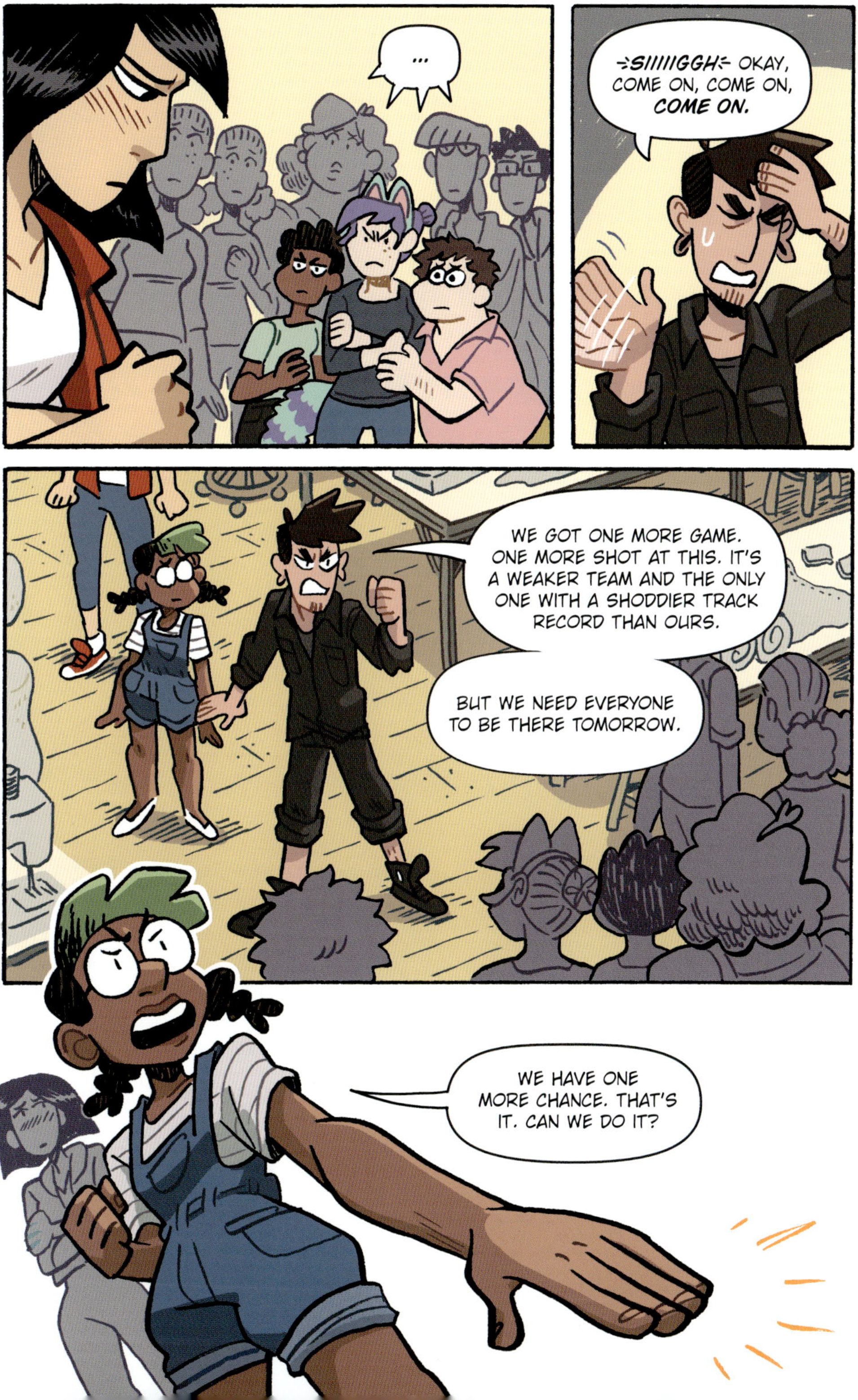
...
-SIIIIGGH- OKAY, COME ON, COME ON, COME ON.
WE GOT ONE MORE GAME. ONE MORE SHOT AT THIS. IT'S A WEAKER TEAM AND THE ONLY ONE WITH A SHODDIER TRACK RECORD THAN OURS.
BUT WE NEED EVERYONE TO BE THERE TOMORROW.
WE HAVE ONE MORE CHANCE. THAT'S IT. CAN WE DO IT?

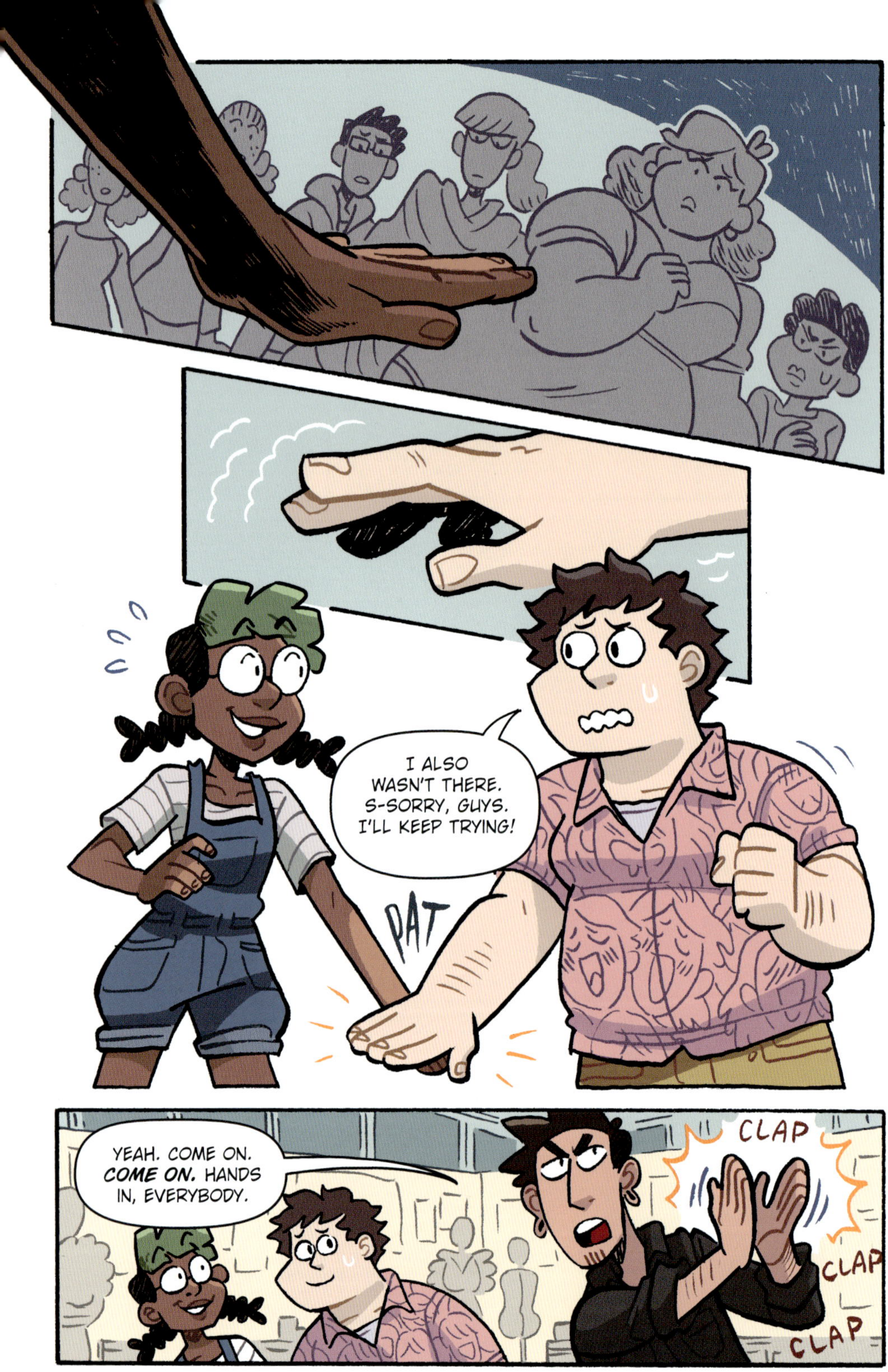
I ALSO WASN'T THERE. S-SORRY, GUYS. I'LL KEEP TRYING!
PAT
YEAH. COME ON. **COME ON.** HANDS IN, EVERYBODY.
CLAP
CLAP
CLAP

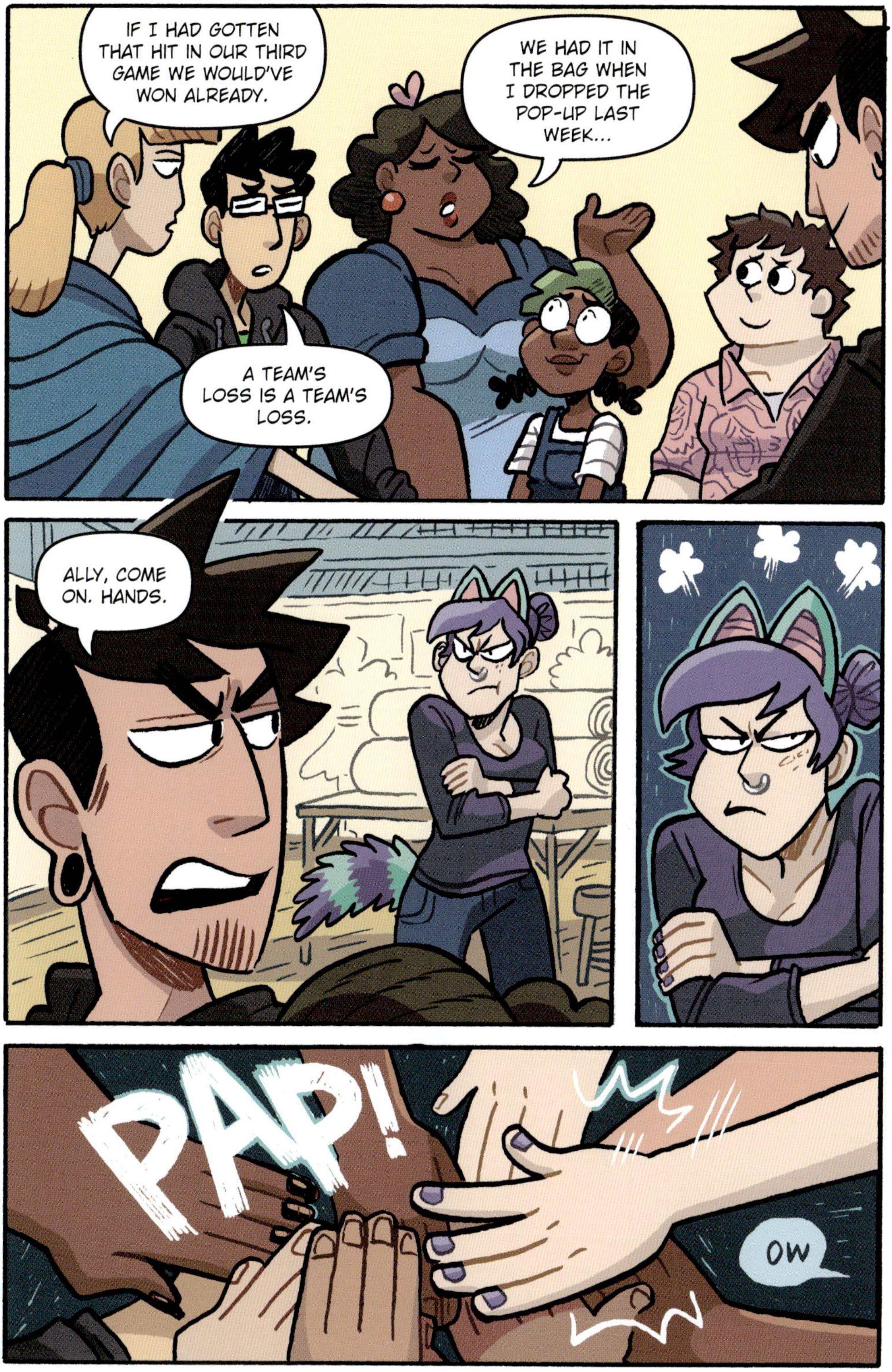
IF I HAD GOTTEN THAT HIT IN OUR THIRD GAME WE WOULD'VE WON ALREADY.
WE HAD IT IN THE BAG WHEN I DROPPED THE POP-UP LAST WEEK...
A TEAM'S LOSS IS A TEAM'S LOSS.
ALLY, COME ON. HANDS.
PAP!
OW

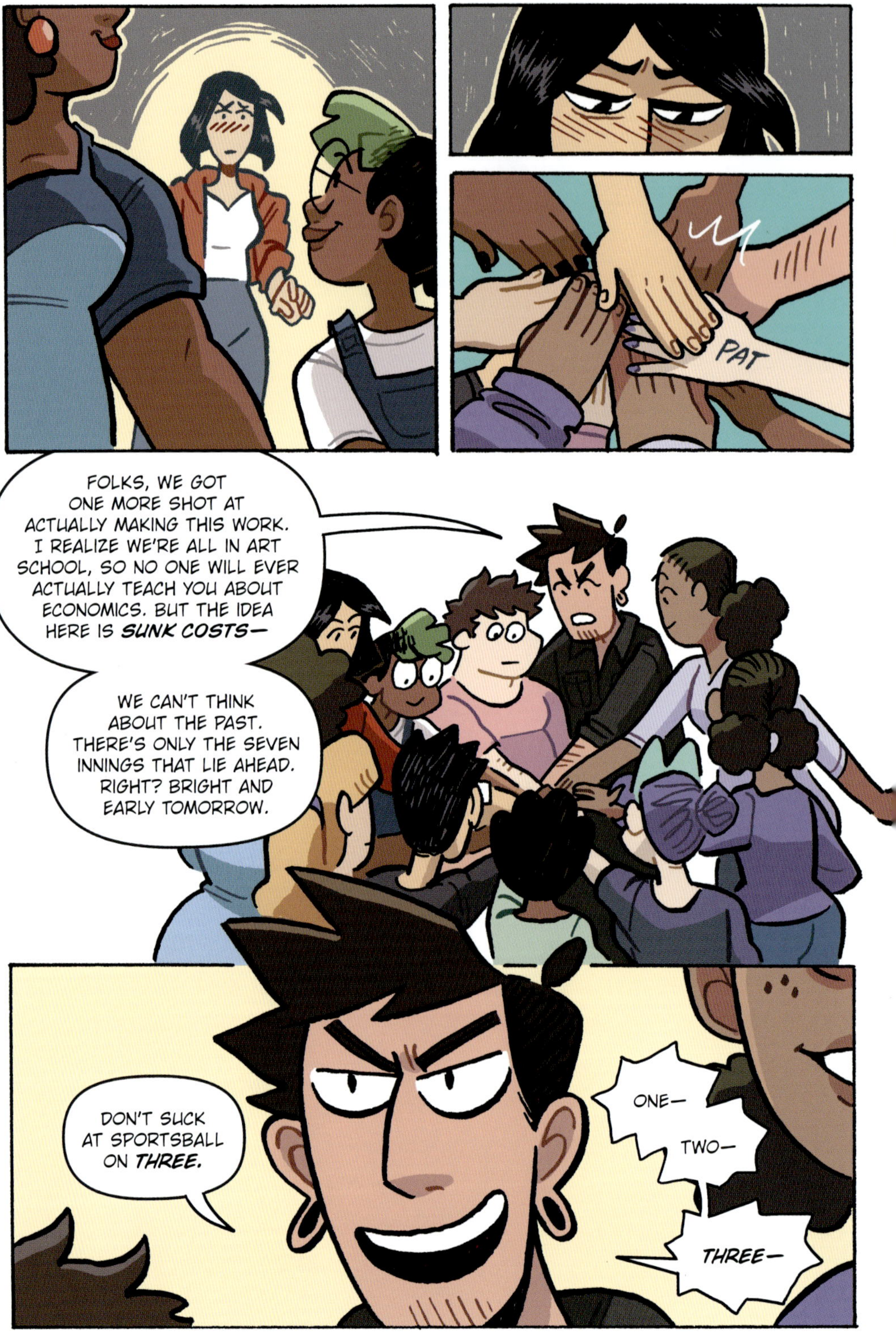
PAT
FOLKS, WE GOT ONE MORE SHOT AT ACTUALLY MAKING THIS WORK. I REALIZE WE'RE ALL IN ART SCHOOL, SO NO ONE WILL EVER ACTUALLY TEACH YOU ABOUT ECONOMICS. BUT THE IDEA HERE IS *SUNK COSTS*—
WE CAN'T THINK ABOUT THE PAST. THERE'S ONLY THE SEVEN INNINGS THAT LIE AHEAD. RIGHT? BRIGHT AND EARLY TOMORROW.
DON'T SUCK AT SPORTSBALL ON *THREE.*
ONE—
TWO—
THREE—

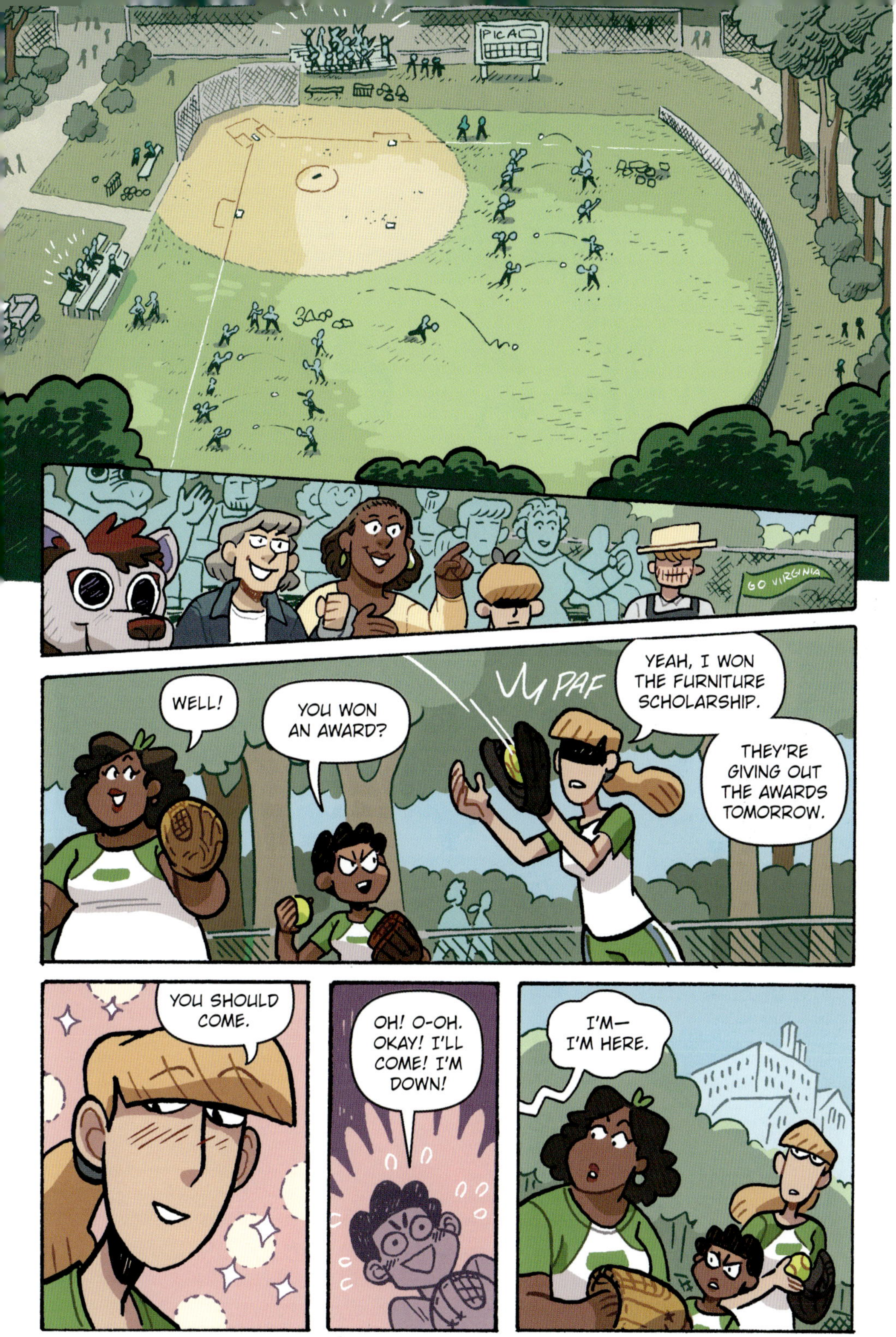
PICA
GO VIRGINIA
WELL!
YOU WON AN AWARD?
PAF
YEAH, I WON THE FURNITURE SCHOLARSHIP.
THEY'RE GIVING OUT THE AWARDS TOMORROW.
YOU SHOULD COME.
OH! O-OH. OKAY! I'LL COME! I'M DOWN!
I'M— I'M HERE.

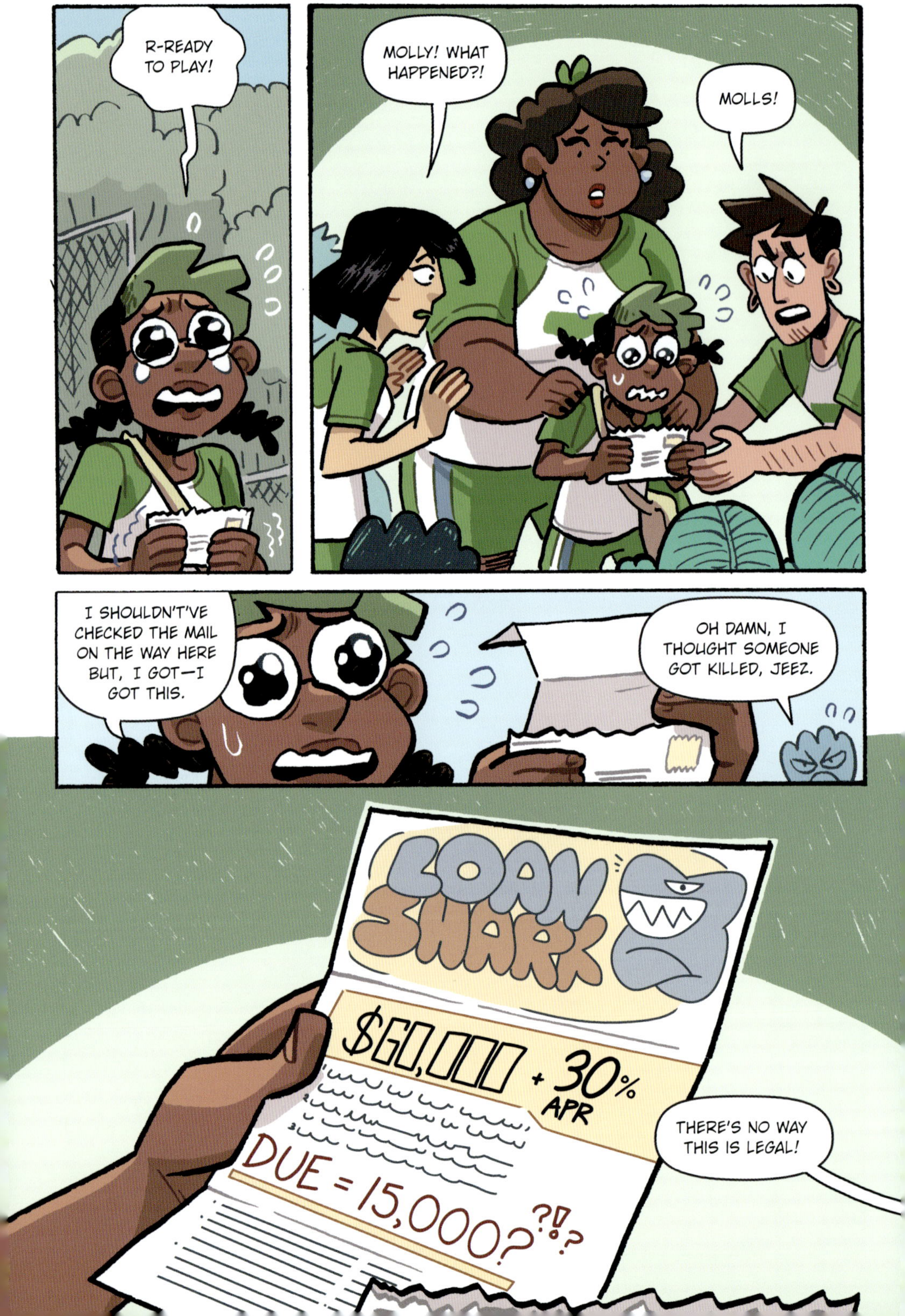
R-READY TO PLAY!
MOLLY! WHAT HAPPENED?!
MOLLS!
I SHOULDN'T'VE CHECKED THE MAIL ON THE WAY HERE BUT, I GOT—I GOT THIS.
OH DAMN, I THOUGHT SOMEONE GOT KILLED, JEEZ.
LOAN SHARK
$60,000 + 30% APR
DUE = 15,000?
?!?
THERE'S NO WAY THIS IS LEGAL!

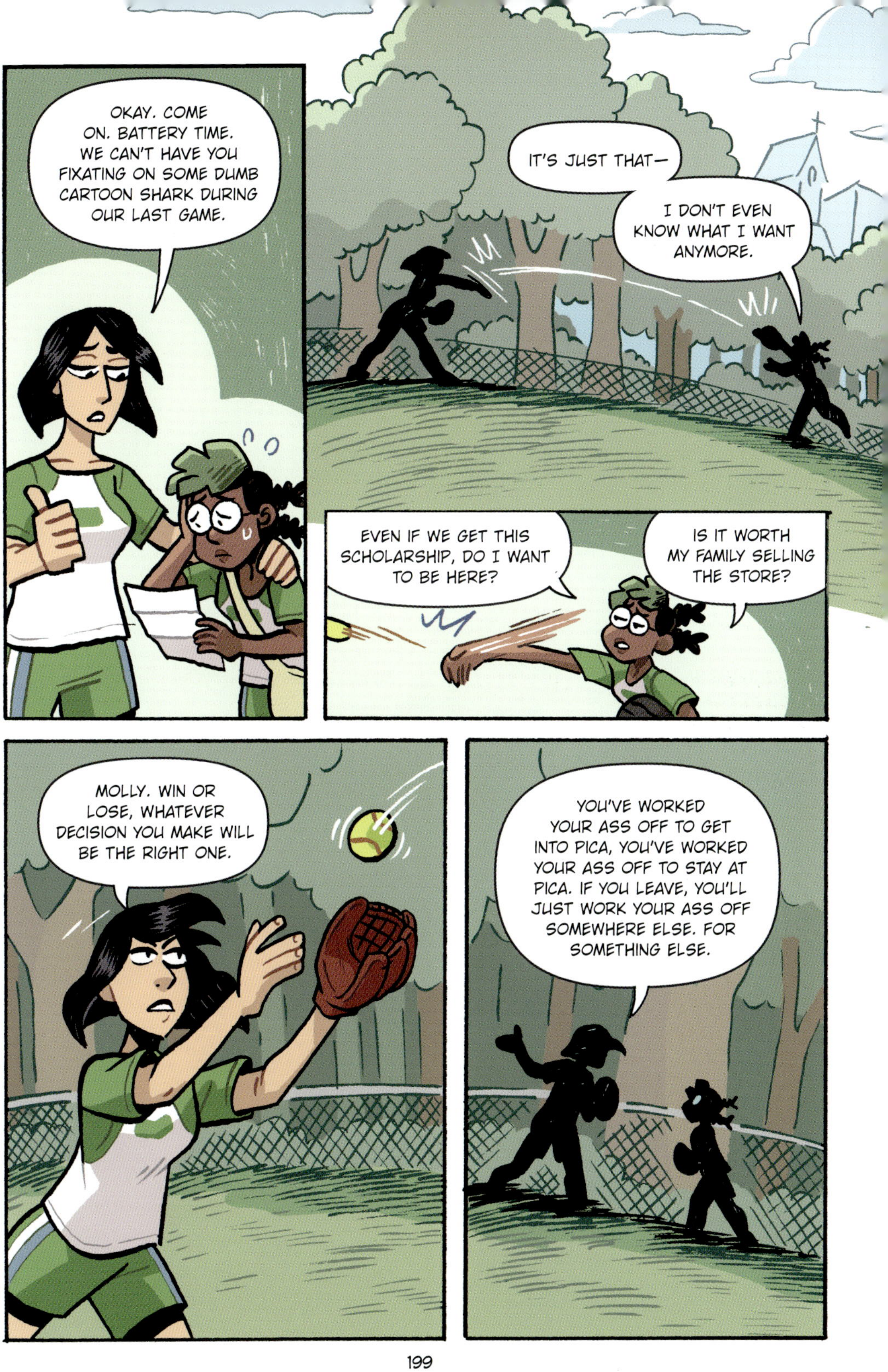
OKAY. COME ON. BATTERY TIME. WE CAN'T HAVE YOU FIXATING ON SOME DUMB CARTOON SHARK DURING OUR LAST GAME.
IT'S JUST THAT—
I DON'T EVEN KNOW WHAT I WANT ANYMORE.
EVEN IF WE GET THIS SCHOLARSHIP, DO I WANT TO BE HERE?
IS IT WORTH MY FAMILY SELLING THE STORE?
MOLLY. WIN OR LOSE, WHATEVER DECISION YOU MAKE WILL BE THE RIGHT ONE.
YOU'VE WORKED YOUR ASS OFF TO GET INTO PICA, YOU'VE WORKED YOUR ASS OFF TO STAY AT PICA. IF YOU LEAVE, YOU'LL JUST WORK YOUR ASS OFF SOMEWHERE ELSE. FOR SOMETHING ELSE.

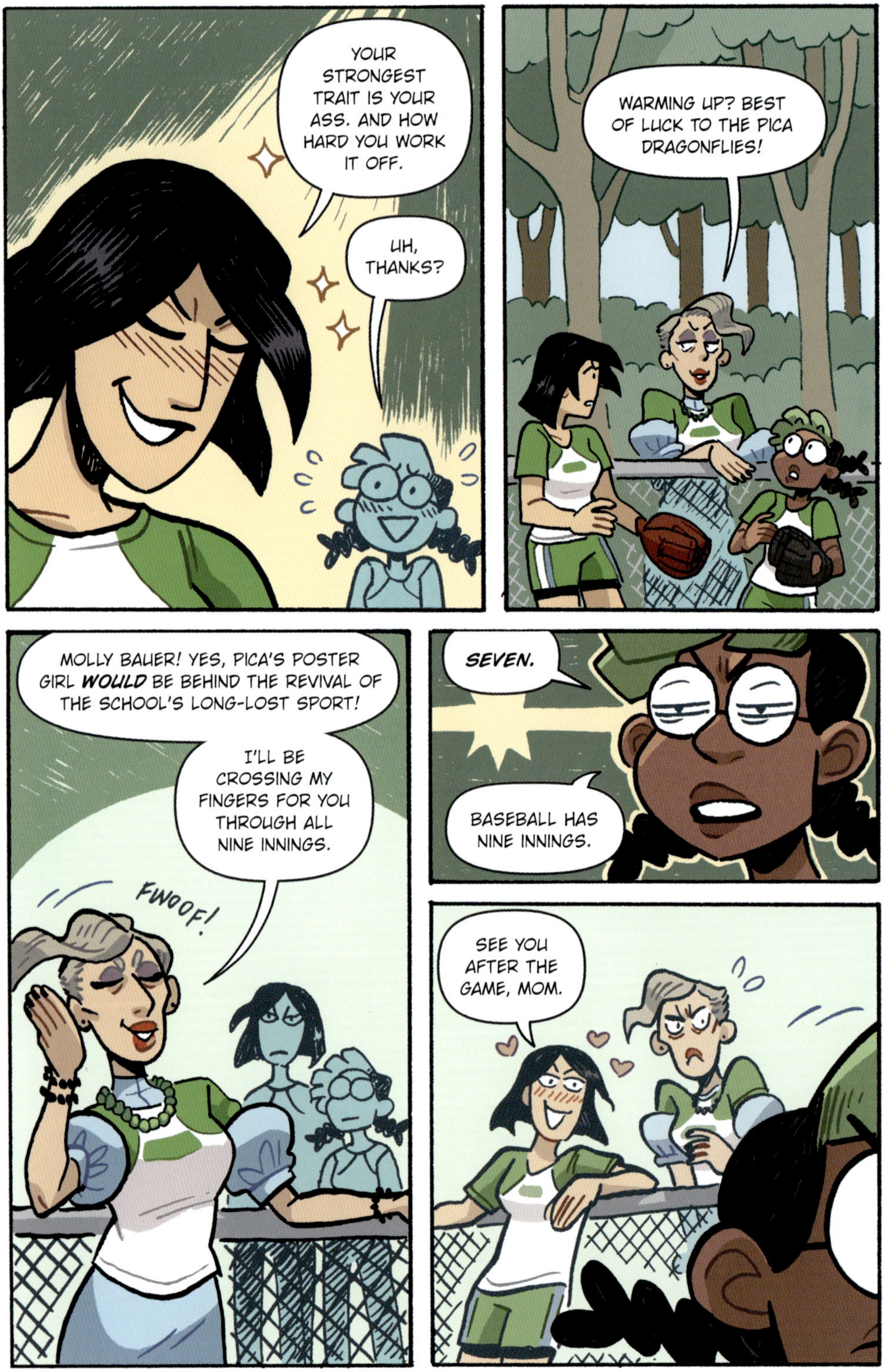
YOUR STRONGEST TRAIT IS YOUR ASS. AND HOW HARD YOU WORK IT OFF.
UH, THANKS?
WARMING UP? BEST OF LUCK TO THE PICA DRAGONFLIES!
MOLLY BAUER! YES, PICA'S POSTER GIRL *WOULD* BE BEHIND THE REVIVAL OF THE SCHOOL'S LONG-LOST SPORT!
I'LL BE CROSSING MY FINGERS FOR YOU THROUGH ALL NINE INNINGS.
FWOOF!
SEVEN.
BASEBALL HAS NINE INNINGS.
SEE YOU AFTER THE GAME, MOM.

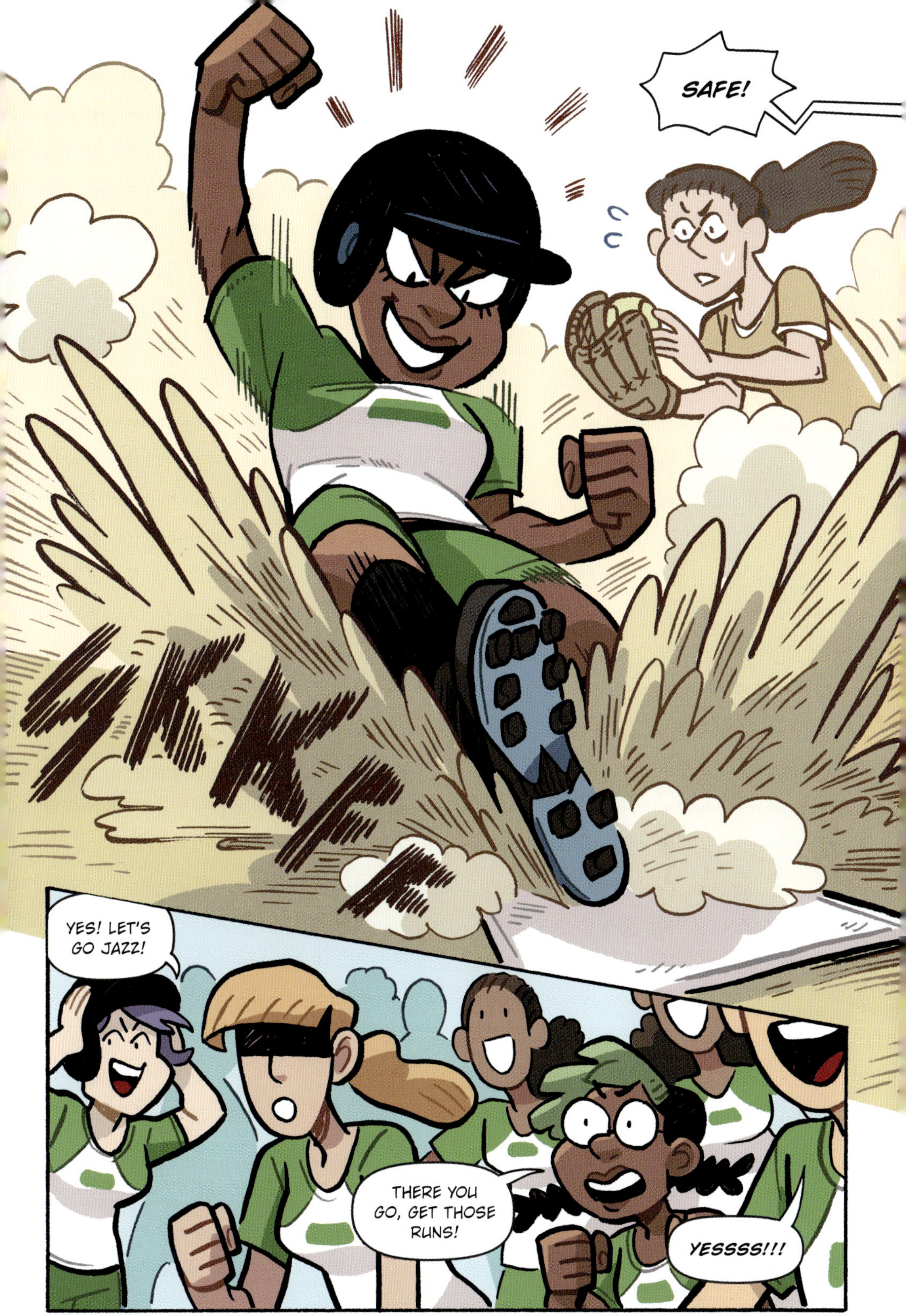
SAFE!
SKKF
YES! LET'S GO JAZZ!
THERE YOU GO, GET THOSE RUNS!
YESSSS!!!

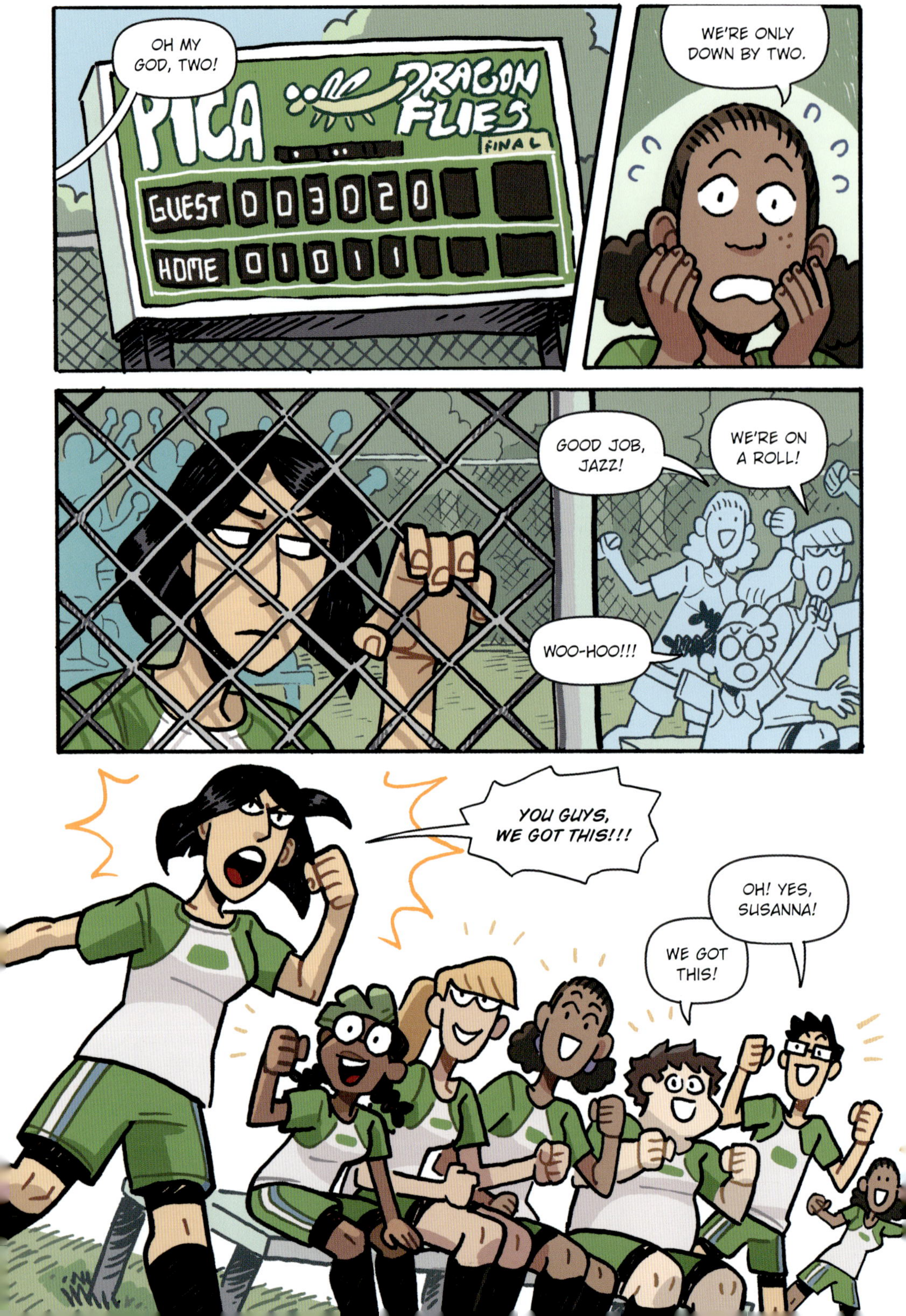
OH MY GOD, TWO!
PICA
DRAGON FLIES
FINAL
GUEST 0 0 3 0 2 0
HOME 0 1 0 1 1
WE'RE ONLY DOWN BY TWO.
GOOD JOB, JAZZ!
WE'RE ON A ROLL!
WOO-HOO!!!
YOU GUYS, WE GOT THIS!!!
OH! YES, SUSANNA!
WE GOT THIS!

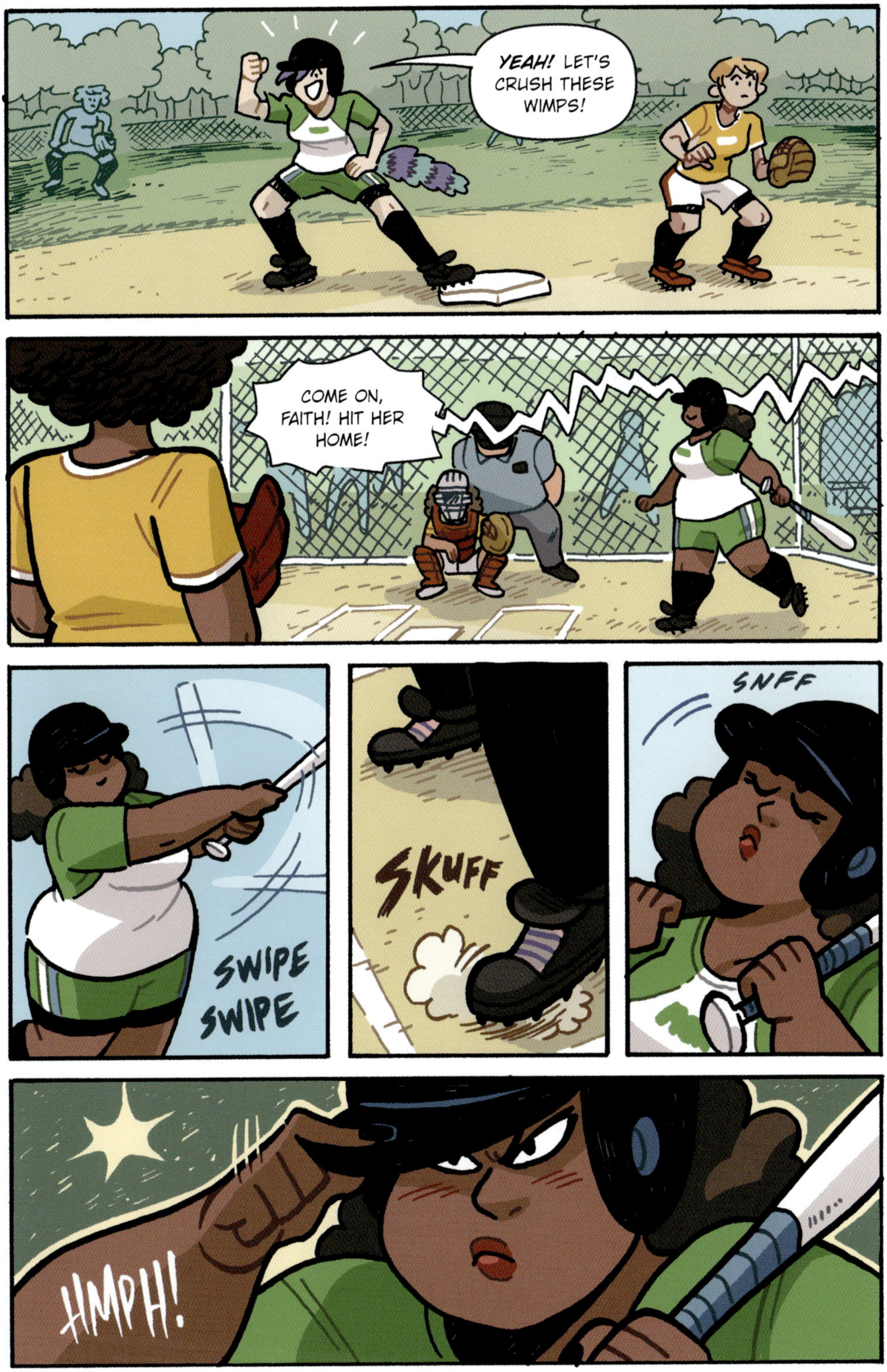
YEAH! LET'S CRUSH THESE WIMPS!
COME ON, FAITH! HIT HER HOME!
SWIPE SWIPE
SKUFF
SNFF
HMPH!

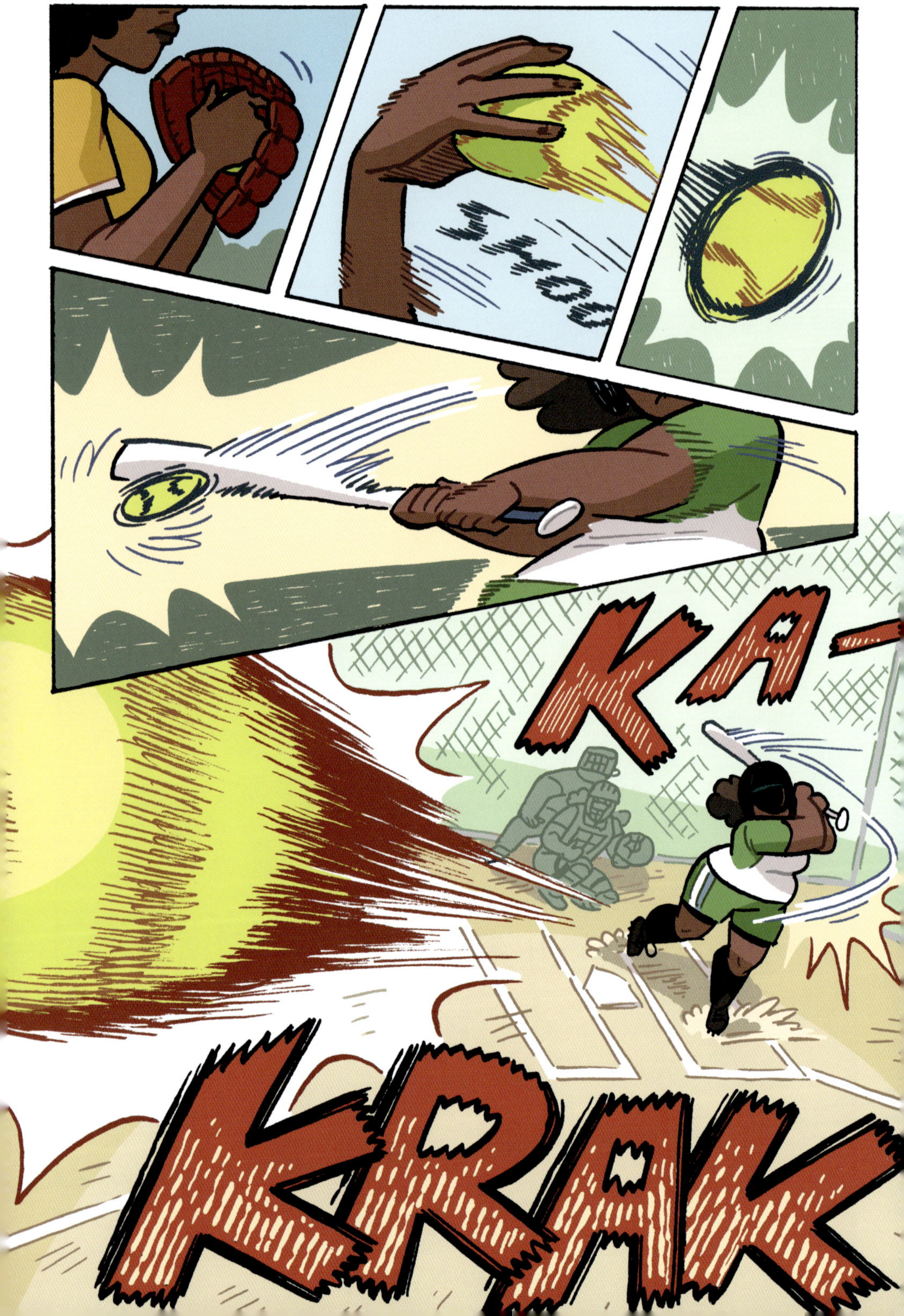
KA-
KRAK

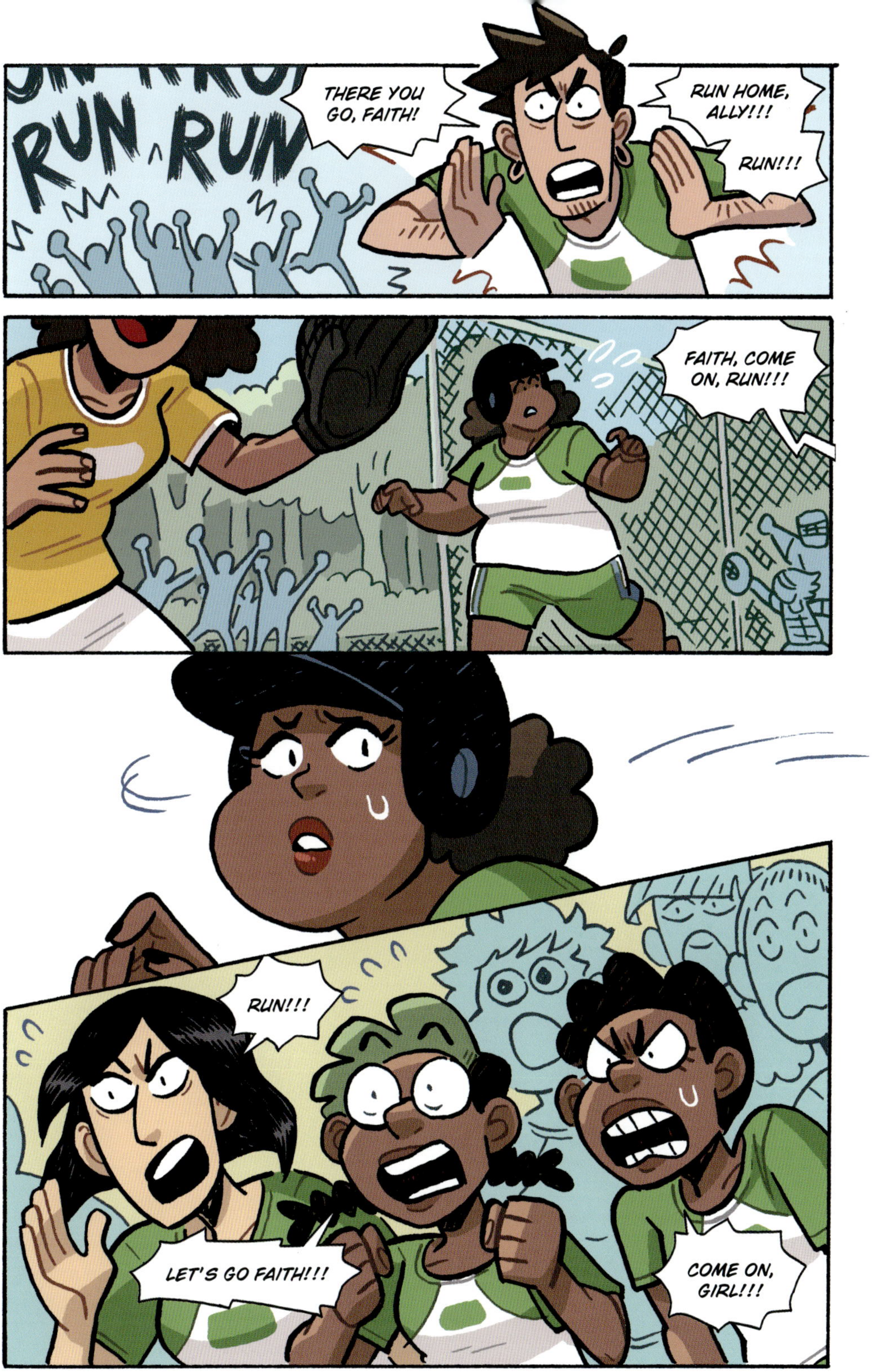
RUN RUN
THERE YOU GO, FAITH!
RUN HOME, ALLY!!!
RUN!!!
FAITH, COME ON, RUN!!!
RUN!!!
LET'S GO FAITH!!!
COME ON, GIRL!!!

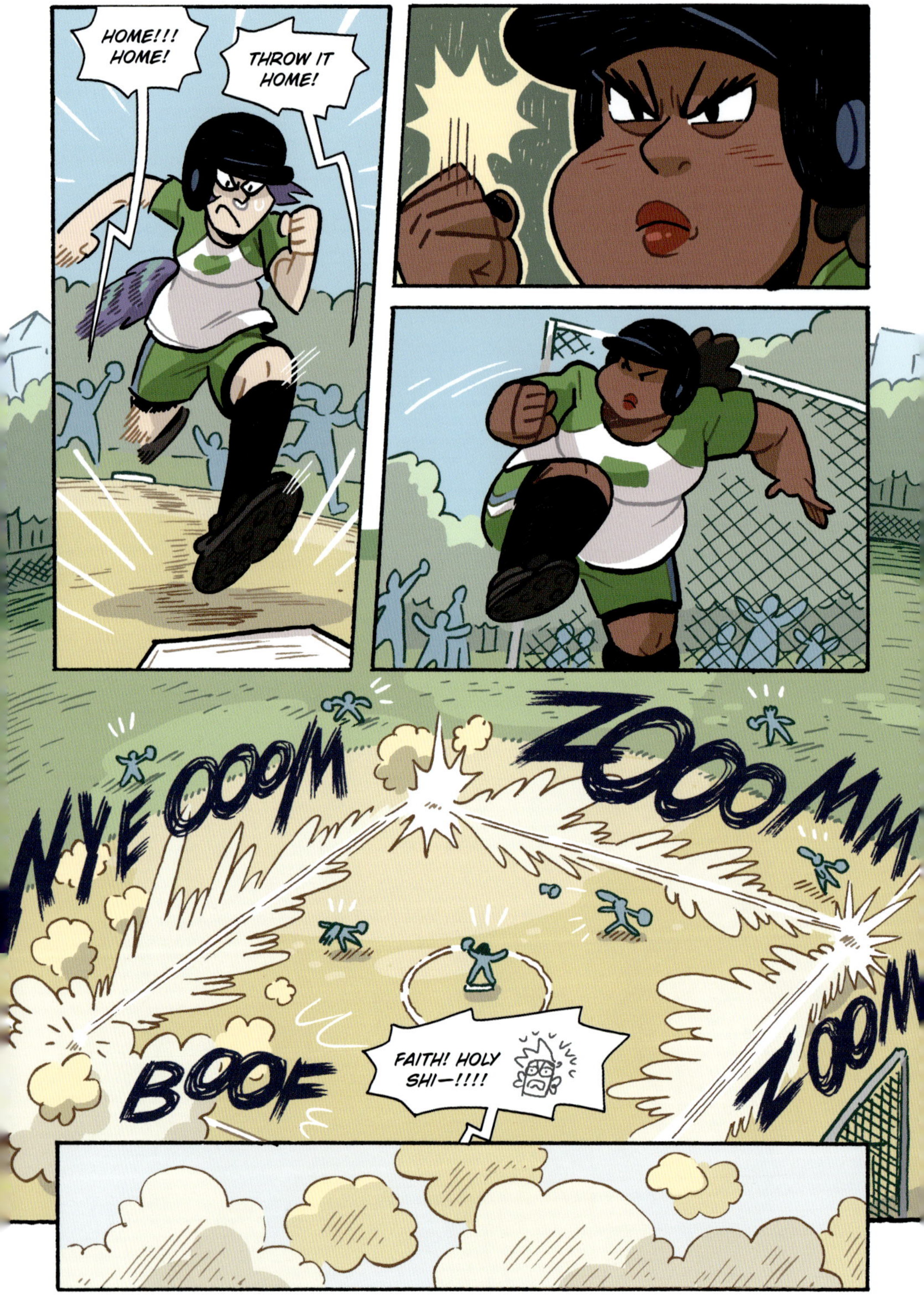
HOME!!! HOME!
THROW IT HOME!
NYEOOOM
ZOOOMM
BOOF
FAITH! HOLY SHI—!!!!
ZOOM

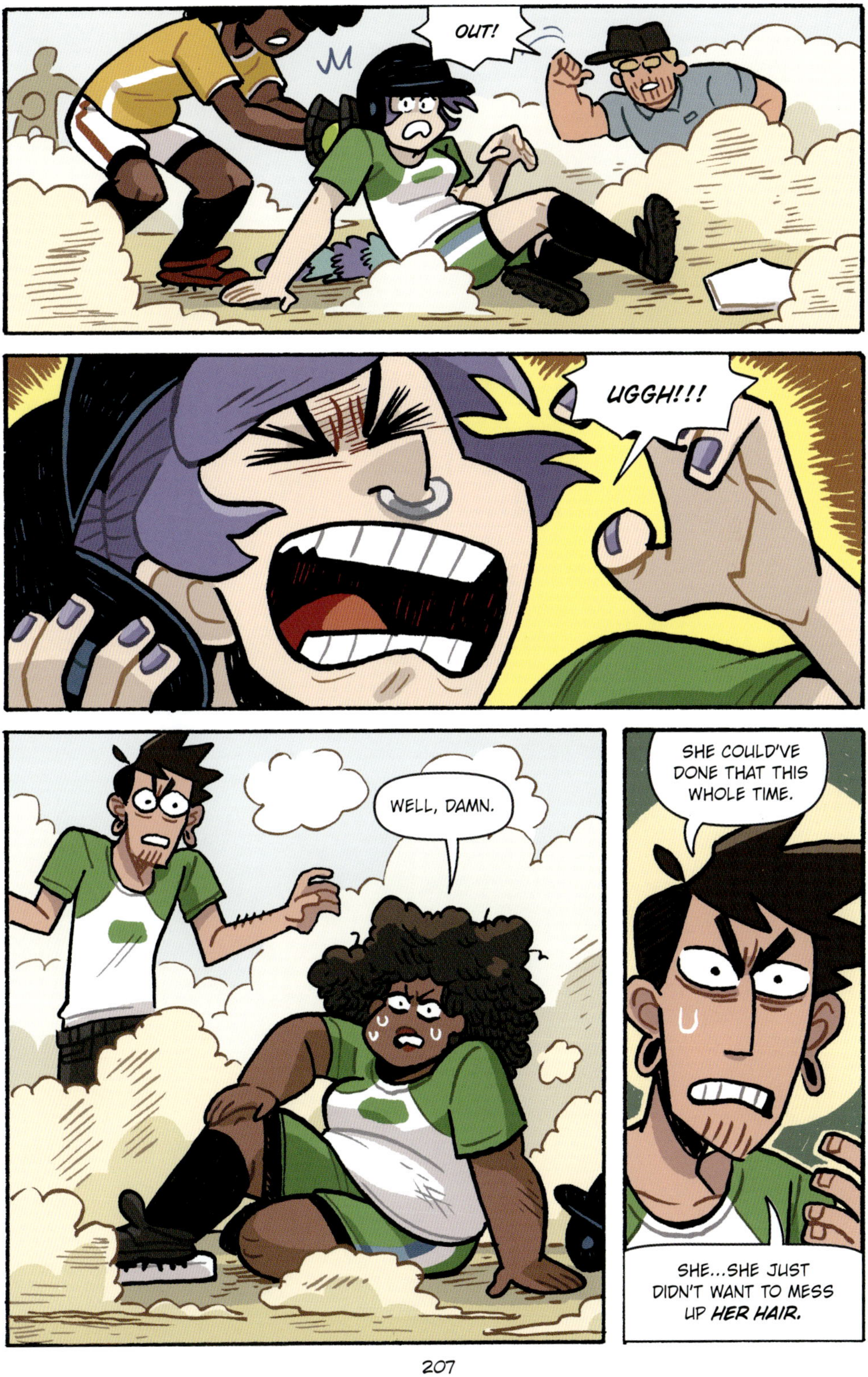
OUT!
UGGH!!!
WELL, DAMN.
SHE COULD'VE DONE THAT THIS WHOLE TIME.
SHE...SHE JUST DIDN'T WANT TO MESS UP HER HAIR.

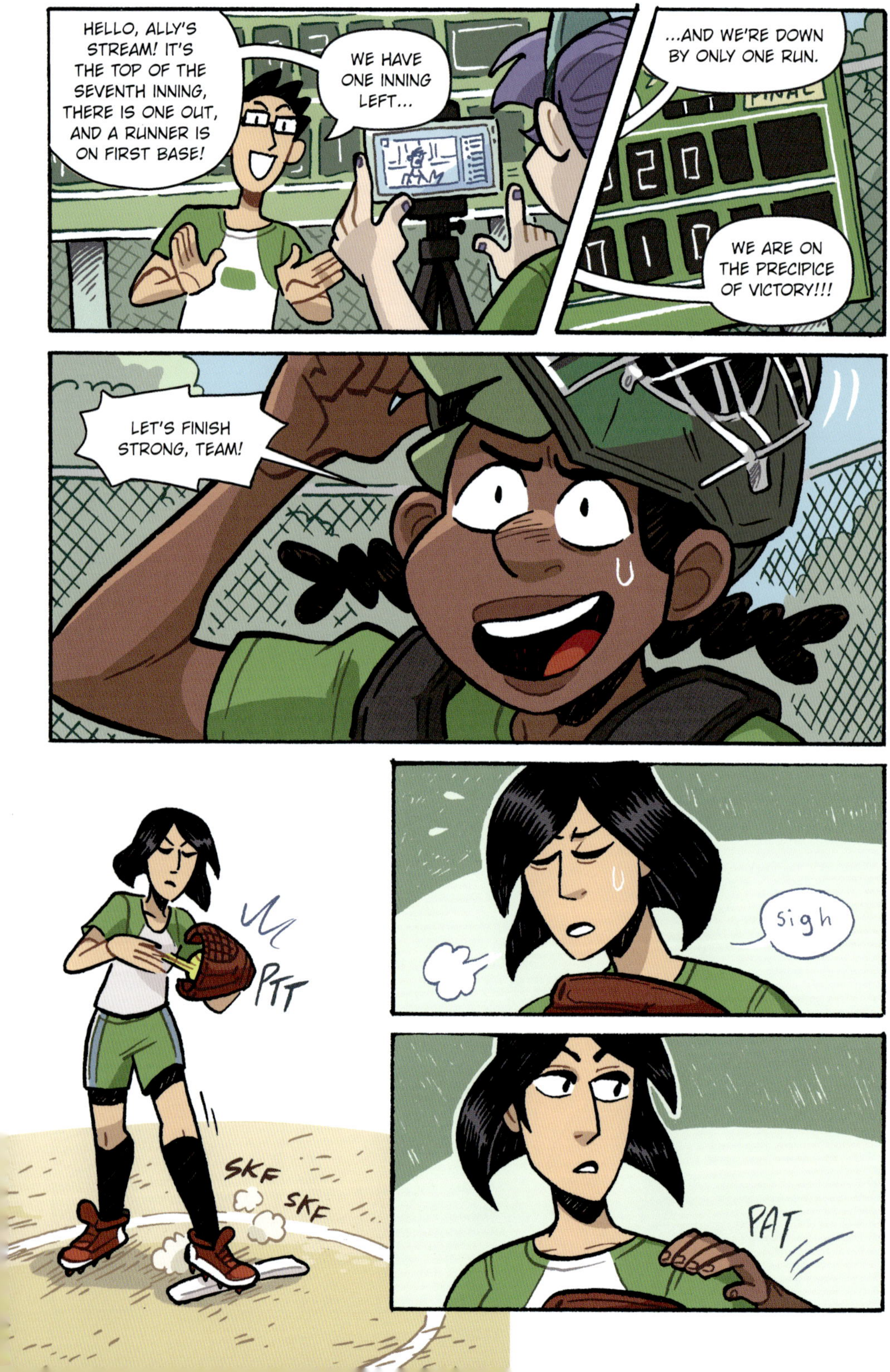
HELLO, ALLY'S STREAM! IT'S THE TOP OF THE SEVENTH INNING, THERE IS ONE OUT, AND A RUNNER IS ON FIRST BASE!
WE HAVE ONE INNING LEFT...
...AND WE'RE DOWN BY ONLY ONE RUN.
WE ARE ON THE PRECIPICE OF VICTORY!!!
LET'S FINISH STRONG, TEAM!
PTT
SKF
SKF
sigh
PAT

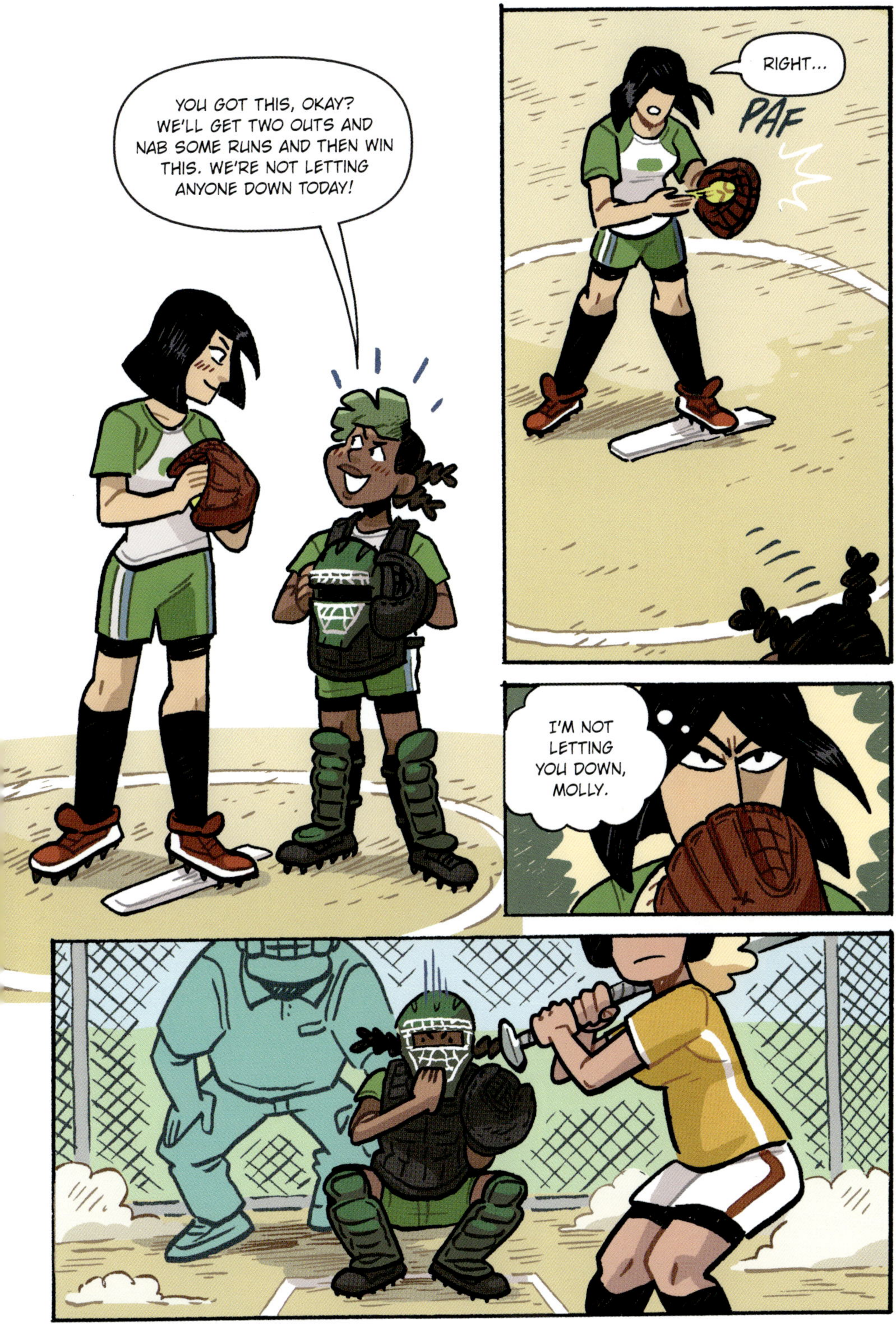
YOU GOT THIS, OKAY? WE'LL GET TWO OUTS AND NAB SOME RUNS AND THEN WIN THIS. WE'RE NOT LETTING ANYONE DOWN TODAY!
RIGHT...
PAF
I'M NOT LETTING YOU DOWN, MOLLY.

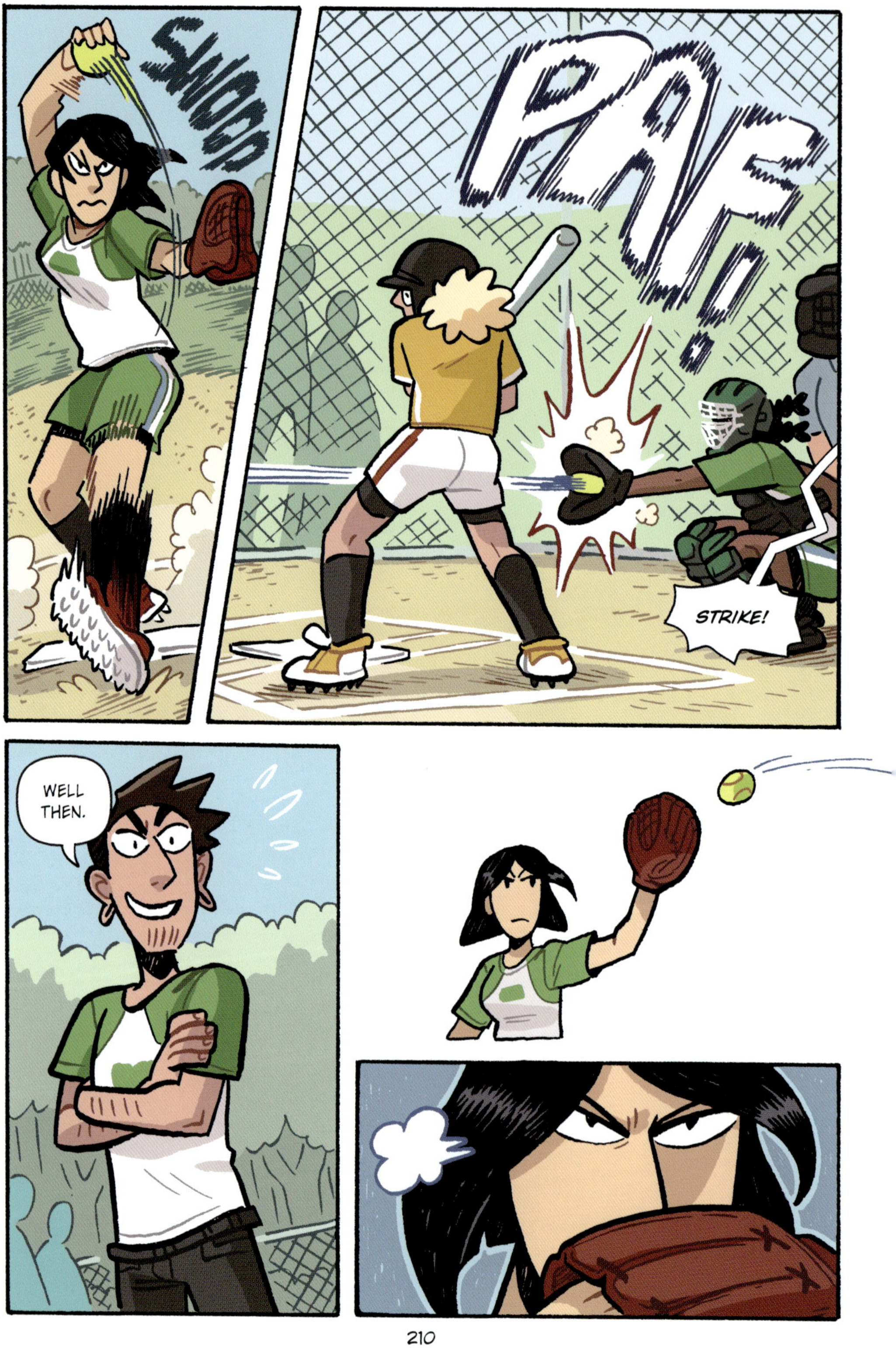
SHOOP
PAF!
STRIKE!
WELL THEN.

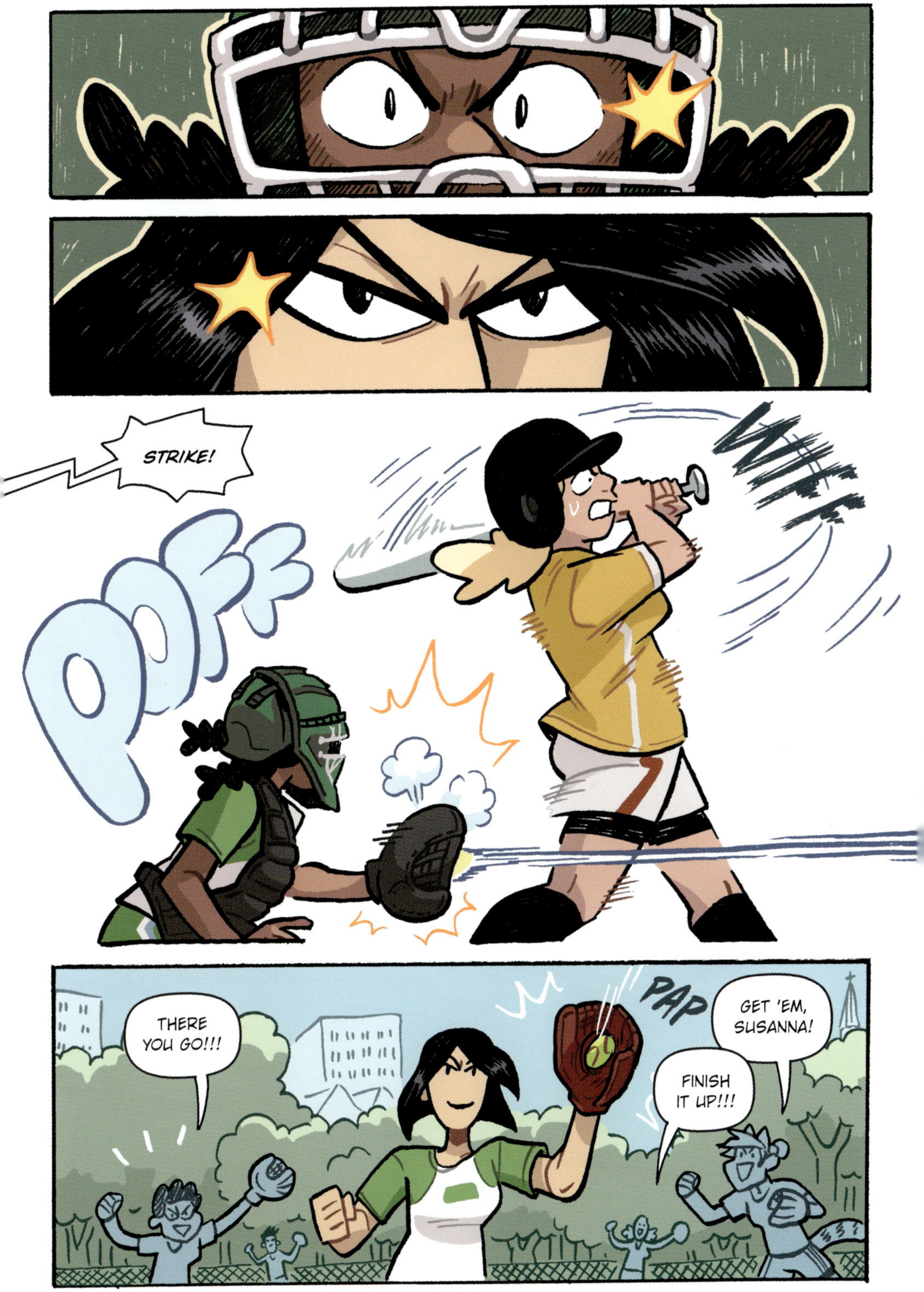
STRIKE!
POFF
WIFF
THERE YOU GO!!!
PAP
GET 'EM, SUSANNA!
FINISH IT UP!!!

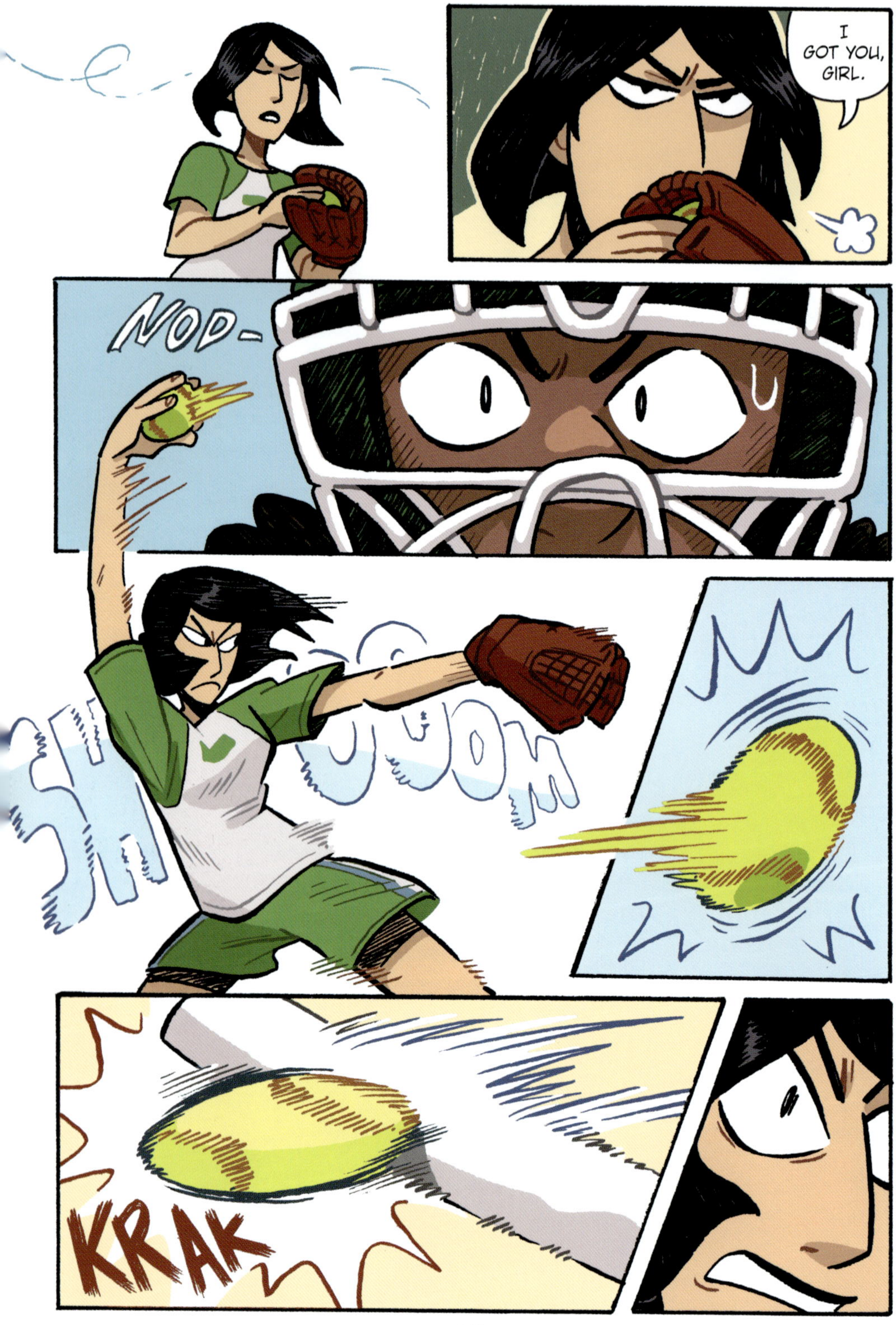

I GOT YOU, GIRL.
NOD-
WHOOOOM
KRAK

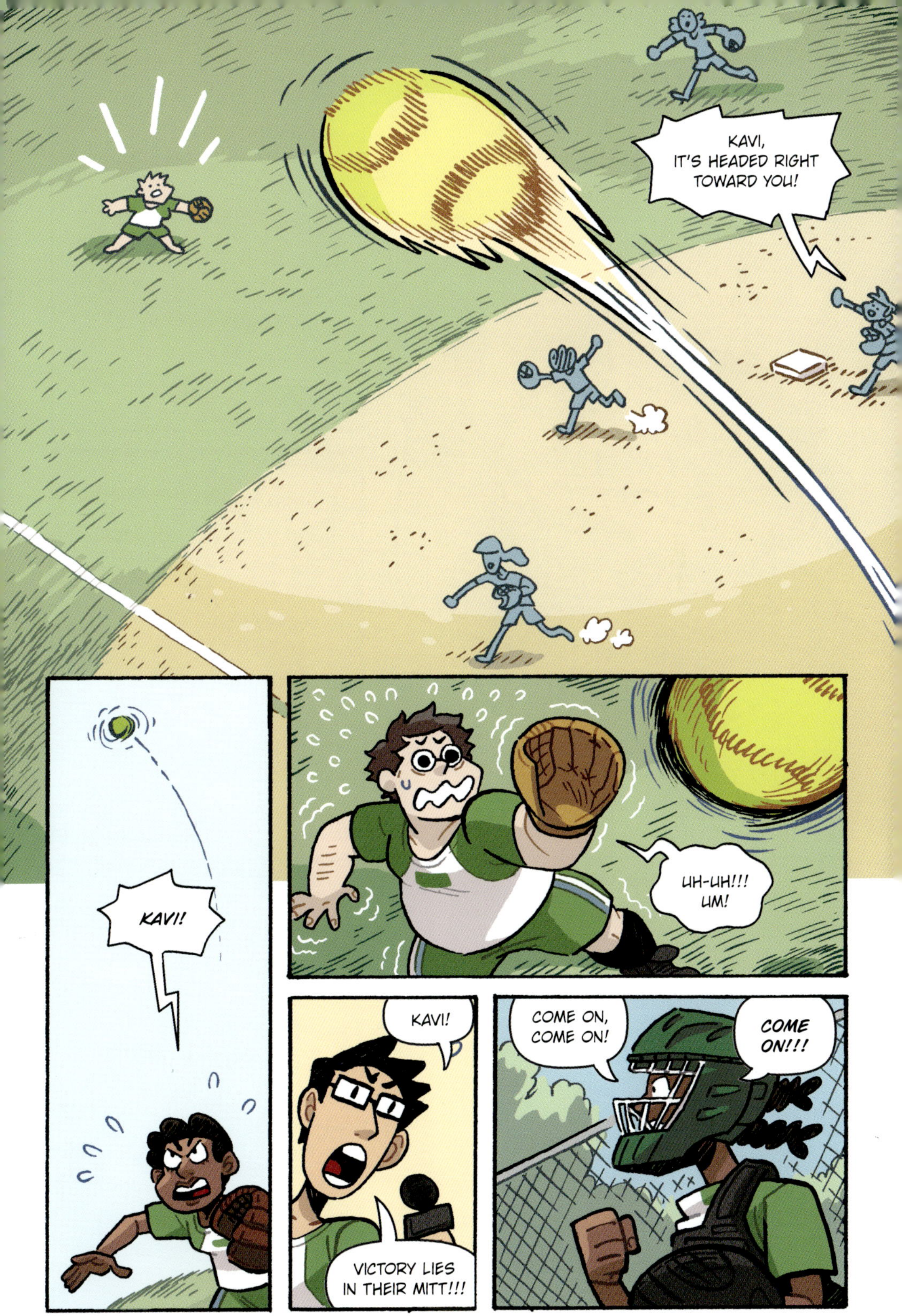
KAVI, IT'S HEADED RIGHT TOWARD YOU!
KAVI!
UH-UH!!! UM!
KAVI!
VICTORY LIES IN THEIR MITT!!!
COME ON, COME ON!
COME ON!!!

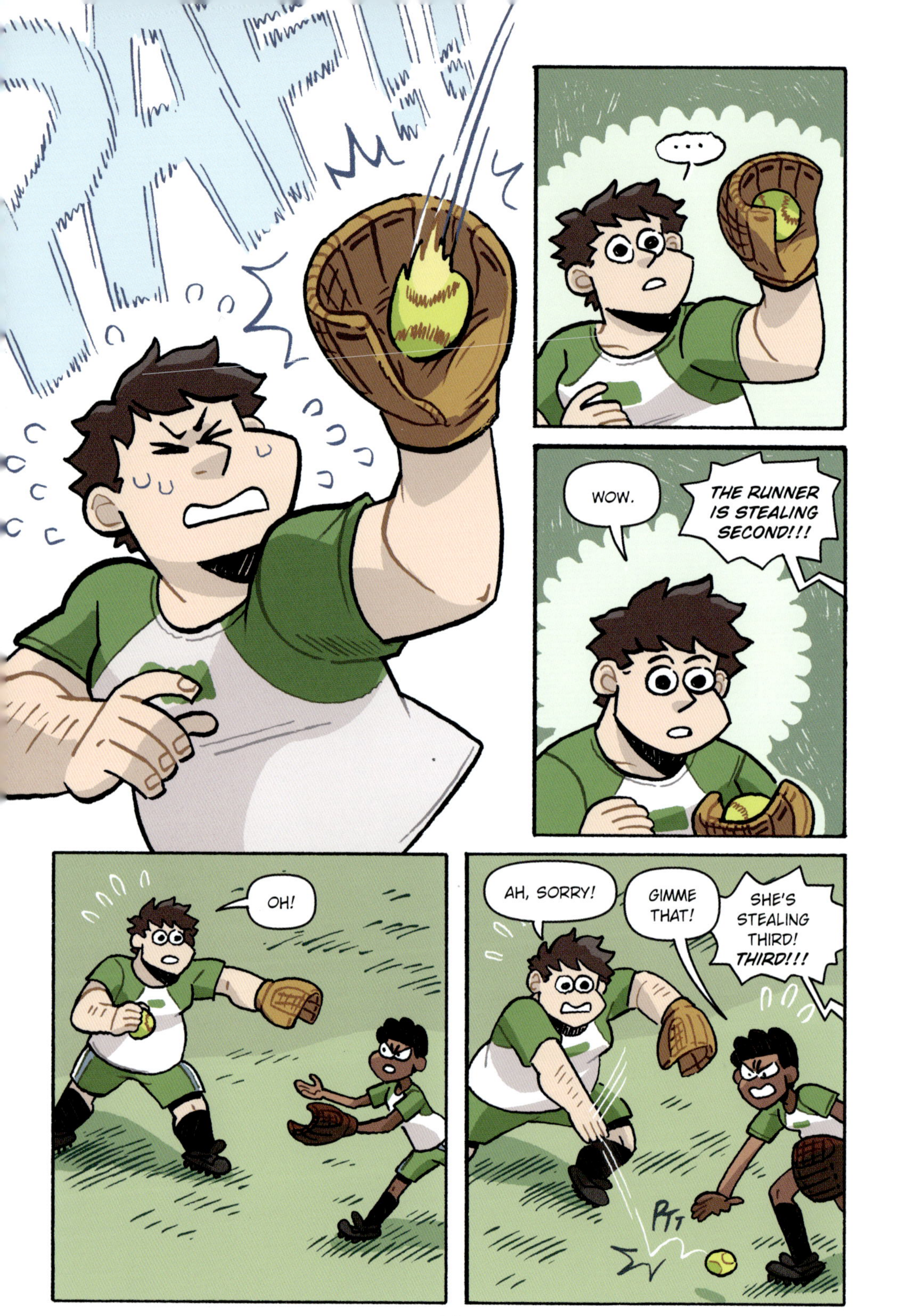

...
WOW.
THE RUNNER IS STEALING SECOND!!!
OH!
AH, SORRY!
GIMME THAT!
SHE'S STEALING THIRD! THIRD!!!
PTT

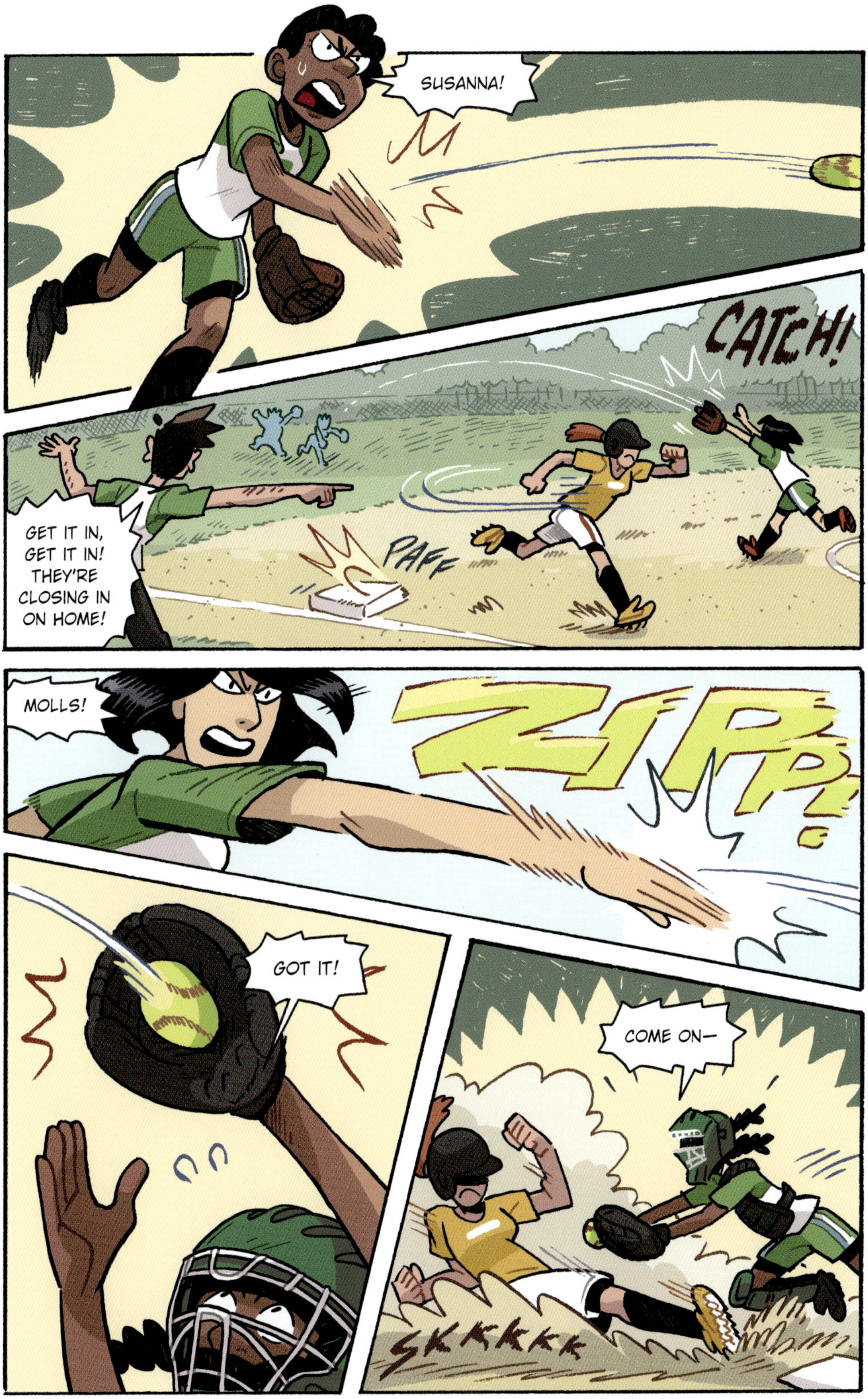
SUSANNA!
CATCH!
GET IT IN, GET IT IN! THEY'RE CLOSING IN ON HOME!
PAFF
MOLLS!
ZIPP!
GOT IT!
COME ON—
SKKKKK

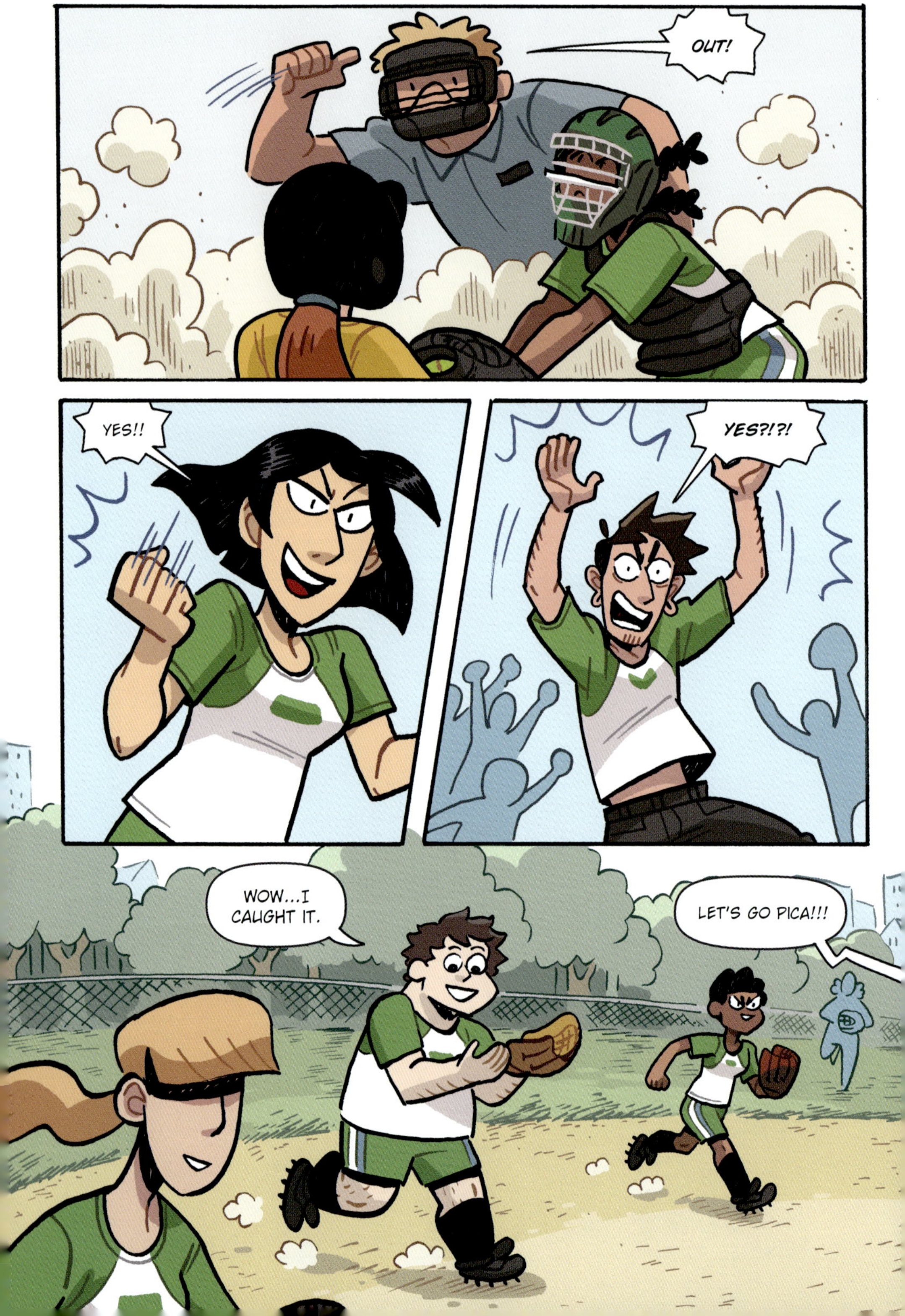
OUT!
YES!!
YES?!?!
WOW...I CAUGHT IT.
LET'S GO PICA!!!

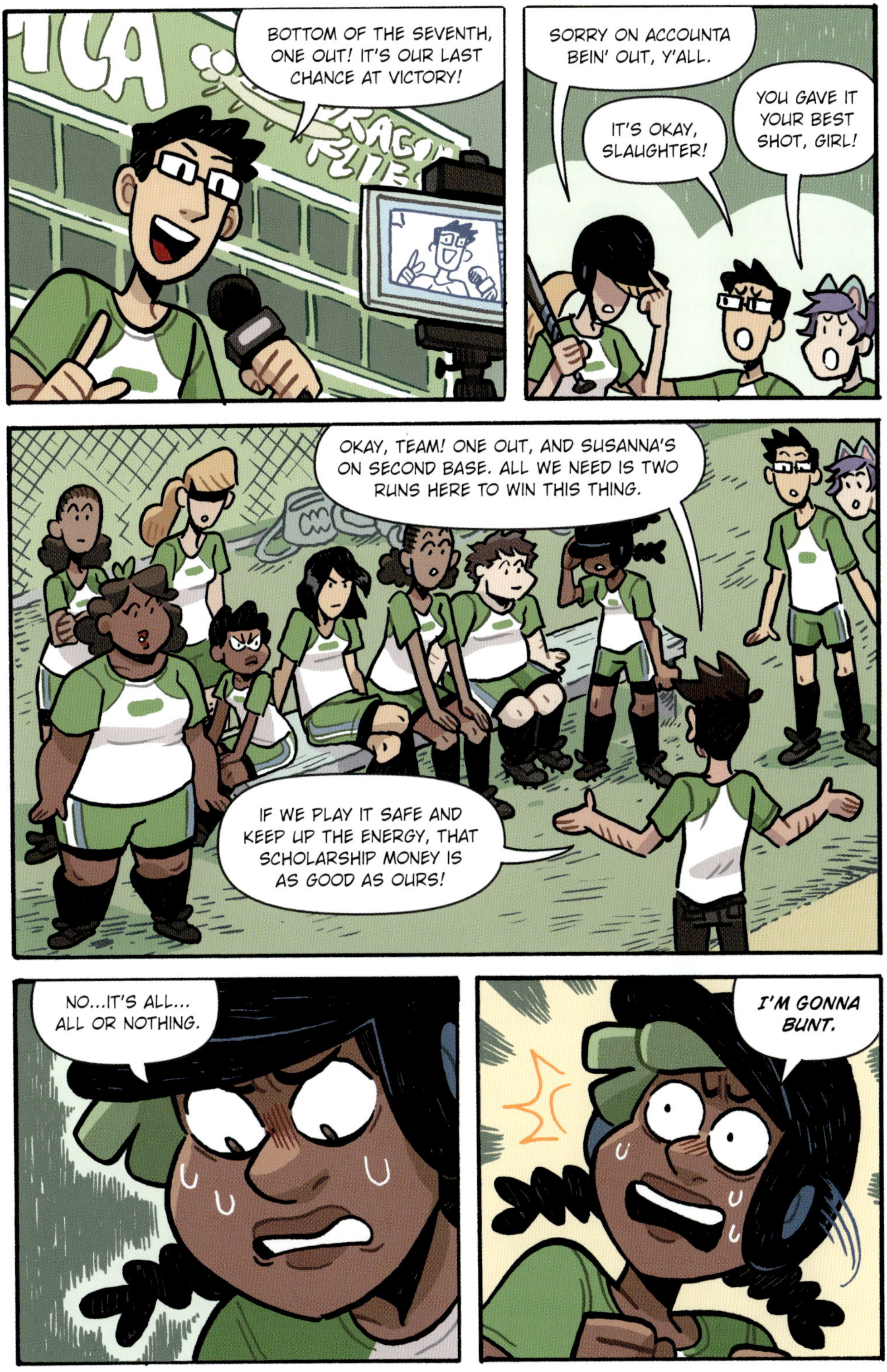
BOTTOM OF THE SEVENTH, ONE OUT! IT'S OUR LAST CHANCE AT VICTORY!
SORRY ON ACCOUNTA BEIN' OUT, Y'ALL.
IT'S OKAY, SLAUGHTER!
YOU GAVE IT YOUR BEST SHOT, GIRL!
OKAY, TEAM! ONE OUT, AND SUSANNA'S ON SECOND BASE. ALL WE NEED IS TWO RUNS HERE TO WIN THIS THING.
IF WE PLAY IT SAFE AND KEEP UP THE ENERGY, THAT SCHOLARSHIP MONEY IS AS GOOD AS OURS!
NO...IT'S ALL... ALL OR NOTHING.
I'M GONNA BUNT.

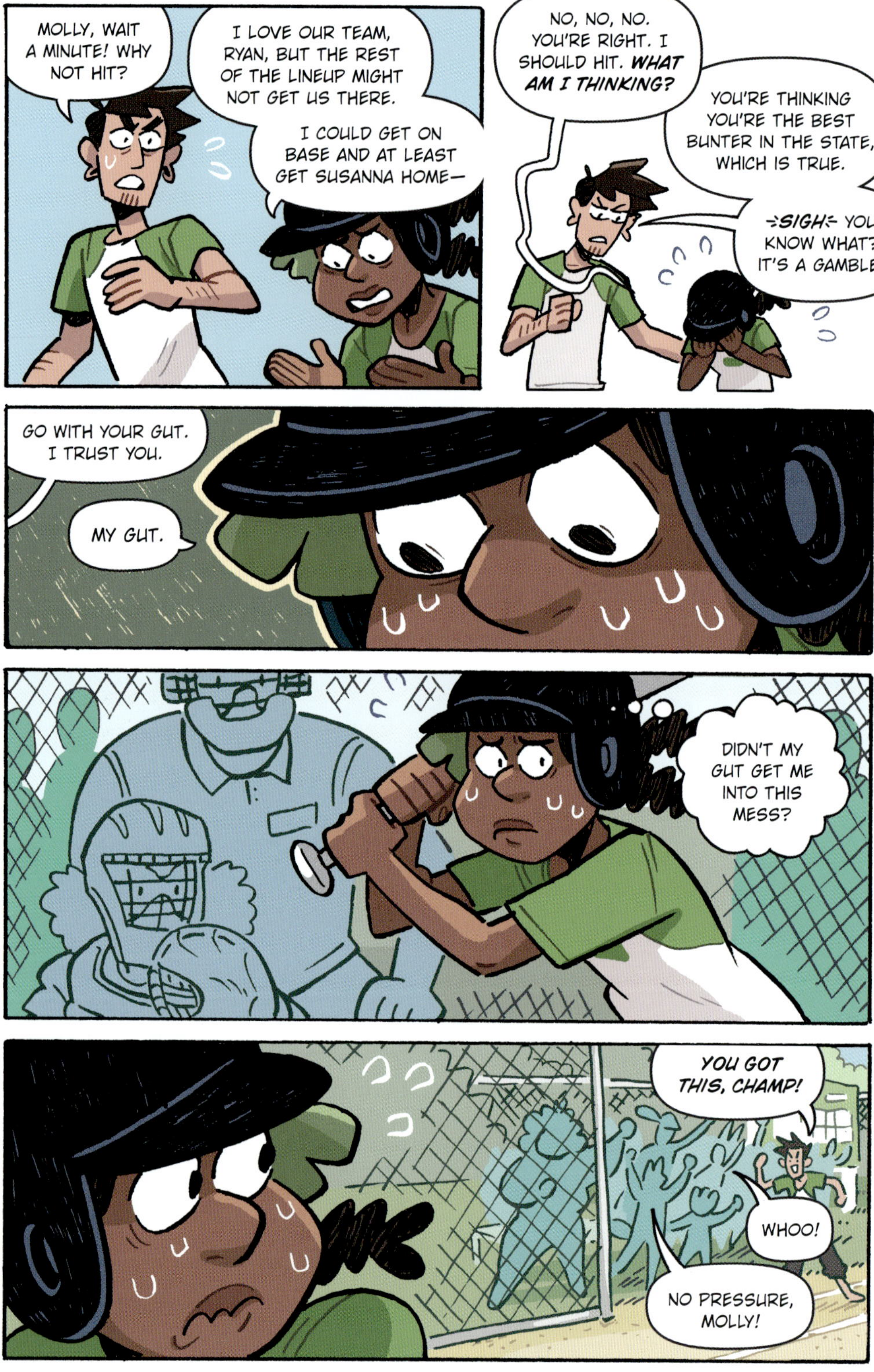
MOLLY, WAIT A MINUTE! WHY NOT HIT?
I LOVE OUR TEAM, RYAN, BUT THE REST OF THE LINEUP MIGHT NOT GET US THERE.
I COULD GET ON BASE AND AT LEAST GET SUSANNA HOME—
NO, NO, NO. YOU'RE RIGHT. I SHOULD HIT. *WHAT AM I THINKING?*
YOU'RE THINKING YOU'RE THE BEST BUNTER IN THE STATE, WHICH IS TRUE.
SIGH YOU KNOW WHAT? IT'S A GAMBLE.
GO WITH YOUR GUT. I TRUST YOU.
MY GUT.
DIDN'T MY GUT GET ME INTO THIS MESS?
YOU GOT THIS, CHAMP!
WHOO!
NO PRESSURE, MOLLY!

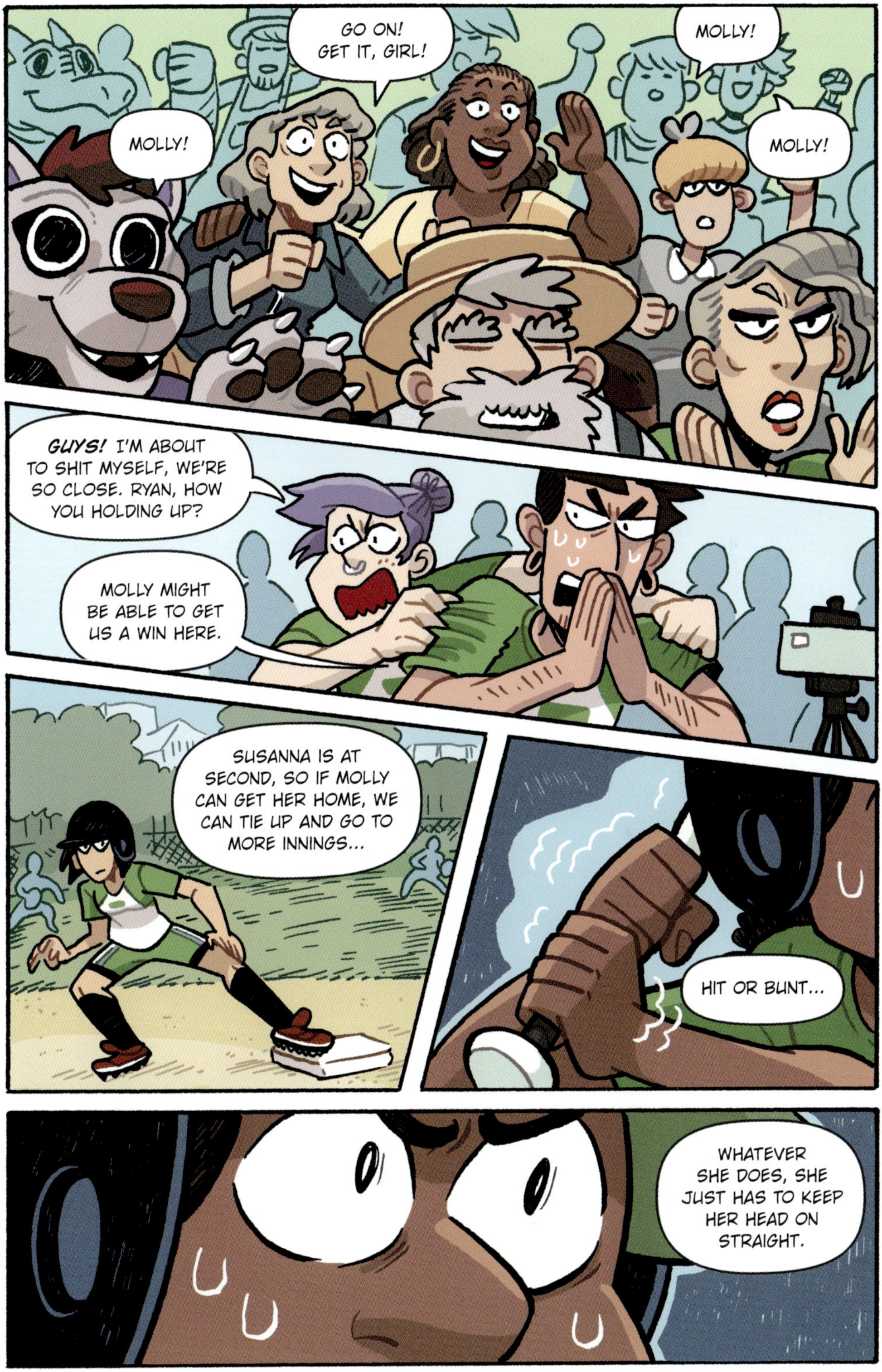
GO ON!
GET IT, GIRL!
MOLLY!
MOLLY!
MOLLY!
GUYS! I'M ABOUT TO SHIT MYSELF, WE'RE SO CLOSE. RYAN, HOW YOU HOLDING UP?
MOLLY MIGHT BE ABLE TO GET US A WIN HERE.
SUSANNA IS AT SECOND, SO IF MOLLY CAN GET HER HOME, WE CAN TIE UP AND GO TO MORE INNINGS...
HIT OR BUNT...
WHATEVER SHE DOES, SHE JUST HAS TO KEEP HER HEAD ON STRAIGHT.

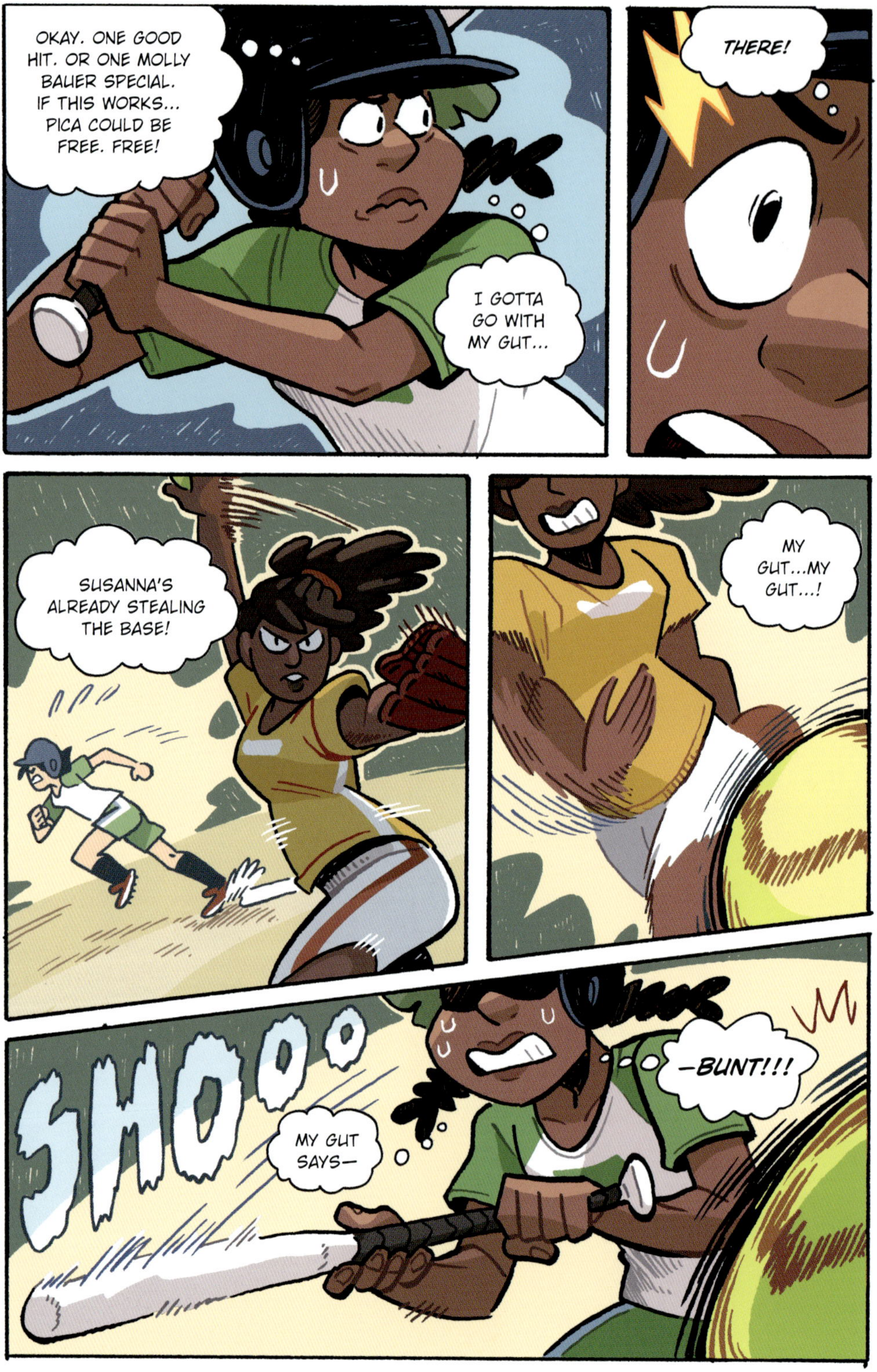
OKAY. ONE GOOD HIT. OR ONE MOLLY BAUER SPECIAL. IF THIS WORKS... PICA COULD BE FREE. FREE!
I GOTTA GO WITH MY GUT...
THERE!
SUSANNA'S ALREADY STEALING THE BASE!
MY GUT...MY GUT...!
SHOOO
MY GUT SAYS—
—BUNT!!!

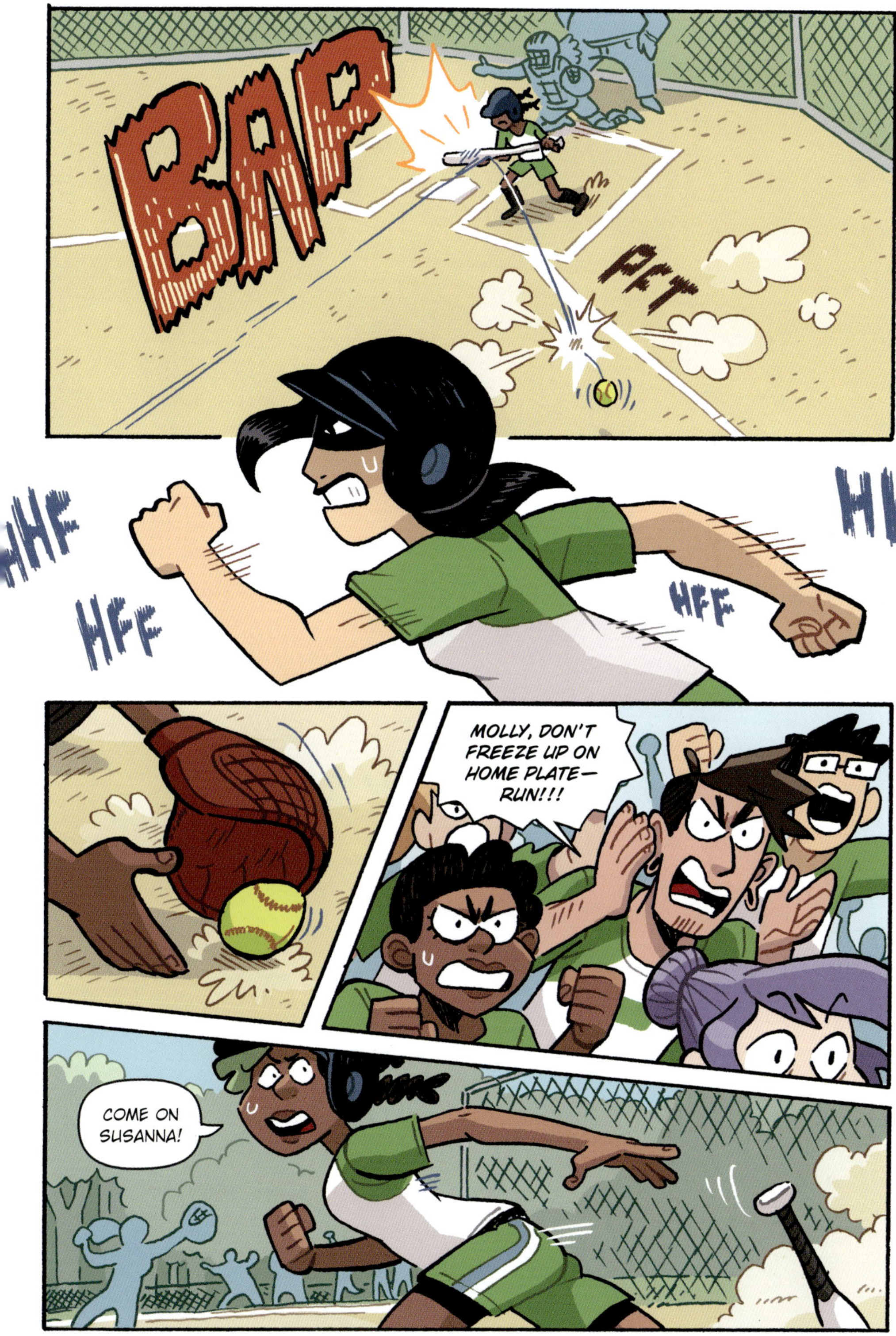
BAP
PFT
HHF
HFF
HFF
HHF
MOLLY, DON'T FREEZE UP ON HOME PLATE— RUN!!!
COME ON SUSANNA!

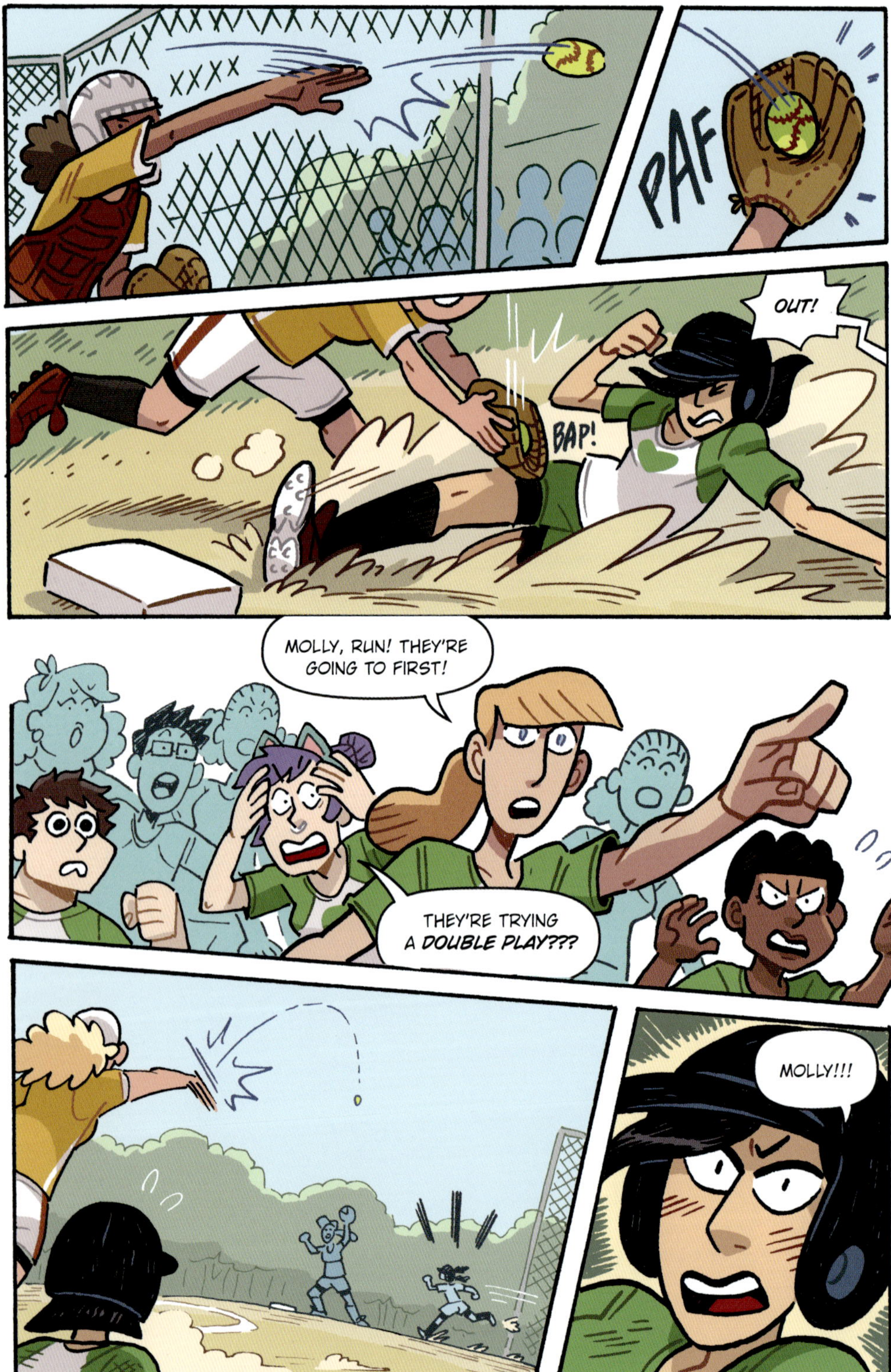
PAF
OUT!
BAP!
MOLLY, RUN! THEY'RE GOING TO FIRST!
THEY'RE TRYING A DOUBLE PLAY???
MOLLY!!!

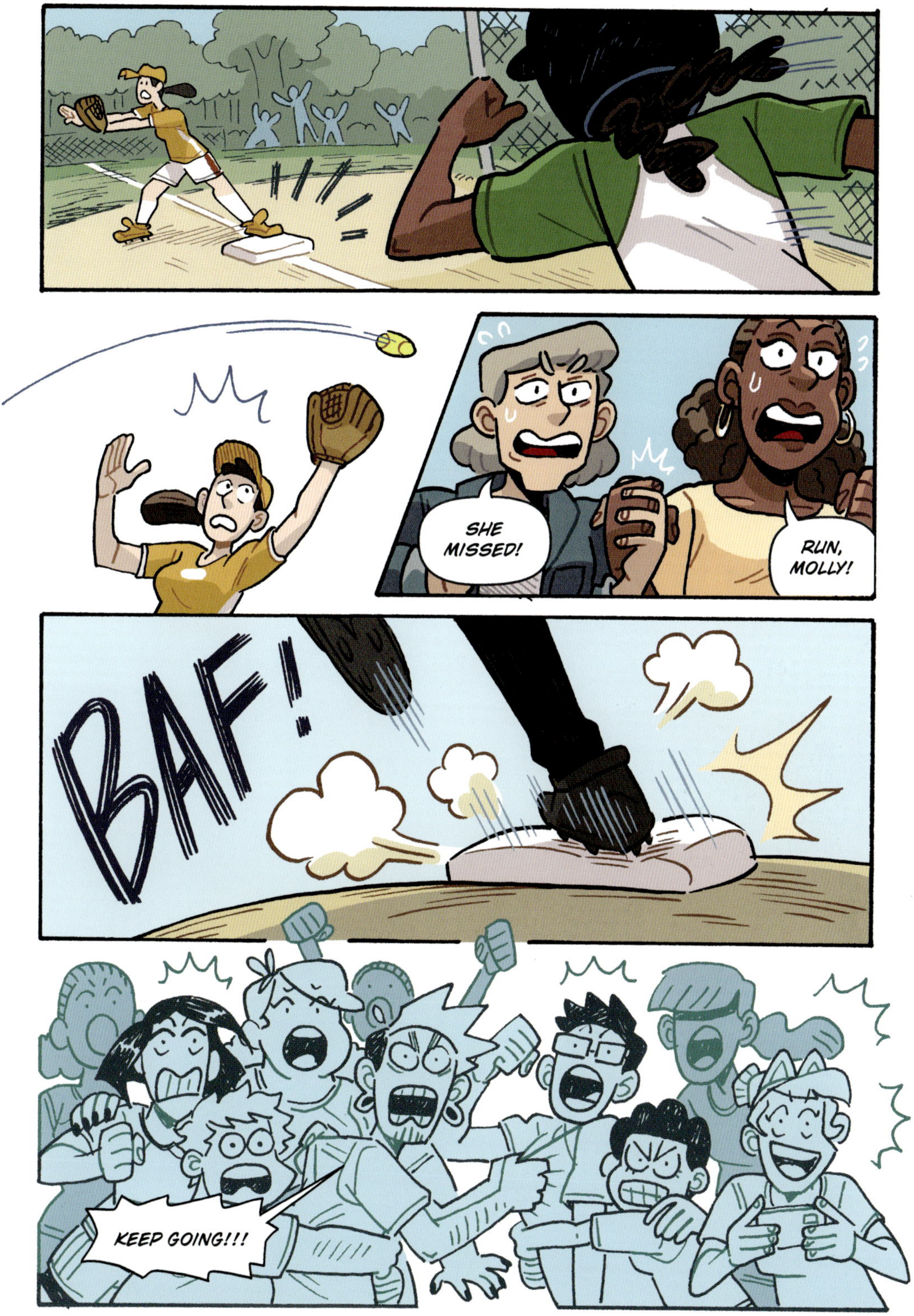
SHE MISSED!
RUN, MOLLY!
BAF!
KEEP GOING!!!

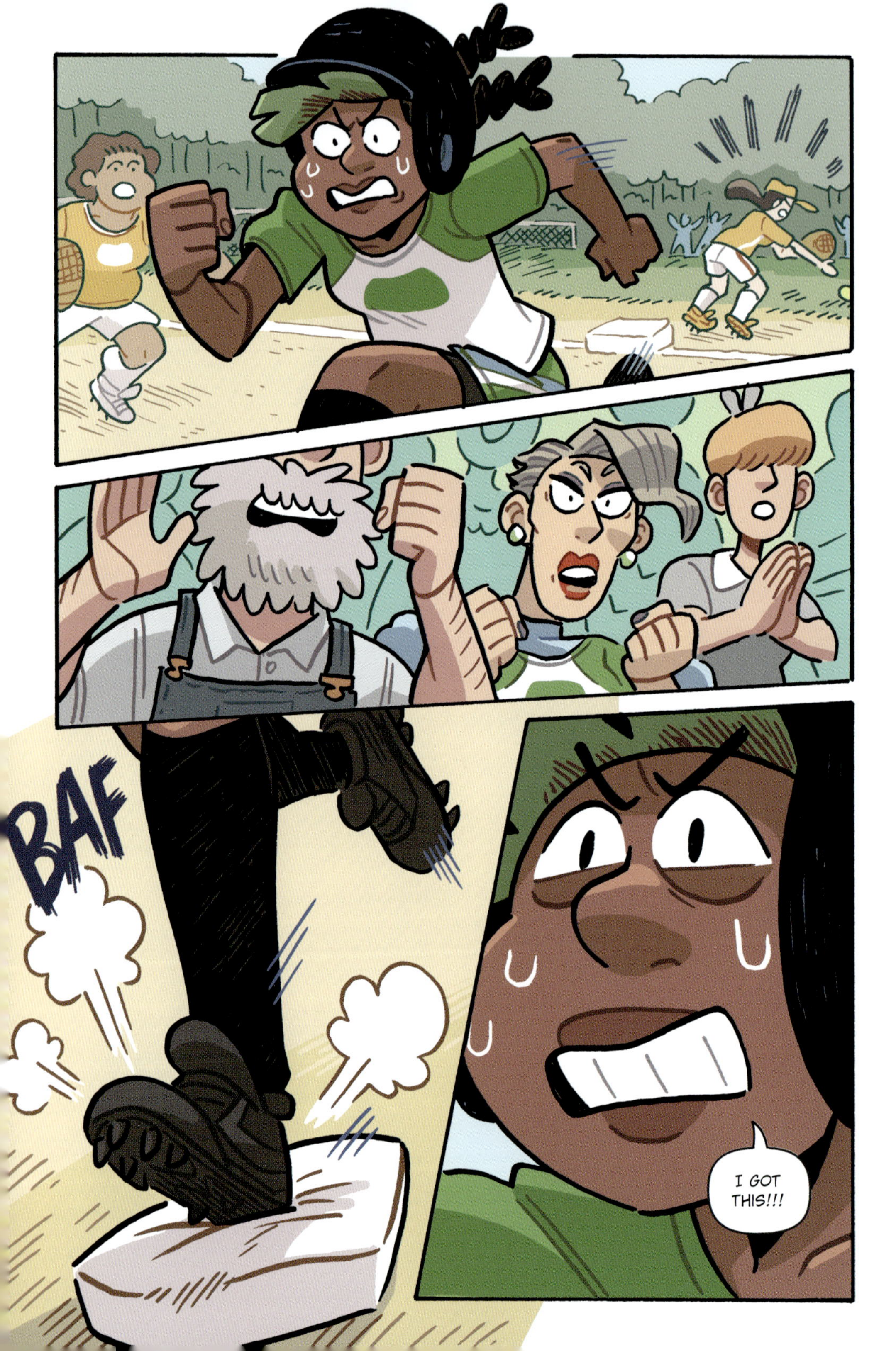
BAF
I GOT THIS!!!

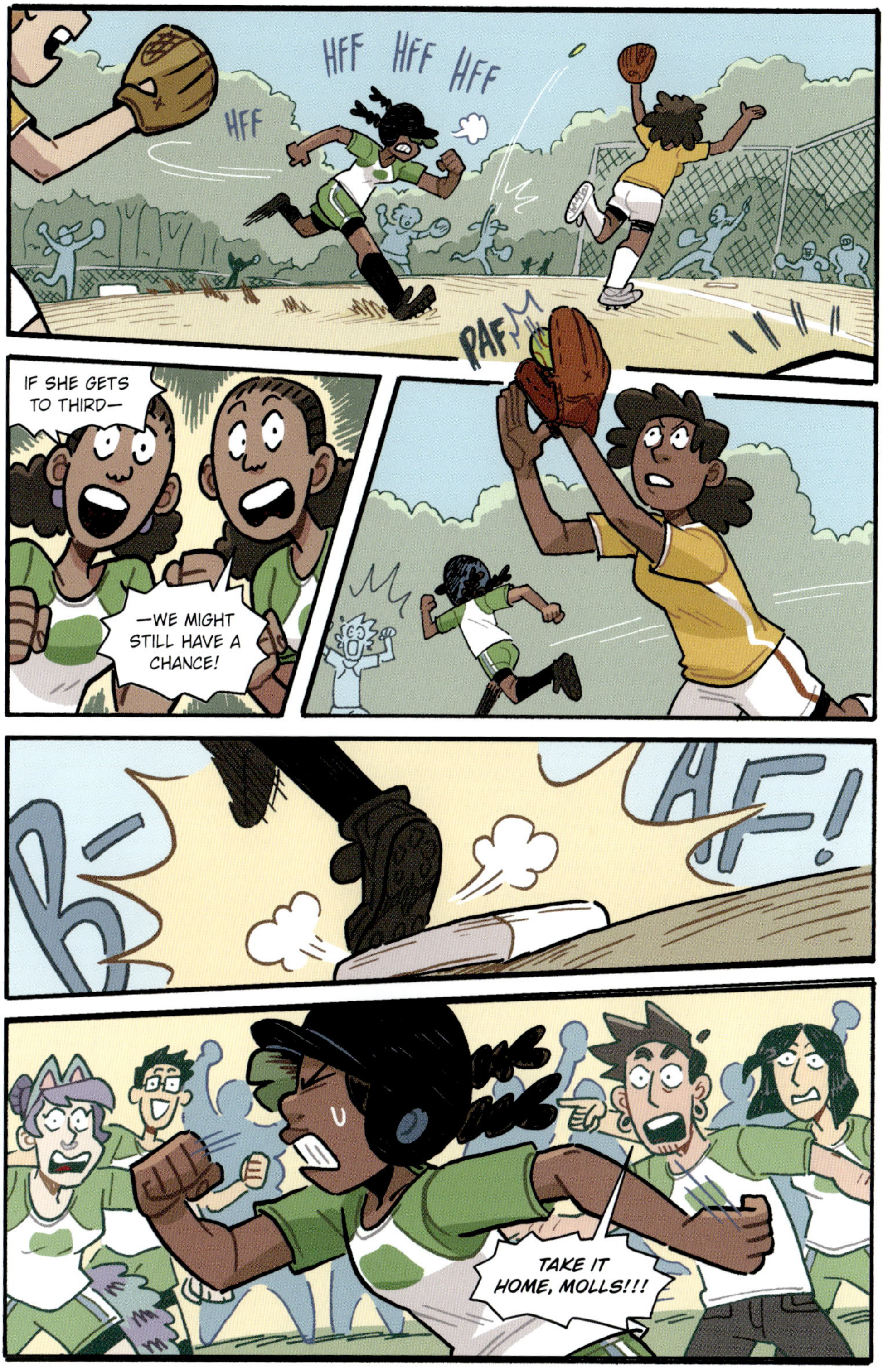
HFF HFF HFF
HFF
PAF
IF SHE GETS TO THIRD—
—WE MIGHT STILL HAVE A CHANCE!
B-
AF!
TAKE IT HOME, MOLLS!!!

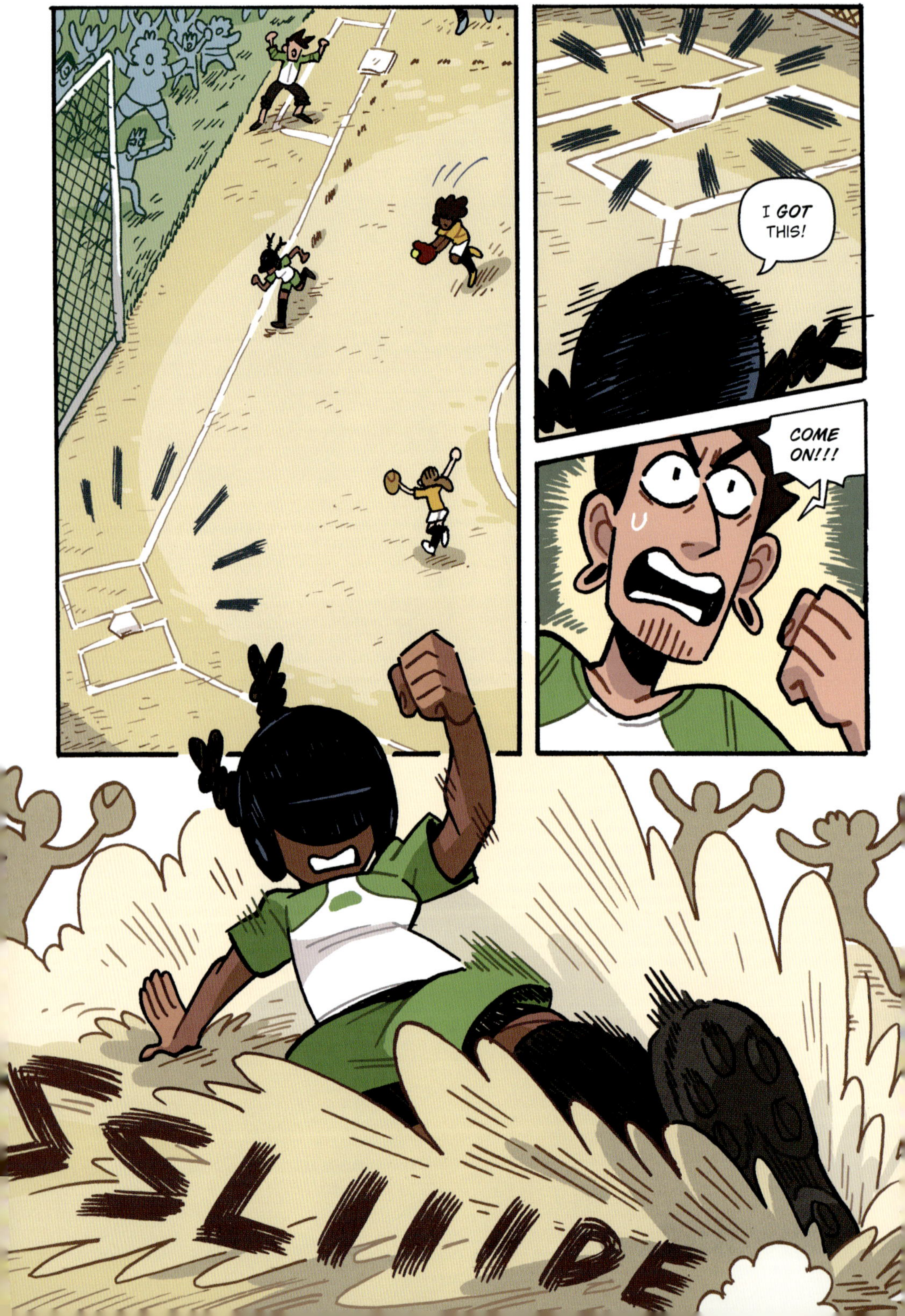
I GOT THIS!
COME ON!!!
SSLIIIDE

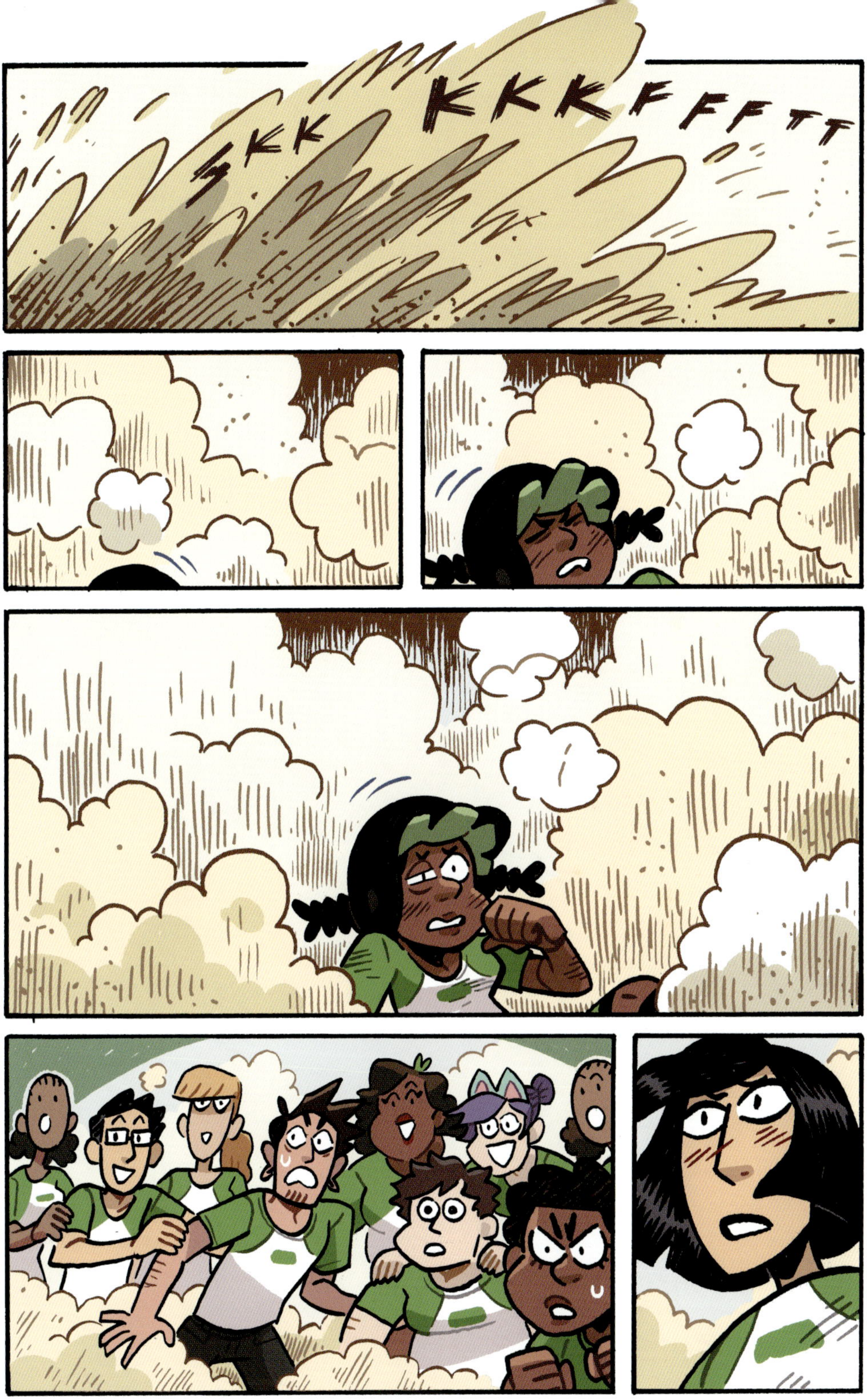
SKKKKKFFFFTT

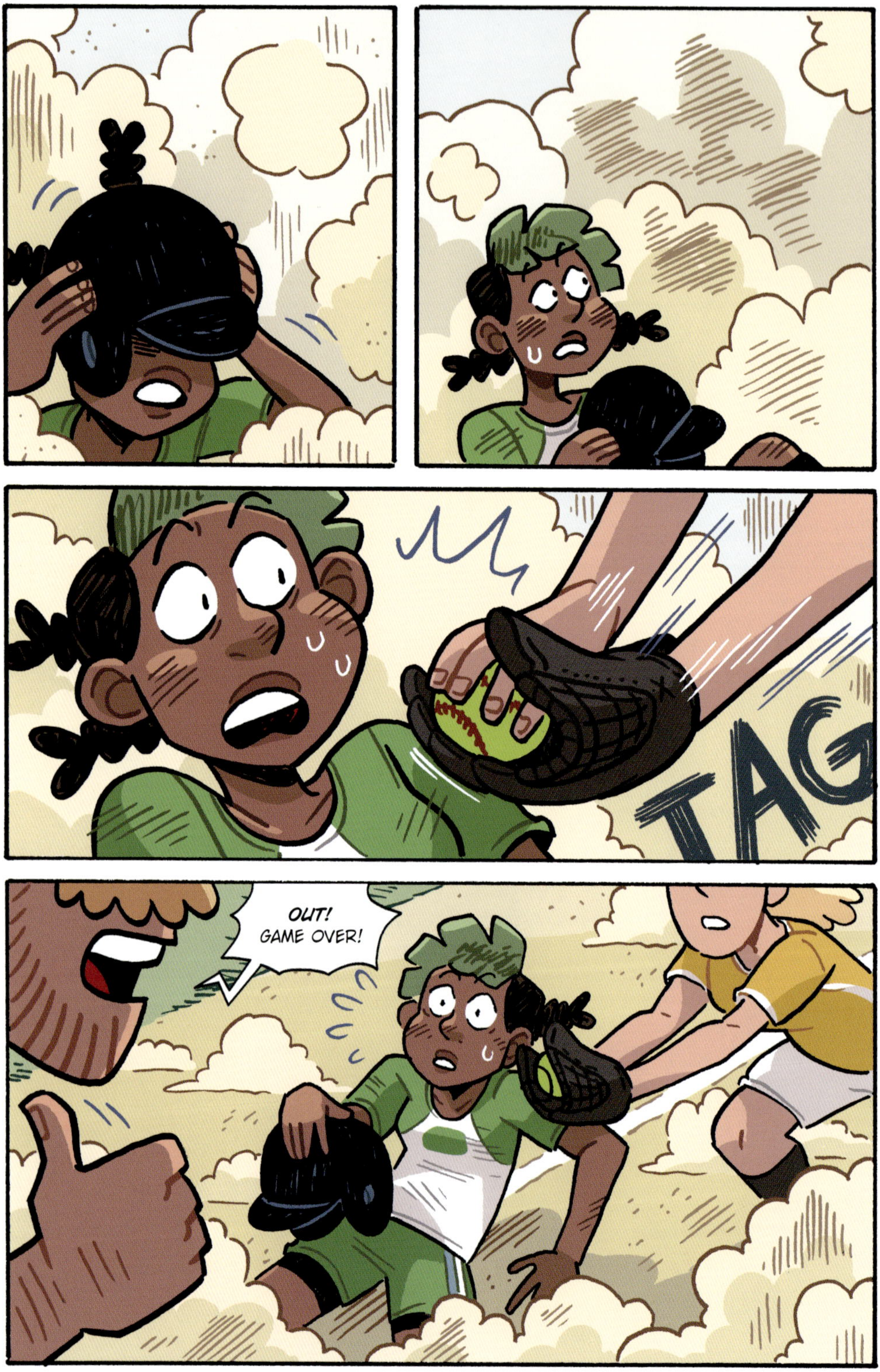
TAG
OUT!
GAME OVER!

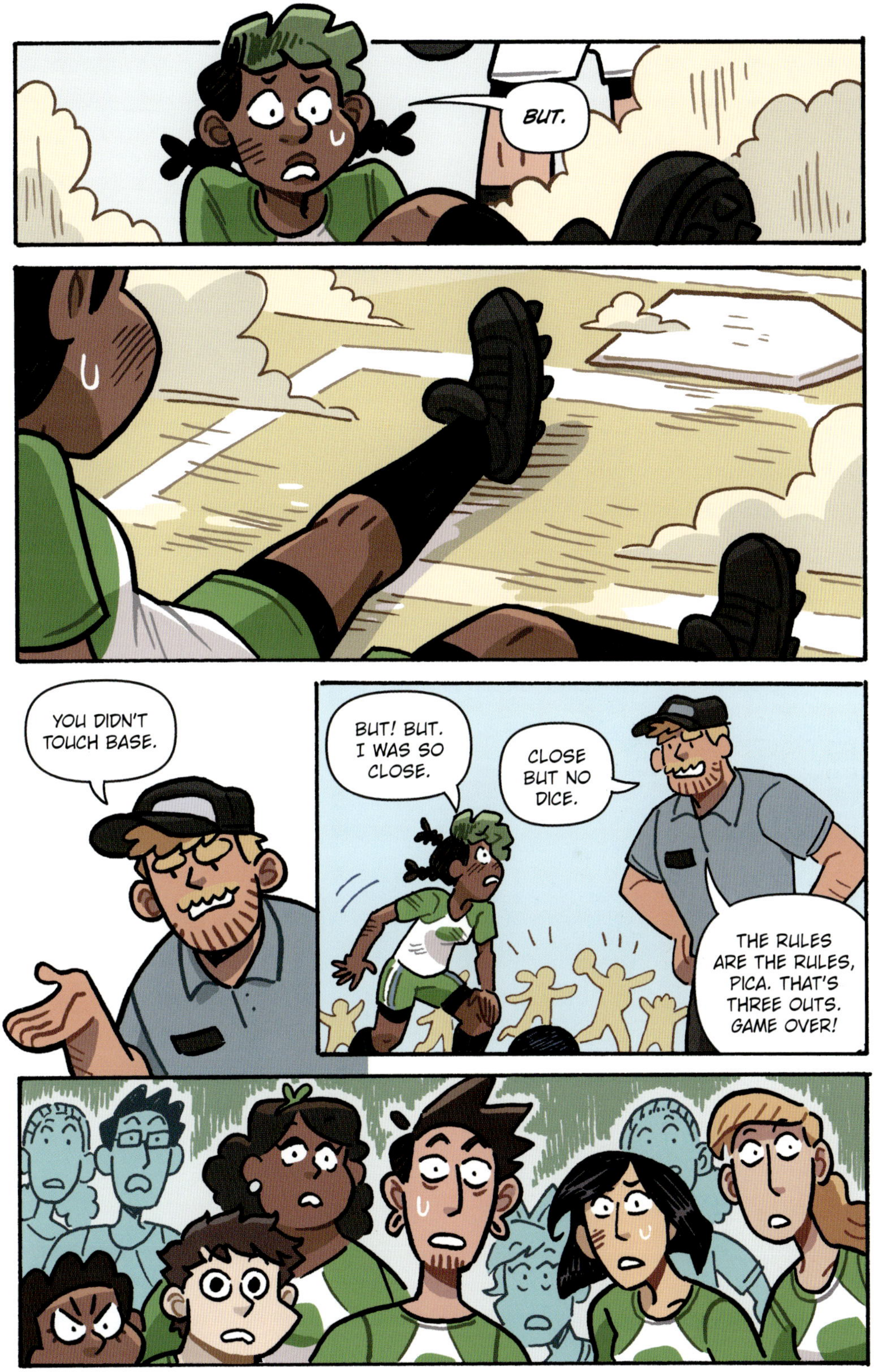
BUT.
YOU DIDN'T TOUCH BASE.
BUT! BUT. I WAS SO CLOSE.
CLOSE BUT NO DICE.
THE RULES ARE THE RULES, PICA. THAT'S THREE OUTS. GAME OVER!

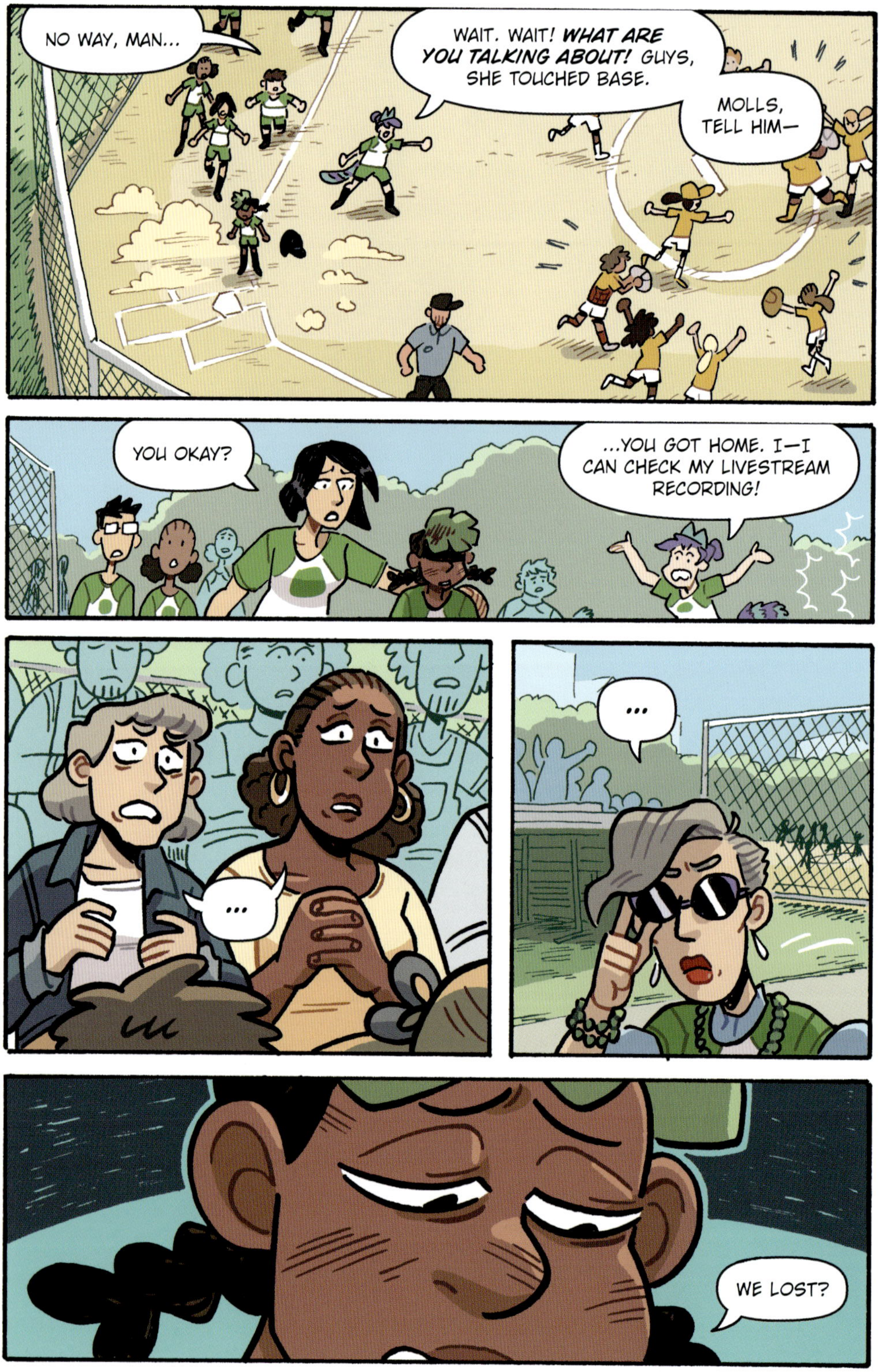
NO WAY, MAN...
WAIT. WAIT! WHAT ARE YOU TALKING ABOUT! GUYS, SHE TOUCHED BASE.
MOLLS, TELL HIM—
YOU OKAY?
...YOU GOT HOME. I—I CAN CHECK MY LIVESTREAM RECORDING!
...
...
WE LOST?

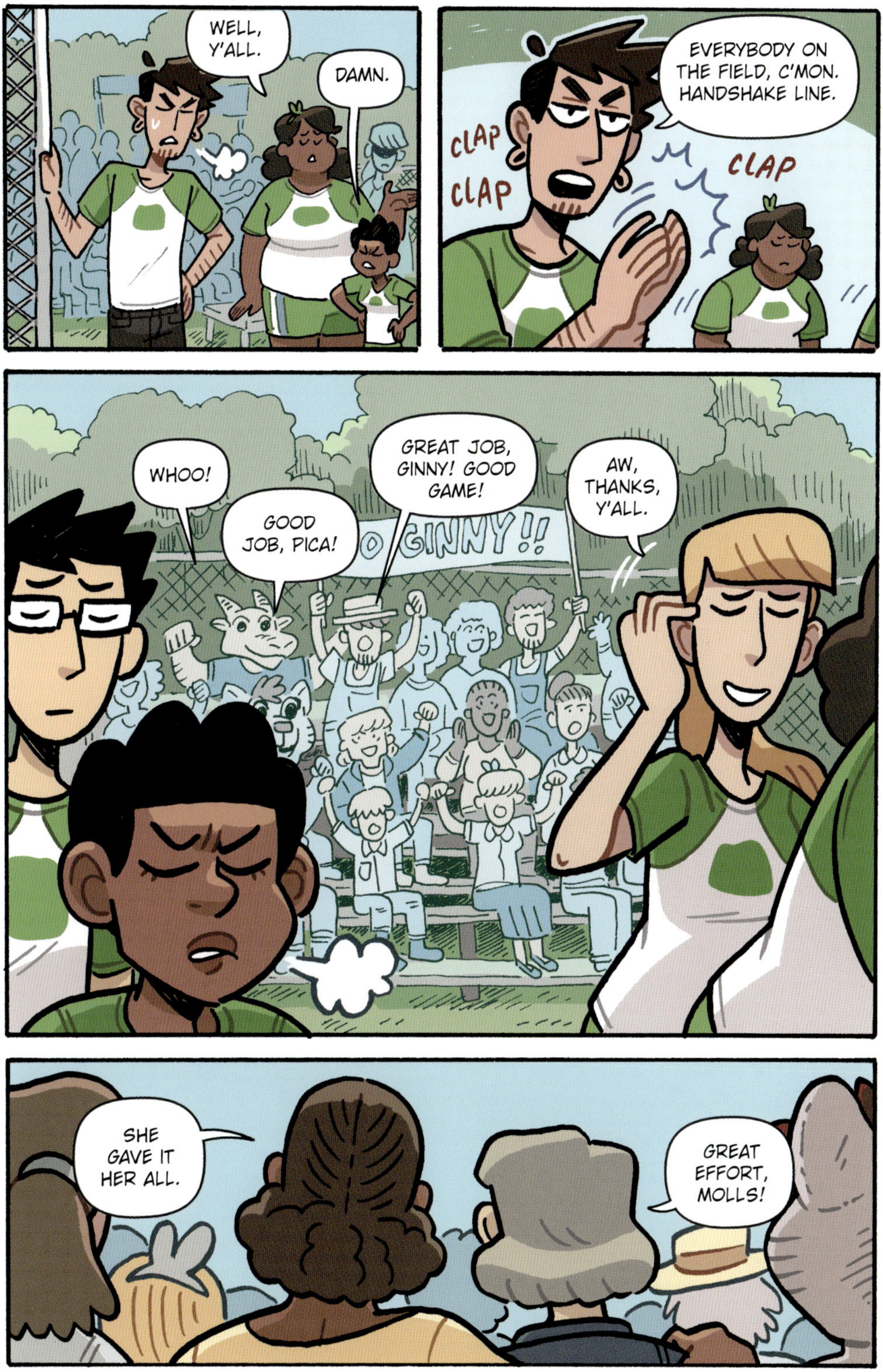
WELL, Y'ALL.
DAMN.
EVERYBODY ON THE FIELD, C'MON. HANDSHAKE LINE.
CLAP CLAP
CLAP
WHOO!
GOOD JOB, PICA!
GREAT JOB, GINNY! GOOD GAME!
AW, THANKS, Y'ALL.
O GINNY!!
SHE GAVE IT HER ALL.
GREAT EFFORT, MOLLS!

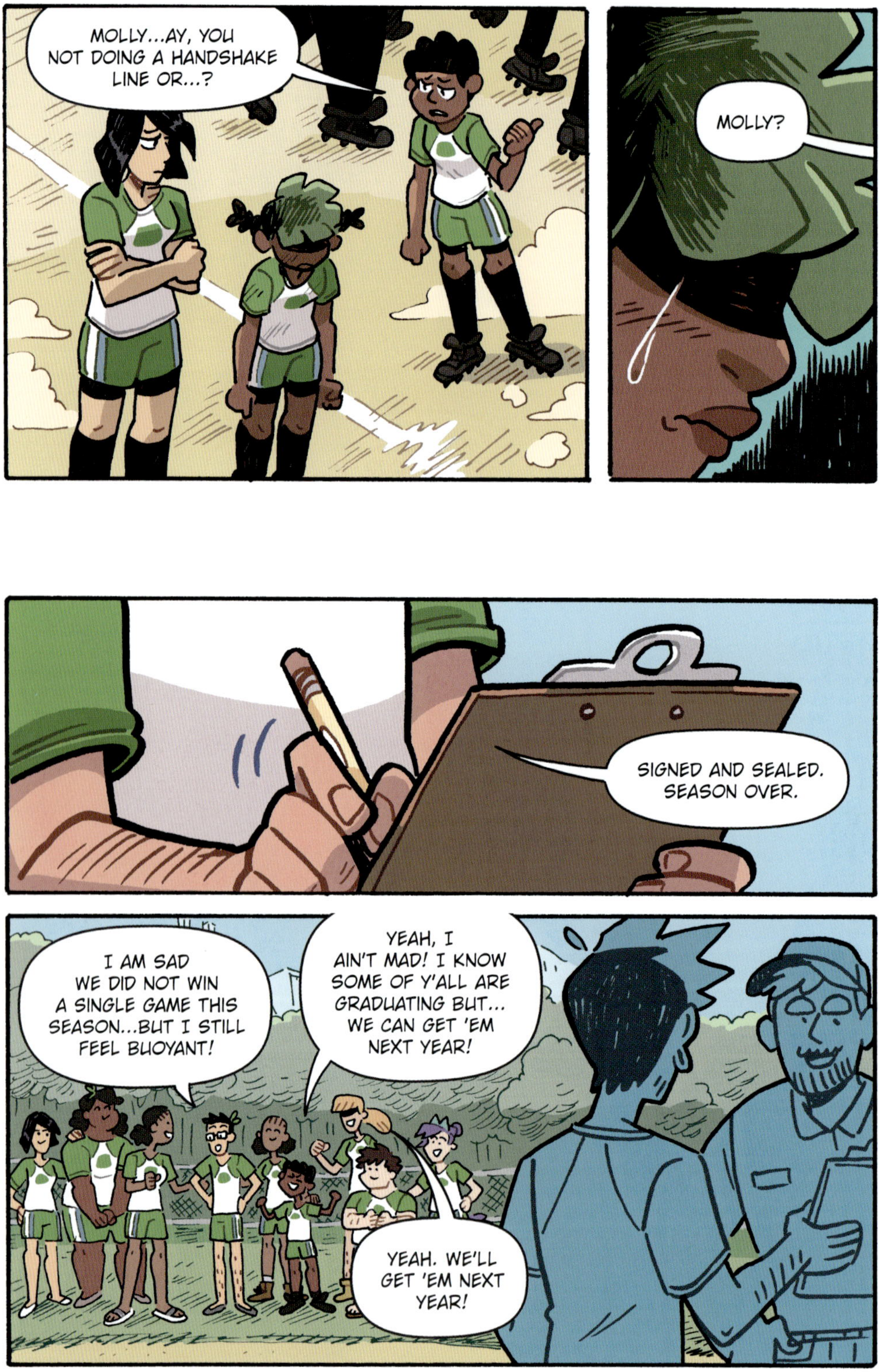
MOLLY...AY, YOU NOT DOING A HANDSHAKE LINE OR...?
MOLLY?
SIGNED AND SEALED. SEASON OVER.
I AM SAD WE DID NOT WIN A SINGLE GAME THIS SEASON...BUT I STILL FEEL BUOYANT!
YEAH, I AIN'T MAD! I KNOW SOME OF Y'ALL ARE GRADUATING BUT... WE CAN GET 'EM NEXT YEAR!
YEAH. WE'LL GET 'EM NEXT YEAR!

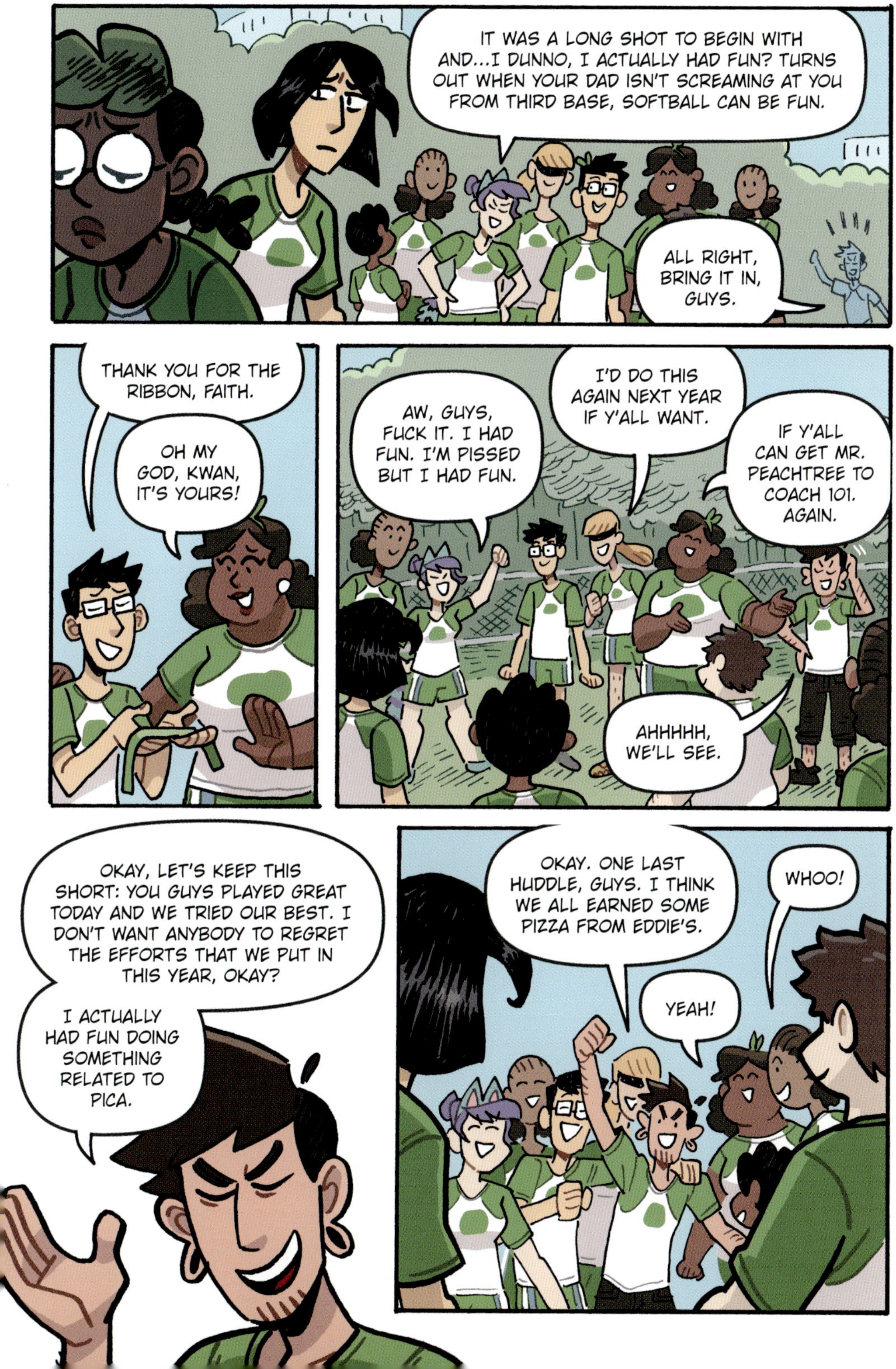
IT WAS A LONG SHOT TO BEGIN WITH AND...I DUNNO, I ACTUALLY HAD FUN? TURNS OUT WHEN YOUR DAD ISN'T SCREAMING AT YOU FROM THIRD BASE, SOFTBALL CAN BE FUN.
ALL RIGHT, BRING IT IN, GUYS.
THANK YOU FOR THE RIBBON, FAITH.
OH MY GOD, KWAN, IT'S YOURS!
AW, GUYS, FUCK IT. I HAD FUN. I'M PISSED BUT I HAD FUN.
I'D DO THIS AGAIN NEXT YEAR IF Y'ALL WANT.
IF Y'ALL CAN GET MR. PEACHTREE TO COACH 101. AGAIN.
AHHHHH, WE'LL SEE.
OKAY, LET'S KEEP THIS SHORT: YOU GUYS PLAYED GREAT TODAY AND WE TRIED OUR BEST. I DON'T WANT ANYBODY TO REGRET THE EFFORTS THAT WE PUT IN THIS YEAR, OKAY?
I ACTUALLY HAD FUN DOING SOMETHING RELATED TO PICA.
OKAY. ONE LAST HUDDLE, GUYS. I THINK WE ALL EARNED SOME PIZZA FROM EDDIE'S.
WHOO!
YEAH!

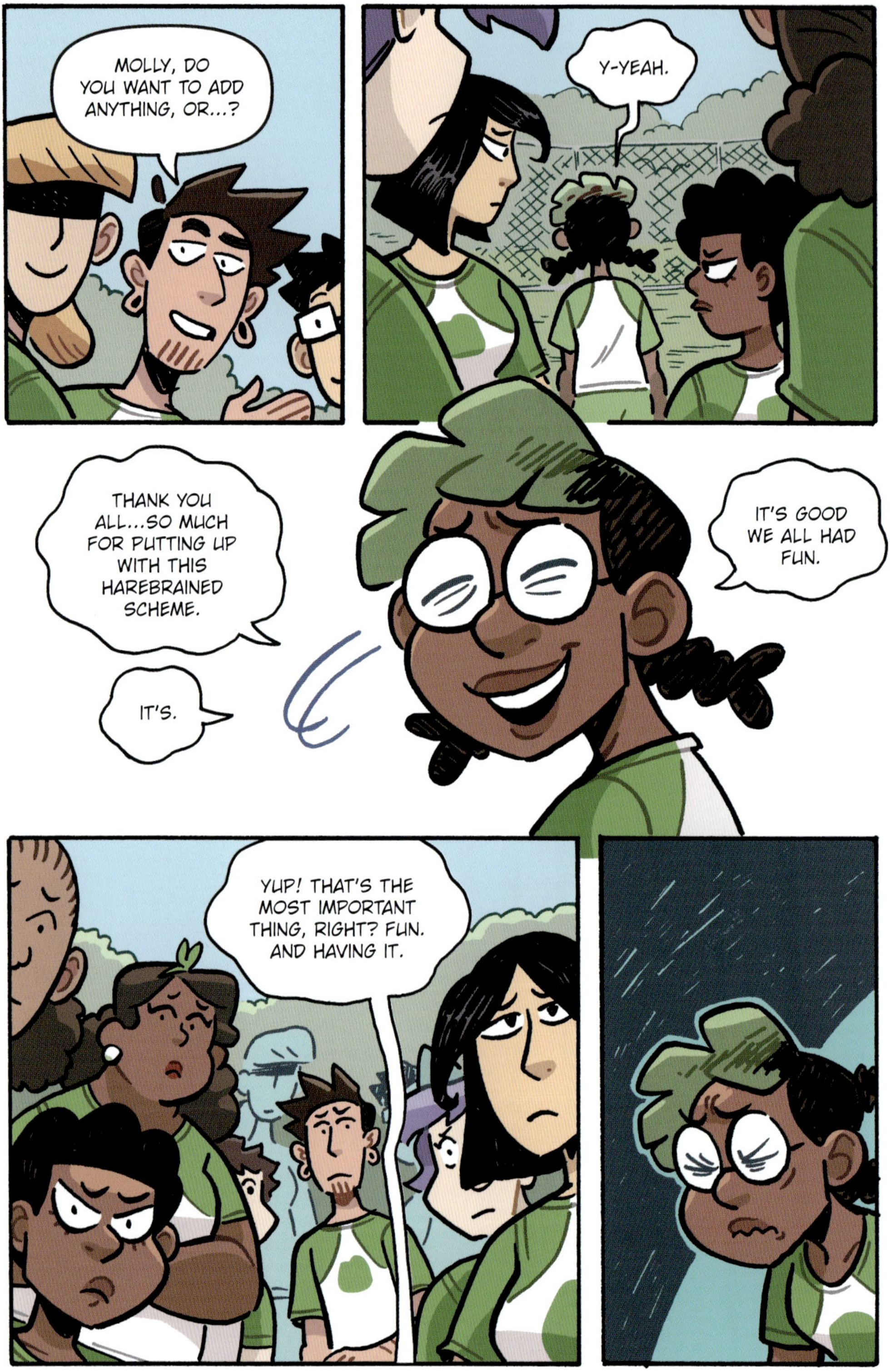
MOLLY, DO YOU WANT TO ADD ANYTHING, OR...?
Y-YEAH.
THANK YOU ALL...SO MUCH FOR PUTTING UP WITH THIS HAREBRAINED SCHEME.
IT'S.
IT'S GOOD WE ALL HAD FUN.
YUP! THAT'S THE MOST IMPORTANT THING, RIGHT? FUN. AND HAVING IT.

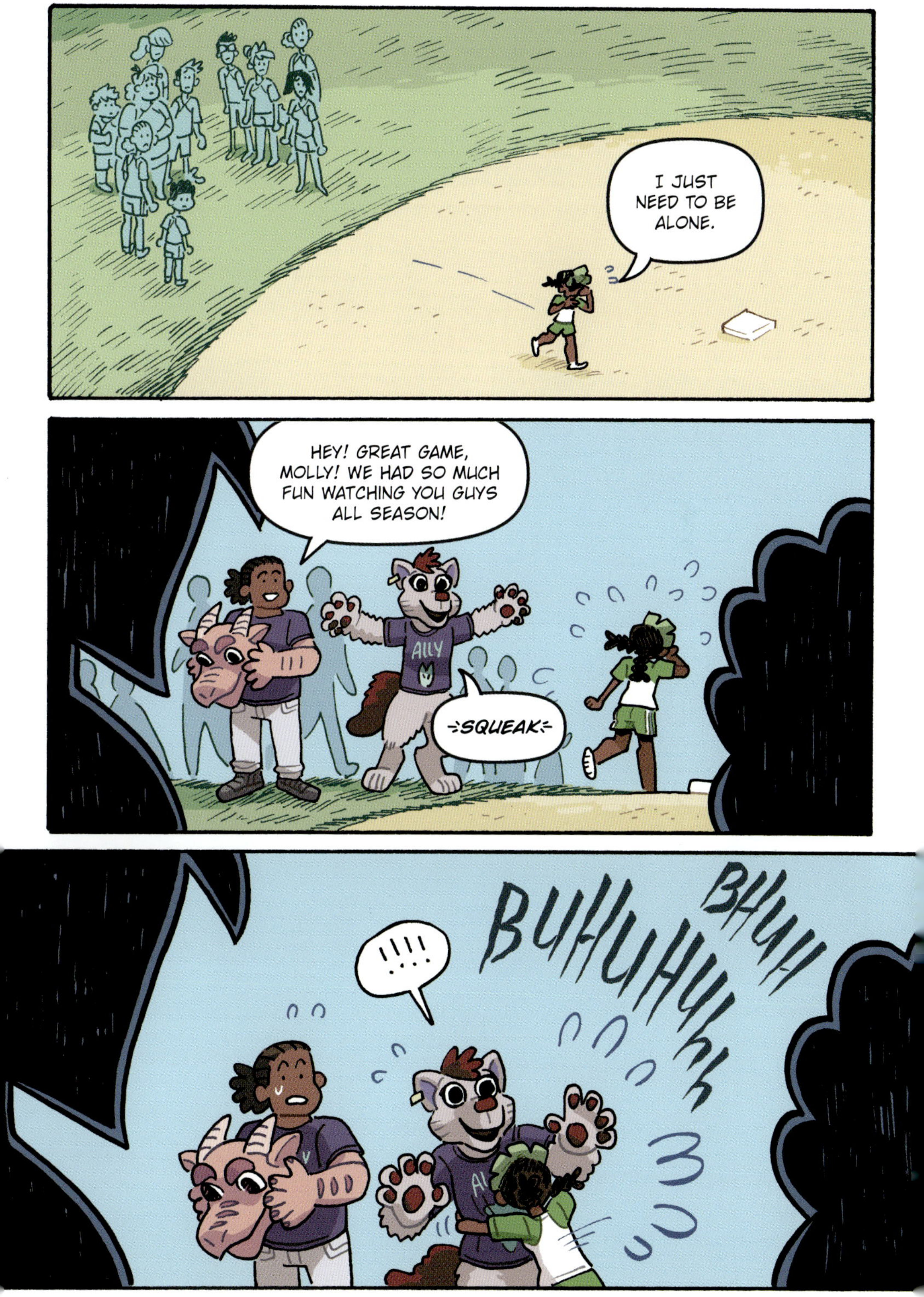
I JUST NEED TO BE ALONE.
HEY! GREAT GAME, MOLLY! WE HAD SO MUCH FUN WATCHING YOU GUYS ALL SEASON!
ALLY
SQUEAK
!!!!
BUHUHUHUHH
BHUH

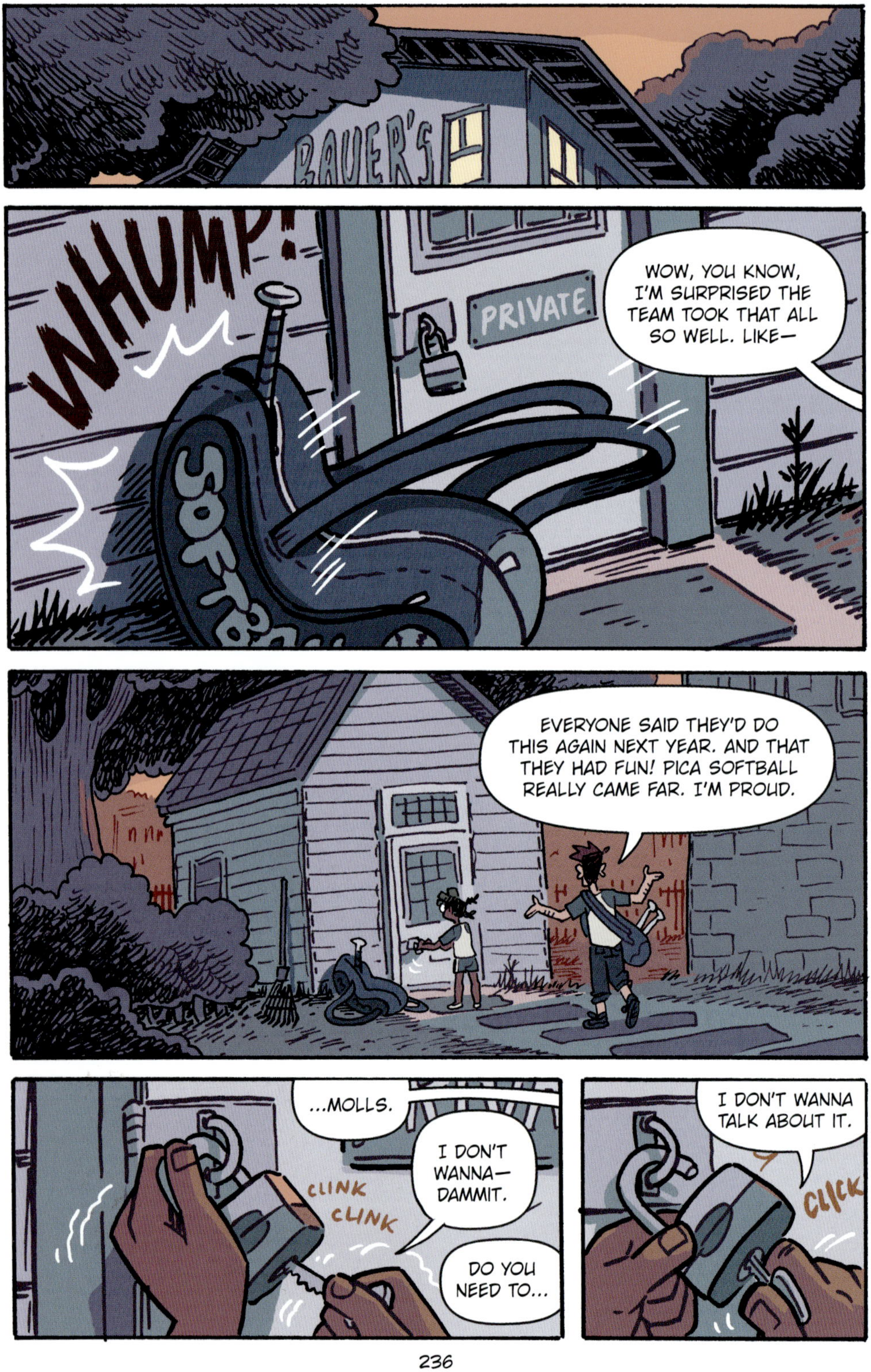
BAUER'S
WHUMP!
PRIVATE
WOW, YOU KNOW, I'M SURPRISED THE TEAM TOOK THAT ALL SO WELL. LIKE—
EVERYONE SAID THEY'D DO THIS AGAIN NEXT YEAR. AND THAT THEY HAD FUN! PICA SOFTBALL REALLY CAME FAR. I'M PROUD.
...MOLLS.
I DON'T WANNA— DAMMIT.
CLINK
CLINK
DO YOU NEED TO...
I DON'T WANNA TALK ABOUT IT.
CLICK

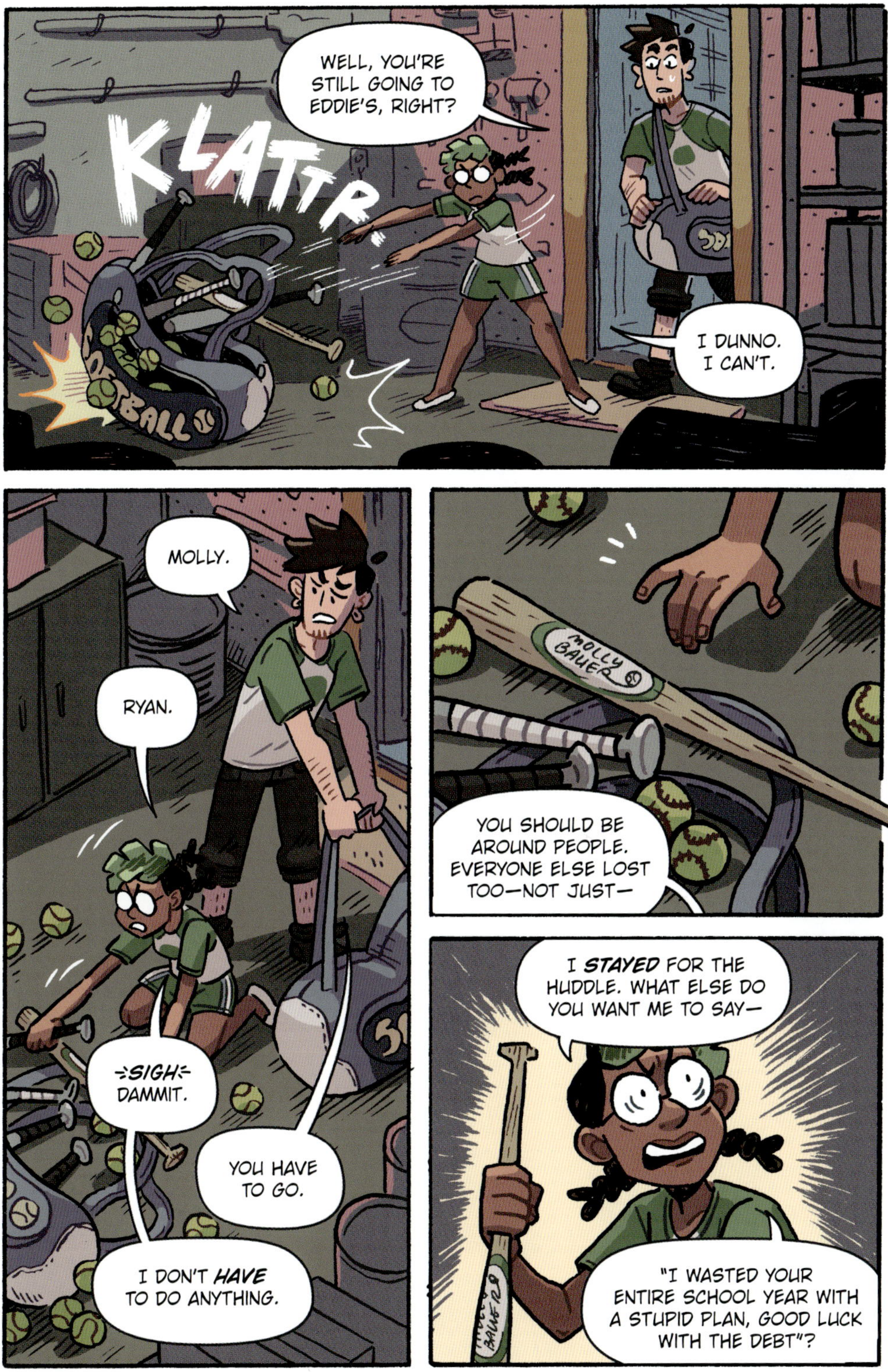
WELL, YOU'RE STILL GOING TO EDDIE'S, RIGHT?
KLATTR
SOFTBALL
I DUNNO. I CAN'T.
MOLLY.
RYAN.
⁼SIGH⁼ DAMMIT.
YOU HAVE TO GO.
I DON'T ***HAVE*** TO DO ANYTHING.
MOLLY BAUER
YOU SHOULD BE AROUND PEOPLE. EVERYONE ELSE LOST TOO—NOT JUST—
I ***STAYED*** FOR THE HUDDLE. WHAT ELSE DO YOU WANT ME TO SAY—
"I WASTED YOUR ENTIRE SCHOOL YEAR WITH A STUPID PLAN, GOOD LUCK WITH THE DEBT"?

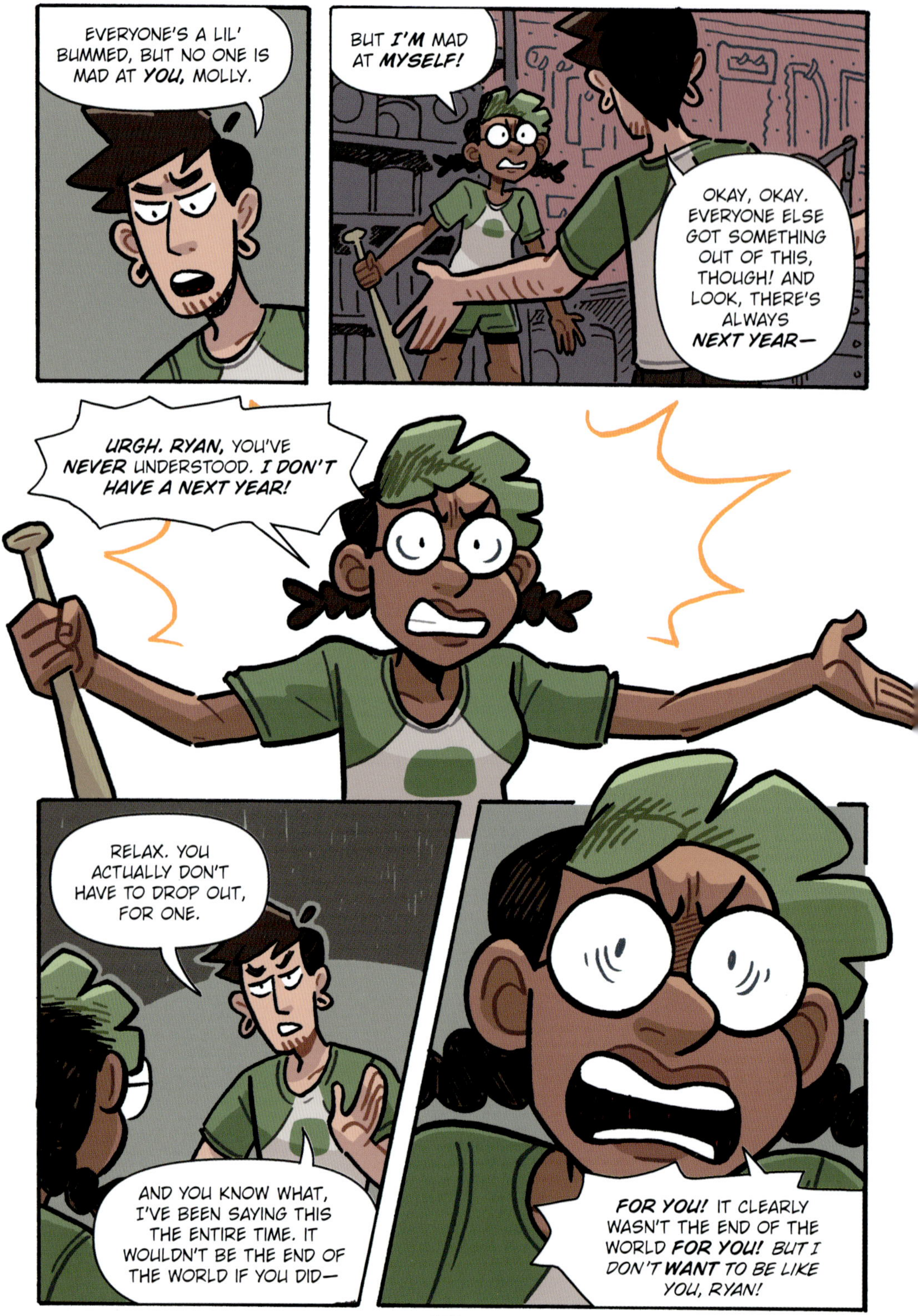
EVERYONE'S A LIL' BUMMED, BUT NO ONE IS MAD AT *YOU,* MOLLY.
BUT *I'M* MAD AT *MYSELF!*
OKAY, OKAY. EVERYONE ELSE GOT SOMETHING OUT OF THIS, THOUGH! AND LOOK, THERE'S ALWAYS *NEXT YEAR—*
URGH. RYAN, YOU'VE *NEVER* UNDERSTOOD. *I DON'T HAVE A NEXT YEAR!*
RELAX. YOU ACTUALLY DON'T HAVE TO DROP OUT, FOR ONE.
AND YOU KNOW WHAT, I'VE BEEN SAYING THIS THE ENTIRE TIME. IT WOULDN'T BE THE END OF THE WORLD IF YOU DID—
FOR YOU! IT CLEARLY WASN'T THE END OF THE WORLD *FOR YOU! BUT I DON'T* ***WANT*** *TO BE LIKE YOU, RYAN!*

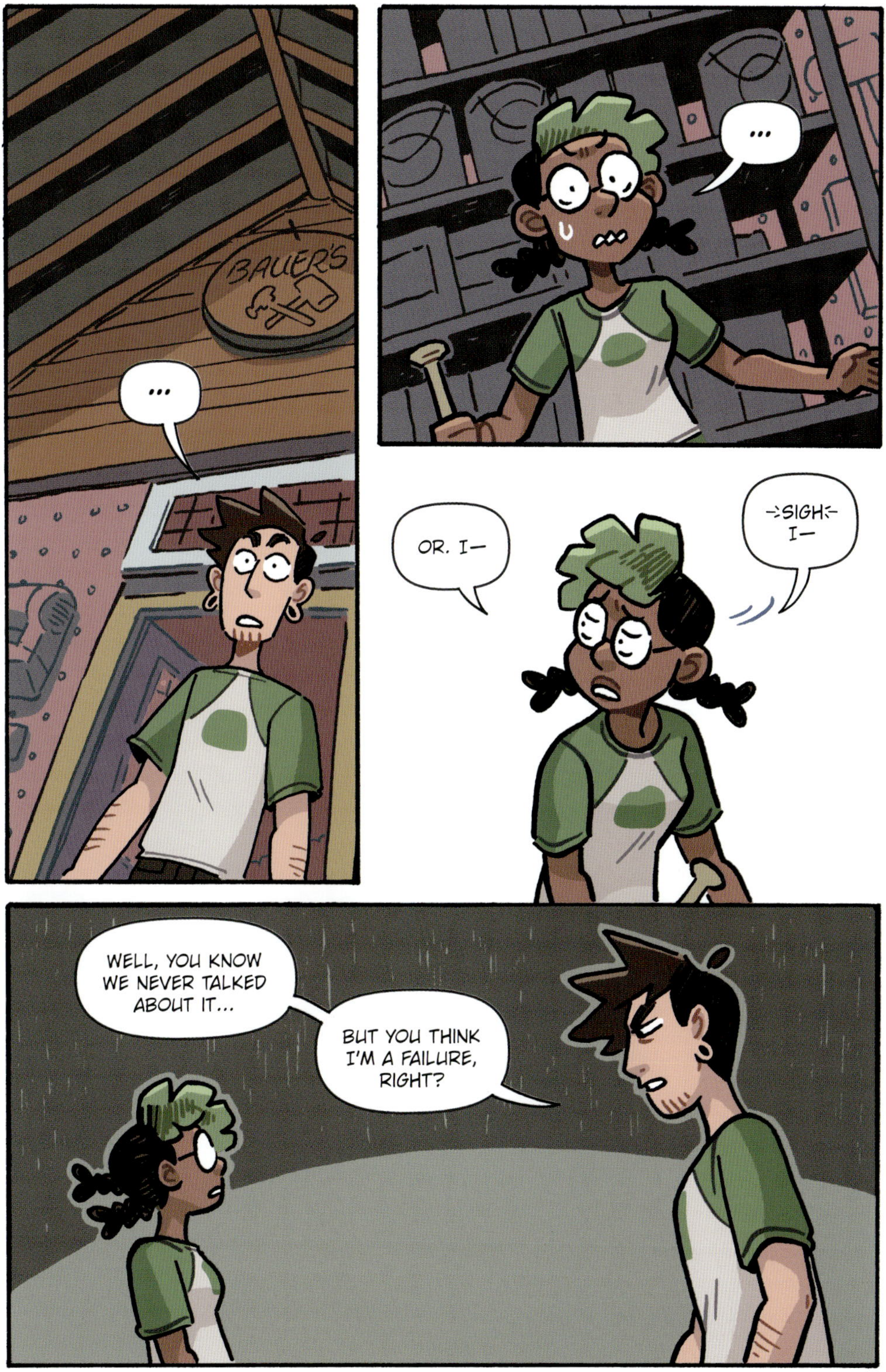
BAUER'S
...
...
OR. I—
-SIGH-
I—
WELL, YOU KNOW WE NEVER TALKED ABOUT IT...
BUT YOU THINK I'M A FAILURE, RIGHT?

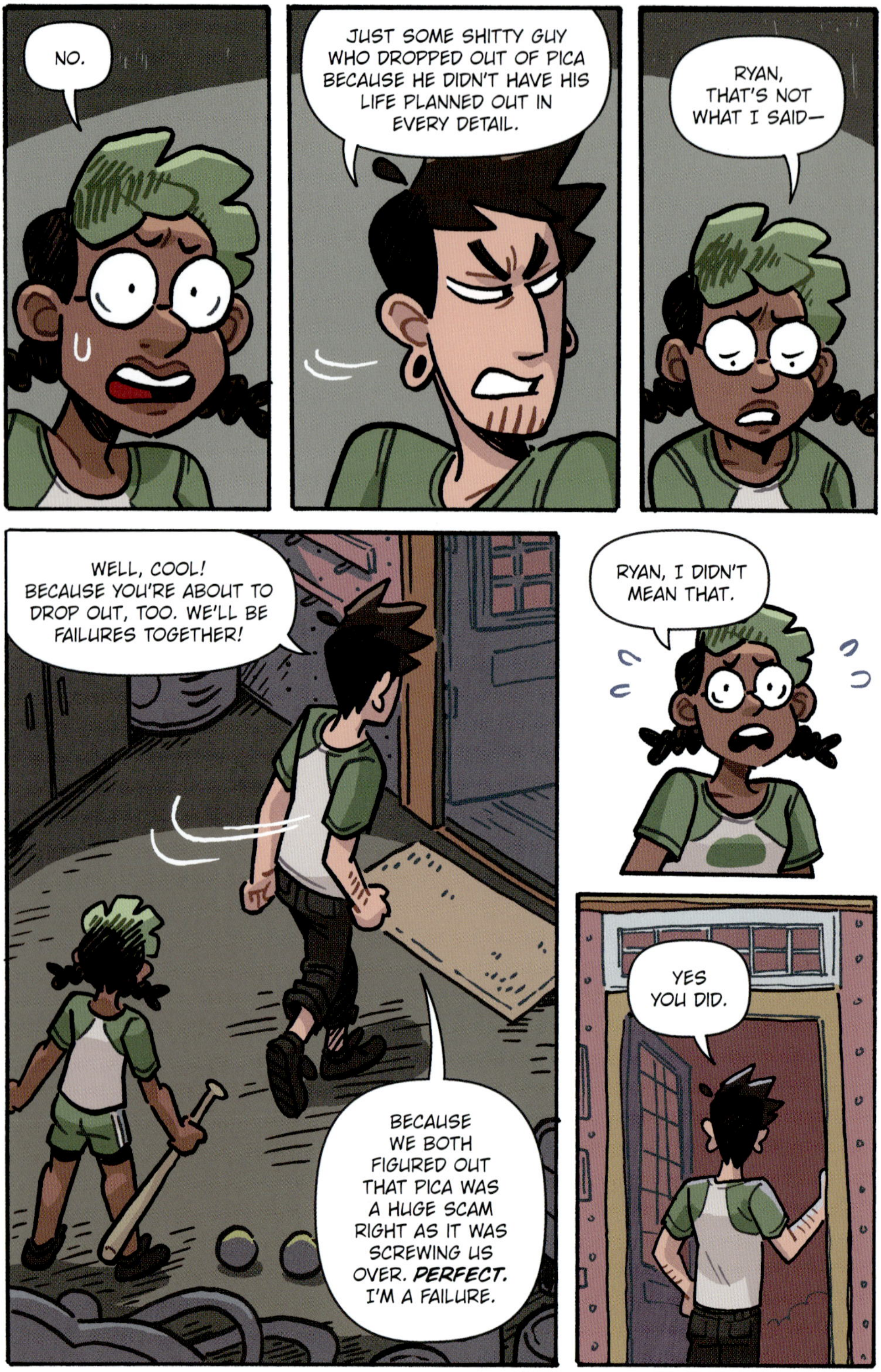
NO.
JUST SOME SHITTY GUY WHO DROPPED OUT OF PICA BECAUSE HE DIDN'T HAVE HIS LIFE PLANNED OUT IN EVERY DETAIL.
RYAN, THAT'S NOT WHAT I SAID—
WELL, COOL! BECAUSE YOU'RE ABOUT TO DROP OUT, TOO. WE'LL BE FAILURES TOGETHER!
BECAUSE WE BOTH FIGURED OUT THAT PICA WAS A HUGE SCAM RIGHT AS IT WAS SCREWING US OVER. *PERFECT.* I'M A FAILURE.
RYAN, I DIDN'T MEAN THAT.
YES YOU DID.

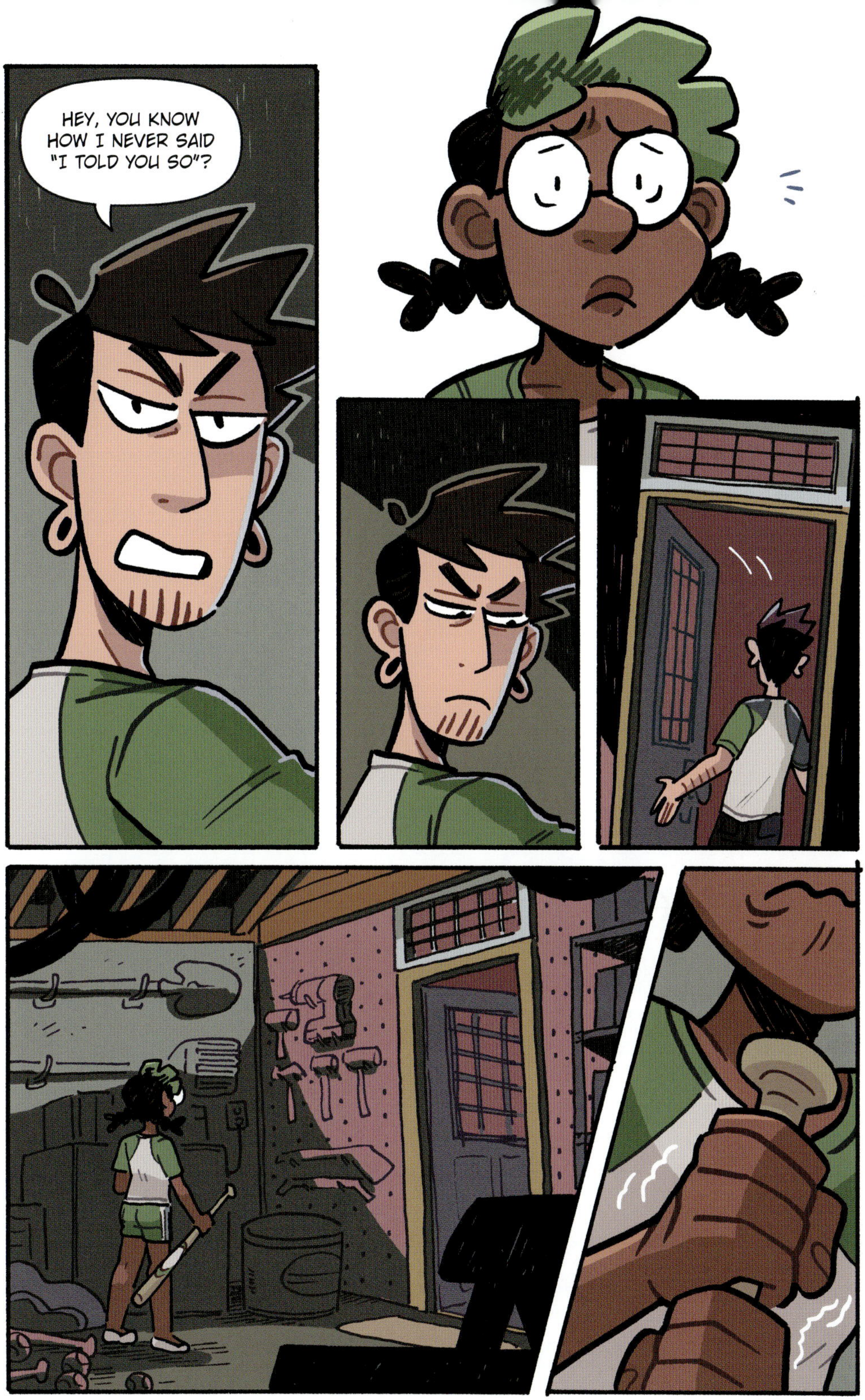
HEY, YOU KNOW HOW I NEVER SAID "I TOLD YOU SO"?

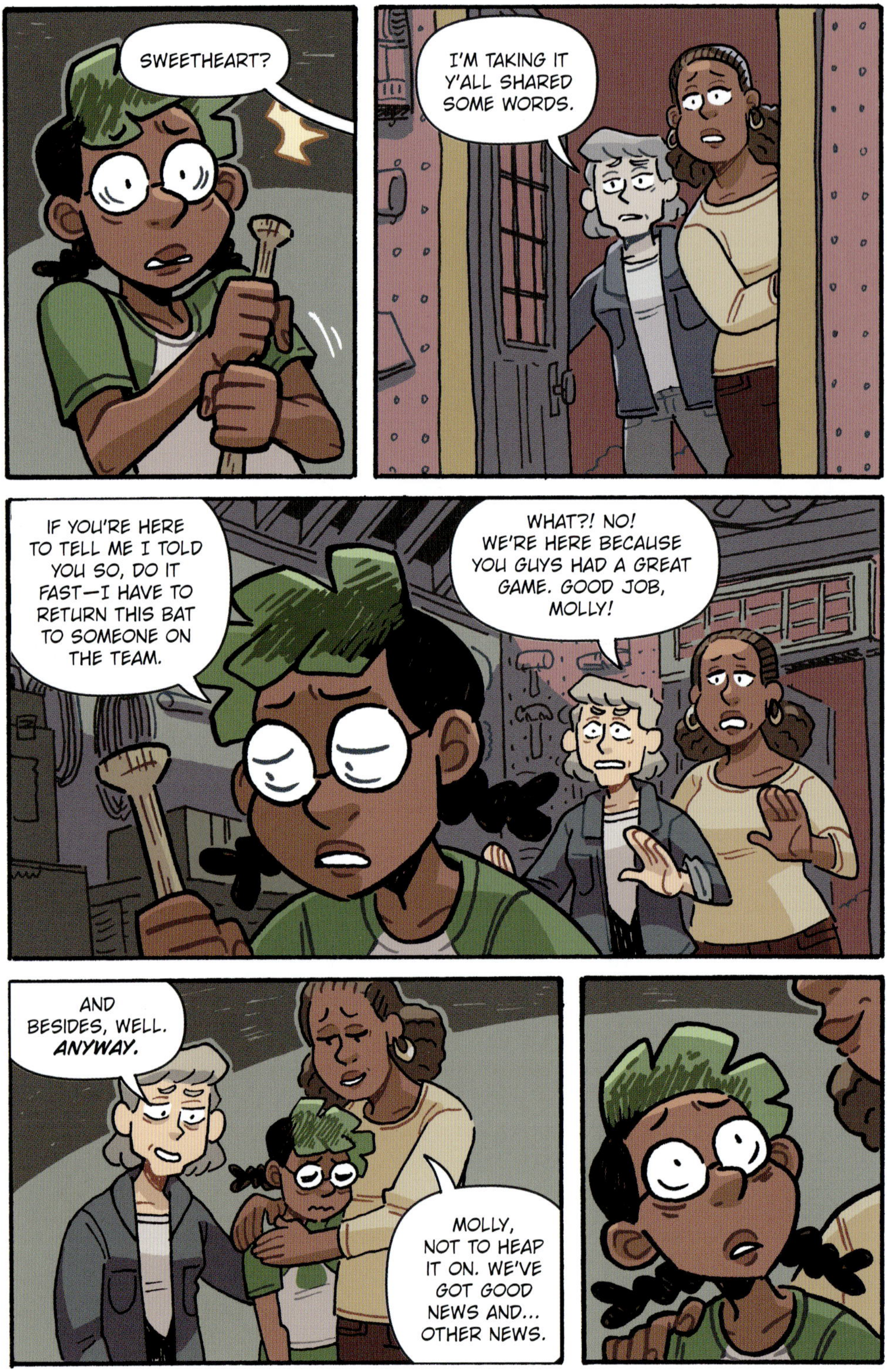
SWEETHEART?
I'M TAKING IT Y'ALL SHARED SOME WORDS.
IF YOU'RE HERE TO TELL ME I TOLD YOU SO, DO IT FAST—I HAVE TO RETURN THIS BAT TO SOMEONE ON THE TEAM.
WHAT?! NO! WE'RE HERE BECAUSE YOU GUYS HAD A GREAT GAME. GOOD JOB, MOLLY!
AND BESIDES, WELL. *ANYWAY.*
MOLLY, NOT TO HEAP IT ON. WE'VE GOT GOOD NEWS AND... OTHER NEWS.

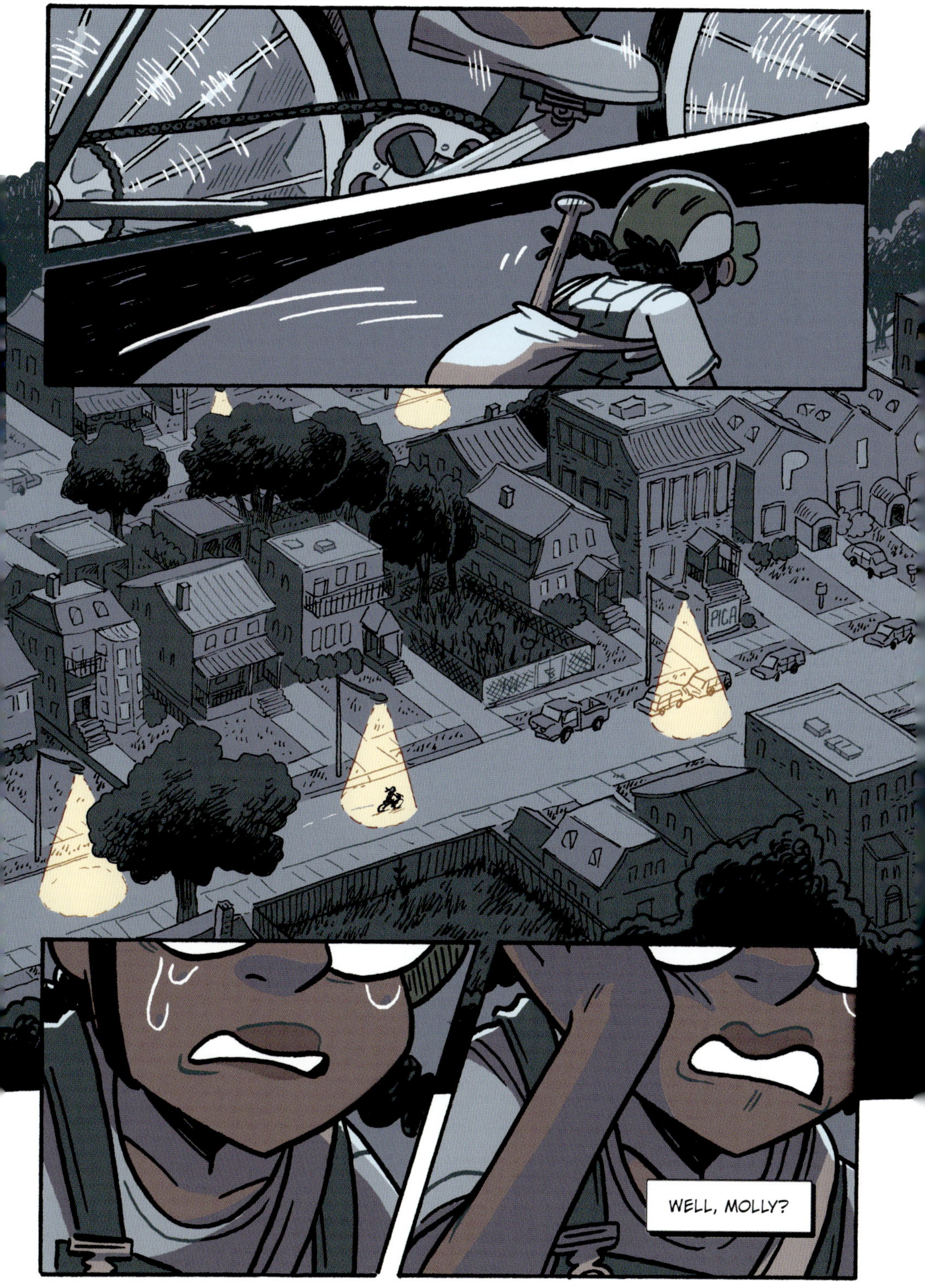
PICA
WELL, MOLLY?

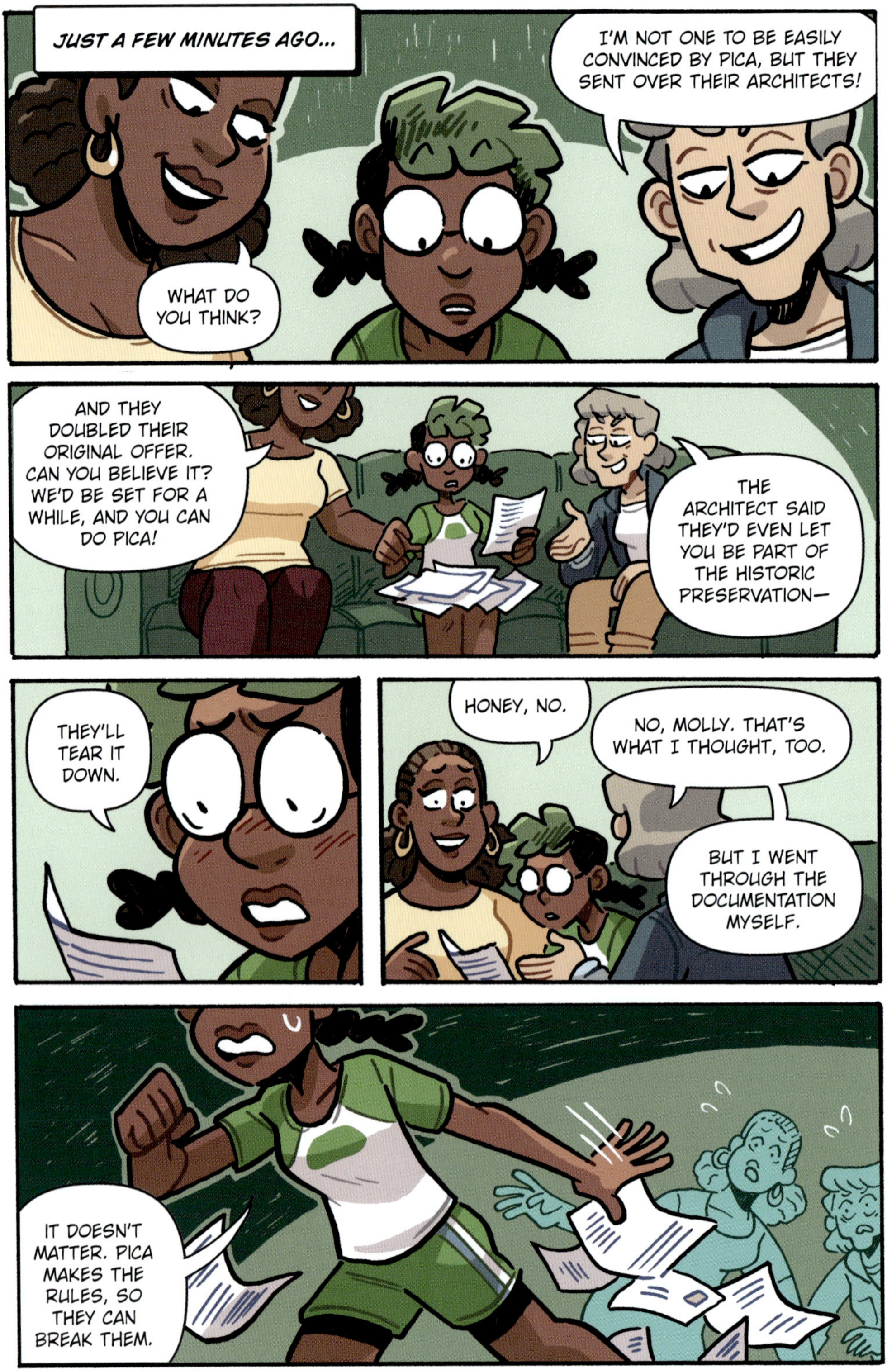
JUST A FEW MINUTES AGO...
I'M NOT ONE TO BE EASILY CONVINCED BY PICA, BUT THEY SENT OVER THEIR ARCHITECTS!
WHAT DO YOU THINK?
AND THEY DOUBLED THEIR ORIGINAL OFFER. CAN YOU BELIEVE IT? WE'D BE SET FOR A WHILE, AND YOU CAN DO PICA!
THE ARCHITECT SAID THEY'D EVEN LET YOU BE PART OF THE HISTORIC PRESERVATION—
THEY'LL TEAR IT DOWN.
HONEY, NO.
NO, MOLLY. THAT'S WHAT I THOUGHT, TOO.
BUT I WENT THROUGH THE DOCUMENTATION MYSELF.
IT DOESN'T MATTER. PICA MAKES THE RULES, SO THEY CAN BREAK THEM.

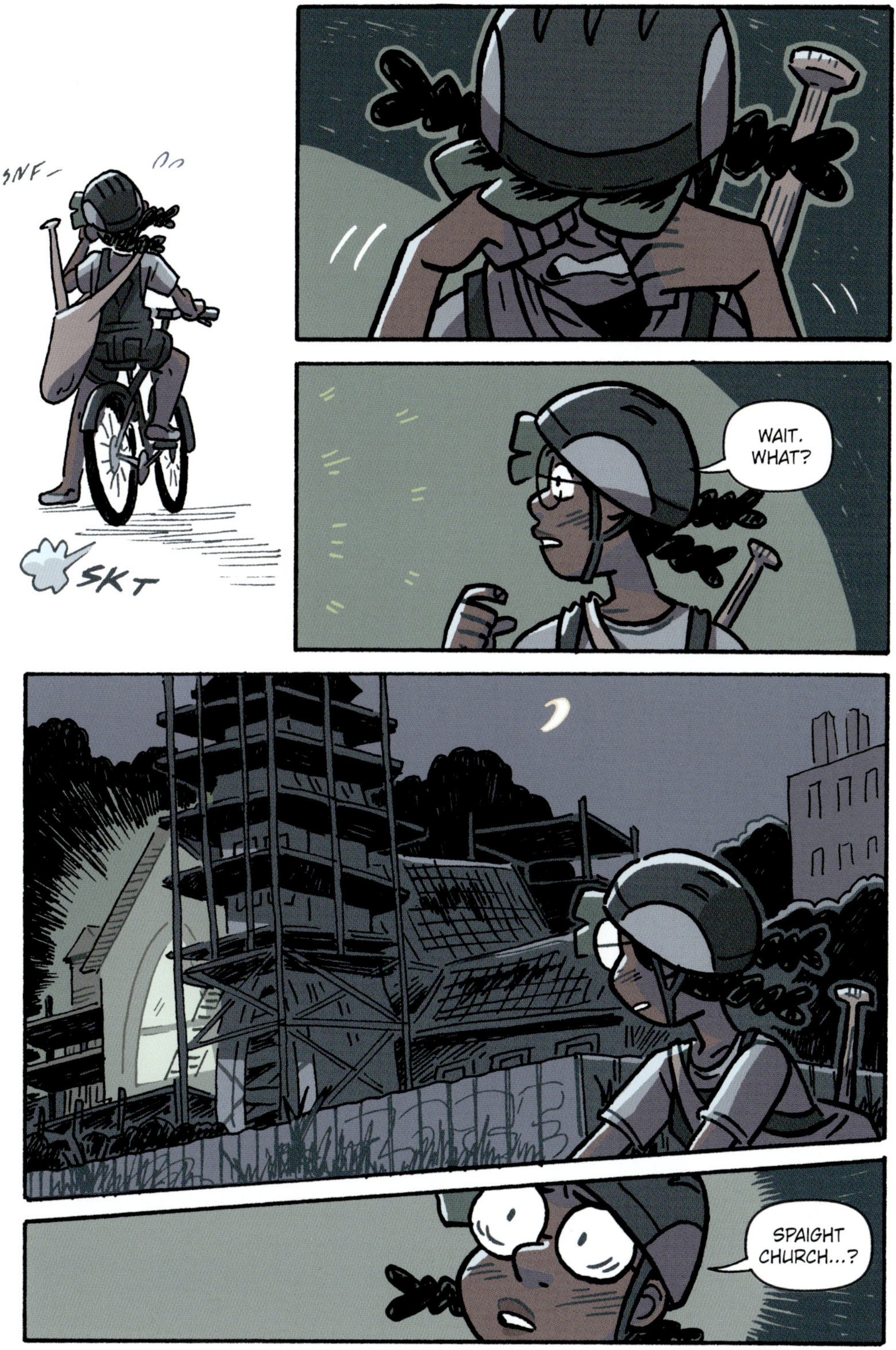
SNF-
SKT
WAIT. WHAT?
SPAIGHT CHURCH...?

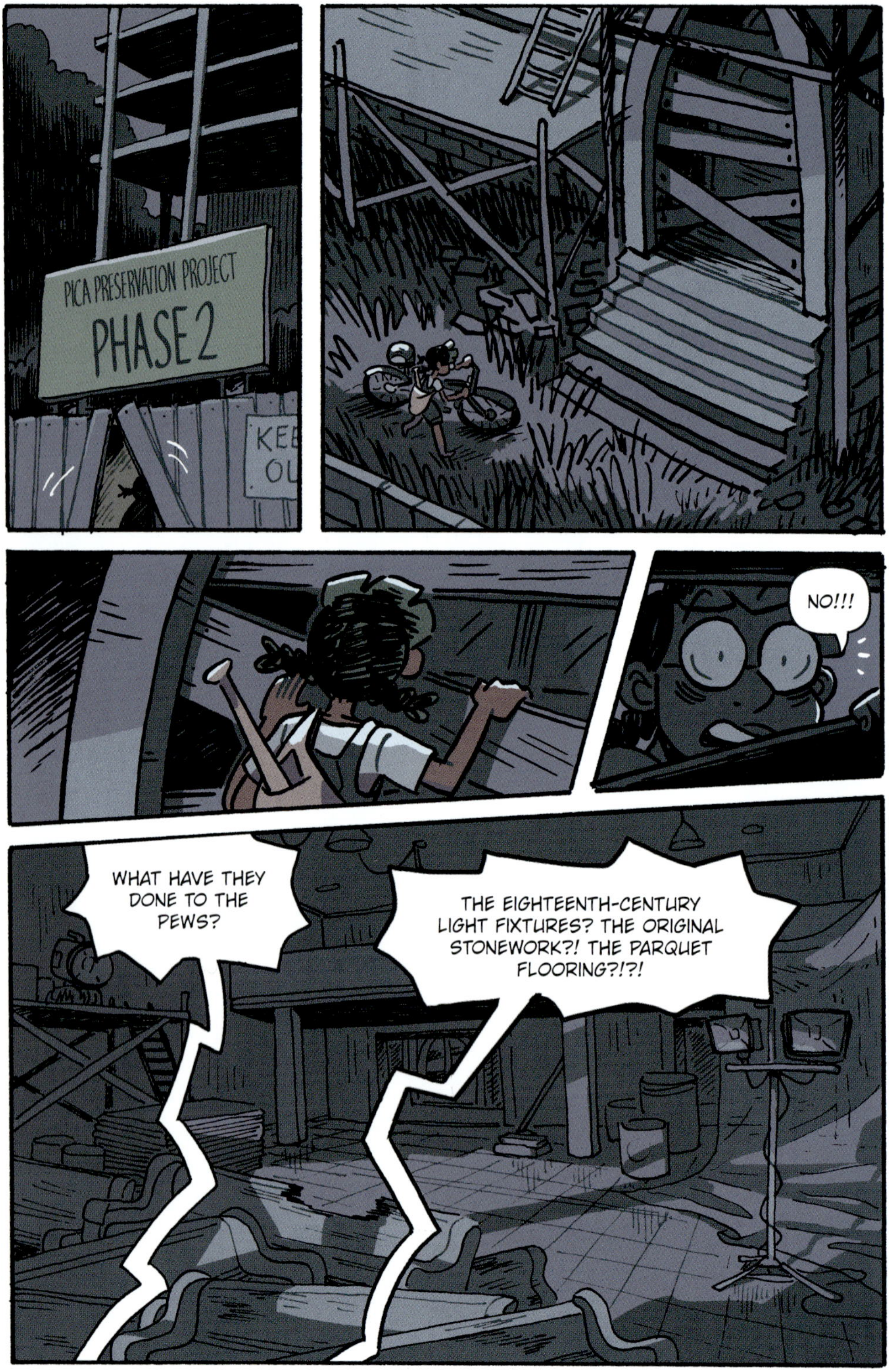
PICA PRESERVATION PROJECT
PHASE 2
NO!!!
WHAT HAVE THEY DONE TO THE PEWS?
THE EIGHTEENTH-CENTURY LIGHT FIXTURES? THE ORIGINAL STONEWORK?! THE PARQUET FLOORING?!?!

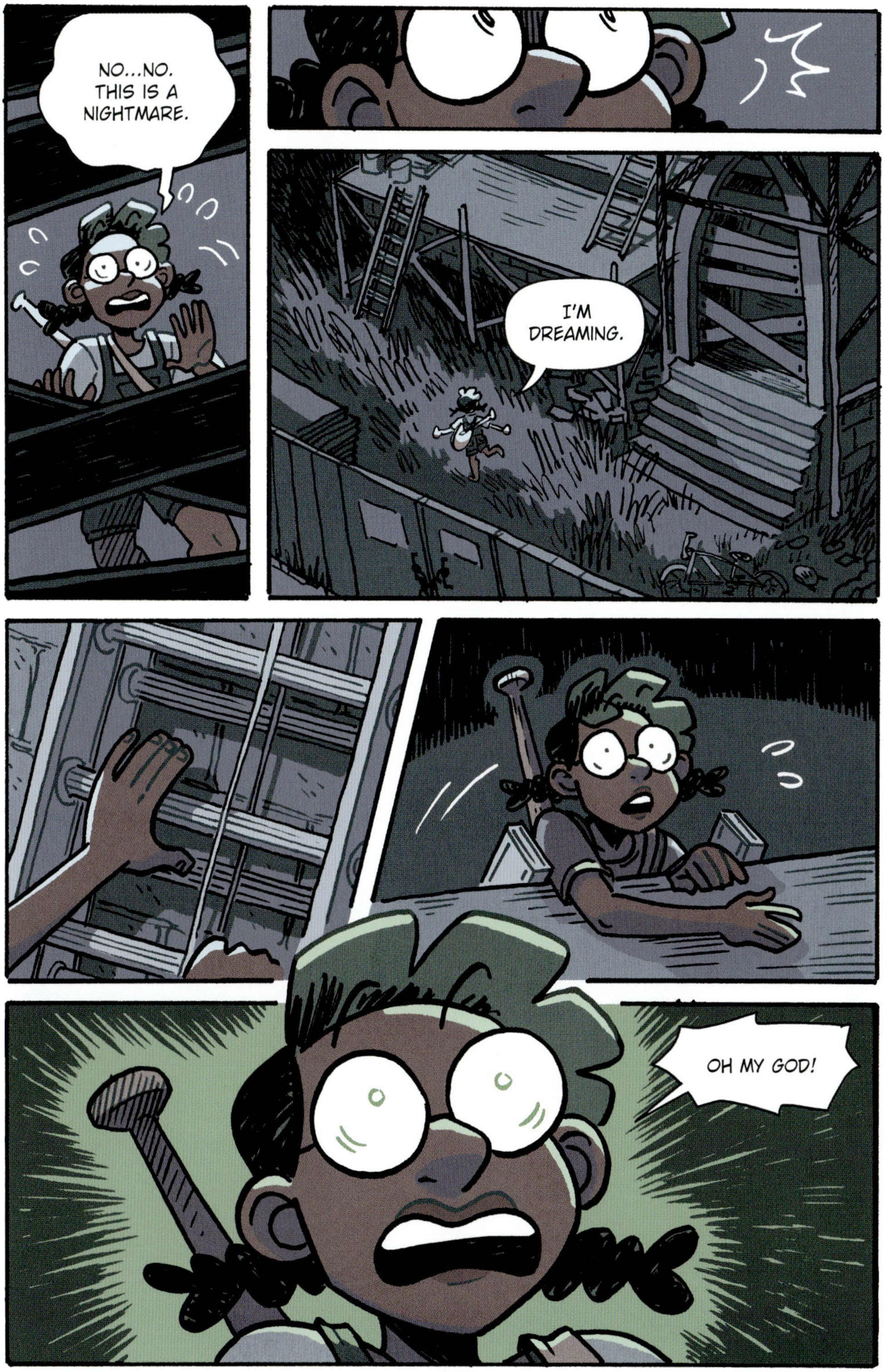
NO...NO. THIS IS A NIGHTMARE.
I'M DREAMING.
OH MY GOD!

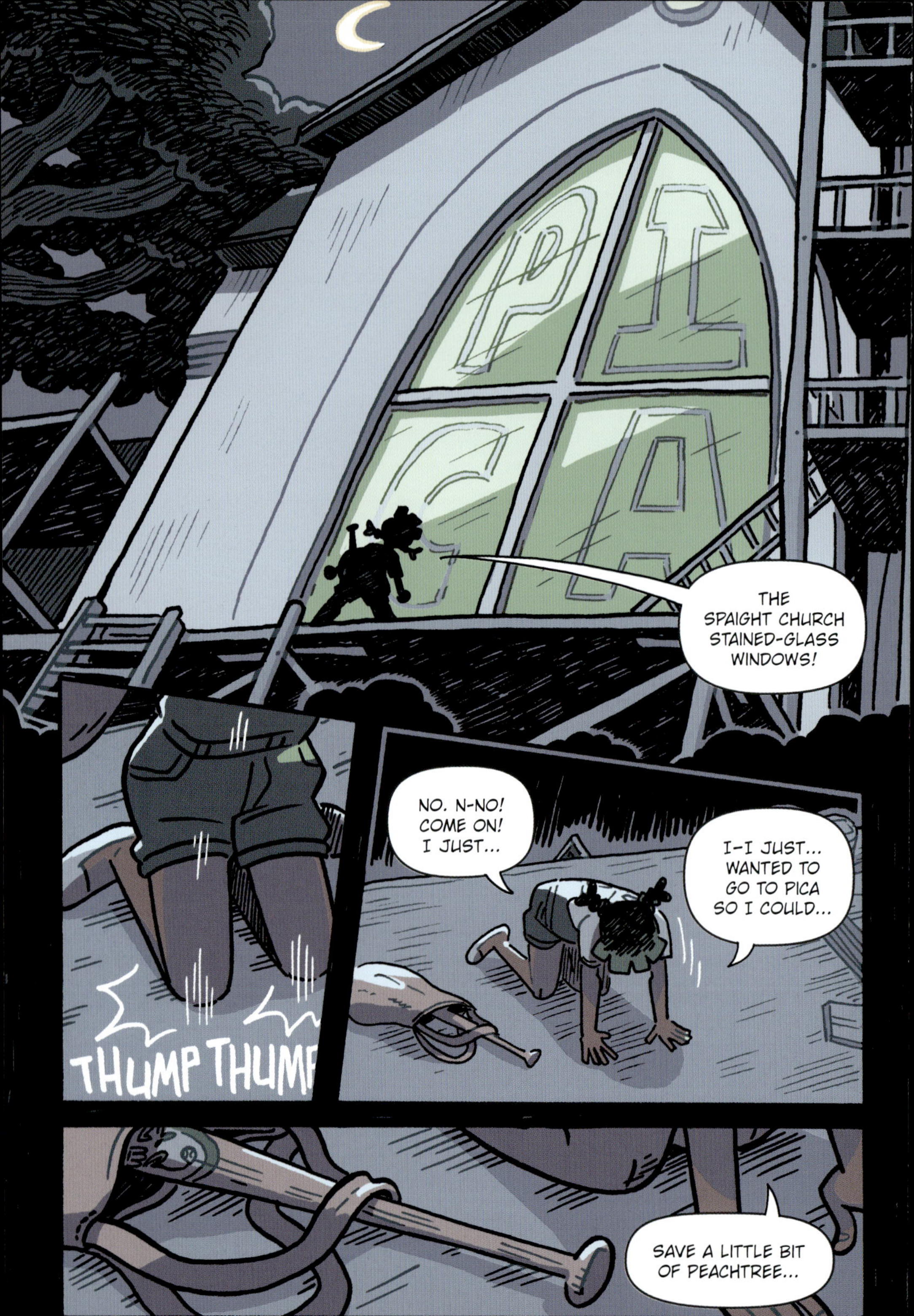
THE SPAIGHT CHURCH STAINED-GLASS WINDOWS!
THUMP THUMP
NO. N-NO! COME ON! I JUST...
I-I JUST... WANTED TO GO TO PICA SO I COULD...
SAVE A LITTLE BIT OF PEACHTREE...

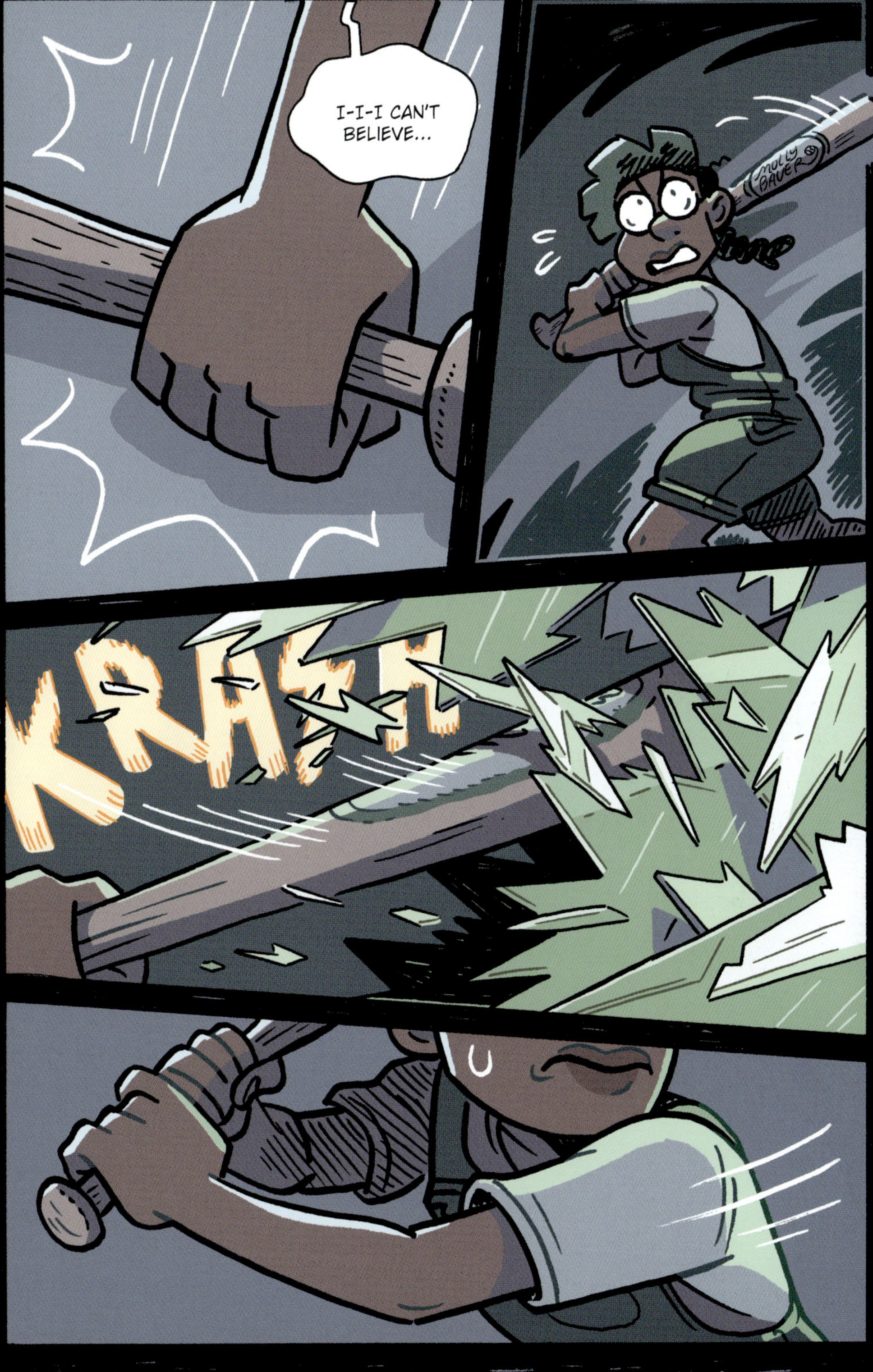
I-I-I CAN'T BELIEVE...
MOLLY BAUER
KRASH

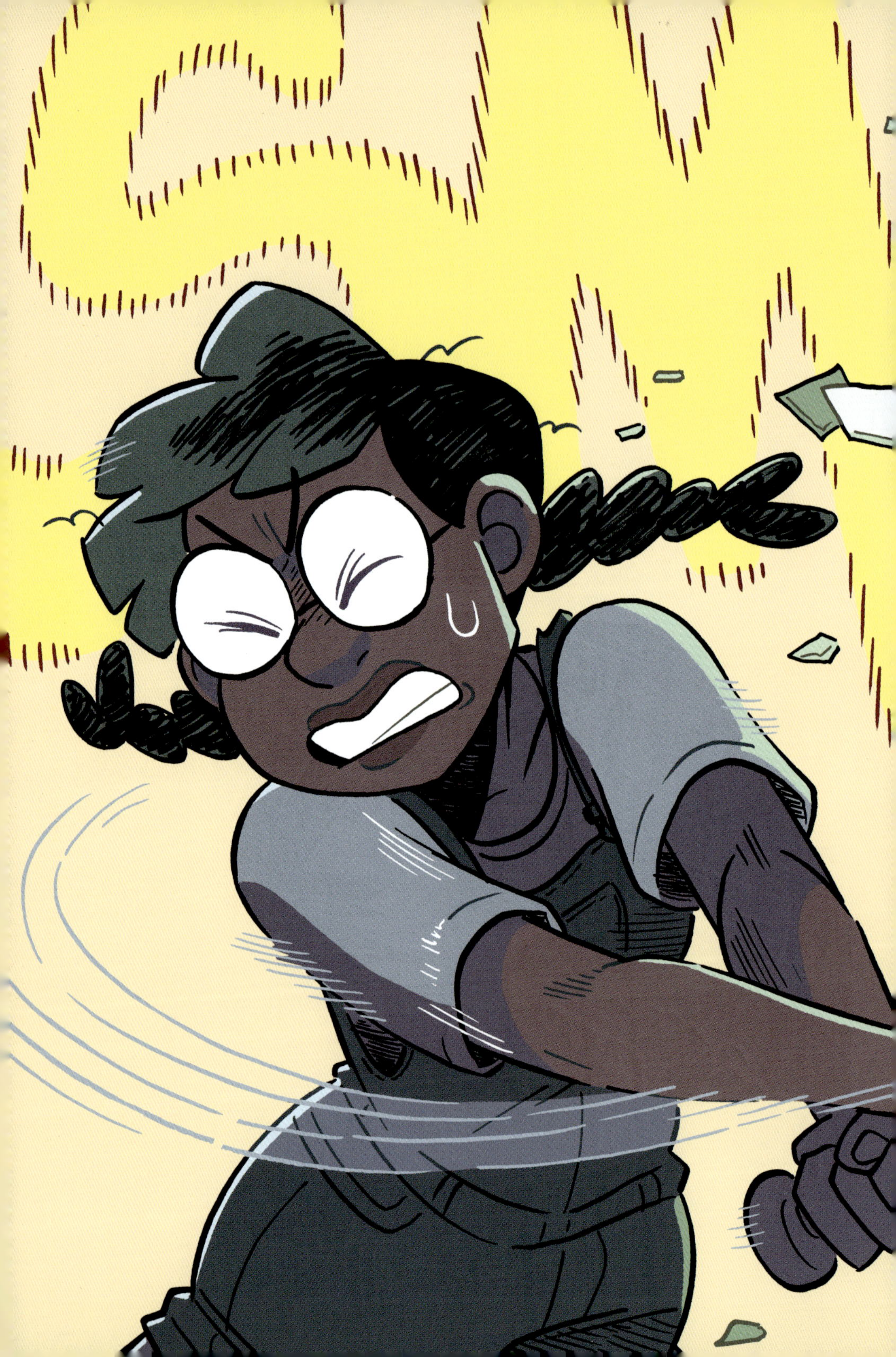

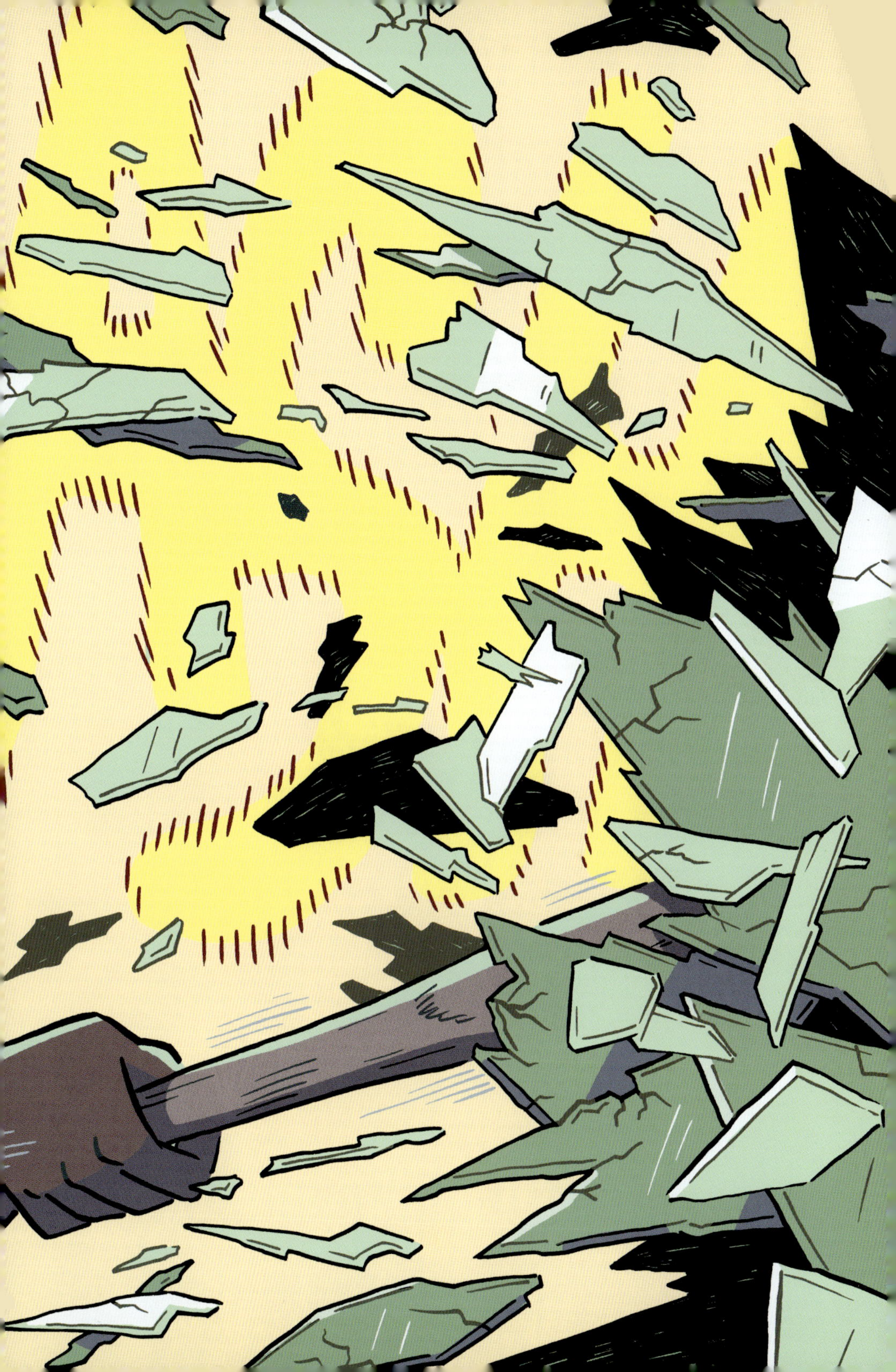

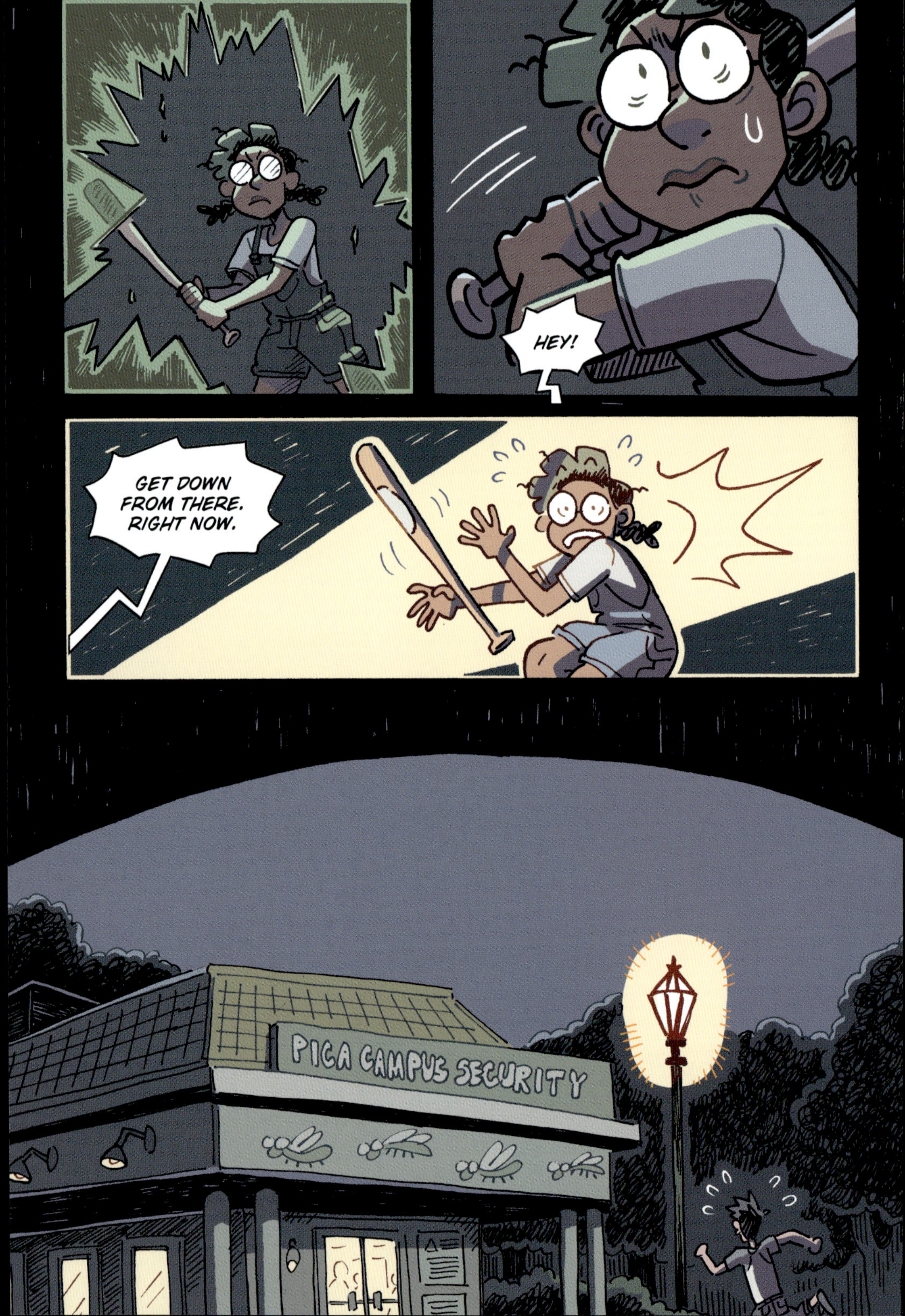
HEY!
GET DOWN FROM THERE. RIGHT NOW.
PICA CAMPUS SECURITY

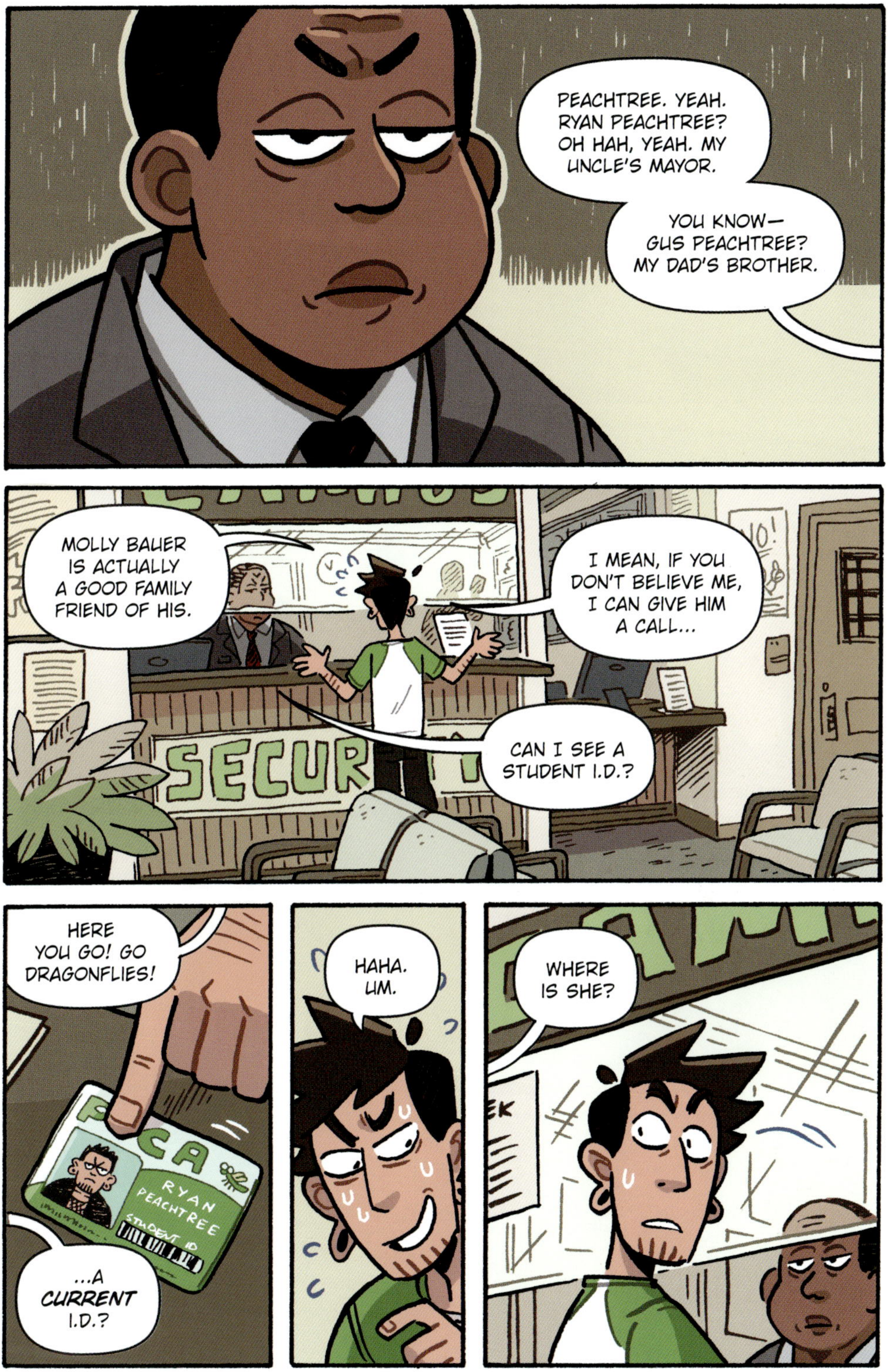
PEACHTREE. YEAH. RYAN PEACHTREE? OH HAH, YEAH. MY UNCLE'S MAYOR.
YOU KNOW— GUS PEACHTREE? MY DAD'S BROTHER.
MOLLY BAUER IS ACTUALLY A GOOD FAMILY FRIEND OF HIS.
I MEAN, IF YOU DON'T BELIEVE ME, I CAN GIVE HIM A CALL...
SECUR
CAN I SEE A STUDENT I.D.?
HERE YOU GO! GO DRAGONFLIES!
RYAN PEACHTREE
STUDENT ID
...A *CURRENT* I.D.?
HAHA. UM.
WHERE IS SHE?

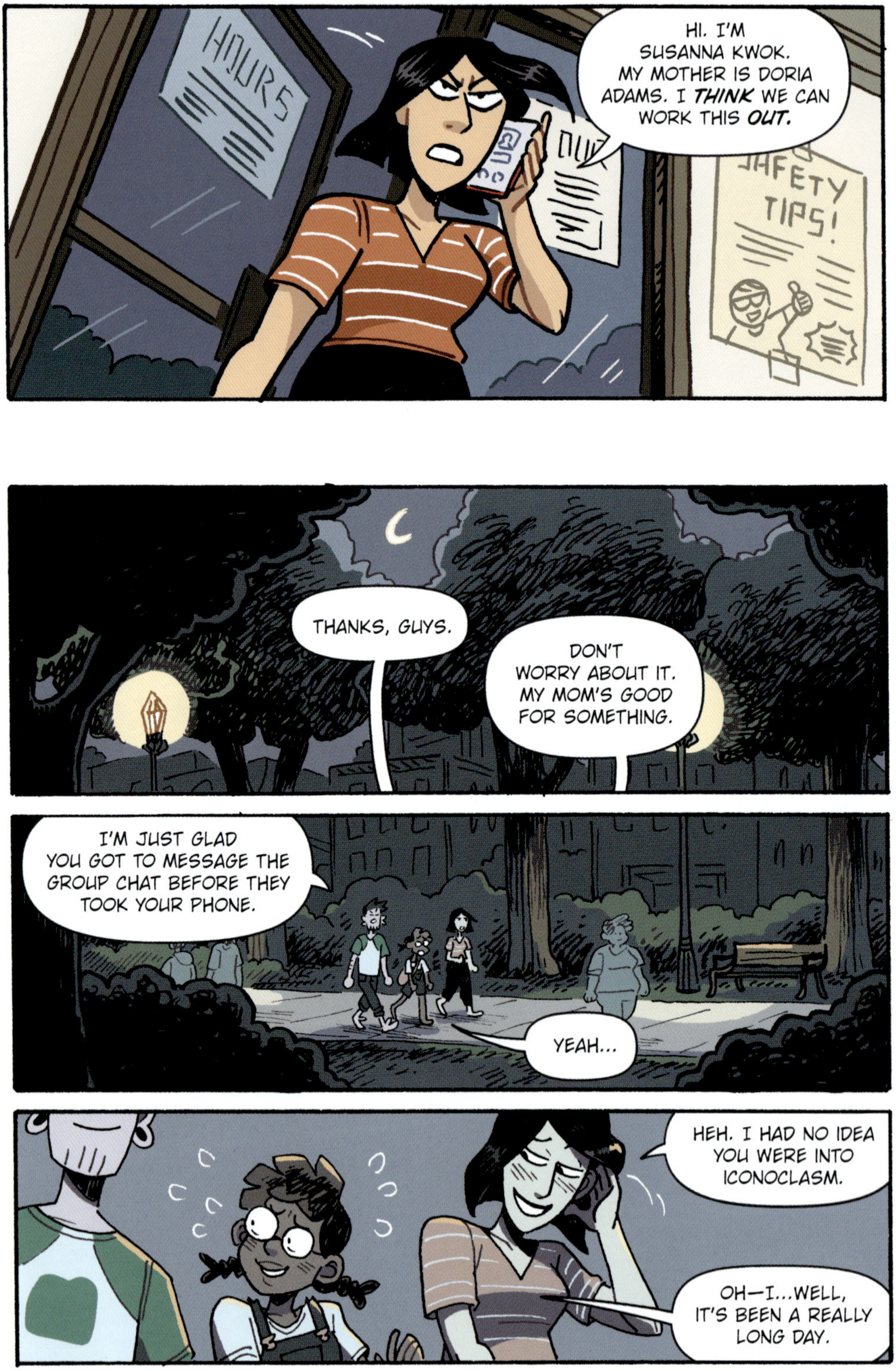
HOURS
HI. I'M SUSANNA KWOK. MY MOTHER IS DORIA ADAMS. I *THINK* WE CAN WORK THIS *OUT.*
SAFETY TIPS!
THANKS, GUYS.
DON'T WORRY ABOUT IT. MY MOM'S GOOD FOR SOMETHING.
I'M JUST GLAD YOU GOT TO MESSAGE THE GROUP CHAT BEFORE THEY TOOK YOUR PHONE.
YEAH...
HEH. I HAD NO IDEA YOU WERE INTO ICONOCLASM.
OH—I...WELL, IT'S BEEN A REALLY LONG DAY.

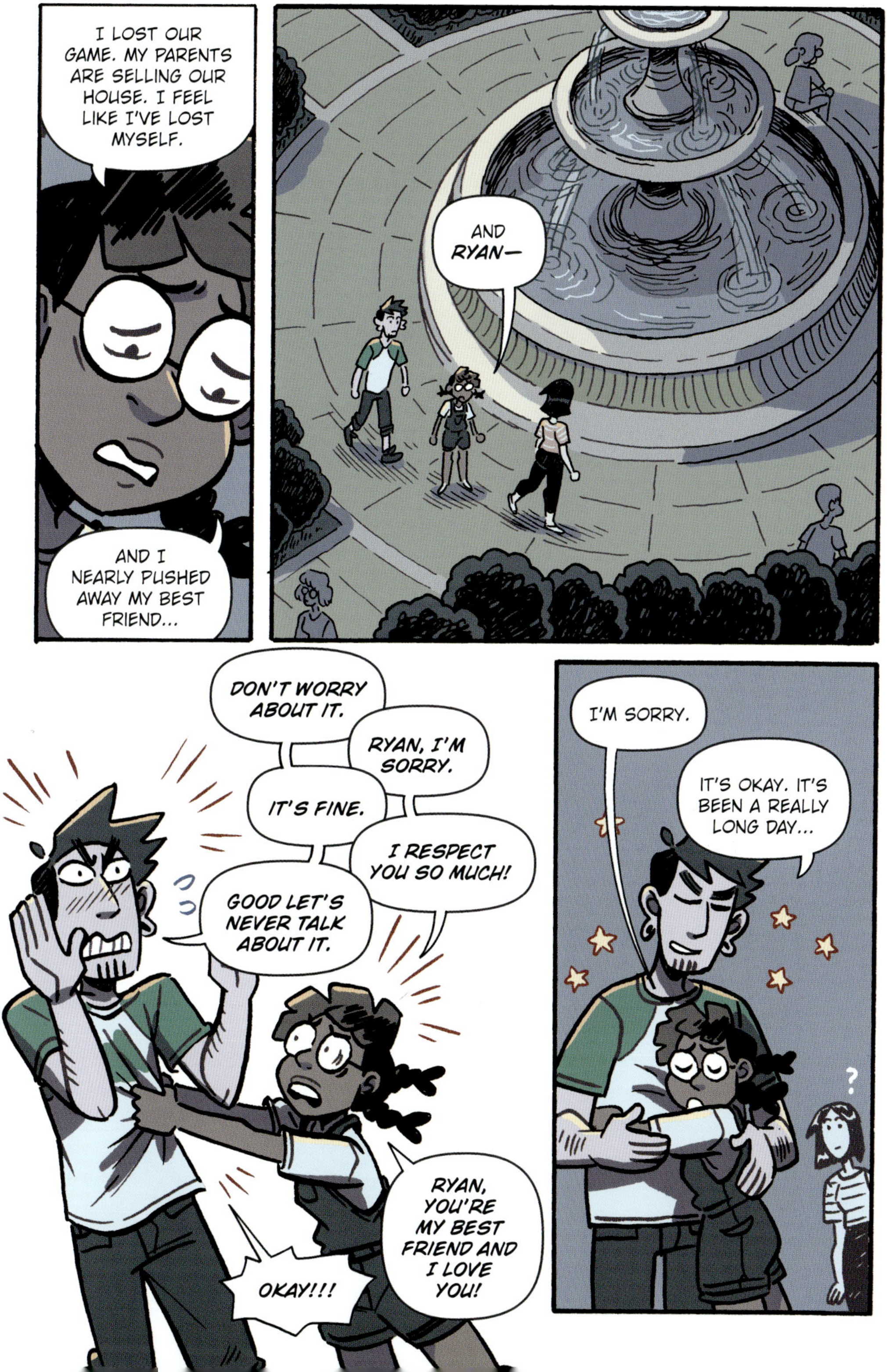
I LOST OUR GAME. MY PARENTS ARE SELLING OUR HOUSE. I FEEL LIKE I'VE LOST MYSELF.
AND I NEARLY PUSHED AWAY MY BEST FRIEND...
AND *RYAN—*
DON'T WORRY ABOUT IT.
RYAN, I'M SORRY.
IT'S FINE.
I RESPECT YOU SO MUCH!
GOOD LET'S NEVER TALK ABOUT IT.
RYAN, YOU'RE MY BEST FRIEND AND I LOVE YOU!
OKAY!!!
I'M SORRY.
IT'S OKAY. IT'S BEEN A REALLY LONG DAY...
?

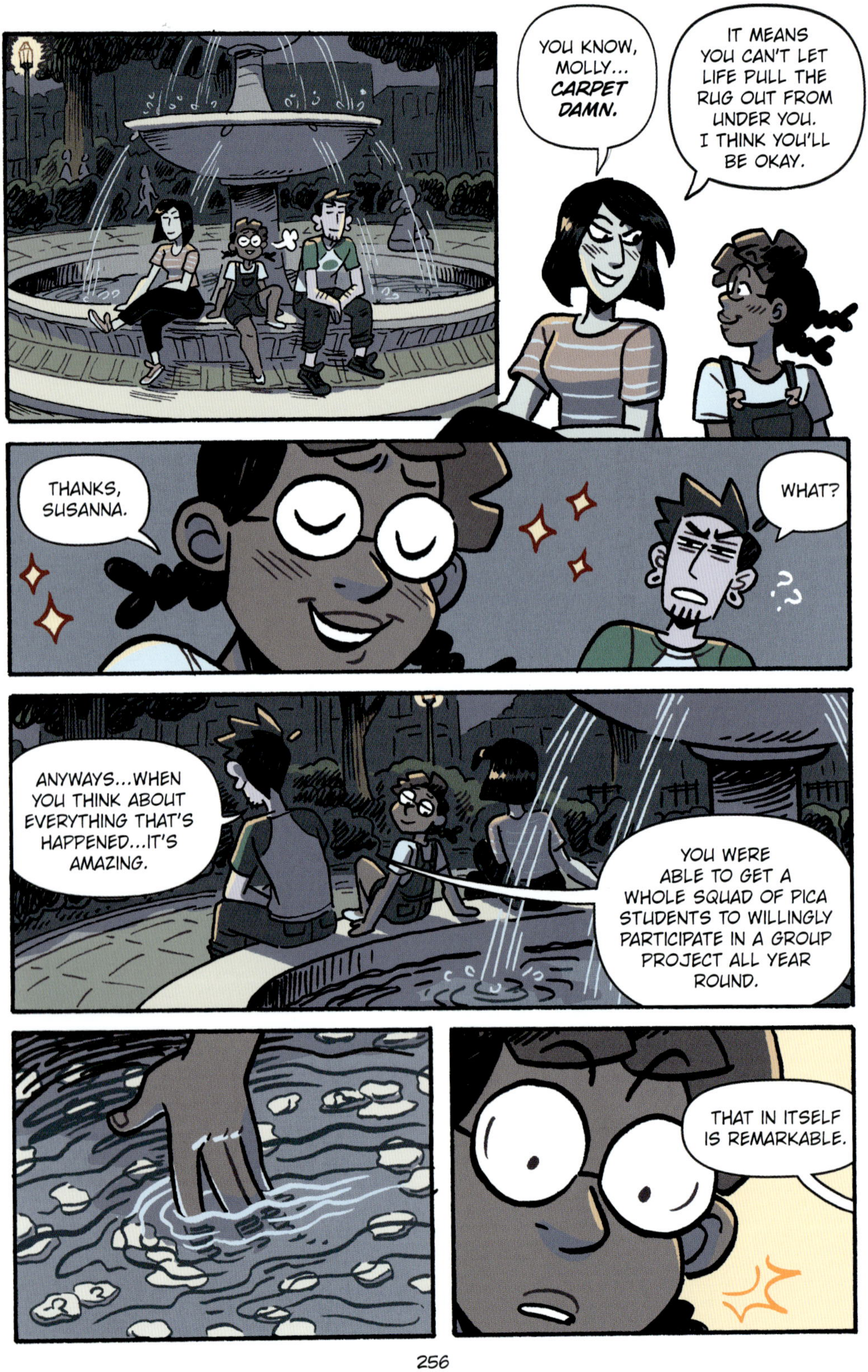
YOU KNOW, MOLLY... CARPET DAMN.
IT MEANS YOU CAN'T LET LIFE PULL THE RUG OUT FROM UNDER YOU. I THINK YOU'LL BE OKAY.
THANKS, SUSANNA.
WHAT?
ANYWAYS...WHEN YOU THINK ABOUT EVERYTHING THAT'S HAPPENED...IT'S AMAZING.
YOU WERE ABLE TO GET A WHOLE SQUAD OF PICA STUDENTS TO WILLINGLY PARTICIPATE IN A GROUP PROJECT ALL YEAR ROUND.
THAT IN ITSELF IS REMARKABLE.

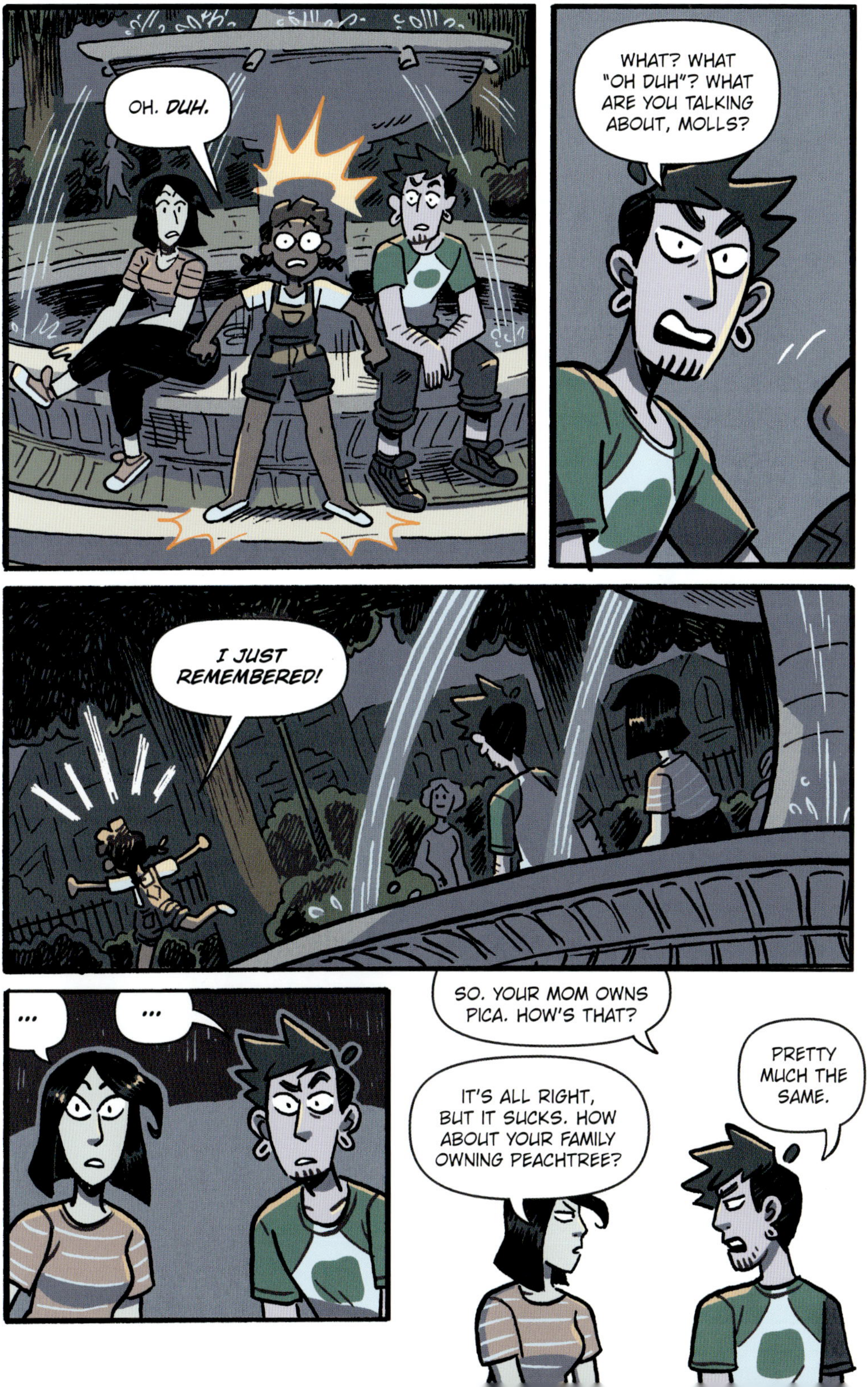
OH. DUH.
WHAT? WHAT "OH DUH"? WHAT ARE YOU TALKING ABOUT, MOLLS?
I JUST REMEMBERED!
...
...
SO. YOUR MOM OWNS PICA. HOW'S THAT?
IT'S ALL RIGHT, BUT IT SUCKS. HOW ABOUT YOUR FAMILY OWNING PEACHTREE?
PRETTY MUCH THE SAME.

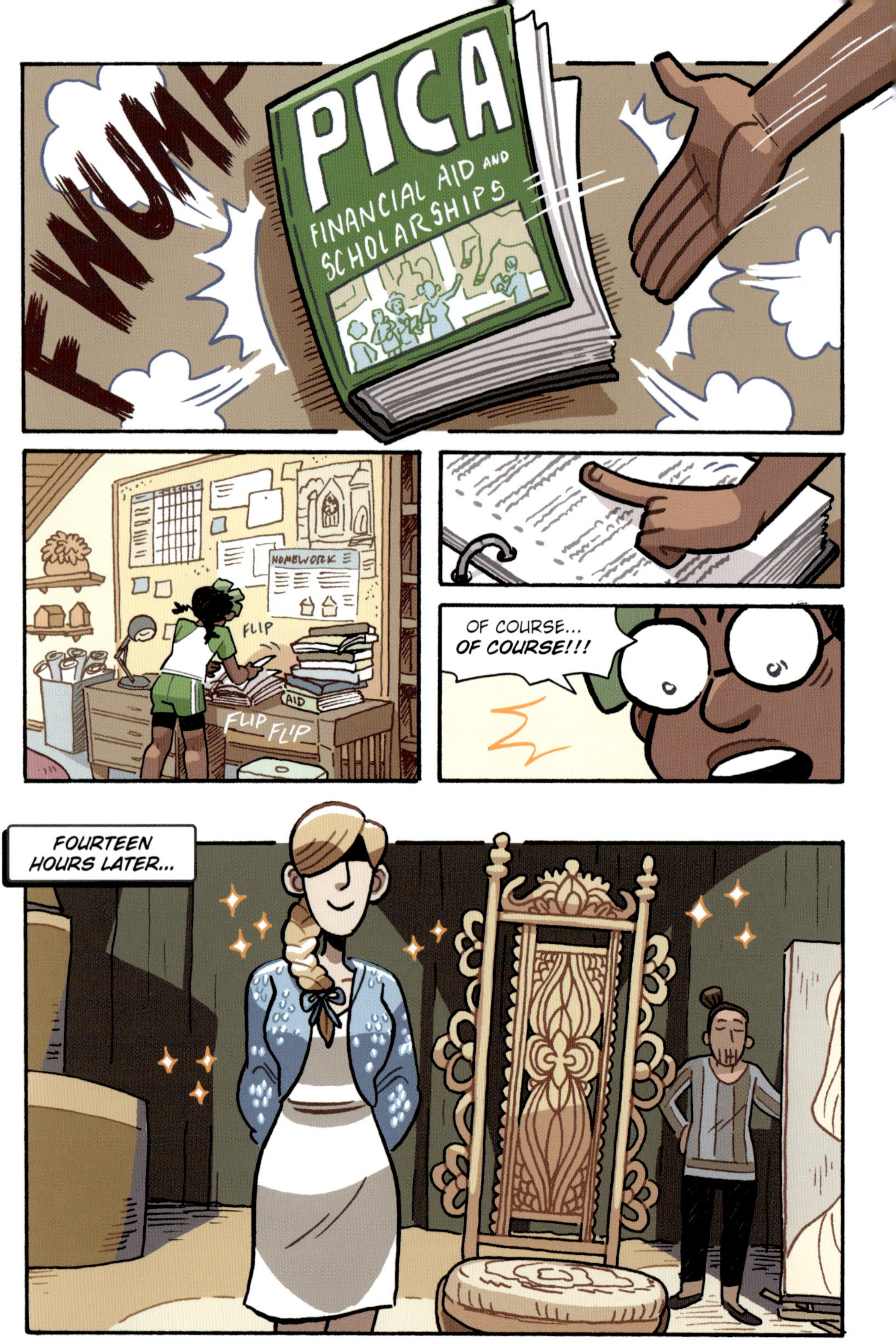
FWUMP
PICA
FINANCIAL AID AND SCHOLARSHIPS
HOMEWORK
FLIP
AID
FLIP FLIP
OF COURSE...
OF COURSE!!!
FOURTEEN HOURS LATER...

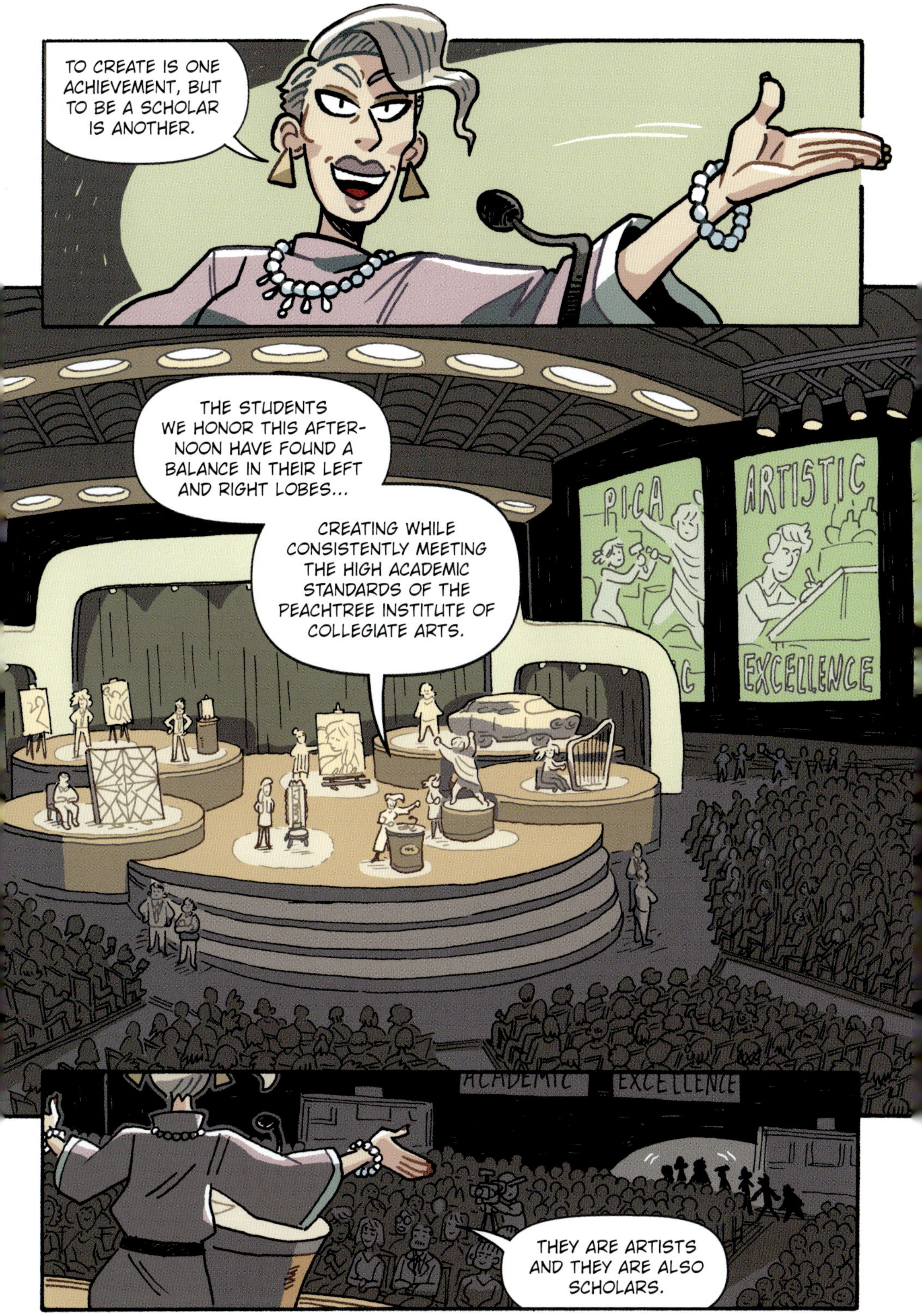
TO CREATE IS ONE ACHIEVEMENT, BUT TO BE A SCHOLAR IS ANOTHER.
THE STUDENTS WE HONOR THIS AFTER-NOON HAVE FOUND A BALANCE IN THEIR LEFT AND RIGHT LOBES...
CREATING WHILE CONSISTENTLY MEETING THE HIGH ACADEMIC STANDARDS OF THE PEACHTREE INSTITUTE OF COLLEGIATE ARTS.
PICA
ARTISTIC
EXCELLENCE
ACADEMIC
EXCELLENCE
THEY ARE ARTISTS AND THEY ARE ALSO SCHOLARS.

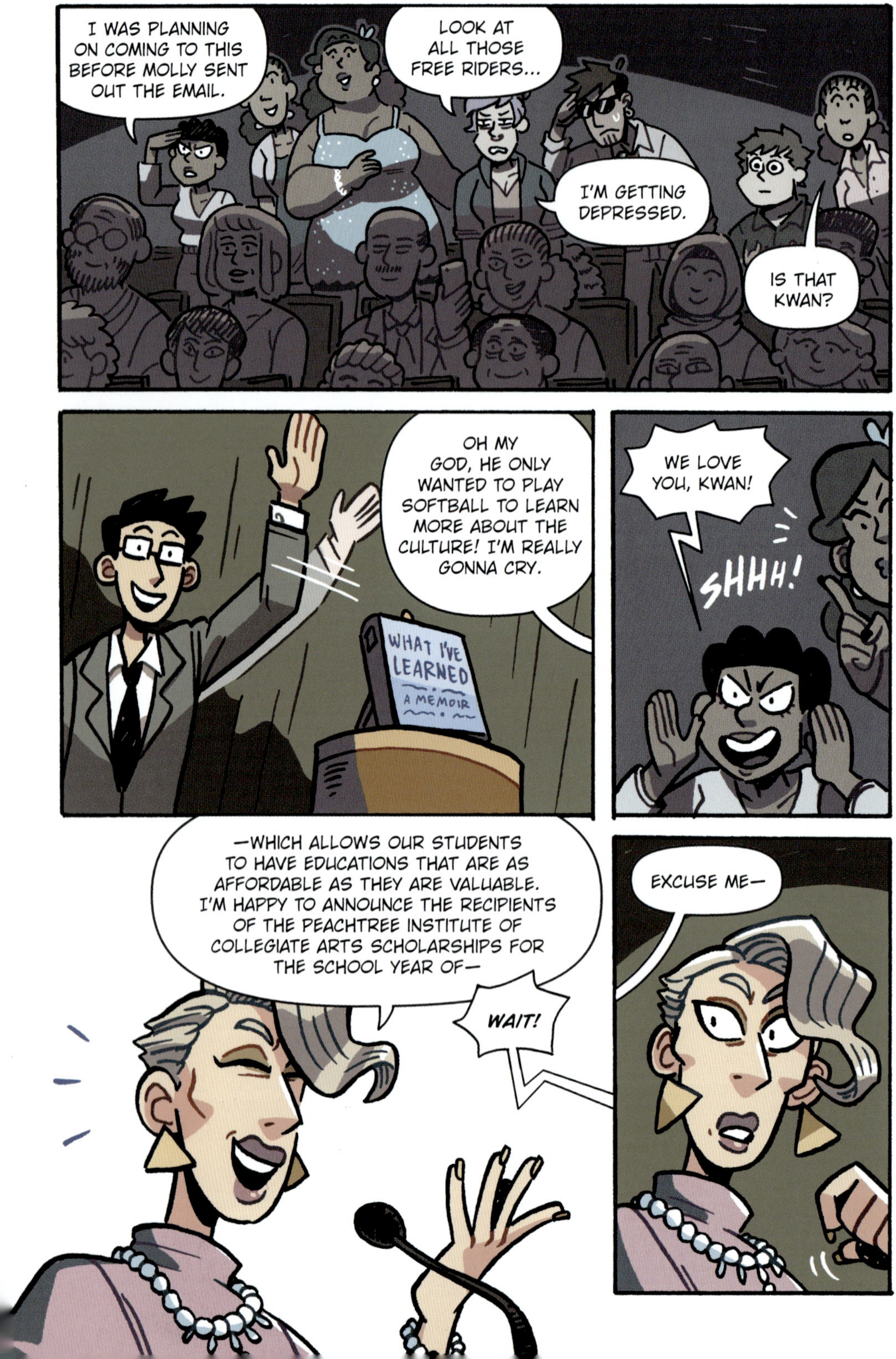
I WAS PLANNING ON COMING TO THIS BEFORE MOLLY SENT OUT THE EMAIL.
LOOK AT ALL THOSE FREE RIDERS...
I'M GETTING DEPRESSED.
IS THAT KWAN?
OH MY GOD, HE ONLY WANTED TO PLAY SOFTBALL TO LEARN MORE ABOUT THE CULTURE! I'M REALLY GONNA CRY.
WHAT I'VE LEARNED
A MEMOIR
WE LOVE YOU, KWAN!
SHHH!
—WHICH ALLOWS OUR STUDENTS TO HAVE EDUCATIONS THAT ARE AS AFFORDABLE AS THEY ARE VALUABLE. I'M HAPPY TO ANNOUNCE THE RECIPIENTS OF THE PEACHTREE INSTITUTE OF COLLEGIATE ARTS SCHOLARSHIPS FOR THE SCHOOL YEAR OF—
WAIT!
EXCUSE ME—

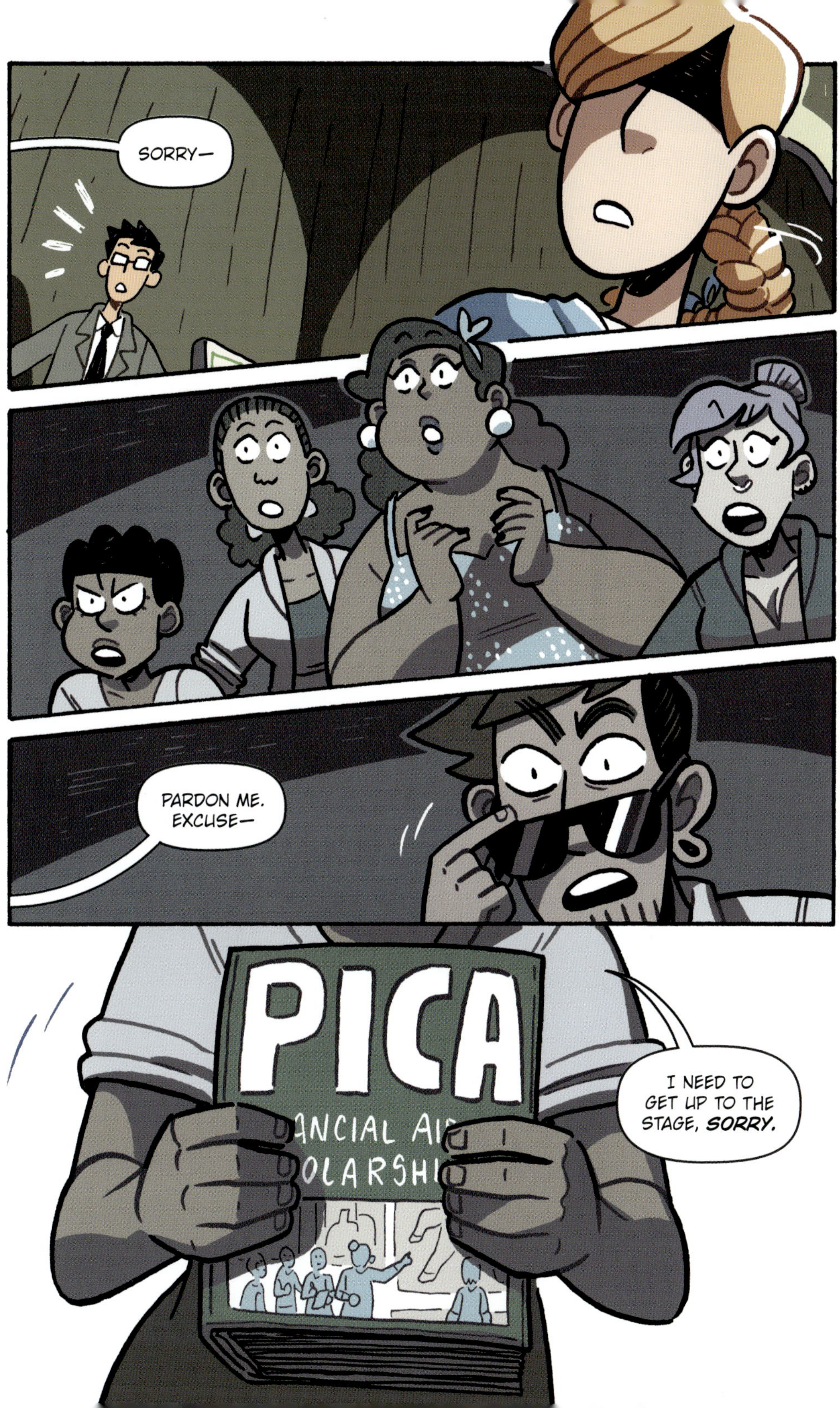
SORRY—
PARDON ME. EXCUSE—
PICA
I NEED TO GET UP TO THE STAGE, *SORRY.*

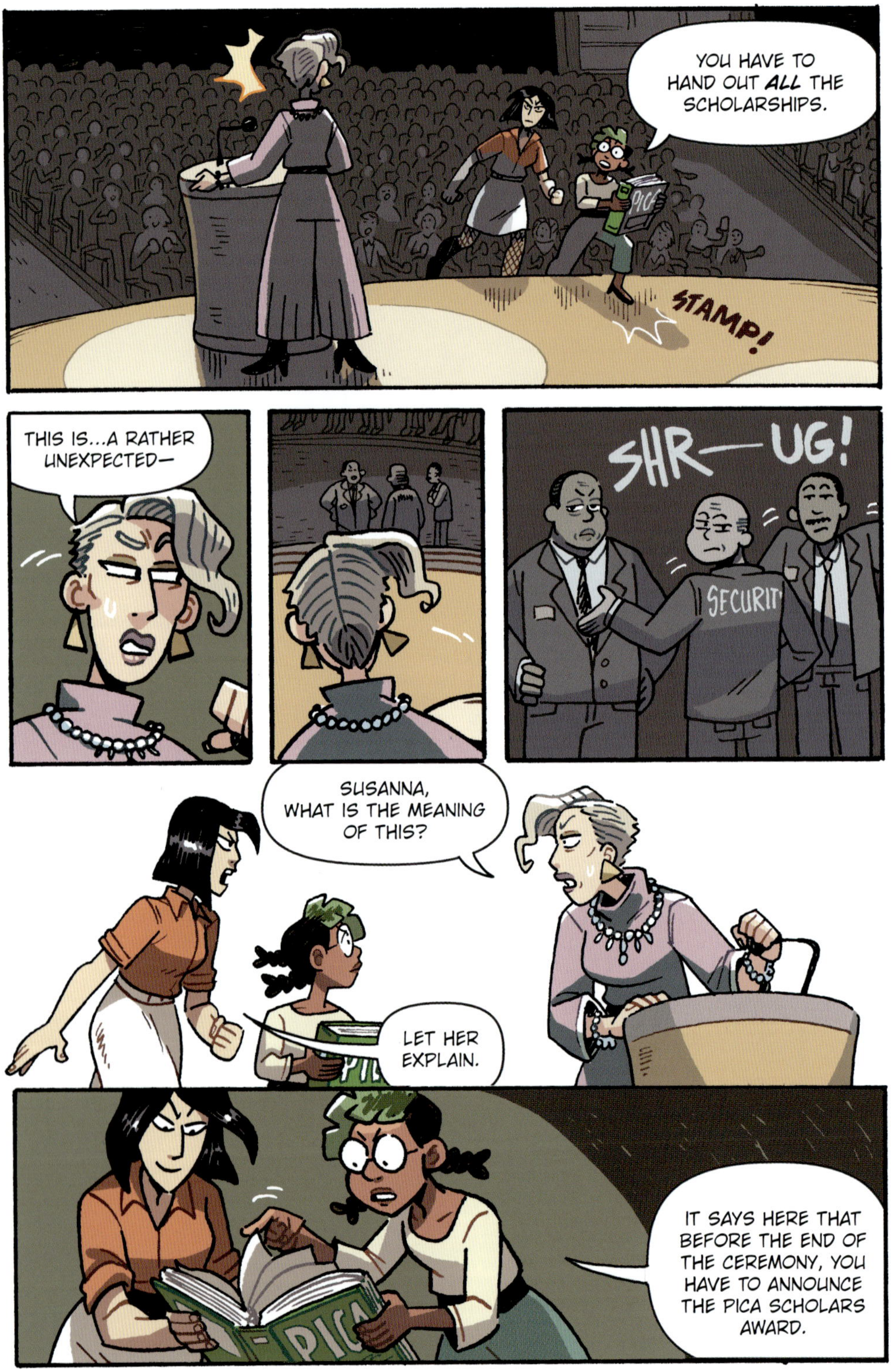
YOU HAVE TO HAND OUT ALL THE SCHOLARSHIPS.
PICA
STAMP!
THIS IS...A RATHER UNEXPECTED—
SHR—UG!
SECURIT
SUSANNA, WHAT IS THE MEANING OF THIS?
LET HER EXPLAIN.
IT SAYS HERE THAT BEFORE THE END OF THE CEREMONY, YOU HAVE TO ANNOUNCE THE PICA SCHOLARS AWARD.

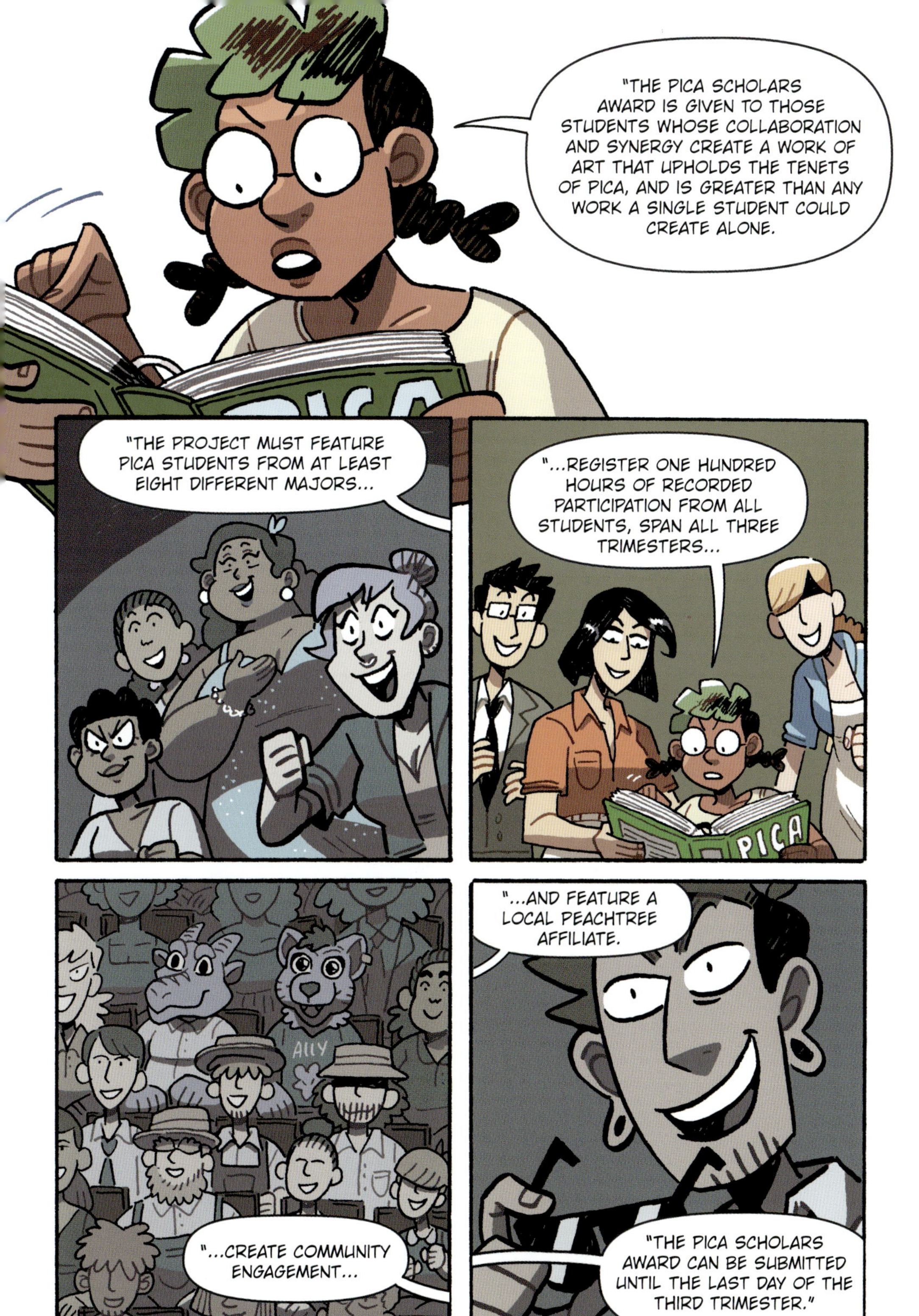
"THE PICA SCHOLARS AWARD IS GIVEN TO THOSE STUDENTS WHOSE COLLABORATION AND SYNERGY CREATE A WORK OF ART THAT UPHOLDS THE TENETS OF PICA, AND IS GREATER THAN ANY WORK A SINGLE STUDENT COULD CREATE ALONE.
"THE PROJECT MUST FEATURE PICA STUDENTS FROM AT LEAST EIGHT DIFFERENT MAJORS...
"...REGISTER ONE HUNDRED HOURS OF RECORDED PARTICIPATION FROM ALL STUDENTS, SPAN ALL THREE TRIMESTERS...
PICA
ALLY
"...CREATE COMMUNITY ENGAGEMENT...
"...AND FEATURE A LOCAL PEACHTREE AFFILIATE.
"THE PICA SCHOLARS AWARD CAN BE SUBMITTED UNTIL THE LAST DAY OF THE THIRD TRIMESTER."

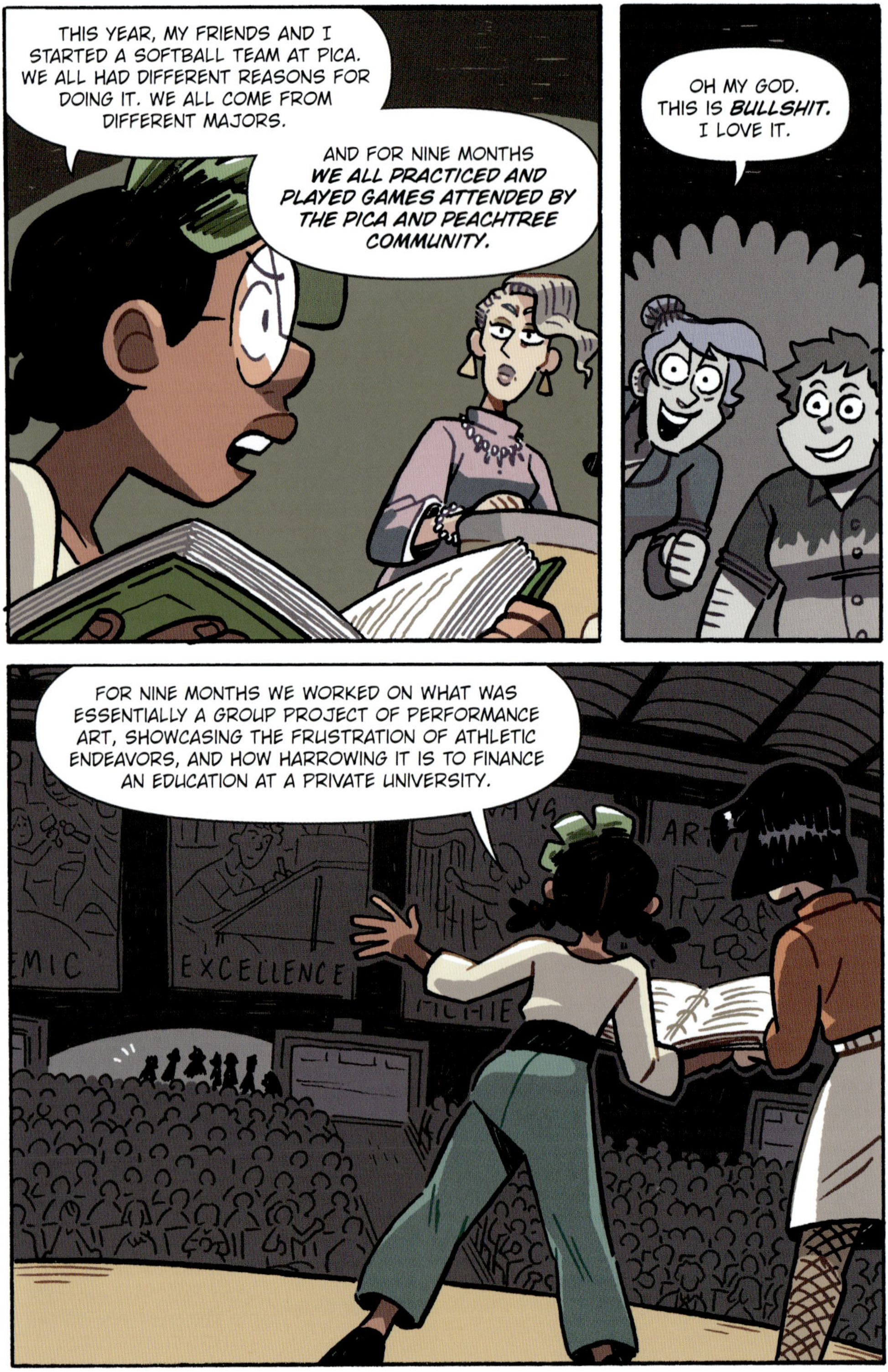
THIS YEAR, MY FRIENDS AND I STARTED A SOFTBALL TEAM AT PICA. WE ALL HAD DIFFERENT REASONS FOR DOING IT. WE ALL COME FROM DIFFERENT MAJORS.
AND FOR NINE MONTHS ***WE ALL PRACTICED AND PLAYED GAMES ATTENDED BY THE PICA AND PEACHTREE COMMUNITY.***
OH MY GOD. THIS IS ***BULLSHIT.*** I LOVE IT.
FOR NINE MONTHS WE WORKED ON WHAT WAS ESSENTIALLY A GROUP PROJECT OF PERFORMANCE ART, SHOWCASING THE FRUSTRATION OF ATHLETIC ENDEAVORS, AND HOW HARROWING IT IS TO FINANCE AN EDUCATION AT A PRIVATE UNIVERSITY.
EXCELLENCE

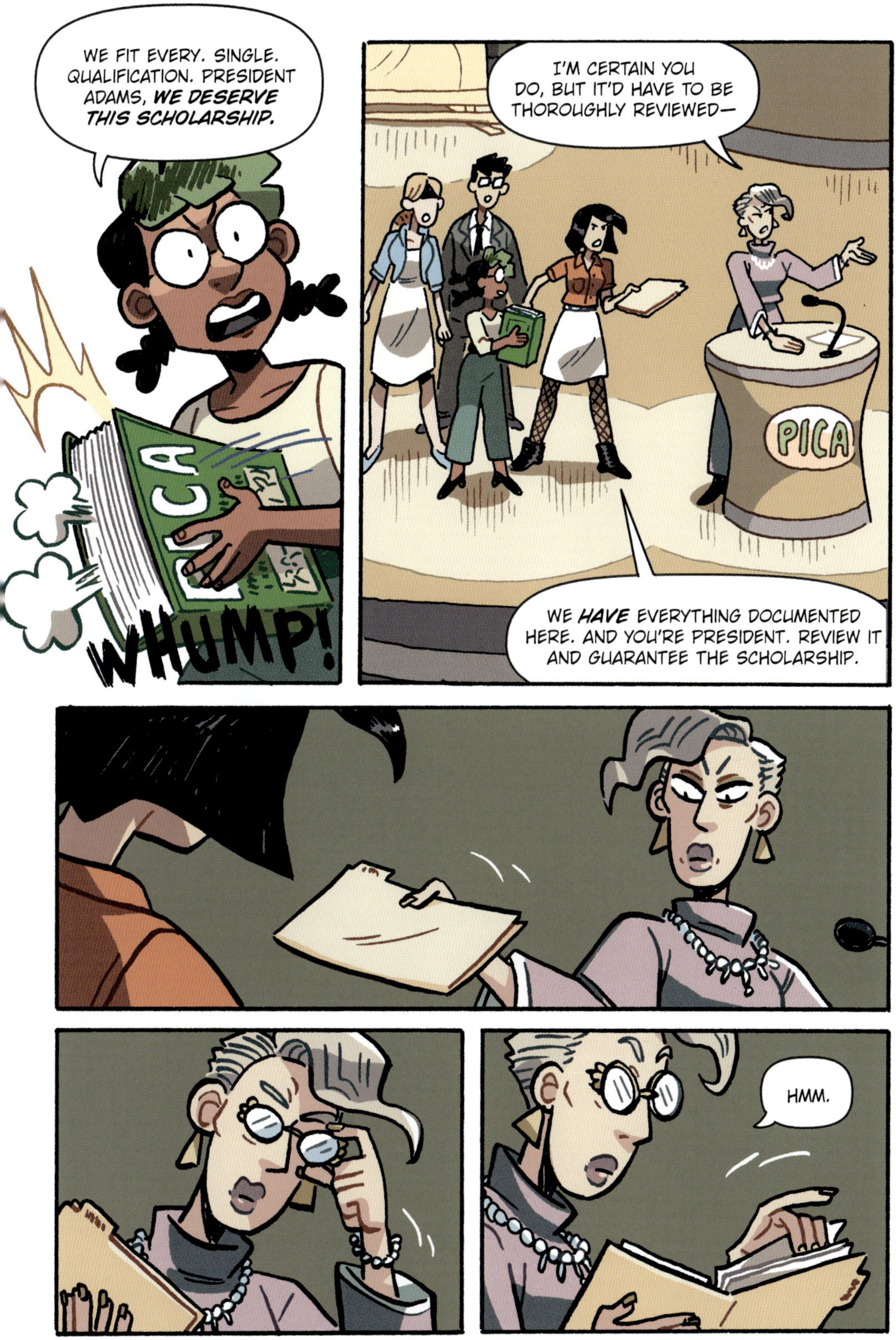
WE FIT EVERY. SINGLE. QUALIFICATION. PRESIDENT ADAMS, WE DESERVE THIS SCHOLARSHIP.
PICA
WHUMP!
I'M CERTAIN YOU DO, BUT IT'D HAVE TO BE THOROUGHLY REVIEWED—
PICA
WE HAVE EVERYTHING DOCUMENTED HERE. AND YOU'RE PRESIDENT. REVIEW IT AND GUARANTEE THE SCHOLARSHIP.
HMM.

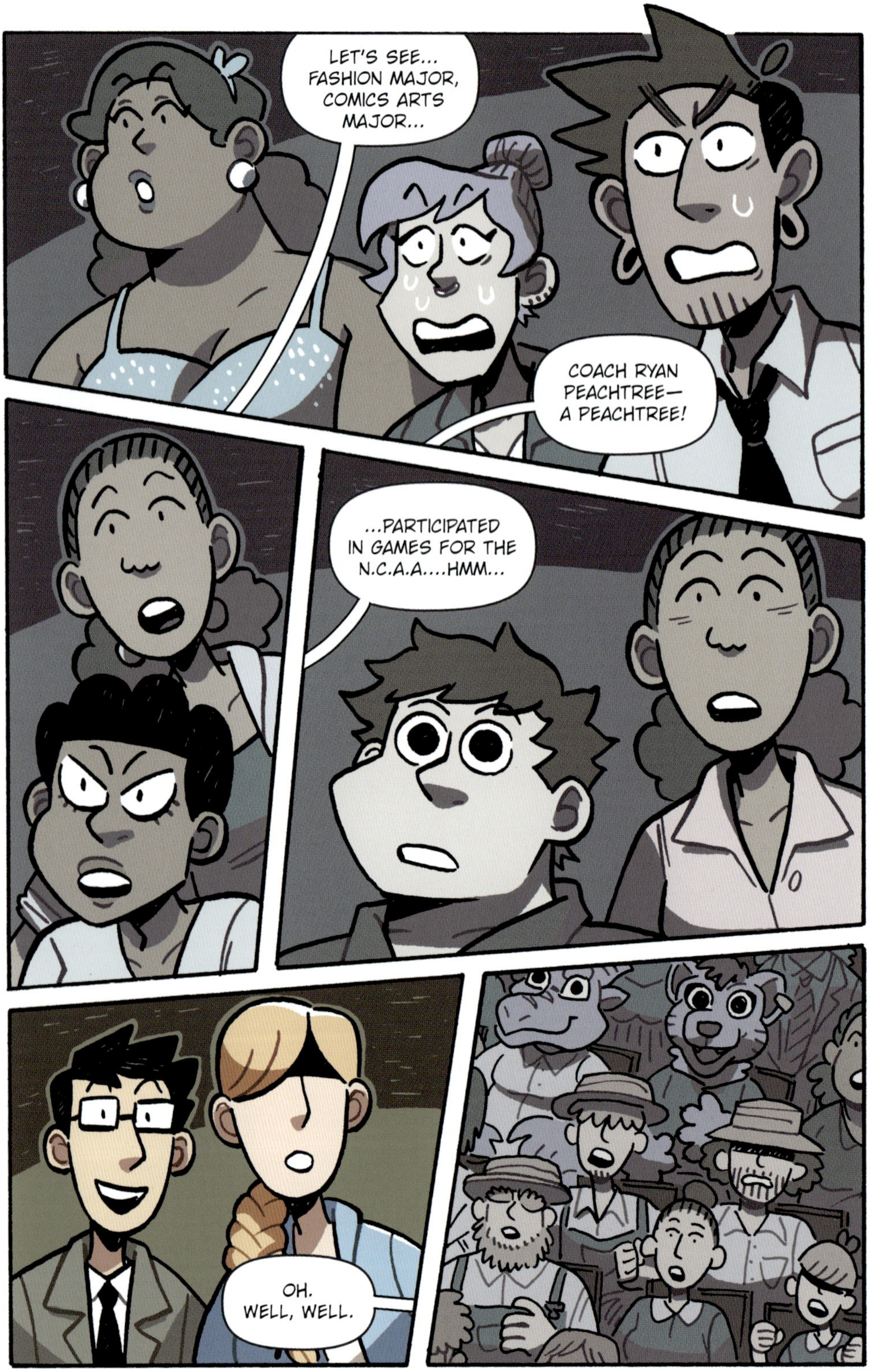
LET'S SEE... FASHION MAJOR, COMICS ARTS MAJOR...
COACH RYAN PEACHTREE— A PEACHTREE!
...PARTICIPATED IN GAMES FOR THE N.C.A.A....HMM...
OH. WELL, WELL.

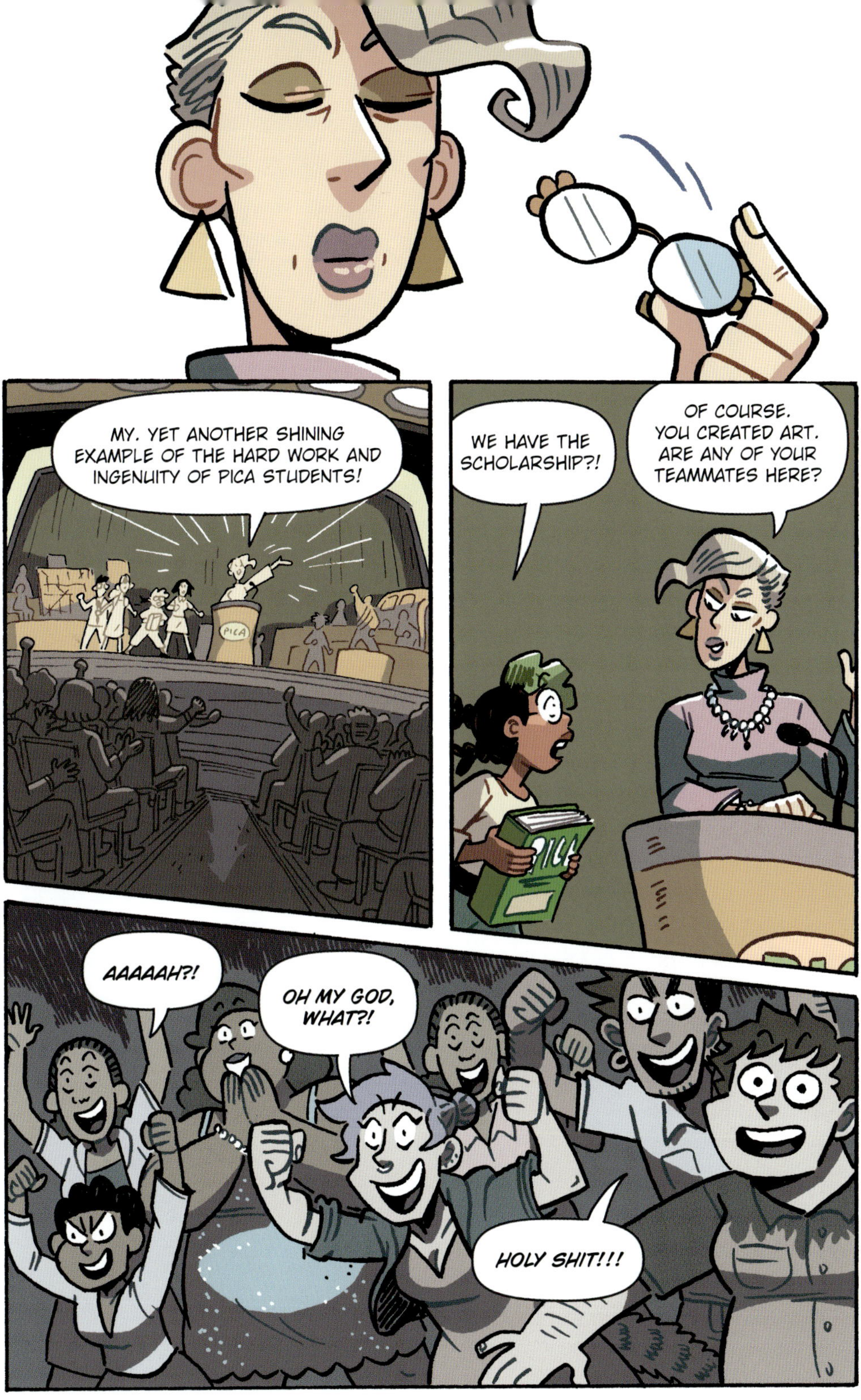
MY. YET ANOTHER SHINING EXAMPLE OF THE HARD WORK AND INGENUITY OF PICA STUDENTS!
PICA
WE HAVE THE SCHOLARSHIP?!
OF COURSE. YOU CREATED ART. ARE ANY OF YOUR TEAMMATES HERE?
AAAAAH?!
OH MY GOD, WHAT?!
HOLY SHIT!!!

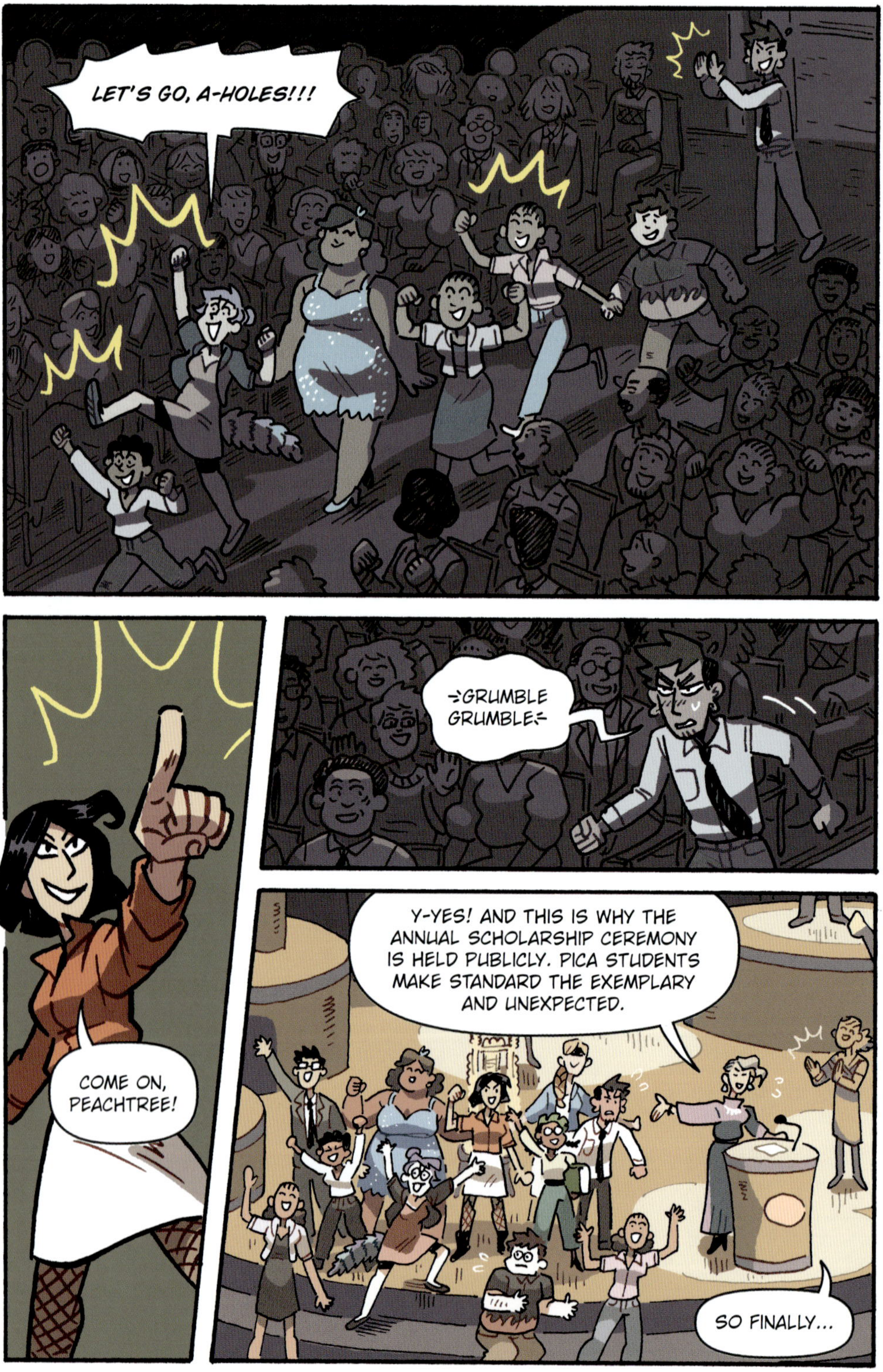
LET'S GO, A-HOLES!!!
COME ON, PEACHTREE!
GRUMBLE GRUMBLE
Y-YES! AND THIS IS WHY THE ANNUAL SCHOLARSHIP CEREMONY IS HELD PUBLICLY. PICA STUDENTS MAKE STANDARD THE EXEMPLARY AND UNEXPECTED.
SO FINALLY...

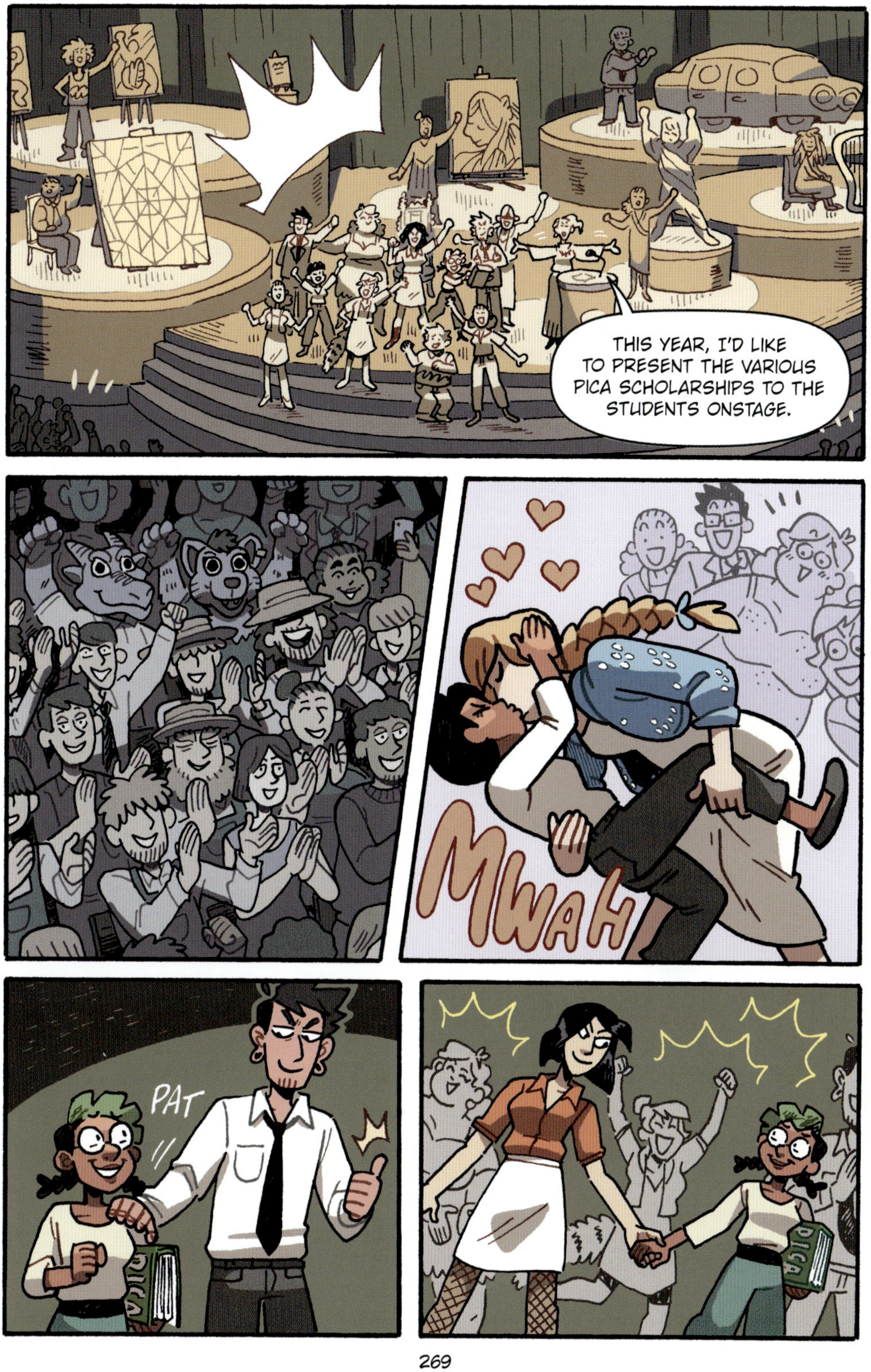
THIS YEAR, I'D LIKE TO PRESENT THE VARIOUS PICA SCHOLARSHIPS TO THE STUDENTS ONSTAGE.
MWAH
PAT

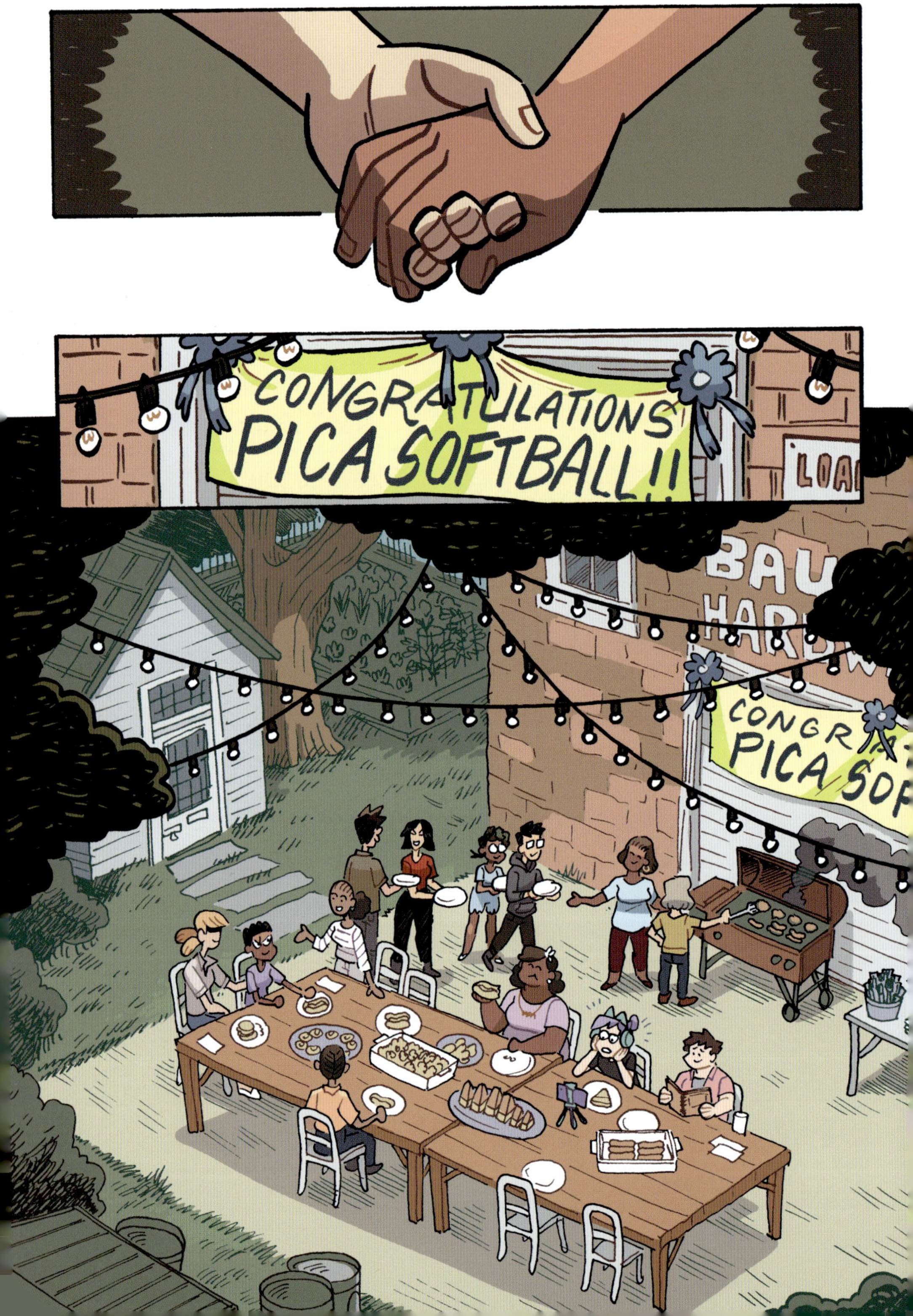
CONGRATULATIONS
PICA SOFTBALL!!

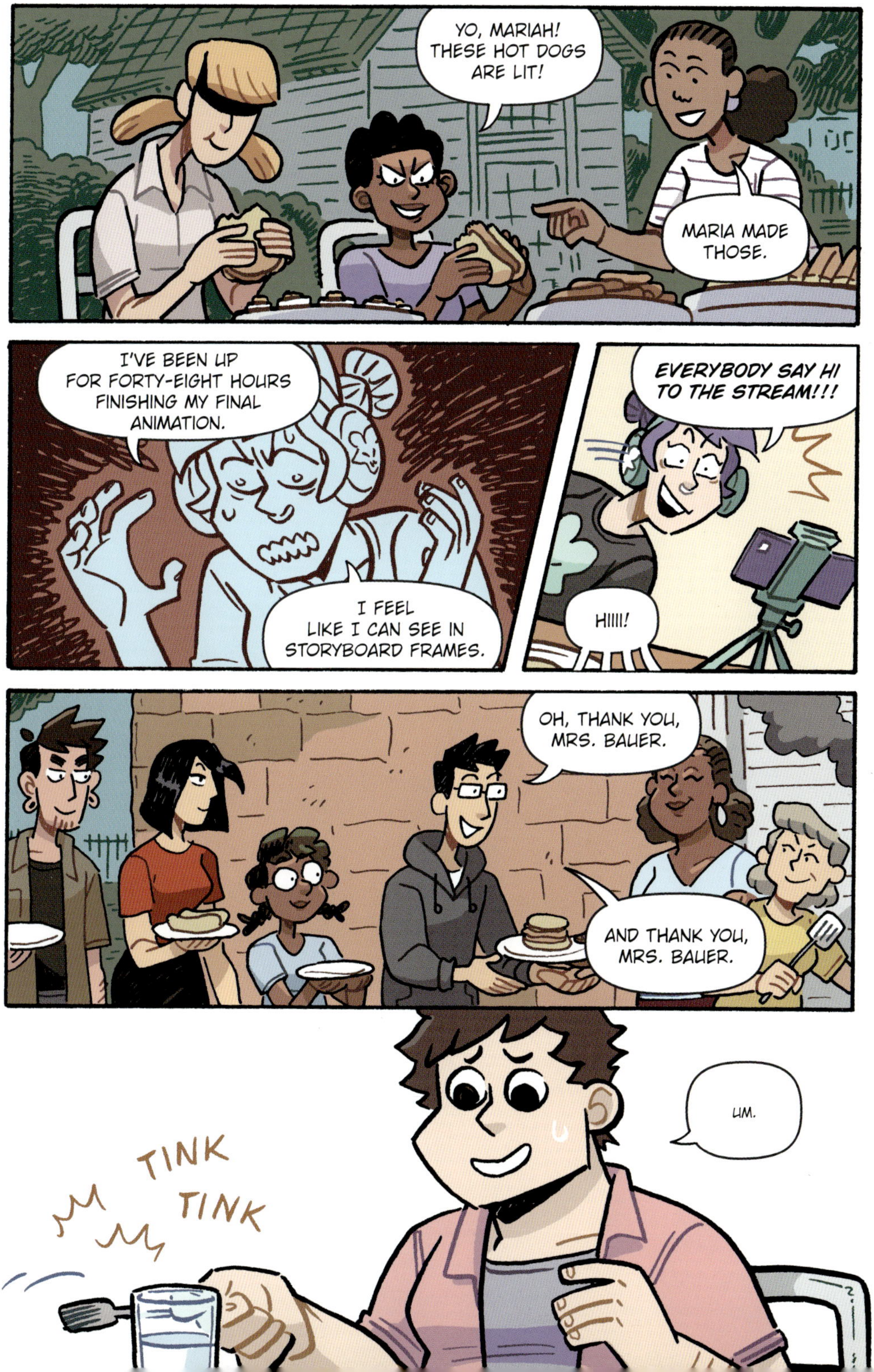

YO, MARIAH! THESE HOT DOGS ARE LIT!
MARIA MADE THOSE.
I'VE BEEN UP FOR FORTY-EIGHT HOURS FINISHING MY FINAL ANIMATION.
I FEEL LIKE I CAN SEE IN STORYBOARD FRAMES.
EVERYBODY SAY HI TO THE STREAM!!!
HIIII!
OH, THANK YOU, MRS. BAUER.
AND THANK YOU, MRS. BAUER.
TINK
TINK
UM.

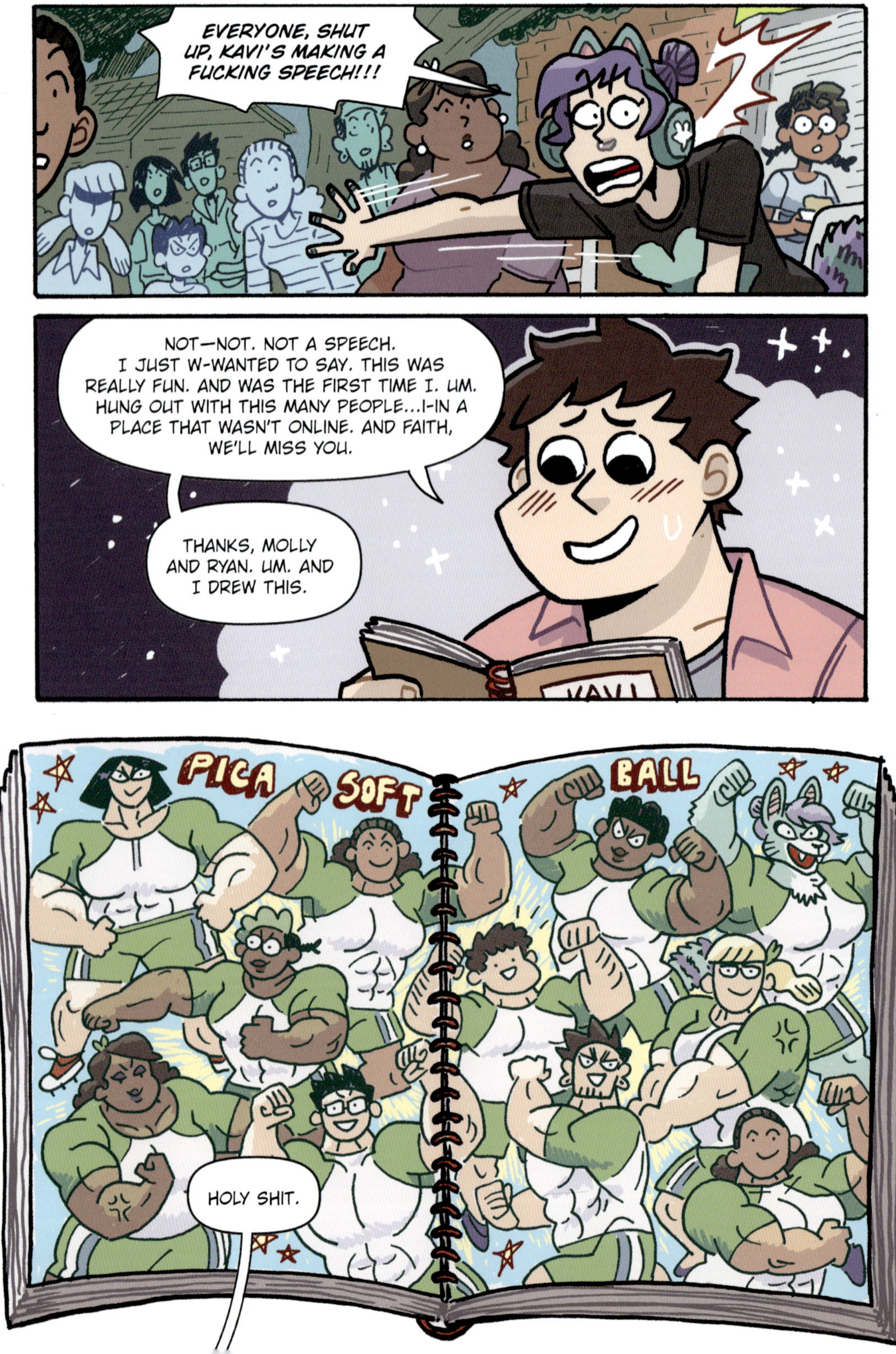
EVERYONE, SHUT UP, KAVI'S MAKING A FUCKING SPEECH!!!
NOT—NOT. NOT A SPEECH. I JUST W-WANTED TO SAY. THIS WAS REALLY FUN. AND WAS THE FIRST TIME I. UM. HUNG OUT WITH THIS MANY PEOPLE...I-IN A PLACE THAT WASN'T ONLINE. AND FAITH, WE'LL MISS YOU.
THANKS, MOLLY AND RYAN. UM. AND I DREW THIS.
PICA SOFT BALL
HOLY SHIT.

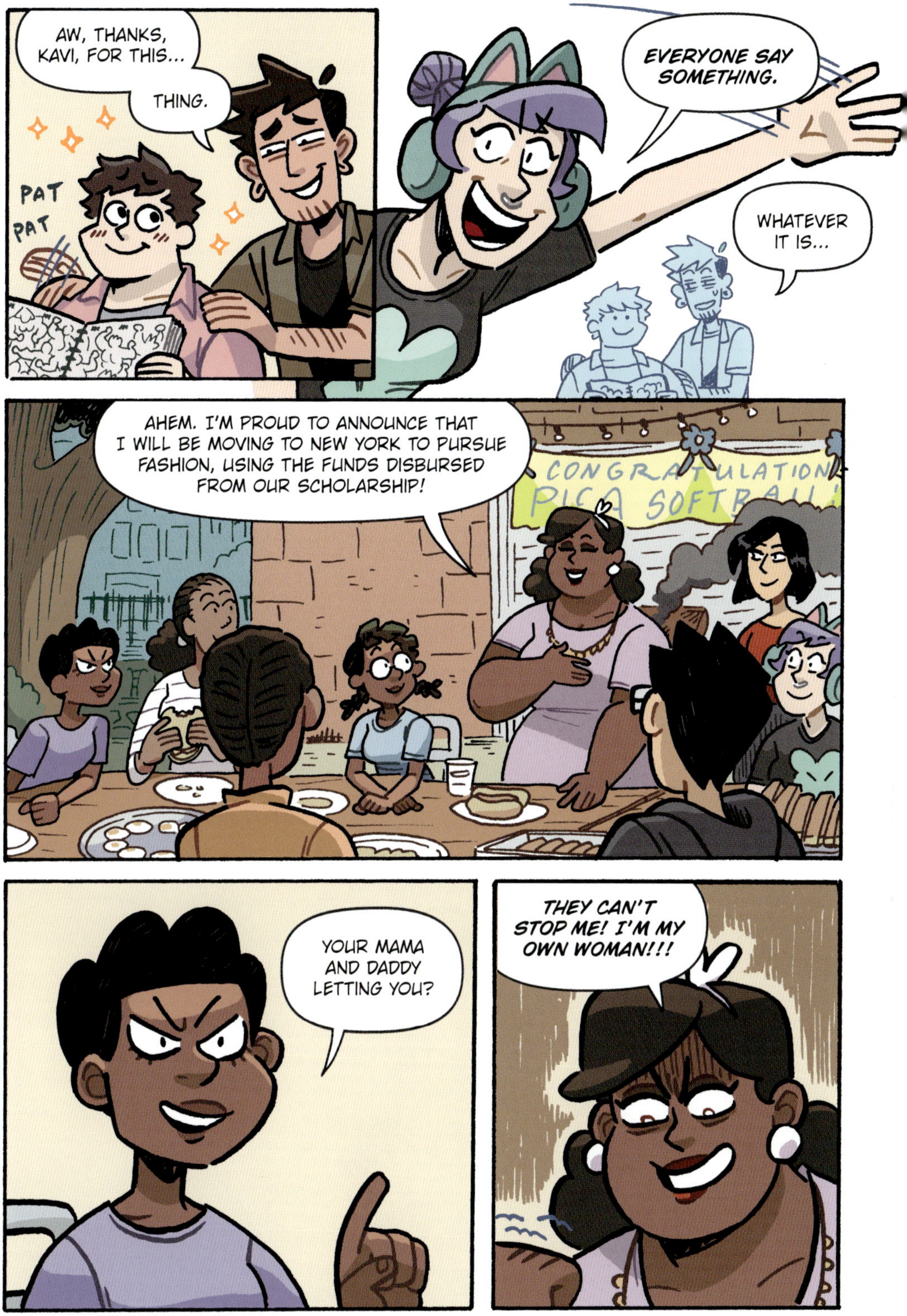
AW, THANKS, KAVI, FOR THIS...
THING.
PAT
PAT
EVERYONE SAY SOMETHING.
WHATEVER IT IS...
AHEM. I'M PROUD TO ANNOUNCE THAT I WILL BE MOVING TO NEW YORK TO PURSUE FASHION, USING THE FUNDS DISBURSED FROM OUR SCHOLARSHIP!
YOUR MAMA AND DADDY LETTING YOU?
THEY CAN'T STOP ME! I'M MY OWN WOMAN!!!

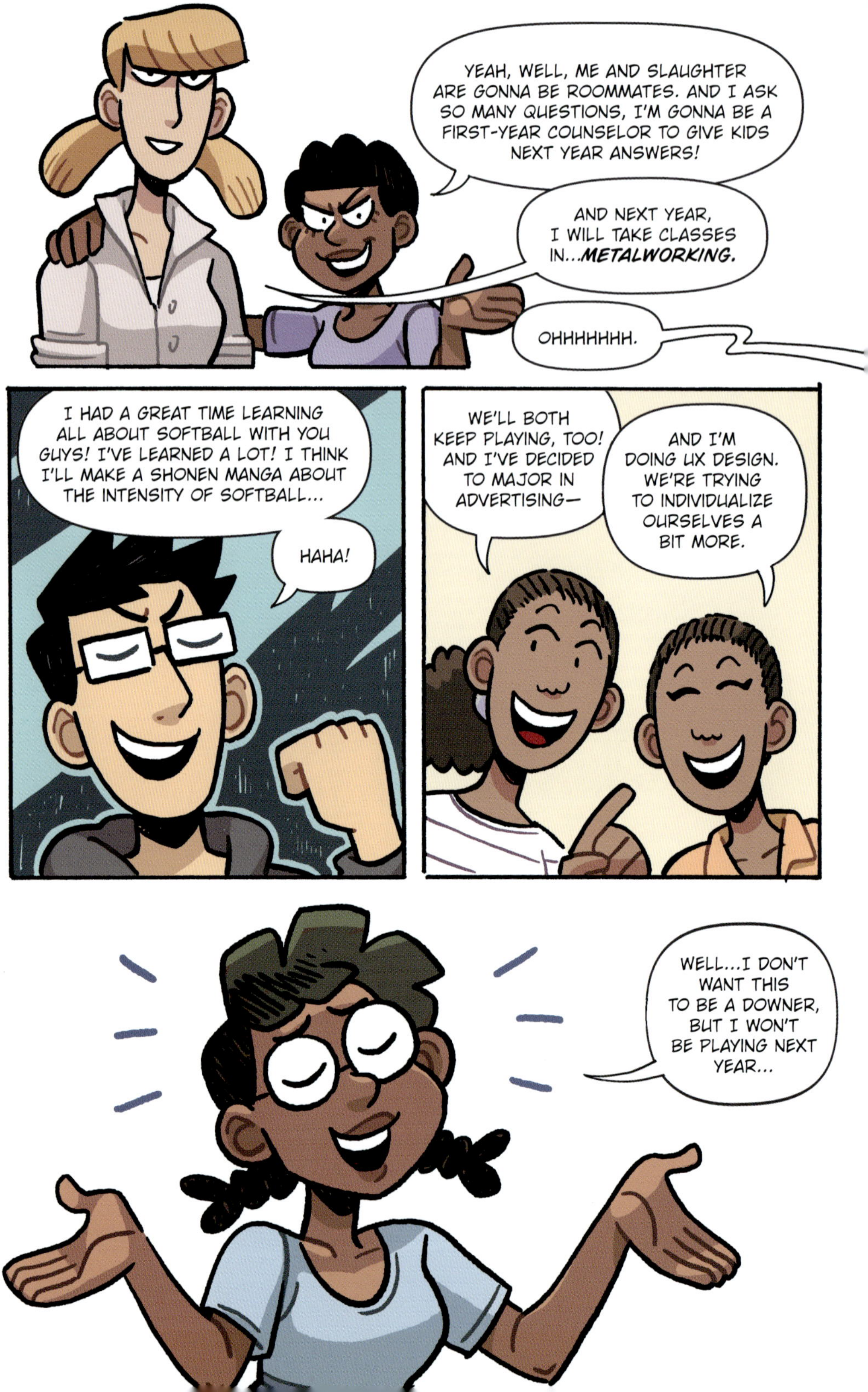
YEAH, WELL, ME AND SLAUGHTER ARE GONNA BE ROOMMATES. AND I ASK SO MANY QUESTIONS, I'M GONNA BE A FIRST-YEAR COUNSELOR TO GIVE KIDS NEXT YEAR ANSWERS!
AND NEXT YEAR, I WILL TAKE CLASSES IN...*METALWORKING.*
OHHHHHHH.
I HAD A GREAT TIME LEARNING ALL ABOUT SOFTBALL WITH YOU GUYS! I'VE LEARNED A LOT! I THINK I'LL MAKE A SHONEN MANGA ABOUT THE INTENSITY OF SOFTBALL...
HAHA!
WE'LL BOTH KEEP PLAYING, TOO! AND I'VE DECIDED TO MAJOR IN ADVERTISING—
AND I'M DOING UX DESIGN. WE'RE TRYING TO INDIVIDUALIZE OURSELVES A BIT MORE.
WELL...I DON'T WANT THIS TO BE A DOWNER, BUT I WON'T BE PLAYING NEXT YEAR...

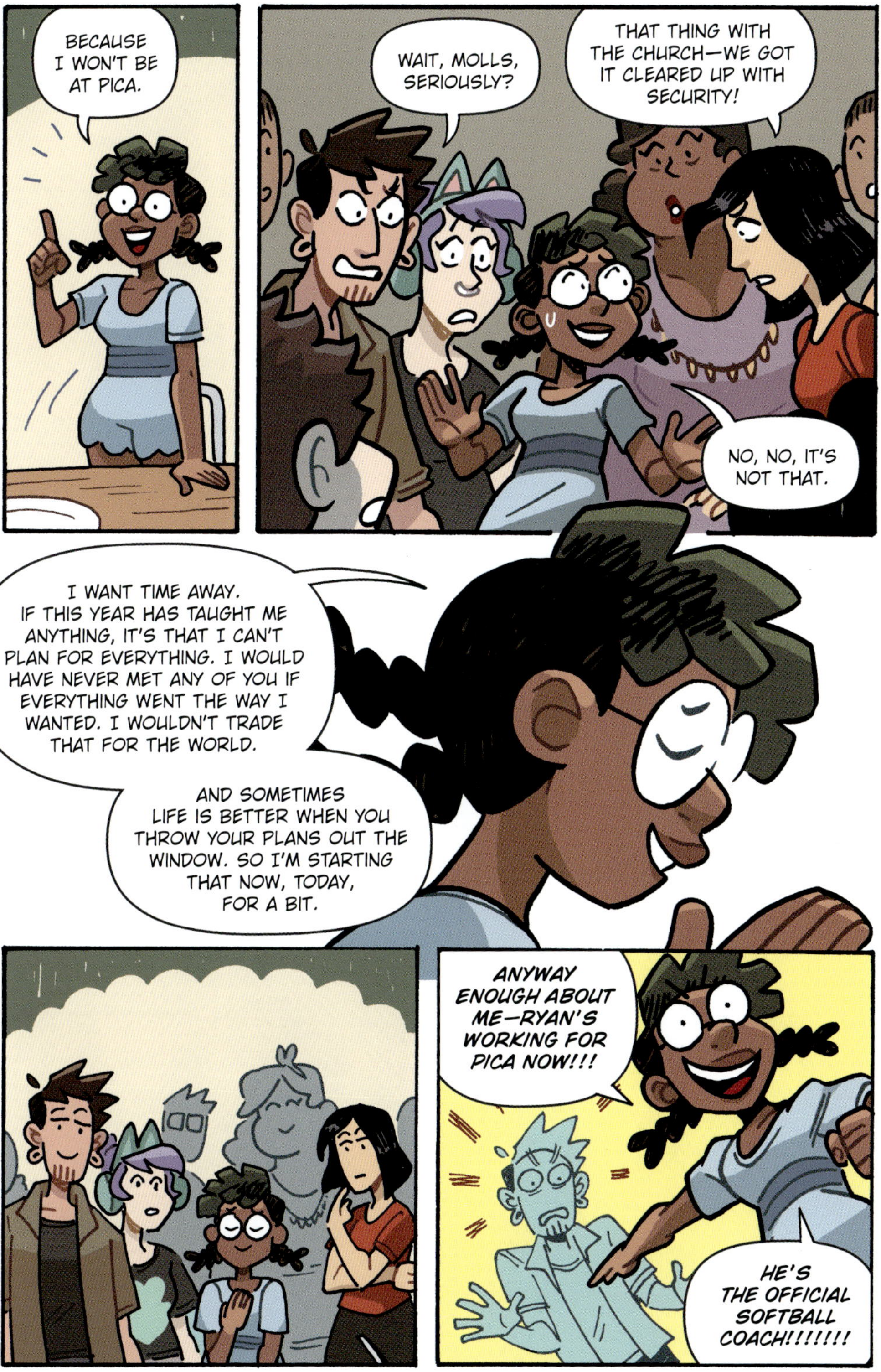
BECAUSE I WON'T BE AT PICA.
WAIT, MOLLS, SERIOUSLY?
THAT THING WITH THE CHURCH—WE GOT IT CLEARED UP WITH SECURITY!
NO, NO, IT'S NOT THAT.
I WANT TIME AWAY. IF THIS YEAR HAS TAUGHT ME ANYTHING, IT'S THAT I CAN'T PLAN FOR EVERYTHING. I WOULD HAVE NEVER MET ANY OF YOU IF EVERYTHING WENT THE WAY I WANTED. I WOULDN'T TRADE THAT FOR THE WORLD.
AND SOMETIMES LIFE IS BETTER WHEN YOU THROW YOUR PLANS OUT THE WINDOW. SO I'M STARTING THAT NOW, TODAY, FOR A BIT.
ANYWAY ENOUGH ABOUT ME—RYAN'S WORKING FOR PICA NOW!!!
HE'S THE OFFICIAL SOFTBALL COACH!!!!!!!

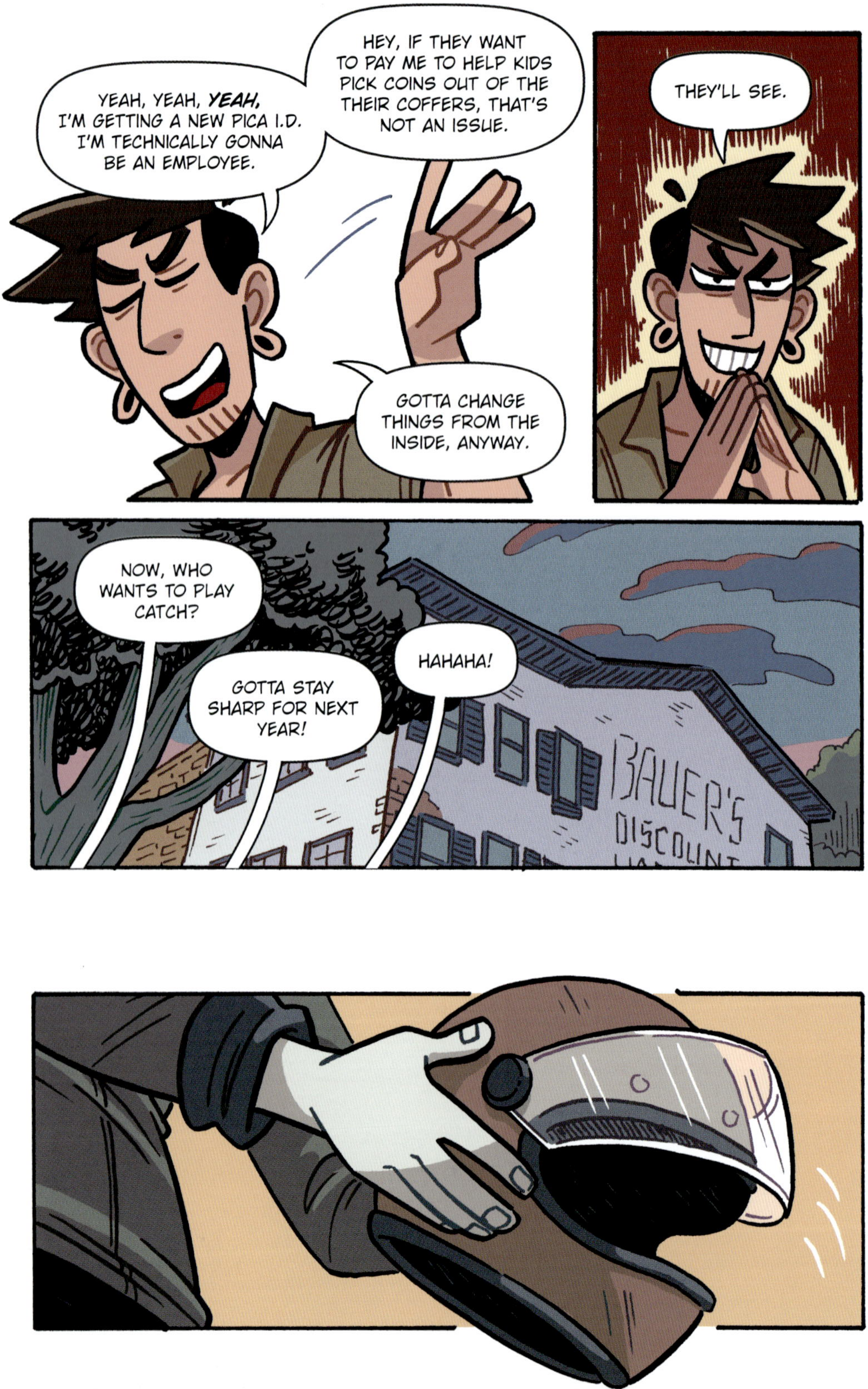
YEAH, YEAH, ***YEAH,***
I'M GETTING A NEW PICA I.D.
I'M TECHNICALLY GONNA BE AN EMPLOYEE.
HEY, IF THEY WANT TO PAY ME TO HELP KIDS PICK COINS OUT OF THE THEIR COFFERS, THAT'S NOT AN ISSUE.
GOTTA CHANGE THINGS FROM THE INSIDE, ANYWAY.
THEY'LL SEE.
NOW, WHO WANTS TO PLAY CATCH?
GOTTA STAY SHARP FOR NEXT YEAR!
HAHAHA!
BAUER'S
DISCOUNT

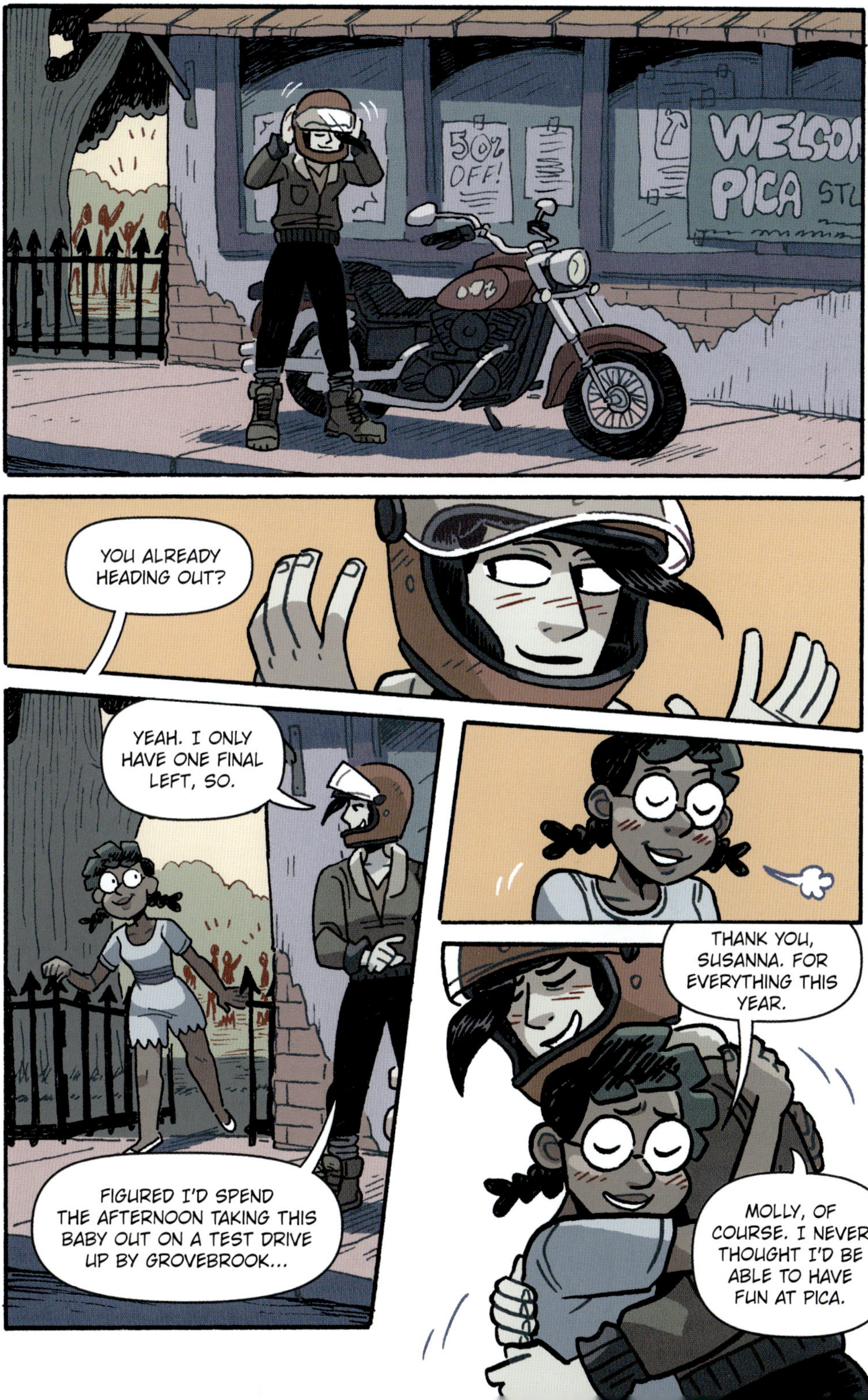
50% OFF!
WELCO
PICA ST
YOU ALREADY HEADING OUT?
YEAH. I ONLY HAVE ONE FINAL LEFT, SO.
FIGURED I'D SPEND THE AFTERNOON TAKING THIS BABY OUT ON A TEST DRIVE UP BY GROVEBROOK...
THANK YOU, SUSANNA. FOR EVERYTHING THIS YEAR.
MOLLY, OF COURSE. I NEVER THOUGHT I'D BE ABLE TO HAVE FUN AT PICA.

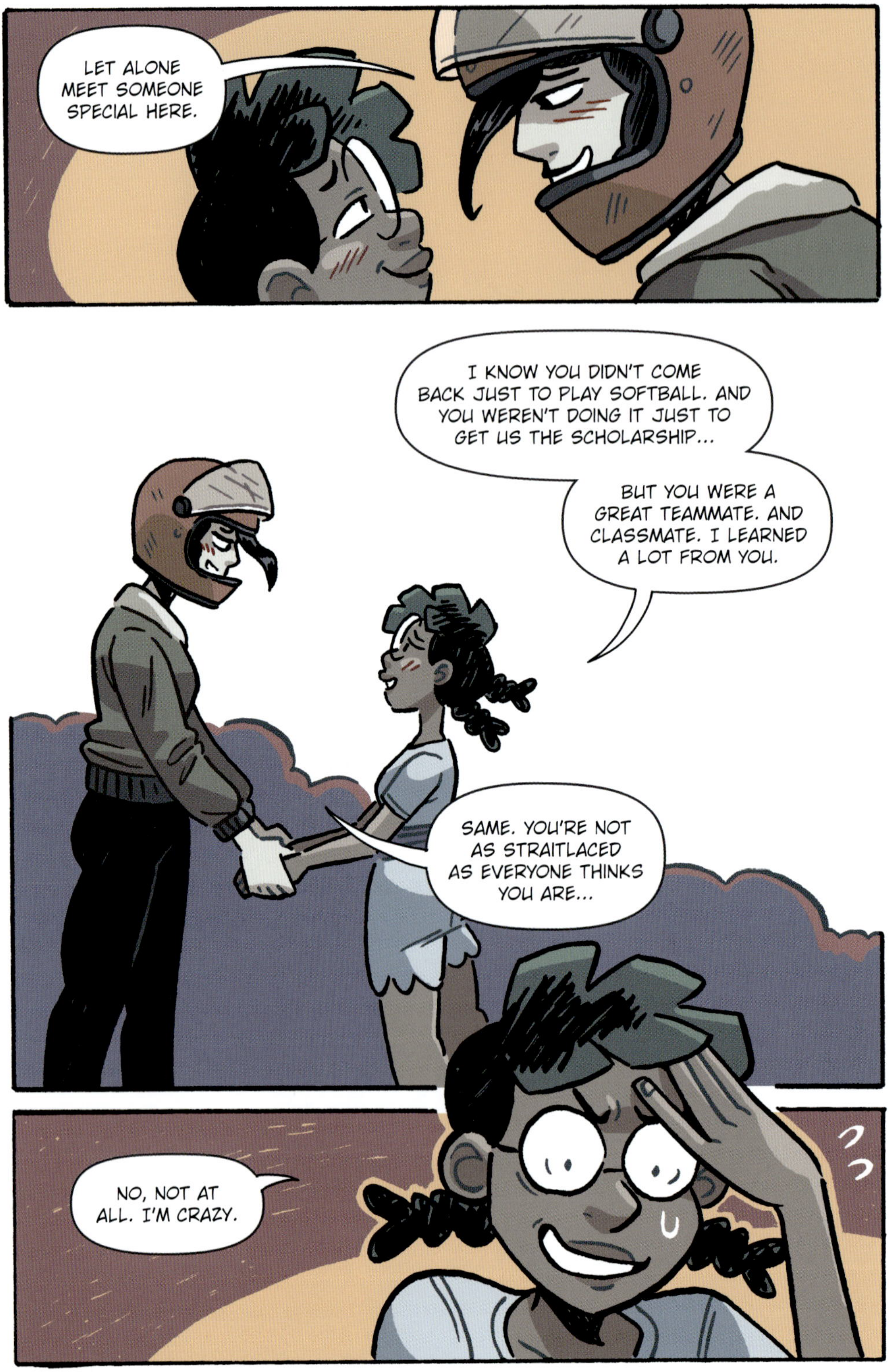
LET ALONE MEET SOMEONE SPECIAL HERE.
I KNOW YOU DIDN'T COME BACK JUST TO PLAY SOFTBALL. AND YOU WEREN'T DOING IT JUST TO GET US THE SCHOLARSHIP...
BUT YOU WERE A GREAT TEAMMATE. AND CLASSMATE. I LEARNED A LOT FROM YOU.
SAME. YOU'RE NOT AS STRAITLACED AS EVERYONE THINKS YOU ARE...
NO, NOT AT ALL. I'M CRAZY.

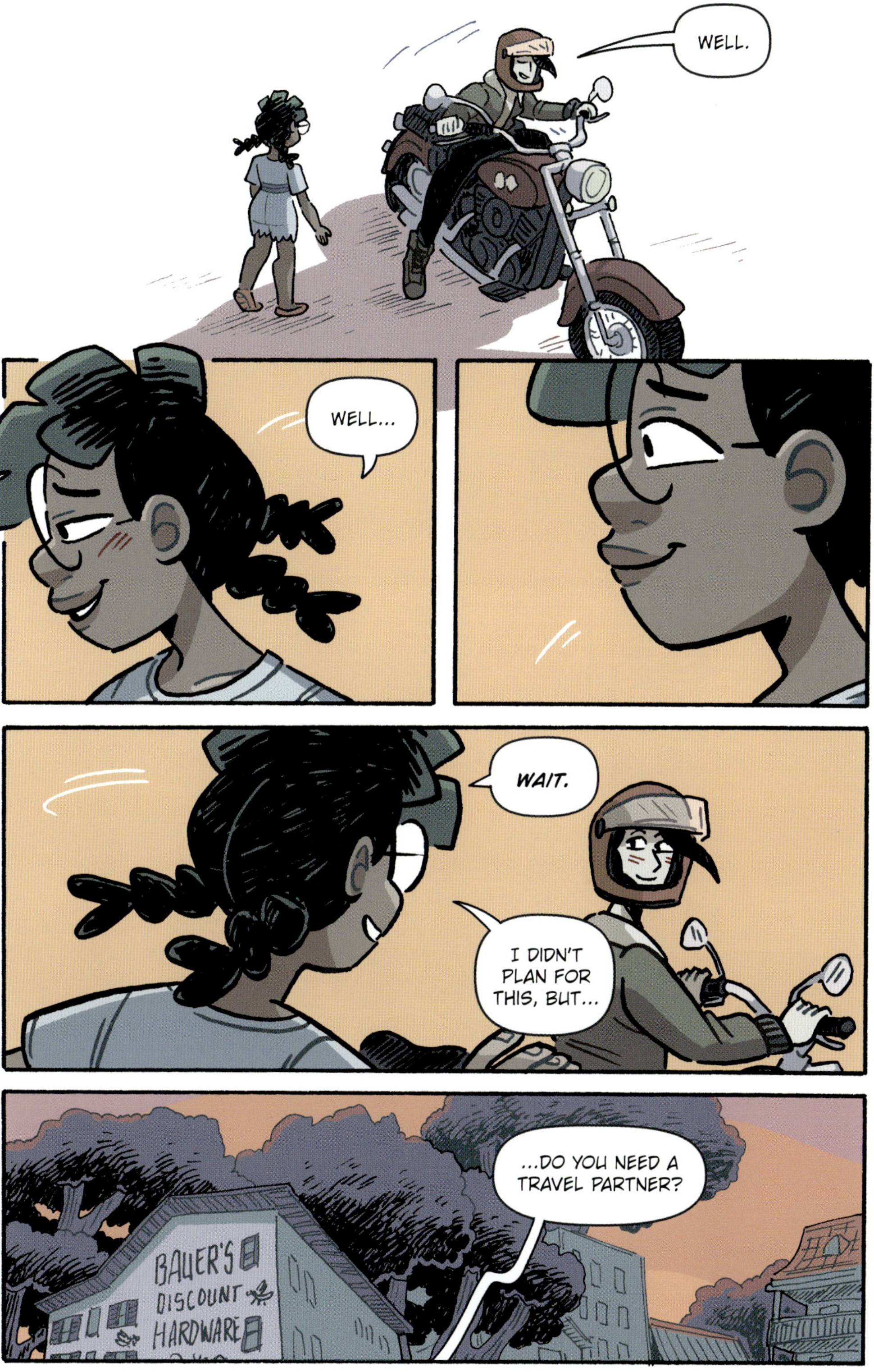
WELL.
WELL...
WAIT.
I DIDN'T PLAN FOR THIS, BUT...
...DO YOU NEED A TRAVEL PARTNER?
BAUER'S DISCOUNT HARDWARE

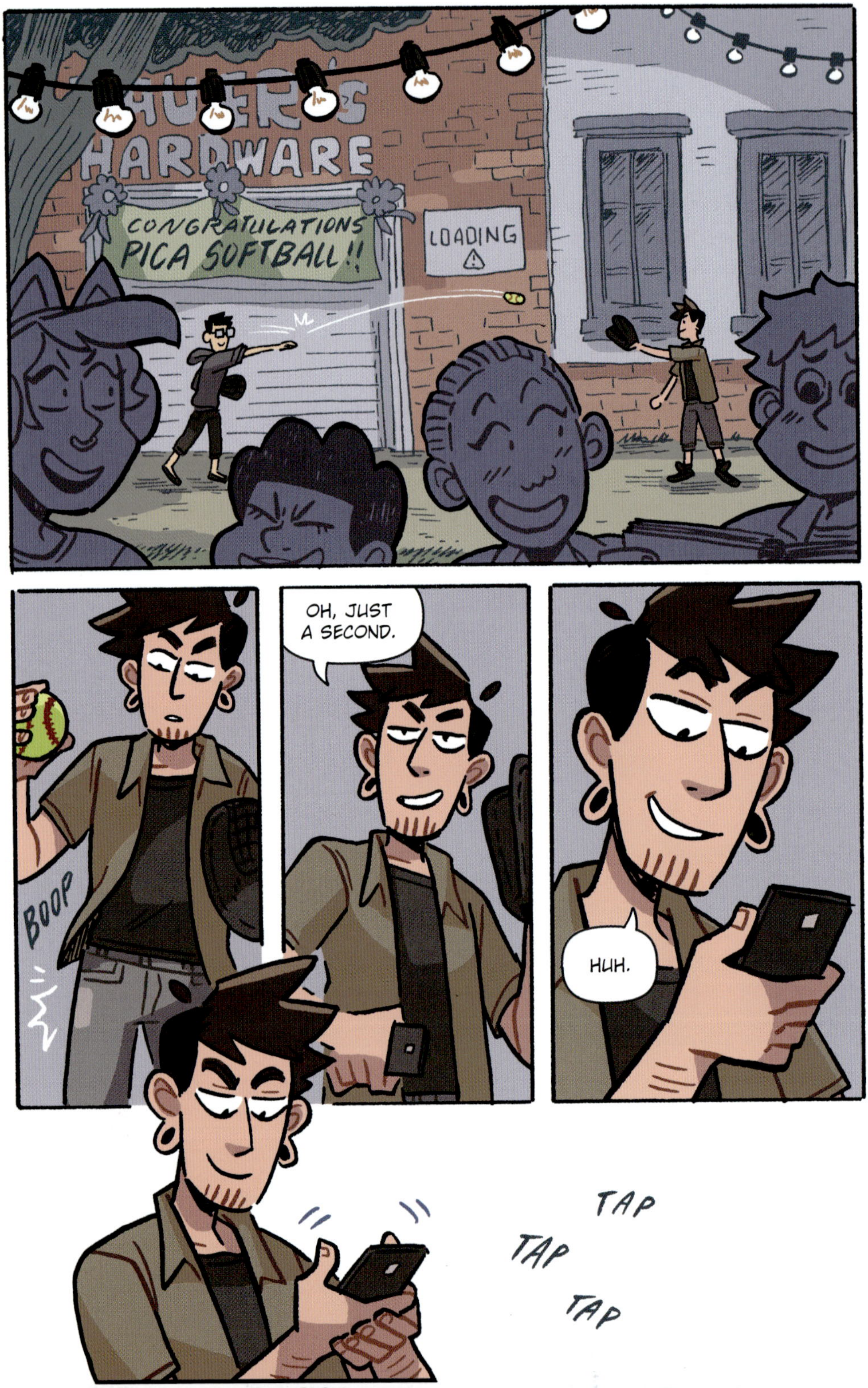

HUBER'S HARDWARE
CONGRATULATIONS PICA SOFTBALL!!
LOADING
BOOP
OH, JUST A SECOND.
HUH.
TAP
TAP
TAP

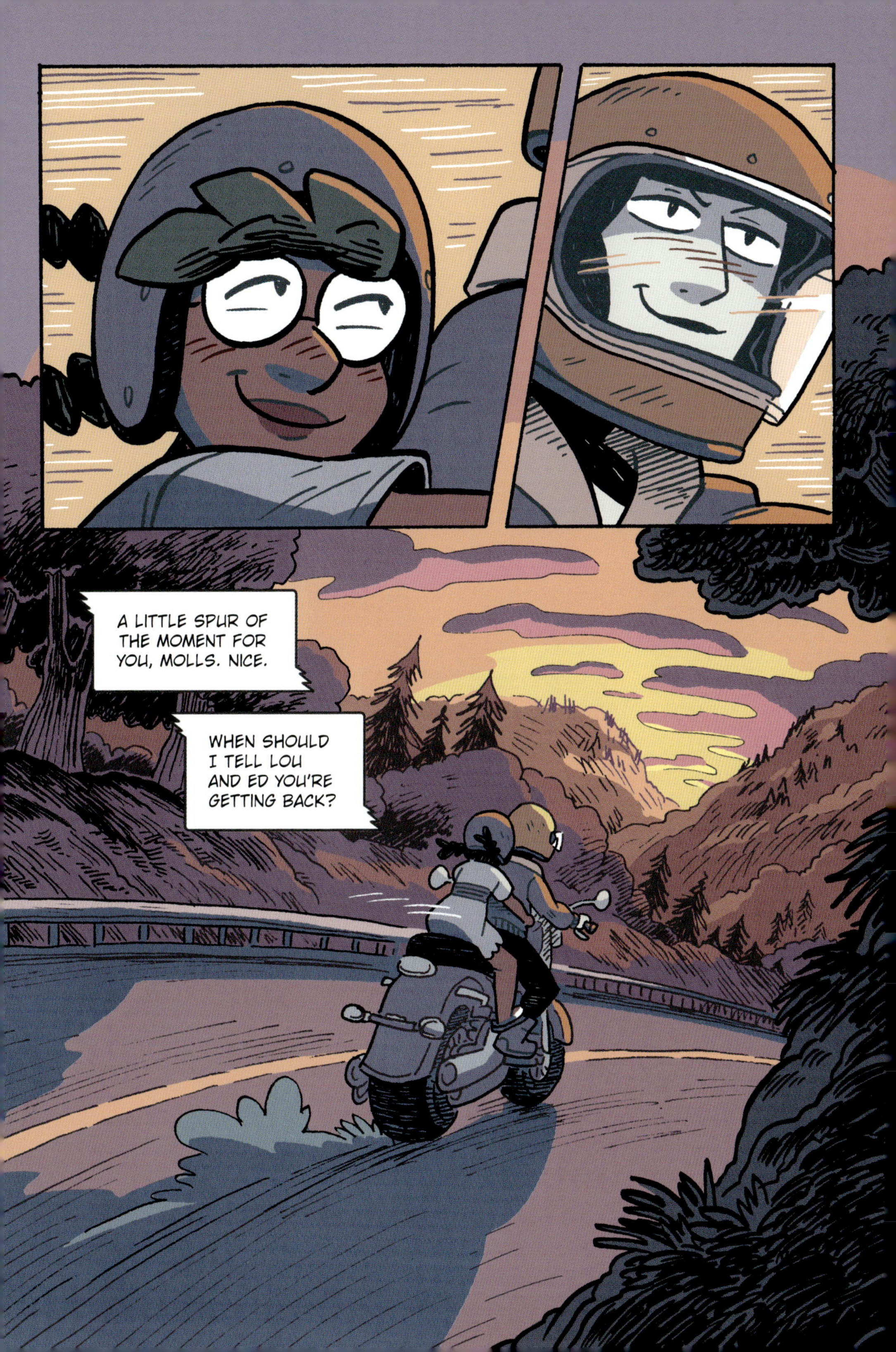
A LITTLE SPUR OF THE MOMENT FOR YOU, MOLLS. NICE.
WHEN SHOULD I TELL LOU AND ED YOU'RE GETTING BACK?

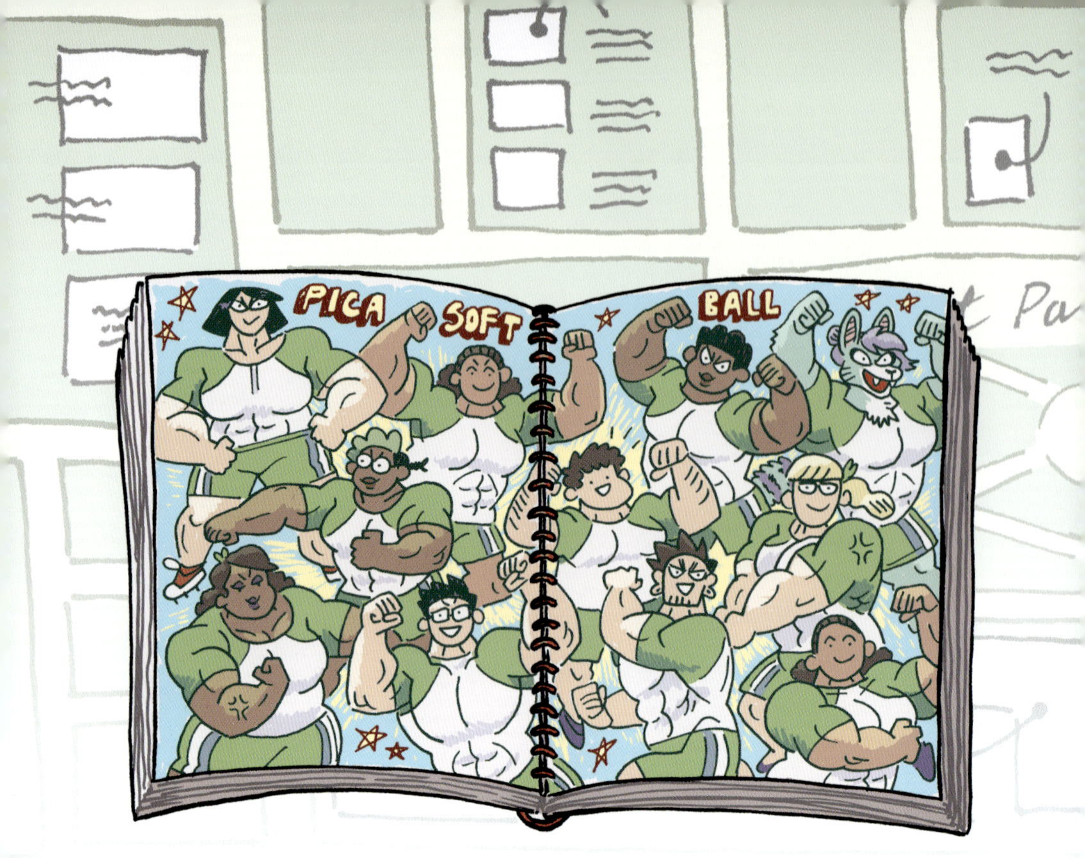
PICA
SOFT
BALL

Thank you to Kiara Valdez and First Second for giving us the space to finish this silly tale. Thank you to George Rohac for setting this project in motion, and to Chelsea Eberly for guiding us to the finish line. Rachel, Gale, and Dave—I've learned more from you all than I have from art school. (Thank you, Kneece!)

I'm lucky to have the most creative and supportive siblings in the world—Ogechi and Ikechi. Thank you to my parents for teaching us kindness and hard work.

And thank you to Madeline Rupert Jaspering. This book would not exist without your diligence, your insane sense of humor, and your raw, crackling artistic talent. I am grateful to be your friend. I am pained that we no longer share a middle name.

–NGOZI

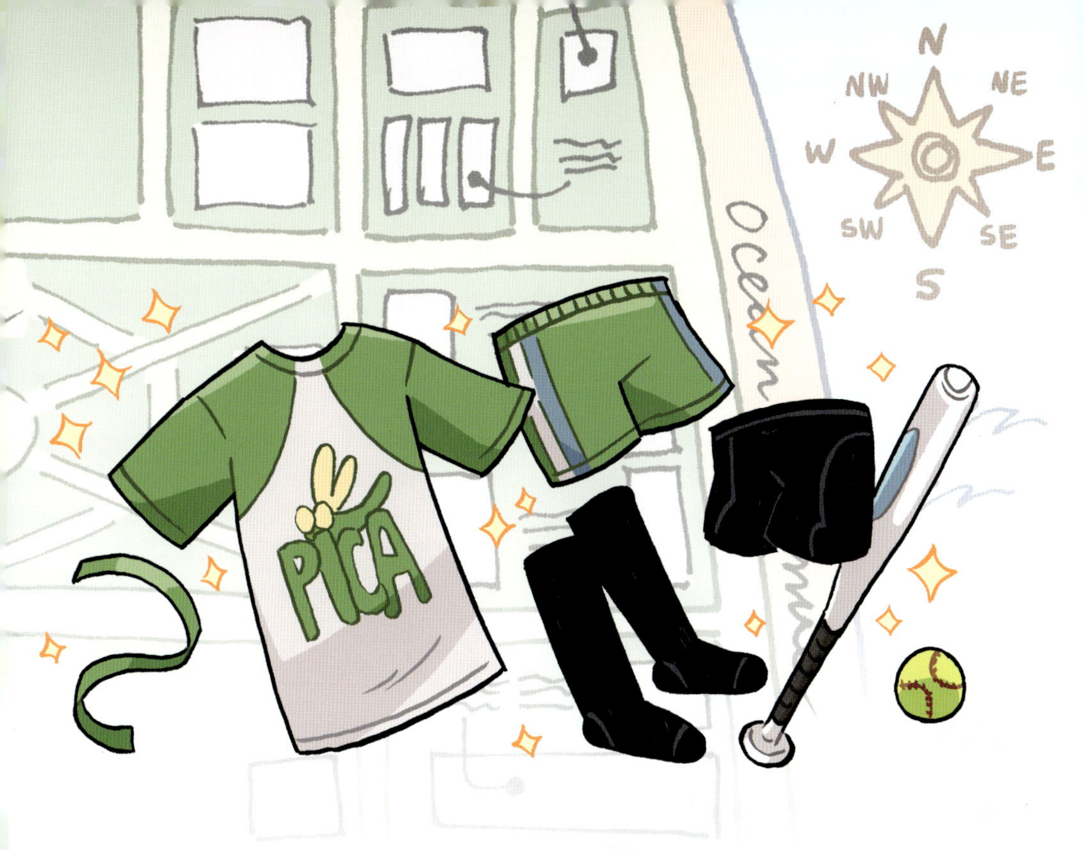
N
NW
NE
W
E
SW
SE
S
Ocean
PICA

Firstly, thank you to Ngozi for roping me into this project and for always being there to workshop ideas, talk through feelings, and cheer me on. I couldn't ask for a better collaborator or friend!

Thank you to my wonderful partner, Gannon, whose patience and enthusiasm for my very chaotic art career has kept me going all these years. I love you!!

Thanks to my parents and my brother, who have always been very supportive of my silly little drawings. And to my dad especially, for all those years of travel softball.

Finally, thank you to my editor, Kiara, the staff at First Second, and to everyone else who's supported me as a friend, student, peer, or creator.

–MAD

Published by First Second
First Second is an imprint of Roaring Brook Press,
a division of Holtzbrinck Publishing Holdings Limited Partnership
120 Broadway, New York, NY 10271
firstsecondbooks.com

Text © 2024 by Ngozi Ukazu
Illustrations © 2024 by Mad Rupert
All rights reserved

Library of Congress Control Number: 2023937811

Our books may be purchased in bulk for promotional, educational, or business use.
Please contact your local bookseller or the Macmillan Corporate and Premium Sales Department
at (800) 221-7945 ext. 5442 or by email at MacmillanSpecialMarkets@macmillan.com.

First edition, 2024
Edited by Kiara Valdez
Cover design by Molly Johanson
Interior book design by Molly Johanson and Casper Manning
Production editing by Avia Perez
Color by K Czap
Lettering by Tess Stone

Penciled with Photoshop, printed on cardstock and inked with Kuretake Fudegokochi
and Micron pens. Scanned, cleaned up, and colored digitally in Photoshop.

Printed in China

ISBN 978-1-250-19351-3 (paperback)
10 9 8 7 6 5 4 3 2 1

ISBN 978-1-250-19352-0 (hardcover)
10 9 8 7 6 5 4 3 2 1

Don't miss your next favorite book from First Second! For the latest updates go
to firstsecondnewsletter.com and sign up for our enewsletter.